THE CITY OF TREMBLING LEAVES

THE CITY OF
Trembling Leaves

WALTER VAN TILBURG CLARK

RANDOM HOUSE · NEW YORK

for R. C. C.

Contents: B O O K   O N E

BOOK TWO

Book One

Prelude

THIS is the story of the lives and loves of Timothy Hazard, and so, indirectly, a token biography of Reno, Nevada, as well. Now, whatever else Reno may be, and it is many things, it is the city of trembling leaves. The most important meaning of leaves is the same everywhere in Reno, of course, and everywhere else, for that matter, which is what Tim implies when he calls moribund any city containing a region in which you can look all around and not see a tree. Such a city is drawing out of its alliance with the eternal, with the Jurassic Swamps and the Green Mansions, and in time it will also choke out the trees in the magic wilderness of the spirit. In Reno, however, this universal importance of trees is intensified, for Reno is in the Great Basin of America, between the Rockies and the Sierras, where the vigor of the sun and the height of the mountains, to say nothing of the denuding activities of mining booms, have created a latter-day race of tree worshippers. Furthermore, to such tree worshippers, and Tim Hazard is high in the cult, the trees of Reno have regional meanings within their one meaning, like the themes and transitions of a one-movement symphony. It would be impossible to understand Tim Hazard without hearing these motifs played separately before you hear them in the whole.

The trees of the Wingfield Park-Court Street region dispense an air of antique melancholy. You become sad and old as you walk under these trees, even on a bright, winter day when all the leaves are gone and the branches make only narrow shadows across homes covered with sunlight.

The park is not large, yet it feels like the edge of a wilderness of infinite extent, so that if you lie on the grass there on Sunday, or sit on one of the green benches (this is in the summer now), you don't even have to close your eyes to believe in a great

3

depth of forest and shadow of time. In part this is due to the illusion that the treetops of Reno are continuous, one elevated pampas of stirring leaves, unconcerned with houses and streets below, so that the park, actually a ledge between the Truckee River and the bluff of Court Street, does not seem set apart. Even more it is due to the spacious shadow and the quiet under the trees. No rush of wind and leaves, no slow snowing of cottonwood-down, or cries of playing children, or running on the tennis courts can really disturb this quiet. It is an everlasting late-afternoon somnolence, the mood of a Watteau painting, if you can imagine the beribboned courtiers much smaller under their trees, like Corot's wood nymphs, and completely dreamy, not even toying with flutes, mandolins, fruit or amorous preliminaries. This applies only to the older part of the park, of course. The newer part, on the island breasting the Truckee, is out in the sun, and its trees are younger and more susceptible to vagrant airs. It is like a light motif dropped into the melancholy central movement in anticipation of the theme of the outskirts.

The mood of the Court Street trees is heavy with the homes, some of which can be seen from below, staring northward from the bluff out of tired windows. Among their lawns, shaded by their trees and their pasts, these houses do not wholly despair, but they have reason to. Their doors seem closed, their windows empty and still, and they appear to meditate upon longer, more intricate and more pathetic pasts than any of them could possibly have accumulated. The vitality of these houses, compounded of memory and discontent, is inconsiderable compared with their resignation. Even though it would not be statistically accurate, you must think of all the houses in Court Street in terms of high-ceilinged rooms with the shades drawn in late afternoon in summer, or with the shades up but the windows closed in a windy, moonlit night in winter. And you must be alone in the room and in the house. It makes no difference any more who lives in these houses, or what they do; they cannot change this nature, which has been accepted and expressed by the trees of Court Street.

Beyond Court Street to the south, this mood goes through a

gradual and almost constant brightening. The Court Street theme still dominates the region of Flint, Hill, Liberty, Granite and California, all that height and slope between Belmont Road and Virginia Street, the region of big rooming houses and apartments, which owes allegiance to the Washoe County Court House, and may be called the Court House Quarter. Even the private homes of this region are sunk under the Court Street theme, and its big and beautiful trees give the impression that they should be motionless, even in a plateau gale, and that only their topmost leaves should accept sunlight, and tremble. Tim's best friend, Lawrence Black, whose life will at times seem almost synonymous with Tim's, lived in this quarter when he was a boy, and Tim says that his home echoed the theme, and was gently and completely haunted from attic to basement. Its livliest time was the bearable melancholy of six o'clock in the afternoon in June. Tim's great single love, Rachel Wells, also lived in this quarter, in a big house with a porte-cochere and an air of dark yesterdays, until she had finished high school.

From here out, to the south and west, spreads a high region of increasingly new homes, bungalows, ornamented brick structures of greater size, a number of which it would be difficult to describe fairly, and white, Spanish houses. This region seems to become steadily more open, windy and sunlit as you move out, and at some point you will realize that the Court Street theme has become inaudible, and that you have truly entered what may be called the Mt. Rose Quarter. Here there are many new trees, no taller than a man, always trembling so they nearly dance, and most of the grown trees are marching files of poplars, in love with wind and heavens. Here, no matter how many houses rear up, stark in the sunlight, you remain more aware of the sweeping domes of earth which hold them down, and no matter how long you stay in one of the houses, you will still be more aware of Mt. Rose aloft upon the west, than of anything in the house: furniture, silver, books, or even people. Even at night, when the summit of the mountain is only a starlit glimmer, detached from earth, it is the strong pole of all waking minds in that quarter.

I do not mean to celebrate newness as such, any more than I would celebrate oldness as such. Temporal age is unimportant. There is a strong likeness between many old houses, brownstone, brick and Victorian frame, and the brand-new gas works, factories and warehouses which quickly create moribund districts in a city, districts from which life, if it has any choice, shies away. It is rather that this Mt. Rose region is more open to the eternal and reproductive old. It may be significant, for instance, though doubtless it galls a few property owners, whose interest in earth is in marking it into salable squares, that part way out Plumas Street, which is the main thoroughfare of the Mt. Rose quarter, there is still a farm, with a brook in its gully, cows on its steep slopes, and a sign on a tree saying EGGS FOR SALE. It may also be significant that Tim Hazard and his gentle, golden-brown wife Mary, live in one of the small bungalows about halfway out Plumas, not far beyond the Billinghurst School, and on the east side of the street, so that Tim can sit on the front steps and look at Mt. Rose while he waters the lawn, and Mary can see it through the kitchen window while she works at the sink. It may even be significant, for that matter, that the Hazards live in a bungalow. Such houses, the easiest in the world to forget, are infinitely mutable under the impact of the thoughts, dreams, desires and acts of the people living in them, while in houses like those on Court Street there is great danger that the shaping will be reversed. Houses are incipiently evil which have been intended to master time and dominate nature. That is a moribund intention. It feels death coming on all the time, and, having no faith in reproduction or multiplicity, tries to build a fort to hold it off.

On the north side of the Truckee River, the Court Street theme continues, but in a higher and sharper key, interrupted by short, ominous passages from the middle of the city. Also it moves toward the north edge more rapidly and with a quickening tempo, for in this district of the McKinley Park and Mary S. Doten schools, the dominant houses are, from the first, the dying miniature Victorian and the bungalows, and they don't influence the trees.

6

When you reach the little trees of the north edge, where Virginia Street becomes the Purdy Road, or the region of upper Ralston Street west of the hilltop cemeteries, there is a new theme, higher, clearer and sharper than that of the south edge. Here the city is thinner, and not expanding so rapidly, for it is already on the mountains. From windows on the heights, University Terrace, College Drive, Fourteenth and Fifteenth Streets, you look down across the whole billowing sea of the treetops of Reno, and feel more removed from the downtown section than in any other place in the city, because you are off any main streets, away from the sound of them even, and because you can see the tops of downtown places, the Medico-Dental Building, the roof sign of the Riverside Hotel, the gray breasts of the Catholic Church, like strange and tiny islands in that sea, and realize how far you are from them.

There is another difference, too, which indirectly affects the meaning of the trees. The University of Nevada is on the climbing north edge, and it is an even better place than any of the parks for glens and stretches of lawn, and clumps and avenues of trees. It has a tone of active, enduring quiet, and is big enough to impart much of this tone to all the north end except the eastern corner, which is drawn into the influence of the race track. For Tim Hazard, after his boyhood, the university quarter was foreign country, the city of the hills seen from the plains. He went up there only once in a while, to hear some music, or see a play, or watch a game in the gymnasium or on Mackay Field. Yet he says that he always felt that in going north, toward the university, he should walk, but in going south, until he had passed the last service station on the South Virginia Road, he should drive, and drive like hell.

A further and, perhaps, in the course of time, even more important, difference between the high north edge, and the low south edge, is that Mt. Rose is the sole, white, exalted patron angel and fountain of wind and storm to south Reno, while in north Reno, her reign is strongly contested by black Peavine Mountain, less austere, wilder, and the home of two winds. Mt. Rose is a detached goal of the spirit, requiring a lofty and difficult worship. Peavine is the great, humped child of desert. He is barren, and often lowering, but he reaches out and brings unto him, while Rose stands aloof. He is part of the great plateau which is the land of the city, while Rose is part of the western barrier. Rose begets reverence, but Peavine begets love. There is a liveliness in his quarter which gets into everything.

It is up in Peavine's quarter that Tim's friend Lawrence lived, on and off, during the best years of their conversations. He lived in a cabin in an alley on top of the hill. There is a telephone pole, with many cross arms, beside the cabin. Lawrence once did a dark pastel of this telephone pole, with a small moon racing through a scud above it. It is deeply moving. You cannot see the wires, but you can hear them cry in the wind. Behind you, as you look at the picture, you can feel Peavine brooding in the immense night of the plateau. Also in the best years, it was here more than anywhere else, excepting, perhaps, Pyramid Lake, that Lawrence's dark and beautiful wife Helen was one of a triumvirate, to which I sometimes added a fourth, that had formed against destiny; Helen who was wild to be doing, and had no patience with the limitations of words, or of thoughts, or even of the body, though she trusted the body most.

Tim tells me that for him the theme of the north edge is identified with a little aspen that grew in the yard by Lawrence's cabin. The yard was surrounded by a high board fence and was very small, and only the aspen and sturdy weeds grew in it. Tim and Lawrence and sometimes Helen would sit out there in the sun for hours. If the wind blew from Peavine, bringing dust along the alley, they could take shelter against the fence and still hear it in the telephone wires and in the aspen. All their thoughts and words were touched by the twinkle of sun on the aspen and by the whispering and rushing of its leaves.

The north-east quarter of Reno, with the ranching valley on the east of it and the yellow hills with a few old mines on the north, is drawn out of the influence of the university and Peavine into the vortex of the race track. Even in Tim's boyhood the race track was alive only two or three weeks out of a year, yet it seems a fast-moving place. The trembling of the leaves in its sphere rises easily into a roaring through tall Lombardies set in rows in dust and open sunlight. This quality of thin, hasty brightness persists clear down through the quarter, where the trees close in and the small, white houses fill the blocks, in the lumber yard beyond, and even down to the Western Pacific Depot and the grimy edge of Fourth Street. It is a theme almost strident, and saved from being as intolerable as persistent whistles only by the yellow hills, like cats asleep in the north, and by the greater and darker Virginia Range in the east, through which the Truckee cuts its red and shadowy gorge. Sunset on those hills is also a very important subduer.

It was in this quarter that Tim Hazard lived when he was a boy, on the street right next to the track, so that he got to see a good many horse races and rodeos, and even circuses that set up their tents outside the fence. He lived in a square, white-board house with a shallow porch with a dirt walk and three big poplars in front of it. His bedroom was upstairs in front, and when he was in bed he heard the poplars, winter and summer, windy and quiet, and saw them, morning and night, cloudy and clear, moonlight and starlight and dark.

Tim's father worked in the lumber yard, and on Saturdays, and sometimes after school, Tim worked there too. His mother worked in the house, and in her garden behind the house, and at keeping her troublesome males living together. There were three of these males, the third being Tim's young brother Willis, who started to smoke, drink, stay out late and play seriously with girls when he was smaller than most people would believe, and who wanted to be either a jockey or a prize-fighter. Then there was also Grace, Tim's older sister, a gentle, dreamy person, with whom he could talk more easily than he could with Willis, who regarded conversation as another form of fighting or racing. Grace married a kind, steady fellow she had met in high school, and they went first to Stockton, where he ran a service station, and then to Bakersfield, where he worked with the highway department. They have three children, one of whom promises to be a lot like Tim.

The south-east quarter of Reno combines the qualities of the north-east and south-west, yet has a quite different, quieter and more uniform tone, because it is dedicated to the valley, into which it is slowly spreading, and is not much influenced by any mountain. Daybreak and sunset are the test times of any region's allegiance, and at daybreak and sunset the south-east quarter thinks toward the valley, where the light spreads widely, and is more aware of that level spaciousness than of the mountains beyond it. None of the themes of Reno is isolated, however. They merge one into another, and so one corner of this quarter, the Mill Street toward Virginia Street corner, echoes the Court Street theme and the rumbling and cries of the center of the city.

Reno began with Lake's Crossing on the Truckee, and in its beginnings was divided by the Truckee, but as it grew the activity of men quartered it by the intersection of Virginia Street, running more or less north and south, and Fourth Street, running more or less east and west. Virginia Street and Fourth Street are what is commonly called the main arteries, or the purveyors of the life-blood of the city. They are the streets which continue on out and tie Reno into the world, as the others fade away or blend into each other. The only important difference between them and the purveyors of the life-blood of any city arises from the fact that Reno has sheltered itself in the north-west corner of its valley, so that it has stretched along Virginia Street only to the south, where it becomes the highway to Carson, and along Fourth Street only to the east, where Reno and Sparks have become practically one city. It is more important, however, to the Reno of Tim Hazard, that on the west, Fourth Street plunges quickly into the foothills of the Sierras, and that North Virginia Street promptly becomes the Purdy Road, which goes away lonesomely across passes and great desert valleys into a land of timber, fine cattle, deep upland meadows and secret lakes. It is notable, for instance, that on the Purdy Road hawks, and even eagles, may be seen perching for long periods on fence posts and telephone poles.

Mary Turner lived in a frame bungalow on North Virginia Street, opposite the university, while she and Tim were going to the Orvis Ring School. The Orvis Ring is the school for the north-east quarter. The Western Pacific tracks run right behind it, but the Western Pacific there is a quiet, single line, and doesn't disturb the school, or have much effect on the quarter, except as a dividing line between the university region and the race-track region.

This is not the case with the big Southern Pacific lines, but since they run through the downtown section, and only a block south of Fourth Street, they don't create a separate zone. Aside from the fact that they make a railroad street of Commercial Row, their effect is one with that of Fourth Street. Yet they have a subtle influence in Reno, whether it is heeded or not, aside, that is, from the obvious results of carrying thousands of people and cattle, and thousands of tons of freight, into and out of and through Reno. The gigantic freight engines of the S.P., often two to a train when headed into the mountains, gently shake all the windows in the city in their passage. At night their tremendous mushrooms of smoke, lighted from beneath by the center of the city, may be seen from the hills of the north edge, swelling above the trees. Their wild whistles cry in the night, and echo mournfully all round the mountain walls of the valley. Thus Reno is reminded constantly that it is only one small stop on the road of the human world, that it trembles with the comings and goings of that world, and yet that the greatest cry of that world is only a brief echo against mountains.

Mary told me once that the whistles of the big steam engines were so sad that when they woke her at night, in the bungalow on North Virginia, and she heard their echoes still slowly circling the valley and dying, she would sometimes even cry a little, and would invariably begin on long thoughts of loneliness and mortality. This confession is significant, because Mary is a contented person, wise in the small, permanent ways, and her childhood home was much more peaceful than Tim's. Her father was a short, quiet man, who worked on the university grounds and did a little business in taxidermy in a shed behind the house. Her mother was a plump, affectionate woman, and a very good cook, whose chief interest, aside from her family, was in several varieties of roses, which she made to grow over the house, over the green-lattice fence between the house and the shed, and in clumps about the lawn and the steps. It is enough to indicate the peace of Mary's home that her father took up taxidermy for the secret reason that he hated to think of so many lovely creatures leaving no tangible memories, that her mother always wrote for a dozen seed catalogues when the first thaw came in February, and that the three of them often sat together silently on the front porch in the summer evenings and watched the last light slowly ascend the trees on the university campus.

There is also, of course, the treeless center of the city, which we have worked all around, though not without hearing it several times, in sudden, shrill bursts from the brass or deep mutterings in the rhythm section. This, however, is the region about which the world already knows or imagines more, in a Sunday-supplement way, than is true, and it will do, for the present, to suggest that it is not unlike any moribund city, or the moribund region of any city. It is the ersatz jungle, where the human animals, uneasy in the light, dart from cave to cave under steel and neon branches, where the voice of the croupier halloos in the secret glades, and high and far, like light among the top leaves, gleam the names of lawyers and hairdressers on upstairs windows. In short, this is the region which may be truly entered by passing under the arch which says, RENO, THE BIGGEST LITTLE CITY IN THE WORLD.

Yet there is one important difference between even this region and the truly moribund cities of the world, the difference which makes Reno a city of adolescence, a city of dissonant themes, sawing against each other with a kind of piercing beauty like that of a fourteen-year-old girl or a seventeen-year-old boy, the beauty of everything promised and nothing resolved. Even from the very center of Reno, from the intersection of Virginia and Second Streets, and even at night, when restless club lights mask the stars, one can look in any direction and see the infinite shoals of the leaves hovering about the first lone crossing light.

CHAPTER ONE: *Mostly About Lucy, the Golden Tart, But Also About Gladys, the Skull, the Trinity of Heroes, and the Influence of Mrs. Boone*

THE body of Tim Hazard was not born in Reno, but within hearing of the steamer whistles, ferry bells and waterfront drays of San Francisco. This, however, is a fact of no importance, since from the first Tim was what is generally called a fool or a dreamer. That is to say, he was a personality which automatically sought meanings rather than manifestations, so that mere habitat did not seem to him to matter. With the instinct of a bloodhound, he pursued the fainting traces of previous passage all over the stony ground of life. Like a bird upon a nest when the eggs begin to work from within, he responded with great throbbings in the breast to every inner movement of his imperishable and impersonal past and future, as one might remember with sharp nostalgia an old incident of profound pleasure or grief. Since the years in which he was most completely the bird and the bloodhound, making his ceaseless excursions with only an occasional awareness of existing in the flesh, since these sniffing and shell-breaking years were spent entirely in Reno, he considers himself to have been born there, although actually he was old enough to start school within a year after his family moved into the house near the race track.

Tim went to the Orvis Ring School, the school by the Western Pacific tracks, which were the dividing line between the university and race-track sections of the north-east quarter. The children who attended this school came about equally from under the two signs, and not being aware at this stage that there were any differences between their respective parents save differences of spirit, which were individual, not sectional, they mingled in absolute, cruel, lively and unembittered democracy.

13

Neither was there any recognized difference between dreamers, or, as Tim would call them, primary realists, and factualists, or secondary realists, which latter, for purposes of not seeming to quibble, I will continue to call realists. The realists were in their usual numerical superiority, and Tim sat at the feet of the leaders among them, which he now thinks was a good discipline for him, though he thought nothing about it then.

Throughout school he was two or three years younger than most of his classmates, small for his age, and skinny. Mary, who has an affection for past existences, and who was in the same class with Tim for two years, has saved her class pictures. They show Tim as a small, thin, big-eyed creature, with a habit of dodging haircuts as long as possible. In the seventh-grade picture he is seated cross-legged in the front row between two of his heroes, Beefy Stone and Tony Barenechea, and behind him stands a third hero, Dutch Adams. There is no denying the fact that in this position Tim, called Timmy then, looks like a pip in the teeth. He was eleven years old, and weighed seventy-nine pounds. Beefy, who wasn't quite bright, was seventeen and weighed one hundred and eighty-five. Tony, who was a Basque, whose father was a sheepherder, was fourteen and weighed one hundred and forty-five. Dutch was much shorter than these two, but was the strongest and quickest boy in school. He was sixteen, much too old for his grade, but this was not because there was anything wrong with his head, but because his father was dead and he had been working at night since he was nine years old.

If you can remember specific incidents from the improbable era when you yourself were a spontaneous savage in the enchanted forest of life, let's say when you were eleven years old, you will recall that the spiritual difference between seventy-nine pounds and one hundred and forty-five or fifty, to say nothing of such an improbable mass as one hundred and eighty-five, to say nothing of the additional difference between eleven years and fourteen or sixteen or seventeen, is very great. Tim was perpetually in the position of the humble disciple, unduly exalted by the word of praise or the morsel of recognition. Fortunately, two of his masters, Tony and Dutch, were considerate dictators, and Beefy's trouble was so noticeable that he never received the adulation, even from dreamless boys as small as Timmy, that would enable his slight tendency toward bullying to blossom into terrorism. It remained only a minor meanness, without organization or direction, satisfied by an occasional passing poke in the ribs to someone who knew too many answers in class, or by recitations, in the sun in the courtyard at recess, of extremely adult achievements with beer, cigars and lively girls. Tim says it was probably a good thing for him that neither Dutch nor Tony often showed interest in Beefy's narratives, but emulated what they believed to be the traits of selected heroes among the athletes of Reno High School and the University of Nevada, and were advocates of strict training. They would laugh sometimes at one of Beefy's more subtle jokes, such as, "What the hell do you guys know about what you can do in the bushes? Your trousers ain't never had no bumps in them, have they?" but most of the time they paid no attention to him except as a useful dead weight on their teams.

Only once, in his seventh-grade year, Timmy felt that both Dutch and Tony were stirred by something which he did not understand except that it was in the realm of Beefy's adventures. It was a sunny, spring day, and when the upper grades emptied for recess, Timmy came running out, waving his fielder's glove, and all set to sprint, take the several steps from the court to the sidewalk in one jump, and tear around the school to the field of dirt and stone, where the slabs marking the bases were already sunk in dusty wallows. Then he saw that most of the boys who usually played were gathered in the sun by the low, stone rail of the court. Perceiving by their quiet that something of intense interest was being talked about, he slowed to a walk, and approached the outside edge of the group. Beefy looked around and saw him.

"What you doing here, pip-squeak?" he asked, grinning. His grin was very convincing, because he had lost his front teeth. This also made him lisp sometimes, which was fascinating rather than funny in a boy of his dimensions and past and dislike for washing.

"Go on away," he said, still grinning. "You can't do yourself any good here, pip-squeak."

Some of the others laughed. The unknown was in their mirth.

A boy called Henry, who lived on a small, poor farm outside the city, and whose father was also a groom during racing season, was in the inner circle on the other side, and had been doing the important talking.

Henry said, "Who's that? Timmy?" and when he saw that it was, said, "Beat it, Timmy. This ain't any beeswax for you."

"It's a free country," Timmy said.

"It's free enough," another boy said, and they all laughed again.

Timmy would have left, except that now it was harder to go than to stay. He didn't want to stay.

"Oh, leave him have a try, Hank. It'd be fun to see him try," somebody else said.

"Geez, look at him," Beefy said. "It ain't no use. What could he do?"

Everybody laughed again.

A boy called Harold Ashby said, giggling, "You don't even know what we're talkin' about, do you, Timmy?"

"Well, I don't guess it amounts to too much," Timmy said.

"You oughta try it some time," Harold said, and there was more laughing, although it wasn't so spontaneous, and a number of comments were made which were more informative, but didn't mean any more to Timmy, whose practical vocabulary was small.

Dutch put an arm around Timmy's shoulder. Dutch's arm was stubby and hard as wood.

"Don't pay any attention to 'em, Timmy," Dutch said. "They're just a bunch of dirty-mouthed bums, anyway."

Nobody was offended. Henry grinned and said, "I guess you ain't interested maybe, huh, Dutch? Oh, no, I guess not. Look, Timmy," he said in a quieter voice, "you gotta find out something about life, some time." He practically whispered, "Lucy and Gladys are gonna give out at noon hour, up in the jungle."

The jungle was the acre of willows by the railroad tracks north of the school. Timmy thought of the jungle with unintelligent excitement, and asked, "Give out what?"

This time the laughter was stunning. Boys slapped their knees. They turned against the wall and hammered it with their fists. They repeated with vaudeville inflections, "Give out what?"

"You come on up in the jungle, noon hour, and you'll find out," Henry told him finally.

"Don't you do it, Timmy," Tony said. "Not if you don't want to. Just like you said, it ain't anything so much. Anybody can do it."

Tony was serious, but for some reason or other this seemed to be the best joke yet. They kept repeating, "Anybody can do it," as they had, "Give out what?" and one of the boys even had to sit down against the wall and close his eyes and hug his stomach because he couldn't stop laughing.

Timmy was only a little encouraged by Tony's support, though. He knew that he wasn't worthy of it. He wanted to be like any of them, a man strutting independently in the dust and sun of spring, making his choice with understanding. Instead he was miserable, because he knew he would shrink from whatever it was they were going to do. It would be impossible to expose his ignorance.

While they were still laughing, some of the boys began to describe what would happen to Timmy if he entered the jungle. Harold Ashby gave the loudest description. Harold was a smooth, brown boy, not much bigger than Timmy, but nearly all his talk was about girls. He described in detail how Timmy with the girl Lucy would be like a sailor overboard in mid-ocean. He laughed all the time he talked, so that it was hard to understand him. For some reason, whenever Harold started laughing about girls, he would soon be the only one laughing.

"For Chrissakes, loud mouth, shut up," Hank ordered. "Ain't you got any brains? The windows is all open. You want old lady Henny-Penny out there snoopin' around all noon hour?"

"Oh, bushwah," Harold said, but not loudly, and his face became very red and then very pale, and such a strange expression, as of terrible loss, filled his eyes, that some of the boys stared at him curiously and others, like Timmy, couldn't look at him at all.

Old lady Henny-Penny was the out-of-the-presence name of the principal of the school, a woman whose bent and white-haired person was actually revered little short of idolatry because of her sternness, fairness, patience, incredible energy and gift for knowing what nobody could know. She signed herself Henrietta P. Boone, and for years had been called just Henny, but when she received an honorary degree from the university for fifty years of unflinching teaching, her full name was read, revealing that the P. stood for Penelope, after which Henny-Penny was inevitable. It was also a sound of cabalistic efficacy. The gathering of the vultures was dissolved.

After recess, Timmy looked often at the girls named Lucy and Gladys. They didn't look any different. Gladys was a tall, thin girl, whose dresses were always too long and loose and were made of clinging material with big flower patterns. She was much older than Timmy, but how old he didn't know. She looked older than most of the girls, because she used powder and lipstick, and did her blonde, wavy hair in a knot on the back of her head, like a woman. She had long, thin hands and feet, and her legs were just shin bones around which her cotton stockings were always twisted in spirals. She was quiet in class, and always appeared to be studying hard or listening closely, although she never knew any of the answers. She was intent on her geography book now, an elbow planted each side of it, and her forehead in her hands.

Lucy was a different sort. Lucy was fourteen, and said so, and was short, womanly of body, and always neatly dressed in tight skirts and white blouses. She had an olive-colored face and dark hair and thick eyebrows for a girl. The calves of her legs, covered by smooth, silk stockings, were as muscular and bunchy as a boy's, her ankles were thin and hard, and she wore high-heeled shoes. She was a loud, good-humored talker, and had a wit too sharp and realistic to be tampered with. She was a good student too, when she wanted to be, and never caused any more disturbance than Gladys did, since she was never caught in her continual note writing and small, preparatory activities. She failed to be one of the leading students only because she was too busy.

It seemed to Timmy that, if all this about the jungle was not just a hoax of Henry's, these two girls should be greatly changed after that recess, but they weren't. Once he saw Gladys slowly and carefully turn her head to look at Beefy, and when Beefy winked, make a slow smile at him, as if she felt sick. Once Lucy caught Timmy looking at her, and suddenly thrust her head out toward him, puckered her mouth, made several little quick kisses in the air, and then, just as quickly, drew back and sat hugging herself, leaning over her book and jerking with silent laughter. That was all, and how much that meant was uncertain. Gladys always looked sick when she smiled, and Lucy was always making quick kisses at people. Lucy was stimulating. Those kisses helped the imagination, and so did the way she hugged herself, especially when your grasp of the subject, like Timmy's, was limited to a few variations of the arrangement of a hug and a kiss, and was purely academic even there. He discovered that it was impossible to imagine voluntarily hugging and kissing Gladys. He believed she would smell sour.

At noon hour he took his lunch out onto the north steps of the school. From there he could see the jungle, which was beyond the school yard, the dirt road on which he usually went home, and a patch of tumbleweed. The willows grew right up to the edge of the railroad embankment. Above them lifted the pale tops of a few poplar and aspen saplings. The willows were motionless and shamefully important. They showed nothing. The lightly attached leaves of the poplars and aspens, however, though the air seemed perfectly still, stirred constantly, as if some activity went on below, against the stems. The air danced like water above the tracks and the cinder embankment. Timmy didn't see either of the girls, or any of the boys who had been plotting so boldly, but he couldn't get over his excitement, or his burden of mortification and the conviction of unmanliness. He was not hungry, either. His food seemed dry, and stuck in his throat. At some point in his watch, everything turned unreal. The thin voices and playing bodies of the other children in the school yard were in another and distant life. Even the glittering leaves of the saplings over the jungle seemed merely dancing lights in his own eyes. Once he thought he heard faint laughter from the jungle, but he couldn't be sure, because many of the children in the yard were laughing, and their voices also sounded far away. At last it became impossible for him to sit still with his strange shame and confusion, for which he could find no real reason except that he was being left out of something. He put his lunch back into its tin box and went around to the front of the school, where the jungle would be out of sight.

In the afternoon class he knew that something had happened. The boys who had understood what was going to happen kept grinning at each other, Gladys fell asleep with her head on her arms, half an hour before school ended, and even Lucy was very quiet in a dull way that had no gleam or promise.

CHAPTER TWO: *About the Influence of the Divine Mary, and About Kisses and Prayers*

EVERY person is also a jungle himself, a forest primeval, a prehistoric swamp in which life is rich, various and reproductive, in which it is very easy to get lost, but absolutely impossible to see everything. Tim maintains merely that he must have changed in some way, because after that hour of dark wonder on the north steps, he remained constantly in the presence of Lucy and Gladys through the rest of that spring, and all through his eighth-grade year. He remembers, for instance, that when the class was sent to the blackboard for arithmetic problems or grammar diagrams, both of which he dreaded, he would be a little excited if he stood next to Lucy, and would sometimes even try to stand next to her, if it was impossible to stand next to Mary, but that he would always manage to get somebody between him and Gladys. He also had an adventure that may have begun while he was looking at the secret willows in the sun.

He was standing at the blackboard, miserably failing to place his adverbs and adjectives in probable positions. Lucy was beside him. Mrs. Boone was correcting a diagram on the opposite side of the room. Suddenly Lucy put an arm around him, hugged him hard, and blew on his neck inside his open shirt collar.

"What do you care, Timmy?" she whispered. "Who ever got anywhere diagramming any old sentences, anyway?"

"I'll have to stay after school," Timmy whispered.

Lucy comforted him further, while swiftly laying out her diagram with true, ruled lines. "So will I. I didn't study my history. I'll see you in the cloakroom after school. I'll give you something nice to think about, Timmy." And she made two of her puckered kisses at the adverb "rapidly" while she put it in its place.

Timmy was very nervously curious about what Lucy would give him. Her hug, short and playful though it had been, strengthened this anticipation. But he was also troubled. He was being true to his true love Mary at this time. In fact he had already, though without reward, been true to his true love Mary for more than a year. Her people had moved to Reno in the summer before his seventh-grade year. She had come to school, new and lonely, the first day that fall, and sat in the seat two ahead of his own, but in the next row. A condition of adoration had been attained in three days, and maintained ever since as a direct line through Timmy's pursuit of life, all other experiences being entered like notes above and below the staff. Thinking about Mary was an act of devotion. Such disturbances as the day of the jungle and this promise of Lucy's were accidental confusions without future. Nonetheless, they were confusing. Timmy had yet a long way to go before he discovered that he had an ego to maintain as a guide in all matters of moral confusion, and at the time was only sure that if Lucy wanted him to do something, he would probably do it, whether he wanted to or not. The question was what she wanted him to do.

Mrs. Boone's examination of his diagram, which looked like a Van Loon drawing of the Amazon and its tributaries, fulfilled his defeatist expectations. What happened after school was also what he expected. He was given ten sentences to diagram, beginning with a very simple one, "I ran home" (on which, nonetheless, he floundered because of a nightmare similarity between objects and predicate words) and progressing gradually, in the saintly hope that he would progress with them, to a very complex-compound sentence. He stood there making unconvinced, wavering scratches, and erasing them, and telling himself a story in which he was a strong and capable hunter in the mountains, who awoke in every dawn with a heart eager for life because there was nobody around to talk at him about anything that must be done. This story was interrupted frequently by Mrs. Boone's patient exasperation, by fragments of other stories he had been working on, in which he and Mary lived up to all except the real expectations of the readers of *Love Stories*, and by moments of looking at Lucy and wondering about the cloakroom. He was afraid Lucy would get out before he did, and be too impatient to wait, and he was also afraid she wouldn't.

While he was still wandering in the mazes of the fifth sentence, Mrs. Boone having been worn into abandoning each of the first four, or rather into demolishing them herself, by way of demonstration, Lucy closed her book, raised her hand, talked in a low voice to Mrs. Boone for ten minutes, and got up. She tucked a note into Timmy's off-side hand as she went by. He got a chance to read it after Mrs. Boone had surrendered the sixth sentence, because the telephone rang in her office.

"Hurry up, slow poke! I'll be in the auditoreim at five P.M., unless old dodo kicks me out."

Lucy was wise. At five o'clock Mrs. Boone, weakened by internal revolt, and her natural resources exhausted, hung out a white flag while the eighth sentence was scarcely breached and was still held by a conjunction, two prepositions and an entirely fresh company of adjectives and adverbs.

Timmy innocently went to the front door of the auditorium. Old Dodo, the school janitor, in his black-cloth sleeve protectors and striped engineer's cap, was locking the door.

"What de dickens you do aroun' here dis time de day? You bin in soom trooble, I bat. Now you want more, huh?" Dodo complained.

While Timmy was going back out through the dark hall, he heard Dodo going slowly down the stairs into the basement, muttering about dese fool keeds, and all night next, I bat.

Lucy herself let Timmy into the auditorium by the north door from the playground.

"I hid back-stage," she said. "Old Dodo locked up and never even knew I was here."

In the large and shadowy hall, divided by a tall, blue drape into a classroom and a theatre, Timmy was overwhelmed by a conviction that he was probably about to learn more than he wanted to. His bones, breath and vision were shaken.

Lucy took his hand. "Let's go in the other part," she said. "Somebody might come in here." She seemed simultaneously excited and moved by secret mirth. She kept looking at Timmy and giggling.

They went into the theatre half, up the steps at the side of the stage, and into the gloom of the north wing. Timmy stood there, smiling defensively at her.

"Oh, throw away those old books," Lucy said.

Timmy put the books down very carefully. Lucy stood watching him, with her hands on her hips.

"Timmy, you're a honey," she said. "Only, you don't know what anything's about, do you?"

"Oh, I don't know," Timmy said. "I guess I know enough."

"Well, why don't you prove it?" Lucy asked.

She came close to him, and touched his belt with her hand, and held her face out to him with her eyes closed. There developed in Timmy's mind a whirl of excursions and retreats which finally organized into a paralysis. It was as if a sheet of clear but very thick glass stood between them. He looked at Lucy's face through this glass. Lucy opened her eyes.

"Am I poison?" she asked. "Do I look like I would bite or something?"

"No," Timmy said.

"Oh, my heavens," Lucy said, and stamped and walked away from him. He stood quite still. If he moved he would be seen again, or he might even fall apart. Lucy came back and stood looking at him.

"Honest to God, Timmy, you ain't ever even kissed a girl, have you?"

"Maybe you think I haven't," Timmy said.

"Then what's the matter with me?" Lucy demanded.

Timmy was in a terrible position, for here was Lucy, always as generous as the sun, and she sounded hurt.

"Nobody's gonna see us, Timmy," she said. "Come on. Give us a kiss."

She took his hand. Her touch broke the intervening glass, and Timmy leaned forward. At once Lucy snuggled against him, and when he tried to escape after a quick token-kiss, she grasped him around the waist and warmly and openly fitted her mouth over his. With her free hand she tried to put his arms into more pleasant positions. When they were more or less locked, she took her mouth away.

"Timmy, honey," she murmured, "be yourself. Give us a little loving. Honest, Timmy, you're sweet."

Timmy did his best to help her, in the fainting hope that it would end the matter. They worked through several thunderous kisses. Lucy let him go.

"I know what's the matter with you," she said, pinching his chin. "I shouldn't oughta of done this, should I, Timmy? You're being true to Mary, ain't you, Timmy?"

Timmy saw that she was hurt again, for some reason which escaped him. "Gosh, I don't know," he said. "I like you a lot, Lucy."

"Sure you do," Lucy said, patting his face as if she might slap it in a moment. "You're just crazy about me, ain't you, Timmy?

"O.K., Timmy," she said, stopping the patting, "I won't tell on you. Wait a minute," she added, and drew a handkerchief out of her blouse, wet it with her tongue, and began to dab and rub at his face. "If Mary was to see you like that," she said. "You look like somebody'd been throwing rotten strawberries at you."

When she had cleaned him up, she gave him one more, very light kiss. "There you are, practically new goods."

She got her own books in a very businesslike manner. Timmy also picked his up. They were bound by a belt, which he slung over his shoulder.

"Timmy," Lucy said, "will you tell me just one thing?"

"Sure. I guess so."

"Did Mary ever let you kiss her?"

"Well," Timmy said, "I don't know. I didn't ever try."

Lucy shook her head. "What some people think is fun," she said. "What do you do over at her house, eat sody crackers and play with blocks?"

Tim was glad of the dusk back-stage. He could feel the fury of his blushing. He was also sweating. "I don't know," he said. "I've never been over to her house."

Lucy laughed suddenly, throwing her head way back. "Goodness' sakes, Timmy," she said finally, still laughing, "you gotta get going. Life isn't for always."

Timmy understood that she was being very nice with him when she said "goodness' sakes" and "my heavens." He was hurt, but he tried to smile.

Lucy laughed again. "O.K., Timmy," she said, and patted his face again. "I guess you just naturally don't know anything. I guess you're just naturally a sweet little lamb and a angel. I shouldn't ever of kissed you even. It might give you ideas. I'll claw hell out of anybody else that tries to kiss you. Except maybe Mary, of course," she added, and laughed again.

When they were at the outside door she hesitated and looked at him. "You ain't mad at me, are you, Timmy?"

Timmy shook his head.

"Well, I'm the one oughta be mad, I guess," she said. "There's plenty of boys like to kiss me. But I ain't, either. Give me one kiss, will you, Timmy? Just to show you ain't mad. Just a nice kiss?"

Timmy leaned forward to kiss her, and she made the kiss exactly equal.

They peered out the door. The playground and the road were empty. They went down the steps quickly and separated at once.

"So long, Timmy," Lucy called. "You be good." And she laughed.

Timmy was a sailor home to the sea, out in the great spaces and master of his own thoughts. He felt exceedingly free and light as he walked along the road across the tracks in the shadow of the late afternoon. All heat and motion were out of the air. Only the mountains across the valley and the tops of a row of poplars ahead of him reached up into the silent sunlight. A few of the top leaves of the poplars very gently stirred.

Luckily his father was late coming home, too, and supper wasn't on yet. He went up to the bathroom, undressed, doused himself with cold water, scrubbed his lips with a wash rag and rinsed his mouth out. This purification completed, he went into the bedroom and closed the door. There he knelt by the bed and prayed until he felt that, so far as Mary was concerned, it was as if he had never kissed Lucy. But because he didn't want to hurt Lucy's feelings either, he concentrated on a prayer about her, too. He didn't think any words for this prayer, because it wasn't clear what he wanted for Lucy, but when he felt she wouldn't mind his having washed her kisses off, he considered the prayer successful, rose and dressed and went downstairs.

Such prayers were the whole of Tim's religion until the summer he was seventeen, when Rachel Wells and a moss-agate first shook his faith in ecstasy. He prayed every morning and every night, and often, if he could get by himself, three or four times during the day. He would never pray with anyone else present, because then nothing happened inside him, and the prayer felt foolish or false. A prayer was a failure that did not end in soaring joy. Sometimes he would try to think a prayer in words.

His best prayers of this kind were compositions of praise in ecstatic and very free verse. Several times it happened that one of these eulogies gradually assumed a fixed form, but then it lost the power to move him, and he dropped it. He memorized the Lord's Prayer once, but had to drop it for the same reason. Sometimes he prayed to God and to Christ by those names, and when he was thirteen, he included Saint Francis for a few months, because he had read that Saint Francis loved birds and animals and the sun and the moon. More often, however, the word God, or the words Our Father, or the words Great Spirit floated loose in a sensation of something all-pervasive and benevolent, and he tried his best to keep this sensation from assuming a limited and deceptive form, which would really be, for instance, that picture of Moses on Mt. Sinai, with his hair and beard blowing in the dark wind, which appeared in the book of Bible tales his mother had given him. Such an image always prevented the mood of perfected prayer, the mood which meant that, for a moment, he had touched what God really was. Usually, when the tide began to move up through him toward success, rapid images would replace all words: Mt. Rose at dawn, Mary walking toward him on an empty sidewalk in the dusk, the wild stallion he had seen galloping on the Pyramid range, the shining flocks of birds that rose from the islands in Pyramid Lake at sunset, things like that. At the ultimate moment these images too would vanish, consumed in an all-inclusive light which was filled with music and the wordless cheers of his mind, like the hosannas of an invisible multitude.

By the time Timmy was twelve, he had read the Bible clear through, and although he was really interested only in some of the stories from the Old Testament, and in the crucifixion and a few of the miracles, like the walking on water, in the New, he held the entire volume in physical reverence, as an object sacred to the touch. It was not until he was well along in high school that he consciously questioned the Bible as an authentic account of the activities of God, and it was not until he had been out of high school two or three years that he saw the irreconcilable difference between Jehovah and the God whom Jesus preached, but even so, there was practically no connection between his prayers and his reading of the Bible. The reading often made him feel holy and penitent, but the two processes went on separately. And long before he really thought about the Bible, he was troubled by certain stories about a mess of pottage, peeled wands, and gain by the hoarding of grain in a starving land, and most of all by the flood and the tower of Babel. Even if all of humanity except Noah's family did deserve to be drowned, why were all those innocent creatures, barring a sample couple of each kind, drowned with them? The Bible just avoided that question in a way that made him uneasy. What about the poor deer and elephants, the oxen and horses, crowding in mortal fear onto the last mountain tops, only to be swept remorselessly away? What about the vast flocks of birds flying and flying over that endless sea, until they could fly no longer, and fell, one, two, a dozen, a hundred at a time? What about the butterflies, soaked and driven down by the rain till they littered the gray waves like pitiful bits of colored paper? In the same way he pictured a great deal about the tower of Babel, so that he was always surprised, when he returned to the Bible, to find how little it told. The idea of all the people working together on that magnificent tower filled him with hope, and the vengeful confusing of the tongues and scattering of the races made him gloomy and rebellious.

Nor were his religious thrills and wonderings limited to the Bible. He knew nothing about them save that they were the great prophets of other people, but the names Buddha and Mohammed aroused in him something of the same indefinite aspiration that the name Christ aroused, and he was not much differently stirred by the wonderfully present deities of the American Indians, and only a little less by the Greek and Nordic gods and heroes. He didn't bother to sort out or relate this heterogeneous pantheon. They just got along together. He went to church sometimes, with his mother, who was religious in much the same way he was, but he never, even for a moment, felt that the peculiar sanctity of churches had any connection with the exaltations of lonely prayer. In fact, he felt more as if he were attending the funeral of someone he didn't know, and was intent only on remaining inconspicuous so as not to offend those who were really afflicted.

CHAPTER THREE: *About Divine Mary, and the Pagan Goddess Who Taught Art, and Jacob the Terrible Fiddler*

ONLY one other of Timmy's mental love affairs was such as to cause him to do penance. It is probable that this affair would never have blossomed beyond wondering anyway, but the fact that Harold Ashby was made the emissary of passion doomed it from the start, and Harold's failure was made the more certain by the moment he selected for making his proposition. In order to understand this incident, however, we must first trace the preceding history of Timothy Hazard in the arts.

There were only three subjects in which Timmy got A: reading, music and art.

His skill in reading reached a climax in the eighth grade. Mrs. Boone said, one day, that they would commence to read *The Lady of the Lake* aloud, each reader to continue until he made an error. Anyone who heard an error was to raise his hand. Under the pressure of such excitement, errors were like dragons' teeth. No one read more than five or six lines. Usually there would be a forest of arms waving after a line or two. Timmy desired to avoid this test. He concentrated upon becoming invisible, and at one moment believed he had succeeded in blending with the shadow in the back corner. But he hadn't. He heard his name, the forest of arms sank away, and he arose and stood like one tree upon a scorching plain. The book trembled in his hand, and for the first ten lines he proceeded with meticulous care. The most unnerving thing was that even a false pause, due to fearful failure of breath or a glance ahead at a tough word counted as an error. After the first ten lines, however, the rhythm caught him. When the hunt really began, the story caught him also. Filled with a fierce sympathy for the stag, he nonetheless rode with the hunter and died with the steed, and all deep in the heart of Scotland. When Mrs. Boone's voice first told him to stop, he heard it vaguely, but it was outside actuality and not aimed at him. When her second order came, with laughter, he really heard it, and stopped, although he didn't want to. It seemed foolish to come back to that brown room and the light of ordinary day from the gathering dusk in a highland forest. The enchantment dissolved, and it was discovered that he had read fifteen pages.

Probably the climax of his art career came in the sixth grade, where the teacher finally had to forbid him to draw pictures of cars, airplanes, football players and fellow students on the blackboard at recess and noon hour, because everybody stayed in to watch him and make requests. He recalls this, at least, as his only period of popular fame. He tried once, just after Mary came, to revive these chalk talks in the seventh grade, but the dangers of his skill had been noised ahead of him, and he had only succeeded in converting the letters C-H-I-N-A in a vertical column into a full-length portrait of a mandarin in a robe, when the teacher said he could draw all he wanted to after school, but not at noon or recess, and naturally that ended the revival.

However, another important, if undecipherable, experience came to Timmy in connection with art in the seventh and eighth grades. The art teacher, Miss Frost, who came only once a week for an hour, was so inspiring personally that Tim says he still hasn't any idea how good or bad she was as a teacher, though it wouldn't have mattered much anyway, at one hour a week. Most of the teachers in the school were veterans, and dedicated to their labors like nuns, and probably to no more exciting extra-curricular activities. Miss Frost was another kind of creature, young, miraculously and glitteringly blonde and waved, slender all over but perfectly protuberant, tightly and variously garbed, high heeled, and given to a savage delight in huge and colorful bracelets, necklaces and earrings, and to sharp and sweet perfumes. She carried with her the atmosphere of many strange places and adventures, and of the probability that they would never cease to lure her. To Timmy it was exaltation that she should touch his hand to guide its stupid pencil. Elevation unto bliss took place when she stood beside his seat. Celestial light swam in the room when she walked in the aisles and turned with a gentle tapping of the high heels. Even Beefy really tried to draw Easter cards for Miss Frost. Timmy labored for hours at home, with high and throbbing heart, over complicated peculiarities in water color, in spite of his brother Willis. Willis would come in, hitch himself up onto the table, make a thrust of his chin and a sound as if spitting into the corner (his mother had cured him of realism in this art) and say, "Geez, what a mess! What you want to spend all your time making a mess like that for? I guess I don't know, huh? You got a crush on that Frost dame, that's what. Why the hell don't you get wise to yourself? You don't think she cares what the hell you do, do you? Let me tell you something, buddy; and I keep my eyes open, too. Don't you forget that. That Frost dame ain't really nothin' but a floozy. I seen plenty of floozies, and she ain't really nothin' but another floozy."

Timmy's love for Miss Frost was not as that for Mary, of course. Mary provided him with a steady sensation of delightful rarity. The sensation produced by Miss Frost was wilder and more spasmodic, and never gave rise to convincing dreams of intention. He tried, a few times, in solitude, to imagine himself being drawn by Miss Frost's white, slender and sharply manicured hands, against the strong forward curve, like a bow, like the chest of an Arab horse, of Miss Frost's hard thigh, or even against the silk- or satin-covered heavenly peaks of her breasts, whence arose, as from a temple, the swooning incense. Once he even tried to imagine himself breaking the bondage of time and rapidly adding height, years, wisdom and earning power to his already sufficient worship, in order that he might marry Miss Frost and have her splendor forever in his house, probably a small, white house under cottonwoods or poplars and pretty well separated from the rest of the world, to which he would return with his prize only at rare intervals, to bask in the universal masculine jealousy. More often he would try to whittle Miss Frost down to his size without loss of fascination. But none of this necromancy worked very well, and its greatest illusion of success was always dispelled, like mist before the star of day, by the next entrance of the real Miss Frost. Her enduring position in his mind was that of a physical ideal, a minor deity, a Diana, solitary, enchanting, chaste, vital and unchanging, toward which, for instance, one might hope a Mary, at present likable but pale and tame, lacking in white dazzle and unbelled by the hounds, might slowly develop. He worked a good deal on the problem of bringing himself and Mary to a marriageable age, say fifteen or sixteen, with the reality of Mary and the divinity of Miss Frost neatly merged. It was a great shock to him when, one day after art class, he followed Miss Frost, at a decorous interval, out into the court and saw a naval officer waiting for her. The officer was of that indefinable age between the teens and white hair, a tall, dark-faced man. His uniform was white, with blue bars on the shoulders, and he stood waiting for Miss Frost with his cap in his hand. At once Timmy knew the depth and breadth of the chasm between himself and Miss Frost, but along with all earthly probability, peculiarly, she also lost the attributes of divinity. He even felt faint inclinations toward Willis' theory. After that, although he did not altogether cease to relish Miss Frost's physical presence, he did stop trying to make dreams about her and trying to blend her with Mary.

Music was a greater, and for a time, therefore, a more secret, matter with Timmy than either reading or art. From the time of his first thoughtful experience with music, it became almost synonymous with successful prayer in his world, which was very much a world of feeling. His own voice had great volume for his size, but he was timid about using it with other people around, and didn't like the way it felt when he suppressed it, so he remained musically anonymous. The school music was as sketchy as the art, but the teacher did notice the speed with which Timmy mastered the system of notation, and at recess often helped him with it, so that he got far ahead of the rest of the class, excepting Jacob Briaski. She also began to bring records for him to hear, operatic solos, violin solos and parts of symphonies and of piano concertos. Sometimes she would even bring a score for him to follow while he listened, and then would talk to him about the use of the instruments, and give him hints on what to listen for. By the time he was in the eighth grade, he automatically read a score by hearing it instead of seeing it, and could follow some scores which were not altogether simple, though with a tendency to listen closely to the melodic line only, allowing the rest to surround it with a somewhat hazy glory.

However, the most important step in Timmy's musical beginnings was his friendship with Jacob Briaski. Because their approaches to life were very different, because Timmy loved sports and wandering by himself and Jacob didn't, and because they lived in different parts of town, this friendship didn't ripen and spread beyond music, and in high school, when even their ideas on music were separating, degenerated into a mere acquaintance. But at the Orvis Ring Jacob was an important part of Timmy's life.

Jacob was a small Russian-Jewish boy, who was lonesome. His father kept a combination clothing store and hock shop on Commercial Row, down among the speakeasies, flop-houses and taxi-dance joints, none of which had anything to do with what Jacob had made up his mind to wrest out of life. Fortunately, or perhaps, in the end, unfortunately, neither his father nor his mother, both of whom were short, fat, sad people, who spoke broken English, had any deep-seated demand in their souls for the pleasure of running a hock shop. They both loved music, and his father was, in addition, addicted to reading and pondering over the philosophers and over the Talmud, which he did not, however, approach from a superstitious point of view. The Briaskis' small and stuffy apartment, upstairs over the hock shop, was full of records, sheet music and instruments, including a piano. Mr. Briaski couldn't get himself to sell a really good instrument that came into his shop. He had even been known to lend the owner of such an instrument the money he wanted, without taking the instrument. In other cases he would simply keep the good instruments in places where they were hard to see, and eventually they would work their way upstairs. There were all kinds of instruments in the apartment, a trombone, a trumpet, two cornets, flutes, clarinets, a saxophone, a bass viol, two cellos, three guitars, a mandolin, half a dozen violins, and even a harp. Mrs. Briaski played the harp a little. Mr. Briaski really played the cello, but he had a try at all the others too, and could give himself pleasure on the violin and the flute. When too many of any one instrument accumulated, he would look for people to give them to. If Mr. Briaski's soul was dedicated to any one thing beyond waiting, pondering upon the infinite sorrows, and loving his wife, it was to spreading the gospel of music.

So it was no wonder that Jacob, at an early age, had decided to become a famous concert violinist. He was impelled about equally by his mother's hopes and by his dread of the hock shop, and of Commercial Row, where he was always having to dodge drunks with their clothes half undone, stubble on their faces, and red, rheumy and sagging eyes, or to pretend not to hear the mocking endearments of girls from the taxi joints, some of whom, having moments of eclectic desire, really propositioned him by the time he was ten years old. Jacob was a slender boy with a very white and beautiful face, large, dark eyes, and black, wavy and shining hair. His mother often said, shaking her rather small head dreamily, "Ah, that Jacob, he will be nice with a violin in all those lights, no?" If it was his father who gave Jacob his music, it was his mother, in her mundane, comforting way, who gave him his hope, for Mr. Briaski, although usually very gentle, attentive and considerate, had no real hope, about Jacob or anything else. Jacob told Tim, on a night years later, after they were both out of high school, how at one time he had not touched the violin for five days, because he had overheard his father tell his mother, "That Jacob will never play the violin good. He is a good boy. He works very hard with his practice, and everything the mind can learn about music he will know. But he does not have the ear. Every time he plays, some time he is out of tune and does not know it. I have been thinking for a long time now I should tell him." It was his mother who finally guessed that he must have heard, and gradually coaxed him back to his playing, and maintained that often such an ear, which was really just a little off, was cured by a great deal of music. Actually his father never could bring himself to tell Jacob directly, and after a while Jacob was more than ever set on proving up. But sometimes, when his father would come in and stand there looking at him sadly while he was playing, the terrible feeling of defeat would come back, and Jacob held it against his father. At such times he would take his violin to school, and not play it at home again until his mother would point out to Mr. Briaski what was going on, and Mr. Briaski would try to sound cheerful and unaware when he invited Jacob to play duets with him that night.

All of this Jacob told Tim in one rush, between numbers at the club where Tim was playing then. Tim still blames himself for not realizing that such a confession from proud Jacob, and even the fact that he was in the club at all, where nothing but popular jazz was played, and years after the two of them had been intimate, was serious. Afterwards he remembered many things about the way Jacob had chain smoked, and drunk whisky, which he had never used to touch, and not looked up as he talked, but watched the end of his cigarette or his other hand picking at the tablecloth. The signs were there plain, for anyone to see, but Tim had been preoccupied by his work, and troubled about his own music, and besides, it had been like talking to a stranger, so he couldn't be sure what any little habit meant. Jacob had been away for two years, studying with a famous teacher in San Francisco. It was only the next day that Tim remembered all the signs clearly, and saw that he should have tried to say something to Jacob that would matter. The next day he heard that Jacob had gone home that night and shot himself through the head with one of the old six-shooters from the shop window. The famous teacher had finally been compelled to tell Jacob the same thing he had overheard his father say.

Tim had gone down to see the Briaskis. Mr. Briaski had met him, and they had sat and talked, and Mr. Briaski had seemed the same as ever, except that he wouldn't look Tim in the eyes, but kept looking all around the room instead. Mrs. Briaski, though, wouldn't even come out to speak to Tim. It wasn't that she blamed Tim for anything, at least any more than she blamed everybody who had ever been connected with Jacob, herself most of all. It was more than a year before she would talk to anybody except Mr. Briaski. If a customer came in while she was in the store talking to Mr. Briaski, she would go upstairs without even finishing what she had begun to say, and without looking at the customer. She would never listen to violin music again, either, or touch her harp.

But all this, which now influences Tim's memory of Jacob, was still in the future when they were at school, and was only faintly foreshadowed, not at all to Timmy, of course, by Jacob's fanatical determination, and by his father's sadness, which made the Briaskis' apartment, surrounded by the life of Commercial Row, feel like a bit of transplanted moribund city.

Timmy's friendship with Jacob began one afternoon in the fall, when Timmy had been kept after school for fractions and the battle of Salamis. Outside, the end of the year was beginning, and the poplars along the front walk were quietly letting go yellow leaves which came down twirling, or dipping like heavy feathers, making a sound, when you listened to enough of them along the walk, like the scattered beginning of rain. When the Persians were finally annihilated, Timmy went out into the courtyard, and stood staring at the water in the round basin of the fountain, and listening to the drops that fell upon it from the flowering spray. You know that mood, like a trance, in which suddenly all other sounds and considerations are shut out, and some little, repeated note will become very clear and important? In just that state Timmy stood there listening for the single meaning of the drops from the fountain and the tapping of the leaves. Through these he finally began to hear the sound of a violin which had been playing for some time. It was playing Offenbach's *Barcarolle*, which moved Timmy as being perfectly suited to the expression of the end of the day and of the year, to the falling of water and leaves, and to the silence following the battle of Salamis, when the five-o'clock sun slanted across an empty terra-cotta plain, and the blackened hulks, far apart upon the still, blue bay, sent wisps of smoke straight up.

He followed the *Barcarolle* into the auditorium, and found Jacob, who always wore both a jacket and a necktie in class, in his shirt sleeves with his collar open, playing earnestly with his entire body. He didn't want to startle Jacob, or to appear to be sneaking, so he tiptoed up front, and sat down by the flag beside the stage, where Jacob could see him. After he had told Jacob how much he liked the *Barcarolle*, they talked, and Jacob played him other things, like *Humoresque, The Glow Worm*, the *Melody in F* and Brahms' *Lullaby*. He made Jacob play Brahms' *Lullaby* three times. They stayed there until Jacob couldn't see his music, and Dodo came and kicked them out.

After that, whenever Jacob brought his violin to school, Timmy went in to hear him play. He even missed football sometimes, to hear the violin, and Jacob brought it to school more often. Some time in the winter Timmy began to take lessons on it, with Jacob earnestly and patiently teaching him. Timmy could hear only too well that Jacob didn't always play in tune. Sometimes it was terrible to hear him go rippling and skimming dexterously along, always a little off. It was worse than if he had not been skillful with his bow and fingers, and made it hard to give the praise that Jacob wanted so much to hear. Sometimes, though, Jacob would get started right, and go all the way just as cleverly without a bad note, and then Timmy would be all admiration and pleasure, and often Jacob would stop playing for several minutes, and declaim almost fiercely about his intended future. For that matter, Timmy felt so humble before Jacob's technical mastery that he sometimes wondered if it was his own ear that was bad.

One day, after they had been practicing together for some time, and Jacob had started Timmy on the third position,

Jacob, rather defiantly, and while he was putting the violin into its case so that he would not have to look at Timmy, invited him to come to the apartment Saturday afternoon and play. From then on, Timmy went to the apartment often, though he never got used to it, and had to be invited each time, not only because it was so far downtown, but also because he didn't like it. He felt very melancholy and uneasy in its stuffy and cluttered front room, where the trains, rumbling by, shook everything. In the Briaskis' apartment there seemed to be a thin, gray film over life, and all but Mrs. Briaski was muted and had the quality of a dusty antique. But on one of those visits he got his great and bewildering early treasure.

While Timmy was playing, Mr. Briaski came silently up from the store below, and stood in the door, looking at him, listening, and keeping time with one finger. Timmy was going to stop, but Mr. Briaski shook his head so that his jowls trembled, and said, "No, no, you are doing it fine. Go ahead now, play that." He nodded very gravely when Timmy was done.

"Reba," he called.

Mrs. Briaski came in.

"You take the shop, please, a little while. We are going to play a trio."

Then he got his cello, and another violin for Timmy, and they had their trio for more than an hour. When they were done, he gave that violin, which was a registered one, with its case, a new bow, resin and a mute, to Timmy. Timmy protested that he couldn't take so much. If he could just borrow it, he said.

"Nah, you take it," Mr. Briaski said. "I want you should have it. Many kinds of a fool I am, but about music is not one of them. You have music. Besides," he said, mopping his brow and the throat of his cello with his handkerchief, "without the violin how are you going for our trio to practice? It must belong to you. To borrowing, it is not the same thing."

So Timmy took the violin, and there were more trios, and he and Jacob worked up several duets at school.

It was when he came out of the auditorium one afternoon after a fine duet with Jacob that this other mental love affair was introduced by Harold Ashby. It was a very bad time for it, because Timmy had attained to the mood of successful prayer in that final duet, and the after-glory filled his mind and colored the world when he came out.

CHAPTER FOUR: *Presenting Harold, the Panderer, and Dorothy, the Dangerous Lorelei*

HAROLD was being accidental. He was standing on the front walk with his hands in his pockets, looking the other way and whistling. He pretended to hear Timmy coming down the steps, and turned, and looked foolishly surprised and excited to see him. Harold was always too excited.

"Hiya, Timmy?" he said, loudly and quickly. "Just the guy I was looking for."

"Hi," Timmy said.

"Going my way?"

"What way you going?"

"Over to Dorothy Wade's."

Dorothy lived only about three blocks from Timmy's house. It was shorter to go by the dirt road, but not enough for a polite excuse.

"Guess I am."

They walked half a block without speaking. Timmy wasn't going to start the talk. He didn't care what Harold had on his mind. He wanted to keep the music, and it was ebbing fast already.

At the first crossing Harold said, "Dorothy's throwing a party tonight."

"Is she?"

Harold began to sell it. "It'll be some party, too. Her folks ain't home."

Timmy didn't say anything.

"She wants to know will you come."

"No, thanks, I guess not. I got a lot of algebra and stuff to do."

Most of the class would have hooted at that excuse. There were half a dozen of them, including Mary and Jacob, who always did their home work, but Timmy wasn't one of them. In fact Timmy wouldn't have dreamt of using that excuse to most of them, but it came out quite naturally to Harold. Harold had the concentration upon one interest which, in any other field, might have meant genius, or at least a fanaticism like Jacob's. He couldn't turn it on and off, like Lucy. It was on all the time, and burning him up. Not that Timmy understood this. He just felt that excuse would do for Harold, and it did. Harold thought it was silly, but probably real, in which he was exactly wrong.

"You could let it go for once, couldn't you? There's gonna be everything. I got some cigars, and Dorothy swiped some cigarettes from her old man, and Beefy's gonna bring some beer. This ain't gonna be no little old drop-the-handkerchief."

When Timmy still didn't answer, he said, "I bet you're scared to come. That's whatsa matter with you. Old scaredy-cat."

"I am not scared. I got my studying to do, and besides, I'm in training for football."

"Beefy and Hank are playing football too, ain't they?" Harold said. "And they're both coming. Don't be an old sissy."

"They don't ever train anyway," Timmy said. "Beefy can't even run ten yards without getting all out of wind."

"They could either of them lick you quick enough."

"What of it? That doesn't prove anything," Timmy said, with an unhappy feeling that it did. He took refuge in the example of superior heroes. "I bet you anything Dutch isn't coming."

"Old Dutch has to work, or he would. He said he'd like to."

"I bet he did. I bet you Tony isn't coming either."

"He is if he gets done work in time. He said so."

Timmy didn't say anything. They had turned the corner, and were passing the lumber yard on the other side of the street.

"Look, Timmy," Harold said, suddenly very friendly, "I got something to tell you. Let's go over in the lumber yard."

"I don't know. I got to get home."

"You'll be sorry if you don't know, I'm telling you."

"Well, I gotta make it snappy, though. My old man'll be home."

Timmy never called his father his old man, except to keep up a front like this. He felt bad about doing it, and also because he was going into the lumber yard at all. Whatever Harold was going to be so secret about, it was going to be dirty and make his face burn. They found a place where they were out of sight from the street and the office and the sheds, and sat down with their backs against a pile of lumber. Harold took two cigars out of his pocket.

"Have a smoke."

"No, thanks."

"Scared it'll make you sick?"

"I'm in training. I already told you that once."

Harold bit the end off a cigar, lit it and began to puff and expertly tap the ash off the end before it had formed.

"Now, listen, Timmy," he said. "You gotta come. You're supposed to come for Dorothy. Listen," he said confidentially, leaning toward Timmy, "Dorothy told me to tell you something."

"What's that?" Timmy asked, feeling the confusion of the jungle begin.

"Jeez, can't you guess what? You ain't blind, are you? She's got a crush on you."

"Oh, yes, she has. She hasn't ever even said anything to me."

"She's scared you don't like her, that's why. She's got an awful crush on you. She's talking about you all the time."

"What do I care?" Timmy said. His face was burning, all right.

"Yeah, what do you care. What are you blushing about? Jeez, Timmy," he went on, reasoning patiently, "you ain't gonna be tied to Mary's apron strings all your life, are you? She's nothing but an old teacher's pet anyway."

"You lay off Mary."

"Oh, I didn't mean anything," Harold said quickly. "Mary's all right; sure, she's all right. Only, what fun is it? And she don't even care anything about you. She said so."

"When did she say so? I bet you can't tell me when. You're making it all up."

"I am, am I? She told me just the other day, at recess. I was teasing her about you having such a crush on her, and she said all she wished was you'd mind your own business. If you don't believe me, you can ask her."

"I bet she did," Timmy said, but he was wounded as with quivering lances. He had always suspected that whatever Mary thought of him, it was nothing they could get married on, but as long as nothing was said, the dreams weren't much damaged. Now his foolishness was right out to be looked at. Probably all the kids in the school yard had heard her tell Harold that. He began to pick at chips on the ground, watching his hand. "Anyway, what's that got to do with Dorothy?" he asked.

"Well, it isn't gonna hurt you to come to just one party, is it? Dorothy ain't so bad, anyway," he added wisely.

"I didn't say she was. I didn't say anything about her."

He had never paid any attention to Dorothy. She was just another girl in the class, not revolting, like Gladys, or exciting, like Lucy, or worshipful, like Mary, but just another girl with nothing particular about her except she was very clean and shiny and starchy-looking, and had a thick mouth that looked soft and dry. She had pretty hair, though. It was thick and pale gold and hung down to her waist. It was part of what made her look so shiny. All he wanted now, though, was to get by himself and see if he could pull his dreams about Mary back together.

"Anyway," he said, "even if she does have a crush on me, that doesn't mean I gotta have one on her."

"You oughta try going with her awhile," Harold said. His

voice sounded different. He wasn't even answering what Timmy had said. "Listen, kid," he said. "She knows how to do it, see? She likes it. She likes to do it all the time."

Timmy was shocked, so that he looked up and stared. In an academic way, he knew now what "it" was. He had gradually come to understand a good deal since the noon hour of the jungle and that time back-stage with Lucy. He could believe that sort of thing about Lucy now, but Dorothy wasn't an old-looking girl like that. It shook the orderly autumn world into chaos to hear a thing like that about a shiny, starchy girl like Dorothy, who didn't look any older than Mary.

Harold went right on talking. He was practically talking to himself, though loudly. "She likes a boy to do anything," he said hungrily. "Last summer I found out she really wanted to do it, see? Jeez, when I think about it." He began to talk more rapidly. "Her bedroom's on the first floor, see, right back by the kitchen. I used to go up there darn near every night, and she'd sneak out the window, and we'd go out in the woodshed or in the bushes across the ditch and do it. I used to get so pooped out I couldn't hardly walk, but she didn't never get pooped out. She always wanted to do it again. It don't poop a girl out the way it does a boy, see? Sometimes I'd think, 'Oh, the hell with it,' but then every night I'd get to thinking about how she did it, and I'd go over there again. Kee-roust, you oughta feel her without any clothes on, Timmy. Wow!"

He remembered a lot about it, for a moment. "Kee-roust," he said again. "You know what she knows how to do?" and he began to explain Dorothy's amazing skills rapidly and plainly. His eyes stood out and sometimes he stammered, and finally he was even trembling. Timmy could see the cigar in his hand trembling. The cigar had gone out.

Timmy tried to appear to understand, but also to appear unmoved, and not to show how looking at Harold when he was like that made him feel like hitting him, or even kicking him when he was down. When Harold asked, "Jeez, Timmy, did you ever try that?" and really waited for an answer, Timmy got up, and pretended to be busy dusting the chips and sawdust off his pants. He felt thick-headed and confused, and the old lumber yard in the autumn sun was a different place.

"I gotta beat it," he said. "It's nearly supper time."

Harold walked half the length of the lumber yard beside him, still trying to argue him into coming to the party, saying now that Dorothy wasn't always like that, that she was a swell kid too. Timmy just kept walking, and suddenly Harold stopped.

"You could come easy enough, if you wanted to," he said.

"All right, then," Timmy said, staring directly at him for the first time, and all at once angry himself, as if he wanted to fight. "All right, so I don't want to. There."

That bewildered look, as of a terrible loss, filled Harold's eyes. Timmy had gone on nearly half a block before Harold called after him, "Oh, all right for you, sissy." Timmy turned around and dropped his books and started for him, but he stopped after he had run a few steps, because Harold was running away. He picked up his books and started home again. He didn't even look around when he heard Harold yell, "Yay, sissy, couldn't even catch a flea," from way up by the corner. After all that yelling, he wished he didn't have to pass Dorothy's house, though. He would have gone all the way back to school and home by the dirt road, but Harold would see him doing it. He didn't look at the house. He was afraid he would see Dorothy. He thought how Dorothy would probably look, coming out of her bedroom window in the dark with nothing on, and also of going out into the shed or into the bushes by the ditch with her. It seemed more possible, thinking of it by himself, and passing her house, where he could see the shed and the willows along the ditch, out of the corner of his eye. In time, this new insight changed even the incidents of what he imagined to have taken place in the jungle. If Dorothy knew that much, think how much Lucy must know. Gladys became an unimaginable monster.

The next day, when he saw Dorothy again, though, he didn't know what to believe. At noon hour she stopped him right in the middle of the front walk, where anybody could see them.

"Harold told you a lot of things about me, didn't he?" she asked.

"Well, I didn't ask him to," Timmy said, his face burning.

"Well, don't you believe him," Dorothy said. "He's an awful liar, and he thinks every girl likes him." She was very red herself. She turned away quickly and joined two other girls and walked on, being gay and indifferent. She looked back from the porch of the little store across the street, where they sold ice cream and suckers, and tops and jacks and marbles, and she wasn't being gay or indifferent. She was scared about what Harold had told on her.

She seemed to think the ice was broken, though. Timmy had to make a lot of unconvincing excuses for not coming to her house after school to drink lemonade, or after supper to play phonograph records, and often he caught her watching him in class with a look in her big blue eyes that reminded him of Gladys smiling at Beefy. She finally assumed, in his imagination, a place of provocative unreality halfway between the dark earth that was Lucy and Gladys and the cloud-bastioned sky where Mary dwelt.

CHAPTER FIVE: *About the Small Things Which Can Create and Maintain a Major Alliance, and About the Virgin Mary of Pyramid Lake and Willis the Worldly*

THE Hazards and the Turners began their alliance on a thin but sufficient bond.

It would be hard to conceive two men much further apart in the ways they felt about life than Mr. Hazard and Mr. Turner. Mr. Hazard believed that life was a kind of trick on him, and that the only way to get anything out of it was to beat it out. Mr. Turner believed that he was himself an incorporated and only hazily defined part of life, and that there was, therefore, nothing to be got out of it, in Mr. Hazard's literal sense, so that he existed quietly, by a kind of constant osmosis, the fluid of life passing evenly and without interruption into him and out from him. Not that either of them had any formulated philosophies of this sort. On the contrary, they were both piece thinkers, reacting only emotionally and to immediate stimuli. The sum of a sufficient number of their reactions, however, could have been simplified into such philosophies. But they had two great and fundamental loves in common: pitching horseshoes and getting away from it all. Mr. Hazard counted getting mildly drunk and explaining himself loudly, with or without audience, as one means of getting away from it all, while Mr. Turner, in hours of the same kind of unhappy necessity, would play solitaire on the kitchen table with his eyes and hands, while his damaged being retreated inward and awaited refreshing contact with universal evenness. Against common wear and tear or less serious injury to the ego, they both liked to go out onto some wild and unpopulated acre of the earth and pitch horseshoes.

There was yet a third, though minor and paradoxical, bond between Mr. Hazard and Mr. Turner. Mr. Hazard also liked to get away from it all on the wild acres of earth by hunting and fishing, and delighted in lifeless trophies of his prowess or luck, while Mr. Turner, who suffered when any creature was hurt or killed, took a secretive and even mystical pleasure in restoring the victims to a condition reminiscent of life. As their alliance developed, greatly strengthened by the almost complete agreement in all basic matters of action and attitude, between the industrious, somewhat sad, wholly idealistic Mrs. Hazard and the industrious, cheerful and wholly materialistic Mrs. Turner, Mr. Turner did quite a bit of taxidermy for Mr. Hazard, at cost of materials.

The immediate cause of the union, however, was horseshoes. Mr. Turner came down to the lumber company where Mr. Hazard was a kind of yard boss, to order lumber for a movable bleacher for the Mackay Field. When the lumber had been selected, it was already eleven-thirty, and there was no use in moving the planks until after lunch. On the way back to the office, Mr. Hazard saw the horseshoe pits where he and others among the yard workers played during noon hour, or after work, or while nothing was moving. Mr. Hazard was a good horseshoe pitcher, averaging about one ringer out of every two shoes by the use of the flat rotation method. He was so consistent that it was no fun for him to play with anyone else in the lumber yard unless he gave him a handicap, which is unsatisfactory to a man who likes his sport clean cut. So it was only to make talk that he asked Mr. Turner if he ever played horseshoes, since at eleven-thirty there was nothing to do but play when Mr. Turner said yes, that as a matter of fact it was his favorite game. It turned out that Mr. Turner also averaged about one ringer out of every two shoes, and sometimes better, and that he had a provoking but stimulating habit of capping ringers whenever he shot second, although he used the method of making his shoes turn over once on the long axis and plunk straight on. This difference in style added a pleasant theoretical antagonism to the fundamental contest of man against man, and by twelve o'clock they had played three games, Mr. Hazard managing to salvage only one of them, and that by the extra point score of 25-23. Having the habit of victory, Mr. Hazard was politely infuriated, but since it was impossible to be personally aggrieved with a man as monosyllabically friendly as Mr. Turner, who gave no sign of taking an insulting pride in his triumph, the result was a series of prearranged duels. When this series turned out, over a considerable time, to be quite evenly divided, it was continued for years, and led to everything else, including practically the only chances Timmy ever got to be alone with Mary.

A favorite place for the Hazards and the Turners to get away from it all was by the castle-like tufa formations which they called the rocks, on the edge of Pyramid Lake, just north of the ranch. Here they would spread a tarpaulin in the shade of the smaller and separate formation against which the fire was built. Sitting on the tarp, in harmony about a wealth of hamburgers, buns, potato salad, cold sliced meats, lettuce, jelly, pickles, cake and watermelon, they would eat and encourage eating by admiration, generosity and example. The adults would talk in fragments of small inherent interest but of great value to the spirit of inter-family communion, and the children would be almost quiet until they could escape. The women drank coffee from the smoky pot, in tin cups, and the men drank home-brewed beer from a variety of bottles.

Then the women would sit on the tarp and watch single gulls, or alternately gliding and flapping lines of white pelicans, go slowly by in the air far out over the blue water, making points of light against the sun-hazy mountains, or else they would go slowly down and walk slowly north along the beach, picking up colored pebbles or minute shells, and constantly conversing with each other in gentle and happy voices, about what they picked up, what they saw in light or color or space, and about housekeeping, personal affections, philosophies in nutshells, and the miraculous curative effect of coming to Pyramid Lake.

The men would take another bottle apiece of home brew up onto the small, level arena where Mr. Hazard's old bulldog of a Dodge touring car was parked, put the bottles on the running board on the shady side, set up the stakes and begin their attentive combat. In the time-laden silence of this place the shoes would make tiny, slowly rhythmic thuds and clinks. In the unstinted light, the radiator cap of the Dodge and the nicked heads of the stakes would glitter preciously. At intervals determined by treaty or by the ends of games, the men would go over to the Dodge and stand there taking a few slow swallows of beer, looking down at the trembling cottonwoods and poplars around the ranch house, and discussing the care of lawns and shrubs, the damned foolishness of young workers who didn't know better than to smoke cigarettes around a lumber yard, and the politics of Reno and Nevada, and sometimes even of the nation, though seldom beyond that. To both Mr. Hazard and Mr. Turner there was little difference between Europe or the Far East and the *Arabian Nights*, and Mr. Hazard didn't care for fairy tales, while Mr. Turner made up so many of his own that he didn't bother to read any.

While the grown-ups thus renewed themselves at the fountainhead of peace, eternity, verity and awe, the children entered their own world.

Pyramid Lake and its mountains now have the naked grandeur of an old planet, and the profound indifference to everything mortal which is part of a planetary sense of time. But to understand the world of the children, you must imagine Pyramid also in its childhood, when it was part of the swarming seas of the globe, invaded, when the ice crept south, by those racing submarines of the Arctic, the killer-whales, and when the fire crept north, by those indolent islands of appetite, the giant mantas. You must imagine that when the killer-whales came, the forests receded onto the mountains and became small and tough, and the saber-toothed tiger crouched to watch the tiny, three-toed horses trooping in the windy grass, and that when the mantas came, the waters rose and the trees grew until the mountains were tropical islands, and pterodactyls swept down from the palisades and tore great, snapping fish like serpents from the water, while Brontosaurus made thunderous explosions in the swamps. You must imagine also, to bring it closer and quieter, that these rocks, where the Hazards and the Turners have just had lunch, are like coral reefs, far under water and bristling with infinitesimal, communal life, and that they open blue grottoes and green channels to the slow explorations of legions of painted fish. If this childhood seems to you somewhat confused or fabulous, so much the better. So is the life of all children, and, besides, Pyramid has long since ceased to keep even its millenniums straight.

Within this wilderness, you must imagine the children as tiny creatures upon the border of intellect, darting, hovering, hiding, listening, peering all the time, inside and out, aware of the hungry omnipresence of death, and always hungry for life themselves, because they never dare take more than one peck at a time at it, like a bird at a hanging apple, lest two pecks mean no more. Remember also that size and the date have nothing to do with the intensity of this life. Perhaps it would help, as we drain the ancient seas, burn off the ancient forests and raise the barren mountains so returning Pyramid to its present bald and awful age, to conceive, without other change of a single detail, the lizard Tim is going to meet later this afternoon, as blown up to the size of a dragon, and the humming-bird which is at this very instant hovering upon invisible wings and piercing the trumpet-flower on the side of the ranch house with its needle, as blown up to the size of a roc.

The children had eaten too much watermelon, and the heat made them feel as if they were floating, so at first they gathered in a shady hollow under the big tufa castle, and sat around, and fiddled with notions and pebbles. Willis, inspired by having Mary and Tim there at the same time, did most of the talking. Tim experienced sudden, winged hopes that Mary would believe selected portions of these insinuations, but Mary could only pretend not to hear them. There were too many passages she didn't understand. Grace tried repeatedly to rebuke Willis, or to change the subject, but Willis could not be distracted for long, even by horse-racing, and direct attack merely stimulated him. When even the memory of the adults had evaporated, Mary stood up and asked Grace if she'd like to take a walk. She couldn't look at Timmy by then, but Grace smiled at him to show she knew the apple in his wilderness, and to promise that he might have it before too long. Then the girls put their arms around each other and walked down to the shore and north, as sedately as their mothers before them, save that their murmurings were concerned entirely with the future, and were designed to beget excitement, not peace.

Timmy couldn't help going part way down with them, though walking off to one side, by himself, and apparently concentrating on throwing stones. In the last shadow of the castle, he could no longer bear the sensation of Willis watching from above, and climbed onto one of the boulders and sat there with his arms around his legs, watching the girls get smaller on the beach. Grace wore a pink dress and Mary a white dress. Grace's hair was dark brown and short; Mary's was light brown and hung long and smooth down her back, and changed like watered silk in the sunlight, showing copper and gold. Their bare arms and legs were golden brown. The heat attacked the edge of

Tim's shadow, and the ancient, terraced beach became watery at a distance, so that the stalks of bleached weeds, standing up sparsely out of the stones, rippled like living seaweed. Finally the girls began to waver in it too. Mrs. Hazard and Mrs. Turner had gone so far toward the point in the north that they were merely flakes of light against the edge of the water, like gulls floating at a distance.

In the other direction the dark mountain of Anaho Island appeared to be a peninsula of the far shore. Like the higher mountains over there, it was dusty with sun and distance. Near it the pale Pyramid shimmered on glassy water, so that it appeared suspended in air. Far in the north, on the horizon of the lake, the white Needles shone in the sun like temples and minarets. Yet in that clarity nothing looked really far off except the tiny, receding humans and the birds.

The silence had weight. Timmy's ears rang, as if he were too far under water, and stretched till their gristle ached, trying to detect the meaning of any actual sound, like the faint droning of a fly, or the single, plaintive squawk of a gull two miles away. His body felt small and temporary upon its boulder, and he squatted there, apparently quiet, while his heart coursed wildly after Mary, and his many un-unified souls hid, scampered, crouched or fought valiantly because of the tremendous desolation.

Willis became as active as a lizard. He darted up to where the men were playing horseshoes, and began a campaign of blackmail against peace and his father. He stood at the side of the horseshoe court, halfway between the two stakes, and followed the entire flight of each shoe with his head and one raised arm. When it landed, he would either comment upon the lack of skill, or say, "Nuts. You're just lucky." His father showed great patience, saying nothing through four or five shoes, and then only, "Shut up, Willie." Later he said, "You heard me. Now shut up, or I'll tan your britches." Finally he came to the desired point, dropped the shoes he was about to throw, and advanced, saying, "I told you to shut up. Now, beat it. Go on. Beat it."

Willis retreated to the front of the old Dodge and got ready to keep it between the two of them.

"Gimme a beer?" he asked.

"No," Mr. Hazard said. "Now beat it. We're trying to play a game here. We don't want any more pestering from you, you hear me?"

"For one beer."

"I said no. How many times . . ."

"Gimme one beer and I'll beat it."

"My patience is about wore out, young man. A kid your age wanting beer and telling me what he'll do. Now you get, and quit pestering around, or I'll take a hand to you."

"Oh, all right," Willis said, surprisingly, and shoved his hands deep into his pockets and dawdled back toward the rock, appearing, from the rear, to be deeply dejected. This retreat did not signify a defeat, however. It was a strategic withdrawal. Willis had just remembered that the whole campaign was unnecessary.

"Gawd Almighty," Mr. Hazard said, with receding wrath, and while he returned to pick up his horseshoes, "that brat's enough to drive you crazy. His mother can't do a thing with him."

Mr. Turner meditatively said nothing, and the game began again, after a brief debate about the score.

Willis maintained his slow pace, occasionally kicking with dramatic irritation at a pebble, until he was out of sight below the parking place. Then he sprinted to the cave under the fire rock, dropped onto his knees and began to dig. He uncovered four more bottles of beer, wrapped in wet newspapers. He removed two of them, smoothed the sand back and, still under cover of the rise, crossed to the big castle with his take. He saw Timmy perched on the boulder below, and said aloud, "Jeez, this puppy-love. It gives me a bellyache." He worked his way to a cave which was an old haunt of his. There he buried one of the bottles again, and took an old package of cigarettes out of the same hole. He scraped the cap off the other bottle on a rock, and sat there, humming *The Sheik* to himself, slowly sucking the beer, and smoking two cigarettes. He laughed sardonically several times, and in the most sardonic moments, pasted the cigarette to his lip and let it dangle. He also drew the smoke up his nostrils now and then. Finally he began to wonder what was going on, and finished the beer a little faster, in order to start scouting.

When the women had disappeared around the point in the north, and the girls were as small as the women had been, Timmy suddenly felt deserted upon his rock, and became restless of body also. He returned to the picnic place, got three pieces of bread from the basket, and went down onto the beach. There he took off his shoes, in order to feel the hard-packed black sand, which was as fine as emery dust, and the crunching water-row of tiny white shells. He made his tracks in a circle upon the sand and shells, and moved off, trying to walk lightly enough to leave no tracks, which didn't quite work, and looked at the circle. The footprints contacted neatly, heel to toe, all the way, but the circle was lopsided. He made another, which was better, and while making it began unconsciously to hum a tune which was reminiscent of some others, especially of the down-sweeping violin theme from the first movement of the *Pathetique*, but which was much more restless and changeful of mood than any of its sources. Still humming, he waded knee deep into the water, which had a yellow and creamy lip of foam left by wind in the morning, and stood there staring at nothing, suspended in cool liquid and blazing air, until a gull came coasting over, observing him with cocked eye. He saw the reflection of the gull coming at him, and then looked up at the bird itself. Its breast was blinding with the sun on it. Timmy tore off a piece of bread and tossed it up at the gull, which sheered off but then swooped back down and plucked the bread from off the water deftly, merely dimpling the surface with its beak and wing tips. They did this twice more together, and then the gull coasted down onto the water a few feet away, fussily settled his sharp wings back, and prepared to take in this sucker more comfortably. The lake had appeared naked and the sky over it empty, but the gull's maneuvers in the air had been seen.

Other gulls materialized out of the void. This minor miracle always happened. To prolong the fiesta of wing and web, Timmy waited until each piece of bread had been won, and the whole flotilla had settled back and was swimming attentively about, before he threw the next piece. Very slowly, the three pieces of bread worked down to empty hands in alternate drifting peace, and splashing, flashing, squawking, cross-lacing flight. This alternation of tempo was very pleasing, and yet maintained a single mood. The quiet upon the water was as alert as the white dance in the air. The pattern of the dance broke and floated down like dropped petals after each piece of bread had been snatched and swallowed. Timmy set the melody he was humming to the flurry and ebb of the game. When the bread was gone, he showed his empty hands to the gulls. Some of them came quite close in curiosity and greed.

The girls were returning along the shimmering sand. Timmy went back up onto the beach and absent-mindedly erased the two foot-printed circles while he waited, not wanting to be obviously watching them come. Gradually, one or two at a time, the flotilla of gulls dwindled back into the secret vastness.

When they arrived, the girls were also a little stunned and dreamy from sun. The three sat on the sand and spoke softly together, which permitted Timmy the illusion that Mary, though her words were as to anyone, spoke tenderly. He was greatly irrigated by the waters of life after the long drouth upon his rock. The melody and the light in his brain from watching the gulls blended more closely into a new bliss which he kept silent. Gradually the three dedicated themselves to a swim. Into this holy peace Willis, in a gray bathing suit too big for his angular and gesticulating body, popped himself atop the big white boulder that stood out into the water, and began to chant loudly,

Last one in would suck eggs,
Last one in would suck eggs.

Timmy ran up and got the three bathing suits and the girls' caps from the Dodge. Grace drove Willis off the boulder because she and Mary wanted to get into their bathing suits in the shadow of its overhang, right by the water. The tufa, even when it was not hot, was cruel as broken glass to bare feet, and they didn't want to walk down across it.

Willis scampered off like a tickled monkey toward the sunny southern side of the castle, ducking about amongst the confusion of great boulders. His frantic shadow swelled and shrank, appeared and disappeared among the shapes of the boulders. He was yodeling in an energetic falsetto which echoed on the formation.

Timmy went to the place higher up, where the boys always undressed. Willis' clothes were dropped there, all over the place, his shoes ten feet apart. Willis' yodeling stopped, and in the ringing shadow the half-warm air stirred a little, and the sound of humming flies was distinct. It didn't take Timmy long to get into his bathing suit. He had on only a shirt, pants and shoes. He waited, because it always took girls longer to get undressed, and he couldn't pass the boulder until they came out. He was humming and scuffing sand with his foot, letting the cool grains trickle between his toes, when Willis appeared around the corner of a boulder and signaled excitedly for him to come.

"What's the matter?" Timmy asked. His voice was low, but Willis made frantic signs at him to be quiet.

"Want to see something?" he whispered, when Timmy came over.

"What?"

Willis flapped a hand at the boulder below. "They're both bare nakedy," he whispered exultantly. "Hurry up, or they'll have their suits on."

"What you want to go sneaking around spying on girls for?" Timmy asked loudly. He didn't think of Grace in the picture at all, but was heavily shamed by the idea of Mary being watched by the sly Willis.

"Shut up," Willis whispered fiercely, coming up behind the rock.

"O.K., old maid," he said, relaxing. "They probably got them on by this time, anyway.

"You shoulda seen them, though," he added after a moment.

"You didn't see them," Timmy said.

"Oh, no, I guess not. Right out there in their birthday clothes, giggling like hell. Mary's the best, though," he said, watching Timmy closely. "She looks kinda funny 'cause she's all white where her bathing suit covers, but she's got what jiggles already."

"You didn't see them. You're just making it up," Timmy said weakly.

"Oh, yeah? Well, I'll tell you something else you don't know. Mary's got hair, and it's red. I don't give a damn," he said complacently, "about seein' Grace. I seen her plenty of times. But Mary, oh boy, oh boy."

He dodged away and stood out of reach, grinning. "Timmy's sore 'cause I seen his girl; Timmy's sore 'cause I seen his girl," he began to chant.

Timmy knew better than to try to stop this by direct attack. Willis started going barefooted as soon as the snow was off the ground, and he could run like a centipede on the sharp rocks. Besides, under pressure, he would resort to broadcasting and dictate his own terms for silence.

"You didn't see nothing," Timmy said.

Willis stopped chanting. "You think so?" he asked, grinning and still alert. He saw through this indifference.

"Maybe it was you saw 'em, then," he said. "O.K., I'll tell Mary you saw her all bare nakedy."

"If you do," Timmy broke, and moved.

Willis darted away down, zigzagging among the rocks and yelling, "Mary, Mary, Mary."

Full of shame and confusion, Timmy stood out where he could watch, but waited until he heard what Willis would say.

The girls were already on the beach in their bathing suits. Grace's suit was red, and Mary's a bright blue. They both had white caps shaped like close-fitting helmets. Down against the sand these colors were very bright. Mary was just pulling on her cap.

"What?" she called up.

"Timmy loves you, but dasn't tell you; Timmy loves you, but dasn't tell you," Willis chanted.

"Oh, you hush," Mary said.

Willis kept on chanting it as he skittered down past the girls. Mary pretended to make a desperate effort to catch him, and he splashed out into the water, fell flat, and then swam away under water.

The true crisis averted, Timmy himself became excited. He exhibited, for Mary, dives from the boulder and astounding stays under water. He felt tenderly solicitous toward Mary in a bathing suit, with drops of water on her face, and started a battle of splashing with her. When she retreated into deeper water, he dove for her feet and upset her, until she finally ran up onto the beach. But she was laughing, so he attained to his happiest illusion, a belief that Mary felt about him just the way he felt about her. This illusion grew stronger, until he was deeply and solemnly moved, and invited her under water to see how the sunlight came down in broken angles through the green, and illuminated the saffron base of the boulder. He held her hand during this submarine journey, and she didn't try to take it away from him. When their heads emerged once more, she agreed that it had been wonderful, like looking at the windows in a church. Timmy was at once convinced that this miracle of water, stone and light had been of his own making, and that Mary also felt the new and marvelous splendor of the wilderness that joined them, a splendor which made his ribs strain outward with joy till they came near cracking. The joy was solemn and tremendous, however, and he didn't feel like playing games any longer.

Willis had already scrambled out of the water and disappeared among the boulders, and Grace was going out onto the beach on the north side. Timmy and Mary, not looking at each other, splashing water with their fingertips, climbed slowly up onto the beach on the other side. They walked a long way south from the boulder and lay down in the hot sand, propping themselves on their elbows. To Timmy this was a rare, sweet intimacy, and he had thoughts which made his head swim and his heart exult but work uncertainly, though his *Song of Songs* remained in the realm of pure, unsounded music. They talked about everything else instead. Timmy talked a good deal about sports and his part in sports, not because they seemed to him very important right then, but because he couldn't remain silent without exploding, and couldn't have found words to say what he meant, even if he had dared to try.

After a while there came a moment when they realized that a strange sound had been going on for some time. They gave it their attention then, and recognized it. From somewhere far off, Willis was chanting, "Timmy loves Mary, Mary loves Timmy." This chanting continued without faltering, "Timmy loves Mary, Mary loves Timmy." It was terrible, like flashing swords upon them in that naked quiet. They finally discovered Willis. He was a tiny figure standing straddle-legged on the very top dome of the big formation, and waving something in his hand to accompany the chant. They couldn't tell from there, of course, what he was waving, but it was the other bottle of beer. His voice was a choir of gnats and a cloud of mosquitoes. They couldn't lie still under it, and its faint, tireless whining wholly drowned out the *Song of Songs*. "Timmy loves Mary, Mary loves Timmy," it went on, rising to the Mary and falling to the Timmy.

"Don't pay any attention to him," Timmy begged Mary. "Don't pay any attention to him." But his own throat was constricted, and his voice sounded wild and uncertain.

Mary sat up, intent upon brushing the sand from her elbows. "I wonder what Grace is doing all alone," she said distantly. "I guess I'd better go and see if I can find Grace," she added, and got up, and brushed the sand from her knees, and began to walk away toward the boulder, slowly and with a heart-breaking simulation of solitary thought.

"Ho-ho, ha-ha, lookit Mary's runnin'," the gnat voice intoned from the heights. Timmy endured a blinding desire to hit Willis rapidly, a hundred times, with increasing ferocity.

MARY disappeared behind the big boulder, and Willis disappeared from the sky, which became silent and empty. After a few minutes, two gulls, several yards apart and flying in counter rhythms, cruised slowly past. Timmy went back into the water and played porpoise by himself. When he came out again, he practiced a few sprint starts in the sand. Then he walked south on the beach. The joy of solitude filled him suddenly, and he began to sing aloud the air he had constructed while making the circles and feeding the gulls. Soon his walk became a strut, and he was singing very loudly, using a language of liquid, meaningless syllables, which suited the notes and sounded Italian or Spanish. When he came to a weathered dock which the lake had abandoned, he stopped before it and addressed to it, in a voice outrageously loud and sometimes falsetto, a portion of his song which then began to take the form of a kind of Ave Maria, inspired by the thought of riding home beside Mary in the back seat of the old Dodge. The final image, a combination of the lights of Reno under the dark mountains and Mary's shoulder against his arm, was fulfilled by a new air, akin to the *Evening Star*, at the end of which he sang the word Mary three times, with clear, descending pathos. Then he made a grand, free gesture of one arm, and three dignified nods of his head toward the dock, after which he let the song return to its universal celebration, and went on.

A large, gray lizard, with a black collar and a tail as long as a snake, fled across in front of him and up the sandy slope, and stopped abruptly, coiled about a rock and glared at him over the top of it. Then he saw that there was a horned toad hanging cross-wise in the lizard's jaws. Its pale, soft belly, turned upward, was punctured by the grip, and it hung motionless, with drooping tail. Timmy stopped singing. The flat, watchful head of the lizard became, in miniature, the mask of all evil. If the lizard had been alone, Timmy would have stood breathless and watched it as long as it was in sight, and gone on full of the love of lizards. Now he wanted to kill it, and to rescue the horned toad, if only for honorable burial. He began to stalk the lizard, glancing about for a stone to throw, but each time looking quickly back at the lizard. Lizards had a way of dissolving during the wink of an eye. The lizard, however, had craftily fortified himself in the first row of stones at the top of the beach. Timmy began a flanking movement, intended to reach the stones a few yards to the right of the lizard. The lizard flipped about twice on its stone, to keep this maneuver under observation. Just as Timmy leaned over to pick up his missile the lizard shot off, over and among the rocks in a frenzy of energy which curled its tail aloft like the stern of a Viking ship, and so rapidly that Timmy was always seeing it where it had just been. It was out of sight before Timmy could straighten up again. He dropped the stone and went back down to the beach. He stopped there to look at the lizard's track, a long, fine line fretted along the edges by small, slender footprints, so that the whole pattern looked like a fern just leafing out. Timmy developed no theory from this observation, but went on without singing because of the strange dissonance of the beautiful track and the deed which had made it.

Ahead of him a wavering line of dead willows and weeds marked the old channel of a creek from the hills. The creek was cut off at the ranch now. Tim knew that beyond the dead willows there was a sun-shelter where the Indians drew and split their fish and laid them out on top to dry for the winter. The shelter had four posts of juniper and a thatch of dusty poplar boughs. The sun had gone far enough west now so that only about half the shadow would be under the thatch. The other half would extend into the open toward the lake, like a porch floor. It was pleasing to sit on this shadow-porch and be cool and yet out under the open, blazing sky. Tim was thirsty, and also, after seeing the lizard with the dead horned toad, Mary's desertion had come back to him like an agony of final loss. He wanted to pray. He decided to sit on the shadow-porch of the shelter until a prayer succeeded, and then take another swim to wash off the implications of the lizard. He stopped idling along and began to struggle purposefully up through the loose sand toward the shelter. The sand was hot around his ankles, and pebbles in it burned like bits of hotter metal. He stopped a few yards from the shelter, because somebody was already there, sitting cross-legged in the shadow. At first he thought the person was a thin Indian. Then he saw it was not an Indian, but a white boy, probably about his own age, but even thinner, so that all his ribs showed distinctly, and burned even darker. He had black hair, like an Indian, but his eyes were larger and rounder than Indians' eyes, and a strip of white skin showed on the thigh where his shorts were pulled up. The shorts were all he had on. The boy sat there and returned Timmy's stare seriously and calmly. Finally he spoke.

"Hello," he said.

"Hello."

Timmy began to see that the boy's hands, which were long and narrow, were covered with gray clay and sand, and that he was surrounded by objects of great interest. A water bag hung upon one of the juniper posts. There was a bucket near the boy's right elbow, and, on two old, sun-silvered boards before him, a mound of partially modeled clay. Near his knee, and between him and Timmy, lay a venerable desert tortoise. It was wrinkled like an accordion where its body joined the shell. Its little elephant hind legs and its knobby flippers were extended and set, and its serpent head, with the upper lip like a beak, was also out. But some understanding had been reached. The tortoise was content to remain where he was. Timmy was going to ask about the tortoise when the boy spoke again.

"Was that you singing a while ago?"

Timmy grinned and then looked away. "I guess it was."

"It sounded grand," the boy said, "out here like this." After a moment he asked, "What was it you were singing? It sounded like something from an opera."

Timmy felt shy and ignorant when he heard the boy speak. He spoke very softly and yet clearly, with a distinct, unwestern accent that slurred no part of any word, but turned each out perfectly, like a work of art, suggesting a mind used to thinking that way, and probably full of strange lore.

"Oh, no," he said, "it was just something I was kind of making up. I didn't know anybody could hear me."

He felt an unusual wish to be honest with this boy. "I was just kind of pretending it was opera," he said. "That's why it sounded like that, I guess."

"It sounded fine," the boy said again.

"Is that your turtle?" Timmy asked.

"Well, I found him."

"Can I look at him?"

"Certainly."

Timmy came into the shade and squatted in front of the tortoise, and looked.

"Does he bite?"

The boy shook his head. "No, he's very gentle."

Timmy extended a hand slowly. The tortoise saw it coming, and withdrew his head, and pulled his flippers in a little. Timmy felt of the shell. It was hard and smooth, and gave the impression of covering great weight. Timmy touched one flipper, which had big knobs on it, where it had been injured long before and had lost the nails. The flipper felt almost as hard as the shell, as if petrified.

Timmy drew his hand back, and after a moment the tortoise let his head out again, gaped, and lay still, observing the world steadily.

"Gosh, I bet he's old," Timmy said.

"I guess he is."

"Did you find him here?"

"No. We found him in the road. We nearly ran over him with the car."

The boy was still asking questions, by means of things he didn't say, but his hands had strayed back to shaping the clay. Timmy watched, his own questions fading in his mind, and the boy began to work more steadily. His hands reshaped the clay strongly and quickly.

"You're making the turtle, aren't you?" Timmy asked.

The boy nodded.

After a moment he asked, "Do you want to make a turtle too?"

That was just what watching the boy's hands had made Timmy want to do. He had faith in his own skill. It looked so easy.

"Sure."

"There's some clay in the bucket still. There's not enough to make a turtle this big, but you could make a smaller turtle."

Timmy found himself a board lying out in the brush and brought it back.

"You have all the clay you need?"

The boy nodded. "You take the rest. If you get stuck, you can have some of mine. I'm going to have more than I need."

Timmy scooped the rest of the clay out onto his board.

"Where'd you find the clay?"

The boy pointed to a place some distance south. "Down there in the edge of the water. Quite a ways down. It's not very good clay, though. There's too much sand in it."

Timmy's confidence departed when he began to work the clay. It was not as easy as the boy's hands made it look. The idea was clear. He could see just what he wanted. But the clay kept going wrong, and then the idea began to lose shape too. He felt very clumsy, as he watched the boy dexterously reproducing the malformed flipper, leaning over the tortoise to look closely at the part he was working on. A new idea came to Timmy from idly breaking a lump of clay he was holding.

"I know what I'll do. I'll make a lot of little turtles for babies for your turtle."

"That would be fine. We can put them all together in a family."

"Maybe we can fool the real turtle," Timmy said, laughing. "Maybe we can make him think he really has a family."

The boy paused in his work and looked at the tortoise whole, and briefly explored its probable past. "Maybe," he said, "but I don't believe so. He must know nearly everything."

Then they worked silently for some time. Only once the boy said, "Little turtles wouldn't have such deep grooves, would they?"

"No, that's right," Timmy said, and made the grooves shallower with his thumb. Because Timmy's turtles were very small, filling only the palm of his hand, he couldn't put much detail into them, and the two finished about the same time. They placed the little turtles, of which there were thirteen, around the big one on its boards. The big one was impressive, with bits of flint for eyes, wrinkles on its neck, and even the warts on its flippers.

However, the living tortoise, when set face to face with this unnatural and sudden heritage, was not interested.

"Maybe he can smell they aren't really turtles," Timmy said.

He asked a question which had been troubling him. "What you going to do with the real turtle?"

"Let him go," the boy said. "He wouldn't be happy if I took him home."

"No," Timmy said. He was relieved by this decision, which exactly agreed with his hopes.

"We'd better put him where he can hide," the boy said. "He's so slow getting anywhere."

"Can I carry him?"

"Certainly, if you want to."

Actually, since the tortoise was heavy, and they decided to carry him clear up the slope and across the road, and leave him where the sagebrush was thick, they took turns carrying him.

When they got back to the shelter, the boy took down the water bag. He offered it to Timmy, who had forgotten about it, but now had a hard time not to drink greedily. The bag was dark with the water it had soaked up, and was sweating coldly. It felt wonderful in the hands. The boy drank also, holding the water bag high, so that Timmy could see when he swallowed. Then he corked the bag and hung it up on the post again.

"You want to take the turtles home?" Timmy asked.

"I don't know. Do you want yours?"

"I don't know," Timmy said also. "They'd just get busted."

"If we just left them out in the sun here, they'd get baked good and hard," the boy said.

"Let's," Timmy said. "We'll put them where we're the only ones that know," he went on, excited by the idea of secrecy. "Then we can find them again, when we come back."

They chose a low peninsula of broken tufa to the south, a long way from where the Indians usually camped and the fishermen came down to the boats. They started off with the boards between them. On the way Timmy told about trying to kill the lizard with the horned toad. He didn't tell it as he would have to most of the boys he knew, as if all he had wanted was to hit the lizard, and maybe take a look at the horned toad, but just as it had happened, including everything he had felt about it, even, though not very clearly, what he had felt when he found the beautiful track of the lizard. He was justified in this act of faith, for again they agreed. He felt very happy about meeting the boy. It seemed important that they should be slowly stumbling along the beach in the hot sun, carrying their treasured turtles between them, to hide them from everyone else.

Out nearly at the end of the white peninsula, they found a circular arena with a floor of black sand. It was five or six feet across, and protected all the way round by an escarpment of the tufa two or three feet high. It looked as if it might be the last weathered remnant of a small dome such as made up the large formations by joining in numbers, like bubbles out of a pipe. They carefully placed the big turtle in the middle of this arena, and set the little ones beside it and behind it, so that they appeared to be marching all together toward the lake. The boy rearranged the little turtles several times, until they made a pattern he liked. Then they threw the boards away and went out to the end of the peninsula, where the water lapped among the tufa fragments and swung the bright green hair of the water weeds. They squatted there, washed the clay and sand from their hands, and felt that the affair of the turtles was ceremoniously completed.

"It'd be fun if we found those turtles again, some time a long time from now," Timmy said. He felt that such a discovery would somehow circumvent the chanciness of life.

"I don't believe anyone else will find them," the boy said. "I'll bet they last forever."

"I'll bet they do too," Timmy said.

On the way back up the beach, Timmy finally asked, "What's your name?"

"Lawrence Black. What's yours?"

Timmy told him, and said, "I live in Reno, really."

"I do too, now. We haven't been there very long, though."

They told each other where they lived and, discovering how far apart their homes were, talked about how they would get to see each other again, aside from happening to come out to Pyramid at the same time.

When they got back to the beach below the shelter, they designed and built a harbor city in the sand. It was projected as a vast work about a central stronghold or cathedral on a hill, the lower city divided by many streets and canals, and surrounded by a wall which left it open only to the water. They discussed what kind of people lived in it, and populated each area of the city as it was completed, even naming the most important members of each family. It was to be a peaceful city, in which everybody loved music and art, and there were many wonderful gardens with running water and all the streets were lined by flowering trees, represented by leaves from the thatch of the fishing shelter, and there were many pleasure boats, twigs, on the canals. There was no need of an army, a navy or a police force; commerce was a matter of delight because of the beautiful things handled, the merchant-marine vessels and the fishing fleet all had painted sails, and the mayor was a cheerful fat man who played the cello for the fun of it.

The building of this Utopia, however, was far slower and less perfect than its projection, for the fine sand at the edge of the water was shallow, and the sand from higher up was so coarse that it wouldn't pack very well, even when wet. The towers of the cathedral on the mount, for instance, kept crumbling, and it was impossible even to start its spires, so that they finally settled on a kind of terraced Pyramid of the Sun. The work was far from complete when they saw the boats coming in and began to hurry, and wasn't much farther along when they stood up to watch the landing.

There were two boats, one white and one green, with two fishermen in each, and one big-faced Indian rowing each. The Indians pulled sharply at the very last, and the two prows crushed up into the sand and stopped suddenly. The boys stood together and silently watched the men climbing out and hauling the great, inert cut-throats out by the gills. Two of the men were short and fat and wore white-cloth hats with floppy brims, which hadn't saved their round faces from being burned red. A third was short, lean, gray haired, and already very brown. The fourth, who came out last from the stern of the white boat, was tall and thin and very dark. He looked like Lawrence. As he stepped out onto the sand, he grinned and said, with a slight and courtly bow of his head, "Black, how are you?"

"Fine," Lawrence said.

The man looked at Timmy and said to Lawrence, "And what did you do with yourself all day?"

"Oh, I made a clay turtle, and we've been building a city. Father, this is Timothy Hazard. He's been making things with me."

They spoke like two men who admired each other, but were not very well acquainted. Mr. Black was holding a big cut-throat in each hand. He had to bend his right arm to keep from dragging the fish on that side in the sand. The armor of the fish shone in the low sunlight, and their great eyes were very staring and empty.

"Timothy, I'm glad to know you," Mr. Black said, making the same little bow.

"It must have been fine to have company," he said to Lawrence. "And what became of the tortoise?"

Lawrence told him.

"I'll take 'em, Mr. Black," one of the Indians said. He was a broad, heavy man, and his big face had deep lines, like chisel cuts in dark wood. He was wearing a blue shirt which had been washed and sunned until the color was very pale, and a pair of faded Levis rolled up around his thick calves. He was bare-footed.

"Ah, Jesse," Mr. Black said, bowing in agreement and offering the fish, "that would be fine. Thank you very much."

He stuffed and lighted his pipe while he asked more questions about what the boys had been doing. His voice was deep and husky, and his words were cleanly made, like Lawrence's. He looked at Timmy often from the corners of his eyes while they talked.

"I see," he said finally. "Well, Black, it's too bad not to finish your city, but I'm afraid we must be going."

He was very polite and friendly, but now that he spoke of going Timmy felt lonesome with him and the other men there. He understood that his planning with Lawrence had been imaginative, and that, considering their addresses, they probably wouldn't see each other again. The group standing on the beach, already up to their knees in the shadow of the mountain, with the pale, quiet lake behind them, suddenly became a clear picture to him, a picture full of sad, elusive meanings.

"You must come and see us some time, Timothy," Mr. Black said.

"I'd like to," Timmy said.

"Ah, good," Mr. Black said. "We'll be seeing you shortly then, I hope."

He started up the beach toward the ranch, but then waited while the boys said good-bye. The boys felt shy now. Good-bye was all they said.

"Could we give you a lift somewhere, Timothy?" Mr. Black asked.

Timmy said no, thank you, his folks were over at the rocks, and then stood there watching Lawrence and the men climb up until they were full length in the sun again, and the big fish shone when they were turned at the right angle. The Indian who had been rowing the green boat wore an orange shirt. It was bright against the shadowed mountain. Lawrence stopped at the top of the climb and looked back and raised one hand solemnly. Timmy replied quickly, in the same way. Then the party went out of sight toward the trees which showed over the ranch, and Timmy started back up the beach.

The mountains across the lake glowed softly, their canyons and ravines, and the fluting of the escarpments toward the north, a smoky amethyst. The still water was opalesque, and brokenly reflected both the mountains and the sky. When he was halfway up the beach, Timmy heard voices calling him. He wouldn't answer. He didn't want to make a loud noise. At first he didn't want to run, either, because he was heavy with sadness about losing Lawrence, and full of questions about him to which he was imagining answers. It was a slow time of day, anyway. Even the gulls going home to Anaho flew slowly. But he made himself begin to run, and after he had run a few yards the questions and sadness were out of him, and he felt a great joy about the afternoon, and ran with a wonderful feeling of being light and fleet.

Grace met him by the big boulder and gave him his shirt. She said Mary had waited under the boulder for half an hour while Grace had hunted for her dress. Grace had found it finally, on top of the boulder, tied into a well-soaked knot with Timmy's shirt.

Timmy didn't get to sit beside Mary on the way home. He and Willis had to sit on the floor in back. But at least he got to sit on the side where Mary was sitting, so that he often touched the feet from the golden path, and, after Willis fell asleep, even touched her knee with his shoulder. Above the side of the old Dodge, the peaks of the near mountains swam slowly by, and grew darker, and became, at last, faint silhouettes from which the fountains of stars sprang up.

MOST of the horses which came to the Reno race meet arrived just long enough before it to get the train or the trailer out of their legs, but there were always a few which came earlier. It was this pre-season which furnished Timmy and Willis with the friends around stalls, paddocks and gates, who later let them into all the races for nothing.

It was a season more exciting to Timmy than to Willis. Willis had a terrible racing instinct which made him unable to eat any lunch on race days, and Timmy didn't. Except for a strong personal devotion to certain horses, which led him to watch their races in agony, the crowds, the noise, the flags, all the gigantic drama of race day overwhelmed Timmy, whose excitement about the outcome of most races wasn't sufficient antidote. Willis was all business on race days. The crowd was just something to force his way through. The only sounds he heard were the bugle and the official announcements. He was as intent as a bookie, not on the love and luck of one horse, but on the relative chances of the field in any event, and the amount of money to be won according to the quotations which kept changing on the big blackboard in the infield. Willis never picked a winner for such an idiotic reason as passionately hoping that horse would win. On the contrary, he would concentrate on one horse, even if he hadn't managed to see it, which was improbable, and just to show, if all the dope proved it would show and make more money than could be made by betting on the winner. Having this kind of focused attention, and a ferocious interest in seeing his analysis sustained by the race, and also a craftsman-like interest in how the horses were handled, Willis, in spite of being unable to eat, was never practically annihilated by race day, the way Timmy was. On the contrary, by the time he was nine he had the true racing soul, and was intent on everything which happened during the training days, only because of what it would mean on race days, which remained for him the real goal, the mountains toward which the barren plains stretched.

Timmy's heart, on the other hand, truly went out to the track only in the preliminary days. Then it seemed to him a friendly universe, spacious in the sun, yet comprehensible. He loved its empty and resounding grandstand, its clubhouse where important politicians and horsemen and their guests and women sat in the shaded seats of the mighty on the upper veranda on race days, its long line of stalls against the west fence, and its city of stables at the south end. All of this was so scoured, bleached and powdered by sun and weather that it seemed akin to the dusty poplars that looked over from the outside and to the wavering yellow hills in the north. The dozen or fifteen or twenty early horses and their grooms and trainers and·jockeys were the perfect quantity of animated life in this natural quiet. They moved around, far apart in the great, hot arena, and touched it with bits of color and motion, and yet everything could be seen without confusion.

Yet to those who didn't know them, Willis would have seemed far more excited than Timmy during the preliminary days. Timmy would shortly fall in love with a particular horse, and hang about this horse's stall until he was accepted, and then help with the watering, the feeding, even the grooming, or simply sit or stand where he could look at the horse's beautiful, prick-eared, delicately veined head hanging out and turning in the sun. He would become a knight for this horse's colors, imbued with irrational faith in its power.

Willis, on the other hand, would be on the move all the time, seeing every horse and every man, taking it on himself to help, clambering onto the half doors when the horses wouldn't come front to be looked at, or he couldn't see enough to satisfy himself. He would have to take it all in every day, following all the horses through their workouts, groomings, feedings, blanketings.

Timmy would never speak to those infinitely wise and

worldly men, the grooms and the jockeys, unless they spoke to him first. Willis was always asking them questions, and often telling them answers, and sometimes bumming smokes from them. When the horses were walked in the paddocks under their bright blankets, Timmy would be hoping in silent agony to be set upon his chosen horse, to feel with terror and delight its heat and promissory fury beneath him, and to wish into its great shoulders, through his knees, all the luck in the world. Willis would try for a ride on every horse that was out, and even get some rides when the horses were saddled and about to be run, and he would be intent all the time upon a weirdly mature calculation of the comparative merits of the horses, as well as upon all the tricks of riding them. When the early horses ran trial heats, Willis would be among the attentive men, heckling them to know what the watch said. Timmy would be by himself, hanging over the rail. As the days passed, and the stables filled, and there were more and more men walking about in the dusty streets of this city of royal horses, Timmy would stick closer and closer to his chosen horse, and Willis would become more and more violently omnipresent. Timmy, in all the years of his attendance, was never allowed to handle a racer alone. Willis was jockeying in trial heats when he was eleven. Yet it was Timmy who came home from these days exhausted and quiet, while Willis would tear into the house as wildly and noisily as he had left it in the early morning. The difference lay in this: that Willis was intent upon making all horses contribute to his fortune, while Timmy was unswervingly intent upon giving himself to the fortunes of one horse, although he sometimes had secondary favorites, and at any rate would pick a horse to hope for in every race. Willis was always collecting; Timmy was always paying out.

One particular race, which is most important because Timmy's great love began while it was beginning, was typical of what horses meant to the two of them, because it happened that they had the same favorite, a small and delicate sorrel mare from Southern California, Sunday Wind. Sunday Wind was running under silver and blue, which influenced Timmy because those were the University of Nevada colors, but influenced Willis because they were also the colors of Skate Regan, an ex-jockey owner and a first-rate fixer.

Sunday Wind was practically unknown. She was running in the fourth race. Before the third race went on, Willis came to her stall and stood with his hands on his hips and his legs apart, looking at her. Timmy was sitting on the bench by the door.

"For once, stoop," Willis said to him, "you picked a horse. She's drawed a little fine though, ain't she?" he asked the trainer, a thin, red-eyed man with a gold tooth.

The trainer grinned. "The hell she is, sonny," he said. "She was never better."

"You think she'll take it?"

"Like Grant took Richmond," the trainer said.

"I still wouldn't take your word for it, Toothy," Willis said, "only there's better men think so too."

"The hell you say," the trainer said.

"The hell I don't," Willis said.

"You gonna put up the dinero on her?" he asked Timmy.

"I haven't got any," Timmy said.

This was true, but also he had a superstition that to bet on his favorite horse would spoil its chances, though he never would have admitted that, at least not to Willis.

"For Chrissakes," Willis said, "are you gonna let that stop you?"

He departed on the run in the direction of the paddock.

Timmy felt unreasonably encouraged by the fact that both he and Willis preferred Sunday Wind. He began to talk softly and sentimentally to the mare, who couldn't keep her feet or her ears still.

Willis began to talk to Skate Regan in the paddock.

"Your mare gonna win, Mr. Regan?"

Skate took a toothpick out of his mouth and looked at Willis with his head on one side.

"You don't see me feeding any losers, do you?" he asked.

"Not unless you want to."

"No," Skate said.

73

"Gimme a coupla bucks to bet on her, Mr. Regan."

Skate put the toothpick back into his mouth, and watched a horse being led into the paddock. "Now why," he asked gently, as if meditating, "should I give you two bucks to bring down the price on my horse?"

"You ain't scared she's gonna lose, are you, Mr. Regan? And if she don't, you get your two bucks back, don't you?"

"I might," Skate said, "if you just didn't happen to forget where you got it. Nope, I don't do business thataway."

"What's the deal?" Willis asked wearily. "I gotta have the two bucks."

"I get half the take," Skate said.

"Jeez, what a big heart you got. O.K., gimme the two plunkers."

"And if she don't win, you clean out all my stalls."

"O.K., O.K., I'll risk it. Gimme the two bucks."

Skate gave him two silver dollars.

"Remember, I'm watching the board," he said.

Willis found Trury, the apoplectic-looking balloon-and-pennant man, hawking by the grandstand gate.

"You place my bet, Trury, and I give you a buck off the take."

"If there's any take," Trury said, and yelled, "Here's all the colors. Get a balloon, folks; take a balloon home to the kiddies. Show your colors, folks," and jerked at the spray of balloons flying over him and over the pennants on canes. The balloons had shining cheeks in the sunlight.

"Whaddya want, a lead-pipe cinch?" Willis asked him. "Ain't you got any gambling spirit?"

"You'll want me to cash it too, won't you?" Trury asked.

"Well, I sure as hell can't myself."

"Two bucks," Trury said.

"Jeez, what a Shylock," Willis said. "It ain't hardly worth bettin' with all you guys cuttin' in."

"That's my price," Trury said, and yelled about balloons and pennants again.

"O.K.," Willis said, "if I take twenny-five or over. If I get less, one buck." He observed Trury's indifference carefully. "I gotta split with Skate Regan the way it is," he added.

Trury looked at him. "Regan?" he asked. "Well," he said, "what do you want?"

"Fourth race," Willis told him. "Sunday Wind on the nose."

"You're crazy," Trury said. "Sunday Wind, with Valley Jack, Gloriosa and Marble King in there?"

"I'll wait here for my ticket," Willis said.

When Trury brought him the ticket, he clutched it in his hand. He wouldn't trust anything so promising and so elusive to any of his pockets.

"Who's riding her?" Trury asked.

"Brandon."

"Well, he's good."

"You're goddam right he's good. You don't see Skate Regan pickin' any losers, do you?"

He waited till the soft-drink and hot-dog vendor was busy at the other side of his booth, took an orange pop, and elbowed and ducked his way up to the rail to watch the finish of the third. He told the man behind him, when the clods had returned to earth and the dust had blown down after the uproarious passage, that the winning jockey didn't know his mouth from a hole in the ground about riding, but that that horse could win under even a worse jockey.

When Sunday Wind had been led out, and the crowd had thinned to bet the fourth, which was the feature, Timmy found a place beside him at the rail.

"Did you bet?" he asked.

"Sure I bet," Willis said. "What the hell you think I been doin' all this time? Pushin' peanuts with my nose?" He was very tense and belligerent. Timmy didn't say anything more.

The bugle sounded and the parade began. It was led by a heavy, gray-haired marshal, whose face was an indoor red. He wore a white Stetson and a sky-blue silk shirt with white piping on the cuffs, collar and pockets, and a white-silk tie. He was mounted on a heavy palomino with wavy tail and mane, its bridle, saddle and tapaderos ornamented with silver. The marshal turned the parade directly in front of the boys.

The controlled mettle of a parade, promising the storm to come, but never letting out, pleased Timmy more than anything else on race day. He then unwittingly adored all the horses, although regarding all but one as potential enemies.

First after the marshal came Marble King, a tall horse, queer-looking for a racer, with obvious signs that his wasn't all hot blood. He had a gray, lusterless coat, flecked with black. His legs and neck were long, stringy and flat, and his chest was deep but peculiarly narrow. His head was oversized, narrow and Roman nosed. He walked without much spring, but with a forward surge of suppressed energy. He was giving his rider no trouble, yet he suggested something piratical and untrustworthy. He was a kind of equine work of El Greco, provokingly elongated, malicious, distorted and violent. His rider wore dull black and shining red in even halves.

Behind Marble King came Valley Jack, the sentimental favorite because he was a Nevada horse, ranch raised, and because everybody felt sure that no tricks were ever played with him. He was put to every race with all he had, and was undefeated in five starts in this meet. He was a big, shapely black with a high gloss, a white star and three white socks, and was the only stallion on the day's card. His colors were white with a gold band.

"He's got a heart," Willis said contemptuously, "but that ain't gonna make him no big-time runner. He's too hefty. 'Fore he's done he'll just kill himself tryin'."

Next came Duchess Molly, a medium bay, going nicely with a little spring and almost no head motion. She was even more an outsider than Sunday Wind. Her rider wore a single color, bottle green.

Gloriosa, the money favorite, came fourth. She was as small and perfectly tapered as Sunday Wind, but rounder, and the black satin of her haunches made little lightnings of muscle-play in the sun. Her jockey wore silver and rose in even halves.

The crowd couldn't help laughing at the fifth horse, and

men's voices called advice to the jockey: "Take him out of there, sonny, and let him catch up on his sleep." "Look out, buddy, he's liable to go off under you." "Somebody page the S.P.C.A." On the card the horse was Sunfish. He came from Arizona. He walked like a mustang in a bad drouth year, with a long, flat reach and his neck sticking out straight in front, with no lift or pride. He was a sorrel with a fair shine, but narrow as a knife blade, stringy muscled and sparse of tail and mane. His jockey wore white with red sleeves.

"Just the same, he ain't as dopy as he looks, I betcha," Willis said. "He's got good legs and he's deep. Only they musta been feedin' him on sawdust. Godawmighty, jockey," he yelled, "pick his head up. Don'tcha even want him to come out?"

Sunfish was right in front of them, and the jockey looked down at Willis. He was old for a jockey, with gray hair at his temples, and his thin face looked tired and hardened only by nerve, as if he couldn't care about anything any more, except getting a long rest, but couldn't afford that.

"Don't you fret yourself, sonny," he said with an edge. "He'll come out all right."

"Yeah," Willis yelled after him, "if he ever gets in."

Sunday Wind followed Sunfish. She was beautiful, but she was really making Brandon work, tossing her head all the time, and traveling along sideways, like a trotting pup, but in a high-lifting, jittery dance. Sometimes she waltzed clear out of line, and then she was hard to put back.

"For Chrissakes, Brandon," Willis yelled at him, "talk to her; let her know you're around."

Brandon was working without expression, everything slow and firm, but he was nervous. He didn't answer, but he looked at Willis for an instant, and his eyes were furious.

"For Chrissakes," Willis said privately, "Brandon's jittery himself."

Coming around for the back-parade, Sunday Wind ran clear out, as if taking to the track, and when Brandon held her, whirled twice around, like a cow pony pressed to show off. She came back across sideways, and part of the time even backwards, so

77

that the jockey on the last horse, a dark bay gelding called Ring-Around, had to check him and pull him over to let her in. People in the stands began yelling at Brandon to handle her. Willis was furious and incoherent. Once Sunday Wind was back in line, though, she went better, dancing and sidling a little, but not breaking any more, or messing up the parade.

"That's better," Willis muttered, "that's better. She'll save it now. She's still the class of the field. I'll still take her. Only that goddam Brandon."

Willis couldn't stop talking. He was shifting around restlessly against the rail, too.

Ring-Around walked steadily and springily, strictly all business. He'd tossed off a little as Sunday Wind sidled by, fighting the bit, but had settled again at once. Willis was taken by this indication of both edge and control. He talked about it, making out an ardent case for Ring-Around's young, blond jockey in green and gold, against the experienced Brandon. But he kept saying, "Even with Brandon, she can. She's the class."

Except when the parade was passing right in front of him, Timmy watched Sunday Wind all the time. The rest of the field became alternately ghosts and monsters. He was silently and fixedly as excited as Willis.

At the barrier Sunday Wind began to act up again. She refused the stall repeatedly. Once Brandon worked her in and she tried to climb out in front. Timmy was paralyzed for fear she would hurt herself. Willis softly and continuously cursed Brandon. Brandon had to pull her out again, let her go a little, and bring her back. As far as the boys could tell at that distance and over the barrier, she wasn't lamed, anyway. Once more she refused and, in spinning, knocked against Ring-Around, who was suddenly stirred up too, and wouldn't stand. The boys couldn't hear anything from there either, but they could feel how furious Ring-Around's jockey must be. People at the far end of the stands, near the barrier, began to yell advice and condemnation. People in the near end stood up and craned their necks and told each other what was happening. Gloriosa got nerves for a moment, and had to be let out and brought back.

All the horses were stirring restlessly except Sunfish, who was next to Sunday Wind's stall on the inside. He had his head up now, but he was standing. His jockey was just sitting there, relaxed. Some man with a deep voice and a self-important tone was rebuking Brandon through the loud-speaker: "You'll have to put her in there, Number Six. We can't wait all day for you. You'll have to put that mare in there, Brandon. You're holding up everything."

The nervousness of the little mare had spread into everybody there. It became a kind of growling and yelling madness, and gave a new and predatory significance to the bare track leading down from the barrier into the first curve, as if something about everybody's fate were implicated in the trouble, and would be resolved in the rush of the race when it came.

When Sunday Wind refused again, a man stepped across the low rail from the infield and approached her cautiously. Another man followed him. Then the mare stood still, and the boys could see Brandon shaking his head. He was arguing about something. Then he stopped shaking his head. They could see his upright body, in the shining silver and blue, sliding along the top of the gates behind the other jockeys, toward the outside of the track.

"They're gonna take her out," Timmy lamented. "Oh, Jeez, they're gonna take her out."

"The hell they are; the hell they can. They can't do that," Willis said rapidly. "They're walkin' her, that's all. They're just walkin' her. Oh, the bastards," he said suddenly and loudly, because he understood what was going to happen. "Oh, goddamit," he said over and over again softly and despairingly. "They're gonna start her outside the barrier," he explained to no one in the same moan. "It's soft out there. There's no bottom out there. Brandon'll never get her back in, the bastard."

It was true. Sunday Wind was coming up outside the barrier. One of the men stayed there to hold her.

It was at this peak moment of anticipation that Timmy, who couldn't bear to stare at his heart's darling out there alone and being held, turned and saw Rachel Wells for the first time.

He and Willis were at the rail right next to the entrance to the stands. The girl was seated in the front row of the second box, not twenty feet from him. She was small, and her brown, round face was fixed apprehensively toward the barrier. There was no wind, and her Dutch bob lay flat at the side of her head. Her hair was a soft, medium brown, brushed so that it shone, but without showing any other color. Her round face and the Dutch bob made it seem that her body should be chubby, but it wasn't. It was small and slender. She was sitting very straight and still, with her hands clenched in her lap and her knees and feet tensely together. She had on a shining yellow dress, with short sleeves, and her arms were golden brown, like Mary's. She appeared alone, maybe even lonely, no matter who was around her, and in spite of the throng in the ascending tiers above her. Such aloneness was a sensation which Timmy was already expert in diagnosing. He didn't have to study the girl to decide that about her. He wasn't even really thinking about her, not with Sunday Wind standing down there in shame before all those eyes, under all those loud voices. At the moment what he felt was that the girl was also out of the world for Sunday Wind.

The front of the box was in bright, hot sunlight, which gleamed on the yellow dress. The older women on either side of the girl were also watching the barrier, but quietly, with mild curiosity. Three of the men in the back row of the box were also sitting, but the fourth was standing and watching the doings at the barrier through a pair of field glasses. All the motion was in the grandstand behind the box, where everybody was stirring or standing up and yelling, or making angry gestures. There were great, vague and broken patterns of colored dresses and white shirts in the stands, but subdued by the shadow of the high roof. The figures in the very back were just jumping-jack silhouettes against the wide bar of sky and sunlight. This mass and motion made the group in Box 2 appear lifeless, like a wax-work group, and yet, because of the shadow, became just a background for its spotlighted intensity.

The crowd made a unanimous, moaning sigh, as for the end

of something, and began to settle back. Only isolated, angry voices kept yelling, "About time." "Take that no-good filly out of there." "Brandon, who ever told you you could ride?" Timmy looked back at once. All the horses were in and standing, except Sunday Wind. She was still out in the soft edge, with the strange man holding her.

There was another burst of impatient yelling as Gloriosa began to rear, and had to be let out again, but she went back in under her jockey's hands, and the noise died.

Willis was still pattering his monologue. He was intoning it. It was a prolonged and repetitive curse against Brandon and the officials, and even against Skate Regan for letting Brandon up. Then he yelled, "Brandon, you get her the hell out of there. You get her across there, you son of a bitch. They put her out there. To hell with 'em. Cross 'em all up, the bastards."

A man beside him said angrily, "What you expect them to do? Wait all day for her? She ought to be scratched. That's what ought to be done."

"Yeah?" Willis asked. "Screw you, mister," he said. "She's the best damn horse on the card today. It ain't her fault. It's that goddamned Brandon."

"At sixty to one?" the man said.

"What does that prove," Willis asked him loudly, "except there's a hell of a lot of other guys here don't know any more than you do?"

"You're a fresh brat, aren't you?"

"Well, I don't bet because I think the colors is sweet, anyway," Willis said.

There was a moment in which the whole scene was quiet in the sunlight. The only motion was the slow, relaxed snaking of the long pennants on the edge of the roof. The only sound was the hoarse and distant voice of one vendor, "Ice cold sody-pop. I have it here, everybody. Here it is. Ice cold sody-pop."

The flag was up. The man at Sunday Wind's head let go of her and went over the outside rail. She plunged a little, but Brandon held her. The flag came down and the gates were sprung. Sunday Wind settled slowly and plowed out. To Timmy it looked as if she were coming away in slow motion. It was impossible to tell from there, but the field must have had two lengths on her, no matter how it was among the rest of them. Then Brandon was lying out on her to make it up from the start. The crowd was all standing, and roaring and screaming the horses' names. Sunday Wind was halfway up on the field when it came abreast of the boys and suddenly appeared to be really running, but then she wouldn't come in, but went at the first curve still way on the outside. Gloriosa led at the rail. Marble King, with a great leaping stride, was slowly showing his head up along her side. Then came Ring-Around on the rail, Sunday Wind abreast him outside, running two for his one, Valley Jack coming up on his haunch, Duchess Molly following half a length and Sunfish tailing. The dust went across slowly behind them. They began to sort themselves out on the curve, and the monotonous voice of the announcer started to repeat their names, numbers and changes of place as the trample faded toward the back stretch. They straightened out and were only rocking heads and bowed backs in bright silk gliding along the far rail.

"Good God Almighty," the man beside Willis said, "lookit that Sunfish go."

Sunfish *was* going, too, coming up as if he had just started to run. In the first half of the back stretch he slid past Duchess Molly, and then past Ring-Around, who had fallen back of Valley Jack. The crowd screamed about it, and some of them, who were probably betting on Sunfish or on Valley Jack, kept screaming as he came up alongside Valley Jack. The rest of the crowd let out another roar, for a different reason, but the desperate boys didn't know why, because the race fled back of the rodeo fences and chutes in the infield, and they could see only tiny bits of color flying past the openings between the boards. There was another roar while the race was still hidden from them, and then it broke into the open, way up on the north-east curve and tiny under the dusty hills. The announcer explained. He had dropped the numbers, and sounded excited himself. "It's Sunday Wind in front by a length now," his voice boomed and crackled. "Sunday Wind. Two is Marble King. Marble King two. Three, Gloriosa, four, Sunfish, and he's still coming, that Sunfish. Then it's Valley Jack, Ring-Around and Duchess Molly, in that order."

The storm of yelling increased as the field came onto the last curve, the foreshortening suddenly making it appear that they were running desperately in one place, like hobby-horses. The jockeys' whip arms could be seen working, tiny and rhythmical.

The announcer began to reel off the order of the race again, but all at once said, "Oh-oh," into the mike, so it came out like a gigantic private surprise. At almost the same instant the crowd, Timmy and Willis with it, cried out. Sunday Wind had gone wide again, clear to the outside, as she came off the curve. Willis moaned and cursed Brandon, who wasn't whipping, but just lying to her to straighten her out. As at the start, it was hard to tell how the horses stood, but it was clear that Gloriosa, in a sudden spurt, had pulled up beside Marble King, and that Sunday Wind's lead was practically, if not altogether, gone. Then Gloriosa fell back and in, and it was Sunfish coming up through, and Valley Jack showing right on Marble King's tail at the rail, but not coming out. The announcer stopped trying to say anything in that roar. The field reached midway of the stretch and appeared to be moving again instead of just rocking up and down. Valley Jack finally came out without the whip. His jockey hadn't used the whip all the way. Marble King's jockey was flogging him at every jump, and because he was on the pole, and farthest out to the boys' vision, the big, ugly gray appeared to be clearly pulling away. Sunday Wind was refusing something, or threatening something, for suddenly Brandon began to whip too. Sunfish was coming right up the middle of the track, laid out flat like a dog, the jockey with his chin nearly between the horse's ears, but giving slack rein and clenching the whip unused and upright.

Because it was now plain that the race would finish with its front clear across the track, and never stretch to the rail again, the crowd went mad. Yet for an instant the roar went even higher into a scream, and Timmy, not making a sound, just stared as Sunday Wind sheered off, struck against the grandstand barrier, and came on down by herself at an idle canter, her head high and tossing. Willis wasn't saying anything either. The field, four nearly abreast, fled to the post and past, going long and very fast when again seen from the side like that. The jockeys took off the whips, braced themselves high and began to draw slowly, going for the curve. The thunder slackened and widened, and the dust went slowly across into the infield, sifting down golden as it went. It was Sunfish, Valley Jack, Marble King in that order, Gloriosa right on them, and then, close but one at a time, Ring-Around and Duchess Molly. Brandon wouldn't let Sunday Wind out again, but just let her lope onto the curve to take the nervous curse off the break.

Slowly, like the dust, the after-yelling faded away.

Timmy's chin was jittering, and there were tears in his eyes. "She ran farther than any of them," he said thickly. "She ran on the outside pretty near all the way. She'd still have beat them, if Brandon knew anything."

"Nuts," Willis said. He was very calm and savage now. "It wasn't Brandon's fault. It was just like I said. She was drawed too fine. Croust," he said, "a hunnerd an' twenny bucks down the drain, jus' like that."

His mouth was drawn up into a sneer right under his nose, the upper lip trembling with fury. He tore his ticket up into small pieces and threw the pieces at the back of the man turning away from him.

"She's still the best horse," Timmy said. "If Brandon . . ."

"Oh, for God's sake, dry up," Willis said, suddenly squaring at him as if about to start a fight. "What the hell do you know about it, drivel-puss? You wouldn't know Man o' War from a cart horse. Best horse my eye. No horse with any bottom ever pulled a run-out like that last one. She's no damn good. She never will be.

"Brandon's no good either," he said more quietly, "but it wasn't his fault this time. They oughta shoot that mare for dog meat. She ain't never gonna be any good for anything else.

"A hunnerd and twenty bucks, the little bitch," he said, and walked off, strutting like a jockey in boots and tight pants.

The track again became unreal to Timmy, color, sound and motion moving off into the realm of illusion. He was overwhelmed by the desolation and loneliness that must now be borne by Sunday Wind. The world had ganged up on him and Sunday Wind. He understood that all the world would pass the same judgment on her that Willis had. He had recognized at once that Willis had spoken the words of the world against Sunday Wind and himself—"shoot her for dog meat."

He watched Brandon bring her up under the stand, brandish and hand down his whip, dismount and go off stiffly with his saddle. Brandon was a good jockey. He didn't show anything. He would have come up and walked off the same way if he'd won by five lengths. It was one bad race to Brandon. But Timmy was thinking that Brandon probably felt the same way, that Sunday Wind was no good.

He turned to go out to the avenue of stalls and be there when Sunday Wind came home. Somebody must be there who believed forever in the heart of Sunday Wind, and the man with the gold tooth wasn't that kind. He didn't want to see another race anyway. No race mattered as much as the way Sunday Wind was feeling.

In the lane leading to the betting booths, he saw the girl in the yellow dress again. Her party were all talking, and laughing a little, and shaking their heads, probably, he thought angrily, making fun of Sunday Wind, but the girl's face had the same still look. Her chin was lifted. Her arms were down straight at her sides, and her hands were clenched. She didn't look around. She was walking by herself among all of them, as she had sat by herself among all of them. Timmy believed that she too was harrowed by the disgrace of Sunday Wind.

As he sat in the shade on the bench beside the stall, watching the groom walk Sunday Wind slowly back and forth under her blue blanket, he thought about the girl in the yellow dress also.

TIMMY'S transition from Mary, the worshipful symbol of all womankind, to Rachel, a personal deity, was assisted by other changes and events, which combined to lead him from the sunny fringe of the wilderness into its shadowy and more complicated depths.

In the first place, he began to grow as if he had been transplanted into more fertile earth or set out nearer water. By the end of his sophomore year in high school, this sprouting had transformed him from a nimble-footed, scurrying creature five feet tall and ninety pounds in weight, to a drifting, incomprehensible being six feet tall and weighing one hundred and fifty. Even on that September day when he first went down there to the edge of the center of town, and approached, with somewhat watery knees, the two flights of steps, the concrete steps and the wooden steps, and then the two great, brass-bound doors above them, this change was well along. From the first of it, so much of his energy went to lengthening his bones and enlarging his hands and feet that he could never eat or sleep enough. His own plate would be filled two and three times at a meal, and after he had devoured all that, he would clean up anything left by the rest of the family. Often he drank a quart of milk at breakfast or supper, and worked another in some time between. His mother cheerfully called him the family garbage can, and left odds and ends out on the kitchen table for him to pick up after school. With sleep it was even worse. When his father woke him in the morning, for school or work, he felt a dread of moving his arms or legs, and a great depression about everything he would have to do that day. He stretched cautiously, with an all-over tingling like that of a foot being walked on after it has gone to sleep, blinked at the sun in the tops of the poplars, and endeavored to close his nerveless hands into fists. He always succeeded at last in making the fists, and feeling the strength spread slowly through him, as if slow, chilled blood had thawed and begun to trickle a little, but often his mind would be only partially fired after a whole day, and would go out the moment he lay down again or sat still. It was more to combat this reluctance of his brain than to overcome his body that he began the Spartan practice of dousing himself with cold water every morning, after driving himself through a half-hour of ferocious exercises accompanied by quick tunes in his mind. Yet in spite of these efforts, he moved through the thin air of Reno, for the most part, like a water-logged vessel cruising a weedy sea. His hair, like the lion's mane, was the outward sign of his inner state. When it was cut, he always had it shorn down to a fine stubble, but he still would let it go for weeks, till it hung out over his ears and collar and its curls became too tangled to comb.

He took pleasure in driving his body when he was outdoors too, in forcing himself further miles up Galena or Hunter's Creek or among the yellow hills, when his legs already ached and the slopes swam before his eyes, or in continuing to carry too many slabs at a time, in the lumber yard in the sun and the smell of resin and sawdust, long after he yearned to sleep in the nearest shade. Yet he was likely, more often, to wander dreamily, or stand and stare, upon his journeys, and to drift without knowing it between jobs. The older boys who also helped in the lumber yard during the summer called him dopy, and frequently, at supper, he endured long verbal beatings from his father. It stung to be called dopy by boys he knew at school too, but he soon learned to make his father's voice only a noise in the kitchen, to sit still in an attitude of listening, and think about something else. Usually his father became so interested in salutary illustrations drawn from his own somewhat mythical youth that he fell into complete autobiography, with the object forgotten, and never penetrated the false attention. Once in a while, though, he became suspicious, and without a break asked, "What did I just say to you?" and then the lesson ended abruptly. Mr. Hazard stood up, banged his chair into place against the table and stood there, little demons of fury dancing in his eyes. "What the hell I waste my breath on you for, I don't know," he would say loudly, and then tramp loudly out of the room, down the hall and up the stairs, muttering about brats, no good, and why the hell a man is ever idiot enough to get married.

Sometimes, when Timmy went up to bed, he'd hear his father's voice behind the closed bedroom door, still taking it out on Mrs. Hazard in a deep and continuous rumbling. Mrs. Hazard had everything taken out on her, except what she could share with Grace while they did the dishes or the ironing or hung out the long rows of wash in the back yard. Yet she remained the cement of affection that kept the unlike males of her home together. Once in a while, especially when he had settled down with his beer on Saturday night, Mr. Hazard would drop politics and demonstrate to her, at length, how her improvidence kept them on the verge of shameful poverty and her lack of a strong hand was letting Willis go to the devil already, and how her own weaknesses were reproduced in Timmy and would prevent him from ever amounting to a tinker's damn. These explanations, when he overheard them, hurt Timmy more than anything Mr. Hazard said to him, for he couldn't understand, as yet, that his mother had a gift like his own of not really hearing them. He didn't know, for that matter, that he had the gift himself. It wasn't until much later that he realized the simple and enduring significance of the long summer evenings when his mother and father sat together on the front porch, watching the sunset perform subtly and flamboyantly among the western thunderheads and the Virginia Mountains in the east, or the times they went off to the movies in the old Dodge and didn't take any of the kids.

Willis was always saying, "What the old lady don't know, won't hurt her, and she don't know plenty," yet Tim believes now that he cost his mother more than Willis did. She saw her own nature, long blurred and unsatisfied because she lacked the selfishness to protect it, beginning its course over again in

Timmy, and she yearned toward him terribly. He never opened fire against her battered defenses, as his father did, or slipped by her nodding sentries, as Willis did, but he was that harder thing to bear, an ally who never came to counsel. He wandered alone in a world she could have enjoyed too, and fled intently upon the scent of hopes which had vaguely been hers, and didn't even know he was excluding her from the only life she had left.

Along with his big body and his dreamy mind, Timmy developed a deep voice and a new way of talking. Until the sprouting began, except when he was among boys who raised his hackles, or with girls like Lucy or Mary, he had said, directly and in a treble, just what he thought and felt, and in his inner world, of which he was not fully aware, had never bothered about what anybody else would think. Now he began to defend himself against what others would think even of thoughts he never expressed, sometimes by argument as sophistic and elaborate as a church father's, or by false enthusiasm, and sometimes by a curt and slangy simulation of indifference.

Still another change came over him by way of his first pair of long pants. To forgetful adults, the donning of long pants may seem merely a minor and symbolic investiture, but actually it was an important factor in Tim's transformation. He had grown so long that he felt conspicuous and ashamed in his knee breeches, and bound by them to a past he had outgrown. He had taken to walking next to walls, so that one side of him, at least, would be free from observation, and to sitting down as quickly as he could when he entered a class room, because the short pants weren't so obvious when he was sitting down. In classes where the students had to stand to recite, he always contrived to push his seat up with his legs and stand behind his desk instead of standing out in the aisle. Now, all at once, the burden and the dodges were dropped; the past was put by, and he was dedicated to the future.

His first long pants were stiff, yellow cords, with sharp creases. In time they would become an honorable garment of experience, like those of older high-school boys and the university upper classmen, washed limp and nearly white and covered with the record of life, school initials, class numbers, favorable football scores, signatures, hearts-and-darts and cartoons. In their new, bright, rigid state, the material smelling strongly, like a wet hide, they were the lower half of what Timmy wore to his first late party. The upper half was a coat of his father's, much too big around the middle, but all right over the shoulders and arms, so that it worked if he didn't button it.

The event which finally prepared this transformed Timmy for the encounter which took place at that party was the trial by inquisition and battle through which the freshmen passed each year into the body of the high school. The battle was a formal affair, marking the end of their trials, but the inquisition went on from the day school began until the afternoon of the battle, and was a much more fluid and nightmarish process for Timmy, who had no particular fear of being hurt, but an almost paralyzing dread of being shamed. In imitation of a university tradition, all the freshmen were compelled to carry little books containing the school songs and yells, the history of past athletic achievements, the student-body constitution, and lists of officers and team captains. All of this they had to memorize, and upon the demand of any sophomore or upper classman, they had to open the little book to the required page, present it courteously to the persecutor, stand or kneel, as instructed, and recite or sing without error, under pain of further indignity. The boys also had to wear little red caps with blue buttons, and raise them to their betters. These disciplines, however, had some point, and were conducted with reasonable fairness. It was a more random form of terrorization which darkened the first weeks for the newcomers, and made many of them only too serious when the day of battle finally came. Every morning, every noon-hour, and sometimes even between classes and for a few minutes as school was letting out, freshmen boys and girls were arrested in the halls and made to perform acts about which they had no choice, at the top of the steps which led up into the study hall from the lofty and shadowy main hall. Recalcitrant victims were hauled up bodily, kicking and squirming. In the meantime, during all their daily coming and going, they might be stopped anywhere and forced to entertain or adore, and to hear of terrible things, most of them apocryphal, which had happened to freshmen in past years, during the final ceremony of humiliation, which took place in assembly just before the battle, and during the battle itself, and all over the city in weird hours of dusk and darkness. Tales of broken bones and unconsciousness, of stone-throwing and kicking with boots on, were remembered aloud in their presence, and they swelled the rumors among themselves.

The worst of all these torments, to Timmy's mind, was proposing on the study-hall steps, with the whole school watching, to some girl he had never seen before or, even worse, to some girl he knew well enough to imagine her feelings. It shook him cruelly to see the inquisitors deliberately choose, as they sometimes did, a very homely girl, or a very shy girl from one of the ranches, who still didn't dress quite the way the city girls did. She would have to stand there and bear it, trying to smile, trying to be a good sport, while the kneeling suitor, red and stumbletongued or forcedly brazen, declaimed terribly false praises of her charm and satirical oaths of devotion. Sometimes the suitor, too embarrassed even to think of the girl's humiliation, would try to postpone kneeling by blurting out, "Oh, my God," or even, "Jeez, couldn't you do any better for me than that?" In spite of all she could do, it would show in the girl's face then that the hurt went much deeper than mere confusion. And because these love pranks always stirred and embarrassed the audience too, more than any of the other acts, like singing or dancing or making a speech or begging pardon, there was always more laughter about them, sudden, shrill, raucous laughter, that struck the girl like a slap in the face. The laughter was always the worst when the boy said something that made it harder for the girl, too. It wasn't so bad for the pretty or popular girls, because they knew they were really being admired, and besides, they could always manage to carry it off. But when it happened to the lonely girls, it was like half a death. Tim saw one of them, an hour after her shame, crying by herself in one of the end class rooms, and it made him feel desolate and hopeless about the whole human world. There was no way of avoiding these persecutions, either. If you tried hiding out or coming late, you were sure to be noticed and haled up. The best thing was just to mingle with the mob in the hall and hope. Actually, after all his agonies, Tim was never called. His feeling that he stood out like a pine among pinon trees had no basis in fact. He wasn't even noticed.

This war of nerves reached its peak on the day of the battle. All the oral propaganda was stepped up; single freshmen boys who were considered rugged enough to make trouble were drawn aside and told in detail what would be done to them, and one of the sophomore boys, a quick, clever cartoonist, was conducted from room to room by a numerous bodyguard while he populated the blackboards with a sub-normal, gnomish race, which was the freshmen. These creatures had spindly arms and legs, huge, thick hands, feet like turned-up snowshoes, and enormous heads with receding chins, protruding front teeth and almost no foreheads. The hair of the males started at a crown near the base of the skull, swept forward, and stood out stiffly, like eaves, over the bulging eyes. The hair of the females stood up in short pigtails, like clusters of bobbins. Their effect, in such numbers, in white and colored chalk, was of tiny, deformed ground-dwellers, forced up into an unfamiliar immensity of sun and wind, and their holes blocked, so that their activity was unceasing but aimless and their only emotion a pop-eyed, hair-on-end fear. The few quiet figures among them were not superior. They stood about as if bereft of even leg-energy, and sucked their thumbs or lollipops, or clung to dolls which looked exactly like them.

This general comment was sharpened by the cartoonist's knack of suggesting individual peculiarities without greatly changing the racial type, and by rapidly printed warnings. Promising athletes were shown on the football field in diapers and befuddled agony. A couple of incipient scholars grew foreheads, wore huge spectacles, and were still more attenuated of body and limb than their brothers. Recognizable couples appeared in attitudes of infantile adoration, accompanied by trenchant suggestions that going steady was bad for yearlings, tending to limit their knowledge of life, besides making them disgusting.

All morning the freshmen stared at themselves as the cartoonist saw them, heard their individual and collective fates specified, assayed the indubitably superior confidence of the lolling sophomores, and themselves gathered and flowed apart, plotting feebly and promising fierce restoration of equality when the battle came. They were advised by important juniors and seniors, boys in blue sweaters with big red Rs on them, heroes who had battled in the far climes of Elko and Fallon, Lovelock and Winnemucca, and even Sacramento and Stockton, who had attained the sepia Valhalla of the team photographs in the library and the inky fame of the sports pages of the *Nevada State Journal* and the *Reno Evening Gazette*, they were advised by these condescending giants to get organized if they didn't want to be rubbed out. The sophomores always won, the giants said, because they knew each other and were organized and worked in teams. So the freshmen made knots in the halls and talked organization. They passed notes in class about organization. They drew up twenty different lists of sophomore champions who must be knocked out early, and thirty different lists of freshmen who could do the knocking out. They established a score of signs and calls by which they should know each other, and none of the signs got beyond its group of eight or ten conspirators. Earnestly they strove after organization and created confusion. When the bell rang for assembly at one o'clock, and the tide flowed up the steps and into the huge study hall, strangeness passed in with the freshmen, stronger than ever.

Save for the clothes of the freshmen and of the sophomore boys, the fact that the gruesome rites were performed more formally under the guidance of the student-body president, and the fact that it was longer than any previous period of trial, there was little difference between this last assembly and the things that had been going on for weeks. The freshmen girls flocked in the back of the room on the left side, clad in rompers, short dresses and half-socks, with their hair tied up in bows or in pigtails such as the cartoonist had promised, some of them with lollipops, most of them with dolls or teddy bears. The freshman boys sat in the back on the other side in battle dress, old pants and sweaters, Levis and torn shirts, boots and basketball shoes. The sophomores, just ahead of them, were dressed the same way, but there was no trouble telling the difference. The freshmen were marked with green and the sophomores with red, green and red shirts and pants, arm-bands and sashes and painted numerals. Now and then a sensational marking would cause a shout while the assembly was still settling, and everybody would stand up to see. One big sophomore raised his hands and shook them in the air, and they were blood red with streamers of red down the arms. Another stood up over near the north wall, and drew back his unbuttoned shirt to exhibit a huge red '25 painted across his chest and belly. Roars of nervous laughter followed one very fat freshman up the aisle. Across the ample seat of his pants were printed the green words, "Kick Me Here It Don't Hurt." A very small freshman had his hair painted bright green, and kept explaining to those around him that the top of his head was all anybody could see, and that if his head had to be broken, he didn't want it done by friends.

Gradually the uproar was reduced by the president's gavel, the names began to roll forth ominously, and the freshmen rose as they were called and stumbled up the aisles to the platform, sometimes falling over suddenly thrust-out feet. Timmy got his breath again only after each list had been read and laid down without the sound of his name. Rachel Wells was called up, froze like a rabbit, and was unable to perform the Charleston required of her. She was finally let off with a little embarrassed laughter, after she had apologized three times for her stupidity and clumsiness, and was on the verge of weeping. She had to repeat her apologies because nobody could hear them, not even the officers on the platform with her. Tim didn't recognize her, though he remembered later, and made up stories in which he rescued her. At the moment he was sitting way in the back, practicing the old art of disappearing, and pulling constantly at the two worn neckties and the pieces of rope he had brought for the tie-up. The hour passed, his name wasn't called, and he came up like a diver who has been down too long. The assembly broke up with a roar like the surf about him.

In cars and on foot, singly and in small groups, the school streamed along the streets and up to Whitaker Hill. There was constant cheering and yelling of insults and waving of rags and ropes. Timmy was walking by himself, lacing the armor of his insides, when Billy Wilson slowed his bug alongside and yelled, "Hop on and save your strength." Billy had gone to the Orvis Ring too, but his folks had moved during the summer to a place way out the South Virginia Road. He was a short, bow-legged boy, with tremendous energy, a huge voice and a love of any kind of tool work. It was hard to get on the bug, because it was only a bodiless framework with an engine, four wheels, and a gas tank set right behind the open seat, and there were already five boys on it.

"Hop on the hood," Billy yelled. "I kin see around you O.K."

Timmy climbed onto the hood and sat astride, and Billy set off again. The bug did a lot to restore Timmy's bravado after the assembly. The hood was bright red and the wheels canary yellow, and there were signs all over it. One side of the hood said "Danger, High Explosives," and the other said "Engine Room for Rent." The gas tank said "Rumple Seat." The right side of the seat said "Women Only" and the driver's side said "For Fun, Inquire Within." There was a big cardboard sign dangling off the tail, which said "To Hell with '25." The bug charged noisily up the hill, scattering walkers right and left, and was finally stopped by the curb of the cross street, because there were practically no brakes.

The hill, which was to be the battlefield, was a dome sloping down toward the city. It was only fringed by trees, and there was some sagebrush on it, and a lot of dirt and rocks and tumbleweed. The wind was blowing up there, and Timmy could see its slithering courses over the treetops of Reno below, as over a summer prairie. The afternoon sunlight made everything clear as crystal from the hill. Timmy felt its warmth alternate with the cool wind from Peavine as he also chilled and burned within. The two temperatures blended into a physical numbness in which it was impossible to think, though everything visible was unnaturally distinct and memorable and every sound strangely important. The girls gathering along the edges of the field, their hair and dresses tossing in the wind, became singular and lovely, so that he wanted a long time to look at each of them. The cries of challenge were like cock-crows, and near-by talk about nothing demanded his attention. He worked out among the milling warriors, looking for some signs of order that would tell him where to go. The voices of the marshals began to resound from their megaphones as they strove to get the two classes behind their starting lines. Once begun, the division continued of its own accord, with increasing speed. Nobody wanted to get left alone among the enemy. The sophomores gathered behind a line at the west side, and fell into orderly groups. The freshmen gathered and milled behind their line on the east. Upper classmen ran down the center and placed seven footballs at even intervals across the field. The senior marshal came out, his hair jumping in the wind, and gave loud instructions, first to one side and then to the other, but nobody paid any attention to him. They knew the rules. The most balls, in possession or across the opposite line, won, and nothing else mattered.

Massed on the field as they were, the freshmen could see their superiority in numbers, but they could also see that the sophomores knew what they were doing. There were just seven of those groups, one opposite each ball. It wasn't far across the field, maybe forty or fifty yards, and Timmy, standing in front of the third ball from the right, could see that the sophomores' faces showed cockiness and even elation, as if they were pleased by something that was going on. The freshmen around him were now developing a strained courage and a last-minute unity. He could hear them encouraging each other loudly. A few of them were running around yelling for order, shouting at their fellows to form groups, but nobody paid any real attention to them. Groups took partial form but dissolved into a chaotic common front again as soon as the self-appointed generals were gone. There was a moment of near silence. The wind drew off from the trees below, and then poured back over them like a wave.

In this last moment two boys ran out in front of each sophomore group, knelt quickly, side by side, and kicked themselves little starting pits, in which they braced like sprinters. Tony Barenechea thought he understood the tactics. He began to yell at the freshmen, through his hands, "Get your fastest men out front, '26; get your fastest men out front." Between yells he pushed at Timmy, saying, "You can run like hell, Timmy. This is one ball they ain't gonna get, by God. You hang on if it kills you." Then he kept saying, "We're right behind you, Timmy; we're right behind you."

But the whistle blew before the freshmen were set, and Timmy started badly. He saw that the first runner was going to beat him to the ball by yards, and slowed up to be able to go either way for the tackle. But the first runner came right past the ball, and the second, with plenty of time now, scooped it up. Then Timmy understood, and yelled, "Pass." It was happening everywhere. All the freshmen were yelling, "Pass." As Timmy balanced there, Tony hurtled by him, and made a diving tackle. The passer, who had been watching Timmy, was caught off guard. He went down flat and hard and the ball bounded high into the air. It struck again and the two armies flowed together over it. In a moment there were five big dogpiles on the field. Two of the passes had succeeded. Dust rose over each pile, like smoke from wet leaves burning, and blew into one shining haze across the field. Now and then one of the piles broke and streamed a little way toward one line or the other, and then was gathered again. It was all a phantom action in the golden dust and the gull cries of the girls. Timmy was still down in the bowels of the second pile when the final whistle blew and the upper classmen came charging in, tugging at arms and legs, yelling, "All over, all over; cut it out, you guys." He hadn't even touched a ball. All that was left of his shirt was the collar loop and the button band, and he was sweaty and dust-caked and covered with little red maps drawn by tumbleweed stickers and pebbles, but he still felt more silly than anything else.

The boys rested in clusters all over the hill, stretched out, or on their knees and hunched over, trying to get their breath. Somewhere in the mêlée, two boys had really been hurt, and the others curiously and impersonally watched them being helped off the field and driven away in a car. The marshal announced that the sophomores had won the rush five balls to two. Tim felt a little ashamed, but otherwise not much concerned. He wished he could get mad. Somehow it seemed much later in the afternoon, now, than it really was. Small, separate clouds, like fish with bright edges, swam slowly in the west over the Sierra. The wind made more pale serpents across the savanna of the treetops. The calling through the megaphones began again, and the two sides formed slowly for the second event, the tie-up. This time the sophomores showed a solid front too.

"Stick together," Tony kept saying. "Stick together and they can't get none of us."

"Both wrists and ankles have to be tied when you carry them over the line," the marshal called through the megaphone. "Freshmen carry them over on the north side, sophomores on the south. Wait till the checker has the guy's name. Most tied and over wins. Listen," he yelled, turning the megaphone up and down the field and toward both ends, "listen, you guys. No slugging, no knees, no kicking, no strangle holds, no ropes on the neck."

While he yelled, the freshmen kept telling each other fiercely, "Stick together, stick together." They were beginning to get angry because the sophomores had outsmarted them so easily in the first rush. Some of them were really angry because of personal encounters, and were swearing, and trying to see where their individual enemies were in the opposite ranks.

Timmy felt better than before the first rush, anyway. He wasn't nervous, and at least his blood was hot, and he felt a disgust with himself that was almost as good as rage. He and Tony and six other boys from the Orvis Ring were going to stick together. He looked around. Yes, they were all together.

The whistles blew, and he charged forward. He didn't even understand why this was a mistake until Harpy White, a senior, explained it to him on the way home. The sophomores didn't charge. They came forward slowly, separating into compact squads as they came. One of these squads closed around Timmy, and he didn't see his own bunch again. In a minute the field was covered with small, struggling groups, each with its cloud of dust. Sometimes shadowy figures broke from one group and charged across to another, their choked voices shouting encouragement. Others wandered indecisively, and then were suddenly yanked down into dusty turmoil, or swarmed under by four or five triumphant boys charging back in after lugging out a bound victim. Upper classmen who couldn't see enough of the battle through the dust filtered out and encircled the wrestling bunches. Voices husky with exhaustion and dust called out for help, called friends' names from skirmishes hidden by the crowd. When the marshal and the checkers were busy, prisoners who had worked off their bonds stole back into the battle.

In his first charge, Timmy grappled with a boy he didn't even see clearly. At once he was hit in the legs by another. A third was on his back, pulling him over by the throat. His neckties and ropes were snatched from him. For an instant he strained fiercely to stay on his feet, and then another weight heaved against the side of the pile and he went over. Hands began snatching for his wrists and ankles and he worked quickly to keep them free. It was funny, weighed under like that, not even to see who was working on his wrists and ankles, so that every touch and change was unexpected and mysterious. When he had finally counted four working on him, and seen no other freshmen, he kept up the struggle only as a matter of honor. It occurred to him, though, that this was not only futile but ridiculous. It would be much more sensible to lie still and allow himself to be bound and carried across, and then take it easy. He pictured himself, limp and philosophical, riding out between two sophomores, and began to laugh.

A circle of upper classmen had drawn around his prone indignity, and this made it even funnier, somehow. He went on laughing, but kept flipping over and back like a landed fish. He saw Harpy White watching him, and laughing too. "Attaboy, Timmy," Harpy yelled. "Give 'em hell, kid." It looked very funny to Harpy too. He choked and spluttered because of the dust when he laughed.

The four had him tied once, but before they could lift him, he kicked free of the noose on his ankles. They tied him again, but his wrists were bound only by a necktie, and while they were dragging him, he broke it, and managed to bring down one of his captors and pin him with a body hold which buried his own wrists beyond reach. While they pried him loose, he kicked his ankles free again. He even managed to get to his feet once, and had to be wrestled down once more before they could start all over to tie him.

The upper classmen were all laughing now, and yelling at the sophomores to hurry up and tie him, were they going to be all afternoon tying one frosh? One of the sophomores, the one he'd had the body hold on, lost his temper. When Timmy was down again, this boy sat on him, and bounced his weight up and down to knock the wind out of him, and leaned into his throat with a forearm, forcing his chin up and strangling him.

Timmy twisted his head to the side, trying to breathe. "No strangle holds," he wheezed, "no strangle holds."

At the same time he could feel the invisible work recommencing on his wrists and ankles. It was a rough rope on his right wrist, and it kept sliding and burning as it was tightened. He felt as if he were wrestling five matches, one each at his ankles, belly, throat and two wrists. The boys on his arms were pulling them together under the boy who was sitting on him.

"The hell you say," this boy growled. "Lay still, frosh, or I'll really give it to you, goddam you." He dug his elbow in under Timmy's ear, and leaned harder.

It was at this point that the rush changed from a silly game into a battle. The curse and the dig were like a charge of new energy to Timmy. He forgot that anyone was on his legs and arms, and threw himself over furiously. The boy astride him was pitched to the ground. Another was kicked by the driving feet, and sat off, bent over and holding his stomach with his arms. Timmy struggled to his knees, flailing blindly right and left with his bound fists, and heaving away from every grasp until he got to the boy who had been sitting on him. The boy was only half up. Timmy threw his whole weight against him, knocked him over again, and rolled heavily on his head. When the boy came out from under, he was wild too, and weeping. Timmy's hands pulled free, and he slugged at the red, crying face. The boy went down, and Timmy swung about on his knees and tackled another who had been tugging at his neck from behind. He thrust his shoulder in, hoping to break the knees. He wanted more than anything to hear the knees splinter when he hit them. The boy went over backwards, flat and hard. The weeping boy and two others closed over him again. "Now," Timmy thought, "a lot of time has passed. They don't have time to get me." With this return of a formulated idea, a recognition of limits, he felt a rush of fierce exultation. The three weren't even trying to tie him now, but just to hold him and punish him. But they couldn't do it. He didn't feel anything. He wrestled and slugged and tackled, and only felt the change of weight when they fell or came back. He could hear the circle of upper classmen, not laughing now, but yelling fiercely. He couldn't tell what they were yelling, though. There were too many of them yelling. The dust was blinding and stifling. In the center of the cloud he kept breaking up out of his besiegers and getting another free crack at one of them. The ankle rope came undone and pulled off, and sometimes he even got to his feet and swung two or three times before his legs were knocked out from under him again. Every time he was hit like that, so that it jarred, he would go berserk again and struggle only to get at the boy who had hit him last. It pleased him, like a wonderful gleam in his mind, every time he saw the red face of the boy who was cry-ing. The boy's nose and mouth were bleeding. He thought that probably his own were too. They'd been hit often enough. That idea pleased him too. He thought curiously, as if it were one more thread of restraint broken, "Now there's nothing to keep clean; now it's the works." Once, as he was pressed down from behind, he saw that his chest and belly were smeared with blood in which the dust was sticking darkly, and he wondered, like a very clear idea spoken in words, whether it was his own blood, or blood from the boy who was crying.

Toward the end of time, another big freshman, Teddy Munn, pushed his way through the watchers. He was trying to yell encouragement to Timmy, but was making only a loud, hoarse croaking. Together they actually got the weeping boy and the boy who had been kicked tied and carried across. This was a kind of triumphant joke. They were coming back in, looking for another, when the whistle blew.

Harpy White found Timmy standing in the middle of the field, staring at the ground. Harpy put an arm around him.

"Pooped?" he asked.

Timmy nodded. He couldn't talk. The fight was over, and suddenly all his seeing red was gone, and the new energy that had come with it and kept him from feeling anything was gone too. He was so weak he trembled, and didn't want to try to walk for fear he would fall down. It was a detached, slightly in-sane matter of pride that he should not fall down.

"Jeez, were you doin' battle," Harpy said.

"You got any way to get home?" he asked.

"Walk," Timmy whispered finally.

"On your hands and knees," Harpy snorted. "You go sit in my car and take a breather. I gotta find Alice. Left her around some place. Then we'll take you home."

Timmy finally saw Harpy's car, and very slowly walked to it, but his hand was too weak to open the door. He couldn't close his hand over the handle, or think of anything else to do about it. This seemed silly, and he laughed feebly to himself. He sat down on the running board and let his head hang. Once in a while, with an effort, he looked up. The golden dust had swept from the field and dissolved among the trees. There were scraps of rope and pieces of cloth all over the field. Some of the pieces of cloth gathered and rolled in the wind. Some of them had fluttering corners where they lay. The marshal announced that the sophomores had won, fifty-five to forty. It didn't matter. It was a satisfying victory for Timmy Hazard over the numerous forces of his conception of Timothy Hazard.

Harpy and Alice Maley, the girl he had gone to find, came over, and Timmy looked up when he saw their feet, and then stood up slowly, using his hands against the car.

"My God, Tim, you look like a bad dream," Harpy said, staring at him.

Alice was staring at him too. She wet her lips a little, but didn't say anything.

"See," Harpy told her, "I told you his eyes were green."

"Are your eyes really green, Tim?" he asked.

"No," Timmy whispered, feeling as if he were arranging a difficult paragraph into exact prose, "they're blue."

"Well, they aren't now. They're green, like a cat's."

"I got sore, I guess," Timmy whispered.

"You guess," Harpy said, and laughed. "Sore?" he said. "You were nuts."

He stopped laughing and stared at Timmy. Timmy was staring at him too, trying hard to see him clearly. His eyes kept wanting to get out of focus and blur everything and put it far off, the way they did sometimes in a day-dream.

"O.K.," Harpy said. "Don't start on me. I didn't do anything. Pile in."

"I can't open the door," Timmy whispered, and giggled.

Harpy opened the door, and then had to help him in. All the way home Harpy explained the tactics of the battle, and how the sophomores had won the tie-up by coming out slowly and keeping their groups, instead of charging and getting scattered, the way the freshmen had, but Timmy was thinking mostly that Harpy had called him Tim, without any diminutive, and that Alice Maley was afraid of him the way he looked now. He wondered, too, what happened to eyes to make them turn green when they were really blue.

When he got upstairs into the bathroom, he looked at himself in the mirror. He was a mess, all right, plastered white with dust, so that his face was a mask. Part of the blood had been his own, too. It made black streaks all around his nose and mouth, and his lower lip was huge. But his eyes were the queer thing. Not much wonder Harpy and Alice had stared at them. They even frightened him a little, they looked so big and wrong. At first the whole face looked like somebody else's, but even after he had touched it with his hands and made it his own, the eyes were still wrong, because they didn't look the way he felt. He felt weak and mildly happy and very sleepy and relaxed, but the eyes stared out fiercely, like those of a feeding hawk which has been disturbed, and they were really green, a kind of pale, jade green, like Pyramid Lake in the right light. He couldn't make them seem like his own eyes, or feel that he had any control over them. If he closed one of them, the other still glared bleakly at him. If he closed both and then opened them again, they were still coldly murderous. He wondered if they would ever be the right color again.

It required three slow baths to get the dirt out of his hair and hide. He had to make them slow, because he was too limp to move quickly. He seemed to have to think about it, and slowly direct energy to the desired region. Sometimes, when he tried to move faster, nothing happened. He would decide to pick up a piece of soap, and the hand wouldn't close over it, and when he had pushed the soap into place with the other hand, the arm wouldn't rise with it. Then, after a while, it would. Nevertheless he felt steadily and gently a new and satisfying power. He would lie there indolently, minutes at a time, observing complacently the intricate scratches upon his body and arms. Then he would come to, just before he fell asleep and slid down into the water. He had to wipe himself slowly too. When he looked at his eyes again, after that, they were the right color.

He fell asleep naked on top of his bed at five o'clock. At nine he woke. He was still slow and drowsy. He put on a shirt and trousers, went downstairs, ate a bowl of bread and milk in the kitchen, and went out onto the front porch. He sat there for an hour, feeling the cool wind through his shirt and on his bare feet and ankles, and listening to it in the poplars. The wine of conquest was gone out of him, but in the cool emptiness remained a nuclear conviction.

CHAPTER NINE: *About the Possible Significance of a Small Aspen as an Intermediary*

BILLY WILSON gave his party a couple of weeks after the battle. It was a long way from the race-track quarter to the Wilsons', out in the open meadows by the South Virginia Road, but Tim's mother had patiently nagged her way to a bicycle for him. The party was to start with supper, and the sun was still up when Tim pedaled out onto the highway. The beneficent fingers of the poplar shadows were laid upon the pavement and the meadows. The light and the air were one stillness, and the far-off twanging of the red-wing blackbirds in the tule marshes was clear though faint. The horses and cattle in the fields moved quietly, a step at a time, cropping with short jerks of their heads. The isolated mountain, which must once have made an island in the valley to the east, burned softly, and the influence of Mt. Rose, lengthening her shadow with those of the trees, finally to absorb them, was strong and steady, and made a gentle excitement of promise. Tim, wheeling slowly along the edge of the highway, looked constantly around, near and far, as he always did when he got outside the city, and was exalted by the spacious peace. He wasn't sure that he wanted to go to the party. He didn't know who else was going. He didn't know what they would do after supper, but he guessed, with some trepidation at the thought of such intimacy with strangers. He was happy now, by himself, and whatever happened at Billy's, he knew it would disturb him.

He turned into Billy's driveway, and left his wheel out back against the new garage. There were chickens in a fenced yard back there, and rabbits in a double-decked hutch. The chicken house and the hutch were made of new, unpainted wood. There were still deep and hardened ruts in the driveway and the back yard, and the red and purplish brick and white woodwork of the house had new, strong color. The house was wide open to the valley and the mountains, because its trees were also new, and seemed to huddle about the house rather than to defend it. Tim talked to the chickens and the rabbits. He felt that they were with him in a league of dumb adoration of being, opposed to strangeness and to first parties.

Finally he went slowly around to the front porch to expose himself. It wasn't bad. There were only boys there so far, and he knew them all. Billy took him in to see the house, which had pale, shining, hardwood floors, a smell of fresh plaster, and furniture that wasn't yet sure it was in the right place. While they were still inside, they heard the voices of the first girls.

"Well, there's some skirts finally. Always late," Billy said. He didn't sound as indifferent as that, though. He felt the same change in the air that Tim did. Something was coming to flower. The calm, clear and lonely air of autumn became springlike, full of the soft, distant thunders of flooding waters, and of intimations of mysterious and ancient futures. Thoughts took erratic wing, like swallows hunting in the air in the early evening. Immediately there was a great deal more talk and laughter on the front porch.

Billy was about to take Tim upstairs, but he said, "Well, that's about all there is worth seeing," and they went out onto the porch. There were four girls. They looked at Billy and Tim with bright, quick, experimenting eyes and laughed a great deal at something bold which Billy said, which wasn't very funny. Billy at once entered into the jockeying for preferment which was the real purpose of the rapidly shifting talk about school, dates, the house and the coming football season. Tim didn't know any of the girls, even by name. He had seen them in the halls at school, that was all. Billy never slowed things up with introductions, so Tim leaned against the concrete rail of the porch and appeared to be earnestly laughing at the jokes and insults, while he really thought about Mary. He became lonesome for Mary, without realizing that this was the first time he had thought much about her since high school had opened. It seemed to him that he had spent most of his life being separated from Mary by mere circumstance, and all of his life feeling lonely for her.

When Billy took the girls in to see the house, the other boys trooped after to protect their gains, and Tim was left alone. He sat down on the top step and looked at a very small aspen on the lawn. The aspen was standing out in the deep sunlight, beyond the shadow of the roof, which pointed at it like the shadow on a huge sun dial. Tim could feel no motion in the air at all, yet a few of the little aspen's eighteen or twenty leaves were constantly shivering and twinkling. It made Tim feel that he was in the presence of some vast, benevolent and very gentle force which he was too dull to perceive. Once in a while all the leaves would tremble at the same time, making a faint rustling, as if in an access of joyous but nervous expectation, and Tim would feel a sympathetic ascension. The heavier world of mountains and the house, of the voices inside and the burden of his own body, receded beyond the perimeter of his mind as beyond a very far-removed horizon, and he was full of the motion and light of the little aspen.

Perhaps this five-minute communion, stirring nearly forgotten leaves of the magic wilderness within him also, gradually becoming one tremulous expectation of something, performed the last preparation for Tim's conversion. He has compared it to another brief interlude, which came upon him years later:

"I was sitting on the front steps of a ranch house in an orchard. It was the first warm night in the spring. I sat there, barefooted and in my shirt sleeves, enlarged and unthinking. There was a full, white moon just up. I could see shining fragments of it among the leaves of a big cottonwood on the other side of the orchard, and it made a gleaming path on the irrigation pond beyond. The light was as soft as the air, and powdery where it reached the ground among the trees. Near the door stood an almond tree in blossom. Whenever I think of that night, I remember the sweetness of the flowering almond. Three of the ranch dogs lay in the dust under the almond tree. These dogs usually took a great delight in chasing anything that stirred, and sometimes made trouble by running the horses in the pasture after dark, but that night they were as quiet as I was. The only motion anywhere, save the majestic rising of the moon, was the soft coming and going of bats.

"Out of this absolute quiet, a whippoorwill dropped before me like an apple from the stem. He lit without a sound, in the center of a moonlit patch of dust, and at once my senses were wide awake. He huddled there so long that I began to wonder if he had been stricken by something I'd neither seen nor heard, but I didn't move for fear I'd start the dogs and they'd jump him.

"Suddenly he fluttered up a foot or two, and dropped back again. The movement gave me a sharp impression that he'd been hurt, as if I'd felt the injury myself, but a moment later he leapt again and when he continued to rise and fall silently in that moonlit space, I realized that he was hunting insects. I watched the hypnotic dance as if hunting myself. Once the bird dropped within a few feet of the nose of a chow bitch who was the quickest and most intelligent of all the dogs. I held my breath, but the bird rested there for a long minute, and the bitch didn't lift her nose from her paws or change her breathing. She wasn't asleep, either. I could see the faint glitter of her watching eyes. The whippoorwill rested there, scanning the dusk. None of the dogs moved. Either the bird was invisible and inaudible to them, which didn't seem possible, since I, with my far poorer senses, could both see it and sometimes hear its feathering, or there was some universal truce in force that night.

"It was in this moment that I felt the birth of the world, and the deep, sad kinship of everything in it. I had considered this kinship, of course, innumerable times, but I knew it then, beyond question. It was revelation. It was in me without an idea. All that I had ever considered, argued and doubted about universal kinship, by bones and by atoms, by the seasons of fruiting and of death, by the immortality of generation, by the universes of space and of the grain of dust, was in that instant established and yet made a childish tinkering with notions.

"The bats still flew, like small, vague ideas among the trees of the orchard. The moment endured without losing intensity, and became an illusion of dissolution. I was partitioned among all things, and free of the limits of any of them, or of time or of space. I felt so near the center of what is, the answer, that a little fear, half joy, raised the hair on my neck. I actually felt that if I held out my two hands, the answer would be in them, and I was hungry for it and afraid of it at the same time.

"Then the whippoorwill rose again, dropped off to one side in the air, and fled away among the trees and up and over them, and I lost him against a clump of cottonwoods down by the pasture. The dogs lay still, as I sat still, and the sensation of immensely important nearness ebbed slowly. For a moment, nevertheless, I had belonged. I had the talisman."

CHAPTER TEN: *In Which Tim Feels the Touch of the Quaking Aspen*

SO TIM sat there alone on the steps, looking at the young aspen trembling in the sunset, and five minutes went by.

A Cadillac sedan drove up and stopped at the edge of the road in front of the house. A small girl got out of the front seat, closed the door and stood talking to the driver, a man who wore glasses and had a deathly weary expression. The girl's arms were straight down at her sides, and her hands were closed into fists. She was wearing a brown-and-gray plaid skirt, with thin lines of red and yellow in it, and a brown-velvet jacket with a high, close collar, like the collar of a Russian blouse. The collar and cuffs of the jacket were red and yellow plaid, and the jacket came just to her waist. She wore no overcoat and no hat. Her fine hair, cut in a Dutch bob, stirred a little, like the lesser movements of the aspen, in some faint passage of air. Tim guessed, from the way she stood, that her apprehension about coming here was even wilder than his own had been, and his own returned when he remembered that he was alone on the porch to meet her.

The man to whom she was talking nodded, said something final, and started the car. He turned it around in the next side road and drove back past. The girl was still standing there, and the man smiled at her and waved one hand gently. The girl quickly raised her hand halfway. Not until the car was almost out of sight did she turn around and start up the walk.

Tim knew her then; that is, he remembered having seen her at the race track and in her mortification before the school assembly, and it seemed to him that she had been very dear to him for years. When she reached the steps, he rose, and she stopped and looked up at him and made a quick, difficult smile, and then quickly looked away from him and stopped smiling. All her movements were quick, like those of a bird. Tim didn't put it that way, of course, but he realized that she also was devouring the apple of life a peck at a time.

"Am I too early?" she asked.

Tim was trembling, but said casually, "Oh, no. There's a lot of them here. They're all inside now."

"Oh," she said.

Tim looked at her, and then at the aspen. She looked at the steps.

"Aren't there any other girls here yet?" she asked.

"Oh, yes," Tim told her. "They're all inside too. I guess they're just looking at the house," he added. "They'll probably be back out in a minute. Billy's just showing them the house."

She nodded.

"It's a brand-new house, you know," Tim said.

"Yes."

"They just moved in. It's all brand new."

She nodded quickly once. She always nodded once only, like a peck.

Tim had an inspiration. "I guess the party's a kind of house warming," he said.

She looked at him, and then away, across the meadows to the south.

"Do you want to go in and see the house?" he asked her.

She shook her head once.

"Well, don't you want to sit down?" he asked, after a long silence. "You might as well come up and sit down. Billy'll be out in a minute."

She came up the steps quickly, and pulled herself up onto the rail and folded her hands in her lap. Her feet didn't reach the floor of the porch.

Tim remembered the boldness he had discovered in battle, and how Alice Maley had looked at him in fascination, but it didn't help. He was more confused and doubtful now than he had been before the football rush. It wasn't the same, of course. He was also having bright instants of delight, although they didn't last. He was in a great hurry to do something; he didn't know what. He only knew the world had begun to revolve twice as fast, that night after night was advancing apace, and he must do something, or at least say something, before it was too late.

"It's nice out here, isn't it?" he said.

"Yes," she said. She looked up quickly at the mountains across the valley, and then down again. Most of the valley was in shadow now, but the mountain like an island and the range along the east were glowing more quietly and fervently than ever.

There was a loud giggling and some scuffling going on upstairs in the house. Then there was a loud thump and a burst of laughter. The girl darted a look at the screen door, then looked at her hands again.

"I guess there's some monkey business going on," Tim explained. "There's most always some monkey business going on when Billy's around."

She didn't say anything, and he asked, "Do you know Billy?"

She glanced at his eyes, and then looked down at the bronze buckle saying RENO HIGH SCHOOL on the belt of his new cords. He felt that the words on the buckle were probably writhing.

"Not very well," she said. "Do you?" she asked, glancing at his eyes again. Each time she looked straight at his eyes that way, there was a shocking fierceness in her own.

"Yes. We went to the Orvis Ring together. We were in the same class at the Orvis Ring."

"Oh."

The crowd inside was coming downstairs, clattering and laughing. The world again accelerated toward night.

"Which school did you go to?" Tim asked desperately.

"The Mt. Rose," she said.

Billy came out the screen door, slamming it clear back against the wall. The others came pouring out behind him and spread all over the porch. There were new guests coming, too. Another car had stopped out front. Practically the whole world had surrounded them all of a sudden, and now the important words would never get said.

Billy assumed a swashbuckling stance, with his hands upon his hips. "Well, well, look who's here," he said loudly.

The girl slid down to her feet and stood there, and said, "Hello."

"Why didn't somebody tell me you were here?" Billy roared. "What do they think I been waiting for? Tim, you old double-crosser, what you think I been waiting for anyway?

"You're gonna be my partner," he told the girl. "You're gonna be my girl."

He held his hand out to her as if to shake hands. She put her hand into it quickly. He pulled her over beside him and drew her arm through his. "Anybody else that double-crosses me," he said, and thrust his chin out. Everybody laughed, and the girl laughed quickly too, glancing at them and flushing, and then becoming pale.

Two couples came up the walk from the car, and another car came right behind theirs. Billy had to let go of the girl to meet them. He led everybody inside. The girl often disappeared in all the moving around them, but, when Timmy could see her, she seemed to be feeling better. Often she was laughing. It was brief laughter, and she bent over a little and threw her head back to make it, but while she was laughing, she would look longer, terribly long sometimes, at whoever it was had made her laugh, and her eyes would be narrowed by delight, and shining. Tim didn't think about where he was, or even remember that he existed as a recognizable body, but he was thinking about the girl all the time in a hunting swallow way, and kept finding himself in the same part of the room she was in. Billy was always there too, though. Often Billy would have hold of her arm, as he had on the porch, and once he even had his arm around her.

Tim saw Mrs. Wilson, a small, quick woman with a big smile and glasses, lighting the candles on the table in the dining room. He began to hope so strongly that he would sit beside the girl that soon he believed it would happen that way. When they all went into the dining room, and he saw that she was going to sit on the other side of the table, and clear up at the other end, beside Billy, he felt sharply wronged.

Big shadows of the party moved on the new, bare plaster walls. Through the window, blue dusk showed over the valley. Against the light of the yellow candles inside, this blue was a very deep, periwinkle blue, which looked too heavy to be in the air. There were three bowls of stiff, bright yellow-and-orange flowers on the table between the candles, and red, yellow and orange cracker favors by the plates. The silver and glass and the water in the tumblers gleamed and twinkled in the candle light. The linen was new, and its pattern of ferny foliage gleamed like silver too.

Billy snapped his favor in the girl's face, so that she winced and jerked her head back, but then he immediately leaned over and put his ear against the one she was holding. She laughed, and then, with her lips set in apprehensive primness, snapped the favor in his ear. He pretended to be in agony first, and then to be partially deafened. When she said something to him, he would lean forward with his hand cupped behind his ear, and say loudly, "What was that, hey? You'll have to talk louder. I'm a little deaf, you know. Explosion in my youth." Each time he did something like this he would put his face close to hers, as if inviting her to put her lips right against his ear, and she would lean away from him a little and get very red, but then double over in a quick spasm of laughter. Tim felt accompanying changes course through him every time her expression changed.

Colored tissue-paper caps came out of the favors. Everybody put them on and assumed poses, or made deals to exchange them because of their color or shape or to indicate choice and hope. The caps were shaped like fezzes, cocked hats, dinks and dunce caps. There were paper tassels or plumes or feathers on all but the dinks, which had little cardboard buttons on top. Everybody laughed at the others in their caps, or made loud insults about the way the wearers' personalities or physical characteristics were exposed by the caps. Tim saw Billy make the girl trade caps with him. She received a yellow cocked hat with a red plume, which looked ridiculous and wonderful on her. The one she gave Billy was a red fez with a drooping black tassel. Billy set it on at a forward angle, jumped off his chair, squatted until his knuckles dangled on the floor, and then started looking around at everybody with quick jerks of his head, and scratching his ribs with an upturned hand.

"Who'll be my organ grinder?" he asked in a falsetto voice. "Who'll be my organ grinder?"

Everybody laughed, and two or three boys began to sing loudly, and out of tune, songs the organ grinder might have played.

Tim felt his own cap yanked from his head. He looked around, and the girl beside him was holding it away from him, behind her, and offering hers. She was leaning way over toward him, as if she expected to be kissed. She had a big mouth, and was grinning very broadly. There was something in her eyes and mouth that made Tim think of oil. He didn't know her. He made a laborious grin, and called her a thief, with a depressed sensation that he hadn't made it sound very funny or friendly, but more as if he meant it, and took her cap and put it on. It was a blue dunce cap, and he tried to make up for calling her a thief as if he meant it by making an idiotic face with crossed eyes.

He wasn't very successful at that either. He didn't even feel funny. The girl, however, was nearly crippled by laughter.

"Oh, you're just a scream," she gasped. "Positively a scream," she shrieked.

Later the girl on the other side of him kept putting her arm through his, forcing the two of them into an appearance of intimacy. Each time she would confide to him something about what one of the others was doing, something any fool could see for himself. This embarrassed him, because she had a large, soft body, like a mature woman's, with heavy upper arms and breasts, and he could feel her give like a warm pillow under the pressure of his shoulder and elbow. But when he looked at the girl in the yellow cap, she was never watching him after all. She was usually looking with sober determination at her plate, though too often she would be curled over, laughing quickly and blushing at something Billy had said. Tim was trying all the time to hear what Billy was saying to her. He wanted to hear her name. He wanted to hear what she said too, because it might show how much she liked Billy. But he couldn't hear anything, because first the cushiony girl would cotton onto him and whisper, "Look at Sheik. He has a silver cigarette case. Doesn't he think he's something?" and squeeze his arm, and then the oily girl would seize his arm on the other side, and shake him, and gasp within two inches of his nose, "Lookit what Benny's doing," and then rock back, pulling him with her, and shriek, "Isn't he a riot? Oh, I think he's a scream." Tim felt all mixed up.

It was the oily girl who told him what he wanted to know, though. She suddenly decided that she wanted to say something to the girl in the yellow cap, and she leaned out over the table and yelled, "Rachy," and when that didn't penetrate the hubbub, went up an octave and screamed, "Rachel, hey, Rachel, Rachel, Rachel," until everybody else stopped talking and laughing, and Rachel looked at her, and so did everybody else, and then all she did was point at Billy Wilson and shout, "Don't you believe him, Rachel. He's just an old sheik himself."

This made Rachel very red, and she apologized to Billy with her eyes and then looked down. But it wasn't quite as stupid as Tim felt it was. He didn't understand that it was really meant as a compliment to the boy called Sheik, who was sitting right across the table from the oily girl. Sheik understood, and grinned at her. But anyway, that was the name, Rachel. Tim sat there and watched her and thought about the name.

After supper, Billy led them all into the living room. "Let's play something," he said.

"What?"

"I know," one of the girls said. "Drop the handkerchief."

There was groaning. She was reminded that she was in high school now, and was questioned about her age and mentality.

"Charades," another girl said, and there was more groaning.

There was some hope about musical chairs, but Billy said they couldn't play that because of the new floor, and anyway there was no piano and the new phonograph hadn't come yet.

There was more groaning about Teakettle.

"Oh, let's play something some fun," Billy said. "I'll tell you what. Let's play spin-the-bottle."

Tim didn't know what spin-the-bottle was, except that it was probably a boy-girl game and embarrassing, because several of the boys whooped and laughed, and the girl with the big mouth suddenly clutched him by the arm, as if to save herself from falling in a paroxysm of laughter, and when she got barely enough breath, squealed, "He *would* want to play that."

Tim saw that Rachel also either didn't know the game, or was afraid of it. She was standing like a soldier by herself at the other end of the couch, trying to smile and look as if she understood. There was a row of many, small, red-and-yellow plaid buttons down the front of her velvet jacket. They bound the jacket closely over her sharp, small breasts, and he could see how quickly she was breathing.

Some of the boys were pushing the couch out of the way against the fireplace. Tim helped to roll the rug and put it against the wall. Billy stood out in the middle of the shining floor with an empty pop bottle in his hand.

"O.K., here we go," he yelled. "Everybody get in a big ring. First a boy, then a girl, all the way round like that."

He came over and dragged Rachel into the ring, and then went back out in the middle. "O.K.," he said again. "No moving. You gotta stay right where you are."

He laid the bottle down on its side, and spun it between his thumb and finger. The bottle twinkled rapidly, glittered as it slowed down, and finally lay still and gleaming, with its neck pointing at a boy. There was lamentation, as if this were a disappointment.

"Be a fish," Billy told him.

The boy lay down full length on the floor, and vaguely imitated some sort of a swimming creature. He was mildly applauded and heavily insulted.

"You spin now," Billy told him.

The game went on. The modest purpose of its first stage was to inflict upon the person chosen by the bottle a physical maneuver entailing some indignity. The transition period began when the dark boy called Sheik, who wore a college-cut suit and a red necktie, was told to go around the circle and bow to each girl and kiss her hand. There were fake protests from the girls and cheers from the boys. One boy yelled, "That ain't nothin' for you, is it, Sheik?" When Sheik went around the circle the girls giggled, and posed haughtily, like movie countesses. Rachel became red and then white, and Sheik had to reach for her hand. When he kissed it, she had a spasm of laughter.

After that all the penalties were of the same sort, and everyone watched the spinning bottle intently, and sometimes a victim would try to change his place when he saw that the bottle might pick him. Timmy had to get down on his knees before each girl, and touch his forehead to her right hand, as in token of fealty. When he finished this labor he was sweating, although it wasn't hot in the room, for the door and the windows were open, so that the night breathed in, and pale moths came and quivered upon the screens or drummed against them. He believed that the only hand he could still feel on his forehead was

Rachel's, which was small and cold. He felt that probably there was a sacred mark left by her fingers, their imprint shining like a light.

It was Rachel who ended spin-the-bottle before its possibilities were fully explored. When the bottle picked her, the ringmaster ordered her to go around the circle and kiss each boy on both cheeks. Rachel stood like the soldier. The fields of her soul were given over to battle. Some of the boys offered loud advice. One of them cried that he would take two in the middle instead of one on each side, and everybody laughed explosively, and then stopped laughing suddenly, and only giggled. They all felt their personal futures involved in the battle Rachel was fighting.

Rachel was very red. She made quick little gasping laughs, and looked quickly at different girls, but when she wasn't laughing her lower lip trembled. Her hands were pulling at each other in front of her. Still she didn't say anything. The circle broke up, and she was besieged. She began to shake her head. She was bombarded by arguments, ridicule and doubts of her innocence. She kept shaking her head and trying hard to laugh, but getting further and further from really laughing. Tim was a prisoner watching his own destroyed. Even Billy's powers were weakened by internal dissension. His desire to remain the champion of the liberals was checked by the threat to his personal privilege.

The siege was lifted by accident. One of the boys, intending only to add his bit to the popular pressure, yelled, "I know what's the trouble with her. She wants to play post-office, so we can't see her, don't you, Rachy?" But the suggestion touched a common desire, and at once pressure groups began to form to make it a real plan. A few extremists continued the personal fight though. They agreed to post-office, but worked up a chant, "Rachy has to go first, Rachy has to go first."

Rachel dumbly opposed this action also, and finally the chant died because she could hardly keep herself from crying. The debate shifted to method. One faction insisted that the choice should be personal, and the other that the names should be drawn. Feeling the swing of opinion, Billy voiced the majority preference.

"We'll draw," he yelled. "Then it won't be just one fellow getting all our mail or something." He was cheered, and also accused of fearing to risk himself in open contest. He began to give orders.

"Everybody write his name on a slip of paper," he yelled. He went into a side room and came back with several sheets of paper and a fistful of pencils. While he was folding the sheets together and tearing them into strips, he was assailed as having had the whole thing plotted out beforehand. Tim signed like an illiterate putting his name to a contract before a lawyer he mistrusted. He didn't know how post-office was played either, except that it must be an advance over spin-the-bottle because there was secrecy connected with it. Billy collected all the boys' names in one hat, and the girls' in another.

"First one I pick is post-master," he announced.

There was silence as he drew a slip from the girls' hat.

"Pauline Chester," he announced.

There was an uproar. The bosomy girl in whom Tim's elbow had been buried at supper stepped forth.

"Where do I go?" she asked, when it was quiet.

"The study is the post-office," Billy announced. "You go on in," he said to Pauline. "Then I'll hold the hat in for you."

"No lights," somebody cried.

"No lights," everybody shouted.

"No fakes, either," somebody else shouted. "You have to really kiss. Anybody that won't really kiss has to kiss everybody." This rule was adopted by acclaim, although there were a few skeptics who wanted to know how it was going to be enforced when they couldn't see what was going on. "If they're both a-scared, how do we know what they did?"

This simple game did not grow dull. There was an outburst as each name was read. There was an intense quiet during each interval in which Billy held the hat, and the hand from the dark room reached out and chose a name. There were fleeting expressions of dread or doubt, but also the room was electrical with particular hopes. On a few faces was the blanched agony of the card players in the Suicide Club. As each post-master emerged, he was hailed, belittled and cross-examined. The girls all attempted to appear unmoved by this public prominence. The boys, assuming the license of the double standard, came out in different ways. Some looked knowing and remained silent. Some expressed glee. One skinny youth, blond and freckled, whose pants were too short, came out with his hands clasped before him, his face raised in praise of the Lord who gave such bliss, and his knees sagging and wavering. This interpretation was popular, and was played frequently, with variations. The most successful imitator was practically original. He came out on his hands and knees, rolled over, and expired in jerking agony.

Even though the game was turned over to Fortune, the spear of personal implication was felt often. There was loud booing when one girl chanced to pick the name of a boy who spent most of his time with her anyway. There was laughter and satire when a notoriously unilateral affair attained the secret climax. Loud suggestions for deliberate manipulation were made to Billy, and he pretended to act upon them. Billy himself was called, and somebody else took over the hat. If the door opened too soon, the deed was questioned. If it remained closed a long time, protest, scandalized accusation, and expressions of envy rose into a storm.

Tim kept looking back at Rachel. The davenport had been turned around, and she was sitting on one arm of it. She laughed every time everybody laughed, but never said anything. Tim understood that she was practicing the art of disappearing into the background. He was saying a good many things himself, but they all arose from that same desire to appear inconspicuous, and most of them were just poor imitations of previous successes. Each time it was a girl's hand working around the door, his breath and his pulse were suspended. He took as a sweet if brief reprieve each period during which a boy held office. It was in these moments that he made his few really witty comments which could be quoted. Only one hope, and that half dread, remained constant in him. The numerical chances of entering the study with Rachel were small. Still, he kept thinking how it would be, and each time the chance came up that it might be, suddenly the inside diplomatic preliminaries appeared insurmountable, and a desert without water would begin to expand between his chair and the door of the study.

There were several repeats, one boy being called so often that there were accusations of fixing, and still Rachel wasn't called, and neither was Tim. Tim allowed himself guardedly to begin to hope both ways. He began to look at Rachel even more often, hoping to establish a union by means of their isolation, but she would accept no ally.

The skinny boy who had first swooned was acting as panderer. The dark boy with the red necktie was in the study. The dark hand held up the slip, and the skinny boy took it. He read solemnly, "Rachel Wells."

When the skinny boy said "Rachel" Tim's breath stopped as if it had been his own name. He didn't even hear as far as Wells.

"About time," somebody shouted.

"Do a good job on her, Sheik."

"One ain't enough, Sheik. Take one for all of us."

"Two, you mean," somebody amended.

This became a chorus. "Two for each of us, Sheik."

Finally Rachel got up and walked across to the study door quickly, smiling hard and with her arms down straight. She was cheered and hooted. At the door she stood and waited. She was speaking. Everybody became quiet. She was making a last desperate appeal to Pander.

"I don't have to pick one too, do I?"

She received a great many replies, among which Pander's was lost. It required another moment to quell her own rebellion, and then she entered. The skinny boy put his finger to his lip and his ear to the door. There was silence outside. There was also silence inside. The skinny boy straightened up, shrugging his shoulders and spreading his hands.

The boy called Sheik chose to be non-committal when he came out, and so far as the public was concerned Rachel remained a figure of mystery, as inviolate as upon her entrance. Her hand chose and the skinny boy intoned, "Tim Hazard."

This was also greeted as overdue, and Tim received a good many suggestions. The desert between his chair and the door swelled and sank under him. He entered the difficult portal, and it was closed behind him. He was standing in absolute darkness. He also felt that many-eared silence outside. He waited. Since she was already there, and had seen him come in, Rachel should make the overture. He didn't even know where she was in there. He couldn't even remember what shape the room was, or where the furniture was. He stood very still, except for the roaring in his brain, and listened. Rachel finally made the overture.

"Well," she whispered hard, "don't take all night. I don't want to be in here all night with any boy."

It was impossible to tell from the whisper how angry or tearful or merely matter-of-fact and in a hurry she was.

"Where are you?" he whispered.

This became at once, to him, a question of great significance. The dark study took on the dimensions of a dead planet in eternal night, and across its vast wastes, its tundras and glaciers and cold and whispering seas, he ran and swam and climbed frantically, in quest of a tiny, solitary, lost, perhaps dying, Rachel.

"Here," Rachel whispered.

"Where?"

"Right here," she whispered angrily, "behind the door."

It was shocking that she was so close. Even their whispering had not told him she was so close. He moved only one step, with his hand out, and touched her. He was shivering with expectation, dread and ignorance. It was the velvet jacket he had touched. He was terribly ashamed and bewildered. He didn't know what part of the velvet jacket he had touched. She didn't say anything, or move to help him.

"Is that you?" he asked. The word "you" in his mind began with a capital and from its letters arose tongues of oriflamme.

"It's my sleeve," she whispered.

He ventured to close his hand.

"Hurry up, will you?" she whispered sharply.

He felt that this was an accusation of timidity. He put his other arm around her waist. She was rigid and trembling. It was impossible to pass this barrier of fear. He was the hunter paralyzed by the eyes of the deer that has turned.

The tittering began outside. It had seemed to Tim that the laws of time were revoked. Now they returned in force, at once, and even retroactively. Probably he had been in this darkness with Rachel for a hundred years, and they would never dare to come out. The comments began in the living room.

"Hurry up, will you?" Rachel said again, almost out loud this time. He felt a paroxysm, as of a breath of wind through the aspen, pass down the little body in his arm.

He stammered when he whispered, "You don't really want me to kiss you really, do you?"

"I don't care what you do," she whispered, "only for goodness' sakes do something, will you?"

Tim was bewildered by a great tenderness. He was trembling more than she was. He had no pride and wanted only to do what she wished.

The comments outside had become a clamor.

Suddenly she was pushing him off and whispering, "Let go of me, will you? Let go of me."

She got him loose from her, and scurried past him, and he heard the door knob rattle as she found it, and then saw her in the beam of light as she opened the door quickly. She controlled herself enough to go out slowly, but her face must have given something away about which he wasn't sure himself, because she was met by a sudden outburst of laughter and cries.

Tim started to follow her out, and this brought on another burst of laughter.

"Oh, no, you don't," the skinny boy said, and pushed him back in. Tim remembered that he was supposed to pick a name also.

"What's the matter, Tim? Want more?" somebody called.

Another answered him. "Go on. I bet they didn't even kiss.

I bet it was a fake. They just stayed in there to make us think it was something."

Everybody began to ask Rachel if it had been just a fake.

Tim reached into the hat in the opening of the doorway, and then the slip was taken from him.

After a moment the skinny boy announced, "Pauline Chester."

The bosomy girl, the girl like cushions or a woman, came in. The door closed. There was nothing religious about this encounter, but there was no delay either. There was nothing said. Tim reached out to let her know where he was. She took his hand and worked up along his arm and closed on him. He tried to simulate co-operation, but that probably wouldn't have mattered anyway. It was a long and suffocating kiss. For one minute he forgot Rachel, but not because of any change of heart.

CHAPTER ELEVEN: *About the Many Early Lives of Timothy Hazard*

IT WAS late when Tim got to bed that night, but he began a new variation on the world's greatest story. First he had to depose Mary, in order to make room for the new Isolt; so Mary, now some nameless lady who had plighted her troth with Sir Timothy-Tristram, became unable to bear the stench of the grievous wound Marholt had left in her lord, and ran off before daybreak with a visiting knight who looked quite a bit like the boy called Sheik. This left Timothy-Tristram sunk in despondency, but also honorably released from his vows, and taking with him only his trusty squire, Gouvernail, he sailed forth to seek death or healing at the hands of Isolt in Ireland. After long and stormy mischance, they entered the cliff-bound cove at last, and dropped anchor and sail. The moon stood far down toward the sea, and the cove was sad in its light. Above shone the orange window slits of the King of Ireland's castle, and there, from her chamber in the highest tower, Isolt-Rachel, sleepless with cosmic melancholy, gazed down upon the foreign craft.

While debating whether to call her Isolt and think Rachel, or call her Rachel and think Isolt, Tim discovered that he couldn't remember Rachel's real last name, and put aside the legend for a period of research. He was sure he had heard the name, but he couldn't remember who had said it, or just when. He worked carefully through the party, from Rachel's first hello to the good nights, and two or three times the name glimmered just beyond the light of his memory, but each time he reached for it, it flew softly back into the darkness. The telephone directory would be no help without her last name. He discovered that all he knew about her was that she had gone to the Mt. Rose School, which was in a region as unfamiliar and extensive as Tibet. It was impossible to wait till Monday when this was only Friday night, and besides, he couldn't very well follow her home from school, or ask her where she lived, or ask anyone else either. On the whole, this mystery was stimulating. Sir Timothy-Tristram was going to have real trouble in the pursuit of his one true love. He decided to call her Isolt, though keeping his eye and his adoration strictly upon the face and the form of Rachel, and re-entered the realm of legendary trouble.

Grim with pain, weakness and disillusionment, he sat in the stern of his boat, plucked softly at his harp, and lifted his face and his voice to the castle. Always before, Tim had been content merely to imagine the hearers stabbed to the heart by the beauty and sorrow of the world in this song, and then get on to its after-effect and a whirlwind of incident. This time, however, he felt dedicated to a superior creation, and invented all the words for the song, and came so near to singing its minor and piercing melody that his Adam's-apple went up and down. Admitting a probable improvement due to much later recollection, the words went like this:

You in the great halls, unharnessed after battle,
Easy after the hunt, fed and leaning to the fire with the
cup in your hand while the long dogs sleep,
Hear the wanderer and raise your heads.

I sing of the sea that hissed; my face
Was without sleep that turned to the dawn where the
clouds ran,
My hand grown to the tiller that turned in wind
When the craft stood on the peak of water and leaned
down.
I beheld the shadow of my friend through this sail;
I came as the wind told.
Now wait I here, in need of your words, your hands.

Here surely is the one I seek in the world;
Here is the one who will cleave to me surely.
After the gale, her voice;
After the fist of ocean on the planks, her hand on my
wrist, her fingers on my face;
After the tumult, then in the forest closed from wind
Over us at daybreak the birds beginning slowly
The anthem of our love that grows.

Originally he conceived the last stanza as shifting into a major key and gradually rising to triumph, but, after several experiments, decided it was better to lift only the last two words, like a promise. When the entire song had been rendered once more, without interruption, he went on to his healing by Isolt, his tournament triumphs in her name, the love potion, which he made merely symbolic, feeling the real thing to be a degradation, and the scurvy wiles of Mark. Perhaps because of anticipation, Mark somewhat resembled Mr. Hazard, though it was so hard to imagine Mr. Hazard in velvet and wiles that sometimes the king looked more like Rachel's father, if that had been Rachel's father driving the Cadillac. The legend was subject to some revision during the exile in Brittany, when Sir Timothy-Tristram decided that it would be fairer to strike out that first part where Mary had been a deserter, and reinstate her as Isolt of the White Hands. You couldn't make Tristram look too good where Isolt of the White Hands was concerned anyway, which was true enough, and besides, the change added interest to the exile and built up the fascination of Isolt-Rachel by giving reality to her ascendency. At last, on the way up the dark and clammy staircase to the fatal rendezvous in the tower, Sir Timothy-Tristram fell asleep in spite of himself, so that he was spared the problem of finding a new way out of the trap. He had escaped that trap so often with Isolt-Mary, in spite of the older authorities on the subject, that his resources were running low. His mind had already caught a sufficient glimpse of the lived-more-or-less-happily-ever-after scene ahead anyway, so it didn't matter too much. Sir Timothy-Tristram and Isolt-Rachel would have fled to an empty hermit's cell in the midst of a forest and led a life of simple garments, spare, vegetarian diet, cold-water cleanliness and abundant and innocent communion with God, wild creatures and each other. This was a typical Hazard finale of this period. Occasionally he had slain Mark in the tower, assumed the burden of the kingdom, to the great joy of all the subjects, and been wed with tremendous music, stained-glass light and circumstance, to Isolt-Mary. Once in a great while he had even approached, with sad and tender devotion, the velvet couch upon which Isolt-Mary lay awaiting him. Usually, however, in part out of deference to the proper tragic conclusion he had evaded, but more because of his own inclinations, he and Isolt-Mary, guiltless of blood, had fled the wrath and taken up some simple and anonymous life as religious laymen, village fisher-folk, wood cutters, outlaws of the Robin Hood variety, or wandering minstrels, a life of physical hardship but of spiritual plenty, including a great deal of music, most of it anachronistic.

It was about this time, in fact, that Tim began to undergo a great many strenuous lives, some of them among familiar faces and in such surroundings as the Reno High School, the Wingfield tennis courts, the Pyramid beaches and the university gymnasium, but most of them among strangers and in strange places. Scarcely a day passed in which he did not explore some new region and set forth upon some new quest of Rachel. Mr. Hazard, although his own other lives were limited to the *Gazette* before supper, a Western story or a mystery novel on a winter Sunday, and once in a while, in a nostalgic evening, any sea story handy, even *Moby Dick*, objected only spasmodically to this waste of time. Mrs. Hazard actively abetted it. She carried home books from the library, and even bought the books Tim was always wanting to reread, *King Arthur* and *Robin Hood, Robinson Crusoe, Swiss Family Robinson, Treasure Island* and *Kidnapped, Tom Sawyer, Huck Finn* and *The Connecticut Yankee*, Grimm and Andersen, gods and heroes and saints. One of these volumes, a *Robinson Crusoe* which had pasted-in colored plates, and on its white cover a footprint in rippled sand, even became an object sacred to the touch, like the Bible.

Two of his favorite pictures in this sacred *Robinson Crusoe* are sufficient indication, since he frequently used their scenes just as they appeared, of the strong preference for lonely backgrounds and limited casts which influenced his revision of most of this material. One of these pictures showed Crusoe as the brooding slave of the Moors. Clad in a white burnoose, he sat alone, cross-legged upon the floor, his water jar beside him, one limp hand dangling from his knee and his face nearly hidden. Behind him stretched a long, dark hall to a tiny door open upon bright sunlight and flowers, probably in an inner court. Against the frame of this exit leaned a watchful guard. The other picture was seen from a height, as with the eye of God, or at least of a passing gull, and showed a miniature Crusoe alone on a wide orange beach between a purple sea and towering crags studded with occasional palms. Such themes of lonely unity, in fact, ran second only to the multiple themes of the quest of Rachel. One of Tim's most frequent lives, for instance, was the St. Francis life.

Some time that fall, on one of his first long hikes alone, he came to a little snow-lake in a high meadow south of Mt. Rose. He had meant to climb the mountain, but the lake fascinated him, and he stayed there until he had to start home. It was a still, Indian-summer day, into which the mountain breathed softly and coolly now and then. When the air was quiet it was warm and full of the smell of hot shale, resin and black meadow sod. The water was glassy and black then, and mysterious shapes glowed with a soft gold in its depths. When a breeze came, the color of sky would play lightly over the surface of this dark splendor. At one moment Tim would be drowsing, aware of the big things, the warmth, the silence and the mountains around him. At the next he would be all eyes and shivering delight as the pine needles quivered, the meadow grass and the last flowers bowed and twinkled, and at last the feathery serpents slithered across the water and left the sky behind them. All day nothing of singular importance happened, but he was invaded by a million intimations, as if he had never seen or smelled or heard the world before, and after that day the intimations accumulated into a single memory of great holiness and the little lake became the most frequent scene of his St. Francis life.

In that life he usually built a log cabin among the stunted black trees on the low ridge north of the lake, and never went back to the blind, deaf and pushy world, but dwelt there forever in the presence of a wild and gentle god of the peaks and of the deputies, the old, wise and silent watchers among the white boulders on the hill east of the lake, the tiny, gay sprites of the flowers and meadow grass and running water, and the quick, malicious demons who guarded the upper heights. Each day he swam in the lake at sunrise and at sunset. His possessions were pleasingly few: a bunk, a stove, a table and chair, a lamp, a dozen books and his violin. He wandered everywhere, singing and learning, and became very thin and black and full of a constant energy of joy. There was nothing superfluous about him. He sat on the bench by his door at dusk, and migratory waterfowl settled their feathered bodies down over their webs about him, and told him of their travels. Smaller birds came to his shoulders and wrists by day. Chipmunks played on the cabin floor and gray deer couched beneath his trees. Winter was as wonderful as summer. The wind buried his cabin and made it snug, and carved the drifts and threw glittering plumes from the peaks and ridges, and in the afternoons vast, blue shadows changed their shapes and places slowly in the sculptured white of all the region. It was a life that could never wear out, a life of natural immortality, full of spontaneous hymns of praise and canticles to wonder. Whenever an installment of it had to be ended, the vista remained interminable, awaiting his return. It must be admitted, however, that one of the minor deities to or for whom he prayed there was Rachel Wells, and that often the St. Francis life would begin because he had failed to win Rachel in the tangled world below.

And perhaps Rachel had something to do with another manifestation of this struggle for unity over multiplicity. At least the change came shortly after Billy Wilson's party. Before that time Tim's room in the house by the race track had been a museum and junk yard of his affections. There was sheet music all over the table and bed and dresser. There were books on the shelves, but also on the chairs and the table and the dresser, and under all of them. Scattered around handy were the violin, a dime-store flute, a battered cornet, a cheap snare drum and two or three home-made tom-toms. He drew scores of Reno High School and University of Nevada athletes with colored crayons and cut them out with little stands to support them. He drew and cut out scores of opponents for them, and hundreds of birds and animals, and clipper ships and Viking long boats with shields and warriors to go with them, and mounted knights with carefully copied lions, unicorns, swans and crosses upon their shields, and Indian war parties and tepees. There were Rose Bowls and jungles, battle fields and oceans laid out all over the floor all the time. Pictures of wild places, ships at sea, famous athletes, saints, musicians, Hazards and Turners covered the walls. There were rocks and fossils in the closet and under the bed, pine boughs behind the mirror, dead grasses and flowers standing about in tumblers, pine cones dangling from the head of the bed, a string of sea shells hanging from the light, and a stuffed eagle which Mr. Turner had presented to Mr. Hazard, perched upon a little stand of its own in one corner. Tim had to open the door gently and push his way in, and often he went to bed with pounds of treasure still on top of the covers.

Then he underwent the mysterious conversion, and the room became a cell. The jungles and gridirons, the seas and the wars disappeared. The rocks and shells and grasses were gone, the instruments were put away, there was never more than one book at a time off the shelves, the music was stacked neatly in the closet, and the eagle went downstairs, onto the piano. There were no pictures of any kind on the walls. He even took one chair out of the room because it was unnecessary, and for a while would not have a rug on the floor. It pleased him to come in and see only the bare walls, the bare dresser, the bare table with the one chair drawn up to it, the bare floor and the bed always made up and entirely covered by his Indian blanket. It was a room from which he could have stepped into the St. Francis cabin without a change of mind. Indeed it was the St. Francis cabin, in which he renewed himself to face the multiple world.

CHAPTER TWELVE: *In Which Tim Becomes a Pack of Hounds in the Enchanted Wilderness*

ON SATURDAY Tim was a changed animal. He was up at six o'clock, and not sleepy, but twanging with a new kind of nervous and unstable energy. Usually he read while he ate breakfast, and nobody's talk or activity, not even Willis' flea-hopping jabs at life, got through his fortifications to disturb the chosen world. This morning he didn't even think of a book, although there was an unfinished one under his pillow. He heard everything everybody said, and his walls were breached at a hundred points.

All the family save Mr. Hazard, who was always silent in the morning, wanted to know about the party. Grace was interested in who had been there. His mother asked gentle questions to find out what he had thought and felt about it. Willis, with an interest which set his body jumping and made his voice sharp and his laugh loud, guessed with fiendish accuracy the kind of games that had been played and the way Tim had felt about them. Tim was backed into a corner and forced to battle foes superior individually as well as in number. He was defending a deity and an unformulated but profound faith against heathens who could understand so little of it that to have exposed any part of it would have been a greater act of desecration than any they could perform. He was afraid to tell them even common, public details about dinner and the house, for fear one of them, probably Willis, would penetrate to the existence of Rachel.

He answered his mother with, "Oh, it was all right, I guess," and "Oh, sure. I had a good enough time, I guess."

For Grace he named most of the boys who had been there, and when she asked about the girls, he named two whom she knew, and said he had never seen any of the others before, and couldn't remember their names, which was close to the truth anyway.

He answered Willis, who didn't ask questions, but merely made accusations to be denied, by saying, "Well, what of it?" or, "Maybe they did, and maybe they didn't."

He was so careful to appear casual and unimpressed through all this examination that finally even Mr. Hazard noticed his strange conduct and emerged from his own thoughts to stare at the victim for fully five minutes, while the others worked on him. He didn't say anything, though.

Grace asked, "Wasn't Mary there?"

"No, she wasn't," Tim said. He was pleased. He should have thought of that feint himself. Grace had greatly improved his chances by attacking this abandoned stronghold. When Willis chortled, "Oh-oh, no wonder you didn't think it was so hot," Tim knew he was saved, or at least reprieved. Mary was so much like another sister in the family that even Willis became quickly bored with joking about her unless she was there too, to suffer in person.

"Oh, nuts. What difference does that make?" Tim said. He was careful how he said it, and it sounded so much like his usual pleased attempt to seem indifferent that Willis made only a couple of stale cracks to keep up his own morale, and the siege was raised. Tim did not feel guilty about either the implied falsehood or the sacrifice of Mary. He felt only a frightened, protective joy, as if he had hidden a baby rabbit from a hawk which still hovered overhead. Usually his father had to threaten him out of a book on Saturday morning, before they could start off to work at the lumber yard. This morning, however, he departed alone and unprodded, ahead of Mr. Hazard. He didn't want to be talked to, even as another man with work to do in the world. He wanted to be alone with his magnificent secret.

The sunlight was bright in the tops of trees beginning to turn yellow, but the air was still cold. Breakfast smoke rose vertically from many chimneys, and women with dust cloths on their heads and slippers on their feet were sweeping some of the porches or shaking dust mops over the rails. In this peace, with the whole day ahead, he became an organ hymning the attainment of love and the beautiful vales of a future which would begin in the afternoon. It would be many years yet before he lost the saintly or foolish conviction that the world was what he felt it to be. Even his frequent melancholy was a pleasure. He endured long sadness in his stories because he always felt in it the premonition of the leaping, stag-like joy and freedom which would burst forth at once in the resolution. The longer this joy was kept down, the more tremendous would be its release, going off on the mountains toward the sky in forty-foot bounds.

He didn't take a book to the lumber yard that morning, or even steal any moments behind the stacks to protect the growth of his dreams in this crucial stage. The problem of Rachel was so strong and exciting that he stuck to considering its realities all morning, making only a few starts on stories or songs, and dropping them as less lively than the facts of the situation. This gave him such an intense sensation of contact with the world that everything had more flavor than usual; the sun was brighter, the smell of sawdust and raw wood more penetrating, the changing treetops more miraculous in their flickering. He adored the grind of a truck getting under way. There was delight and manhood in the crawling of sweat down his chest or spine or ribs. The world was very good, bright and palpitating. He wanted to yodel, and did whistle, in a warbling way, full of quick runs and breaks. He had moments of despair about finding Rachel, too. They would both be gray and sick with wasted life if he had to wait till Monday. Also he had qualms which stopped him in his tracks, about what he would really say to her to explain his intrusion, but these ascended quickly into winged happiness when he pictured exactly how it would be simply to see her. At rare moments he remembered that he was a traitor to Mary, but easily defeated these weaknesses by arguing that Mary had never cared what he thought anyway, which he could prove. This was largely true, although it felt to him like an alibi. The amazing completeness of his conversion was demonstrated by the fact that every time he saw he was making an alibi, he felt happier than ever. He was committing the final sacrifice of honor for his love. Because of his excitement, he believed that he was working hard and steadily, and was first chagrined and finally enraged, when the truck driver said, "If you don't watch out, Timmy, you're goin' to lug two or three of them slabs this morning," and later, "Whatsa matter, kid? Didn't you get any sleep last night?" and finally, "For God's sake, if you can't do anything else, at least get out of the way."

Perhaps his mother sensed this other-worldly excitement at lunch. At any rate she asked, "What are you going to do this afternoon, Timmy?"

Willis at once became attentive.

"I guess maybe I'll take a hike up to the Black Panther Mine," Tim said.

"You don't go in those old tunnels, do you?" she asked.

Mr. Hazard looked up and said, "He'd better not."

Tim usually did go into the tunnels. He had gone clear down to the lowest level sometimes, although, or because, it scared him to have to creep and squirm along on his belly to get through the last openings, which were sagging and choked with drift. However, since he wasn't going there at all this time, he said, "No, it's just for the hike. You can make a knife blade all like copper by working it in and out of the dump. The dump's kind of blue-green, but the knife comes out all copper color."

That was all there was to it. He had been afraid of Willis, but Willis had plans of his own, and didn't want to risk diverting the examination. He looked across the table at Tim, from under his eyebrows, to let him know he wasn't being fooled, but he didn't say anything.

After lunch, though, he stopped in Tim's bedroom door and watched him comb his hair, and grinned, and spread his legs and hooked both thumbs in his belt.

"Say, what was so special about that party last night, any-way?"

"Nothing," Tim said. "Why?"

Willis disregarded this ingenuous question. "No, I guess not," he said. "Any day you'd comb your hair and put on a clean shirt just to monkey around that old mine."

Tim didn't answer.

Willis came in and sat down on the bed.

"Jeez, a necktie too," he said.

"What difference does that make to you?"

"None; no difference; no difference at all. Lookee, got four-bits I could borrow?" he asked.

"What you want with four-bits?"

"I wanna give it to the Salvation Army. Whaddya think?"

"Yes, you do not. I haven't got four-bits anyway."

Willis looked at him closely. "I'd make a bet . . ." he began.

Tim turned without finishing the knot in his tie, and Willis realized that there was stronger feeling here than he could see any reason for. He'd missed something, but also he'd better go easy for now.

"O.K.," he said. "You haven't got it. Just thought I'd ask you, that's all."

He got up. "You can owe it to me," he said.

"Black Panther Mine," he said, loudly and skeptically, as he went out.

Then he underwent one of his spontaneous transformations from a con man into a dynamo. He slid down the banister, lit with a bang in the front hall, thumbed his nose at the mild mule deer hanging over the hat rack, simultaneously yodeled and slammed the front door, so that he couldn't hear his mother if she protested or called a question from the kitchen, ran yodeling and leaping to the corner, where he was out of sight from the house, and at once subsided into a slouching and scuffing walk.

He saw his friend waiting for him. "Hey, Barney," he called, "anything doing that ain't marbles?"

"Hay's for horses," Barney said, and spit. "Could be," he said.

They went off together down the street toward Fourth.

The depth of Tim's conversion can be measured by the fact that the university football team was playing St. Mary's on the Mackay Field that afternoon, and that he had not denied himself this game, but completely forgotten it. He remembered it when he saw a bunch of kids playing football behind the Orvis Ring. He felt like a traitor when he came to University Avenue and saw the cars already going up the hill and through the campus gate, and the people walking briskly along on the sidewalks, some of them with blankets over their arms. The varsity would be out warming up right now, in their uniforms with blue-and-white-striped socks and sleeves. Just the thought of these uniforms always stirred a sarcastic and wrathy loyalty in Tim. He could see the field just as it was this minute. Some of the players were throwing and catching passes. Others were squatting and sprinting, squatting and sprinting, to take the kinks out. From all over the turf, punts were taking off, bump, bump, bump. Old Spud himself was standing down by one goal, taking center passes and lifting the best punts of all, the ones that spiraled slowly up into the sky, far above the red roof of the training quarters, and finally dropped into the waiting arms, seventy or seventy-five yards away. Soon the first-string line all together, and the second-string line all together, would begin squatting, and charging when somebody yelled, "Hike." Then the backfields would join them, carrying the balls and sweeping around the ends on each charge. St. Mary's would be out there too, doing the same things in their red-and-blue suits. The stands were filling up with excited rooters, who made loud jokes and called to each other. Cigarette smoke smelled good outdoors like that in the bright fall air. The trees over the little cluster of homes at the top of North Virginia Street were shining and yellow. Honor demanded, especially when the team was playing St. Mary's, that he be up there, working his way along behind the hedge at the south end of the field and up onto the hill in back of the training quarters, where the managers couldn't get at him. From there he could gradually work right down onto the sideline and into the excitement. From the sideline you could see the sweat on the players' faces, and hear their grunts and the slap of their pads when the lines met. You could hear the exact words they said when they swore or encouraged each other, and the long pounding of feet on an end run or a pass play. In fact, down there you were practically in the game. Sometimes you even had to sprint to get out of the way of a fierce tackle, which drove the ball carrier clear over the line, or even out among the reserves on the bench. Sometimes you got to pick up the very ball the men were using, when it fell outside after an incomplete pass. You could feel it with your hands, and turn it over a couple of times before you threw it back in to the referee or the head linesman.

So Tim stood on the corner of Seventh and University and saw the loyal hurry by, and heard the great names spoken, and, from up on the campus, the first thumping and blowing of the band getting ready to march in. He saw and he heard, and yet he went on across Seventh, away from it all, and turned down toward the park.

She went to the Mt. Rose School, which was in the farthest quarter from his own, diagonally across the city. This was exchanging the yellow hills and the race track and gloomy old Peavine for huge, still homes, streets in which he would be conspicuous, and the cold presence of the White Woman, who sent up the pale, tall storms, and offered only a rarefied and uncompanionable peace. He was not in the St. Francis mood today. He couldn't go hunting for Rachel in the St. Francis mood. He had already lied for her.

His heart knocked as he crossed the bridge into Wingfield Park. There he was at the foot of the unknown plateau. She lived up there, where the sad windows stared across the river, across the trees of Reno, and into the north. The air grew sad and experienced around him, thick with history rather than thin and clear with life. He went into the park and pretended to watch the tennis players, even speaking to a couple of them, whom he knew. This was to deceive, or at least propitiate, whatever strange gods kept the plateau, in case they had guessed the precious quarry he came after. When he felt their watch had been relaxed, he went on up the hill and turned west into Court Street.

At once he realized that his trick had been useless. The street was empty and only the fall sunlight shimmered in the yellowing leaves and lay silently upon the fronts of the great houses with the red vines. The houses watched him quietly, thinking their own thoughts in a strange language. The whole region was very quiet, but he felt uneasy and vulnerable. Something knew who he was after, and he would never find her.

He drummed up hope, but then suffered in passing each house from the idea that she was hidden in it, and between houses from the expectation that she would suddenly appear before him, coming down one of the walks, maybe even with somebody else with her, in which case he would be speechless. And if he didn't speak, she wouldn't know him.

He didn't see her or anybody else. He went on out to Newland's Circle, and stood at the wall, as in a redoubt, looking up the river valley toward the Sierras over Verdi. The fur of trees was black and patchy on the sleeping animal shapes of the range, and a faint blue haze of peace lay over it. He went out to the top of the hill and looked down to where the old, gravel road disappeared between the rows of trees under the bluff. He longed to take that road, to walk, or even run, clear out to where the Hunter Creek trail began beside an old shed, and then to climb up and be alone in the canyon. He didn't. He went on through all the streets west of Belmont and Arlington. He didn't see her. He didn't see the Cadillac, which was his other hope. He was late coming home.

He didn't read that night. He went up to his room and sat on the bed and improvised small blues on the violin, and then sat there plucking it like a ukulele and considering his bewilderment. Later a strong wind blew outside, and the black poplars rocked through the stars, and roared, and let many leaves go, which he heard rushing along the street and clicking against the house. This was as it should be. He was full of a new kind of sadness, which made him lie awake for a long time, thinking about the world, without telling himself any stories.

The next day, after Sunday chicken dinner with mashed potatoes, green peas and pie, his father went to sleep on the couch in the living room with the Sunday paper half over his face, and his mother went out and lay in the hammock on the back porch, with a blanket over her, and looked at the sun on the dying garden, and remembered and thought. Tim went out onto the front porch, and stood staring at the street, as if wondering what to do.

Willis was sitting on the top step, chewing a piece of gum and bouncing a ball.

"Going up to the Black Panther again?" he asked.

"Don't you wish you knew?"

"Don't you think I don't," Willis said. He was without animosity. He was too sleepy from last night, and too full of dinner. He was just maintaining his worldly superiority over his brother, who was a dope, but older and bigger, and so possibly dangerous.

Tim understood that Willis didn't know or care. "All right, then, you do," he said. "I should worry."

"Lend me four-bits?"

"Nope."

"O.K. That's a buck you owe me now."

This time Tim went down Alameda Street clear to Fourth before he went across toward Sierra. All afternoon he searched the jungle of the Sunday quiet from Belmont and Arlington east to Virginia, and as far out as the Mt. Rose School again. Phonographs played in upstairs apartments with the windows open. Big cars stood quiet and empty at the curbs. Only once in a while he would hear one of them, a block or two away, start up, and shift gears and depart softly and slowly, or see one of them drift by on a cross street. Maids pushing baby buggies, with older children walking beside them, went past in a sleepy boredom which did not begin to compare with the boredom of the children, who had coats and bonnets on, and had no one to talk to, and nothing new to look at. The wind had already taken off many leaves. They lay on the lawns and in the streets, and because they had fallen, there was more sunlight, but it didn't make the day seem bright there. It was a soft, reminiscent, mildly disconsolate sunlight. Tim did not find Rachel or the Cadillac, but late in the afternoon he turned hopelessly west, to search once more the streets he had searched on Saturday, and found Lawrence Black.

CHAPTER THIRTEEN: *But Flushes Fish*

LAWRENCE was lying on his back on the grass, staring up into the trees. A Springer spaniel lay beside him, its nose upon its fore paws and its hind legs extended. The two of them appeared to be a boy and a dog in Sunday-afternoon lethargy, possibly a trifle discontented. The boy might have had a hangover from going to church and then sitting in his best clothes to eat a long Sunday dinner with many adults. Tim believed, however, that this was not the case with Lawrence Black. He believed that Lawrence Black, like himself in the same position, with trees to stare up into, would be neither lethargic nor discontented, but simply busy. Besides, Lawrence was in his shirt, with no Sunday coat, and looked both comfortable and wide awake.

Lawrence heard Tim's feet stop on the walk, and turned his head slowly on the grass and looked at him, and sat up slowly, as if trying to be quiet, and said softly, "Hello. I wondered when you'd come."

It had been more than a month since they had made the turtles, yet no time seemed to have passed. Perhaps it was yesterday they had made the turtles. The ideas they had started together had not been interrupted.

The spaniel stood up and growled mildly, but also wagged his short tail tentatively, because Lawrence had spoken to Tim first.

"Broccoli, you old fool," Lawrence said. The spaniel stopped growling and wagged his whole hind end. Lawrence stood up.

"Let's go round back, shall we?" he asked.

Tim was abandoning a manifest, though hopeless, duty. He had begun to feel that the rest of his life would be spent wandering along unknown streets, trying to look as if he had a right to be on them, and hoping foolishly to see a Rachel who perhaps wasn't even real. With Lawrence there in front of him in the body, thin and dark in his thin, white shirt, he felt as if he had really been looking for Lawrence's house all the time. He was happy and relieved, free of the shame of appearing aimless.

They walked around to the back, where the lawn became a wide expanse sheltered by hedge. In one corner stood a tool shed covered by vines, and in the center of the lawn, as if in the center of a green stage, stood a round metal table with a beach umbrella over it and four metal chairs waiting around it. There was a light and rarefied tranquillity balanced over this scene, as different from the weary glow of the surrounding region as gentle breathing is from smothering. Mr. Black, in flannels and a dark coat, was holding a hose to water the planting beside the house, and serenely smoking his pipe. The discreet equanimity of Mr. Black was immense.

Lawrence said, "Father, you remember Timothy Hazard."

"Ah, Timothy," Mr. Black said, making his courtly and sagacious nod, "you found us then. Good."

The boys sat down on the grass, and Tim made friends with Broccoli.

"Why did you name him that?" he asked.

"On account of the curls on his ears," Lawrence said.

"He's a kind of vegetable too," he added, stretching out on his back again, and staring up at the trees on the west edge of the lawn.

This merely gave Tim some idea what broccoli must be, and proved that the dog hadn't been named after an Italian opera singer or anything of that sort. There was some constraint about this meeting. It was different from the meeting at Pyramid Lake. That had been a natural accident, which might have happened anywhere on the planet, and at once there had been something to do. This was a conjunction within the arbitrary realm of humanity, and doubtless was subject to certain rules of diplomacy. Tim suspected that these rules were not the same under the sign of the race track and under the combined signs of the court house and Mt. Rose. He wanted this meeting to be a flawless continuation of the first, as if there had been no time wasted between, as he had felt in the first moments it would be, but he had to leave it to Lawrence to achieve this transition. It was funny about being with Lawrence. With most boys he felt himself to be full of sensations and ideas which must be kept secret because they were not hardy enough to be exposed. So much greater was the intent secrecy which lived in Lawrence, and so soft and accurate was his speech, that with him Tim felt large, awkward, and probably capable of many unwitting crudities.

Lawrence dissolved the pause with wonderful ease. "The leaves look like fish in that light," he said.

Lawrence seemed always to say things simply and directly, but the way he said them made Tim feel that each remark might contain many meanings, all folded one within the other, like the petals of a closed bud. He looked at the leaves carefully, and after a minute he saw that where they swam in the expanding shafts of sunlight they appeared free of stems and twigs, and did look like schools of small fish balanced in a medium heavy enough to support them far off the bottom. Slowly this submarine image expanded, and submerged the globe in an ocean of air populated by innumerable leafy fish. Tim had spent many days, in that improbable era before his family came to Reno, standing on a gray pier over the Pacific and watching the multitudes of mackerel sweep, shiver, shift and glitter below. This image fused for a moment with the conception of leaves as fish, to beget a peculiar sensation, enchanting and alarming, of likeness through all creation.

He said, "The sun does look kind of like water, doesn't it?"

They selected leaves which, because of their movement and halos of light, looked even more like fish than the rest. From this exercise they progressed to talking about the turtles they had hidden. Tim asked if Lawrence had modeled any more turtles.

"No. I've been painting some fish. Would you like to see them?"

They got up.

"Father, I'm going to take Tim down to see the fish."

"Ah, yes. Very interesting, Timothy."

When they had started toward the back door, Mr. Black said, "By the way, Timothy, will you have dinner with us?"

Tim said thanks very much, but he couldn't.

"Perhaps a lemonade on the lawn then, when you come up?"

"That would be fine, Mr. Black."

"Ah, good. I shall put in our order with Agnes, then, while you two are busy with the fish," Mr. Black said, smiling and nodding.

They had to descend into the basement, and pass the octopus furnace, and go through a door, as if into a dungeon, to see the fish. This half of the basement had been turned into a studio. At one end there was a cot made up for sleeping. On the wall over the cot hung a plaster bas-relief of figures from the Parthenon frieze. There was a long window bench let into the west wall, and against the opposite wall a long, inclined desk, like a draughtsman's table, with a drop-light over it. Above the table was a single shelf of books, mostly about drawing, painting and sculpture, and along the level ledge at the top of the desk stood an ordered array of paints, ink bottles, and pens and brushes in jars. At the other end from the cot stood a small, square table, on which was a portable phonograph with the lid raised. There was a post in the center of the room, and against this was built an inclined easel, with another drop-light over it. One chair, with a daubed painter's smock over the back of it, stood near this easel. On the wall over the phonograph hung a framed charcoal drawing of a beautiful and intelligent-looking woman who was too old for Tim to recognize these qualities, so that he saw only that the drawing was as clean and delicate as an engraving, and that the woman might not be altogether kind, although she was fascinating, so that he kept looking back at her, wherever he went in the room. Excepting this picture and the bas-relief there was nothing on the walls. The room was long, low, cool and spacious, and full of a shadowy privacy which the drop-light only increased, as the late sunlight, filtering through the leaves outside the narrow windows, increased the secrecy. Tim felt happy in the studio almost at once. It was his kind of room. The St. Francis life would be easy there.

The fish were on the draughtsman's table, under the light. There were a great many of them, arranged in a spacious and moving pattern which Tim did not perceive, except that a sense of freedom about it pleased him. These many but uncrowded fish were suspended in a uniform, pale, aqueous green, which was not interrupted by one bubble, ripple or distortion of a fish to suggest water. Tim's only notion of art was to expect the same reaction to a drawing or painting that he would have had to its subject. Yet his own drawing and daubing had put it into his hand to understand that the lines and delicate hues of these fish, and the transparent unity of the green wash which held them in suspension, were infinitely beyond his powers. He remembered also the crudity of his labors with the small turtles, while Lawrence deftly perfected the big one. He felt that he must say something, but also that it would be better not to.

"It's nice the way they move," he said.

"Yes, I like fish," Lawrence said, as if Tim had not been talking about the painting at all. "They're so easy to draw," he explained, "and you can do almost anything with their shapes."

While he spoke he was winding something which was concealed by his hand. He set this object down on the ledge of the desk. In the room began a faint tinkling, like that of tiny bells. It was so light a sound that it did not seem to have a definite source, and yet so clear that it seemed to come from everywhere. It was another moment before Tim realized that the object was a music box. The notes were very pleasing in a tiny, humorous way that made you want to laugh softly. He and Lawrence stood there, separate, in time suspended and in great amity, and laughed softly at the music box. It was still another few moments before Tim had sufficiently absorbed the humor of the small, springing sounds to realize what a wonderful music box this was. It was not playing the same three or four notes over and over, like most music boxes. It was playing Brahms' *Lullaby* clear through. When he understood this, he laughed out loud with pleasure. Lawrence smiled more. When the melody was done, he took down the music box and handed it to Tim to look at. It was a little barrel with a crank on the side. On top of it sat a wooden peasant woman in a head kerchief and a red skirt, rocking a cradle with a baby in it.

They played the lullaby twice more, and then talked about the music box. In this way the difficulty of discussing the fish was passed over. They went upstairs and through the kitchen, where Lawrence spoke softly to the fat colored woman who was preparing a tray of ware to set the dinner table. The colored woman grinned at him suddenly, almost explosively, and then included Tim in the grin. The abundance of her affection and jollity was alive in the room without her having said a word. It beat back the faint melancholy and secrecy of dying sunlight among the vines which covered the windows.

Outside, Mr. Black was now watering the lawn. On the table under the beach umbrella was a silver tray upon which stood a glass pitcher full of lemonade and ice, with the lemons floating in it, three tumblers and a glass plate heaped with cookies.

"Go right ahead, gentlemen," said Mr. Black. "I'll be with you in just a moment."

Actually he was there in time to serve them. He filled one tumbler and bowed as he handed it to Tim.

"Timothy," he said.

"Lawrence," he said, presenting the other with a bow also.

"Sit down, gentlemen, do," he said, and would not sit down himself until they did.

When they had taken two or three swallows, he said, "And what have you been doing with yourself since we saw you last, Timothy?"

The question made Tim feel as if he were an old friend of Lawrence's, and thus, indirectly, of Mr. Black's also, a friend who had been here on this lawn a thousand times drinking lemonade, but who had been absent for a year or more now, and had been sincerely missed. He felt reassured as to Mr. Black's manner. He had been troubled at the lake and here, at first, by Mr. Black's courtliness, which he had suspected of containing an element of ridicule, the condescension of the wise and experienced to the ridiculously young. Now he perceived that this was not the case at all, but that the courtliness was habitual, and that the ridicule, if it were really there at all, was directed by Mr. Black against his own manner, in order not to make it uncomfortably heavy.

He told them, with a pleasure in this audience which missed nothing, about the beginning of school and the battle on Whitaker Hill. He told it as much more humorous than it had actually seemed. He performed a continual small operation of art upon the crude fact. They seemed particularly to enjoy his exaggeration of the effect upon the freshmen of the campaign of cartoons on the blackboards. They asked questions about these. Mr. Black often laughed heartily but quietly.

When Tim stopped, he asked, "And you saw the fish, I take it?"

He said, filling Tim's glass again, "Fine fish, aren't they?"

One was never forced to expose himself because of the questions asked by the Blacks. Lawrence wound up the music box. Mr. Black answered his own question with another. The talk went on easily. They were three together, quite free of the world. The light became only a faint fringe upon the topmost leaves. The lawn was in deep shadow. Softly, fended off by tree and hedge, the distant sounds of the city came up, and made the seclusion more perfect.

Mr. Black rose and dusted the crumbs from his coat.

"If you will excuse me, gentlemen," he said. "You're sure you won't stay, Timothy?" he asked.

When Tim said he couldn't, that he would have to go now, Mr. Black said, "Don't let me break up the party," and held up one hand as if to settle them back into their chairs.

"It's a shame," he said, looking at Lawrence, "that he didn't find us sooner, isn't it, Black?

"Has Black told you he's leaving tomorrow?" he asked Tim.

"No," Tim said. The lawn seemed much darker.

"It's too bad," Mr. Black said. "He goes away to school. But he'll be back for Christmas. You have a holiday at Christmas, of course, Black?" he asked.

"I guess so. They always do."

"So we can get together then, if not before, Timothy," Mr. Black said, and shook hands, and nodded and smiled, and went off to the house slowly, as if full of thought.

"I hate it," Lawrence said suddenly, but not loudly. "Don't you?"

"What?"

"School."

"Oh, I don't know," Tim said. "It's not so bad."

"Some day I'll run away from it," Lawrence said.

At the front of the house, Tim said, "Well, I'll see you at Christmas."

"I hope so," Lawrence said. His voice was soft and courteous, but he seemed gone off somewhere in the dusk by himself now. Tim was possessed by the sad theme of the Court Street region even before he turned away and left Lawrence standing there, only his white shirt showing distinctly, and the white patches of the dog sitting beside him. Yet he didn't feel as if Lawrence had deserted him, but as if he had deserted Lawrence.

CHAPTER FOURTEEN: *In Which Wingfield Park Becomes the Center of the Universe, and an Important Tennis Match Is Played Which Goes on for Years*

TIM now saw Rachel all the time at school. He saw her coming up the outside steps, carrying too many books for her size. He saw her walking, with her quick, short steps, in the river of students passing from class to class. When he came through the big front door, he would see her sitting on the study-hall steps. At noon hour he would see her sitting in the girls' corner of the main hall, under the stairs that went up to the tower. Where he had not seen her at all, he now saw her all the time. Whenever he saw her, the story he was telling himself at that moment would fall apart. The luminous mist which hung in the halls and rooms of Reno High School, dissolving its walls and ceilings and briefly revealing long reaches into a vast world, mostly archaic, but full of islands of the present, the snow lake, Pyramid, the lumber yard, the lawn at Black's, the race track, this protective mist parted at once and fled her bright presence. The actual swarming which went on around her was likewise withdrawn. He saw her alone, as upon a peak or a sun-struck headland, and his entire self went out to this vision. He didn't know himself alive when he could see her; he was a disembodied attention and adoration. When she disappeared he would return into his body, but feel it changed. A wonderful, sparkling light would be slowly dying out of his mind; his blood, which had been intangible as ether a moment before, would become a heavy and aching liquid.

After an assembly on Wednesday, he found himself coming down the study-hall steps beside her, so close they touched each other. His throat tightened upon an attempt to speak to her. He made a second try, and said "Hello" shakily, in a voice which threatened to go falsetto. She looked up at him and said "Hello" with her quick, defensive smile, but then looked away again quickly. He was startled. For five days now they had battled through inconceivable odds of nature and human hostility to a hundred perfect understandings, and yet it was evident that she had not recognized him. When she disappeared this time, and he slowly returned into himself, he discovered that he was trembling.

He didn't try to speak to her again that week. She was always with other girls. She was alone with them, as she had been alone at the party and at the race track. When they walked in a line, with their arms around each other, she walked beside them, but not touching any of them. When they sat in a cluster on the steps, she would be staring far out beyond them, or looking at her hands in her lap. Still, they were always there. Twice he waited in the front hall after school, hoping to see her start home alone. He didn't see her. He guessed that she must have escaped before he did, and after that he nearly ran out of the freshman boys' session room at three-thirty. He saw her then, hugging her books and making the little, excited laughter, but she was always walking with all those girls. They would trot down the outside steps and troop off together along West Street, talking rapidly and laughing, and he would have to stand there and watch her go, and be doused again by loneliness and helplessness. He gained only a superstitious veneration for the coat she wore, by which he now recognized her at once, even at a great distance. It was a soft plaid coat with a fur collar, and having served only divine purposes, should have been hung in a niche with a candle before it, and worshipped wordlessly by his eyes, that he might gain intimations through it. He practically performed this ceremony several times in his mind.

The next Saturday he had to work all day at the lumber yard. On Sunday afternoon, however, he wandered off helplessly toward the Mt. Rose quarter again. Actually, every evening all week, his heart had run that course behind the gleam, panting with eagerness. His body, nevertheless, went down the traces slowly. He had thought about it so much that he believed his intention must have become conspicuous, and he was intent upon throwing off all possible pursuit by a simulation of indifference, by appearing full of his own thoughts, and going merely where his feet took him. There were hordes of leaves down now. It was a bright day, with small, misty clouds gliding rapidly, high over the world, yet even in this gaiety of the sky there was a premonition of defeat. When the wind came down to Tim's level, it was a cool traitor to sun. The fallen leaves ran in hustling retreat before it on the streets and sidewalks, and crowded in panic into the gutters, or against fences and hedges, where they lay trembling. Tim was an instrument sensitive to such changes in the world. Three cloudy days made him hopeless. The sudden dark blowing and drench of a summer rain revealed to him the inalienable sadness of all life. A still, shining morning, in which the poplars aspired with faint shivering, filled him with sudden hopes, which sprang up and danced and warbled in the air, like meadow larks in the spring. In this whispering afternoon, therefore, he was essentially resigned. It was impossible not to try to find her, but he didn't really expect anything to happen. He crossed the bridge and the island and stopped on the second bridge, where he leaned on the concrete rail and watched the low water working flatly among the stones. Finally he went on into the park to wait out the gods of the plateau. He saw without interest that there was tennis going on. He came slowly onto the lawn by the first court, scuffing among the fallen, golden leaves of the poplars. Then all at once every hound in his soul, belling wondrously, cast after heaven in the wilderness. The small girl in a wide white skirt which lifted out around her as she turned, and swirled snug to her body when she spun back, this girl on the first court, on the side nearest him, this girl he had for twenty wasted minutes half-watched from the bridge, was Rachel. He sat down cross-legged on the grass, moving slowly and with great restraint, in order that she should not be startled or prove an apparition and vanish in the duller sunlight.

Rachel played tennis with that same air of quickly and defiantly resisting the world. After a point she walked quickly, her feet twinkling, to recover a ball. She scraped the ball up quickly with her racket. She walked quickly back to the base line. When she was receiving, she hovered in wait for the ball, like a humming-bird over an open blossom, and then attacked it quickly. She was so short that she almost had to serve uphill, so that her service had no pace, but floated. Nevertheless she served quickly, and at once hovered in wait for the return. Her ground strokes had no more pace than her service. She had no weight or wrist to put behind them. They all floated and cleared the net by a yard or more. Yet she managed to place them all deeply, to work them well from corner to corner, and to use their slowness to skitter back into position. She never let any shot go untried for, and with only a slight narrowing of her eyes and thrust of her chin, succeeded time after time in stopping back shots which should have spun her around or knocked the racket out of her hand. There was no offensive to her game. She seldom attacked, closed in to hold the net, pressed, laid her shots down flatly or stepped up her pace to make use of an advantage. But her fierce, twinkling, unyielding defense would begin, after a while, to work as well as an offense. She never looked around when she was on the court. She seldom even looked at her opponent, except as a moving object whose geographical location must be calculated before her next return. She rarely spoke while playing, except to state the score when asked. She never smiled, and only once in a great while, when a long, straining point had ended in a ridiculous antic, or a final neat dispatch, would she laugh, a brief, bent spasm of agonized mirth, undergone standing still, bending over her racket, which she held with its head on the ground, so that she could lean on it as on a cane.

Not that Tim saw all this the first time he watched her. He had played very little tennis in his life, and had abandoned it, except for those sultry afternoons when nobody can think of anything to do, under the weight of the opinion in his quarter that it was a sissy game. The description is my own. I was playing tennis on the Wingfield courts all those years that Rachel was, and saw a lot of her game, and played with her often. I was a victim, a couple of times, of what followed that first vision of Tim's of Rachel on a tennis court. She never emerged from that defensive game, and I don't believe it ever became any easier for her. Her matches always won the praise of intense quiet from the watchers, but not because they were spectacular. Defensive play, in itself, no matter how courageous, is never spectacular. Yet I have sat through some of her matches, wringing my hands and writhing on the bench, more nervously concerned over the outcome than I ever was over a match of my own, and some of them made me nervous enough. Whole audiences used to do that, sit there and pull their hearts out for Rachel. We literally endured agony sometimes, when the score was crucial and against her. I believe it was because nobody could miss the fact that a very important game was being played out there, whether he actually thought of that, as Tim and I did, or never got beyond feeling it in the air. The big game was Rachel vs. Rachel. While carefully, floatingly, often with lobs, and with unwavering determination, she retrieved and retrieved, actually the high heart of Rachel was slamming cannon-ball drives through the secret soul of Rachel, who wanted to stop all this tortuous struggling and run off and throw herself down on her face under a lilac bush and weep from years of weariness.

One match I remember seems to me a climax to this series of invisible tournaments Rachel played. It was the women's singles final in the state tournament. It was played on the number two court there at Wingfield, late in the afternoon, when the court was all in shadow and yet the light could be seen far off through the trees, so that the Watteau mood in the park was very heavy. Rachel was still in high school then, a junior or senior. She was sick that day, and sat by herself out in the old Cadillac on the park drive until her match was called. Then she came across the lawn, hugging her two rackets, the way she did her books at school. She always hugged anything she carried, if it was big enough, like a child carrying a teddy bear. Her face was white. She kept her eyes down, watching her own toes flickering across the grass.

Her opponent, Mrs. Ray, was no taller than Rachel, but was much older, in the thirties, I guess, and she'd already won the state title three or four times. The first set, Rachel just didn't seem to have any strength in her knees. She made the points long, because Mrs. Ray was also a defensive player, but she stumbled often, served several double faults, kept points going for ten or twelve shots and then feebly dropped the ball into the bottom of the net, fell down twice, getting up very slowly the second time, and lost the set 6-1. Somebody should have taken her home, of course, but never mind the common sense of the matter. That had only to do with the physical tennis match being played, as the bracketings on the bulletin board showed, between one Mrs. Helen Ray, defending champion, and one Miss Rachel Wells, challenger. It had nothing to do with the mortal defiance of Rachel to Rachel.

All of us in the crowd of high-school kids were wonderfully and speechlessly scared. It wasn't only that we were out to make a youth-sweep of this tournament, and had done so in every event up to this one, or even that Rachel was ours. It was because we were in the void, in the unknown. Nothing at all had happened in that set. It might as well not have been played. Not once had we felt the great match of Rachel vs. Rachel beginning. Mrs. Ray was systematically plunking that ball away into nothing, into a great emptiness. This had never happened before. All the rest of us were subject to the usual adolescent fluctuations, the long-limbed, foggy or fiery ups and downs, smashing around like incensed and lucky madmen one day and drifting as indolent as clouds the next. But Rachel, practice or match, had always played that fierce, trembling, pattering, super-attentive game of hers. This, we understood but couldn't believe, was not Rachel. She had stayed at home at last.

I was sitting up on the high chair, calling them. At the end of the first set Rachel came over and stood under me, wiping her hands on the towel which hung from the net post. I saw that her hands were trembling, like those of a nervous old woman. I could see that her legs were trembling, too, because her white skirt vibrated without stopping. After she had wiped her hands, she stood with her head down for a long minute, just stretching the towel out tight between her hands, trying to stop the shaking. I suppose that was the big game beginning at last.

"Why don't you give it up, Rachy?" I asked. "No use killing yourself."

She didn't look up at me, or say anything, but just shook her head. Then she picked up her racket, went quickly across to the other base line, got set and nodded to Mrs. Ray. The Rachel vs. Rachel began in that set, all right. You could feel it like high strings whining and being snapped. I don't remember now what the score was, but it was a deuce set, 8-6 or 9-7 or some such, and very long, point after point going fifteen or sixteen shots. If you hadn't known what was going on, I suppose that would have looked like merely long, bad tennis, because after the set had stayed even for several games, and no point was let go or easily won, Mrs. Ray became cautious too. But when it came to the extra games, the set points, the spiritual ball of that match was traveling like a bullet, and the silent watchers were in a constant uproar. After more than an hour, Rachel, scared to death because she was no good there anyway, twinkled up to the net, took a short, gasping breath, and really smacked the winner away into the far corner. I was watching her so intently that I was slow with the set score. She stood there for probably two or three seconds after that shot, with her eyes closed. Her eyelids were fluttering. Then she walked off the court, and between the benches, and with exquisite care sat down against the trunk of a cottonwood and leaned forward with her face in her hands on her knees. I thought she was done. So did most of the rest of the gang. We believed that we could feel the nervous tension, which must be worse in her than in us, tearing her feelings apart, and leaving her helpless, no matter how she felt otherwise. It wasn't till a long time afterwards, in a mood of reminiscence to which she seldom gave way, that she told me she had experienced practically no feelings at all during those few minutes. She had simply been concentrating intently in order not to faint.

Some of us tried to encourage her. I was begging her to default. She didn't even shake her head at me, but sat there motionless, with her face hidden that way. For a moment I thought she had already passed out.

Finally she said sharply, desperately, and without looking up, "Please, Walt, just let me alone, will you?"

I guess Tim understood then. While the rest of us stood or sat there looking at her helplessly, but not talking any more, he went over to the old iron fountain under one of the big trees, and soaked a towel and brought it back to her. He held it against her hand and said, "Here, Rachy," and she opened the hand and he put the towel into it. She just let it hang there for a minute longer. Then she raised her head, keeping her eyes closed, wiped her face slowly on the cold towel, and leaned forward again, her face in the towel. Tim went over to the soda-pop and ice-cream wagon in the drive and got some ice, and brought that to her. She put some of it into the towel, and put her face against it, and Tim held one piece against the back of her neck.

Mrs. Ray came over and said, "Rachel, why don't we let it go? We can play it off some other time."

Rachel looked up at her and made the quick smile, and said no, thanks, she was all right.

Her doubles partner tried to stop her as she went back onto the court, and Rachel said furiously, without looking at her, "I'm all right, thanks."

She was, too, in the way she meant. She was at that perfect point which is inspiration on the brink of nothing. The great match of Rachel vs. Rachel had been won in that ten minutes under the cottonwood. I knew a little of what she was feeling, from the peculiar way she stumbled sometimes in that last set, the way you stumble when you step up for one more step, and it isn't there. She was playing on air. That expression is usually used, quite wrongly, to express exuberance and a fine, buoyant energy. Actually it is a desperate desire to stop ballooning, to get your feet on the earth and know which way you will go next. Yet sometimes you can play inspired tennis in such a state, because it is impossible to distract your attention. Nothing in your own mind, even, can do it. You are a thin, humming wire of light, like a radio beam, focused upon the ball only. The constant question is at what moment something will cut off the beam, because then there will be nothing left to go on. Rachel could feel how frail, how one, high note fine, her beam was. She played very rapidly, hitting harder than she usually did, almost flat-driving her ground strokes, forehand and backhand. She walked very quickly after balls, and would not lean over or touch her racket to the court, or even touch her hands to her hips when she had to wait a moment, while Mrs. Ray recovered a ball or got into position. She served even more quickly than usual, not hard, but quickly, and the second ball almost too quickly after the first, if she had to serve a second. When she was forced into the fore court by Mrs. Ray's clever drop shots, she would stay there and play the net.

Mrs. Ray stubbornly belted the ball back for two long, running deuce games, and then Rachel's pitiless intensity, which was not directed against Mrs. Ray, but against the time she had left on her beam, was too much. The remaining points, with only a few hitches, ran like sand through the fingers, and Rachel won 6-o. Everybody had that tremendous feeling that something of primary importance to the world had been saved. The match had maintained the intensity of extreme and chancy closeness right up to the last shot, because we all knew that Rachel might go off the beam any second, and that if she did, Mrs. Ray would run it out just as fast as Rachel was running it out then. We also knew that Mrs. Ray was not the mortal enemy thus vanquished. I don't suppose any of us could have told you so, or explained it, but we knew. The applause was spontaneous and extreme. I don't believe Rachel heard it. Mrs. Ray was a fine person. She knew how Rachel had worked to stay on top of that set, and she knew there was no hostility to herself in that unanimous applause after a one-sided set. But the nerves of the freshly defeated are very sensitive. Yet she came around the net at once, and put her arm around Rachel, and said, and she meant it, that she was glad. Rachel only said, very curtly and without looking at her, "Thank you," and stiffened against the arm embracing her. When she was let go, she walked quickly off the court, picked up her other racket in passing, almost ran across the lawn, staring straight ahead, climbed into the car and fainted. She hadn't let go with the rest of us, when Mrs. Ray's last desperate lob struck a yard over the base line. She'd still been on the beam, but she'd had only seconds left, and she'd known it. In order to win the important match, the over-match, she'd had to get both Rachels into the nearest privacy before they could be united and permitted the only kind of truce they ever knew. I think she'd meant to try to get home in the car too, but with the excitement of the match gone, she couldn't manage that.

The qualities of this young and terrible tennis were present in Rachel that first afternoon that Tim watched her. She was playing with a man so old that he didn't need to be considered. His hair was gray around the edges and he wore glasses. At times he would seem to come alive, because he was coaching Rachel, and once in a while, after a rally, he would come to the net, and then Rachel would come to the net also, and stand within a foot of him while he quietly told her something. She listened with respect, and kept glancing up at him and then down again while he talked, and three or four times he even held her hand and turned the racket in it. This would make him seem a person of tremendous importance, but still he didn't have to be thought of as at all dangerous in connection with Rachel, and most of the time he was just a mysterious physical phenomenon, an omnipresent wall which continued to put the ball back so that Rachel could play it.

When they were done, Rachel said, "Thank you very much," and went over and sat on the bench under the big double cottonwood at the back of the courts. There were yellow leaves on the ground around the bench, and she had on a yellow sweater and sat very upright. Her feet didn't reach the ground.

Tim finally worked over to that bench by stages, pretending to be interested in the match on the second court, which could not be seen very well from his place by the first court. He stopped several times on the way, and watched a whole point played out. During one of these entirely thespian pauses, a player on the first court came tearing back after a lob, and then had to let it go because Tim was right in the way. He stood there and glared at Tim, and then finally picked up the ball and went back out onto the court, muttering. His opponent called loudly, "Take it over, Jack," and he answered sharply, "Thanks, if you don't mind." Slowly Tim perceived that he had been guilty of a gross breach of tennis manners, marking himself as either an outsider, full of ignorance, or a boor. Ordinarily this would have subdued him for half an hour, but this time he was hardly affected. At last he sat down beside Rachel. Then, after some time, he even turned his head and looked at her.

She happened to be looking at him also. He rapidly projected two-thirds of a successful future because of this accident, for in this relative privacy, in this bright day in the shadow of the golden cottonwood and the dear, departing year, she smiled at him quickly.

"Hello," she said.

"Hello," he said.

With such deceptive simplicity are the great gates thrown open, and from far up the streets of the city of forever sounds the chorus of exulting trumpets.

They looked at the players running and dancing on the court, and both laughed at something the players also laughed at. Great amity spreads out of laughter together.

"Do you play tennis?" Rachel asked him.

"Not to amount to much," Tim said thickly.

He was being overwhelmed by the results inside himself of the diplomatically and strategically difficult idea that he might walk home with her. This had nothing to do with discovering where she lived. He didn't even think of a house. It was entirely a matter of remaining near her as long as possible, and the flurried conferences going on inside him were considering, one after another, methods of making the approach, all the way from the crudely direct method of simply asking her if she'd mind if he did, to the very complicated one of having her sprain her ankle, so that he could give her his arm to lean on and even, when there was no one in sight, put his arm around her.

He didn't get to walk home with her, because the man with the gray hair and the glasses asked her if she wanted to take winners on the second court, and she did. Tim stayed there watching her run and whirl and twinkle, until there was no one else on any of the benches and it was so shadowy under the trees of Wingfield Park that it was hard to follow a moving ball, and the Watteau melancholy was profound and she seemed to him to be dancing a solo ballet in which her small and moth-like liveliness and wonder was opposed fatally to a pervading, super-human doom. In part this sensation that the end of the world was rushing down came from knowing he should have been home long before. And then, just as the set was about to end, Rachel's father, or anyway, some older man with that sacred right, came for her in the Cadillac.

When she came over to the bench to pick up the yellow sweater, she did say, "Good-bye," though. It was worth the wait.

CHAPTER FIFTEEN: *In Which Mr. Hazard Proves a Poet, and Begets, in His Own Way, the Enduring Image of the Hounds in the Wilderness, and in Which Tim Is Shown in a Musical Practice of Great Importance*

WHEN Rachel was gone, and Tim started home, he became much more worried about how late it was. On corners where the leaves ran and tumbled and he could look west and see the darkening sky over the Sierras, he felt a mortal dread, as if planetary lateness were in the air. When this irremediable passage of time conquered him, he dove within like a frightened fish. Yet all the time he thought also of Rachel and all she had said. When his thoughts became real enough to reproduce her sitting in the yellow sweater among the yellow leaves and smiling at him, then he ascended like a glad duck on swift, small wings. Indeed, during one of these victorious moments, he remembered the ceremony of joy as practiced by the wild birds of Pyramid Lake.

All afternoon the sunlight had lain like burning dust upon the mountains and the palisades, and the still lake had been a mirage. Only a few gulls flew lazily, one at a time and far apart. Others basked upon the motionless waters. Late in the afternoon a high front of thunderheads rose upon the distant west and stayed there. When the sun sank among them, its light was broken, and made dazzling crowns for the domes of cloud, and thrust long, low beams between them, which struck upon the mountains among cinderous shadows. These shadows changed shape slowly, like smoke in the still air, so that in one instant a peak flamed upon the east, and then it dimmed out and after a minute was black against the sky, while a ravine below it was suddenly disclosed as by searchlights. The birds were still. The last of them had beaten slowly back to the islands. There were none of them in the sky and none of them on the water, and they were silent on the islands. Then all at once they went up. They flew in clouds around and around the islands, a huge aerial dance like the little one Tim had started with pieces of bread. They chattered and cried and called in the air, so that the mountains cried back as if, in their canyons, invisible clouds of other birds were also celebrating. They were full of the madness of life. They were trying to relieve this tremendous energy and joy before the dark came and they had to settle. They felt time in the air. Between the broken clouds the light led the mind to such an incredible distance without showing an end, that, somewhere in the shining corridors of sky, the vista became one not of this world, and distance became time. Then the sun was gone and its rays reached only upward and outward upon one plane, making a last and single corona. The ritual cries of the birds stopped. In the dusk their pale cloud fell apart and down, and the islands were still. Time dissolved and the darkened world resumed its measurable distances, and even seemed to huddle, while slowly, and without excitement, the immeasurable realm of the stars reopened overhead. Low over the darkling waters a lone cormorant sped home to Anaho. The sunset ceremony had caught him alone or among strange dancers. He flew with great urgency, his wings making a very rapid, rhythmic whispering.

It was like one of these birds ascending that Tim's spirit leaped up when he successfully remembered Rachel, way back down there fifteen minutes before.

Sometimes, though, the sensation of lateness came with the memory of Rachel. It was ominous, in the Watteau park in the late afternoon in the fall of the year, that he had sat by himself on the bench and she had not once spoken to him or looked at him from the court, not even when she'd had to come back to the fence for a ball.

Yet Rachel had said hello first, and had clearly, with her own voice, been the first to say good-bye. He cherished these portents until they might be examined in solitude, but even while he walked and ran and trotted home, they gathered about themselves implications enough to make a definitive treatise upon the great and religious expressions "hello" and "good-bye."

It was also true that Rachel had asked him a question, but this remained in the realm of mundane torment, along with what his father would probably say or ask, and Willis guess, when he got home and came into the kitchen and they were all done with supper. He had been forced to admit that he didn't play tennis to amount to much, which had felt like a lie, because he knew perfectly well that, in the sense Rachel meant, he didn't play tennis at all. He also understood, since she had said nothing more after asking that question, that she had known he was lying.

Actually the ordeal in the kitchen was a dangerous one. Mrs. Harris, one of the neighbors, had gone for a Sunday afternoon drive with her husband, out toward Verdi, and when she came home she had mentioned to Mrs. Hazard that they had seen Tim wandering across Fourth Street in a day-dream.

The table was cleared, excepting Tim's place. He sat down, and his mother, smiling at him a little fearfully, put his plate in front of him. She had been keeping it warm in the oven. She didn't say anything to him.

Mr. Hazard, still sitting at the end of the table, with his pipe and a glass of beer, became the grand inquisitor. It took more than half an hour for him to deliver his opinion, following the vague and apparently feeble-minded answers which were all Tim could make without revealing the truth, but the opinion may be boiled down to something like this: What the hell was Tim doing wandering all over the unmentionable city without telling anybody where he was going? Why in several sacred names, if all he wanted to do was watch a few people of profanely questionable intelligence and unquestionably profane worthlessness in all the important matters of life, play a trebly condemnable and idle game like tennis, why in all those names over again, didn't he just go up to the university courts instead of worrying his momentarily promoted mother to gray and premature death by traipsing clear down to Wingfield Park? And anyway, if Wingfield Park, for some reason probably not comprehensible even by specifically mentioned inhabitants of spiritual eternity, had become the only place in which he could spend a repeatedly modified existence which probably would have been no more salvageable anywhere else, why in several other names for disturbed Sunday-afternoon tranquillity on the davenport under the newspaper, couldn't he at least have told somebody where he was going? And in final judgment: "And if that's all you can find to do of a Sunday, believe me, young man, I can find you something better, let me tell you!" Pause. "And what's more I will too, and don't you forget it."

Relieved that the questioning was done, and nothing of any importance discovered, Tim just ate and allowed most of this to sail over him. He was stung, however, by one of Mr. Hazard's incidental and more poetic characterizations of the exploit. This followed the confession by torture that Tim had also gone down to the park the previous Saturday and Sunday, which Tim felt to be an exact if incomplete truth, and better than opening up unpredictable discussions about wandering all over the Mt. Rose quarter.

"Anybody would think," Mr. Hazard remarked, in one of his lapses into mere grumbling, "that you were nothing but a damned pup following some bitch in heat."

"Father," Mrs. Hazard said. It was her only remark during the proceedings.

"Well, then, what the hell does he want to go snuffing around like that for?" Mr. Hazard apologized.

Willis gave close and hopeful attention to the examination, wriggling around happily on his chair. Tim understood that it was only a matter of time until Willis would understand everything. Willis lacked Mr. Hazard's adult capacity for getting clear off the track in simple matters. He let it go again, though, waiting until Mr. Hazard had retired to the sitting room with *The Sea Hawk*, before he said anything, and then just asking, "Since when did you get so het up about tennis?" He wasn't going to risk diminishing the pleasure of complete triumph by making an attack over unmapped ground.

Tim was happy to draw out of the battle without exposing the disposition of his main force. So far as he was concerned, this was practically victory in itself. In such an unequal war as that of Tim Hazard against the realists, an escape was a success, even when he knew that the action had been minor and local, and the enemy had used it merely to test out his defenses, or perhaps to mask the opening phases of encirclement.

He went up to his room and got out his violin, and began to compose upon it a melancholy praise of Rachel in the autumn, Rachel loving him with all the great, sad, dear heart in her little body, but forever separated from him by parental malice and stupidity. This praise contained little fluting phrases, very sad and clear, like the whistling of the fate bird in an oriental tragedy. Actually these were repetitions of a statement praising the shapeliness of Rachel's small hand and the rare glances of her wild, shy eyes, recollections which overwhelmed Tim with tenderness, as if, for a moment, he had encompassed her entire rarity in each of them.

His mother came upstairs for something, and stopped in his doorway. She smiled at him with loving sadness because of the attack in the kitchen, because she understood, at least in general, what it was that Tim didn't know he wanted in the world, and understood also that however foolishly and aimlessly he was pursuing it, his conception of the matter was probably quite lovely, and not to be worried about. Also, she was a person quickly moved by any sad or soft music. Her hungry spirit was so thinly covered now by either hope or energy that such music, or even solemn and illusory words with a moving cadence, brought tears to her eyes easily.

"That's very pretty, Timmy," she said. "What is it?"

"Oh, nothing," he said. "Just something I'm making up."

Nevertheless, for the moment he transferred his great sensation of love to his mother, so that it was received and completed, and he went off into a running, climbing, sometimes double-stopping ecstasy. After two or three minutes he returned to the sweet sadness.

Then Willis came up and stood in the doorway with his hands in his pockets. He stared at Tim with very wide eyes, and pretended to spit.

"Holy gee," he said, "put a little pep in it, will you?"

CHAPTER SIXTEEN: *About the Seeming Simplicity of Reaching the Bottom at Lake Tahoe; an Anticipatory Theme*

TIM got started on the importance of tennis to his great and bewildering love one day when we were up at Lake Tahoe together. This was when he had been out of high school three or four years and was in his dark period. He called me up one evening, and said he had to get out somewhere and do some thinking, and would I hike up to Tahoe with him. He didn't explain, but he didn't sound right, even for that time of his life, so I said yes.

We took all day going slowly over the Mt. Rose trail with our packs, and slept that night among the pines by the shore of the lake. It was August, but August is already autumn at that altitude, and it was cold at night. We woke before six o'clock, our blankets rimed with frost and our bodies stiff. The light in the woods and on the water was still gray, for the mountain stood up steeply behind us and made sunrise late. We could see the dome of water clearly, though, and there was already light on the snow-capped peaks on the other side. A long, thin cloud, like a celestial plain, of which we could see only the eastern edge, extended through the sky north from Tallac and was also alight. It was an hour without more weight or motion than the lake itself, and I have always felt that Tahoe, when it is quiet, does not touch its bottom or shores, but is suspended like air, and coldly and constantly refreshed by its true affinity, inter-stellar space. I believe it was this suspended nature, and not any obvious midday reason, like the blue color, which made the Indians call it the lake-of-the-sky. The Indians are subtle in their perceptions of natural qualities, and when the lake is blue it is very heavy in its basin, and not like sky at all. You can be-lieve then that it conceals the weight and power manifest when the wind blows, especially in the winter, when the mountains are white from summit to shore and the water is dark and tor-mented and nearly as mobile and ominous as the snow clouds pouring across it. No, the hour that is Tahoe is this hour of weightless stillness, or such hours as came later that day, when the lake remains motionless and your position with regard to the sun makes it still appear colorless and suspended. It has then a purity which is unique and imponderable, akin to that of Mt. Rose soaring up from it on the east, but not in the same way detached and regal. Mt. Rose is a self-conscious saint and Tahoe in the liquid quiet is an unconscious saint. You may yearn toward the purity of Mt. Rose, but you are finally ab-sorbed by the purity of Tahoe being quiet. It is beneficially alive and all-informing, and your mind becomes filled with quick, cool thoughts which are delightful and of more than mortal implication, but which cannot be retained and completed. What you retain is the way you feel: light, perfect, strong and gentle, which is the sum of the quick thoughts.

Because of the cold, the gleaming peaks and this vital peace, which seemed to have invaded even the rocks, Tim and I couldn't go back to sleep. We got up, and put on our boots and walked on the narrow, tawny road through the trees, and then out onto the rocks on a point. Here the sun reached us, and we saw the lake shine with great beauty, but also assume weight and comprehensibility. Then we went back and made a fire at the edge of the trees and ate bacon and fried eggs, and drank coffee. By then the sun had reached the beach, and was beginning to get hot. There was a lot of gray driftwood wedged in the rocks and scattered along the storm line on the sand. We dragged or rolled some of the biggest logs and timbers together and made a raft. We put food and cigarettes onto the raft, stripped off our clothes and pushed the raft out into the water. Tim got onto the raft and pushed with a long pole, and I stayed in the water. It's great feeling the cool water rise on your body, calves, knees, thighs, the crucial crotch, the belly, and begin to lift you, so that you walk as in one of those dreams where you take off at every step and have trouble getting back to earth, but all the time with your hands on a heavy, slow-moving raft. When I floated, and the pole no longer gave him good leverage, Tim dove in, and we began to swim the raft out together.

We stayed out with it until sunset. First we'd dive and swim and play porpoise, and then we'd climb back out and lie on the raft in the sun, peering down into the water or staring up at the sky. The illusion kept coming over me that I could dive up as well as down. We seemed suspended in the midst of a single substance. The day remained quiet until nearly sunset, and an imperceptible current floated us slowly out.

The water was so clear that it acted as a magnifying glass. While we were still in our cove, we saw something on the bottom which looked like an unblemished tin or nickel canteen. It gleamed very brightly where it lay upon the distinct ripples of the sand. It looked large and near. We decided to dive for it, not because we wanted it, but just for the fun of getting it. That's how you feel about everything at Tahoe when it's quiet.

I drew an ordinary breath and dove easily. When I had gone down as far as I could, the shining object appeared as far below me as ever. When I came up, I told Tim that it was a lot farther down than it looked. He wouldn't believe me until he'd tried too. After that we tried half a dozen serious dives apiece, breathing deeply several times and then filling up with air before each dive. We didn't seem to get any closer. We became enchanted by the idea of the probable depth of this water, and climbed back onto the raft and got the pole. We decided it was about twelve feet long. Tim held the pole straight down into the water. It looked short and stubby. I stood up very straight, looked all around at the mountains, filled my chest and belly with air, and dove again. I passed the end of the pole on the impetus of the dive and then began to work down. I gave it everything I had. My thighs and shoulders began to strain. The pressure closed on my head, especially on my ears. I began to feel numb and dull, and to observe about the core of my purpose, flashing, incomplete and ludicrous ideas. I had to concentrate upon not taking another breath. My body felt sure that even the water would be better in me than the used air that was there. I had no weight, but only tension. My hands felt frail, like fins. I believed that I could probably see through them, and that they were totally ineffective for propelling me on down through this water, which wasn't there at all, yet was as heavy as the center of earth. My eyes would probably pop out of my head in a second, like grapes squirted out of their skins between thumb and finger, yet I didn't look away from the gleam on the bottom. I let out breath to make it easier to go down, but that didn't seem to make any difference. I was still in a thwarting dream. Also, the canteen, if it was that, appeared to remain at the original distance. I gave up. I was so deflated that coming up was soon as hard as going down had been. Besides, my body was lax and resigned. When my head finally emerged, I sucked in air that felt like a shriek sounds. I had to hold onto the raft and keep my head down because the sky was full of black bats at a considerable distance whenever I looked up, and I didn't like them. Also, I was too weak to pull myself up, and was in a delicious state of drowsiness. I just hung there eating and drinking air and feeling my length slowly begin to take interest again.

After that heroic effort, Tim said, "You didn't look as if you got much beyond the end of the pole."

"Holy cow," I said. "The end of the pole? Why ..."

So Tim tried it, and I knew from the way he held on when he came up that he was afraid to see bats, but it was true. He had been grotesquely foreshortened by the water, but had appeared to continue an undignified wiggling at one level, only a little below the end of the pole, and the pole merely pointed at the shiny thing, like a finger, but didn't reach toward it. You might as well have gone diving for the sun.

After that we noticed how close to the top the beautiful, balancing fish appeared, when they came suddenly and hovered under us. Their shadows on the bottom were way below them. Yet when I put an arm slowly in toward a fish, the arm became a stump, and there was the fish, as far below it as the shadow was below the fish. We each did this three or four times. It made us realize, even better than diving or sticking the pole in, that the shining thing was as far away as the sun.

This perception of our limitations didn't disturb the peace and unity of the water and air, and the delight that it was to be there, naked and ourselves, exactly in the middle of it. Rather it cleared the senses like cold water after sleep, and made being alive wonderful and a thing to hang onto by joyous battle.

At some time in the middle of the day, we sat cross-legged upon the raft, feeling the coolness of the water around us and the heat of the sun like a weight on our necks and shoulders, and ate. Then we lit cigarettes and sat there smoking. We had floated far out, and no longer felt linked with the shore we had left, but balanced in solitude within a circle of mountains which preserved us from any touch or breath of a less perfect state of being.

TIM smoked his cigarette down to a butt, flicked the butt out onto the water, rolled over onto his elbow and lay there looking at Mt. Rose. I sat looking at him and waiting for it to come.

The swimming and being on the lake had relaxed him, but even so the way he was living and his fight with himself showed. He was thin and fish-belly white, with big, bruised circles under his eyes. He was trying to live two lives that didn't get along together, at least for him. He had reached the bottom as far as dance bands were concerned. He was playing the horn every night till anywhere from three to seven in the morning, at the Northern Lights, a dime-a-dance joint on Commercial that was really just a vestibule to the Stockade. Some hot bands have come out of places like that, but this wasn't one of them. It was just five guys putting in the time. Most of what they played was thin and sticky, and they played it all from the paper. What sleep Tim got after work wasn't much good either, because he had a downtown room in an office building on Second Street, and it was noisy there in the mornings. Usually by ten or eleven he'd be up in his pajamas, chain-smoking and drinking one cup of coffee after another, even when it was cold, and scribbling and picking away at his own stuff on the piano, with that soupy band fighting it all the time. He'd work all day, and then shave and change, snatch a little supper at Benners' or The Stag, and go back to the Northern Lights. He seldom got out, and then only to walk the streets by himself. He never got out of town, which was the thing that made me sure that something unusual had brought us up here.

I knew also that he was restless about a love affair he'd had the summer before, with a girl named Eileen Connor. He and another boy from the club where he'd been playing then had worked the summer with a beach-club band in Venice or Redondo, or some other of those Los Angeles shore towns, and Eileen had been the vocalist with the band. Tim had been writing to her the way he did write, long letters but not many of them, ever since, and the only picture he had in his room now was a photograph of her, which he kept on top of the piano. She had a beautiful face, almost like one of those idealized Greek statues, but with a gentleness and humor and life in the eyes and mouth that kept it from being anything like a statue. Her hair appeared blond in the photograph, but Tim said it was a pale copper color. He said she had lots of freckles too, which the photographer had been fool enough to rub out. He had talked about Eileen a good deal. He called her "young mother nature," and said that just being with her had made things come back clear, and had made him happy; not excited, just happy and filling up with life again. She liked everybody, he said, and didn't have any plots or plans in the world. He had never known anybody so kind. It was no ideal she was living up to, but just the way she was made, happy and kind and liking it right here and right now. I expected that when he began to talk, it would be about something that had come up concerning Eileen.

Instead he said, still looking at the mountain, not at me, "I saw Rachel Wells the night before last."

Finally I said, "I didn't know she was back."

"Neither did I," Tim said.

"How is she?"

"All right, I guess," Tim said. "She looked the same as ever."

"What's she been doing with herself?" I asked carefully.

"I don't know," Tim said. "I just saw her getting into the car. I didn't get to talk to her."

He glanced at me, and then rolled onto his belly, so that I wasn't in front of him.

"I wrote a letter to Eileen yesterday," he said.

"Oh," I said, and then asked, "did you mail it?"

"As quick as I finished it. I'd already thrown away three starts."

"Was the one you sent any better?"

"No. I guess it was the worst. I got myself explained out very thin."

"You didn't tell her one look at another girl had washed her out?"

"No, but it would have been better that way, I guess. I feel pretty cheap about hedging so much, when it comes out to that anyway."

"Well," I asked after a minute, "do you feel any better now?"

"Yes, I do. But I feel pretty cheap about Eileen just the same."

"You mean to tell me you think one look at Rachel, after all this time, really washed Eileen out?"

"I don't think so. I know so."

I was going to let it go, but after a while he said, "It's funny how sure you are. It was like I'd been out of my mind, or half alive all this time. I didn't think, or remember, or anything. It was just there."

"Did you have all the symptoms?" I asked him. "Did you get weak in the knees, and tremble and lose your breath and get dizzy, and feel as if you were sinking into a pit, and also as if you would take off at any minute?"

"All right," Tim said. "But I did, yes. I was going to the show at the Majestic. It was the first night I'd had free in two weeks, and I was feeling good. I was going to celebrate, Walt. I was going to the show, and then I was going to some hamburger joint that didn't have any music, and then I was going home and go to bed, just to see how it felt. But after I saw her, I went back to my room. Only I got restless, just sitting there, and I didn't want to talk to anybody, so later I walked up to her place. There hasn't been anybody there for nearly two years, you know. Not since her folks were divorced. But there were lights upstairs. It made me feel funny, after seeing it all dark so long."

"So you got to see her after all?"

"No. I didn't go in. It was too late."

"God help you," I said.

"Nuts," Tim said, and buried his face in his arms. It was coming over him again.

Without looking up, he finally said, "All right, so I am a fool. I've told myself that harder than you can tell me. It doesn't matter. I can't help it. That's why I wanted to come up here."

Now I know he was right, and really couldn't help the way those seizures of Rachel shook him, but then I had other ideas. I knew it wasn't faked, but I thought maybe he liked it, and wanted to make more out of it than was really there. I didn't know the way he'd acted with her, and the way it had bothered him.

"Listen, my punch-drunk friend," I said. "You can't go on the rest of your life standing outside Rachel Wells' window looking at the light. You'd better start working on her, or forget it."

"No," he said. "I know better than that now."

"Caesar's ghost," I said, "are you hypnotized?"

"Sometimes I think I am," he said.

"Rachel's a nice kid," I began.

Tim lifted his head and stared at me angrily. "That's got nothing to do with it," he said sharply. "It doesn't matter what she looks like. It doesn't matter what she thinks. It doesn't matter what she says or what she does. It doesn't even matter what I do, as long as I'm with her, though I could kick myself around the block afterwards. Only now I know that while she does that to me I won't do any better, so she can't stand me. Nobody could. In school I was too crazy to know that. I always thought I'd do fine the next time. Now I know better, so at least I stay away."

"My Lord," I said, "I thought that was all in the legends, or anyway not after Lord Byron died."

"Never mind about Lord Byron," he said. "I know what happens to me."

So I went more softly. "But you didn't even go steady with her in school. You had dates with a dozen other girls. There was Marjory Hale, for instance. . . ."

Then he slowly told me, all afternoon, the things I hadn't known. Sometimes, as when he came to the adventure with the moss-agate, I thought he wouldn't go on. He would sit there, or lie there, and not say anything for a long time, but then he would go on after all. Just seeing Rachel for a moment had brought it all back. Anything else three days old was older than everything about her. I'll have to relate those incidents one at a time, though, because other matters attach to them which I knew myself, or which he told me later, and they make a long story that can't be hurried. When he was done telling me about the moss-agate, which apparently bothered him the most, he sat there with his arms around his knees, staring at the raft between his legs. I realized then how late it was, and that he was tired and ashamed at having told so much.

"Well, I'll lay off the fatherly advice after this, anyway," I told him.

"It's all right," he said.

He looked up. "God, look where we are," he exclaimed.

I looked back. We were so far out that I couldn't even be sure which cove was ours. I had to guess by the mountains above the shore, especially by Mt. Rose. There was a chilly wind beginning to blow out of the north-west too, and clouds coming up with it. The sun was low and very red. There was probably a forest fire somewhere on the California side of the mountains. The water was running in small, quick waves, which reflected the red light from thousands of bloody points and angles. The light also glowed evenly upon Mt. Rose and upon the great peaks far in the south-east, and made the forests below their bare summits appear deep and warm and soft. There wasn't really any warmth in that light though. We felt a little of the keen, quickening anxiety any creature feels about night coming on in a bad place. We were already shivering, and we remembered that frost on our blankets in the morning. We noticed for the first time that we were badly sunburned. That frost would feel great on a sunburn.

"We'll have to swim it in," I said.

"I hate to get back into that water," Tim said, but he looked happy about it. Confession was over. He was a free man, or anyway a freer. It wouldn't last, because later, especially in the morning, he was going to feel worse about having told me than about any of the things he'd told, but right now he felt better.

We dove in and began to swim the raft toward the place where we thought the cove was. When the first stars appeared in the east, we lined up a star and a peak to steer by when the light was gone.

CHAPTER EIGHTEEN: *Beginning Revelations on a Raft in the Sky, or About Tristram of the Tennis Courts, and How to Keep the Soul in the Body in One Simple Lesson*

SO TIM, having watched Rachel dance to the flying white ball in the dusk, took up tennis. When he had saved enough money from Saturdays in the lumber yard, he bought a racket and three balls, which he kept in his locker at school, and almost every afternoon he went down to the park and played, and often, at night, he put up marvelous battles, for an unknown junior, against Bill Tilden and Bill Johnson, and sometimes he was the inspired substitute who saved the Davis Cup at Wimbledon or Forest Hills with Rachel watching him and practically praying for him. At first he had to play with the other dubs on the bumpy macadam courts, but because he was quick and loose, and his eye and his rhythm were fine, and because he learned a good deal by a kind of unsystematic bodily osmosis when he was drawn, by Rachel's presence, to watch the better players, and because he strove valiantly by day to come up to the beautiful tennis he played at night, he progressed so well that by the fall of his sophomore year he was often invited to fill in on the first courts. It was then that the bracketings for the school tournament were put up on the bulletin boards in the hall, and he committed the audacious act which would have been his first sharp lesson in realism if he hadn't been able to overcome it by an old religious exercise of his and by the greater beauty of his other lives. Perhaps, also, since she was unpredictably moved by all manner of little events, it was that act which eventually led to the mingling of his inner lives with those of Marjory Hale.

The girls' singles and doubles were posted on their side of the study-hall steps, and the boys' on theirs, and the mixed doubles were posted on both sides. For three days Tim looked at the bracketings every time he went by. He pretended to look at all of them, but it was really the mixed doubles he was watching. Rachel's name wasn't up there yet. In legend he often accomplished the feat of asking her to play with him, and she was pleased, and they went on together to triumphs which even reached the national tournament. But somehow these legends were poor, thin stuff, with no enduring power to please him. There were the actual brackets, for everybody to see, and no blissful pairing, no exalted promise, no Wells and Hazard.

He made a dozen false starts at asking her, but he could never reach her. Sometimes her girl friends would join her before he could. Sometimes she would be out of the building and so far ahead, when he looked for her at noon or after school, that he would have had to run to catch her, and so expose the sacred to public ridicule. Sometimes he would stop simply because the idea of approaching Rachel, when she was actually there in sight, made him dizzy and made his heart beat wildly, so that he knew what would happen if he tried to speak. Instead of shuffling up to her in manly ease, his hands in his pockets, and saying, "Hi, Rachel. How's about we should team up for the mixed?" he would stare, and his mind would be filled by a hundred forms of ecstatic address and a thousand ways of begging that she make him, by being his partner, a god upon the courts for two eternal weeks, and actually the sweat would bubble out upon him, and his tongue would stumble saying something like, "I just thought maybe—well, I didn't see your name up for mixed," or, "I just thought maybe, if you weren't going to play with anybody else . . ." And furthermore, this meeting, which he rehearsed a hundred times, would have to take place right in the main hall, among all those knowing eyes swimming in sardonic thoughts. Still, the time went by.

At noon of the fourth day, with the tournament only two days off, he hurried from his session room and lapsed into careful indolence in the central hall. In spite of the blow it was to see Rachel coming nearer from the other wing, he made his approach in the courtly manner approved in that time and place, heels dragging, thumbs in belt, an expression indicating that if love did not follow this interview, a good yawn would do. Rachel passed a window, and her small face, for a moment, was very clear in the white, sunless light from the court. The paralysis began again, but this time Tim forced it to crouch and wait. And then a girl's voice, a high, harpy piping, called, "Rachy, Rachy, wait a sec," and she turned and waited. Pauline Chester, the bosomy girl, joined her on one side, and upon the other Marjory Hale, who was tall and thin and had a long, slow, sinuous walk, and a long, slow, sinuous look in her cool blue eyes, although the rest of her face appeared soft and young and without energy. Having come this far, however, having put down the inner hordes, Tim would not retreat. He didn't even look at the other two girls, and he spoke like one demanding a manifest right long denied him.

"Can I see you for a minute, Rachel?"

He was right in front of her, so she had to stop. After a wild and silent moment, Pauline and Marjory went on a few steps and waited. Tim could feel them waiting.

Rachel glanced at him fiercely, and then looked at the floor. "Well, what is it?" she asked.

Miraculously, he said, "How about playing the mixed with me?"

"I'm sorry. I already have a partner," she said, and started to pass him on the side toward the wall.

It was not that he didn't believe her. It was never that he meant to argue. It was only that having trusted those bracketings as one trusts the sun to rise, and having succeeded a hundred times in his mind, he was unable to comprehend a mere contradictory fact. He stepped toward the wall also, and blocked her again.

"I didn't see you signed up," he said, "and since we're both sophomores, I thought, maybe . . ."

"Well, I am signed up. Will you please let me by now?"

He didn't intend not to either, but just the same it didn't sound much like a supplication before the altar when he asked, "Who are you playing with?" quite sharply and loudly, in order to be able to say it at all.

Rachel stared directly at him in her tremulous fury. "Ham Brown, if it's any of your business," she said, and then, because he still didn't move or stop gazing at her, "And even if I wasn't, I wouldn't play with you. You have a nerve to ask me, if you want to know it. I'm trying to get somewhere with my game, and you don't even have a school ranking. What made you think I'd play with you?"

Slowly then, and with dreadful reality, Tim saw that this matter should be considered in terms of tennis, and that he was not only a fool, the butt of illusions, but that he must appear to her to be a calculating planner, hoping to get by on her tennis. It was true that he had no ranking. He had never thought of it, but it was true. And Rachel was already the school's number-one player, and the state junior champion. So was Ham Brown. Theirs was the natural alliance of equals. It was based upon reality, and it had a future. He couldn't say anything. He drew back against the wall and let her pass. She went quickly to the bulletin board and picked up the pencil hanging from it by a string, and angrily, in bold, black print, signed her name and Ham Brown's together. Then, without even looking at him, she joined the other two girls. Marjory Hale looked at him with her cool and knowing gaze and turned away, probably to hide a smile. Pauline examined him with a vigorous lack of expression that clearly was going to burst into great expression at the first possible moment. There was no one else in the hall. The three backs went away from him, and around the corner toward the front door, perfection flanked by the Sancho Panza and the Don Quixote of womanhood. When they were out of sight, the laughter came. Laughing, they went out together into the world in the light of noon.

Tim moved, and after a moment his mutilated spirit also disentangled itself from the wall and followed him down into the basement. It waited apart while he took his lunch pail out of the locker, and followed him out into the back court, and with bowed head sat behind him on the steps. It kept touching him coldly and hotly, reminding him that it was there, but he was unable to receive it. All afternoon it couldn't get in.

After school Tim went home and left his books and went out again. He was still uninhabited. He cut across the Experiment Farm to the Valley Road. He felt encouraged for a few minutes, because a man working in the orchard spoke to him in a loud and friendly way, as if he were fit to be known, but this didn't last. The man didn't know the truth about him. He worked through the last fence and went north on the Valley Road, past the small ranches where the long arms of the derricks were lifting the last alfalfa onto the bread-loaf stacks. This work went on in another world, where the men were all in one piece. He crossed the Pyramid Road at the head of Valley Road, and went on north-west through the little yellow hills, and then over the gray hills covered with sage, to the formation which the boys called Castle Rock. He climbed to the top and sat there, with his arms about his knees, and looked abroad, half seeing. The valley was spread quiet and warm in the late afternoon. The smokes of Reno rose vertically from among the yellow trees and were imperceptibly dissipated into a high, faint and luminous mist. Far upon the south-west was the blue Sierra. Close upon the west loomed Peavine, old and lone and dark, slowly and grandly extending his shadow across the pass in which the Purdy Road and the Western Pacific tracks went north. The shadow came up toward Castle Rock, and the chill of evening preceded it a little, and the smell of the sage grew stronger, as if a thin rain had refreshed it. Up here it was undeniable that the shining and only bearably melancholy world was also vast and durable. It stretched away upon all sides of Timothy Hazard, and absolved him by time and space. He felt little bursts of reaching to embrace it. He watched the glory of the light shrink toward its well in the mountains, and his abandoned spirit was less desolate, but still he couldn't bring it in. He knew what he had to do.

He forced himself to move at last, and scrambled down, by crevices and ledges, onto the round hill again. Every sage bush had a long shadow, and the hills and outcroppings cast huge shadows upon one another. The eastern mountains and the high points of rock around him glowed with light. The coolness and the shadows, like his despair, the light and the last warmth like his joys, touched together in him, and made a momentary liveliness. He began to run. By the time he had crossed the dome of the first hill, the running was no effort. He stretched into a longer stride on the downslope, and wove through the brush, or hurdled it, clump after clump. He swung around the curves of hills, labored on the rises, and opened up again as he began to descend. The isolated half-thoughts of his mind fused into a current and became warmer and fell into rhythm with the continuous pelting of his body. He began to see bits of the world around him with great clarity. He was rid of the film of his misery, and his heart leapt at each glimpse. It was a world he could touch. He leapt at the dying sunlight deep in the treetops on the university campus. He saw the fountain of fire that was a mare's tail up the eastern sky, and soared at it. He often ran like this, and always, when he was running his best, he would remember the wild stallion he had seen running on the range north of Pyramid. Now he remembered the stallion, and could imagine that he was running like that. It wasn't exactly that he was the stallion, but more as if he were following it with equal speed and ease, endurance and grace. He could see the stallion rolling away before him down the slope, its long and heavy tail and mane streaming, their flow giving shape to invisible wind, and easy and exultant, he came after. Then he ran even faster, and the stallion was gone. His mind became quick and observant. He thought about his running, not the mere swinging of his arms and legs, but the tactics his pace made necessary. He looked over the field well before him, sharply, attentively, like an officer who almost at once must launch a dangerous attack, picking the places to descend, the places to climb, the best track through or around bad ground or obstacles he couldn't leap. When he came around the last dome, and saw the home region of the valley open below him, he felt the strong and steady joy go up, like a continuous hymn of praise, and knew that he was back together again. It seemed then that he would never want to stop running. He coursed along the Valley Road, exulting and increasing his pace. He ran through the stubble of the farm fields, and swung back and forth among the trees of the orchard for the joy of the curves he was making. Only at the corner of his own block did he begin to slow down, so that he could just walk into the house, as if nothing had been happening. Then there was the cold water all over him, and the clean garments, and combing his hair in the St. Francis order of his room, with the blue dusk in his window, which he understood because he had brought the world in with him.

Yet this unity was only a token, a promise. After supper he studied for a time, full of positive resolutions, but none of the dull matter was clear. His reclaimed spirit raced over the pages and took nothing with it. He went back several times, and tried to concentrate. The joy became peace, and then uneasiness and then discontent. The enormity of his address to Rachel came back over him, a deep, dark tide. At eight-thirty he closed his history book slowly, and went out and began to walk. He walked down toward the middle of the city, skirted the bright center, crossed the bridge and climbed up into the shadows and single street lights of the Mt. Rose quarter. He looked at all the drawn shades, orange with the light through them, and imagined for an instant that each shadow he saw passing across them was Rachel's shadow. He knew where she really lived now, but because of her, yearning and love went out of him to these beings making their brief shadows on the blinds. He went to her actual home too, and stood in the shadow of a tree. Her window, or the one he had decided was her window, was dark, and he imagined her wandering slowly among the trees on the lawn, gently bewildered by night and autumn and the distant, leaf-broken shining of the street lights. Then he went on around the south side, the hound on the tangled and sorrowful traces of humanity. At last the weight of this brooding, the innumerable small, sad thoughts which he could never hold and finish, began to make him angry at himself. Everything that was wrong was in him; he was the fountainhead of all that was wrong with the world. On the way home he began to run fiercely. He had on basketball shoes, and he ran cat-footed, fleetly, along the avenues of dappled shadow toward each little moon upon a crossing and through its light and back into the dark and leafy tunnel of the next block, where shadow and light flowed over him and became quiet again behind him.

CHAPTER NINETEEN: *The Spring Running*

IT WAS after a school dance the next spring that Tim did the night running or angry running which led him to go out for track so that he could run a duel with Red Laughry. Red took Rachel to that dance. Red had been taking Rachel to many dances and movies and parties for nearly two months. It was the first time Rachel had ever gone steady with anybody, and in Tim's other lives, Red often was Marholt of Ireland, and not always as honorable as the Marholt of the original legend, either. In the slower life at the high school, however, it is doubtful if Red even knew who Tim was. Red was the best mile and half-mile runner in school. He was a senior now, and he hadn't lost a race in either of those events since his freshman year. Also, he had a face which made other boys respectful, and made many girls watch him when he wasn't looking at them, a white, tight-drawn, silent-looking face, which would have been very handsome, in a bony way, if the nose hadn't been broken and pushed over. The look in his eyes went well with that nose. Everybody felt that it would be dangerous to disturb the tense and rather haughty quiet of Red Laughry.

The dance was a formal, which meant that the boys wore their best suits instead of cords and sweaters and the girls wore evening gowns and put little, bright ornaments or flowers in their hair. It also meant that there were no robber dances, and that the band played more waltzes and other slow, sweet numbers than usual, and that the stags, instead of rioting and stealing partners, sat in the shadowed alcoves under the balconies most of the time and watched wistfully.

Rob Gleaman's band was working the dance, and Tim sat in the front row beside Rob and blew the fine, shining trumpet which Jacob's father had sold him for much less than he should have asked for it. The band sat on a platform in the middle of the gym floor and tootled along, low and slow, and the dancers circled slowly and dreamily about them through the light and shadow made by a tent roof of woven crepe paper hung with clusters of balloons like huge grapes. There was a great deal of excitement in this quiet dancing, on account of spring and the music. It showed in the dreamy faces going by, and in the liquid eyes of the girls, and in the sudden flowing together of little groups when the music stopped. Tim sat there, holding it in to be soft but clear and true, and watched for Rachel all the time. Usually, when he was playing for a dance, and Rachel was there, he would leave his horn on the chair a couple of times during the evening and dance with her, but tonight, when he went over between numbers to ask Red for a dance, Rachel turned away to speak to another girl, pretending not to see him, and Red said, "Sorry, fella, full up." Well, that was the trouble with program dances. Still, it made even worse the way he always felt about Rachel at a dance, as if he had been with her all of a much longer life than his, but now somebody had taken her away, and he was empty. He kept on watching for her after he had asked for a dance, and whenever he saw her he would be startled, as if it were the first time he had seen her that night. She was always dancing with Red, too, with her head laid against Red's blue coat, and her eyes closed. He had never seen her dance with her eyes closed before, trusting everything to her partner. When her face, sleeping against Red, came into one of the patches of soft, bluish light, something happened to his breath, so that his horn faltered, or failed to hold on a long one, and Rob, swinging his sax with him, would turn and look at him. Then it came over Tim, thinking about it between dances, that Rachel and Red were dancing a straight program. Rachel had never done that before either, not even since she'd been going steady with Red. At first this only made him feel more deserted than ever, but then he got to feeling so bad, so empty and as if he wanted to cry, that by the time the band drifted straight on from the last number into *Home, Sweet Home,* he was angry at himself for caring. He deliberately blew two or three wild, off-key banshee wails into the fade-out, capped the coda with a derisive "over the fence is out," jammed his horn into its case and nearly ran out of the gym, without even saying good night to Rob. The rest of the band watched him go. When he disappeared under the red exit sign, the pianist grinned at Rob, clasped both hands over his heart and lifted a lugubrious face with tragic eyes rolled up toward a cluster of balloons.

"In the spring," Rob murmured. "But he ain't gonna jam my sweet and sicklies for any dame. I gotta take him aside and tell him the facts of life. There ain't really any angels. It's just glandular accumulation." Rob had a lot of older musical friends, who got him into speakeasies and other places with advanced philosophies.

Tim had never smoked before, but he bummed a cigarette outside, and hung around until Rachel and Red came out, and got into Red's car without anybody else along, and drove off slowly, and not toward the middle of town or toward the Mt. Rose quarter either. Then he threw the cigarette away and got his bicycle out of the rack and rode home.

In his room the heaviness of spring, and of the evening of watching, still wouldn't ease up in him. He wasn't angry now, just sad and heavy, but he changed into his old cords and a sweat shirt and a pair of tennis shoes, and went out again, and rode up to the university and past the university gymnasium, where there was a dance still going on, and down into the bowl of the Mackay Field. It was dark and sad and restless down there too. The sky was clouded, only a few stars showing in the tattered south, and the soft wind sighed in the trees at the corners of the field, and sometimes a faint phrase or two would drift down from the band, which sounded big and smooth after Rob's. He had to force himself to begin running, but by the time he had finished one lap, he was angry again, and began to run furiously, not fleetly, as after the stallion, but with driving heel-and-toe strides. He was beating this crazy, sick feeling in him.

As he came around the third time, he was startled by a match flaring up just as he passed the starting line, and he saw that there were two men standing there on the turf. They were still there every time he came around. Now that he knew they were there, he could see them dimly in the light from the gym above. He wanted to run alone, and each time he approached the line, he would run a little harder, to get past them, and then he would hold each increase of speed all through the next lap. Still his breath didn't bind, and his legs didn't get heavy or tight. He began to exult. He was winning something. He felt wild and universally destructive. His feet crunched an accelerating tempo on the cinders, and when he believed for an instant that he was lagging, he would get angry again, and push the tempo up. When he passed the training quarters beside the back stretch, he could hear the hasty pelting of his feet, like somebody racing tirelessly beside him, and he wanted to shout defiance at this ghost runner too. This desire for roaring sound gradually became a blaring and martial quickstep inside him, to which he ran two and even three to one. He went lap after lap. He didn't know how many laps he went.

Then, during one lap, the music in him began to be sadder and slower, and became a big music, like an orchestra, not a band. It was about the spring night now, and not about his little anger against it. He felt a deep content in this music, as if his body slowly turned and plunged in it as in dark, cool and heavy water; it was a turning like the motion of the full boughs of the cottonwoods in the spring night, moving separately, one after another, as the wind slowly played over them. The size of spring surrounded him, so that he was suddenly as nothing in the night, and wanted to cry again, but now with a kind of relief. He must make a quiet ending if those two men were still there. He wished they would go on about their own business. He wished, but not angrily now, that at least they wouldn't stand right where he had laid his bicycle on the grass. He slacked off to slow, springy strides on his toes. The sensation of the swelling music died, and the night was itself. Before he came to the men, he turned off onto the turf and walked softly. They were still there. They peered at him as he came near.

"How far did you run, kid?" one of them asked.

"I don't know," Tim said. "I didn't keep count."

"You're out for track, aren't you?"

"No."

"Well, you oughta be."

"I don't know," Tim said. These men were university students, and they were making a mistake. They thought he was on the hill too. This misunderstanding made it hard to talk to them, as if he were telling them a lie, or at least trying to hide something from them that they had a right to know. The implied praise made him happy, though, as if he had won something by this race.

"How far did you run before we got here?" the other man asked. He was lighting a pipe, and he was a big man with a pink face and blond hair. The first man was small and thin and dark.

"Two laps, I guess," Tim said.

"Then you must have run about two miles," the small man said.

"Tell him," the blond said.

"I've got a stop-watch. We clocked you after the first lap we saw."

"We clocked you for a mile," the big man said. He sounded excited. "You did it in 4:39," he announced.

"Is that good?" Tim asked.

"Is that good? My God!"

The small man, whose face by the match had looked thin and heavy with beard stubble, and ironical in a hard way, was more judicious. "It's good enough for most of the company you'll get around here, buddy, and you can sure as hell do better. You'd already run a couple when we put the clock on you. You oughta cut it plenty on a straight mile. What are you, a frosh?" he asked.

"No," Tim said uneasily. "I'm just in high school."

"Oh," the dark man said. And then, "Well, you're coming up here, aren't you?"

"I don't know. Maybe." Tim didn't think he would be, but it seemed politer to say maybe.

"Well, you'd better go out for track at school anyway. You can run, boy."

"You got spikes on?" the big blond asked.

"Tennis shoes."

"My God," the big blond said.

The two men crossed the track and climbed the hill beside the grandstand. Tim rode his wheel around the end of the track, left it among the spruce trees by the ditch and went to the edge of the water, which gurgled with fullness in the dark. This was the place the boys called Cement Bottom, because, for a few yards, the Orr Ditch flowed here between concrete walls and over a concrete floor. The Orr Ditch is another, though a minor, sacred water, one of the seven secret streams of Reno, which run in great loops through and under the city, linking the snow-feeding mountains upon the west and north with the valley upon the south and the east. Tim had not been in the ditch since he was in grammar school, when the boys had come up there often in the hot days of summer, usually to Cement Bottom, because they could go in naked there, behind the trees and bushes, and because they wouldn't step on the kind of things that were sometimes caught in the muddy parts of the ditch. He undressed and let himself slowly down into the darkness. He was surprised to touch water so soon. The ditch was full and cold with the spring run-off. It made a rushing eddy about his thighs and dragged his legs swiftly downstream. He sank into the invisible water, and let himself be carried away to the bend, where he began to swim back strongly against the central current. When he was over the cement bottom again, he rolled into the slack water and pulled himself up onto the wall. He felt good, chilled and hard and all one. He scraped the water off himself with the edges of his hands, dressed wet, and rode home. He had made up his mind to go out for track. He was going to try for the mile and the half-mile.

CHAPTER TWENTY: *In Memoriam—Sunday Wind*

TIM and Red had it out in the first meet of the season, a triangular meet with Sparks and Carson. It was a brilliant, cloudless day, in which everything stood out with wonderful clearness, the nearest leaf and the farthest mountain, but the air was still chilly, and when Tim came up to the field, a gusty wind from the north was beginning to whirl the sawdust in the vaulting pit. Tim was thinking this would make hard going in the back-stretch, when he saw Red's car parked against the fence at the top of the grandstand, with Red and Rachel in the front seat, and Marjory Hale and Sheik in the back. For the first time he felt really nervous. When he got down onto the field his knees were shaking and his breath came short. He sat down on a bench in the sun until he felt steadier, and then wandered around watching the first events, and looking up often at Red's car. He didn't feel exactly scared any longer, but as if he were floating in an unreal world. He went over to the training quarters before the first call for the half. He didn't want to stay in the dressing room with Red. He was just pulling on his shorts, though, when Red sauntered in. Neither of them said anything, and Tim went out onto the steps to put his spikes on. Often, in practice, when he got into his stride just right, like following the stallion, it had seemed to Tim he could beat Red easily. Now he wasn't so sure. He had only that 4:39 to put against all Red's victories, and how could you be sure of timing in the dark with matches? The coach hadn't let them run against each other, but only against time, and he had kept the times to himself. Tim went out onto the turf and began his limbering-up exercises. Red came out onto the steps and sat down to put on his spikes. He didn't take any exercises, but began to jog around the track, working his arms in the air to loosen his shoulders. Tim finished his exercises and began to jog too. When he passed the stands he saw Rachel and Sheik and Marjory sitting up there in the center section in the sun.

The man with the megaphone made the second call for the half, and the coach signaled for Red and Tim to come over to him. They stood together in front of them, and he looked at them attentively, as if making up his mind how much of what he was thinking he should tell them. Tim looked at Red's legs. Red had hairless, white legs, with flat thighs and ankles, and big calves. He had rub-down on his legs now, and they shone like polished marble and gave off a strong smell of wintergreen. Red also had that say-nothing, who-are-you look on his face. Tim felt hairy and smaller than he was, and awkward beside Red, and hollow, as if Red were full of a valuable power and knowledge he didn't have. He told himself that he ought to be thinking only about defeating the Sparks and Carson runners, but he couldn't convince himself. He was really going to run these races against Red. He heard behind him the thud of the discus and the voices of the officials calling the distances, as if in a dream. It seemed to him they had been standing there a long time, and he glanced at the coach. The coach was chewing gum rapidly, but his expression was as inscrutable as Red's. He stood there in his red sweater, with the wind blowing his fine, blond hair about, and looked at each of them, and then, when he began to speak, looked at Red.

"We've got a good chance for this meet yet," he said. "We may have to give away all but three or four points in the sprints, the hurdles, the high jump and the shot, but we'll cut in enough on the rest so that with Sparks and Carson splitting where they should, we can still do it. But we've got to come in solid on the distances. There's nobody to push you in this half. Just run it for points, not time, and save yourself for the mile. There's a couple of good boys in the mile, but if you go in there fresh, we can have first and second there too."

He looked at them one at a time again, and they nodded. But then he looked at Red once more, and after a moment added, "The mile's your race, Red. This one's Tim's. Save yourself. Tim can take care of it. Just be sure you get your second."

Red looked at the coach, and Tim looked down and dug at the turf with the spikes of his left shoe.

"Got it?" the coach asked Red.

"Sure," Red said.

"O.K. Peel your sweaters and try a few easy starts on the turf."

A good many unfinished, rebellious thoughts flashed in Tim's mind while he made these practice starts, but when the last call came the coach took his elbow and walked to the starting line with him, warning him against being drawn out by anybody jack-rabbiting on him. "Just go to the pole and run your pace, and go out in front when it puts you there," he said.

"Yes, sir," Tim said. It felt like a trust, put that way, like something more important than a personal duel with Red, and he felt better.

When he went to the line, he was nervous again, though. He tried to get in his mind, in advance, that easy, room-to-spare feeling of following the stallion, but it wouldn't come, and suddenly he felt very heavy and scared and out of his body, as if he couldn't predict what his own legs would do. When the gun went off, he didn't leap, but floated out of his pits. The heavy-legged boy from Sparks, on his right, jumped ahead, went away from him in a long-striding sprint, and took the pole yards in front. Red, who had drawn the inside track, went into second place, a dark, thin-legged little Indian from Carson worked into third, and Tim drew in behind him. He could hear the broken rhythms of the other runners following him, and sorting themselves out on the first curve.

A little past the middle of the back-stretch, although he still seemed to be running very hard and without getting his breath even or feeling the track, Tim passed the Indian. Then the wind seemed to be keeping him out of rhythm. The curve into the stretch was sheltered by a sand bluff, and the wind let go of him there. Ten yards ahead, Red was moving out to pass the heavy-legged boy, who turned his head for an instant, but couldn't step up his pace. Tim caught him at the starting post and passed him going into the first curve. The coach was on the curve, yelling something at Red. Halfway around the curve, Red glanced back. But then, instead of slacking off when he saw that Tim was coming away safely, he stepped his pace up almost to a sprint. He wasn't going to take his second, then. Tim felt an upsurge that was almost as much pleasure as anger. As he passed the coach he heard him yelling at him to take it easy, to let Red have it, but he didn't even make a meaning of the words. He could feel his spikes bite into the cinders now. Everything evened off and he rounded the curve fast and leaned and sprinted into the wind. He came onto the north curve only two or three yards behind Red, and they rounded into the stretch running almost lock-step. The coach was up at that curve now, yelling at both of them, but they didn't pay any attention to him. They were frozen into this fight now. They couldn't have stopped it if they'd wanted to. For an instant, as the bluff cut off the wind, Tim came abreast of Red, but his chest was laboring and his legs were tight. Red opened into a full sprint on the straightaway. Tim matched it. Halfway to the tape, Red began to pull away, a few inches at a stride. In his mind, Tim lashed himself like a frantic jockey. He was overcome by despair at inwardly running twice as hard, and yet finding himself falling back. Red took the tape away two yards ahead.

Tim tried to ease off properly, but he staggered as he crossed the line, and then somebody was running beside him and putting an arm around him. He let this boy walk him slowly out onto the grass and then let somebody else force him into a sweat shirt. The sunlight was filled with black and winged creatures. He couldn't get his chin off his chest without his head falling clear back, or lolling on one shoulder. The boy with the arm around him continued to walk him slowly along the grass. He knew vaguely, because of the pressure, that the wind was blowing from behind him, but he couldn't feel it on his skin. He seemed petrified. His legs were stony, and yet they kept buckling at the knees, so that the boy really had to hold him up. He heard his helpers talking to him, but not what they said. Down at the end of the turf they turned him around and started him back. The corporeal illusions passed off slowly. He just felt sick to his stomach and indifferent.

The helpers stretched him on a blanket in the sun, behind a bench. There was another blanket hung over the back of the bench to cut off the wind. All of this had probably taken a very long time, yet the announcer was just calling the results of the half-mile through his megaphone. His voice came loudly, and then faintly, because of the wind and because he kept turning to call to all sides. Somebody from Sparks, one of the runners Tim hadn't even seen clearly, had come in third. The little Indian had finished fourth. Red had tied the meet record, even in that wind.

The coach came over and knelt on one knee and gripped first Tim's calves and then his upper legs. They wouldn't roll or give under his hand.

"Rub him down good. Slap on some extra and leave it to soak in and put him under blankets," the coach said. He sounded angry. He didn't say anything else, but got up and walked away.

The rub-down, with wintergreen in it, going on icy and then turning hot, felt good. Its sharp smell was as needles to his spirit also. His mind sat apart, by itself, drowsy and contemplative, and permitted the active hands to knead his legs, which were of a different and negligible substance, but the sharp smell of the wintergreen cut through this somnolence and began to make him feel alive.

Red was being kneaded on another blanket, a few yards away. His face was very white, a different white than usual, almost blue-white, like skimmed milk. The coach didn't go near him, but went over to the pit where the broad jump was going on.

When they finally went to the line for the mile, he was there looking at them, but he still didn't say anything to either of them.

Tim now felt a steady determination to outrun Red. That was practically all he was thinking about. There was a Sparks runner, a long-legged, bony boy whose jersey flapped in the wind like a sail, who might make trouble in this race, but in Tim's mind, as if he stood at the edge of the track and watched the finish, this runner came in third, yards behind the first two. Tim knew he wasn't ready yet to run his best, but at least he wasn't nervous, and he felt loose and easy from the rub-down. He wouldn't have to run far before he'd be able to imagine his wild stallion. Then he would be all right. A mile was no distance when you felt like that.

The thorn of the coach's silence was in Red. He knew as well as Tim did that the coach blamed him most for all that wasted speed in the half-mile. Also, his confidence had been shaken by the closeness of the race. He let this show by looking scornful instead of just blank when the runners drew for their lanes. Red drew the second lane and Tim the outside one, but still in the first rank. There were three runners in a second row behind them.

Red went away from the start, jumping out of his pits like a sprinter and then not breezing and not calculating, but pushing himself. For a moment Tim felt panic, like a touch of his despair at the end of the half, but then was steadied by his desire to get right, to pick up his rhythm and begin to roll, so that he could go faster each lap, the way he had that night. This could be done only by working up smoothly, until the joy of flight came. He even let the thin boy from Sparks and a stocky, chopping runner from Carson go in ahead of him at the first curve. He stayed behind them all through the first lap, letting them break the wind on the back stretch. On the north curve he could see across the infield that Red was still pulling away, and another seizure of the scared urge to go after him delayed the getting right. It was rhythmically denied him, too, because of the irritating chop-step of the Carson runner right ahead of him. He couldn't work out a syncopation of his own stride with this chopping, so that he felt as if he were running now one stride and now another, like a person walking railroad ties. He passed the Carson runner on the turn into the grandstand stretch, and was at once relieved to fall in behind the Sparks boy's long, though dogged and flat-footed stride. He could match this rhythm and feel the ease coming back.

Red finished the first quarter nearly twenty yards ahead. Tim made himself stay behind the bony boy up the back-stretch of the second lap, but that heavy stride was beginning to clog him too. He knew it wasn't tired running; the Sparks boy could run for hours that way, though not much faster. But there was no release in it; it was a working run. So it was still in irritation, not in freedom, that he set out to catch Red.

The bony boy challenged him all the way down the grand-stand stretch, but finally gave as they came onto the first curve of the third lap. Tim went to the boards without slacking his passing stride, which had already pulled him up a few yards on Red. He wasn't more than twelve or fifteen yards back now. He became fiercely intent on closing that gap without breaking his stride, just by reaching harder. He couldn't get happy. All right then, he'd run angry.

On the turn into the back-stretch, Red glanced over his shoulder. A bolt of joy shot up out of Tim's anger. That was a sign, if an old runner like Red was looking around, and only in the third lap at that. Drums of running began to beat in Tim's mind, though he didn't hear any music for them, no quick-step. He could drum and still keep his mind, with single animosity, on making Red's flapping number 27 grow larger. He could feel that he was running stiffly, that his spikes were jarring him when they hit, but it even felt good to have them strike so hard; it came from eagerness and temper. The wind died off while he was passing the training quarters, and he could hear the echo of his spikes running beside him, in the same rhythm, but about a quarter beat off. Then he passed the building and there was no echo, and after a moment the wind swung back down strongly. It made his eyes water and his lungs labor. He despaired of ever getting right.

Going into the north turn he was still ten yards behind. The ten yards began to look long, but when the turn put the wind onto his shoulder instead of against his chest, this little knotting of the inner runner slipped straight. He thought the drums again, and thought distinctly, in so many words, that if he couldn't run joyously, then he must at least run evenly. He concentrated on evenness, and gradually the tension passed from him. A kind of golden anger of triumph poured into him. Second wind it is generally called, and it is made up as much of smoothness, of getting the inner and outer runner together, as it is of attaining an oxygen balance. Joyously he thought, several times, rapidly and in the tempo of his running, "Now I've got you." He drew abreast of Red at the starting line.

The gun went off for the beginning of the last lap. Tim had forgotten about the gun, and for the time it took the flat echo to bang back from the stands, it blew the triumph and the timing out of him. Then they returned more strongly, a full flood, as if the gun was his send-off, not Red's. He increased his pace, and it was no trouble to do this. The spring sunlight was wonderful. He had forgotten about the sun, the way he had forgotten about the gun, and now it burst open around him. He rode before the wind. It was wonderful too. It made coming down the stretch like running down hill. Now he could imagine his stallion; now he could imagine a pale antelope skimming level backed through the gray brush. He could be lavish with strength now; no silly stride to think about, no miserish idea to cherish, like that of running evenly. Just let go; let go and swing home from the mountains.

Red stayed beside him, and inside, on the pole, but Red's stride was shorter and faster than his now. He wanted to laugh at Red, this futile battler out of the past, trying to make mere determined running do. He didn't really pay any attention to Red. Rather this conception of their duel traveled with them, a mocking, mimicking mote dance in the sunny, windy air around their heads. Tim ran happily on the outside all the way around the south curve, and when they came into the back-stretch, Red began to give. He fell out of sight behind Tim's left shoulder. Only gradually, an inch or two at a stride, using most of the stretch, Tim drew in to the pole. Even the head-wind pleased him now; it was great to breast the head-wind. The poplars in a clump beyond the north-east turn bowed and rushed under the wind, and their great branches writhed sep-arately and turned up the under-sides of their leaves. Tim exulted about the blowing in the poplars. He loved the poplars. They were a shout of triumph whitening against the deep-blue sky, darkening only to take breath and then shouting again, bowing down and swinging.

When the wind let go of him under the sand bluff, he quick-ened his stride. He didn't sprint. He didn't like to finish with a sprint. He liked a gradually swelling conclusion, increasing pace and stride together and coming in like a full peroration, but with plenty left. He came in that way, and took the tape with him.

All the men and boys on the field had gathered along the edge near the finish. They were yelling, but they weren't watching him, but some contest behind him. No one even came out to catch him. He was glad of this; he didn't need catching. He let his exultation and his stride diminish together toward the first curve, and turned back onto the grass, walking. He shone with sweat on his shoulders, and was breathing deeply, but he felt good, only a little hard and heavy, as if he had earned a rest.

Actually the shouting had been going on all through the last lap. Excited boys on the field had been running a few yards on the turf beside their beloved champions, exhorting in a kind of Viking poetry in a very simple language.

"Come on, Ned, come on. You can do it."

"Stay in there, Hank, boy. Don't let him take you, kid."

"The red-head's all tied up, Ned. Go get him, Ned. Atta boy, atta boy, atta boy."

"All the way, Hank. All the way, kid. We want this second, boy."

The solo cries were reinforced by a swelling, conflicting chorus from near the pits and the finish line.

At the beginning of the last lap a tall, black-haired boy with very white legs and a tanned face and tanned forearms, had begun an heroic and laboring challenge from way back. The mysterious duel between Red and Tim had kept everyone quiet; it was brainless and exciting, like a feud. But when Tim began to pull away rapidly, running faster and smoother as Red fell back, the black-haired boy reminded them of the score again, and made a second race of it. He was not running easily, but leaning far forward from the waist and making his legs run after his body. On the south curve he had passed his own stocky, dogged team-mate and begun to close on the thin boy from Sparks. This started the shouting. Going into the back-stretch he had caught the thin boy, and then the tumultuous henchmen had seen that there might even be another race. The Carson boy was sometimes sagging in the knees a little, and Hank from Sparks was chopping right on his heels, and they were both gaining on Red.

Sheik had come down out of the stands to talk to Red before the mile began. Now he raced across the field and came alongside Red as he leaned onto the north curve. Sheik's face was white and pimply. He had begun to smoke and drink a great deal, and the run across the field took all his wind. He could stay with Red for only about ten yards, gasping his exhortations, telling him how the others were coming. Red shook his head at him, without looking around, and then stumbled. He caught himself, and kept going, but Sheik stopped running and stood there, looking after him. Right in front of Sheik, the Sparks boy, feeling the wind let go of him, lifted and came on. Ned from Carson was run out, and didn't even challenge. The thin boy passed him and went after Red. He was on Red's heels at the beginning of the home stretch. He jerked away from the pole to come up beside Red.

It was this duel that everybody was yelling about when Tim finished. Red managed to push himself a little, and for ten yards they came on together, but Red was knotting up, and was already full of black defeat. His race had been lost when Tim passed him on the back-stretch. Hank from Sparks gained a few inches. Then Red staggered and gave away two yards. As Hank clearly left him, the yelling faded, but almost at once it started again. The stocky boy from Carson was sprinting. It was a muscle-bound, up-and-down sprint, but it carried him slowly past his tall team-mate and up on Red. Reno boys yelled at Red. They crowded along beside him, yelling and swinging their fists. Red tried, but his head was wobbling. He couldn't pick it up. The stocky boy drew even with him when there were only three or four yards to go, and Red tried again, but stumbled, and lost the third place also. The holders couldn't even get to him in time. He turned toward the grass, stumbled on the rail, and fell onto his face.

Because of this finish, which also lost the meet, as it turned out, Tim's triumph was spoiled. Standing in the shower, he was crowing to himself, "Next time I'll get you in both of them," and humming *Blue Skies*, and feeling that it didn't even matter what Rachel thought now, that he was free of ever caring what she or any girl thought, when Red came in, with Sheik helping him. Red slumped onto a bench and just stayed there, limp, with his head hanging down, while Sheik and one of the managers pulled his things off. He looked bad. He kept his eyes closed, and his face had those blue shadows again. He had to be helped in the shower too. When Tim was dressed he stood there looking at Red, and trying to think of something to say, but he couldn't, so he went on out. As he came up the hill from the field he saw Rachel and Marjory waiting in the car. They looked unhappy, and he thought maybe they were even worried. Rachel looked worried. Neither of them looked at him or spoke to him when he passed the car. So nothing was changed, after all. He thought, "Oh, to hell with them all," but that didn't help for longer than the time it took to say it. He didn't really feel that way. He felt as if he had cheated Red. He felt as if he had cheated Rachel.

CHAPTER TWENTY-ONE: *Being Mostly Consid-erations of the Power of the Nuclear*

THOUGH the victory over Red seemed to Tim a hollow one, even a defeat of something vague which he did not want defeated, important results came of it in time. It was these rather than the races that we talked about on the raft on Tahoe, for I had seen the races myself.

During the rest of that spring Tim didn't lose a race to Red, or to anyone else, for that matter. Something was gone out of Red. Sometimes he even failed to get into the points. Also, before school was out that same spring, the love affair between Red and Rachel died away. There was no drama that any of the rest of us were aware of. They were just seen together less frequently, and then not at all. Nobody thought much about it. That happened to most of the affairs at school. But looking back from the raft, I wondered if the mile run had had anything to do with it. Tim denied this almost savagely. Rachel didn't go out to pick winners, he said. I granted this, but wondered if there might not have been a change in Red which had estranged her. Red had never been easy to get along with. Tim said, "Maybe." He didn't want to admit even that. It was not merely that he wished to exonerate Rachel of any unkindness, however justifiable, or even that he felt guilty about what those defeats might have done to Red. At the moment, newly ensnared in his memories of Rachel by virtue of one glimpse of her climbing into a car, he felt that the real defeat in that race had been his own, and that Red and Rachel had not been touched by it.

"Sometimes," he said, dragging his hand idly through the water of the lake, "I wish I'd never gone out for track."

"For lord's sake, why?" I asked.

"Oh, sometimes I think that's what started me mouthing off about track and tennis and everything."

"I don't remember your mouthing off about it; not any more than we all did."

"No," he said. "That was the peculiar hell of it. It was only with Rachel I'd get like that. I'd just get started, and I couldn't stop."

He thought about it for a moment. "No," he said, "it wouldn't have mattered. If it hadn't been sports, it would have been something else, probably dance bands. In fact it was dance bands sometimes. It isn't what you get started on that matters, it's that you go on talking when you don't really care about anything you're saying. Nobody can stand that kind of talk. It's instead-of talk. That's why I don't want to see her again. It would just be the same thing."

It was then that he told me about Rachel and the "instead-of" talk. It was only years later, after his dark period, after the pilgrimage to the mountain, after the dream which freed him and perhaps changed Eileen Connor, that he believed he recognized a transformation to have begun in him after that mile run. Nevertheless, the transformation began almost at once. The rest of us at school felt it before his first spring of track was over.

Until that spring, Tim had appeared odd to us, but not much to be reckoned with, a tall, thin kid, sometimes with almost no hair on his head, and sometimes with too much, who sat on the back of his neck and dreamed in class, wandered by himself in the halls, and did nothing that singled him out in our minds, except to play in Rob Gleaman's band. It's true enough that, in spite of his detachment, we couldn't ignore him all the time, and we couldn't make jokes at his expense with impunity, except when he wasn't there. Not often, but often enough to make us uneasy, he would reveal an unexpected sharpness of mind and a satirical perception of our own foibles, which made any answers we thought of seem clumsy and stupid. There was something in his combination which we didn't understand, and we gave it room. But on the whole, given that room, he disappeared from our thoughts.

Then the change began. We didn't notice it going on; we couldn't have picked a moment in which we knew he was different, but by the end of that first track season he was no longer anonymous, but a presence of which we were always aware and much less defensively aware. His jibes were more frequent, and no less acute, but they came out more easily, and were usually humorously put, so that they could be turned again and get a laugh both ways. He was still more by himself than with us, but he sat at ease among us, and we were at ease with him there. If we had bothered to define the change in him, which we didn't, of course, we'd probably have said that he had more confidence in himself, or that he finally "knew what it was all about." Tim himself, looking back, and looking at the change from the inside out, puts it differently.

"I guess it was about then that I started, by way of the bone and the flesh, to evaluate my doings and my thoughts by means of the sensation of the nuclear. Not that I could have defined any such monitor then. I can't remember just when it was, but it was years later, anyway, that I began trying to formulate the sensation of the nuclear as a guiding principle, and to think a lot about men and works and acts which seemed to me to have the nuclear power. I still can't define it exactly. Probably that's the secret of the power, for that matter, that it can't be trapped in a definition or pinned on the cork by a formula. It partakes of the incomplete which is greater than any complete, of the question which remains real while its answers, one by one, are abandoned.

"A lot of words," he said slowly, thinking about it, "mean something of what I mean by nuclear, but none of them quite gets it, and neither does any combination of them. It is a guide toward the whole which is more than any sum we have yet made of the parts. It is an impetus toward the God becoming. People are feeling the power of the nuclear when they call a performance of some kind 'masterful.' But the term mastery excludes the suggestion of the more, and to some extent excludes even spontaneity. Bach was beyond question masterful, but, in my opinion, he isn't nuclear. When critics speak, as they do far too often now, of a composer or painter or writer as seminal, they mean something which is part of being nuclear.

but still isn't all. You and I have argued about Joyce a lot, for instance, and I'll admit that he is probably the most seminal of modern writers. Innumerable imitators stem from him, and many who aren't imitators have gained impetus from him. Yet he isn't nuclear. In himself, he repels more than he attracts. He remains a writer's writer, which is to say, begging many pardons, a corpse for the inquest. Restraint touches what I mean by the quality of the nuclear, but restraint is a negative word, and the nuclear is neither negative nor positive, or rather it's both, the complete cell from which the growth expands, the question by which the search is perpetually renewed. Hawthorne was often marvelously restrained, but he is not nuclear. Emerson, Whitman, Melville, Mark Twain, were all in a great measure nuclear, yet restraint is the last quality you would attribute to any of them. Great is a lesser word than nuclear. Many men, who have truly been termed great, were not nuclear. Washington was great, but Lincoln was, and therefore is, nuclear. If greatness is the ability to make changes which will be remembered, to accumulate about oneself the power of numbers and by means of it extend fear, death, destruction and sycophancy over wide lands and down long years, then Caesar and Napoleon and Alexander were great, but they were direct antagonists of the nuclear. They did not desire all to be; they desired to be all.

"The size of a work, or even the ability to sustain it, doesn't necessarily have anything to do with the nuclear. A short story like Lawrence's *Man Who Died* is nuclear. Debussy's *Hills of Capri* is nuclear. A sonnet by Keats, a few lines by Da Vinci on a scrap of paper smaller than my hand, a *Gettysburg Address*, a paragraph about clouds over a glassy sea in a Conrad novel, a simple folk song, a homely puppet by an anonymous craftsman, an unexpected sentence from the *Voyage of the Beagle*, opening wide ranges of thought, the unconscious selfishness of a child, a single fine gesture by a bad actor, may possess the magic of the nuclear when even great, sustained works, deeds and personalities do not. Buddha speaking gently under his tree, Jesus speaking on the Mount, and not speaking before Pilate, were nuclear, still are, if you can dig back to them, but after them came immense, long-enduring structures, and the magic was destroyed. Freedom of the spirit cannot be produced, like theological Fords, on an assembly line, and authoritarianism is the very antithesis of what Jesus and Buddha were after.

"Let's put it this way. I believe a small boy is near the knowledge when he watches a great athlete perform, and with a sudden access of energy, with a great joy in his face, exclaims, 'Gosh, that guy does it easy.' The athlete's nuclear power, like that of a great singer or dancer or instrumentalist or mechanic, will seem ephemeral because its product, a performance, is ephemeral, and its effects are impossible to trace as one can trace the succession of the popes or the history of a family fortune. Nevertheless, it is real, and more than one man's.

"Ease or naturalness is part of it, margin, room to move in, power beyond determination, or at least that's the sensation by which we can know it, the feeling that the work is great, all that is needed, and yet that the worker could do far more if pressed to it. Yet strangely, if ever it seems he has pressed to his limits, that quality is gone. Then it is clearly seen that the work is not part of life, but an imitation, a separate, exclusive entity. Sharing is no longer possible. The watcher, the reader, the listener no longer believes that he could do it too, that, indeed, he is doing it. He no longer feels wise, gifted, happy, at ease, creative, desirous. Life has ceased. Growth has stopped. Possibly nobody feels that he could write a *Paradise Lost,* but I've never known anyone who wanted to. It's a finished work. It suggests that there is nothing more to say. Everything around it has begun to die. Give it to those unfortunate scholars who are content to collect and repeat. Nobody else wants it. But listen to a lyric by Burns go singing down time. Ah, that is wonderful. It is full of life and life is full of it. Everybody wrote it. Everybody becomes a Burns when Burns is lively, full of joy or sadness. They're wrong, of course, in the sense of so many words on a page. It is infinitely easier to approximate a passage from *Paradise Lost* than a lyric by Burns. Try it, and you'll see.

But in the important sense, they are right. They are Burns while they hear that song. The nuclear is multiple to an infinite degree. It is the drop of water which repeats the cosmos, and yet tricks us into believing that it is entirely comprehensible.

"I know I am vague," he said slowly. "I try to surround what I can't attack directly and bring forth as a prisoner. But isn't that always so when we have finally worked our way back to the beginning? We believe that we share certain truths because we have, in the inexplicable wisdom of our complete beings, experienced certain manifestations which are enough alike so that we may speak to one another with partial understanding. Actually we take it all on trust, and root only in the manifestations, so that, speaking largely enough, we are all absolute fools, but speaking humanly the only fool is that man who, like Kant, having arrived at the point where he perceives the impasse, insists upon completing the structure to fulfill his own desires, or that much more numerous breed which falls into the habit of accepting manifestations which have occurred often enough as explanations of themselves, and ceases to wonder at all, being merely fussily upset when manifestations, which they have come to trust, for some reason or other fail to recur.

"Take mathematics in example. It is called the most exact science, and because of the many material miracles which have been performed through it, it has come to be accepted by the more numerous fools as a form of absolute knowledge. Now no one stands more in awe of the magic of mathematics than I. I am very humble before the beauty and actuality of a Boulder Dam, and the thought of the number of lives it changes, and it passes my understanding how such a manifestation has come to be by way of a legion of closely numbered sheets. Yet I, who know no more arithmetic than will enable me to exercise in counterpoint, am less a dupe, in the final sense, than the learned mathematician who has ceased to wonder because certain calculations, performed without error, will always arrive at the same conclusion. He has fallen into the habit of accepting the manifestation as the explanation, and so has forgotten what I, in my ignorance, never forget, that, although two and two will always make four, I can never know why this is; I can never know what is the true nature, even, of that mysterious and redoubtable digit one.

"So," he said, grinning, "although I can't explain what I mean by the nuclear, I've fallen into the habit of trusting its manifestations, and I believe that it was while I was running that I began to seek the sensation of the nuclear, of being in touch and yet having plenty of room, as the test of doing well. When I felt that core of eagerness and yet easiness within me, what I used to call 'running with the stallion,' I'd know I was going to be all right. From the running it worked over into the music. I began to feel that a band was going badly, shutting its dancers out, when it was working hard, or when I had to think about the music or about what the others were doing. Then I saw that the same quality was present in some music itself, and not in other music. Now I suppose I might say it's the whole philosophy of my life. I sit and listen for the sound of the nuclear."

CHAPTER TWENTY-TWO: *About Telephones and Old Houses*

THERE was another change in Tim's life which was probably due, at least in part, to the effects of the mile run. It was a long-lasting and possibly very important change, the end of which, if such things ever have an absolute end, cannot be discerned. Its beginning, however, for Tim, at least, can be quite exactly fixed. It began at a few minutes after eight in the evening, a few days before Christmas in his junior year. Tim was up in his room, slowly making an arrangement for Rob Gleaman's band. The music paper lay on a board on the bed, and he sat in front of it, testing what he wrote by picking it softly on the violin, which he imagined to have, at various times, the timbre of a trumpet, a sax and a clarinet, as well as its own. He still had to be careful in this way, because he hadn't yet learned to imagine a whole score being played by the many instruments at once. Sooner or later he would always begin to follow some one of them. He was happy sitting there in his hermit cell, slowly doing what he liked best. Coming back to this room, and to writing music in it, was always a comfort to him, even when he hadn't felt particularly in need of comforting. It was like having time to rediscover oneself after struggling for a long time among many strong and different personalities, some of them strangers. He didn't even know that he'd heard the telephone ring downstairs until Grace called up to him, "Tim, you're wanted on the phone."

This was enough of an event to make him uneasy. He disliked talking on a phone anyway. He had often walked as much as two or three miles to see someone about a small matter rather than use the phone. When he did talk on the phone, he liked to be very brief and matter of fact, to say and hear only things which would leave no guessing to be done. "There's a good show at the Wigwam. Want to go?—All right. Meet you at the corner of Virginia and Second at a quarter to seven." That was the only way to use a telephone without feeling that you had relinquished your soul to another's use, the way Indians felt about telling their true names or having their pictures taken.

In the downstairs hall, under the mild, sad gaze of Mr. Turner's version of the head of Mr. Hazard's nine-point buck, he whispered to Grace, "Who is it?"

Grace smiled at him, but the imp of Willis was in her eyes. "I wouldn't know," she said, loudly enough for the phone to hear. "But it's a girl with a dangerous voice. Low down and on purpose."

But Grace never pressed an advantage, and besides, she had graduated and was already engaged to the man who was going to take her to California. She wasn't one really to mock even a young brother's mysteries. The phone was in the hall. She went back into the living room and closed the door.

"Hello," Tim said into the telephone.

"Hello. Is that you, Tim?" He didn't know the voice.

"Yes. It's me."

"I'll bet you don't know who this is?"

"No," Tim said, swallowing and shifting his feet.

"Guess."

Tim heard other voices behind it. They were all girls' voices, he thought, and they were making a smothered giggling noise. So that was it. He had heard about the trick. The voice would make him guess and guess and guess, not even telling him if he was right, to find out what girls he hoped might call him up, and then he would begin to meet girls, and boys too (because the pleasure which comes from such jokes is directly proportionate to the amount of publicity which can be given them), who would ask him how long this one had been his secret sorrow and how long that one had been his pash, but he would never find out whom he had really talked to. Even so, the validity of this kind of test was nearly proven in him. In spite of the fact that he was not at all sure of the voice, everything in him rushed up dizzily and hopefully and wanted to guess Rachel. He throttled the impulse.

"I told you, I don't know," he said hoarsely.

"Oh, please guess, Timmy," the voice begged. He heard the giggling again, and the voice said, away from the phone, "For heaven's sake, hush up."

"No," Tim said. "I don't want to guess."

"Please. I just want to see if you can guess. Don't you know who I am?"

Tim could feel the mounting ridicule of the gigglers as if he stood there in visible awkwardness and confusion before them, and saw all their bright eyes laughing too.

"No," he said. "I don't know. What do you want?"

"Oh, now you're angry, Timmy."

"No, I'm not."

"Wait a sec," the voice said. There was whispering.

Then a different voice said, "Hello, Tim. Do you know who *this* is?"

He knew, all right. He could tell by the constriction in his chest, the roaring in his head and the weakness in his knees. You might wonder if it was the real thing when it wasn't, but when it was, you knew. Then he remembered that she had been among the gigglers. He remembered now that he had heard the little, quick laugh.

"No, I don't," he lied.

"It's Rachel Wells," she said. She wasn't being part of the trick then, anyway. If she wasn't part of the trick, the rest didn't matter. It was silly, but it didn't matter.

"Oh, hello, Rachel."

Then there was nothing for him to say, so he just stood there holding the phone. Rachel didn't seem to know what to say either. There was a long silence. Somebody on the other end was whispering.

"Hello, Tim," Rachel said.

"Hello."

"That was Marjory you were talking to," Rachel said.

"Marjory who?"

"Marjory Hale. We're all down at her house. Just a minute. She wants to talk to you again."

"Hello, Tim," Marjory's voice said again.

"Hello."

"I'm giving a party Friday night. Can you come?"

The whispering and giggling became laughing out loud for a moment.

"Hush," Marjory whispered to them, violently. "He's mad now."

She spoke into the phone again, "Can you come, Timmy?"

"What is this? A joke?"

"No, really it isn't, Timmy. Only they're all so silly about everything. You'll come, won't you?"

"I guess so."

"Well, you don't have to if you don't want to."

"You mean you're really going to have a party?"

"Yes, really I am. You see," she said away from the phone, but loud enough so he would be sure to hear, "now he won't even believe me."

"Sure. I'd like to come, Marjory," he said.

"Well," she said, "that's better. About eight o'clock."

"Who am I s'posed to bring?" he asked. He asked in a spirit of resignation. He was used to being asked to bring one of the left-overs, after all the mutually desirous couples and the girls with secret sorrows had been taken care of.

"Nobody," Marjory said. "You're my partner."

This was so surprising that he didn't reply. It wasn't only that Marjory was giving the party, and so would have first choice, except for steadies. Marjory was a girl who was never left over. He had often wondered what she was really like inside that thin, slowly flowing body and behind that clear stare. He believed that she must possess some dangerous and intriguing quality. Many other boys felt that way too. Marjory had dates for everything that went on.

"Is that so terrible?" Marjory asked.

"No. Gosh, no. That's swell."

"Anybody might think it seemed pretty terrible to you, from the way you sounded."

"No," he said, with a rush of honesty because her feelings were hurt. "Gee, no, Marjory, that wasn't it. I just thought you were making fun of me. All that guessing business, and everything."

"Oh, no, Timmy, really I wasn't. It was just a silly idea some of the girls had. I didn't even want to do it. I'm sorry." She was having a rush of honesty too.

So the ordeal by phone ended in a small, warm triumph of amity, akin to the conclusions of some of his dream stories. He and Marjory between them had established something in spite of the others.

Marjory's house was in the corner of the south-side quarter where the court-house influence dominated, and the valley and the mountains were without power. It was one of the large, frame mansions, with jig-saw rails and eaves, which were common in that quarter, and its once white paint had a smoky look, also common there. Inside it had high ceilings, tall, narrow windows, and tiny fireplaces with huge mantels, suggesting a family which had been successful about the time of the Comstock

Boom. The living room was all Tim knew of the house so far, and there even the ornaments and most of the furniture seemed to have lingered from the beginning. There was an ormolu clock under a glass bell on the mantel, and behind it a mirror in a heavy, gilt frame. There was a beaded portière closing off the second living room, and a gilt chandelier with crystal pendants hanging down from a plaster garland in the center of the ceiling. The fireplace was faced with marble. The phonograph in one corner was modern, and the couch was wide and low and covered with flowered cloth, but one of the tables looked as if the marble slab had just been slipped off it, the desk was a spindle-legged secretary and the straight chairs were upholstered with horsehair or a striped satin, stained with use. The drapes weren't very old either, but they were maroon, to match the all-over carpet, which had once been much darker, and behind them were white lace curtains which completely covered the windows. Even on the brightest days, only a faint, diffused light got in and made wintry glints on the woodwork, the deep, gilt frames of the old portraits, and all the small objects which stood about on the tables, the mantel and the glassed-in bookcase, and the gloom absorbed these little highlights. There was always a musty smell in the room too, as if it were no more open to air than it was to light. Tim had felt, during his few visits, that some very old person, almost too frail to speak, was sitting unnoticed in one of the shadows, and querulously resenting his intrusion upon remembered dignity. It made him feel queer to be in Marjory's living room in the afternoon after school, and hear jazz records playing. It had seemed to him that Marjory was resisting the house that way, and by prowling about the room in time to the jazz and smoking a cigarette, and looking at everybody with that sinuous, adult gaze out of her pale-blue eyes. Yet sometimes, while she prowled, she would caress one or another of the litter of objects, and then it would seem that she was silently rejecting the visitors rather than the room. Anyhow, whichever way her affection tended, that dissonance remained her essential quality, the knowing eyes in the mild and girlish face, the ambling, liquid movements of her body, which yet seemed to be restraining gestures of impatience and discontent.

Perhaps the house had nothing to do with it, though. Marjory didn't really belong to the house. Her mother had come to Reno three years before, to get a divorce, and had stayed. She didn't own the house; she rented it, and she had left it just as it was, bringing in very few things of her own. Marjory was always saying, with a kind of sharp delight, that they might move into another house soon, or even that they might leave Reno soon. She didn't seem to care where they went. It wasn't that she wanted to be in any particular place, but just that she didn't want to be where she was.

Tim had never before been to the house in the evening. It was better in the evening. In the narrow hall there was only one small light on the ceiling in a red globe. In the living room the lights were brighter, the hardwood floor, bared for dancing, shone, and the innumerable highlights had color and warmth. All of this only pushed the shadows back a little and made them deeper, but this night gloom seemed less false and more mysterious, as if it might have arisen from greater tragedy than that of stuffy and isolated decay. The house now brooded not upon its slighted pride, but upon a dangerous and mischievous history, which filled it with contempt for the present.

Marjory didn't show the gloom herself at all. She had on a stiff, rustling, pale-blue evening gown, with gleaming folds, and there was a silver star in her hair and her mouth was painted very red. When she met Tim at the door, she seemed full of repressed excitement. She took his hand and squeezed it and then held it while she peered over his shoulder into the street, where snow lay under the arc light.

"Oh, it's lovely and cold and quiet out, isn't it? Come on," she said, almost gaily, and drew him farther in, and closed the door. He wasn't wearing either hat or coat, and she didn't let go of his hand, but led him into the living room. It embarrassed him to be led in by the hand, yet there was a possessiveness about it which stirred him.

Three other couples were already there. Mary was there with

a boy called Coppy, and Rachel was there with Harvey Brad-
ner. Harvey always wore a suit and a bright tie to school, and
had an effusive but really friendly way of talking too much, and
played classical music on the piano with a good hand but with
too much foot and always with a tendency to go faster and
faster, no matter what he was playing. He was extremely courteous, in an almost codified manner, and he always brought his
partner flowers. The other boy was Sheik, and he had brought
Fay Bailey, a short, beautifully rounded little girl, who seemed
much softer than she was and weightless, because her skin and
her thick, resilient hair were so white that they gave the indefinite impression of something floating in air, of a misty and
lighted cloud. Fay was an albino. Her face was lovely when
you looked at it, but it dissolved from the memory. Something
about her was secretive or aerial, because the same thing happened to your whole impression of her, not only of her body,
but of her nature. You perceived her only by glimpses, even
when she was there all the time. You believed that each enchanting glimpse would be enough to make you remember her
forever, and then you looked away, and your image and your
conception of her dissolved at once, and the next glimpse was
a new discovery. She was very shy, but also very friendly when
you spoke to her, lighting up quickly and softly. You imagined
quick, furtive, gentle feelings darting about in her all the time.
Nothing about her could ever be at rest. No matter how often
you had seen her, Fay still didn't seem real. Yet she was. She
was training to be a ballet dancer, and worked at it for hours
every day. She was really hard, supple and strong.

Other couples arrived every few minutes. Each time the
doorbell rang, Marjory would take Tim by the hand and lead
him out with her to meet the guests.

Harvey was tending the phonograph and maintaining a
steady line of chatter because everybody else was stiff and quiet.
He wouldn't let Rachel get far from him, even when he was
changing records. He had an air of treasuring her, bending to
put his ear close to her mouth when she spoke, holding her arm
when they weren't dancing, stopping his chatter sometimes to

speak very privately to her. Tim couldn't help looking at them often. Sometimes, when he thought Rachel was looking at him, he wished Marjory would stop towing him around that way. Sheik made one attempt to liven up the party by going into the Charleston, but it didn't feel right in that room, and the others only watched, and Fay deserted him, pretending she had to tell Mary something important.

Then Mrs. Hale appeared in the doorway to the hall. She was thin and wide shouldered, like Marjory, but taller, and dark. When you saw the two of them at the same time you realized that Marjory's way of eying the world was only a frail imitation of her mother's. Mrs. Hale stood there in her black evening gown and wrap, drawing on her long black gloves, and looked at the guests, and suddenly they all felt very young and ridiculous. When she looked at Tim, he felt that his ankles and wrists stuck out of his suit, and that he had better not try to get his big feet past each other without some thought.

Once Marjory had said, "Mother doesn't give a damn what I do as long as I keep out of her way," and Tim had thought she was only boasting. Now he wondered if she hadn't been telling a bitter secret.

"Good evening," Mrs. Hale said to them all.

"Marjory," she commanded gently.

Marjory went across to her, and they talked privately, and yet, somehow, as if there were no one else there. The others pretended to go on about what they were doing, but Tim had to stand there waiting.

The outside door opened, without the bell ringing. A tall man, with a white silk scarf and a black overcoat with velvet lapels, appeared in the hall and stood smiling at Mrs. Hale. Mrs. Hale turned her head and smiled at him too, and gave him her hand in a long, straight-armed gesture, and then went on talking to Marjory for a moment, letting the man hold her hand. Marjory nodded.

"Good night, everyone. Have a good time," Mrs. Hale said clearly.

Everyone in the living room mumbled, "Good night, Mrs. Hale," and, "Thank you; we will."

Then the man in the evening coat opened the door, and for a moment they heard Mrs. Hale's high heels tapping down the steps, and then the door was closed again. Harvey hadn't put a record on all the time Mrs. Hale was there. After a minute they heard the car moving away from the curb. It changed gears very softly and evenly out in the cold, muffled quiet, and then they could hear nothing at all.

After that the music worked better, and everybody talked more easily and laughed back and forth while they were dancing.

It was Fay who initiated Tim into the real excitement of the evening. They were dancing together. Her body was very strong and solid in his arm, so that he couldn't get over feeling astonished by her, but it was also light. Dancing with her was so much like dancing with nothing that at first he was worried about having control. Then he discovered that no matter what he was going to do, she always knew about it, and that it was only her perfectly timed acquiescence that made it seem he wasn't guiding her. After that he felt free, and tried many steps and dips and turns he wouldn't have tried with most girls. He didn't know her very well, and she was so shy that they couldn't talk easily, but he became quite happy and confident, just dancing with her.

It was when they danced into the shadow of the doorway to the second living room that Tim was swiftly surprised. Fay stopped dancing and put her hand on the back of his head and drew him down and kissed him, though only on the cheek. It was not being kissed that was the only surprise. The kiss itself was even more surprising. He kept expecting everything about Fay to be cool, airy and unreal, but the kiss was very warm and firm. He just stood there looking at her and holding her hand that he had held while they danced. The others were all laughing. When Tim didn't do anything, Sheik called, "Hey, Fay, try me."

Fay looked up at Tim, and flushed, and laughed a little and pointed up. "Mistletoe," she explained.

Tim looked up and saw the mistletoe hanging from the rod on which the beaded portières had been pushed back. For a moment he felt cheated, as if an act of enchantment, promising a veiled but lovely future, had hardened into a parlor trick with cards or coins or a glass of water. He looked at Fay again.

Fay tried to laugh, and struggled to pull her hand away from him, saying breathlessly, "You're a stingy old meany, Tim." So he caught hold of her with the other hand too, and kissed her quickly, also on the cheek. Fay felt better at once, and they began to dance again. Later, when others were doing it too, he danced her back under the mistletoe and kissed her on the mouth.

A great deal of new, quicker laughter and joking began. There were simulated Pan and Dryad chases. Girls pretended to resist being danced under the mistletoe, and sometimes would even struggle when they were there, after which they would be very strongly kissed. The shadows were completely transformed into desirable places, although nobody used them yet. The dancing was no longer awkward and formal. The excitement of the delectable game overcame all the shy or resistant personal feelings. Rachel was kissed often under the mistletoe, but after the first time this didn't bother Tim. He laughed with all the others when Rachel struggled, and Rachel herself was really laughing, and giving up very nicely each time, when she was finally pinned. Only Tim didn't kiss her. He stole her from Harvey for a dance, and had his mind all made up to kiss her, so that he was trembling violently. He wanted to kiss her, very much, but then he couldn't make himself do it. When he was dancing with her it stopped being a game. He was scared and bewildered, and began to dance stiffly. Then Rachel began to dance stiffly also, and wasn't laughing any more, although she had laughed and twinkled at him at first, all ready to be kissed if he could keep it a game. He tried to joke with her, but they were all bad jokes, and after they had danced around the room three or four times, she didn't even try to answer him. They were two strangers or two people who don't like each other very well. All the others were still dancing and chasing and laughing, but it seemed to Tim that the party had become silent and terrible. He yearned for Rachel until he thought he would break in two, and nobody else in the room mattered any more than if they had not been there, and yet he was afraid even to close his hand over Rachel's while they danced. When the record ended he said, like a mannerly fool, and with the fierce look on his face, "Thank you very much, Rachel," so she just said, "Thank you," too, and turned away, hunting for somebody with whom she could feel free.

Even so the party had worked up its own magic. He danced under the mistletoe with several other girls. He danced under it once with Mary, and they were both laughing, and Mary didn't even try to tease, but put her face up, and they were both surprised because it was a real kiss between their mouths. For a moment that stopped the game too. Tim felt a quick catch of affection for Mary, and he saw her eyes all at once serious, looking up at him, so that he took her in his arms and kissed her again. But then she twisted her head away, and laughed, and cried, "No fair, Tim. That's too much," and they began to dance again.

A long past of dreams poured through Tim. He was like an old man with memories, but much stronger and in more of a hurry. The memories made his emotions remember too, with little, painful, blissful tugs. It was like being in love with Mary again, and yet not quite able to bring the love up to the present. Certainly in the heart of Mary were furled the sunsets from over the mountains at Pyramid, the golden vistas into forevermore, which had also the sadness of nevermore. He remembered riding home beside Mary in the back seat of the old Dodge, one stormy afternoon when the gray hills were like the hills in which Beowulf, Hazard version, battled the dragon and then sat dying proudly. Fine snow swept in separate sallies out of the air, which was cold and full of the smell of damp sage. The snow clouds hid the tops of the hills, but far to the north, in one valley they crossed, slanting beams of white sunlight cut the storm and glorified chosen shoulders and breasts of the eastern range. They had seen that together, and many kindred wonders, and to such intangible splendors the spirit rose freely. All other creation was insignificant, the mind was freed of doubts and debts, and only that inexpressible ecstasy of light had place. Those who truly share such experiences are bound to one another more certainly than the disciples of one prophet.

Even this conversion, however, passed back into the game, and Tim only remembered gladly that he had really kissed Mary, and that she had liked it. Later he really kissed some of the other girls, too. These kisses didn't make him glad in the same way, but they were exciting.

Some time before midnight, everybody ate cake and ice cream. Then Tim carried in the big punch bowl, and when he had put it on the table in front of the east window, some boy, Tim was afraid it was Harvey, but he wasn't sure, turned off all the lights but the one by the phonograph, and turned that one into the corner. Everybody became quieter. Couples formed more definitely, and sat in the shadows and talked in low voices, and gradually sat closer. Harvey took to playing only blues and waltzes on the phonograph, and the couples who danced moved very slowly, and had far-off, dreamy expressions. There was a great, palpitant, expectant softness in the room, and a feeling of loneliness which was already comforted by being there. It was then that Tim danced under the mistletoe with Marjory. They were dancing almost imperceptibly in the middle of the room, and she began to press him gently toward the doorway where the mistletoe was hanging. Tim knew this was going to be still different from any of the other kisses. Marjory was dancing very close to him, and her head was buried in his shoulder. It was almost dark under the mistletoe. He was going to kiss her politely on the cheek, but she put her arm around his neck and drew her face closely across his until their mouths were together. Quickly, but with a little sigh, she let her mouth slide off the other side, but she still clung to him, and she whispered, "Timmy, there's too much light here." She pretended to keep on dancing, but it wasn't just dancing, and it drew them behind the beaded portières into the real darkness of the second living room. Then Marjory stopped even pretending to dance. She had both arms around him, and she was making love to him with her thin, violent body as well as with her mouth. She strove against him to make him kiss her harder. They kissed many times, and only stopped when somebody in the front room made a joke loudly enough so that many laughed. Tim stiffened, and Marjory gradually let go of him. The joke wasn't about them, though. Nobody had noticed them dancing into the second room.

Later Marjory asked him to go to the kitchen with her to pour more punch. When he had put the punch bowl down beside the sink, he had to look at her, and she was staring at him. He felt, uneasily, that he was losing to her a power of independence that he wanted to keep. He thought unsteadily of Rachel, and of the columns of cold sunlight he had remembered after kissing Mary. The thought of the sunlight made him remember a distant pass, with a sunset sky behind it, toward which he had once yearned from a valley way to the east of it, and then that was how he suddenly felt about Rachel, when he remembered that she was really still here, Rachel herself, just one room away. He was excited, wondering what was going to happen with Marjory, and in a way he was fascinated, but he wasn't happy.

"Don't you like me, Tim?" Marjory whispered.

"Sure I do," he whispered.

"Tim, please," she whispered.

She swayed toward him, as if expecting him to come to her, but he didn't move, and she drew herself back and stared at him again. He was reminded of Gladys looking at Beefy Woods in the eighth-grade room at the Orvis Ring. It wasn't really the same, though. Dull, helpless, dirty Gladys wasn't at all the same as Marjory, who looked very new and sharp. There was just something the same, maybe Gladys' expression and the way he felt now.

Marjory backed slowly to the wall where the light switch was, and leaned against it. She let her head fall back, as if it were too heavy for her neck, and her eyes were half closed. She whispered his name. He went across to her. They were close to each other and looking at each other. "Please turn out the light," Marjory whispered, and made a great sigh, and then a little moan, and reached her hand for him. His hand was shaking foolishly, and he fumbled the switch, but then he got hold of it, and the light went out with a click which sounded very loud. Marjory didn't move in the darkness until Tim began to draw her away from the wall. Then she came to him suddenly and as if there were no bones in her, and struggled against him, and kept acting as if her mouth had lost his, and needed badly to find it again. Between kisses, drooping against him, she would whisper. "Timmy, oh, Timmy," she would whisper. "I love you, Timmy; really, I do; really." She would end her whispering almost in his ear, and then let her face slide back against his, hunting for his mouth again. He began to want her mouth all the time, and to try to keep her from taking it away. Each time she whispered about loving him, he would try only to bring her face back where he could kiss her again, and stop the whispering. He couldn't make himself say that he loved her. He knew he ought to say it. He couldn't just stand there holding her and kissing her and hearing her whisper such things and say nothing. She was wrestling him for those words most of all, and he knew it, but still he couldn't say them. They stood there in the dark in the kitchen, engaged in this bewildering battle for a long time, until somebody in the front room yelled for more punch.

It was nearly two o'clock when the party finally broke up. Marjory made him stand with her while she said good night to the others. They stood close together in the hall, and she held his hand against her all the time while she was saying, "Good night. I'm so glad. I'm so glad you did. Good night, Dan. See you tomorrow, Pauline. Good night, Fay, honey." Where she held his hand, he could feel her hard thigh under the stiff, whistling cloth of her skirt. She even pressed his hand harder against it. He didn't pay much attention to most of the good nights. He felt foolish, standing there as if it were his party which had just ended in his house, and he looked away from most of the departing guests quickly, and only said good night when they said good night to him personally. But he couldn't help watching Rachel leave, once she wasn't standing right in front of him. There was a bulb on outside, over the steps, and Rachel, with her fur collar up beside her face, descended step by step in the light, dallying on each step, and then waited on the packed snow on the sidewalk, while Harvey completed his elaborate and whimsical thank-you. Even when she felt it most, Rachel couldn't take long about thank-you. She looked back up once, and the light showed her face clearly, so that Tim's breath nearly stopped, but most of the time she stood with her back turned, looking into the darkness under the trees toward Virginia Street.

When the door had closed after the last couple, Marjory began the kissing again, right there in the hall, against the door itself, in the dim, red light from the one globe. She was even fiercer and hungrier than she had been in the kitchen. She seemed to be trying to make him hurt her against the ridges of the great panels of the door. He kept thinking about Rachel's face looking up, with the light on it, and the fur collar against it, and the snow out there. Suddenly Marjory slapped his face, though not hard, just playfully, and pushed him away.

"Timmy, you're a regular wooden Indian," she said. "Go home. I'm sleepy." Once more she seemed very experienced, detached and malicious. She didn't sound angry. She sounded amused and a little bored.

But the next evening, after supper, she called him up again.

CHAPTER TWENTY-THREE: *More About Marjory, Who Didn't Know What She Wanted, But Wanted It Terribly*

TIM began to walk home from school with Marjory, often slowly and by a roundabout way. After a few weeks they were one of the couples everybody knew was going steady. None of the other boys asked Marjory for dates any more, and if there was a party to which couples were asked, it was just taken for granted that Marjory would come with Tim. He couldn't understand how it had happened. She excited him by her desperate way of making love with her mouth and her body, but when he wasn't with her, he didn't know how he felt about her. Being allied to her was like moving in a fog where something was always hitting you unexpectedly, and you could never see what it was that hit you.

They came home one night from a dance he had taken her to instead of playing for it. There was only one light on in the living room, and Mrs. Hale wasn't home. Tim had played with the band two nights that week already, and had been out another night for a short practice which had turned into a jam session that lasted until three o'clock. He was very tired, in a nervous, unsleepy way that made everything singularly clear and important, but also unreal, almost allegorical. What he really wanted to do was sit still and try to make his mind stay with one thought longer, but Marjory was restless. She took off her coat, threw it over a chair, lit a cigarette and began to prowl. She usually acted this way when they had been out in a crowd, and she always ended by making violent love with him, unless she had one of her unfathomable grudges. Then she would make love to the house instead, touching things, caressing them, and looking at him with those old eyes, as if she knew things about him that made her want to laugh ironically. Tonight she wasn't making love to the house, but she was different. She didn't put on any records; she prowled in silence. She didn't look at Tim, and sometimes she tossed her head, which wasn't a habit with her. She sighed several times, loudly and briefly, as if she were nervous. At first Tim thought she was putting on an act, though he couldn't think why. Then he decided she was really bothered about something. He watched her for a little while, and then his mind stopped paying attention to her, and he only vaguely heard the soft sounds she was making, her pacing and pausing on the rug and the rustle of her gown. He was remembering something they had seen on the way home. He hadn't paid much attention to it at the time, not more than enough to make him grin a little, but now his mind had taken hold of it and was trying to make something important of it, something with a frightening meaning. He couldn't quite get hold of the meaning though. He kept watching the scene go on again in his mind, and the meaning was always out there on the edge, where he couldn't quite reach it.

There were five people in evening clothes, three women and two men, standing on the sidewalk by the court-house lawn. They weren't really old people, but they weren't young either. Four of them were a little drunk, happily drunk, or at least very noisy and gay about nothing for people of that age. They were watching a third man, in a tux and an overcoat, perform on the low fence of iron pipe along the edge of the lawn. They called advice to him, and clapped and cheered when he saved himself, and laughed like everything when he couldn't. The third woman, probably the performer's wife, was standing by herself and weeping silently, as if her heart would break, and every once in a while, when the performer failed, saying through her blubbering, but not as if she expected him to hear, "Please, Joey, come on now, please."

In spite of most of his audience, the performer didn't seem to think he was doing anything funny. He was trying to walk the length of the low fence. The fence wasn't much more than a foot high, but he was working with a serious, determined expression, and when he slipped or began to teeter, he struggled desperately, waving his arms and weaving, and looked really frightened. His mouth came open in a gasp, and his eyes stared. He appeared to believe he was hundreds of feet in the air, maybe walking the cable on a high bridge, and that if he fell off he would be killed. When he actually fell off, which he always did, he closed his eyes to hide what was going to kill him, so that sometimes he staggered about foolishly, and sometimes he sprawled on the lawn or the sidewalk, or sat down hard. Each time he sprawled or sat down, he squeezed his eyes even tighter closed for a moment, and then opened them slowly and stared around in great surprise because he was still there. Each time he slipped off, the four laughed suddenly, and each time he sprawled or sat down, and then opened his eyes that way, they laughed much harder. Then he would start to get up again, and the weeping woman would plead, "Joey, darling, come on now, please." The man who was walking the high cable, however, had a purpose or an ambition, or had made a vow or a bet. When he was back on his feet, he looked at his audience as if they were strangers whose continued presence he couldn't understand. Then he brushed himself off, leaning over very carefully, and went back to the end of the pipe and began again.

Tim still hadn't found the meaning of this scene, when Marjory made up her mind about whatever was bothering her. She moved more swiftly across to an end table, and stubbed her half-smoked cigarette out in a brass bowl, and came over in front of Tim and said, "Timmy, honey, play me something on the piano."

Tim didn't like to play this piano, which was an old, very big and rattly upright, with strings that jangled, but Marjory had made up her mind, and went into the second living room, where the piano was, and turned on the light over the music, and waited for him. He went in and sat down on the wobbly stool, and, after a moment to decide, began to play a blues with a very narrow range, stepping up the tempo from the start. Some of the weaknesses of the piano were disguised when you played it loud and fast. But Marjory said, "No, no, please, Timmy, not that stuff. Play me something nice."

He stopped playing, and asked, "What?"

"I don't care," she said, "but something nice, something sad and nice. Chopin or Debussy or one of them." Her words sounded careless, but the way she said them wasn't careless. She sounded as if it mattered a great deal to her that he shouldn't play barrel-house now. The room, and the two of them waiting for something nice and sad to come out of the old piano, began to take on an elusive, allegorical importance like that behind the man trying to walk the fence. He knew what it would sound like, but he started to play the *Moonlight Sonata*. He would play it slowly, but very softly, and try to slur over the worst keys.

Marjory stopped him again. "That sounds terrible," she said. "The piano, I mean. Let's have a drink, Timmy, a real drink."

Beer was the only thing Tim had ever had to drink, more than to pretend, when he was with the band, and a bottle was passed around. But this wasn't beer; it was Bourbon. It said so on the bottle. Marjory moved restlessly about in the kitchen, prowling even while she mixed the drinks. Then they took the drinks back into the front room, and Marjory turned off all the other lights as she went, so there was only that one light that had been on when they came in. She kicked off her shoes, and curled her legs under her on the couch, and Tim sat down beside her, and they drank slowly and talked. Then all of a sudden Marjory seemed to make up her mind about something again, and finished her drink quickly, and said, "I want another. This was what I wanted, all right. Bottoms up, Timmy, and I'll make us another." So he finished his drink in two or three gulps, although he didn't like it much, and it drew his throat together so he wasn't sure he could speak. They went back out to the kitchen, Marjory pacing along in her stocking feet, more quickly than before. She worked more quickly in the kitchen, too, and hummed one of the tunes the orchestra had played that night, but broke off in the middle of it and turned to him. They kissed for a long time. Then, just as suddenly, she broke away, and finished making the drinks, and turned out the light, and they went back into the other room. While they drank, Marjory kept rubbing her foot and ankle against him softly. In the middle of this second drink they found themselves looking at each other, the talking stopped and forgotten. This look was different too. It went way back in, and was a little frightening. Tim held his breath, and Marjory stopped petting him with her foot. Tim put his drink down and leaned toward her, and she sighed, the way she had in the kitchen that first night, and slowly put her drink down too. But then she held him off, in a way that was like holding onto him too, and whispered, as if there were someone else who might hear her, "Turn the light out, please, Timmy." She began to stretch out on the couch as he stood up to turn out the light. She looked frightened, and her eyes were very big.

It was the first time they had made love lying down like that. In the wildness, when it came on, it seemed to Tim that this wasn't going to be the same. Marjory devoured him frantically with her hands and her kissing and her writhing. She kept whispering to him, not only about love, to make him say so too, but about wanting him. But then it didn't happen. Instead, she began pushing at him, frightened, not angry, and whispering, more wildly than anything else she had whispered, "No, Timmy, no, no, I can't," over and over, and, "Turn on the light, Timmy. Please, Timmy, turn on the light."

He sat on the edge of the couch for a minute, shaken and discouraged and disgusted, but just as glad nothing had come of it, too. Then he got up and turned on the light. Marjory was lying there, huddled up in a ball, with her face hidden, and she was crying. Later, after he had comforted her, she kept saying she was sorry, and starting to cry again. It was all queer and faraway, as if it didn't have anything to do with him at all. When he started home he felt heavy and exhausted, but also devoted to her in a melancholy way, through which came little waves of weary bliss.

After that they made love on the couch often, in the same tormenting way. Tim got to thinking about it when he was alone. If he stayed late at her house, they would both be white and exhausted, saying good night at the door, and although she would still cling to him, she would be quiet in his arms and they would kiss only gently, and her lips would be cool. Then he would walk home feeling heavy and nervous and sadly blissful that way. In this mood, walking through the darkness, or the shadows and moonlight, he would convince himself repeatedly that he was wildly in love with her, but still he was always doing that, convincing himself. Often, when they were kissing in the big, shadowy room, he wanted to cry out or weep, he loved and wanted her so much, and he would tell her this. He had no trouble telling her he loved her any more. He was telling her all the time. But even then a great part of him remained heavy and asleep. There was never anything between them but this unfinished love making, and Marjory's hunger for something, which was always pulling at him. They shared no other yearning. He never discovered anything she was really interested in except proofs that he loved her. They talked most often about getting married some time, and how they would live. She never seemed to think about his music in this planning, but only to have ideas about what they would do when he wasn't working at the music, and even these ideas changed all the time. There was only one thing constant about them. She never imagined them living anywhere except in a city, a much bigger city than Reno, and all the things they were going to do with their time were city amusements. They spent most of the time discussing how they felt about each other, and how the love making would fit into this amusing life in the city. Sometimes this would seem all right to Tim too, and he would have just as many ideas as Marjory, but at other times he would feel very sick and unhappy about it, and keep thinking of how many times they had already said everything they were saying, and then he would have trouble saying the right things, or sounding as if he meant anything he said.

They had many little arguments that didn't matter much, but there were eight or ten times in the year and a half they were seeing each other all the time, when Marjory broke out fiercely against Tim himself, instead of just using him as a lay figure to resist her indefinite unrest and desire. Rachel was the cause of all the outbursts, but they came so far apart, and each incident was really so trivial, no matter what Marjory made of it, that it wasn't until the very last one that Tim himself believed there was something important behind them.

Once, for instance, they were sitting in Mrs. Hale's car at the curb on Virginia Street, and Rachel went past on the sidewalk, by herself, hugging her books. Tim didn't say anything or move. He just watched Rachel until she was hidden by unimportant people coming the other way. Yet something roused up in him and fled out after her, hunting her in and out of the crowd, and for an instant all the little trees in the shining fringe of the wilderness were moved by a brief wind of hope and danced gleefully. In that instant he was also another being, heavy, restless, feeble and left behind, but the moment passed so quickly that he didn't even remember what he had felt. It just seemed to him that all at once the activity of the street had become a sad pantomime to behold, and he thought of big, impersonal reasons for this sadness, like the late sun on the Second Street crossing, and the tangled and dubious destinies of all humanity. Something must have shown in his face, though, in that moment when the chase broke out from him. Mrs. Hale dropped them off at the house and drove on to dinner somewhere, and when they went in, Marjory at once began to put loud records on, with the volume turned way up, and to prowl. She didn't even make an ally of the house. She was by herself, hard and informed and distant in her tight sports clothes, looking at him with the eyes that knew so much, and mocked it all.

Tim tried to draw her down onto the couch beside him and kiss her. He didn't really feel very much like making love to her, but he couldn't stand to have her prowling to that loud noise and staring at him so contemptuously. She braced herself against his pulling, without speaking or struggling, and he let her go, and after this little defeat, he felt guilty for no reason that he knew. Well, he had an inkling, because he was still thinking about Rachel, but he didn't think she could know that. The room became deeply melancholy, as in the autumn that always surrounded his thoughts of Marjory, the late, gray, unmoving autumn in a wilderness without magic.

"Margy," he said finally, "let's play something we can listen to."

Marjory was prowling again, and she didn't stop. "I like this," she said, without looking at him.

He tried again, a few minutes later, while she was putting on another record. "Margy," he said, "what's got into you? Come here." He said it very gently, pleading. It made him feel like a faker, the way he said it.

"Let me alone," she said.

He watched her while the new record started. She went to the other window, and stood there, looking out. He got up to go, and she turned around.

"Do you think I don't see?" she asked.

He stopped in the doorway. "See what?"

"See the way you always look at Rachel Wells; the way you stare at her."

"I don't stare at her. Why on earth should I stare at her?"

"You do. You stare at her all the time."

"When did I stare at her? I didn't even know I was looking at her."

"Oh, didn't you?"

"No," he said.

She shook her head impatiently. "You still have a case on Rachel, don't you?"

"No," he said. "Margy," he pleaded, coming back toward her and getting ready to take hold of her. She moved away from him sharply, twisting her shoulders, as if disgusted at the thought of his touch.

"Don't paw me," she said.

They didn't succeed in mending this rift at the moment, yet Tim, instead of feeling dejected and worn or unhappy, or wise about life while he walked home, wondered if it was really true that he hadn't got over Rachel, and was faintly encouraged by the notion, as if something small were set free in him, and he believed it might grow up and be happy and strong.

But when the phone rang during supper, and Marjory's voice said, "Won't you come down tonight, Tim? Just for a little while, anyway?" he felt that great troubles had been lifted from him. He was devoted, in a stern and monkish way, to his devotion to her. He went down after supper, and Marjory was unusually gentle and affectionate.

IT WAS to this Tim of Marjory Hale's that Rachel could finally speak before she was spoken to. She spoke one Friday afternoon in the fall of their senior year.

They both took physics the last period, in the lecture room and lab in the south side of the tower. The windows of these rooms were large, but being in the tower they showed only the blue Indian-summer sky and the yellow treetops bending slowly in the air, unless you went right up to them and looked down. The lab was brightened by the light reflected from the treetops, and among the slowly moving students, in whom budded vast ideas of space and force, many things shone, excited eyes, troubled eyes, metal wires and instruments of glass and steel and brass. Slow hands printed and figured forth the symbols of intimations and of faith upon blue-lined graph paper, or the special paper for lab reports. The expectations of the week-end, which were always there on Friday afternoon, trembled quietly in the air too, and sometimes brought on little flurries of whispering. These expectations were unusually strong in Tim this Friday, though he wouldn't let himself make much of the reason. He was the number-one tennis player of the school now, and tomorrow the Western Tournament at Carson began, and he was playing all three events, which meant mixed doubles with Rachel, for one thing. Hour by hour, all day, he had felt freer as this expectation grew. He was slow at his experiment with a tuning fork, because he kept looking up to watch Rachel at her table by the French windows in front, and every time he looked down again after watching her, the figures on his paper, and even the careful drawing showing the progress of vibrations in the air, appeared strange, and he had to get acquainted with them all over again. This confusion of the mysteries made him five minutes later than the rest of the class in putting away his instruments and leaving his papers on the desk in the teacher's office. He came out into the hall by himself, and it was there that Rachel spoke first.

"Tim," she said.

So she had been waiting for him. The hall was dark. There were no windows in it, but only the three doors to chemistry, biology and physics, and the doors to chemistry and biology were already closed. The only light, except the little that came up the stairs, entered through the door Tim was closing. Yet it seemed to him he'd never in his life seen anything so clearly as he saw Rachel standing there alone, hugging her books, and speaking his name first. A subdued but golden and commemorative light, like the glow in a cathedral, swam in the hall.

"Hello, Rachel," he said.

"Do you have any way to get out to Carson tomorrow?" she asked.

"Not yet," he said.

She moved toward the stairs, but slowly, expecting him to walk beside her.

"Do you want to ride out with me?" she asked. "We're supposed to play at nine, and nobody else is going out that early, I guess."

"Do you want to?" she had asked. To this delightfully ridiculous question he answered gravely, "Thanks. That would be swell."

In order to walk down the stairs side by side, they had to move closer together. They touched several times, and Tim felt a little shock each time.

"I'll come for you about seven-thirty," Rachel said. "It'll be pretty chilly still at nine o'clock. We'll need a long warm-up. I always need a long warm-up anyway."

"I do, too," Tim said.

This was more wonderful nonsense. Nobody could stand up against the kind of tennis he could play now, without any warm-up at all. But he mustn't startle her out of this unusual confidence, this nibbling in the open meadows of the world, by any hint of the amazing difference he saw between seven-thirty in the morning and eight or eight-thirty.

There was no one else in the main hall when they got down to it. School emptied out fast on Friday afternoons. They stood there for several minutes, talking about their chances in the mixed according to their probable opponents round-by-round, always admitting, so as not to tempt fate, that they might not even get by the first round, and then they walked out together, and Rachel said good night to him on the front steps. On the way home, because of his loyalty to Marjory, he convinced himself that his amazing liveliness, and the fleet running of his heart over the yellow hills was on account of the autumn in the streets of Reno. When he got home, he went up to his room and took out his violin and played a series of tumultuous, flashing improvisations which he told himself represented the dance of the swallows in the infinite, five-o'clock air above the golden trees and the gray streets.

Tim was always nervous before a track meet or a tennis tournament, but the next morning his nervousness was also happy. He got up at six and stood in his bedroom window, looking at morning in the valley. He was full of winged and wordless psalms. The blessing of God was on the hills, and the golden poplars burned on His altar. When Tim had as much of the world outside as he could hold, he bathed quickly in cold water, rubbed himself with a rough towel until he burned, and dressed himself clean from the skin out. Then he put all his tennis things together and took them down into the front hall.

Breakfast was also a kind of sacrament. His mother moved quietly and wearily back and forth between the stove and the table, and his sister spoke softly, full of dreams about her wedding, which was only a month off. His father ate silently and didn't look up. Yet they were all part of the familiar wonder which had turned new this morning. The leaves on the vine over the kitchen windows were a winy red, and glowed like stained glass in the sun. The light entering between them made a mobile pattern on the worn oilcloth of the table and on the linoleum on the floor, and single, dainty beams struck twinkling upon spoons and wet cereal bowls. Tim ate and drank slowly, without saying much, and held down his desire to jump, shout, yodel and embrace his astonished family. Even when the horn blew out front, he arose with apparent calm and even indifference. His mother followed him to the front door, and gave him her benediction before a kind of battle she didn't understand, except that her son was entered in it.

"Good luck, Timmy," she said.

Even Willis was gracious and interested, in his own way. He expressed great contempt for tennis, but actually he took a terrible interest in anything, clear down to double solitaire with Mr. Hazard, which entailed the alternative of winning or being a sucker. His mockery of Tim had entirely changed tone since Tim had become a repeat winner in the mile and half-mile, and had demonstrated to him one evening, with illustrations from an actual race, that there was a lot in common between jockeying and directing oneself through a foot-race. In this realm Willis was even a scientist and a philosopher, and immediately understood the most abstruse theory and analysis. So this communion had improved his opinion of tennis too, although there wasn't a word said about tennis.

Willis always slept naked. He now appeared at the head of the stairs, naked and yawning, his leathery little face queerly old and exhausted from some alley activity which had lasted until two o'clock the night before.

"Good luck, bum," he yelled. "Bring home muchos des cups and stuff."

Tim acknowledged the encouragement almost without hearing it, for the door was open now, and there was Rachel in a yellow sweater, sitting in her blue roadster in the sunlight. It was the same sweater in which, in a previous incarnation, she had sat on the green bench under the cottonwood at Wingfield Park. Rachel was superstitious about the yellow sweater, although she wouldn't admit it. For three days, in her first county tournament, she had warmed up in the yellow sweater, and each day she had won her match. The fourth day she had warmed up in a different sweater, and lost. Now, although the sweater had been mended in many places, and was worn thin and faded, she always wore it before she played a match that mattered to her. With the yellow sweater on, she felt better during the long match of Rachel vs. Rachel which always preceded the real match.

She waved to Tim when he appeared in the doorway, and when he came out she said, "Put your things in back with mine, Tim." Tim opened the turtle-back and carefully placed his old, kicked-about suitcase beside hers, which was small, neat and shiny. He touched her suitcase with his hand, and placed his where it might touch hers all the way to Carson. He placed his rackets against hers also, that they might absorb virtue and become dedicated to the impossible. He contemplated the finished arrangement for a moment, closed the turtle-back and climbed in beside Rachel. He waved to his mother, and Rachel waved also, though she had never seen Mrs. Hazard before. She too was filled with the elixir of this morning. The blue roadster swung round in the bars of sunlight-and-poplar shadow, and fled off along the empty street through the elixir.

"I'll have to step on it," Rachel said. "I was late." She laughed for no reason at all, and even turned her head to look at him, so they could laugh together.

The city was only dreamily astir as yet. Even the downtown section appeared clean and empty and filled with windows which observed the coming day with great hope. At such an hour in such a day, the power of the trees of Reno was great. Their certainty of forever, their knowledge that the river of life was brimming and rippling silently through God's pastures, reached even to the intersection of Virginia and Second.

On the South Virginia Road the shadows of the poplars pointed west, as they had pointed east the evening of Billy Wilson's party. There is a considerable difference between the shadows of poplars pointing west and pointing east. Up in their deep-blue sky, the brown, monster Sierras, drowsy with autumn, reclined upon the edge of the world, and beyond them was the ocean of space. They were resting with thin veins of yellow aspens in their folds. It overwhelmed Tim to be shot forth in the early day to fly through shadow and light under these mountains when he was already dangerously full of delight and ardor. He needed to pour forth, in a sacred service of music, poetry and dance, the ecstasy of being beside Rachel, who sat on a pillow in order to see the road ahead, and drove so lightly and fleetly, although only the toe of her small and holy foot, flexed like a dancer's, touched the throttle. But even if it hadn't been for Marjory, such a festival was impossible. It was a work to wear a genius down to bone, and no creative work will grow in a void. There must be first of all the faith that it is wanted; there must be the earth to its seed, the valley for its river.

Not that Tim thought of his trouble within such narrow limits. When he was beside Rachel like this, he didn't think at all. He didn't even think that he loved her. He couldn't permit the words on account of Marjory, but they wouldn't have done anyway. They didn't begin to express the joyous demolition of himself which took place in Rachel's presence. He felt simply the ungovernable and inexpressible flood rising, as if he were standing in the bottom of a deep canyon and looking up helplessly at a great crack opening across the face of a dam. He felt the imminent doom of that flood which is most terrible, the annihilation of self by shame. He knew that unless something happened which had never happened yet, something which gave him the words to tell her how he really felt in a way she would understand and believe, he was going to begin to talk anyway. If only he could feel all bad about the habit of trying to tell her what couldn't be told, maybe he could hold it, but he couldn't feel all bad. He'd feel the dam cracking, and he'd be in despair, but he'd go right on feeling wonderful and excited because he was with her, and hopeful that this time something would make the words come right.

He said to himself, "Don't talk. You always talk too much when you feel this way. You'll feel terrible afterwards, all washed out. You've got to play tennis, so shut up." He also told himself, "You're in love with Marjory. Besides getting ready to talk endlessly about the first thing you start on, whatever it is, you're already being false to Marjory, and Marjory is already very unhappy about something or everything. She meant a whole lot besides just jealousy when she said she saw you looking at Rachel. She meant that was just another little touch of everything in the world she was always losing or not even finding." More desperately he said to himself, "Which matters the most, anyway, pouring out your insides to somebody who doesn't give a damn for you, no matter what you think of her, or keeping yourself whole for somebody who is dying because things are always falling apart for her?" In the last agony, he cried to himself, "Anyway, don't talk sports. What the hell do sports mean, here where you can see her and hear her, and could even touch her?"

"Remember that St. Mary's game last fall?" he asked Rachel.

Rachel was intent upon silently playing as much of Rachel vs. Rachel as she could before they got to Carson.

"No," she said, "I don't think I saw it."

"Yes, you did," Tim said. "I was there, and I saw you." He was going to tell her all the details of having seen her there, which was the kind of thing she hated even worse than his going on about sports. He never forgot the details of seeing her anywhere. Because of her presence, such details took place in a supernatural light, which awakened an extra and unforgetting sense in him. Rachel stopped him from doing that, anyway.

"Maybe I was," she said stiffly, "but I don't remember it."

"Well," he said, "the thing was that they used a lot of short, over-the-line passes which were really something to see. St. Mary's did, I mean. There were always a lot of players in there, so you couldn't tell who was who, and besides, all the plays started off the same formation and they all looked like they'd be line plunges, and then this passer would rear up back there and let these passes go. They were never very long. They'd make only three, four, five yards a play on them, except for once in a while a break off one of them like they were working for. But they never missed, and even three yards is enough if you can keep on making it.

"There was only once," he went on, "I ever saw anything

prettier. That was in the Utah game two years ago. The Utes had a lot of big fellows, rangy, six feet three or four. They didn't look very heavy, just rangy, with a long reach on them, and smooth, plenty smooth. But maybe they were heavier than they looked. They were wearing those plain, one-color jerseys, you remember, bright red, and a one-color jersey like that, no matter what color it is, makes a man look thinner. The stripes, like Nevada wears, make them look heavier. So maybe the Utes were a lot heavier too. I don't know. But that pass attack of theirs was the most beautiful thing I've ever seen. I still don't see how anybody could stop a pass attack like that. They'd shift in the line just before the play began, and you never knew, when they broke, who was eligible to take the pass. Sometimes even the center would be on the end. They'd go out all distances. It was a kind of buckshot affair, I guess. The passer just picked any man he wanted to and let it fly and . . ."

He went on. He wasn't even clear what he was saying, but he couldn't stop. After such debauches he could hardly ever remember what he had said, except that he had said a lot of it, in almost the same words, before. The only kind of talk anyone can remember is the small, fact kind about something that must be done right away, or the great talk of inspiration, where the outpouring is drawn by a warmth of true desire. Even the way he talked when he got like this didn't sound like himself. Yet against this shame and failure, he could only talk harder, as if by mere volume and energy he could force Rachel to see that it was all a gigantic praise of her. He became a fountain of the names of teams, of dates, of records, of comparisons. He even described games he had never seen, with a wealth of incident and color no mere game ever had. To hear the fervor and massiveness of his eulogies to the great, or to the practically unknown whom he made great by the invention of a single play, you would have thought there was no room in his soul save for the love of athletes.

Rachel said once, like a faint cry in a hurricane, "I don't care too much about football. I just like to see a game once in a while."

Tim didn't feel this as a rebuke to football as a subject, but as a rejection of what he really wanted to tell her. Terribly hurt, and seeing the whole flood coming down now, he still kept going, except that by means of a star quarterback who was also a star forward, he switched to basketball. All over the Great Basin and the Pacific Slope, his gods threw beautiful baskets from the middle of the floor and whipped in one-handers from the corners on the dead run.

"Boy, he was coming down the left side-line, wide open, and he can travel too. He made a push-pass to Hank coming down the center, and then cut in front of the guard and took the pass back, and that was where he pulled it. He sucked that guard clear into the free-throw lane on a fake pivot and then spun around him on the outside and hung up the basket going under. A left-handed shot at that. Holy cow, was it pretty! I thought the old gym would come down for sure. The crowd was all over the floor and gone crazy. That was the shot that won the semi-final from Elko. Remember?"

"No, it wasn't," Rachel said, trembling with the effort of speaking so cruelly. "I saw that game, and it was Hank's long shot won it." She looked straight ahead at the road while she spoke.

Then Tim could not remember, but was sure she was right. Without a word, he prayed for a moment that she would hear back of the words of his traitor mouth. What he meant couldn't be put in any words; it had to be the things themselves, the world that was more beautiful because it was so brief because of her. Eternal night came so fast; came so much faster because of her reprimand.

Actually he covered his wound by going on, after a minute, about a game with Brigham Young. When he had thus obscured the fact that she had trapped him, he switched to track by way of an end who had also been a high jumper. "Remember the high jumps in that meet?" he insisted.

"I hardly ever go to track meets," Rachel said. "They're so dull; all waiting around, or things you can't even see."

"You went to some," came out before Tim could stop it.

"You used to go with Red and sit in his car until his race came, and then come down in the stands." There he was, telling her what she did again.

"Well, what if I did?" Rachel said.

"Anyway," Tim went on heavily, and his mouth described the high jump in eager detail, while he shrank from what it was doing.

"Oh, for heaven's sake, Tim," Rachel burst out, "don't you ever think about anything but sports?" She trembled with the fury and cruelty of saying this. Tim bent double within, torn by the unfairness of her accusation. All the things he really thought about her, the legends, the music, moments of the adoration too vast to take form, poured through his mind, and yet came out as just a last, thin trickle of the same terrible flood.

"Have you ever seen this Oregon fellow play, the one that's coming, the intercollegiate doubles champ?"

"I don't want to hear about tennis either," Rachel said quickly. "You shouldn't talk about it before you play. It makes you nervous."

This blocked the very present moment, and stopped him, and then it was the same as ever in him, exhaustion and black shame. He sat stiffly beside her, trying to keep his hands from giving him away, and looked out on his side of the roadster only, at the weathered ranch houses in the pass, and the bright trees making shadows on them, and the round, brown heads of the hills above, the beautiful, self-contained world from which he was now an exile by his own fault. They sped through the little valley beyond the pass and climbed Washoe Hill. As they came over the summit, Rachel said, "I love this valley."

It was kind of her to say it, because then he could look at the big valley, which was on her side, and indirectly he could look at her. He too loved this big valley with its little lake and its big lake, and the red steers in the meadows that sloped up to the foot of the mountains where Bowers' Mansion kept its unhappy memories behind its yellow poplars. He nodded. Once he was stopped, it was hard to say anything at all. He said very little the rest of the way to Carson, just trying to answer what she said, so as not to seem surly. He had no pride when he was with her, but it was only when he wasn't with her that this fact hurt. He tried to think about Marjory, but she didn't matter now.

As this kind of a slave to Rachel, he played in the tournament as well as he ever had, and sometimes better, especially in the mixed doubles. In the singles there were moments when the game wasn't enough, and the heavy, defeated sadness would come back, not only because she didn't care what happened to him in the singles, but also because his sins spread out, and it seemed to him that he would never be any good at anything. Right in the middle of a rally it would come over him that he would never be any good at anything, and that he ought to kill himself, and so at least stop being in the way and being a fool. Then points, and sometimes even a game or two, would go by before he became frightened by his weakness, and then he would be so nervous for a few points that he would be too careful or would force himself to take risks, hitting hard and trying for close placements while his control was still shaky. In the mixed doubles, with Rachel beside him, he had no such lapses. He was thinking about her all the time; he was doing everything for her. A point won against them became a grievance, and he played for revenge. When Rachel said, "Oh, nice, Timmy," or, "Pretty shot, Tim," or when they rushed the net together and he put one away quickly, and she looked at him with that quick brightness of triumph in her face which meant "We," he would be flooded by a light, joyous strength which would carry him over his head for a game or more. He dropped out in the quarter finals of the singles, but in the mixed doubles they went to the finals, and were defeated by the first seeded team from the coast only after a long, three-set battle.

None of the other wonderful things he had dreamt about happened, though. He didn't sit beside Rachel, or even at the same table, when the players ate at the hotel. He didn't dance with her at the parties, or take her to a show, or even sit in the roadster with her and watch other matches, excepting a couple of times for a few minutes before they were to play together. The tournament lasted for three days, and he knew where

Rachel was all the time, but he was never with her. He sat by himself in the hotel lobby, and brooded about the sins of his mouth, or went up to his room and lay on the bed and brooded about the sins of his mouth. Sometimes he would lie there staring at the ceiling and inventing a series of conversations in which he proved to her that he was really more moved by many other things in life than he was by the deeds of any athlete, and also that it was possible for him not to do all the talking, but only his part, and that very cleverly or wisely. It was hard to start this imagining, because he would begin by remembering as individual sins, for which atonement was necessary but not possible, all the wonderful sporting deeds which he described with conviction and belief, but recognized now as untrue, as just plain lies. When he made them, they were not lies; they were great, spontaneous improvements upon the limited possibilities of the flesh. But when he remembered them, they were just lies, and they made him see how she must feel that everything else he said in such an unquenchable rush was just a kind of lying. He was very unhappy about these lies. He would go over them, and correct each one of them in his mind. Then he would feel better, and could begin to construct the brief conversations which she enjoyed. If he was left alone in his room long enough, he would even succeed in finding words which seemed to declare his love truly, whole passages of great and convincing poetry, or he would compose music which would prove to her how it really was with him. After such a success, he would begin to think hopefully of riding home with her in the blue roadster in the immense and lonely dusk of the valleys, after the last match was played. There was nothing in the world which he wanted so much as to ride home with Rachel in the big dusk. Over every mile of the road, which was much too short, hung the magic of chance. The word, the feeling, the scene they both looked at on such a ride, might perform the nuptial rite of their minds, might send her forth to meet him. He would become so restless thinking about all the places and ways for this to happen, that he would get up and pad around the room in his socks, or put on his shoes and go outside and walk in the night in the dark side streets of Carson, under the big trees under the looming mountains. He didn't think of Marjory very often.

Nevertheless, when the tournament was really over, he got a ride home with Ham Brown, and that night he went down to Marjory's house, with a feeling that he had been away from her for a long time. It was comforting to be where he wasn't always wrong.

CHAPTER TWENTY-FIVE: *False Spring*

IN FEBRUARY came a day that should have waited a month or two. There had been premonitions of it for a week. Old snow on lawns and hillsides sank under its own weight, let the earth show through, and made innumerable, tiny, underground streams, which silently swelled the ditches, the ponds and the river, wearing the ice gray and drawing it away from the banks. People walking along the streets were full of indefinite yearnings and expectations. Sometimes they would stand still and look up at the trees, still bare against a clouded sky, and cock their heads slightly, as if they had just that moment caught one strain of a distant and delectable music which had been going on for a long time. Dogs gathered and ran in erratic packs across lawns and up alleys.

Then there was a night in which fell a quiet snow of huge, wet flakes. Restless sleepers crept out of bed and padded to their windows, and seeing the snow, felt that they had been mysteriously and enormously wronged, and went back to bed unhappy. But it was not the snow which had made them restless and started their dreams. There was something else going on in the night. The snow melted almost as fast as it fell. When daylight reached over the city, there was only a thin covering of snow on roofs and streets, the Truckee flowed black and smooth over its dams, and on the ponds there were left only a few dwindling islands of ice like thin, bad glass. By ten o'clock windows were opened in the school, and a smell of wet sod and pavement was wafted in, and the sounds of running gutters, dripping eaves and sparrows bickering. The waters swelled in the halls and class rooms too, rivers of whispering, chattering, laughing, song snatches and irrepressible bits of dancing, lakes of silent dreaming and staring. Even the teachers turned their heads to look out the windows, and faltered in the middle of sentences when they saw the bright, exultant branches lifted into the blue sky, and then began again to speak of angles, bivalves, participles and amendments in voices which gave those sturdy topics a peculiarly legendary quality. At noon the last snow was gone from the ground, and the last thread of mist from the sky. When school let out in the afternoon, the streets and sidewalks were dry.

Tim left his books in his locker, drifted out onto the front steps, and waited for his irresolution to become a desire, which it didn't. Marjory had been away for two days with her mother, but Pauline had told him at noon that she was back now. She would expect him to come down. He descended the steps and began to walk slowly toward the middle of town. As he turned the corner from Fourth into Sierra, a car pulled up at the curb beside him. It was the blue roadster, and Rachel was alone in it.

"Hi, Tim. Want a ride?"

The sound he had almost heard everywhere all day was now beyond a doubt the fiddles of spring in the streets of Reno. Fortunately he was stricken nearly dumb.

"Sure," he said, and climbed in beside her.

"Where you going?" she asked

Where is there to go when you are already there? "Oh, nowhere in particular," he said.

"I was going downtown."

"O.K."

He had no luck. She found a parking place on Virginia Street the first try, and jumped out and slammed the door. He got out slowly. It was very sad in the shade on this side of the street.

"You going down to Marjory's?" Rachel asked.

"No," he said, which was true now. "No, I've got a lot of work to do. I guess I'd better go home."

"You wait," Rachel said. "I just have to get something for Mother. I won't be a minute. Then I'll take you home."

It was amazing how the shadow on this side of the street glowed.

"Or do you want to come with me?" she asked.

And the glow went off like a rocket. It exploded high above the street and showered the beautiful people on the sidewalk with falling light. Rachel's feet twinkled along the sidewalk in the falling light, and he walked beside her, proud, but embarrassed by the celebration going on inside him. The whole street could hear those explosions. In a moment the whole street would cry, "Oh, look, look. Tim Hazard is shooting off his heart for Rachel Wells." Rachel stopped because of what she saw in a window.

"Oh, I like that," she cried.

"That" was a soft gray dress with a short gray jacket which had loose sleeves, like those of a monk's robe, and was trimmed with a downy gray fur. It was hung upon an evil plaster body which had no head and no arms and an iron pipe instead of legs. The price tag proved that Rachel was considering an offering to spring which was little short of madness.

"Isn't it lovely, Tim?"

Tim stopped looking at the plaster body, and imagined Rachel in the gray dress. "Swell," he said.

She led him in, and he sat on a slippery leather seat and waited. After a few minutes she emerged from among the shadows and mirrors and stood before him, the delicate bones of her ankles together, her arms held away from her body, and looked down at the dress and then looked at him. She even turned once around, slowly, like a mannequin.

"Do you like it, Tim?" she asked.

He wriggled a little and said, "Sure. It's swell."

She assumed an attitude of indignation, one foot forward, and one hand upon her hip. "Tim, you're an old dummy," she said.

"No," he said stiffly. "Really, it's swell. It looks swell on you. Especially the fur. The fur looks swell on you."

She looked at him curiously for a moment, not thinking about the dress. "Tim, you're funny sometimes," she said. Then she swung about once again, but quickly, and said, "Since you're so crazy about it, I'll have to get it," and disappeared once more among the mirrors and shadows.

He sat there, carefully not looking at the girdles and silk underclothes upon dead busts like the one in the window, and silk stockings and high-heeled shoes upon shapely legs without bodies, and took her words apart and put them together again in hopes of making more of them than he suspected she had meant. Nevertheless, having sat in this Parthenon of the female and seen her turn before him, showing him a dress of which he was jealous because she liked it so much, he was full of understanding about the everlasting beauty of woman.

Rachel came out in her school clothes, with the dress in a gray box under her arm. She made Tim carry the box, but also she took his arm, and squeezed it, and laughed at him. They went out onto the sidewalk that way. Then Rachel drove around by Court Street and down through the park so they could look at the tennis courts, but the nets weren't up. Still, they talked about tennis and the coming summer, so that the day felt more like spring than ever, and as they approached Fifth Street, going north on Virginia, Rachel said a thing of great understanding and beauty.

"You don't really want to go home yet, do you, Tim?" she said. "Let's drive out the Purdy Road."

So they drove all the way out to the Dry Lake valley, and Rachel stopped the car there, where the road was built up, like a railroad embankment, and they got out and stood side by side, although not quite touching, and looked at the work of the sunset in the east. The water was probably only an inch or two deep on Dry Lake, but it was spread wide and looked like a real lake. The low hills around it were piebald with snow, and the still air was turning coldly toward night. The hill, the light, the shadows of everything, reached east toward the last white sliver of mountains. The reaching was in Rachel's face also. She looked at Tim shyly, just for an instant, and made the quick smile. If he could have made that instant into an hour, she would have understood. It was that close. But a cold breath from the west came over them and she turned back, and the meaning of everything changed. A bank of dark, revolving clouds was rapidly reaching into the sky from behind the near barrier of the western mountains. It had a cold, brilliant edge, and a sunburst spread up from behind it.

"It's going to snow again," Tim said.

"I guess it is," Rachel said.

Yet the memory of that imminent moment was still with Tim when he got home. It had kept him from even wanting to talk on the way back, and when he came into the kitchen, late for supper, it protected him from his father's comment. But then the phone rang. Once Grace had answered the phone whenever it rang during a meal, because she sat nearest the hall door, but Grace wasn't there any more. It made a great difference not to have Grace at the Hazards' table. Each of them had a whole side of the table to himself now, but there was a bigger space than that. Something was gone that nobody but Mrs. Hazard had known was there before, something which had made them more together at the table. Mrs. Hazard was always searching for this something, and she was beginning to feel very old and tired without it.

The phone rang again. Tim got up and went into the hall and answered it. It was Marjory, and she spoke very quickly and clearly and emphatically. "Tim, I want to see you tonight."

Tim set the phone down on its shelf and pulled the kitchen door shut. He realized now that he had been planning to run or walk all over the city tonight. He hadn't done that for a long time, not to count; only coming and going from Marjory's house, or from band practices.

"Well, are you coming?" Marjory asked.

The old heaviness began to settle in him again. Nobody was talking in the kitchen. Usually, when one of them went to the phone, his mother would lead the others to talk about something, so they wouldn't seem to be listening, but tonight she was too tired, and didn't try. Tim believed they could all hear even what Marjory was saying.

"I don't know," he said. "I have . . ."

"Tim, I want to talk to you. Do you understand? You won't have to stay long, I assure you, if that's what's worrying you."

He could imagine the look in her eyes and the scornful down-curve of her mouth, yet all he really resented was her breaking the peace of the Dry Lake valley.

"I'll see you tomorrow afternoon," he said, trying, for the benefit of the kitchen, to make his voice sound as if he were stating his part of some friendly agreement.

"No, I don't care to wait, thank you. I said tonight."

After a moment she asked sharply, "Do you hear me, Tim?"

"All right," he said. "I'll be down."

She didn't speak again, but hung up abruptly.

When he went back to the table, he could see they all knew the phone call hadn't been the same as usual, but nobody said anything. Even Willis didn't do more than give him a curious look and then go on eating. There had been a queer, blessed, absent-minded streak in Willis lately. Sometimes he even seemed to be looking seriously at Tim and trying to figure out the various strange things about him, and without any militant purpose. He stayed home a lot more than he ever had before too, and sat around in the living room doing nothing restlessly. Mrs. Hazard was worried about this, but she would just say softly to Tim, where Willis could hear, "Timmy, Willis must have found a girl, after all," and Willis would only say, "Nuts," without any heart in it.

Tim went out onto the porch after supper, and Willis followed him.

"What's the matter?" he asked. "Is old coffin-puss griped about something?"

"I don't know," Tim said. He didn't mind the insult to Marjory. Willis was always making them, so he was used to them, but now he wouldn't have minded much anyway. The heavy, tired feeling was increasing so definitely, like a physical burden being let down onto his shoulders, and while he still remembered very freshly how he had felt standing beside Rachel and looking at the distant, snowy mountains, that he was beginning to compare the two sensations.

"Don't bend," Willis pleaded. "For Chrissakes, don't bend," he almost pleaded. "She could haunt ghosts," he added.

But when Tim just stood there looking at the pale curve of the race-track fence in the dusk across the street, Willis said, "Well, don't mind me. It's none of my business." He had changed a lot, all right.

He didn't like it to be obvious, though. "God loves a lot of funny things too," he said loudly, and went back into the house. Only he used to sing or yodel or whistle after a crack like that, and now he didn't.

Tim rode down to Marjory's on his bike, and left the bike against the stoop. He had to ring the doorbell three times before Marjory opened the door. He hardly recognized her then. She was wearing a black, lacy evening gown, very grown-up, without even shoulder straps, and a pair of heavy, black earrings, and she was holding a pair of long, black gloves in one hand. Her eyebrows were changed too, thinner and darker and sharp, like bent blades, and her mouth was painted very red and bigger and more curved than it really was. He was abashed by her strangeness, but she just stood there looking at him, so he spoke first anyway.

"Hello," he said.

That gave her an advantage to begin with, because she didn't even answer, but just turned around and stalked back into the living room, leaving him to close the door. He closed it and went in after her. He could feel that they were alone in the house, except for the secrets between it and Marjory. He had guessed that Marjory was alone when she was phoning, for that matter. There was only the one going-out light in the living room. Marjory sat down in the middle of the couch, very straight and stiff, her ankles crossed and her hands in her lap, and stared at him. Her eyes were different than he had ever seen them before, too, neither dark with hunger nor pale with old wisdom, but full of a shocking anger that didn't belong to any particular age. Because of her manner on the phone, he believed that she had been storing this speechless anger for a long time. Backed by the old house, she was preparing to slay him exactly and neatly for some reason.

Finally she said, too quietly, and like an older person, "I think perhaps you owe me an explanation, Tim Hazard."

Before he could think of anything to say, she asked, still very quietly, "You don't really care very much about me, do you? You never have, have you?"

This was a terrible thing to try to answer, when she was looking at him like that. He had never even answered it to himself.

"Of course I do," he said. "You oughta know I do, Marjory." He didn't care whether this was true or not. He just wanted to say something that would make her more like herself, so they could really talk, if they had to.

"I've made a fool of myself about you," Marjory said.

Tim had plenty of reasons for knowing that this was probably the hardest thing in the world to say, when you meant it, and Marjory sounded as if she meant it. He thought, in order not to feel how terribly she must be hurt to say those words, "Good God, you'd think we were thirty and going to get married, or something. Wouldn't we sound silly if anybody heard this!"

"I don't see what you mean," he said.

"Don't you?" she asked. "Well, everybody else does," she said, letting the anger out just a little.

Rachel stood on the edge of the highway in the late sunlight and looked at the ultimate mountains. She was straight as the little soldier, and her heart trembled for the world. The still, chilly air about her, in which he also stood, was full of the promise of forever, which was like a multitude of soft wings beating. He desired to touch her, but was prevented by the knowledge of holiness.

This came to him clearly, like something which was happening to him again.

"What does that matter?" he answered Marjory, but not as if answering what she had said.

Marjory stood up quickly and said, "If it doesn't matter to you, I'm sure it doesn't to me."

She went across to the phonograph, and stood with her hands upon it, and her back turned to him. He didn't understand what he had said to provoke this open anger. He couldn't even remember his words.

She turned around and faced him. She tossed her head, as if to throw her hair back, although it wasn't in her face.

"Just the same," she said, "I haven't been out with anybody but you since we started going together. I've just stayed here and waited for you, plenty of nights, when I could have gone out with somebody else if I'd wanted to, and you know I have."

She sounded more her own age. She sounded as if she would cry if he didn't find out what to say to keep her from crying.

"Sure you have," he said gently, but then suddenly felt angry, as if he had been caught lying, and said quickly, "But I didn't ask you to, did I? I've said plenty of times you should go out when I have to play."

"I don't want to quarrel," Marjory said, being older again. "Only I'm not going to look as if I were chasing you any longer. I'm sick of it."

"What's this all about, anyway?" Tim asked.

"You don't know, I suppose."

"No, I can't say I do."

Well, he couldn't say he did. Rachel didn't care about him. It didn't mean anything at all, because nothing could come of it. There was nothing real there; only what he felt.

"I was going to come down this afternoon," he began.

"Oh, were you," she said, not asking a question. "Well, you can go to the devil, Tim Hazard, for all I care," she said suddenly and loudly. "I don't give a damn where you go, do you hear? I don't give a damn."

He stared at her.

"Do you hear me?" she asked again.

"I hear you, all right."

"Good," she screamed at him. "Good. I'm glad you do."

She came up close to him, lifting her face almost against his, like another boy intending to fight.

"Do you think I don't know who you were with this afternoon? Do you know where I was? I was in our car, right in front of that store. Do you even help her buy her clothes now?" she asked.

"No. Don't try to tell me any nice stories," she said quickly. "I went in. You didn't see me, but I saw you, sitting there like a dope, while she showed off for you. The little bitch," she said, like spitting.

"All right," she yelled, "go on and hit me. I'd like it. It's the only thing you haven't done. Go on; I dare you to." She thrust her chin out at him, offering her face to be struck. She appeared wildly joyous about this challenge. It seemed as if she really wanted to be hit. Tim was stunned by her grotesque and joyous fury, and her yelling. He didn't move or say anything. He wasn't even thinking anything.

Marjory relaxed. Her hands were trembling. "I didn't think you'd dare," she said. She turned away from him, but she went only a step or two, and then faced him again.

"Pauline Chester called up just before I phoned you," she said.

Still without thinking, he set himself to withstand another attack.

"Do you know why?" she asked.

"No," he said. Because he spoke, he began to feel something. He was overwhelmed by shame. "I don't care," he said. "I guess . . ."

"Well, I do care," Marjory said. "She called up just to laugh at me. Oh, she was my dearest friend, and everything. She just thought I ought to know. Yes, me, and everybody else in school too," she said furiously.

"Know what?" Tim asked.

"That you and Rachel Wells spent all afternoon somewhere out the Purdy Road," Marjory said. She came close to him again, talking into his face. "And don't try to tell me you didn't," she said. "Pauline was out riding with Joe, and they saw you."

"Well, what of it?" Tim said. "Is that any crime?"

He knew he was dreaming himself, but he even started to explain. "She was going to give me a lift home," he said, "and it was nice out, so we drove out to Dry Lake and back, that's all. Is that . . ."

"Oh, yes?" Marjory said quietly.

"Don't you lie to me," she burst out. "Don't you think I know what you go out the Purdy Road for?"

"Oh, nuts," Tim said, because he couldn't think of anything to say that would make any difference. She would just attack anything he said now. "Oh, baloney," he added.

Marjory slapped him across the face with the black gloves. She raised them, and was going to hit him again.

When some time had passed in a void, his eyes cleared slowly, and he could see. Marjory was bent queerly to one side in front of him. Her head was over on her shoulder. She was just standing that way, without moving, and staring up at him. Gradually it came to him that she was afraid of something. Then he saw that she was in this queer position because he was holding her wrist and twisting her over like that. He must have caught hold of her when she started to hit him the second time. He was holding her much too hard, so hard that his knuckles were white. He became frightened. He didn't know how long he had been holding her like that. He wasn't sure whether or not he had done anything else to her. He let go of her slowly. Marjory straightened up, and tossed her hair back. She stood there looking at him, and rubbing her wrist with the other hand.

"That hurt," she said.

"I'm sorry," he said thickly.

"That doesn't help it a great deal," she said.

He tried to find words to explain to her how he had happened to hurt her, but he couldn't. Anything he said would sound like a lie. He had lost the right to say anything, by hurting a girl. When you did a thing like that, there was nothing to say that was not just a bad excuse.

250

Marjory was picking up the gloves, which she must have dropped when he grabbed her wrist. Then she stood there, holding them down by her side, and just waiting. He couldn't look at her face. Finally she turned, and went quickly across the room to the table in the corner. When she was not so near, he could look up. She came back toward him with an old candy box in her hand. She was triumphant. She was celebrating a great event which he didn't understand. She held the box out toward him.

"You might as well take these with you," she said. "I certainly shan't want them."

He didn't want to take the box, whatever was in it.

"What are they?" he asked.

She laughed at him. "A lot of things, all cheap," she said.

"To be exact," she explained, exulting, "everything you've ever given me that I could find."

He took the box, and held it as if he meant to put it down in a moment, or give it back to her.

"Except this," she said gaily, shaking her hair back, and holding out her hand.

It was a silver ring with his initials on it. She had been holding it in her hand all the time. Now she held it out and waited, until he had to extend his hand or just leave her standing there. She dropped it into his hand without touching him.

"Good evening, Mr. Hazard," she said, making a little bow with just her head. She was smiling, and her eyes were full of the cool, knowing look. She was like her mother. She was acting just as she had intended to, now.

He thought of the afternoon in the summer when they had chosen the ring together, and he had felt very young and embarrassed, holding the ring while she slipped her finger into it, and the jeweler stood there watching the ceremony and probably finding it very amusing, although his pale face, with the rimless, pince-nez glasses, had remained serious, and even bored.

Without thinking what he was doing, he carefully put the ring into the box with the other things. He had guessed what they were, and didn't even know that he saw them as he put the ring in. There was a silly little china dog, striped orange and black, like a tiger. There were the yellow, faintly sweet and musty remnants of single blossoms saved out of corsages he had given her. There was one of his track letters and a scholarship pin. There was a silver compact and there were two bracelets and several pins for her hair and trinkets to wear on her sweater and dime-store toys she had seen in the windows. There were some folded sheets of paper which were probably foolish poems he had written for her. It was all stuff like that.

"Is there anything missing?" Marjory asked him.

He realized that he was holding the box partly open and staring at the junk in it. He closed it quickly, as if he had really been caught trying to make sure she had returned everything. His face was very hot. He tried to appear at ease, to be even bored and taking his time, as he went across to the couch and put the box on it, but he felt stiff and ridiculous.

"Will you please take them with you," Marjory ordered.

"I don't want them," he said. "You throw them away if you want to. They're yours."

He didn't look at her, but went out into the hall. She followed him quickly, as if she had thought of something else to say, but then didn't say anything, but stood under the dim red light in the hall. He stood with his hand on the door knob, looking at her.

"Don't let me keep you," she said.

He started to open the door. He ought to say something.

Suddenly Marjory turned and ran back into the living room. He stayed there in the hall, holding the door partly open, and feeling very heavy and sad and undecided about everything. He could hear her crying in the living room. She cried hard and slow, as if the sobs were wrenched out of her at intervals, and she did her best between times to fight them down. It was like a boy crying, who felt even worse about crying than about the grief which made him cry. Finally he closed the door again, and went slowly back into the living room. She was lying on the couch, with her face buried on her arms and her legs drawn up. He was afraid he would start the dreadful noise and fighting all over again, but he couldn't leave her like that.

"Marjory," he said.

She didn't answer him, but just turned her head more away from him and burrowed it harder into her arm, and held the crying in so long that when it came again it was a deep burst that shook her. It trailed out in a little, irrepressible whimpering noise.

He wanted to go. He'd made his try. Why didn't he just go then, and leave her alone, and get this whole trouble over with? It wouldn't do any good to start talking about it again. But he didn't. He knelt beside the couch.

"Marjory."

But when he touched her, she drew up as quickly as a startled cat, and then crowded back from him into the corner of the couch.

"Don't touch me," she said. "Don't you touch me."

The tears were running down her face, and she couldn't look at him long, but quickly hid her face on her knees. She was crying more easily, though.

He was still kneeling there, trying to get her to say something, when the doorbell rang.

"Oh, my God," Marjory moaned.

Tim stood up. "Do you want me to answer it?"

"I don't care," she moaned.

Suddenly she sat up and put her head back and shook it, to make her hair fall straight and free. At the same time she pounded quickly on her knees with both fists. Then she sat there and stared at him fiercely.

"You needn't think I'm crying about you, Tim Hazard," she said. "It's just about everything. I hate everything here."

The doorbell rang again.

"Oh, damn," she said softly. She got up quickly, and shook her head, and wiped her face on her arms like a boy.

"I'm going to marry him, if it's any of your business," she said softly. She sniffed and tossed her head again. "I'm sick of kids."

253

She went out into the hall in the slow, ambling gait that went with the worldly look. Tim heard her open the door.

"I was afraid I had the wrong house after all," a man's voice said.

"Oh, no, quite the right one," Marjory's voice said brightly.

There was a moment of silence, and then the man laughed softly and said, "Well, that's good."

"If you'll just wait in the living room," Marjory said, "I won't be a minute."

Tim heard her feet on the stairs. Then he saw her leaning over the rail. "One of the kids is in there, Tom. He was just going. Mr. Blakeford, Timmy Hazard," she said.

"I didn't break anything up, did I?" the man asked.

"Hardly," Marjory said, laughing. She ran on up.

The man came in. He looked at Tim curiously. Tim wished that old candy box full of trinkets and things was somewhere else. Mr. Blakeford nodded and said, "Hello," and sat down on the couch beside the box. He looked as old as the man Mrs. Hale had gone out with, the evening of that first party. He was a lot like him, too, handsome and easy, but white, and soft, so that his high, narrow nose looked sharp on his full face. He was wearing evening clothes, and carrying a bowler. He laid the bowler on top of the box and drew out a silver cigarette case.

"Smoke?" he asked, opening it, and holding it toward Tim.

"No, thanks."

"It's snowing again," Mr. Blakeford said, after his cigarette was lit. "Pretty discouraging, after a day like this. I had my hopes all worked up."

"Is it?" Tim asked. This man made him feel the way Mrs. Hale made him feel, too big for his clothes, and uncertain of his feet.

"Well, I guess I'd better be going," he said. "I didn't even wear my sweater."

Mr. Blakeford never stopped looking at him, and now smiled a bit, meaning, "So I see, sonny, so I see," but said, "Can we drop you off somewhere?"

"No, thanks. I have my bike. Well . . ."

"Good night," Mr. Blakeford said.

"Well, good night."

It was that wet snow falling again. Mr. Blakeford's car was standing at the curb with the parking lights on, a way nobody left a car in Reno, and its top and hood were already covered with snow. The big flakes floated down black past the street light on the corner, and turned white beneath it. Everything around the crossing looked unfamiliar and improbable, like a movie set for *East Lynne*. So nothing was settled after all. Everything in the hushed world was as vague as Marjory, as unreal as the house. It would all start over again tomorrow.

CHAPTER TWENTY-SIX: *The Economy of the Silver Mill*

NEVERTHELESS, that night was the last time Tim ever saw Marjory. She didn't call him up, she didn't come back to school, and a week later Pauline Chester, watching his face curiously, told him that Marjory and her mother had gone to New York. A month later she showed him Marjory's wedding announcement. This ending was like all the rest of the affair. Looking at the elegant, engraved writing upon the card, Tim wasn't even sure that Marjory had married the man with the silver cigarette case, for he couldn't remember the man's name. The whole thing dimmed out in shadow. Marjory leaned over the banister in the dim, red light, with the vindictive joy in her face, and introduced the man with the silver cigarette case, and then she ran on up the stairs, her long skirt rustling, and disappeared into the shadows. The shadows lingered for a long time. Often they came back over Tim when he had not even thought of Marjory or the house. He would be sitting at the table in his room, writing, and because he looked up and saw a patch of late sunlight lying at an angle upon the wall in front of him, the life would fade out of whatever he was writing. He would lay his pencil down, and sit there staring at the patch of light, and all the labors of mankind through all time would appear to him like an attempt to carve a basalt cliff with a fingernail. He would feel just as he had when he sat on the couch in the front room of the old house, watching Marjory prowling and touching things with covetous affection or satirizing them with the long, cool look; just as he had when he sat there and suddenly, for a moment, the fog dissolved and he understood that the scene was real, and might go on forever.

But even if it is not possible to say when, if ever, Tim was wholly freed of this interminable world, hopeful changes, which made the mood intermittent rather than constant, were soon noticeable. He began to get more sleep. When track started, he was no longer doing a mere stubborn job of running, as he had in the spring of his junior year, but often followed the stallion, attained to the clarifying sensation of the nuclear. Music he heard and books he read came alive again in magical spells which sent him questing eagerly among the chords and images and ideas, and beyond them. His other lives revived as Rachel took up the feminine lead again, and he had four dates with the real Rachel, and although he failed in all of them, they didn't leave him in a sleep-walking misery, but lifted him into heaven for an hour, and dragged him around the bottom of hell for days. They drove him out to walk and run again, in the hills and in the city.

There was another change, too, in the realm of finance. To Tim, finance was represented by a bank he kept on the desk in his room. This bank had the shape of a mining mill, set upon a pyramid of tailings. It was all one color—silver gilt, except the roof of the topmost chamber, which was red. The tailings were silver also. There was a slot in the red roof big enough to slip a silver dollar through, and a door in the back which could be opened to take money out. What Tim had was what was in his pocket or in this mill. He liked silver dollars especially. He liked to hold a silver dollar. The rough circle of the edge felt good, and the weight was just right to be comforting in the hand, and it was pleasant to run the thumb over the smooth, raised figures, and to meditate upon the complex lives of a dollar as suggested by the little date on the face. 1873, the dollar would say. The Civil War was over. In Virginia City the Comstock was booming, and the hill swarmed, and the famous chandelier was blazing in the Crystal Club. The dollar, brand new from the mint and unblackened, was sliding across the dark bar of the Crystal Club to a tall man with a brocaded vest and patent-leather shoes. In that manner the history would begin. No other coin was as pleasing as a silver dollar. The date on a dime started nothing. A fifty-cent piece wasn't heavy enough to feel good. Bills had no life at all. If Tim had more than two or three dollars in bills in the silver mill, he could never remember how much was there. He could never remember how much was there in change, either. But he always knew how many silver dollars there were.

While he had been going with Marjory, there had never been many silver dollars in the mill at once. This was not entirely because of Marjory. Tim had thrifty impulses, but there were too many other matters which were more important. He had bought a portable phonograph, and there was always some new record he had to have. He was always buying sheet music too, and tennis balls wore out fast and rackets broke easily, and sometimes he would even have to spend some money on clothes. He was miserly about this. He hated to spend money on clothes. It was wrong from all points of view. Old clothes felt much better, and were friendlier, and the matter wasn't important enough to remember anyway. But after he began playing two or three times a week with the band, his father made him buy his own clothes. And then Willis was always borrowing from the bank too. That was all right. Willis never thought of returning it, but often he even told Tim he was going to take some, or that he had taken it, and Willis would have been very generous with his own money if he had ever been able to keep any together. There was nothing tight about Willis.

But it had been mostly because of Marjory that the mill stayed empty. Not that Marjory was a gold-digger. She wasn't. She was a collector of reassurances. Sometimes the reassurances would take the form of toys, like the things in the box she had tried to give back to Tim. More often they would be little parties after Tim had not seen her for two or three days, or after he had played for a dance. She would want to go to supper downtown, anywhere. She would want to go to a show, any show. That these activities kept the silver mill empty was the fault of Tim's own conscience. Marjory was willing to pay for them herself. When Tim was broke she did pay, often. But Tim couldn't stand this. He always agreed with her that there was no reason why the girl shouldn't pay for anything they did together, but he wouldn't feel right with himself until he had done something to make up to her for any party she paid for. He would have to take her out on a party which cost more than the one she had paid for, or bring her a present.

Now this contest was over. Also, Willis had nearly given up borrowing from the silver mill. When he did borrow, he would usually take only enough to buy a magazine or to go to a show. Something was happening inside Willis, which made him so different in his habits that even Mr. Hazard, who hadn't noticed the first changes in his manner at all, wondered what was wrong with him. He sat silently in the living room, looking at the carpet and thinking about something, and when he couldn't endure that any longer, he would get one of his magazines and read. The magazines he liked had fiercely painted covers showing mysterious figures with cloaks and masks, or very tough-looking men with slouch hats and tommy guns, or beautiful women on the stocking-ad pattern, with their clothes torn and pulled half off at the important points, because of fierce, rat-in-the-corner defenses against such men. Willis read the way he did everything else. He would start by lying down on his back on the couch, or on the bed up in his room. Then he would change his position every minute or two, sitting up, lying on his side on one elbow, lying on his belly, putting his feet up over the back of the couch, switching around and hanging his legs over the end of the couch. But anyway, there he was at home most of the time, and Tim knew that often, when he did go out, it was only to go across the street and sit in the shadow under the race-track fence and smoke a cigar. He had found Willis doing that at two o'clock in the morning once. He had been coming home from a dance, and had seen the cigar glow and fade in the dark across the street. He had stood in front of the house for a minute, staring to see who was there, and Willis had spoken to him. Mrs. Hazard was really worried now. When Willis was sitting silently in the living room with them, she kept looking at him. She always hoped Willis would tell her something, but he didn't, and she never asked him. Not even Mr. Hazard asked Willis about his business any more. Mrs. Hazard would ask Tim sometimes, when neither Willis nor Mr. Hazard was there, but Tim didn't know any more than she did about what ailed Willis. All Tim knew about Willis was that he was making very bad grades at school, which was nothing new, and that it was only once in a long while, every two or three weeks, that he borrowed several dollars from the silver mill.

It was probably this increase in wealth which first put the moss-agate into Tim's mind. He saw it in a jewelry-store window when he was downtown one afternoon, and he liked it. He didn't form an intention then. He was in no position to. But he did think, at once, how nice the moss-agate would look on the gray dress with fur. After that, whenever he passed the jewelry-store window, he stopped to see if the moss-agate was still there. It always was, and he became very fond of it because of the dreams with which he surrounded it, and the vague hopes it began to represent. If anyone else stopped to look into the window while he was there, he would pretend to be looking at something more reasonable, like a tennis trophy or a pen-and-pencil set, in order not to call attention to the moss-agate.

The agate lay in an open case lined with gray satin. It was made up into a rectangular brooch, and the jeweler must have thought it was an unusual stone too, because it had been set in a delicate frame of platinum, like a true precious stone. It was a pale, translucent gray, and in some lights glowed from within, like an opal, though it never changed color, but only grew brighter. The brightness was like that which spreads through a high, unbroken sea fog in the early morning, and you expected, as you watched, that this mist would gradually dissolve and reveal a blue ocean stretching to a distant horizon. The illusion was reinforced by the singular bits of moss which were trapped in the agate. They appeared to be two tropical islands with palms upon them. One island extended into the agate from the left center, and the other, elliptical and much smaller, lay to the right of it, and just a hairsbreadth above, so that it seemed to be sunk much deeper into the agate, or rather to be many miles farther out on the sea. The distance between the two islands was increased by the palms. The moss on the end of the nearer island formed three distinct silhouettes, with narrow boles and arching fronds, lifted above a mass of lower growth, while on the outer island only a faint fuzziness was visible, which tricked the beholder into imagining a dense wall of palms because he had seen the first three. It was a magic like that of a fine Chinese painting in which air, water and distance are all conveyed by a single soft wash or by the color of the paper itself, because of the clever placement of a few human figures, or sails, or a perspective of serried promontories floating among clouds. The agate was scarcely larger than the thumb nail of a large man, and yet, if you looked at it intently, the rest of the display window faded away around it, and the scene in the agate expanded until the moment came when you were in it, perhaps in an outrigger canoe, paddling quietly toward the first island in the hushed expectancy of the morning. You knew also that other islands lay behind you, and that beyond the tiny one, which was the farthest you could see at the moment, were many more, scattered widely over the face of the serene waters. In short, you were afloat somewhere near the heart of the archipelago of the Secret Isles.

Tim came to have an almost superstitious faith in the powers of this agate because of his many adventures in the archipelago. Due to a tragic misunderstanding over something far more dignified than talking too much, Rachel turned away from Tim and married a man so much older that no honorable vengeance was possible, and Tim, abandoning music, mankind and all but mere bodily life, sailed out on a tramp steamer from San Fran-

cisco and, among the Secret Isles, dove overboard before daylight and disappeared from the world. Years later, Rachel, coming to the only populous island in the archipelago, stood at the
rail of the steamer and recognized him in spite of his breech
clout, long hair and blackened skin. She dared make no sign,
because her husband, a monster whom she dreaded, stood behind her in a sun helmet, smoking a cigar. But at dusk, while
the brute was getting drunk in the village with the trader, she
came running down to the beach where Tim was loading his
supplies. The years were erased in a brief agony of joy, and together, in the outrigger, they set forth toward an unencum-
bered life of guitar music, moonlit beaches, green glades at noon
and long surfs whitening in the dawn. That at least was the
master plot from which innumerable variations stemmed, especially in the last part, which partook of the endless vistas of the
St. Francis life.

Such, then, was the well-nigh incomparable financial wiz-
ardry of Timothy Hazard in the spring before he was seventeen.

CHAPTER TWENTY-SEVEN: *About Such Lessons
in Time as the Revival of the Neglected
Friends, the Victory of the Lost Tournament, the Immortal Flivver and the Incident
of the Misguided Geese*

IT WAS a Friday in late May, warm and windless, the beginning of summer. The trees of Reno stood over the city in
full and heavy leaf, and the year-book was out at school, which
was a great relief to Tim and a great satisfaction to his con-
scientious friend, Fred Waters. Fred was the editor. Tim, for
no reason he could guess, was the business manager. He had no
head for figures, and he loathed his chief occupation, which was
soliciting advertisements from the business men and writing up

in printable form such pieces of their poetry as began, *KOLLEGE KICKS FOR ALL THE KIDS* and *THE MODERN FUNERAL HOME, SERVICE WITH A PERSONAL TOUCH.* Now that was all over, and the year-book had entered into its two or three days of real life. Commencement was near, and everybody was disturbed by its approach. The seniors, especially, were filled with nostalgia, and a little frightened to discover that they had to savor four years in a few days. Everybody carried his year-book around in the halls and class rooms and had it signed by everybody else. Many of the seniors were trying to get all the other seniors to sign beside their pictures, to leave by their own hands small, scratchy tokens of their singular and inviolate beings. It was the great ceremony of the declaration of unification at last. There were still personal differences. Some were seekers and some were givers. Even these differences, however, were tacitly ignored. The meekest seekers, the rabbits and mice of the wilderness, the children of thin hopes and old people's habits, managed to joke like equals as they asked for the names of football heroes, student officers, dramatic stars and girls who always had dates. And if these notables felt that they were giving more than they received, nonetheless they made each earnest joke good with one no better, and wrote their names boldly in ways of great significance, nick-names instead of registered names, and often with additions, "For my friend," or "Best of luck," or "Happy days," and sometimes even with the nick-name of the receiver also, "For Hank," "For Tiny." Through the accumulation of several thousand such small acts of contrition, the ceremony of the year-book acquired the power of a revival. It is true that very few of these converts would even know where the holy books were a year later, and that within two years few but the lost would even care, but for three stirring days, at least, of which this Friday was the last, they were testaments to the overlooked. There is no knowing how much difference this ceremony made in the long run. That would afford a problem even more nebulous than an attempt to trace the influence of Shakespeare or Beethoven, but perhaps, just as an early and indicative instance, it had something to do with Tim's great luck that very Friday.

At noon he and Fred Waters walked back to school together. "We ought to celebrate," Fred said. "Why don't you get a date, and we'll go out to Bowers tonight?"

"Swell," Tim said. "I'll let you know last period."

He spoke as if there were nothing to it, but he began at once to imagine an evening at Bowers with Rachel, and to fumble over the strategy of asking her. Rachel hadn't signed his year-book yet. He had put that off, watching for a time when nobody else was around. He would use the year-book as an excuse to start talking to her, and maybe he would find a way to ask her to go to Bowers. When he got to school, he went into the year-book office, a little room at the end of the main corridor, and his luck began at once. Rachel was in the office by herself. She was a member of the year-book staff too, and it was a privilege of the staff to select what they wanted from among the mounts and cuts and proofs that came back from the printer. Rachel was looking through a pile of mounts on the table. She made it very easy for him. She pretended fright and backed away from him, hugging a mount to her breast.

"First come, first served," she said.

"Curses," Tim said. "Which one is that, tightwad?"

With an air of being about to take wing, Rachel revealed the picture for an instant and embraced it again. It showed the two of them, side by side at the net, shaking hands with the coast team which had defeated them in the finals of the Western Tournament. Tim was sweetly wounded to find himself a part of the picture she was clasping to her breast. He was also pierced anew by the knowledge that their time here was nearly gone, which was all the time that mattered, since Rachel was going away to college. Yet he mastered himself.

"You can have the old thing," he said. "I know a better one." He began to work quickly down through the mounts and proofs on the table. Rachel began to go through them at the same time. They pushed at each other, and their hands touched among the cardboards. Sometimes, when she thought the next picture was going to be the one, Rachel would grab for it with both hands, and try to get in front of him, so that she was practically in his arms. She was laughing all the time.

"I know the one you mean," she cried.

"I'll bet you do."

"I'll bet I do. Anyway, I was here first, you big bully."

When they did come to the picture, Rachel snatched, but Tim got it. He held it up in the air, so she could see it but couldn't reach it. She jumped for it two or three times, and then stood there and made a face at him. "Boor," she said. "Oaf."

It was a posed picture of the two of them in front of the school in their tennis clothes, and holding their rackets. It was a wonderful picture of Rachel, because it had caught the moment of quick laughter, and her eyes, looking right at you, were full of mischief and delight. She was hugging her racket with both arms.

"I didn't want it anyway," Rachel said. "It makes me look like a grinning monkey."

"O.K.," Tim said, "just for that you don't get it. I was going to give it to you, but you can't call the girl I love a monkey." It filled him with blissful dread to find a serious joke like that coming out so easily.

"Don't you try to soft-soap me," Rachel said. "You're still a pig."

They looked through the rest of the mounts more quietly, choosing the ones they wanted and sometimes swapping finds. Rachel stood so near Tim that once in a while they still touched, though they weren't fooling now. He struggled to keep his breath and subdue the orchestral thunders that repeatedly began in him.

At last, and almost naturally, he said, "You haven't signed my year-book yet." He insisted that she sign beside every one of her pictures, and was always finding another. He acted as if these discoveries were accidental, which wasn't true. He knew every picture of her so well he could close his eyes and see them. He knew the numbers of the pages they were on. She declared that all this signing was not only foolish, but a deliberate imposition, and as a punishment made him sign all his pictures in her book. With great restraint, he wrote only "Tim" beside each picture until he came to the posed tennis picture. Then his control failed, and he wrote also, "For my partner," understanding tremendously that, as in the case of "good-bye" and "hello," each of these words had a profound and particular meaning which might be barely suggested by some such definitions as:

FOR: A word signifying the divine privilege of giving oneself entirely, excluding only undesirable traits such as talking too much.

MY: A word often narrowly interpreted to denote the first person singular, possessive, but better conceived as connoting the erasure of self in mutual desire.

PARTNER: A word which, in spite of many mundane, and some practically criminal, uses, may also mean helpmate in bearing forever the marvelous and bewildering beauty of life. Synonyms: beloved, adored, heart's desire, little soldier of the ultimate mountains, etc. Example: "In this one moment, in this one life, in this small room with one window through which may be seen the golden light in the leaves of the trees of Reno, I am about to ask My (see definition) PARTNER (see synonyms) for a date, if only I can speak her name."

He closed Rachel's year-book quickly to prevent her seeing this bold inscription while he was present. His hands trembled.

"You busy tonight, Rachel?" he asked.

"No, I'm not," Rachel answered. Even the tree at the window waited.

"Would you like to go out to Bowers, maybe?" And having said it, he was immediately inspired. "We could have supper, and then go swimming and dance and everything. Fred and Doris are going too."

"I'd love to," Rachel said. "What do you want me to bring?"

"Not a thing," Tim said grandly. "Fred and I have that all fixed." This wasn't really a lie, but just a premature truth.

The first bell rang in the hall outside. Rachel picked up her books and pictures, but she waited, watching Tim, who was hunting through the drawer of the table. He found the shears, and carefully cut his tennis mount in two. He gave her the half with his picture on it.

"Conceited," Rachel said, but she laughed, and she tucked the picture into her year-book. "When should I be ready?" she asked.

"We'll be up about five," Tim said. "About five, in old Tilly."

The first two classes in the afternoon went very slowly. Tim tried to pay attention. He was a good student this year, even on the honor roll. As a compromise he finally began to draw rapidly in his note book. He could listen some while he did that. In the first class it worked pretty well. He covered three pages with ballet dancers, Fred's Ford with four little figures in it, prize-fighters, hurdlers, cowboys, jazz bands, crocodiles in hammocks and deck chairs, saints, mountains, sailing vessels, city sky-lines, vampires, bearded men, lions and opera singers, and bound each page into one design by means of very long dragons and serpents. In the second class, however, he began to draw an outrigger canoe on a lagoon, and it turned into a carefully shaded drawing of himself and Rachel nearing the Secret Isles as the sun rose over the sea and the interminable future. He became immersed in the problem of drawing Rachel with her head turned away, so he wouldn't have to malign her face, and he never emerged. The last class was physics lab, and time went faster there because he and Fred were working together, and first he had to tell Fred about his wonderful inspiration, and then they had to discuss everything they would get, and finally they had to work very attentively to finish their experiment in time.

After school they ran all the way to Fred's house, which was up beside the cemetery in the university quarter. Fred phoned his girl Doris Summers about the change, and then they drove downtown in Tilly and bought pickles, olives, oranges, bananas, bread, cake, four kinds of sandwich spread, potato chips, jam, jelly, lettuce, coffee, four huge steaks and a case of assorted root beer, ginger ale and lemon, cream and orange pop. They took all this up to Doris' house, and she made a great many jokes about the orphans or the conventions they were going to feed, or how long they were going to live at Bowers, while she busily made the sandwiches and kept the boys wrapping them and packing things. She had already made a big bowlful of potato salad, and the last thing, she set the boys to cracking ice into a dishpan and setting some of the bottles in it. Then they started.

Rachel laughed too, when she came out of her house and saw all the wealth piled on the floor in the back of Tilly. They all laughed. They were tickled anyway, by the thought of the four of them in Tilly, proceeding down the long gravel driveway of the Wells' house at five o'clock in the afternoon. The Wells' house was huge and dark and covered with vines. It wasn't on Court Street, but it was in that region, and the ancient and cob-webby sadness of Court Street brooded over the big lawns under the trees which made it like a park. The bright foothills showed between the trees, but they were far off, and appeared unreal, like a back-drop. Tilly didn't belong in such a place, and her air of upright assurance made her very funny.

Tilly was an old Model T touring car with a brass radiator. Billy Wilson would have painted her with circus colors and written jokes on her, but Fred wasn't like Billy Wilson. Tilly was dignified. Hers was the gentle and more enduring humor of an unconscious anachronism. She was painted a thick, shiny black, in which the brush strokes showed, her radiator was polished so that it shone like gold, and there were thin, yellow arrows painted on the spokes of her wheels. Her top had been patched in many places, but was also painted a shiny black, and when Tilly attained her traveling gait, it flapped slowly and heavily, like a sail fallen off from the wind. There was an old brass horn with a rubber bulb fastened to the side of her up-right windshield. Fred drove Tilly in a rigid and elderly fash-ion, and with affection. He would always sound the horn just twice, bonk, bonk. As they came out of the shaded driveway into the sun of the street, he slowed Tilly down until she shuddered and rattled, and squeezed the horn twice, bonk, bonk, and they all laughed.

Tim and Rachel sat on the back seat. The seat was so high that even Rachel's knees were on a level with the top of the door.

"I feel like something in a goldfish bowl," she whispered.

A few moments later she whispered, "I ought to have on a poke-bonnet." She considered. "No," she whispered, "a little black hat with a ribbon under the chin, I guess, and black mitts without any fingers."

"A goldfish in a black bonnet and mitts," Tim whispered, and Rachel laughed, squinting at him with the shining of secret joy in her eyes.

The sun of the long afternoon was warm and golden across the valleys. The smell of cool water came out of the deepening alfalfa and out of the meadows where young stock posed and stared fiercely, and suddenly ran off, cavorting and bucking, and stopped farther away to stare again. Tilly passed along evenly and noisily through the long shadows of trees into the shadows of near hills and out into sunlight again. Sometimes the four talked secretly, in two couples. Sometimes they talked back and forth very loudly. Tilly's top flapped slowly in the wind of her own motion, clop-clop-clop.

There was something settled and gentle about Fred and Doris together. They were like people who have been very happily married for a long time. Theirs was one of the affairs at school which nobody even joked about any more. It was an affair like Fred's nature, which was outwardly slow and unmoved, but inwardly quickly moved by gentle or whimsical thoughts, or by long thoughts about the sweet and earnest intensity of life. The kindness of their love showed in Doris' face too, when she turned around to speak to Tim and Rachel. She was excited by all this fun they were having, and by the magnificence of the preparations, and by the thought of everything that was going to happen. In this same warm and quiet way, Doris could be excited by all kinds of thoughts about living, even when she was just sitting alone on her own porch steps.

The excitement showed only in her blue eyes, and in the tiny, tremulous movements of her lips before and after she smiled. The rest of her face was made beautiful by a tranquil light such as is sometimes seen on the faces of mature women to whose deepest yearnings life has made good answers. It was a pale face, and her hair was pale and shining too. She spoke slowly, and mostly to Rachel, when she turned around. She didn't know Rachel, because they went in different crowds at school, but she wanted Rachel to like her and Fred, and especially Tim, and she wanted Rachel to be happy too about their adventure in holy Tilly. Rachel understood. They expressed affection for each other in girls' talk about other things. Rachel leaned way forward, so they wouldn't have to yell. There was no sign in her of the little soldier mounting guard.

At last Tilly climbed slowly onto the final summit, and showed the Washoe Valley. There was a double feeling in the air here, as if spring weren't so far along. The mountains on the west were already in shadow, and a coolness came from the snow still banked among their heights, down onto the meadows, and brought with it a strong scent of pine. The two lakes were full and still and very blue, and the desert mountains in the east were warmly lighted. Spring was there along an exact line at the edge of the mountain shadows. Rachel was looking out solemnly at the lakes. Her mood had changed.

"Remember the wild geese?" she asked Tim, and smiled at him, and watched him as if expecting something.

That was an afternoon in the winter before Tim started going with Marjory, a cold, still afternoon, under a gray sky that promised snow. Ten of them came out in two cars, to skate on Little Washoe Lake. They parked the cars in the sagebrush on the east side and sat on the frozen ground to put on their skates. They could look up, while they fastened their skates, and see the winter willows by the inlet, and then the ghostly cottonwoods spreading their branches over the last remnant of Washoe City, and then the base of the mountains whose peaks were hidden in the clouds. The ice on the lake was black and glassy, without a mark on it, so that each line cut by a skate had the importance of a first word written on clean paper. Each skater went out by himself first, to make his mark.

Tim and Rachel hadn't come together. Tim started out by himself to skate down the ditch onto Big Washoe, wanting to get out in the middle of the valley, in the middle of all the winter-quiet space. While he was climbing over one of the irrigation gates, he saw Rachel coming down the ditch behind him, and waited for her. They skated together out onto the miles of new, black ice. At first they were only going to go out far enough to get the feel of the space, but then it was so much fun skating along without ever seeing even their own marks, that they decided to skate clear across. Toward the middle of the lake they skated fast, because the ice felt thin and ran in a slow wave before them.

Out in the very middle, east of them, they saw something on the ice, many little mounds scattered over a wide space. They made guesses, and then skated out to see. The mounds were a flock of wild geese, with four wild swans among them. They decided to frighten the flock into the air. This was mean, in a way, but they both felt that it would be like performing a miracle of their own to start that multitude of strong, whistling wings rushing up through the gray air. They would leave right away then, and let the geese settle again.

They came closer, skating fast all the time, and began to yell at the great birds, to startle them up. Many of the geese wailed and beat their wings, but only a few of them actually tried to rise, and they slithered and fell on the ice. Tim and Rachel started to laugh, because the geese looked grotesque, slipping and careening over like drunken old men, and then they stopped laughing at once, because the fear and helplessness of the geese were so plain to see and hear. The whole world became unfamiliar in a moment, and there was present all through it a bewildering dissonance of the laughable and the tragic which reached into a realm beyond their knowledge, so that for a moment they turned superstitious.

It was really simple, though. The geese weren't enchanted or stupefied. They had landed on the ice, probably mistaking it for water in the night, and they were unable to rise from it because their webs slithered on it and they couldn't push off. That was all. Rachel and Tim tried to work them like sheep dogs working a flock, skating around them to drive them to shore where they could get footing. But the birds were so frightened, and cried out and hurt themselves so foolishly, that they had to abandon this driving. Also, the ice crackled under them when they skated so slowly, or paused, or turned short. Long lines of fracture radiated like forked lightning from their blades with each crackling.

"They'll settle down on their breasts and thaw through," Tim said.

So they skated swiftly on across to the beach on the edge of the flat meadows. Rachel's feet were numb, and Tim made a small fire on the beach. The fire was bright and almost red against the snow. Rachel sat down near the fire, and Tim unlaced her skates and drew them off, and drew off her heavy socks and laid them across stones near the fire. Rachel's feet were small and icy in his hands. He chafed them gently with snow before she held them to the fire.

They sat there then, wondering to each other about the geese, and other things the geese made them think of. What was the mysterious mentor in birds that guided and timed their migrations? Why was that mentor occasionally so wrong, as in the case of these geese? It was a short talk because of the cold and the late hour, but it began long thoughts about space and stars and mortal insignificance. Those were tremendous thoughts to share on the edge of the frozen lake in the empty valley, with only snowy mountains in sight and the dusk coming on. It was dark already when they found their way back onto Little Washoe and were guided across it by a big fire on the bank, and the far-away sound of laughing, and the smell of coffee. That was a fine time to remember; nothing at all wrong with it.

"Yes, I remember," Tim said to Rachel.

They told Doris and Fred about the geese, and because of this all four of them were quiet and full of big thoughts when

they came to the tall, stately poplars which defended Bowers'
Mansion from the valley.

CHAPTER TWENTY-EIGHT: *The History of Mankind According to the Poplars of Bowers' Mansion*

THE gray face of the mansion stared out at the valley through
the gap where the driveway entered. The stone fountain on the
front lawn was lifted before it like an admonitory finger. "Go
quietly, go quietly. We remember a good deal here, and we
learned a good deal, though too late. Nobody is of much importance anywhere at any time. Just remember that, and we'll get
along." Tilly passed sedately between the gray face and the
finger and entered the picnic grove. The four emerged from
Tilly by the four doors. Doris stood holding her door open and
looked up, and the others looked up. Everybody looked up
when he first entered the grove. It was inevitable because the
poplars were venerable and lofty, and all their branches reached
upward, closing over one another toward the sky. The shadow
of the mountain lay over the shadow of the poplars in the grove.
Only a few of the loftiest spires reached into the sunlight and
leaned resignedly to movements of the air which could not be
felt below.

This was the sacred grove of a faith which was no longer
even an effective mythology. Yet the great "Why?" always at
the center of the little "whats" and "hows" that make religions
into mythologies is often stronger in dead temples than in living. Mortality gives the Why its power, and mortality is undeniable in the sacred grove of Bowers' Mansion. Tim thought
of Sandy Bowers and Eilly Orrum as he and Fred started a fire
in the old stove against the bank where the wild grass went up
and then out onto the open slope. Only Sandy and Eilly of all
the mansion's ghosts remained individually present. The in-

numerable mocking roisterers from Virginia City, Gold Hill, Silver City, Johnstown, Carson, Washoe, who had fed upon Eilly's vanity and Sandy's blind generosity, came and went like autumn leaves before each breath of the imagination, but it seemed to him that Eilly and Sandy were still presences in the mansion, presences which withdrew before the intruder, but always left some disturbing essence of themselves to make him uneasy. At this hour, when the shadows came, the picnic grove was also theirs, though they could never come out on the other side, to the swimming pools and the dance platform. Here, upon the dusty paths, in the quiet gloom, Eilly paraded slowly and haughtily, taking the air of the past, and poor Sandy crept behind her. Most often, when Tim imagined them in the house, he saw them posed like an old photograph, Sandy, in the high collar and elegant boots he hated, seated before the east window of an upstairs room, sometimes coughing slowly and weakly, staring out at the valley and dreading the moment when he must go downstairs and play host to guests he now knew for what they were; Eilly standing behind him, one hand upon his shoulder, holding him, not because she wanted him, but because he was her property, seeing herself at last as the jest of Europe and the butt of the silver camps. Those were their everlasting moments.

Tim thought of these things only in fragments, but the big Why was constantly present in the grove, only the more so when he and Fred spoke with mortal voices while they made the coffee and cooked the steaks, or when he heard the girls laughing softly together, speaking in their light voices, making little sounds of glass and silver as they set the table and spooned out the salad. Three small children from another supper party at the other end of the grove played tag among the trees, making little flitting patches of color, laughing breathlessly as they ran, calling out where they were hidden, squealing when they were caught. They alone seemed oblivious of the shadow, quick as birds in a world without a past or a future, and their sounds disturbed the quiet no more than bird notes.

When the four sat down to their feast, Tim and Rachel on

one side, Doris and Fred on the other, Tim felt the great Why of the grove very strongly. It made Rachel's small, white face, laughing beside him, appear terribly important, desirable and temporary, against a background of many dark tragedies from which he couldn't protect her. This life of a moment, as if he could foresee their sufferings and their lonely deaths too near behind them, was also in the faces across the table. It made him sad, and at the same time very happy that he was there, looking upon these three, hearing the words they spoke. The sunlight slowly left the last spires of the poplars. Little winds before night rustled the leaves and turned up the corners of the paper napkins on the table. The four of them, sitting there and drinking their coffee and laughing softly together, were snatching something of inestimable worth from under the nose of time. He kept this secret to himself.

Doris got up, saying, "I'll have to take a walk before I dare go swimming."

There was a great deal left to be taken home, or eaten later, if they were hungry again. They stored it away in Tilly, putting the dishpanful of ice and pop bottles on top because they would be more likely to want that than anything else. Then Doris and Fred walked away among the trees toward the mansion. Tim and Rachel went in the other direction, climbing up the bank into the wild grass, and taking the narrow path toward the base of the mountain. The trees were pines out there, and far apart. Passing them was like passing people to whom you should pay some attention. The poplars in the grove made a wall, protecting the memories in the mansion from the valley, in which they could not live. Out here the valley was open. Tim and Rachel found a big boulder on the side of the mountain, and sat on it and looked at the valley. The lakes were in the shadow now. There was still sunlight among the mountains in the east, and above them and above the shadow of the Sierra, it streamed across the sky. Coming up here from the grove was almost like coming outdoors. They talked quietly, with long pauses, about Rachel going away to college, and about what Tim wanted to do with his music. When the light went off the last mountains, they walked back down the path, and through the grove, and around the mansion to the swimming pools. They walked slowly and dreamily. They stood by the deeper pool and looked dreamily at the water. Already the bats were hunting in and out among the poplars and over the pools.

Fred and Doris came out of the dressing rooms with their bathing suits on. Rachel and Tim got theirs too. When they came out of the dressing rooms, there was darkness in the valley and blue gloaming in the sky. The little lights on lines around the pools and the dance platform went on while they were looking, and made the sky as dark as the valley. The night air moved under the lights, and played with their half-naked bodies. Rachel looked even smaller and more perfect and more separate in her bathing suit than in her clothes. Tim was newly filled by a great rush of sad adoration, the beginning of songs and legends about her. She saw him looking at her, and made the quick smile, but wistfully. It was all working in her too. They walked slowly and silently, side by side, to the edge of the deeper pool. Rachel put on her cap there, stood poised for an instant with her arms back, and dove in. Tim watched her feet disappear under the little cloud of bubbles which rose and glittered in the light, and then he dove in too.

At first their swimming was also dreamy. There were other people in the water, and Tim stayed near Rachel, but felt as if he were kept from going to her. He would float on his back, attacked by this grief of separation, and think brief, disconnected thoughts about the bats that dipped quickly into the light, onto the water, and then fled softly up into the dark again, and about the stars he could see in the east between the treetops, and about Rachel, whose wonder not his heart or his mind could define or withstand. When several thoughts about her had passed through him, he would feel a little fear, because a great deal of time must have passed, and he didn't know where she was. He would roll over and look for her white cap, and see it fifteen or twenty feet away, at the other end of the world, perhaps even with the heads of strangers between. He would swim softly toward it. When he came close, Rachel would see him, and smile at him, and sometimes make the fireworks in his heart by gently splashing a little water in his direction. Once, when he rolled over and looked, he couldn't find her anywhere on the water. He was filled with despair and the emptiness of loss. Then he saw her. She was standing by a tree between the two pools, and looking up intently toward the sky, probably trying to see the stars over the electric lights. His love shot up with joy, and celebrated her.

Later the four of them played tag in and around the pool. They were all good swimmers and divers. They pursued each other across the dark water, through the splintering of the little lights on the ripples, and clambered out dripping, and raced around the edge, and dove back in again. They laughed in fine water battles, and competed to see who could slip into the water most quietly from a jack-knife dive. Tim and Rachel had a race across the pool and back. Rachel was a smooth little swimmer. She slipped through the water softly and evenly, only her fluttering feet making a swift, whispering churning. Tim beat her only because of his reach and strength.

They didn't notice that the orchestra was tuning up on the platform until there were only the four of them left in the pool.

Then it was so big and free to have the water to themselves, that they began another game of tag. After that they swam together in a kind of water dance to the music the band was playing. This was deeper fun. There was something which searched them and then made them happy, in gliding along, four in a row, all right arms gleaming slowly up together, and then all left. They swam in circles, one behind the other. Then they swam in a kind of square dance in couples, back and forth, splitting couples as they met and swinging wide on the turns. Then they lay on their backs in a four-pointed star, with their feet together in the center, and revolved slowly, and then swam apart to the wall, and turned over and swam back until their heads were together. Doris was the slowest swimmer, so they let her set the pace where it was easy for her and she could keep it up, and when they wheeled in line, she was the pivot.

It was Doris, while they were pulling the star apart, who

first saw the moon rising, and called in a hushed voice, "Oh, look," and stopped swimming and stood there looking.

They all swam over to the east side of the pool, and hung with their chins over the edge, and watched the moon. The moon was huge and white, and its ascent was so tremendous an event that the silence and ease with which it happened made them remember how far away the moon was, although it appeared to be just above the mountains across the valley.

"It looks so close, but it isn't," Rachel said.

Then they all felt that the world was rolling over to expose the moon, and when this sensation finally expanded their space conception immeasurably, they were suddenly aware of the incredible speed with which the world was spinning and at the same time swinging bodily through emptiness. With their fingers on the edge of the pool, they clung to a flying world and felt confusedly the beauty and unhappiness of mortality.

Then, between the spires of two poplars, the moon rose high enough to light the valley, and the gleam came across Big Washoe, and this near beauty was more bearable. Tim turned his head and looked at Rachel's face. The moonlight was stronger on it now than the glow of the electric lights, which had become pitifully small and yellow.

"Let's get dressed and dance," he whispered.

They danced slowly, and without talking. The moonlight came in among the poplars and lay in patterns with the shadows. The number of the poplars was multiplied by their own shadows. The band played two waltzes to every other kind of number, and whenever they played a waltz, the little lights around the platform were turned off, and there were only the shielded lights on the music racks. The faces of the players were pale and isolated above these lights, and the dancers moved slowly and steadily around the floor in the darkness and through the gently stirring patches and beams of moonlight. The band played *Moonlight and Roses* again and again, and when they didn't play it for three or four numbers, some of the dancers would ask for it. They didn't want the fast, jazzy numbers. When the lights went up, and the band began a loud, fast number, only a few couples stayed on the floor. More of them sat down on the benches around the edge of the platform, and some left the platform entirely and wandered about in the shadows in the grove. They came back when the lights went off, and the band began to play *Moonlight and Roses* again. Always the same thin, dark boy, with a high tenor, stood up in the band and sang the refrain.

> *Moonlight and roses*
> *Bring wonderful memories of you;*
> *My heart reposes*
> *In beautiful dreams so true——*

Many of the dancers sang with him, softly, or hummed the melody. Their voices made a murmuring undertone, above which the voice of the singing boy flew slowly, by itself, like a gull above the sea of their murmuring, like the moon above their darkness.

His voice wasn't really good, but thin and shallow, like a falsetto, and also the playing of the band was thin and methodical. Nevertheless, small among the feet of the poplars, lost in the vast night under the moon, carried upon the soft singing of the dancers and the hushed scraping of their feet, this music had a plaintive beauty.

Tim even felt that it was good to have all the other dancers there. They were all the rest of the human world, and to be loved because they could all be together, quietly and happily, and yet each couple alone. They must all be in love too, he thought. They were the dark history of the race, moving obscurely under the lofty spires of the poplars, which were struck by moonlight, and sometimes shivered in it, not as if the air stirred, but as if the air were perfectly still and the trees themselves shivered because of the moonlight and the things they were remembering in the moonlight.

Here and there on the platform, a single face would pass into the moonlight and be clear and wistful for an instant and then turn slowly away or fade back into the shadow. It was these little passages which made the dark history true. True history was the incalculable sum of single faces showing whitely for an instant and then gone. True history was not to be told by events or by nations, or by the names of kings and presidents and dictators. This moon hung also over the desert, softly leveling the dreamy hills into the dreamy valleys and raising up the peaks of the great ranges in their snow, the peaks of the Sierras, the Wassuks, the Shoshones, of the Toyabes and the Toquimas, of the Monitors, White Pines, Rubies and Rockies, all the great blades shearing up from the great plateau, the peaks which in snow and in the moonlight were brothers of the moon. All humanity like one frightened, migratory tribe, filed in a thin dark line across this empty land, bending up into the passes and down into the valleys, into the faint mist of the moonlight over the lakes in the valleys, where they knelt and drank, and turned up their faces to the moon, and then went on, and were gone. How long the great ranges had lain under the moon before the line began to cross them; how long and little changed they would lie there yet, riding vastly eastward in the night, after the line had passed, and the sun had dimmed, and the earth become a huge, faint moon, and time itself had grown old in the everlasting.

This vision, like a symphony in Tim's mind, brought on a fierce access of love for Rachel, of yearning for her inestimable worth and courage and her tiny bit of time. Since her head was on his breast now, since her hand was in his, and he held her in his arm, this yearning became joyous, and was a moment of successful prayer. In such space, in such multitude, in such unimaginable time, the whole meaning of life for him was never to be where he couldn't touch Rachel. He must always be able to touch her among mountains and moons and time. Out of the dark, strong, minor symphony of mankind, cried out suddenly, clear, high and resounding, the trumpets of the adoration of Rachel.

He was very careful, in order not to startle her, but he drew her closer and closed his hand a little upon hers. Rachel moved her head, but not away from him. Perhaps she too was hearing history according to the moon in the poplars of Bowers' Mansion. They danced slowly into a beam of moonlight, and turned slowly in it, and Tim, bending his head, being the tender sentry to guard her from the universe, saw her face against his sweater. Her eyes were closed.

He began to hear the orchestra again, gently and automatically thumping and crooning *Moonlight and Roses*. As they danced along the side of the platform in the darkness, he saw an area of the bare face of the mansion through the trees, bold in the moonlight. He thought of the dark window in it, and of Sandy Bowers sitting in the window, and Eilly standing behind him, like a photograph in an old family album. He chuckled softly. Comedy was such sad stuff.

Rachel's head moved against his sweater. "What are you laughing at?" she asked.

"I was just thinking that probably Sandy and Eilly are sitting up in the window now and listening to *Moonlight and Roses*. I was just wondering if they got on any better together on a night like this."

After a moment, Rachel said, "Oh."

Then she asked, "Don't they get on together by now?"

"I don't know," Tim said, "but I don't see how they could. Eilly always wants so much, and old Sandy doesn't want anything, or if he does, he doesn't know what it is."

Rachel said, "Oh," again.

It was a soft oh, as if she were happy. Tim was very happy about the way she said oh.

Moonlight and Roses ended, and the lights went on around the platform. Tim didn't want to let go of Rachel, but he had to in that light. The dancers were moving around, making little groups and talking, sitting down by couples on the benches, going down by couples into the grove, but even in the light the spell wasn't broken. Tim could see by their faces that all of them were still feeling the spell. As they passed him, going down into the grove, many of them were still humming the tune softly. He saw Doris and Fred going away together among the poplars, toward the back of the mansion. They were holding hands, but trying to walk close enough together to hide this weakness from anyone coming behind them.

"Maybe they won't even haunt tonight," Rachel said.

"What?"

"Eilly and Sandy. Maybe they'll get some rest."

The band began to play *Brown Eyes, Why Are You Blue?* rapidly and jerkily.

"No rest," Tim said, grinning.

"No rest," Rachel said, smiling quickly.

It was wonderful how much they understood because of Eilly and Sandy. Rachel smiled as if she were happy and feeling gentle. Tim was very happy about the way Rachel smiled.

"Let's take a walk around, till they get done with that thing," he said.

"Let's," Rachel said.

They strolled between the trees toward the front of the mansion, because Fred and Doris had gone toward the back. Tim thought of holding her hand, or taking her arm. He even thought of putting his arm around her. But he didn't touch her, or even look at her too often. She walked along beside him, and the trumpets of the human symphony blew high and clear and challenging within him. Every thought about her, or impulse toward her made him strong, daring and joyous. He believed he could do anything she wanted him to do, anything. If he could pity the human race, and not lose hope, if he could return from among the stars and the terror of their time, and find that he loved her more than ever, then that was a great love. That was the kind of love that could do anything.

They came out in front of the mansion, where the trees opened to the road and the valley, and hesitatingly stopped walking because the night felt so different here. The fountain, caught between the moon and the lights of the mansion, made confused shadows, which passed through one another upon the circular lawn. The night was open over them, and the moon was rising on it, and the greatest stars. The open hall door and the four first-floor windows made yellow rectangles in the moonlit face of the mansion, but the upstairs windows and the four dormer windows in the roof were closed and dark, and reflected the moon.

In the white light inside the white living room there was a silent scene taking place. On the corner of the table sat a beautiful young woman, with her long legs crossed and swinging. Her face was white, clear-featured and austere. Her black hair was parted in the middle and drawn back into a knot. She was seen in the interval between two young men standing with their backs to the window. A third young man, in profile, completed the semicircle before her. The young man in the middle was performing slow endearments to the long legs. The beautiful young woman did not appear to be aware of these endearments. With detached and haughty mien, she was raising a glass to her mouth. She was raising the glass carefully, but also lifting her head away from it. The young man in profile held his hands out toward her, in suppliance or explanation, and began speaking rapidly. His lips moved hurriedly, and his face was pale and sharp with eagerness. The young man who was begging of the shapely legs, ceased moving, and stood with his hands folded upon the young woman's knee, and appeared to listen attentively. The third man, who had not moved until now, turned his head and watched the man in profile. His face was heavy and red, with thick, black eyebrows. It was also puzzled and sullen. He disliked the eloquence of the young man in profile, or else he could not understand it. The beautiful young woman held the drink in the air before her, and slowly turned her head, and stared at the eloquent young man, and said something brief and decisive. Her lips moved with precision as she spoke, and closed firmly when she was done. Nothing that was said could be heard, because of the band in the grove, which was still playing *Brown Eyes, Why Are You Blue?* loudly and jerkily. The scene was a stately and grotesque pantomime, framed by the window. Its background was a white plaster wall upon which appeared, with an effect of ridiculous formality, a closed door in the center, and upon one side a dark oil painting of Eilly Orrum, and upon the other a dark oil painting of Sandy Bowers.

To the two children standing in the driveway, staring at it, this scene made a great and confusing change in the meaning of the night. They both looked away from the scene, and away from each other.

"Shall we go in where the piano is?" Tim asked.

Rachel didn't answer, but began to walk forward by herself, and to climb the stone steps. Tim followed her. He felt that he was now pleading with her for something, though he didn't know what. They entered the hall. The door of the room in which the beautiful and austerely drunken young woman was perhaps holding at bay her three lovers, was closed, but now the voices were audible. One of the men was saying something in a deep voice. Before he had finished, the woman began to laugh shrilly. While she was still laughing, two of the men began to speak at the same time. They sounded angry. The laughter continued, but it became broken and gasping, and was made up of giggles and little shrieking spasms, as if one of the men were playing with her in a way which tickled. The little, shrieking spasms became words. The beautiful young woman was crying out repeatedly, "Harry, stop it. Stop it, Harry. Harry, if somebody comes in."

Rachel went into the other front room, and Tim followed her. The room was not large, but it had a high ceiling, and was empty, and it echoed. The floor was bare and bright and waxed for dancing. The only object in the room was an automatic piano in one corner. The piano had a front of opaque, green glass, set in wooden arches, so that it looked like a church window.

The laughter across the hall stopped with impressive abruptness, but after a moment the voices went on arguing.

Rachel stood in the middle of the room. She was the little soldier. She looked slowly about the room, and up at the ceiling. Everything was going wrong.

"Want to play something?" Tim asked.

"All right," Rachel said.

He put a nickel into the piano, and it grumbled to itself and then began to play. It was out of tune, and tinny, and sounded very loud in the empty room. It immediately took possession of the empty room. The keys jumped sharply, by themselves, all up and down the keyboard. Rachel stood in the middle of the room and stared at the jumping keys. She was getting farther and farther away. When Tim came toward her to dance, to see if he could hold her, she continued to stare dreamily past him at the jumping keys, while she slowly raised her right hand for him to take. She moved stiffly and mechanically in his arms, and held her head away from him. There was nothing in the room at all but the two of them dancing stiffly and slowly around the outside of the floor, and the piano hammering away, yet the room felt crowded with embarrassing presences. When they passed the north window, which was also open, the band, playing another tune in another rhythm, contested with the piano. Tim thought that if someone else, newly come from the grove into the open moonlight, were to stop out front and look at the mansion, he and Rachel, dancing slowly, like courteous enemies, in the bright and empty room, would make a pantomime to balance the one in the other room.

"Holy cow, what a noise," he said, making a face.

"Let's not dance," Rachel said quickly, and at once stopped and took her hand away from him, and went out of the room with rapid, nervous steps. He followed her. The door across the hall was still closed, but with the piano playing, the voices couldn't be heard. Rachel went through the hall to the court in back, and waited for him there. It was better in the court, in the soft light, laced with shadows, and with the mountain going up, steep and near, into the moonlight, but still they could hear the ruthless piano playing by itself, far away in the house, with nobody there to dance.

Tim had to do something to change what was happening. He had to do something right away, because he was losing her, and felt as if he might start talking to keep her. He wanted to explain to her that what had just happened didn't mean a thing, and then to prove to her that it didn't mean a thing, by telling her all he had thought about the history of mankind and about the time when the world itself would finally be a moon, and how, after all this wandering through the universe, what had really happened was that he loved her even more than he ever had before, if that was possible. But he couldn't explain, because he didn't know what had happened to them. Nothing had happened, really. He hadn't said anything or done anything. And he knew he couldn't tell her how he loved her. The first terrible words were already filling his mouth: "Do you remember that four-forty in the Western meet this spring?"

The door of the old bar-room in the north wing was standing open. A warm, orange light came out of it, and made a long, distorted rectangle upon the flagstones of the court.

"How about a root beer, or something?" he asked loudly.

Rachel nodded more emphatically than a root beer was worth.

They went into the bar-room. An old man was asleep in a round-backed chair beside a small round table with a marble top. He was slumped over, with his chin on his chest. A white cat with a black patch on one side of its face was curled on his knees. The cat watched them enigmatically out of wide, amber eyes. A thin man with gray hair, and wearing a white, starched jacket, stood behind the bar and watched them too. He was no more curious than the cat. He didn't say a thing when Tim asked for two root beers, but just poured them, and put a lot of cracked ice into them, and pushed them across. Tim and Rachel stood there and drank their root beers through straws and sucked the ice. They didn't try to talk, because it was so quiet in the bar-room. The mechanical piano must have stopped playing by now, but if it hadn't, they couldn't hear it. All they could hear was the old man in the chair, breathing slowly through his mouth, as if sighing, and very distantly, because the windows were closed, the band in the grove playing *Lover, Come Back to Me*. The bar-room was old. It seemed older than the white rooms in the house. More of what had happened in there had soaked into the dark walls. There were no ghosts in there tonight, though, not old ones or new ones. Everything began to get better in the bar-room.

When they went out into the court again, Rachel stopped and laughed.

"What's the matter?" Tim asked. He was experiencing the interior fireworks because she had laughed.

"Do you know what we've done?" she asked, giggling.

"No, what?"

"We've just bought two root beers," she said, "and there's still five or six bottles of root beer in Tilly."

This was very funny, and he couldn't understand what he had been so worried about, a few minutes before. They had seen some drunks making fools of themselves in a kind of queer combination, and the mechanical piano had sounded terrible. That was all.

They walked slowly around toward the dance floor. When they came up onto the platform, the dark boy who sang *Moonlight and Roses* was waiting for them. He took hold of Tim's elbow.

"How goes it, Tim?" he asked.

"'Lo, Paul. You know Rachel Wells."

"I don't, but I'm going to, right now. Monty wants to know will you take a fiddle solo on the next number."

Tim felt shy about these dreamy dancers. This wasn't his band. He became awkward and reluctant. Also, he didn't want to leave Rachel, not even for a minute, not even with Paul, who was all right.

"I don't . . ."

"Monty has a fiddle here. He says everybody's softened up fine, and with a fiddle solo now, he can make 'em swoon. He wants you to swoon 'em."

"Well, I . . ."

"On *Moonlight and Roses*. If you'd never heard it before tonight, you'd know it now, wouldn't you?"

"Sure," Tim said, "but . . ." He looked at Rachel.

"Go ahead, Tim," she said, laughing quickly. "Make us swoon."

"I'll see she doesn't miss out on the dance," Paul said. "She can swoon on me."

"Well . . ." Tim said, and looked at Rachel, and then went over to where the band was waiting.

The violin was on a chair beside the piano. Monty was sitting at the piano. He was a thin man with a white face, a patent-leather hair comb and spectacles. They said hello, and Tim opened the case and took out the bow and tightened it and put the resin on. Then he took out the violin, and pinched it under his chin. Monty gave him the A, and he tuned to it with open string chords and short runs to get the intervals. The violin had the little differences from his own which made it feel strange in his hand. The throat was bigger and the bridge was higher and more steeply arched, so that the fingering was harder than on his own, and he had to roll the bow more than he liked. The whole violin was heavier, too, and felt stiff and thick, as if it wouldn't build up the sounds from the strings. Tim stood out of the light, with the violin tilted down, and played soft runs in different keys until he had the intervals. Then he held the violin up and did a couple of bars from *Avalon Town*, and finally swept down his beloved strings an air from the first movement of the *Pathetique*. He had a superstition that you could tell what kind of soul a violin had by playing that air on it. This violin had a heart after all, and a mouth. It could sing. It still felt stiff, as if the melody came off the strings only, but it didn't. It came out of the inside of the violin, a sweet, mournful sweep that had depth. He fingered rapidly through *Moonlight and Roses*.

Monty put him out front, with the lights behind him, and the band began to thump and croon *Moonlight and Roses*. The dancers weren't in the dark now; they were in the moonlight. The moon was overhead, and its light came down the length of the poplars. Tim was nervous about playing, and he didn't like this. He liked to feel anonymous and impersonal when he played, just part of his instrument and part of the music made by all the instruments. Here he was a stranger to the instrument and to the band. Rachel was part of it too, probably. He was listening for the refrain, but he kept looking for Rachel dancing with Paul, and thinking that he was playing for Rachel, as if this were a command performance, and he had a lot staked on it. He raised the violin. The band didn't lead him in at all, but thumped right on into the refrain. He took almost a quarter beat delay, and then went through the refrain that way, just a little behind the band, so that it seemed he was playing more slowly and fully than the band. He wasn't with the violin yet, though. He was just playing on it. But he brought the band to him. They began to draw the tempo out a little, and to go more softly, and build him up. The second time through, he played the whole song, and when they reached the refrain, he and the violin were together. Then he forgot everything else, and played. He was joyous, and wanted to play tricks with chords and runs and high climbing, but he held all that to the line, and let it come out in making the strings sing sweetly and strongly in the vocal range, swelling on the rising phrases, taking the refrain away from the introduction, the way it should be. He wasn't even thinking about Rachel now. He wasn't thinking about anything, but bursting with the hope that he could make the violin strong and soft and sad-happy enough to belong out there under the sky and down there among the poplars as in a deep well of moonlight and leaves. He felt everybody listening and dancing and loving, but they were all one, and he was part of the same great love and listening with them, and he and they were all part of the same great thing without a name that the leaves and the moon were part of too. The third time through, he was right all the way.

There was real applause. Dancers called out to have it again. Monty turned around and looked at Tim, and Tim nodded. He was happy with the violin now. He could go on playing all night, only not *Moonlight and Roses*. He wanted to improvise. He wanted to compose on the violin, with some kind of a magical orchestra to keep up the background for him. He wanted to tell everybody, with the violin, how wonderful the night was, and how it was to be in love, and what he thought about the moon and the leaves. He was full of ideas for weaving all around the first part of *Moonlight and Roses*, which was dead, and just waiting. Instead, he let that part go by again, and then let himself softly and tremulously into the refrain.

They had to play *Moonlight and Roses* for a third dance,

even. When Tim went back to put the violin away, Monty looked at him curiously, but only said, "Good going, kid. Thanks."

"Any time," Tim said. "It's a swell fiddle."

He wrapped the violin carefully in its silk cloth, and put it to sleep, thinking about Rachel again. That was his secret he would have to keep from Rachel, that when he and the violin were together, he wasn't thinking about her, but about everything at once, and wanting only to say it all with the violin. It was funny he hadn't thought of it before, but it was really that way whenever he played what he wanted to, or was going well with a band that was going well, or was writing a song or a poem that moved him. They would nearly all begin with Rachel. In his mind he would be playing or writing for Rachel, but when the creation took hold of him, he was for everybody, or perhaps even for nobody. That happened even to the songs about the Secret Isles. He would still see Rachel, but she would be everybody, all the girls in the world in love and full of wonder, and he would be there in the story too, singing the song, but he would be all boys amazed by the beauty of their girls and by the fierce and wonderful mysteries of the universe. Somehow, this secret from Rachel made him happy. He was worth more when he went back to her.

It was again only Rachel he wanted, though, when he went about looking for her and Paul. He found them by the stairs, where Paul had stopped him.

"O.K., boy," Paul said. "You are the star. It's a good thing for you, you got back, though," he said, looking at Rachel and grinning. "You were breaking my heart. I was falling in love with somebody, and who was there here?"

Rachel laughed too.

When they were alone, she said, "It was swell, Tim. It made the whole band sound different. I don't know. It got everybody."

They stayed there dancing until the band was done. The crowd was smaller toward the last, and many faces had the tired-dreamy kind of look, but they were happy, and they all sang *Home, Sweet Home* quietly together when the band played it.

The lights went off over the pools. They were off in the mansion too, and the moonlight was on the roof, but the face was in shadow. Tim wanted to be very quiet, and treasure tenderly everything he had. They walked slowly together to the picnic grove, and this time he did take Rachel's arm, and then, with her arm inside his that way, even took her hand and laced their fingers together. She didn't seem to mind.

Only a little moonlight penetrated the picnic grove. The great shadows were everywhere. Tilly was in a shadow. They found Fred and Doris sitting on Tilly's running board, drinking ginger ale. They squeezed over, and all four of them sat on the running board, and Tim and Rachel had root beers. They were all quiet and happy and not sleepy. They didn't want to go home.

They went home very slowly, even for Tilly, so slowly that the top didn't go clop-clop, but only flipped gently once in a while. The moonlight was all over the land, and the mountains were soft and dreamy in it, and seemed to have tender, personal memories. But their dreaminess wasn't sleepy. It didn't seem to Tim that anything could be sleepy that night. The animals in the fields weren't asleep. They stood at the fences and watched Tilly go by, and their eyes gleamed in the moonlight, and in Tilly's headlights.

Fred had one arm around Doris, and only the pale crown of Doris' head showed over his shoulder. They spoke to each other seldom and in whispers. For a long time Tim didn't dare, but finally he put his arm tentatively about Rachel's shoulders. It was a moment of suspense. The splendor of the night was at stake. Rachel moved closer to him, and laid her head in his shoulder. The moonlight was dazzling. The motor of Tilly was a symphony. In the silence and awe of the night, millions of small, lovely, winged creatures fled softly about in the air in ecstasy. They circled the mountains in worship. With great crescendos of affection, they swooped down over the heavenly fields. With tiny cries of desire, they soared at the moon. They were the many million parts of the bliss of Tim Hazard, which he couldn't contain. When Tilly turned upon a hill so that the moonlight came in, and he could see clearly how Rachel's hands lay together in peace in her lap, he wanted to weep for happiness. He didn't dare to move. He didn't dare to speak.

Rachel lay so still against him, that finally he was afraid she had fallen asleep. This thought made him feel more protective than ever, but also strangely unhappy and lost. All the motion in the night stopped when he thought that Rachel might have fallen asleep. He had to know.

"Asleep?" he whispered.

She shook her head a little against him.

In the night the silent and glittering flight was resumed.

"Tired?" he whispered.

She shook her head again.

That was all they said on the way home, and then Rachel said good night twice. She said it once as they stood outside the door, and then, when the door was almost closed, she opened it part way and said good night again, very gently.

CHAPTER TWENTY-NINE: *Oh, My Brother, My Brother*

TIM asked Fred to let him off downtown, and when Tilly was a block away, he stopped idling along the sidewalk and nearly ran to the jewelry-store window. He was afraid, now that he saw what he had meant all along to do with the moss-agate, that it would be gone. It wasn't. There was no light in the display window, and he couldn't see the agate very well by the street light, but it was there. He didn't have to see it. He knew the world of the moss-agate better than he knew the white house by the race track. He would come down and get it the next day.

On the way home he became very busy testing out different plans for presenting the moss-agate to Rachel. It mustn't look like trying to give her an engagement ring or a frat pin or anything like that, but maybe, after tonight, it could be a little more than a going-away present, a kind of till-you-come-back present. He finally got the party all planned. The family car was in the garage with serious trouble. All the better, then; he'd rent a drive-yourself car, not one of the old, rattly, taxi-cab sort, but a fine one, a big Packard or Cadillac sedan. They would drive out to dinner at one of the clubs on the river, and then go to a show, if there was a good one, and then go to one of the clubs downtown and dance. He had friends in most of the bands now, who could get him in. When he had all these details settled, he tried to foresee the conversation which would lead up to giving Rachel the agate, but here the planning failed. He couldn't decide which place would be the best, and he couldn't imagine with any confidence what Rachel would say when he said something. That would just have to wait till the time came. He only hoped Rachel would wear the gray dress. That would give him an easy lead. It would take a lot of money for such a party, though. There would be a big deposit on the car he wanted. He'd count the money in the silver mill when he got home. If only it could be very soon, even tomorrow night, while there was still this moon, while they both remembered whatever it was that had made Rachel say good night twice. He began to create the marvelous future of which this was hint enough to make his heart beat wildly whenever he thought of it.

When he reached the house, he stood on the porch, looking at the moonlight on everything, until he had brought this future safely to the point of the interminable vista. Then he went in and tiptoed up to his room. He turned on the reading light above his table, and carried the silver mill over to the table from the dresser, but then delayed the counting because Rachel's graduation picture, in the gray dress, with her name signed across the corner, stood on the desk. He sat looking at the picture, and entered into the near reaches of the interminable vista. He was seated beside her in the moonlight on a great rock, and the south sea lapped softly around them.

"Hiya, fella," Willis' voice said behind him.

He sat very still for a moment, relinquishing the moonlight, and then turned around. Willis was standing in the doorway.

"Have a good time?" Willis asked.

"Sure. All right."

"You mind if I come in?" Willis asked, and then came in, and after standing there with a queer, uncertain grin on his face, sat down on the edge of the bed. He looked at the floor. Then he looked up and started to say something, but only held his mouth open, and closed it again without saying anything.

The religious trance, and the resentment at having it disturbed, ebbed in Tim together, and he was frightened. Things weren't right with Willis, not when he hesitated like this. He saw now that Willis not only wasn't stripped or in his pajamas, but that he even had an overcoat on over his other clothes, and was holding his cap in his hands. He sat there, leaning forward, trying to make up his mind to say something he didn't want to say, or couldn't figure how to say, and kept turning his cap over and over in his hands. And Willis was frightened too. It was because everything added up to show that Willis was frightened, that he himself was frightened. Tim had never seen Willis grin like that before, so that his lips trembled, and he appeared to be about to make an apology. His face didn't have its old, wise look, but was very young. Tim's great love of everything that night shrank, but was intensified by fear, and was all for Willis, tough, quick, all-by-himself Willis, sitting there on the edge of the bed, afraid. Willis had never come wanting anything before, anything more than a buck or two from the mill, nothing real.

"Did you just get in, Willie?"

"No," Willis said, looking at the cap. "I been waiting up for you."

He tried to sound like himself and feel like himself. He looked up, and tried to grin, and said, "That must have been some party. It's pretty near two-thirty. What did you do, get married or something?"

"We went out to Bowers," Tim said.

"Oh," Willis said, and let it drop.

Tim wanted to tell him everything about the night, and what it was like to be in love with Rachel. He wanted to give himself all away like that, so that they would be brothers, and together, and Willis could tell him what it was that was so hard to say, and made him want to cry.

"I took Rachel Wells," he said. "We went out with Fred and Doris. It was a swell night."

Willis looked at his cap and nodded. "Yeah," he said. "She's a nice kid, I guess, only kind of snooty sometimes."

Then he apologized even for this almost extravagant praise. "Don't mind me, my friend. What would I know about life in high society? Anyway," he said, looking up and trying to grin, "she don't sleep in a coffin. That's something."

Tim also tried to grin. They sat there, trying to grin at each other, and waiting till it got so that Willis could tell what was on his mind. Willis kept putting it off. Now he became practically maudlin.

"You've had a crush on her for a hell of a time, ain't you?" he asked.

"Oh, I don't know," Tim said. He was bewildered by the humility of these remarks.

"No?" Willis asked. "Go on," he said. "I can see through you like through a window."

Tim felt, uncomfortably but without resentment, that excepting for some silent and intricate movements of his soul, this was probably so.

"Well," Willis said in benediction, "she's a swell kid. She's smart, and she's got a lot of guts."

Once more he began to say what was really on his mind, but couldn't, and got out a cigarette and lit it. He was trying to make his face hard and old now. He was trying to assume the outward aspect of the man who knows all the answers in the world, and is not encouraged by them. But his hand, lighting the cigarette, was trembling. He sucked in a big lungful of the smoke and let it back out in two jets, through his nostrils. Then he felt better. He had assumed the attitude, and been granted the spirit.

"Listen, Tim," he said. "I gotta beat it."

Tim looked at him, trying to find out. "What's the matter, Willie?"

"Nothing," Willis said. "Nothing much. I got the itch. I wanta see some country. I'm sick of this going to school and hanging around home all the time, listening to the old man jawing."

Then he said, "I wouldn't've said nothing, only, I don't know. I just got to thinking about Mom, I guess. This is gonna be tough on Mom, I guess, and she isn't so good these days anyway. I don't know."

He took a drag on the cigarette and snorted at some joke with himself. "Mom thinks I'm still wet behind the ears," he said.

"I was gonna write a note for her," he went on, "but I don't know. I couldn't figure what to write. Everything I thought of to say sounded kind of mushy. So I figured maybe it'd be better if you'd just tell her for me. Then it wouldn't be so much like running out on her, anyway."

He sat there, thinking, and holding his cap still for a minute.

"Poor Mom," he said. "She's lonesome enough, with Grace gone, and Mrs. Turner gone too. They were about the only ones she ever really talked to."

He stood up. "Well," he said, "you tell her so long for me, will you? And take care of yourself, kid."

Tim thought about trying to tell their mother, in the morning, that Willis had run away. He thought how she would feel about Willis going away in the middle of the night, by himself, without saying why, or where he was going; without even saying good-bye to her. She was tired all the time now. Sometimes she had to stop working in the kitchen, and go into the living room and lie down on the couch. She would lie there with a gray face and with her eyes closed. If he went in where she was, she would open her eyes and look at him, and her eyes would look bigger and darker, and he would feel that she was thinking big, strange things. The way she looked frightened him, because usually, when she looked at him, or at Willis, or at their father, she would just be seeing whichever one of them it was, and showing her love, but when her eyes were dark that way, he would feel that she was looking at something much bigger, something he didn't know anything about.

He stood up too. "Willie," he said, "you wait and see Mom, and talk to her."

Willis shook his head. "Not me. I just didn't want her to think I'd run out on her without saying good-bye, that's all. You tell the old man good-bye for me too, will you?" he said.

"I can't just tell them that, Willie, and you know it. You're crazy for sleep. Why don't you go to bed, and see how it looks in the morning?"

"No. I got to beat it now. You just tell her not to worry about me, because I got it all figured out. I'll be all right."

"Tell me where you're going, anyway, Willie. I have to tell them something besides that you beat it in the middle of the night. I can't just tell them that."

Willis shook his head. "If you don't know, then you don't have to lie," he said. "You never could tell a decent lie. You just say I said I was all right. I got it all fixed up with a guy I know, to be a jockey for him. You tell her I'll write when everything's fixed up."

Willis meant it, and if he meant it, there wasn't any way to stop him. Many notions for stopping him came and went quickly. They were all ghostly and useless.

"Willie," he asked, "what have you done? What's wrong?"

Willis grinned in that way that hurt to watch, as if he were going to cry. "If you don't know, you don't have to lie," he said again.

"Sometimes," he said, "it don't matter if you've done anything or not. If you get some guys after you, you're just as bad off if you're an angel."

It must have been something awful, real trouble, not just kid trouble, that Willis had been worrying about all this time. Tim felt sick for Willis. It seemed as if he himself were to blame, as if all these years he hadn't seen what he saw now, that Willis was his little brother in the world. It seemed as if now all the other people in the world, except their mother, were angry at Willis. He felt desperate, and furious at all the other people in the world for picking on Willis.

"You don't have to look like that," Willis said. "It's not as bad as all that. I didn't kill anybody. There's plenty of guys around this town make their living doing worse than what they say I did, only they're big-shots, or they got big-shots to cover for them. Hell," he said scornfully, "there ain't hardly anybody in Reno, except poor guys, suckers like Dad, that don't know plenty they ain't telling. Yeah, only just let some kid do some little ole thing, like they been doing a hundred times worse all their lives, and you'd think they was all preachers or saints or something.

"Oh, I been around in this man's town. Don't you think I ain't. It ain't what you do that counts, it's do you get caught. If you're big enough to do the catching, then you don't get caught, that's all. Well, I'm no big-shot, and I got no big-shot friends, and I talked with three, four of the kids been to Elko, and I'm not having any of it."

He became ashamed of the fear his anger was showing.

"What the hell," he said. "That's all right too. Every guy for his own self. Only I ain't gonna be one of the suckers, that's all."

Tim was still standing there looking at Willis, trying to guess what Willis had done. If he knew what Willis had done, maybe he could think of something to do, or at least something to say that would keep Willis from running away. He'd always thought he knew a lot about what went on in Reno. There were some things everybody talked about, and being in Rob Gleaman's band, you knew about a lot of other little things that went on in the clubs and down on the line and so on. He knew that a couple of the older fellows in the band were hop-heads already. For a little while they'd be better than ever, really hot, if they didn't have their stuff, but then, if they had to wait too long, they'd go kind of crazy, and wouldn't be able to play at all. He'd heard a lot of opinions about where they got the stuff too. But now he realized that he didn't really know where they got it, and that everything else he knew about Reno was the same way. He didn't know what was behind it. He didn't know where it began. He couldn't even guess what kind of trouble Willis was in, or who was after him. He didn't know anything about where Willis went at night.

Willis said, "Honest, it ain't so bad, kid. They wouldn't give me the little house in Carson, or anything. Only I heard tonight this particular guy figured I was in on it, and the son of a bitch says he's gonna make something of it, so I figured I'd give him time to cool, that's all. It ain't so much. He'll cool.

"Anyway," he said, making the uncertain grin, "I'm sick of school and just hanging around two-bit joints. Where does school get you? Oh, maybe it's all right for you. Maybe with the things you like, you'll get something out of it. But I don't see it makin' any jockeys, do you?"

"If it isn't so bad, Willie, Dad can fix it up," Tim said. "You'll really get in trouble if you run away, Willie. Willie," he said, making up his mind, "you wait, and I'll wake Dad up, and you talk to him."

"Nothing doing," Willis said. "Oh, the old man's all right, but what can he do? Pay through the nose, maybe. Maybe not even that. This bastard's gunning for me. If I stick around, there'll be a lot of trouble. If I beat it, and the old man don't know anything, well, they can just suck air, that's all.

"Look, Tim," he said reasonably, "don't take it so hard. All I want to do is ride horses. Horses are all right. So I'm gonna ride horses."

He laughed a little, but the laugh was shaky too. He talked like a hard man who knew the easy way around, but he looked like what he was, a scared kid.

"You look like you seen a ghost," he said. "Relax, kid, relax. I got it all figured out, I tell you."

"Well," he said, as if it were all settled, but still stood there.

"Tim," he said finally, "I hate to ask you, I bummed so much off you already, but . . ." He waited.

Tim remembered the moss-agate, and everything he'd

planned about giving it to Rachel. He'd forgotten about that when he became scared for Willis, and thinking that he had to let the moss-agate go, made him feel very lonely and defeated in his love for Rachel. But thinking about Willis running away to nowhere in particular, and about all the millions of strangers in the world, made him feel like just one of the millions himself, like nobody in particular, but just one, the way Willis was just one. They had to stick together, against all those millions. He couldn't be one of the kind Willis was afraid of.

"How much you think you'll need?" he asked, making a last fight with himself. He was ashamed of the question at once. How could Willis answer such a question?

"I don't know," Willis said. "Oh, nuts," he added, "forget it. I'll get along. God knows I've chiseled you long enough." He started for the door.

"No," Tim said quickly. "I got plenty. Really."

Willis stopped. "You're saving it for something, ain't you?"

"Well," Tim said, "part of it. But there's a lot more than I need."

He got the silver mill off the dresser, and opened the back, and poured the silver out onto the table, and then fished the bills out.

Willis came over and stood beside him. "You keep out whatever you was counting on, and some extra," he said. "All I need is a few bucks to eat on till I get set. Five or six bucks would put me in the gravy."

"I don't need any of it," Tim said. "What I was saving it for doesn't matter."

He wanted to make it sound like a joke, so it would be easier for Willis to take the money. "It was a matter of absolutely no importance," he said, "a luxury, a foppery. You take it. You can't tell what you'll need."

He scooped up the silver dollars and the change, and then picked up the wad of bills, and held it all out to Willis.

Willis wouldn't take it. "I got enough on my mind," he said, grinning. "Don't you make a heel out of me too. You keep what it was you wanted."

It was hard to talk about money like this. It made you feel cheap and a tightwad to talk about it at all. It had been better the way it was before, when Willis just took what he wanted. Tim felt miserly and traitorous because he wanted so badly to save enough for the moss-agate. He kept holding the money out.

"No," Willis said. "You keep what you need." He was ashamed too. "Hell," he said, "am I J. P. Morgan, with a yacht to run, or something? What do I need of a pile like that?"

Tim counted the price of the agate onto the table, and gave the rest to Willis. It still wasn't so bad—over thirty dollars.

"Thanks, pal," Willis said. He folded the bills into a snug wad, and put them into his watch pocket, and put the change into his side pocket. He seemed to take courage from the money. He joked without so much trouble.

"If you wait long enough," he said, "maybe I can do something for you, too; stand you a beer or buy you a five-cent cigar." He grinned.

"How are you going, Willie?" Tim asked. "Hitch hike?"

"Side-door Pullman," Willis said importantly. "They come through slow from Sparks, and you can hook on easy, east of the Lake Street crossing, only you got to keep on the Plaza side till you're across Sierra, so they don't see you from the station."

Tim could see Willis, runty and a kid and alone, no matter how tough he thought he was, sitting in the dark in a box-car, with everything banging around him, going up through the mountains in the night, and on his first time away from home. The picture made him sad and desperate again.

"Willie, chuck it," he said. "It can't be as bad as all this. Why don't you tell Dad, anyway, and see what he says?"

"Nix," Willis said. "What I really like is horses. I'm going where I can ride me horses."

He was embarrassed by a sudden springing of nearly tearful affection in himself. He put his knotty little fist against Tim's chest and shoved gently. "Don't you worry about me," he said. "You worry about yourself. Hell, you still think the world's a garden, or something." He started toward the door again.

"I'll walk down with you, anyway," Tim said.

"Go on to bed and dream about her," Willis said. "There's another guy going with me."

He put on his cap, and held out his hand. They shook hands. It was funny not really to become brothers until the last time, perhaps, you'd see each other. It still didn't seem like the last time, of course. It seemed as if Willis would come out of his room in the morning, the same as usual, with his face looking old from not sleeping enough.

"Don't forget to write Mother, will you?" Tim said stiffly. "You might drop me a line too, if you have time."

"I'll think about it," Willis said.

He stopped in the doorway and looked at Tim again.

"And you tell her I'm sorry, will you? I mean, about not seeing her."

"I'll tell her."

"Well, so long, fella."

"So long."

After a moment, Tim had a great, frightened urge to go after Willis and stop him, or to go in and get his father up in a hurry, before Willis could get down there and catch the train. At the same time, he knew he wouldn't do either. He would let Willis do what he'd decided to do, and it was going to be very bad in the morning. The impulse took him as far as the rail of the stairwell. He heard the front door close softly. He realized that they had been talking very quietly too, almost whispering.

Outside, before he reached the corner, Willis began to whistle one of the marches the band always played at the race track. He whistled it loudly and clearly. He was telling the world that so far as Willis Hazard, called Willie, who was really tough, was concerned, the whole wide world was about to become one big race track. Then he must have gone around the corner, for the whistling faded, and finally Tim couldn't hear it any longer.

Tim went back into his room, and turned off the light, and stood in the window looking at the moonlight. The moonlight had changed. It looked thin and old now, and afraid of dawn.

The trees, rustling slowly and individually, were dark and secret. Finally he turned back, and undressed and got into bed, but he couldn't sleep. He heard the trains whistle in the sacred, the eternal, the home Truckee Meadows, and echo on the mountains, and thought of Willis in the box-car, going slowly up into those mountains.

CHAPTER THIRTY: *The Token of the Eternal and the Touch of the Moribund*

TIM didn't sleep at all. He was awake when daylight came into his room. He was still lying there, thinking, when he heard his mother down in the kitchen, moving the stove lids. Then he heard his father stirring around as he always did, shaving and dressing, sometimes mumbling to himself. Finally he went downstairs too. It was morning in the house of Hazard, but Grace was gone, and now Willis was gone. Something was happening to the house of Hazard that felt like the thin line of people creeping in the wilderness in the moonlight.

Tim got dressed and went down into the kitchen. He didn't want to eat, but he didn't know how to begin about Willis, either, so he'd have to act as if nothing was changed. His father was sitting by the window, reading the *Journal*. Tim could see the pattern of sunlight and leaves through the paper. His mother was frying the bacon and eggs. After what Willis had said, Tim thought about how she looked. She looked very tired and gray and inwardly silent. Her hair hung down beside her face in gray, untidy strands.

Mr. Hazard ended the pretending quickly, anyhow. When Tim sat down at the table, he looked up and asked, "Isn't Willis up yet? Or didn't he bother to come home at all last night?"

So Tim told them. His father slowly let the paper down onto his knee and sat staring at him. His mother stood very still in front of the stove when he first said Willis was gone. Then she carefully pushed the frying pan onto the back of the stove, and came to the table and sat down across from Tim, and looked at him, trying not to believe it. When he'd told them how he'd tried to argue with Willis, and how he'd given him some money when he'd seen there was no use arguing, and how Willis had said he had a job waiting, he looked at the table because of the way his mother was watching him, and told them good-bye for Willis, as Willis had asked him to.

"Why in hell didn't you stop him?" Mr. Hazard said. "Why in hell didn't you come in and rouse me out? Huh?"

Then he took out his worry and fear on Tim. It would have gone on for a long time, probably, except that once, when he paused for a breath, Mrs. Hazard said faintly, "Please, Father." He looked at her, and stopped talking, but then, after a moment, hammered furiously on his knee with one fist.

"Where did he go, Timmy?" Mrs. Hazard asked, and Tim had to admit he didn't know.

"What did he do? What in hell did he do, to have to go running away like that, a damn fool kid his age?" Mr. Hazard asked.

Tim had to admit he didn't know that either. He'd tried to find out, but he didn't know.

"Is there anything in God's world you do know?" Mr. Hazard roared suddenly.

Tim kept staring at the table, and said, "Willie promised he'd write."

Mr. Hazard looked at the clock on the shelf, and said "Hell," and got up. He didn't believe Willis would write either.

In the doorway, he said, "You'll have to come down to the yard with me. Willie was s'posed to be working today." He went on down the hall, talking softly to himself, and making motions with his fists.

Tim stood up. He hated to leave his mother sitting there, looking like that.

She looked up at him, with that big darkness that went beyond him in her eyes. "You'd better eat some breakfast, Timmy," she said. "You can't work all morning with nothing in your stomach."

"I'm not hungry, Mom."

"I know, Timmy," Mrs. Hazard said, getting up, "but you'd better try and eat something." She went to the stove, and pulled the pan with the bacon forward, and broke a couple of eggs into it.

"I should have stopped him some way, I guess," Tim said. "I'm sorry, Mom."

"It's not your fault, Timmy," she said. "Willie was a very strong-headed boy. I've been afraid for a long time he was in some kind of trouble, he's been moping so. But he wouldn't tell me about it either. Your father's just upset. He knows you couldn't stop Willie, if he had his mind made up."

When the eggs were ready, she put them and the rest of the bacon on a plate and set them in front of Tim, and poured him a cup of coffee, and then she went into the living room and lay down on the couch. Tim gulped the food and coffee. It was bad eating alone in the kitchen, with his father moving around upstairs, and his mother lying in the living room, thinking about Willis. Slowly Tim began to hope about the moss-agate again. The way he felt about Rachel was something he could use against all this trouble and shame, and the great, invading dread it started for no real reason, the dread that went out beyond, like the look in his mother's eyes. He went upstairs and changed into his jeans and blue shirt. He stood looking at the money, and at the picture of Rachel. When his father yelled at him from downstairs, he put the money in his jeans and went down.

After work, he went downtown and bought the moss-agate. It didn't mean everything to have it, and to think about giving it to Rachel, as it had so long seemed it would, but it meant something. He went over to the Park, to see if Rachel was playing tennis. He believed that if he could sit on one of the green benches and watch Rachel playing, and speak to her, and see what showed in her face today, and all the time be holding the moss-agate, in its case, in its wrappings that made it look like any small box, he would discover what it still meant. He would perhaps discover something important about what it meant against the heaviness and the loneliness.

Rachel wasn't there. There were only two people, a man and a woman he didn't know, playing bad tennis on the first court in the melancholy late afternoon. Early summer was quiet in the domes of the trees. The vista, made very long by the light, showed under the trees across the lawns and across the river. He could remember the vague unhappiness of all the summers of time. He was holding the moss-agate, and it wasn't for anybody now. He sat down on a bench back under a tree by the first court and watched the bad tennis. The man was heavy, and wore glasses, and ran stiffly. The woman held the racket out in front of her, and pushed at every shot. When the man stood still, and patted the ball past her with an air of great care and decision, she would always squeal, and then cry out, "Oh, Henry, how do you do it?" and the man wouldn't say anything, but he would look very pleased.

When Tim got home, he heard his father speaking loudly and angrily in the living room. At first he thought it was his mother being yelled at, but then he heard another man's voice.

"Listen, Hazard, once, I let it go. Twice? No. I got the proof it was your kid, and this young Blair, and Tony Guielmi's boy. Now, I want to know where they are, or do you pay me one third of what they steal? You take your choice, but don't give me no more of your lip. I got Jeff here to back me up, and he's been over the whole business."

"My lip," Mr. Hazard said.

"Please, Father," Mrs. Hazard's voice said.

"You keep out of this, Anne," Mr. Hazard said. "You go on out now, and let me talk to these guys. Listen, you bastard," he said angrily.

"I don't take these names," the man said.

"The hell you don't. Sit down. Go on, sit down, before I bust you one."

"I got the law . . ." the man began.

"The law," Mr. Hazard roared. "This old bag of pus? No, and you sit down too," he said. "Sure you got the law," he said. "And what kind of law? For once I'll get it off my chest, and you'll hear it for once, too."

Tim was standing in the hall listening to this. His mother came out into the hall. She looked as frightened as he felt, and sick.

"Oh, Tim, he'll get himself in some awful trouble. He won't make it any better for Willis, and he'll just get into some awful trouble."

She sat down on the second step of the stairs, with her hands twisted together in her lap, and looked at Tim, as if pleading with him to do something about it. She knew he couldn't.

"I'll tell you what kind of law you got," Mr. Hazard was yelling.

"Who is it?" Tim whispered.

"Nick Briasi and a policeman," she whispered. "They say Willie and two other boys stole two slot machines and took the money out of them."

"You got two speed cops who do all the work," Mr. Hazard was yelling, "because that's the only kind of police work you want done, and about forty old wrecks like this one, that don't see anything more than a kid stealing nickels, if they see that, friends of the mayor's, that can't do a real job any more, if they ever could, so he gives 'em uniforms and pensions 'em off. And where do you find them if anything really happens?"

Mr. Hazard told Briasi where he could find the police. Then he told him a lot of things he must have been storing up for a long time. He mentioned a murder in Douglas Alley, a minister who had been forced to leave town because of a drunken speech the mayor had made from his pulpit, unexplained fires in out-of-town night clubs, prohi raids from San Francisco that busted up some clubs, but never touched others, dope peddling that nobody could trace, even in a town as small as Reno, the finances of the red-light district. Twice Briasi cleared his throat and started to interrupt, but Mr. Hazard shouted him down. When finally he paused, Briasi asked, "And what's all that got to do with me?"

"You tell me that," Mr. Hazard said. "Something, or your joint would have been padlocked a long time ago. But I'll tell you one thing for sure." And he argued loudly, standing in one place, by the sound, that one thing the rackets couldn't get away with, if somebody wanted to stand up and make it a case for the people to hear, was framing kids; that one law even the big-shots were jumpy about was the law against selling kids liquor and letting kids gamble. "You push this, you two-bit, back-alley Capone," he yelled at Briasi, "and I'll open it up if it costs me every nickel I've ever made. And if I do, your friends will drop you like a hot potato, and you know it. You aren't big enough to matter that much."

"You're talkin' a lot for no evidence," Briasi said.

"Yes?" Mr. Hazard asked, with savage joy. "This is once somebody's got the evidence, Briasi," and he told Briasi some of what he knew about kids in Briasi's place. "And the very thing you're belly-achin' about, Briasi, is all the evidence anybody needs."

"So you admit your kid swiped them machines, huh?"

"I don't admit a damned thing. I don't know, and I don't care. All I know is you've scared a fourteen-year-old kid into runnin' away from home, and if he does come back, you ain't gonna do a thing to him. And you ain't gonna do a thing to those other kids, either. And nobody's gonna pay you for your goddam slot machines, either.

"That's what you came to find out, isn't it?" he asked more quietly. "All right. Now you know. Now get the hell out of here."

The chair creaked as Briasi stood up. "All right," he said, "now you've shot your mouth off . . ."

"Take it easy," Mr. Hazard said, breathing hard, "take it plenty easy, Briasi; I'm just achin' for an excuse to knock your teeth in." The cop started to say something. "And yours too, fatso," Mr. Hazard said.

"O.K.," Briasi said. "I was just giving you a chance to settle quiet, that's all. Now I'm tellin' you. Either you pay me that two hundred, or your kid goes to Elko. Come on, Jeff."

Tim had to move back into the hall to let Briasi and the policeman get to the front door. They were both short, square, fat men, but Briasi had thick, black, oily hair, and a kind of sloppy, animal power, while the policeman was white haired and had all his weight settled down toward his hips. Neither of them looked at Tim or Mrs. Hazard. They went out, Briasi first. The old policeman shut the door with great care, as if there were somebody asleep in the house and he didn't want to wake him up. After a minute their car turned around outside and drove off.

Mr. Hazard was standing in the living-room doorway. "I told the bastard a couple of things, anyway," he said.

Mrs. Hazard was standing up now, holding onto the newel post. "Could he really put Willie in the reform school for that?" she asked.

"No, he couldn't," Mr. Hazard said. "Not a first time, anyway," he added, looking away from her and rubbing the back of his neck. All the delight of battle was gone from his face. He appeared dazed and tired. "But he could make trouble, maybe," he said. "You never know what ways these guys have of getting at you."

"But Willie could come back?" Mrs. Hazard asked.

"Sure, Willie could come back, if . . ."

But Willie never did come back.

CHAPTER THIRTY-ONE: *The Disappearance of the Secret Isles*

THE night of the moss-agate materialized as accidentally as the night at Bowers, though with ominous premonitions rather than with such happy omens as those of the year-book office.

The premonitions were first sounded at the tennis courts on a Saturday afternoon nearly a month after Tim and Rachel, among dozens of other white-clad girls, all lovely and promising that evening, and dozens of other boys, all dark-clad and sweating and awkward, had marched across the stage in the gymnasium, to receive from the principal an enormous handshake, a couple of curt, nearly tearful nods, and a blue-leather diploma, stamped with gold, which at the moment convinced them only of the fact that their world of four stormy and beautiful years was right then, at that touch, abruptly and wholly dissolved. It was a hot, still afternoon. The big cotton-wood at the back of the courts seemed to droop like a weeping willow. Tim and Rachel had just finished three sets of doubles. They were going to play again, against Ham Brown and Peggy Hammil. They were thirsty, and went out to the ice-cream and soda-pop wagon in the road, and Tim bought two root beers. They went back into the shade on the lawn to drink them.

"When do you go?" Tim asked, not really thinking about it.

"Next week, I guess," Rachel said.

"Next week?" Tim asked. The hot, real afternoon was gone, and they stood in the shadows of the Watteau park.

"Uh-huh," Rachel said, nodding and sipping at her straw.

"Not for good?"

"Well, hardly," Rachel said, laughing. "My family lives here."

"I mean, you'll be back before college starts, won't you?"

"No, not till Christmas vacation, I guess."

Hurry, Tim Hazard, step on it. Time goes by like the leaves of November, and death is the wind that drives them. Was there enough money in the silver mill? There had to be.

"Are you busy tonight?"

Rachel laughed. "I wasn't fishing, Tim," she said.

"I know," he said, with terrible seriousness, "but are you?"

She stopped laughing. "No," she said. "I guess not, unless . . ."

"Could you go out to supper and a show with me, maybe? Maybe we could go somewhere and dance afterwards, too. If you'd like to."

After a moment she said, "Thank you. That would be nice," without looking at him. Already she was receding. The old need to declare himself, to prevent her from vanishing utterly, began to well up in him.

"We could go out to the River House," he began rapidly. "I know a guy in the band will get us in. It's Arty Meyer's band playing out there now, you know. Arty's is about the best around here, now. Arty blows a pretty hot horn himself, when he really gets going."

"I know," Rachel defended. "I've heard him."

"Of course there's Ollie Blake out at the Glass Slipper," Tim went on, "but he can't hold a high one, and clear, the way Arty can, and Arty . . ." and he explained Arty's art, and from that worked into the art of Arty's pianist, who made good arrangements without phony symphony introductions and perorations or section stunts that kept a number from taking hold solid, and from that into the art of Arty's drummer, to whom he was giving amazing skills when Ham and Peggy arrived, and Rachel greeted them with great joy and began at once to talk to them about a party Tim hadn't even heard of. Then Tim sat there silent, and stared at the grass between his feet, performing the black penance of counting his lies, and feeling that he could never be the equal, the fit companion, in the flesh, in the spirit, in the world, of these three who sat there talking so casually, a sentence at a time, as if nothing mattered too much. It was only in the last set of their match, when he began to go well and not angrily, that he could feel hopeful about the evening again, and he was nearly home, running because it was late, before the fatal sin became merely a bad habit which might be cured.

Even so, after he had shaved and scrubbed himself, he stood naked in the middle of his room for several minutes, his face lifted and his eyes closed, and tried to make a successful prayer for silence by means of calling up images of vast and quiet or ancient things, like Pyramid or the stars or the council rock of the lost people in the Truckee gorge, and when they failed, by words about the same things: "Great Spirit, Thou Who art all things, and in all things, give me to remember that I have beheld Thy eternal waters, that I have stood before the rock of time and numbered my little years, that I have seen the cities of man, and lo, their lights died in the darkness, and the stars were no older and shone. Grant me the peace of this understanding. Make me the well of this silence."

When it seemed to him that at least a sort of fatalistic calm might be retained, he dressed, polished his shoes, put the bills from the silver mill into his wallet and the coins into his watch pocket, where they wouldn't jingle, brushed his short hair till his scalp tingled, and fixed in his lapel a little rose from Mrs. Hazard's vines on the back fence, which made the yard so sweet in early summer. Lastly he slipped the moss-agate in its case into his jacket pocket, pulled the jacket into exact place, and gazed for one critical yet hopeful moment at his image in the mirror. Then he darted out of the room and down the stairs, already tremulous with expectation.

The family car was home now, but he had made up his mind to the luxurious sedan. He rode his bicycle down to the drive-yourself garage. Two of the fine cars were there, but the man grinned at him, and said, "Fifty dollars deposit, son," and he had to take one of the old taxi kind, after all. It had worn, imitation-leather upholstery, was stiff in the places where it should have been loose and loose in the places where it should have been stiff, and too slow to the gas and too quick to the brake. He comforted himself with the thought that at least it was a sedan, and wouldn't muss Rachel's hair the way the Hazard family car would have, and drove it around for a while, to get used to its oddities. He looked at his watch every minute or so. Rachel had said seven o'clock. At two minutes to seven he arrived under the Wells' porte-cochere. He switched off the ignition, slipped the moss-agate case into the pocket of the car, so his coat wouldn't bulge, and sat there for a minute, reminding himself to be a well of silence. He rang the doorbell with a trembling hand at exactly seven o'clock.

He was let in by the maid, and had to wait in the hall at the foot of the stairs, a big hall, nearly a living room, with thick rugs, soft lights, and a multiple gleaming of mirrors and polished furniture. There was no one else in the hall, or in the actual living room which opened from it, but through a wide doorway on the far side of the living room came the sound of quiet voices and the clinking of silver and china. After ten minutes, Tim heard a door close above, somewhere toward the back of the house, and the quick, light steps coming to the head of the stairs. He rose, and stood looking up. The prayer for silence was forgotten. He trembled and began to vanish outward from his own mind. Rachel, wearing the gray dress, with a gray cloak over it, appeared in the shadow of the upper landing and descended quickly into the glow of the hall lights. He didn't realize that he was staring until she looked into the living room to avoid his gaze. She spoke to him from the lower landing, paused for an instant before one of the hall mirrors to pat her hair and draw the cloak closer about her throat, and went on toward the door. He always was shy and awkward in her house, and now her every motion made him feel still more clumsy, and a little as if he were kidnapping her. He fumbled the handle of the car door as he helped her in, and they were quiet all the way out to the River House.

Tim was quiet enough while they were there too, though not with the wise quiet of proportion for which he had prayed. They took their places at a table for two in the back corner, and he got off to a bad start by forgetting to take Rachel's order, so that she had to give it herself. After that he began to worry again about how he was going to give her the moss-agate. Here, in her presence, and among worldly and much older people in evening clothes, it seemed to him often that even the intention of giving it to her was preposterous. Also, as he looked at her sitting just on the other side of the little table, her eyes watching her plate, her small, slender, brown hand rising and falling with the shining spoon or fork, he was assailed by waves of possessive tenderness in which many of the events of his legends became confused with the present, and then, when the moment became itself again, he would seem to be holding time off by the strength of his single will, or rather, by the bewildering intensity of his yearning. He would be on the verge of telling her everything she meant to him. He could never begin cleanly, though, as one might strike a true note with the first, sharp down-bow. Instead, he would ask her if her soup was hot, or if she wanted a special salad dressing, or if she wanted something else to drink, since she wasn't drinking her coffee, or if she wanted him to get her cloak, since there was a window open in their corner. He would find himself helplessly insisting that these changes could be made, and when the tiny fury darted in her eyes as she said, "It's all very nice, Tim, really," he would see at once how she would loath to have him say what he was really leading up to, and the urge would ebb away, leaving him as naked as a tidal rock out of water. He was flooded with equal swiftness, however, as when Rachel said, laughing, "You don't seem to be eating very much, Tim," and he perceived that he had been sitting there staring at nothing. All his hopes were set in motion again because she had noticed this. So he was nearly silent all through dinner, but only with an inwardly roaring alternation between the flood and the ebb.

While they were having dessert, the rest of Arty's band came in, and the dance music began. Arty stood in front of the band and got each number under way, and then turned around, his trumpet under his arm, and conducted vaguely with his free hand, while he watched the dancers and listened for his cue. He was watching for someone to smile at. Arty's smile was famous. It was no toothy, professional grin, but a slowly widening, almost tremulous salute to some one person. He would lean over and speak and smile like that, and the event was portentous. He would seem to be paying no attention to the band, but when his break neared, he would lift the trumpet slowly, but pointing it high and tensely, as if he were about to blast the roof off, and then, just a bit behind the beat, would come in with a very soft, high, clear note, which he held for an unbelievably long time before he tumbled down into the melody, or went off on his own all around it. That hold-note entry and the hold-note smile were practically Arty's personal signature. In spite of his abortive lecture in the afternoon, or perhaps partly because of it, the whole performance, even the careful but sweet simplicity of the band, seemed as stagy and false to Tim as a Paul White-man introduction. Nevertheless, it was good dance music, with a strong, unbroken rhythm that took hold, and he and Rachel danced.

The second time they danced, they passed close to the platform, and Arty's great, sad eyes, in the white, sad, almost homely face, selected them. He leaned over and asked, "How are you, Timmy?" in the slow drawl that worked like the smile. He began the smile for Rachel. They had to stay there, dancing in one place, looking up at him.

"Ah'm glad you came out," Arty said, and looked at Rachel again.

"Miss Wells, Mr. Meyer," Tim said.

"What was the name?" Arty asked.

"Wells," Tim said stubbornly.

"Please, you tell me," Arty said to Rachel. "He's keepin' secrets."

Rachel blushed and whitened, and laughed quickly and said, "Rachel."

"That's better," Arty said. "I'm Arty, and glad to know you, Rachel. Not that I blame Timmy here for bein' a bit close." He moved along the platform beside them when Tim started to dance on. "How's about takin' the fiddle break on a couple with us, Timmy? Huh?"

"No, thanks," Tim said. "Not tonight, I guess, Arty."

"One, maybe? *Moonlight and Roses?*"

"I don't feel like playing," Tim said.

When they went back to the table, Rachel didn't sit down. "Let's go," she said. "It's getting too crowded to dance," and she started toward the door without waiting for him to answer. He caught up with her in the entrance to the lounge, where the cloak room and the gaming tables were. He took hold of her elbow.

"Did you want me to play that, Rachy?" he asked.

"Of course not, if you don't want to."

He let go of her arm. "I'd just as soon play, if you want me to."

"Heavens, Tim, what difference does it make? Will you get my wrap, please?"

"It's just that it all sounds so phony tonight," Tim said. "I didn't feel like getting up there and playing stuff like that, on your last night, and everything."

"It's not my last night, whatever that has to do with it."

"I mean for me," Tim pleaded. "I didn't want to get up there with all that lousy jazz, and . . ."

Rachel stared right at him for an instant, with the little fury in her eyes again. "Tim Hazard," she said shakily, "you're the most conceited boy I ever knew."

Then Tim was staring at her. He was astonished and deeply hurt, and bewildered. How could she think that of him, of all things?

"Please," she said again, "will you get my wrap?"

It wasn't until they were outside that he remembered he hadn't tipped the check-girl. He was mortified by the oversight. Everything was going wrong. It wasn't until they were nearly in town, and he had to find out what they were going to do, that he could speak again.

"We could still see a second show," he said.

Rachel didn't want to see a show. She didn't want to go anywhere else to dance, either. She said she had a headache. He knew she wanted to go home, and he knew he would only be making things still worse if he didn't take her. The black ebbing began in him. But he couldn't take her home like this. How could he ever start to give her the moss-agate when it was like this between them?

"We'll just drive for a while, then," he said. "Maybe the air will help. It was awful stuffy and smoky in there. Where do you want to go?"

"I don't care," Rachel said.

"Let's go out the Pyramid road," he said. Wonderful places on the Pyramid road came to his mind, big places with barren mountains and long, empty valleys. There would be a moon before long, too. It came to him that they could even go all the way out and look at the moonlight on the lake. It would take an hour to get out there, and maybe the moon would be up then, and he could give her the agate while they looked at the lake. It wouldn't seem so important or so hard to do out there. The pain and joy rose in him, thinking of being with Rachel and looking at the moonlight on Pyramid.

"All right," Rachel said, sighing. She looked out the window on her side. "But I can't be out late, Tim. Really, I can't."

They passed through the city, and out the familiar road beside the race track, and around to the fork by the ranch house that looked like an old roadhouse. Tim swung the car up into the hills. When they were over the first summit, and the lights were gone, and the big darkness was around them, and stars over the mountains, he spoke.

"What makes you think I'm so conceited?"

"Oh, Tim, please. I'm sorry."

"If it was on account of what I said about Arty's band . . ."

"Tim, I didn't mean it. It doesn't matter."

"Yes, it does," he said. "It does to me to have you think that. I didn't really mean Arty's band was no good."

Rachel clenched her hands in her lap and looked down at them.

Tim saw that, but still he was drawn on. "Arty's got a swell band. It wasn't anything about Arty's band. It was just because it was your last—my last night with you, and I didn't want to play that stuff. I don't know; it just was all wrong. You always make me think of big music, like Beethoven or Tschaikowsky, or Debussy's *La Mere*. Even *Moonlight and Roses* is all wrong; too kind of soupy; too much make-believe." This was true, as far as it went, but he didn't go on because just that much, with Rachel sitting there looking at her hands, sounded like a pose or even a lie.

"Anyway," he said, trying to laugh and sound as if he were joking, "I didn't want to let you go for even the time it takes to play one number. Not tonight." But that didn't lead anywhere either, because Rachel just looked out at the first moon-glow beginning over the mountains, and didn't answer. He began to drive faster, hoping that if it didn't seem to take too long, she wouldn't care how far they went. They came off the humping road between the near hills set with junipers, and into the Spanish Springs Valley. They fled across the flat, through the soft, wuthering gloom. The Spanish Springs turn-off came into the headlights.

"Will you please turn around here, Tim," Rachel ordered.

He slacked off, but couldn't wholly believe she had said that.

"Tim, I have to go home. Turn around, please."

He turned into the Spanish Springs road. It was a little longer way home, and it would be one big valley, anyway.

"We can go back this way," he said. "It's hardly any farther."

"All right," Rachel said. "If you want to."

The moon came up, immense and pure and white, while they were in the valley. Its soft light stole down the western hills, and lay at last over the brush all about them. Hurry, Tim Hazard, step on it. Time can no more be held than moonlight. On the hills it is forever, but in the heart it is a moment, and death is the moon that casts it. Cattle lying in the brush slowly lifted their white faces to watch the car approach. The car passed the lone ranch house at the center of the valley. The windows were all dark. The people were asleep in there, full of the wonderful peace of their valley. The moonlight twinkled in the leaves of the trees, and lay like frost on the haystacks. Rachel didn't speak.

The moonlight, in little patches, lay on the lawn under the trees at Wells', too, and there was no light in the porte-cochere, but only a dim glow showing in the window above the door. Tim stopped the car, and then, hesitantly, shut off the motor. After that he was powerless to move or speak. Rachel sat there too, poised on the edge of the seat, waiting for him to get out and open the door for her. "Well," she said finally, and laughed a little, and took hold of the door handle.

"Rachel," Tim gasped, "Rachel," as if he were going on headlong, but then couldn't say anything more. He leaned toward her.

"I have to go in now," she said quickly, and opened the door.

"No," he said. "Just a minute; I have something." He fumbled hurriedly, and managed to get the case out of the side pocket. He hadn't thought before that it was unkind to give her the case without any wrapping on it, so that she would have to open it in front of him. He hadn't thought of it in the light of manners at all, but most often had imagined, with quickening pulse, how she would open the case and look at the moss-agate, and be pleased and touched, and then look at him with questions in her eyes, and begin to understand. Now he wished the case was wrapped, but it was too late to mend that. He thrust it at her, so that she took it almost in self-defense.

"Here," he said.

Rachel sat holding the closed case and looking at him.

"It's nothing," he said. "I just got it to go with the gray dress." Then he said, foolishly, "You have the gray dress on. I'm glad you have the gray dress on."

Rachel looked down at the case. Finally she opened it slowly, as if afraid something detestable would spring from it. Tim held his breath and watched her face eagerly. The little light on the dash showed clearly her knees, and her hands holding the case, and obscurely, with softened outlines, her face looking down at the case. Now she would begin to understand.

Her face didn't change. She turned her head, but didn't look at his face, but at his shoulder.

"But I can't take presents like this, Tim," she said.

"Why can't you?" he asked. The question sounded harsh and rude. He hardly knew that he had asked it.

"Because I can't," she said. "I couldn't take a present like this from any boy," she said more rapidly, and snapped the case closed and put it on the seat between them. She was going to get out. He could feel that she was going to get out and run up the steps too quickly for him to follow, and go in, and close the door.

"Rachel," he begged, "it isn't anything. I didn't mean anything. It was just on account of the gray dress, and you were going away."

She was poised on the edge of the seat again, but the way he was begging stopped her, though she couldn't look at him.

"Please," he begged, "please take it," and held the case out to her.

"I can't, Tim," she said sharply, tremulously.

He slid across the seat toward her and took her hand. She tried to draw it away, and he wouldn't let her. He held her. He didn't try to put his arm around her. That would be acting as if he wanted to neck or maul her, when what he really wanted was to beg for his life. Even in his dreadful confusion he understood that. Already he felt debased and vile, because he had held her against her will. Yet he had to hold her; he had to make her understand. He was shaking, as if from a strong chill, and everything he did was clumsy. He dropped the case in her lap and took her hand with both his and kissed it. This act of subservience, and the touch of her hand against his mouth, overwhelmed him. He wished actively to debase himself before her, to be grossly humble. He didn't know what he was thinking or doing. He kissed her hand again and again. Rachel struggled once more to take her hand way from him.

"Stop it," she whispered sharply, and then, "Please, stop it," with a little panic. When he still wouldn't release her, she sat stiff and motionless, waiting for him to know what he was doing. He didn't understand what she whispered, but he felt the still, hostile waiting of her body. With her hand yet against his mouth, he bowed his head into her lap, and lay there, half curled onto the seat. Even with his body, he was debasing himself. He was pleading with her physically. It didn't seem to him that he would ever be able to think of a word to say to her again, unless she were kind to him now. She sat still. He felt the soft dress, which had been cool when he put his face against it, grow warm from her thigh beneath it. Then, for the first time, he knew that he desired her also.

The desire must have been there for a long time, but he had never known. In sultry day-dreams which came on him sometimes when he was alone, he had imagined possessing many girls. He had tried, several times, to imagine possessing Rachel. It had been very different from imagining the others. They were all girls he knew had given themselves to more than one boy, or women he saw in places where the band played, about whom it was easy to imagine anything. Often, in thinking about them, he had invented ugly or humorous or violently importunate, or even cruel introductions to the act. When he had thought of possessing Rachel it was always in one of the

legends, and came as an exalted union which they both wanted
desperately and tenderly, after a long period of restraint and
proof of one another, and he had touched her as if she were
sacred and fragile. More than that, although it was easy to
imagine the entire act with those other girls, or with any girl
who attracted him at all, even if he knew she wasn't easy, it was
impossible for him to imagine the consummation with Rachel.
He had imagined her, in many tales, as ready to give herself to
him, and had even written her some love songs which weren't
purely idealistic. He had imagined her waiting for him in a
great shadowy bedroom, with moonlight in the windows and
on the floor. Two or three times he had succeeded in seeing her
on the bed, naked and small and delectable, and full of a death-
less love for him. But when, even with the greatest reverence,
and he never approached her otherwise, he was about to enfold
her in his arms in a corner of moonlight from the window, in a
world of tragedy and loneliness, and in an ecstasy of yearning
which was only as near desire as the idea of God is near man,
he would no longer be able to see her. Either the vision would
disappear entirely, or he would find that he was pressing to him
one of the other girls, with whom he could imagine actually
doing such a thing. A familiar face, in no way like Rachel's,
would materialize beneath him where hers had dissolved, and
be laughing or weeping or strained with the urge. It had been
literally impossible for him to imagine possessing Rachel, and
he hadn't even dreamt of doing so except in the legends.

Yet now he desired her terribly, with a kind of cherishing
violence which pierced him like the far cry of a trumpet. He
contained this desire and his ecstasy of adoration and humbleness, and his dread at the intolerable idea of losing her. No
longer kissing, he pressed his face more deeply into her hand,
so that his own hand was pressed deeper into her thigh. There
began to be repeated in his mind an image in which he had
slipped to both knees beside her on the floor of the car, and was
embracing her knees, with his face buried against them. He
could feel this coming. He had a convulsive desire to accede to
this foresight, and make the final gesture of worship and of

desire which was not brutal. He must not let himself. To resist it was as difficult as struggling against the repetition of an old vice.

He lifted his head, feeling it very heavy, as if it were made of stone. It was still harder to let her hand go, but he did. He moved back behind the wheel of the car, and buried his head upon his arms, and muttered that he was sorry.

Rachel didn't answer, but neither did she get out of the car.

"But I didn't mean to do anything you wouldn't like," he said, raising his head. He sat up straight and pounded softly on the steering wheel with his fist, and stared at the steering wheel. He began to talk quietly, in fragments, without looking at her. "It's because I love you. I always have loved you. I always will. Only I've never been able to tell you. I can remember everything about you. Do you remember when we first met?" He looked at her.

She was watching him as if half fascinated, but when he looked, she stared down at her hands and shook her head.

"I do," he said. "I remember everything about you. That wasn't the first time I saw you. The first time was out at the race track. There was a horse called Sunday Wind running. You were sorry for her too."

He went on telling her all that he remembered about her. He began it as an apology, in those short sentences, with waits between. But then he began to speak more easily. He even told her how he had felt about her at times. He couldn't bring himself to explain why he talked so much sometimes, for that seemed peculiarly shameful, as it would have been to tell her that he had tried to make love to her on a bed in his mind, and besides, he wasn't sure why he talked so much. He knew that being with her started it, and that often he couldn't stop it, though he felt the dreadful black shame, as at a form of cowardice, but he didn't understand that he did it because he couldn't say what he meant. He thought of telling her, and then remembered that she didn't like what he was doing now: reminding her of all the times he could remember, but she couldn't. He flowed into telling her about poems and songs he had written for her. He was pleading again, and almost hopefully. He still spoke with some confusion, but he was rushing; he was trying to get it all out. Before he knew what he was saying, he was proposing to her.

"I know—not now," he was stammering. "Some time—when you're done college—only to know you would—I'd wait till the end of my life if I knew you would. We could be engaged, Rachel."

"No," she said, "I'm not ready to be engaged to anyone."

"Rachel, I've always loved you. There's never been anybody . . ."

"What about Marjory Hale?" Rachel asked.

The question was curt. Suddenly he came out of the fog and saw that actually she was still just waiting for him to finish and let her go.

"You don't believe me, do you?" he asked incredulously.

"Of course I don't," she said. "Why should I?"

He had no answer for this. He had said everything. He had believed he was making everything very clear.

Rachel got out of the car and stood in the driveway, with the door open. She was holding out the case with the moss-agate, and appeared to have been goaded into fury by something incomprehensible, for she said distinctly, "I couldn't use it, anyway. Nobody wears things like this any more."

He was crushed by the scorn of this rejection, and yet not angry at her. His defeat and loss were too great for anger. He didn't even understand, really, what she had said. That final revelation of his dream-bound blindness, the knowledge that he had reverently presented her with an ornament that was actually in bad taste and unusable, could come only later, when he was alone. Now she didn't seem to be commenting on the gift at all, but rejecting him, making her final declaration that he was a person from whom she could not accept gifts. If only she would keep the agate, he would save something; he wasn't sure what, but something.

"Please," he said, with the dignity of admitted defeat, "I wish you'd keep it. I got it for you."

"Well, thanks," Rachel said at last, and turned toward the steps.

He started to get out to go to the door with her.

"Never mind, thanks," she said quickly. "I'll let myself in."

So, with his face burning at this last mistrust, he sat where her words stopped him, on the end of the seat, with one foot out on the running board, and watched her run up the steps into the heavy shadow under the fanlight, and saw her silhouetted against the light beyond the opening door, and then the door closed behind her.

CHAPTER THIRTY-TWO: *The Fall of the House of Hazard*

MRS. HAZARD failed rapidly that summer, though it was a long time before Tim and Mr. Hazard understood that there was anything wrong with her besides weariness and worry about Willis. It required a shock, and an event which changed the routine of their lives, to make them see. Tim told me something of this period during that afternoon when we sat on the raft at Tahoe, and mentioned incidents from it and thoughts about it a hundred times during the dark years. He has also told me more about it quite recently, though, so that probably, in the main, it is the older Tim Hazard, with his longer perspective and changed sense of values, whom I quote, as nearly as I can, in his own words. Needless to say, I didn't sit there with a pencil and a shorthand notebook while he talked, nor am I a Boswell, any more than Tim is a Dr. Johnson. In fact the idea of telling Tim's story came up during a conversation with Lawrence Black, years after most of its events had taken place, and I actually started to put it together not because it is unique, or because there is anything world-shaking about any of its inhabitants, but rather for the very contrary reason. But at least, if I don't get down Tim's exact words, I'm quite sure of the important matters, his attitude, and the incidents he considered significant.

"Most men," Tim said, "as the more thoughtful of them, and all women, know, are essentially loners, and when domesticated are prone to a kind of preoccupied blindness to their immediate surroundings. It doesn't matter whether heaven or the stock exchange is their destination; the result is the same. And Dad and I were even blinder than usual at the time, I guess. I was staggering around in the world of the realists which Rachel had left me, fighting off my desire to dream as if it were a mortal sin, and still dedicating my future to her memory, so to speak, although it had become painfully clear to me that so far as actually spending any of that future with her was concerned, it was ruled out by a dilemma which neither dreams nor hope could any longer obscure, to wit, that only if I ceased loving Rachel would I have any chance of becoming a being Rachel might love. I was constantly pondering this dilemma, and the nature of the world into which it led me by the asses' bridge, as if every other problem which confronted me were dependent, at some point in its working, upon this first one."

Tim thought for a minute, and said, "As, of course, they were," and went on.

"Dad was preoccupied too. It began with the business of Willis and Briasi, I guess, though I'm judging only by symptoms. I never learned what came of that matter, if anything. Nothing, I suppose. At least nothing ever happened to the other boys who had been involved with Willis. But the Briasi business wasn't all there was to the change in Dad. It reached far back of that, as I learned the following winter. At any rate, he changed, changed until even I noticed it. He had always taken the offensive in his monologues before, using Mother or me as his other self, and he had always picked individual targets by name, some lawyer, politician, mine owner, rancher, union organizer or liquor racketeer, or just some man with whom he had argued at the lumber yard about the curing of white pine. Now he drifted onto the defensive and into generalities, complaining in detail and with considerable sophistry and alarmingly little profanity, that it was inevitable that things should be like that in Nevada, considering its barrenness, its small population and its history of fortune-chasing. I suppose this enlargement from the personal to the general, from the specific 'what' to the theoretical 'why,' might be considered an advance in thinking, but it wasn't in Dad's case. It was simply a loss of power. Sometimes this loss of power showed even more plainly. He would just sit there by the kitchen table, with his hands folded between his knees, as if trying to make himself small, not touching his beer, letting his pipe go out in the saucer he used as an ash tray, staring at nothing, saying nothing. There would be a hopeless, far-away, muddled expression on his face, as if some inner goal toward which he had been working or hoping had disappeared or been removed beyond reach.

"Poor Mother was worried about him. I'd catch her watching him when he sat there like that. She'd try to make talk with him about the lumber yard or his horseshoes or hunting or going out to Antelope Valley, or she would get him into a game of double solitaire or two-handed pinochle, or cribbage. Mother didn't like cards herself; they bored her; but Dad was like Willis. Everything in the world was win or lose with him, and he loved cards.

"It seems strange, and kind of terrible now, to think of Mother worrying about him, and about Willis, and about me too, for that matter. She would sit there at the kitchen table, gray with weariness or pain, and deal the cards and make mistakes, but keep trying until some of Dad's combative spirit returned, and he boomed out a challenge or two at her, and began to drink his beer as if he liked it. Then she'd laugh at him, and dare him back, and they'd be quite foolish and happy together for an hour or two.

"Well, anyway, Dad had his obsession, and I had mine, and neither of us really saw what was happening to Mother.

"Then, one night, when I was up in my room, Dad called me from downstairs. His voice was strange, frightened and too loud. I was working on a score, and usually, when I was doing that, I'd say I was coming right away, and think I was too, but I wouldn't budge for an hour. This time I piled right downstairs. Mother was on the couch in the living room, where Dad had placed her. She had fainted and fallen out of her chair while they were playing cards in the kitchen. Dad had poured water on her face, and taken off her shoes, and tried to force a drink of whisky on her, and now he didn't know what to do. He was standing there looking at her, and twisting his hands together.

"Well, there's no use going into all that again. The doctor came, and took her to the hospital that night, and a couple of weeks later they operated on her for abdominal cancer. She stayed very weak, but the pain was gone, and for two or three months she seemed to be getting better. She couldn't do anything, though, and her mind tormented her. All her life she'd been used to working all the time, at a never-ending procession of the same little tasks, and by that time such content as she won came from her work. Rest and thought had been pleasures to her only because of the work. Now she had to watch Dad or me doing the work, clumsily or slowly, or some woman Dad would get in once in a while, and she had too much time to think and feel. She had a big reaching and yearning in her all the time, and had no art to be tranquil by philosophy. That big quality in her had never had a chance to be satisfied or disciplined enough for that. Without her work, it only made a tumult in her. Sometimes, when Dad and I were both away, she would try to work to quiet herself. We'd find her on the couch, exhausted, when we came home, and she would smile at us, and confess. The hardest thing for her to confess, I think, was that she couldn't last at any work for more than a few minutes. A haunting feeling of uselessness and loneliness, and of error in her past, overcame her.

"She was all right when the three of us were together in the evening, just listening to the radio or playing cards. Having us there seemed to fulfill and excuse her. She liked to hold Dad's hand, and would reach for it sometimes even when we were playing cards. She would look at me in the same way, as if she wanted to hold me. But once in a while, even during such evenings, her eyes would change; the darkness inside her would show through them and she would look about the room as if she had never seen it before, and look at Dad and me as if we were strange too, and were only small figures in the foreground of what she was really looking at. In those few months her hair had finally turned quite white, and her face was white too, and thin, and the old lines were graven more deeply in it, and there were new ones, fine, intricate, indecisive traces, like the beginnings of crumpling, between them.

"We talked to encourage her all the time, making plans for the week-end trips we would take when she was well enough, and for renting a place on Tahoe for a whole summer, but I believe she knew, after that first operation, that she was dying. She would smile at our lusty planning, and add a few ideas of her own, and describe what she liked best about the places we were discussing, but never as if she were really going to them again, and suddenly, in the midst of our busy cheerfulness, she would sink back into herself, and we could see that she wasn't listening, and that what she was watching came from way back."

Tim sat remembering, and then said, "There are a number of little incidents I recall very clearly, so it's not hard to guess the rest now, in spite of how little she said and how much I must have missed.

"Once I came in to dust the living room. She was sitting in Dad's big chair by the front window. When I had worked around close to her, I stopped to kiss her. Usually, when I did that, she would just smile. This time she took my hand with both hers, and held it, and looked at me. She wanted something terribly; her eyes tugged at me more than her hands. But I guess what she wanted was something nobody has words for. She didn't say anything until I had kissed her again, and she had let go of me. Then she said, 'I like this time of year so much. Don't you, Tim?' and looked out the window again, so that I looked too.

"It was late fall. The light was clear and mellow, and there was only a gentle warmth and stillness in it. The leaves had thinned out on the poplars, and those that were left were yellow. You knew, without seeing, that the Indian-summer haze was on the mountains, and that Pyramid would be so quiet that you could hear every wing-clap of a pelican for miles. The melancholy wanderlust is in that time of year, as the gay and savage one is in the spring. I told her yes, I liked it too.

" 'It seems to make everything so much truer,' she said.

"Another time she asked me how my music was coming, and we talked about it. That is a very good time to remember. We had never talked so much about the music before, and she was happy about it. It wasn't until she had asked me various questions about my music at a dozen different times that I saw what she was after. She was trying, without talking about the money in it, to assure herself that I would be happy and able to make a living with my music. She had been secretly with me against my father, in this, all the time, but only because she saw what I didn't see myself, I got into such agonies over it sometimes; she saw I was happiest when I was at my music. I believe she was afraid that my father was right, that I could never live by it, yet that if I couldn't, I would be unhappy, lacking something big and central to give meaning to the rest, as she had lacked it. When I understood that, I was really frightened, because I saw that she was knotting the ends of life together in her mind, getting ready to leave the whole work, yet with that terrible, empty feeling that she hadn't finished.

"Once she asked me about Rachel, too. I had never talked about Rachel at home, except diagonally, describing how she had played in some match, something like that, and then only when Willis wasn't there. But I suppose I had shown more than I realized; I was no poker-face, and Mother never missed anything that was going on in any of us. She wasn't a thinker, or a good talker about thoughts, but her emotions, her instinctive understanding of emotion, reached all about into life, like the roots of a forest. I talked to her about Rachel, but she knew something was wrong, and never asked me about her again.

"Sometimes, when I was in bed, I could hear her and Dad talking in their room, long after they were usually asleep, or after Dad was, anyway, and I would fall into a kind of raging despair in which I hated God, so to speak, because I knew she was knotting up more ends.

"Once in a while I played the violin for her in the evening. She liked it better than any other instrument I more or less played. She would smile and say that the piano seemed to her like a person who kept on talking when you had something else on your mind, and that no wind instrument seemed to mean anything to her by itself, but that it rested her, 'smoothed her out,' she said, to hear a violin. I could never play it very long, though, because it made Dad uneasy, and after about so long, usually, he would get up and go out to the kitchen, and begin to play solitaire, and Mother would worry about our driving him off.

"I remember twice, between the operations, when I think she was really happy. The first time was when the note came from Willis. It was the only note he ever wrote home, and it was very short and stiff. It was written in pencil on one side of a piece of gray scratch paper, and said that he was at a ranch on the edge of a town in Texas, training quarter-horses, and riding races, and the people and the wages and the food were fine, and he had been in the money better than half the time in his jockeying, which gave him quite a bit in bonuses. His closest approach to a word of affection was to tell Mother not to worry about him, because to train horses you had to train yourself too, and he was being good. It was hard for Willis to speak truthfully when he was moved. But after letting Dad and me see this letter, Mother kept it with her all the time, and she wrote to Willis every day, even when she was unable to get out of bed, right up until she couldn't keep her mind clear because of the pain and drugs. Even then, when she had an easier spell, she would ask me to write to him for her, and I would sit by her bed and write while she told me, a little at a time, what to say.

"The other time I remember came late in her last summer, when we took her up to Tahoe one Sunday. We found a sheltered place under the rocks on a beach near Incline, where she could sit in the sun and look at the lake and at the mountains on the California side. She didn't even want to talk, and we left her alone most of the time. Dad sat in the car up in the woods, and smoked a cigar and read the Sunday paper, and then went to sleep. Mother was tired from the ride, and we had fixed her with a blanket and pillows so she could go to sleep too, but she didn't. She slept very little during those last months, even before the pain returned and prevented it. She would lie there silent and motionless, but wide awake, feeling things strongly, remembering, always hunting for something, the answer which would bring real quiet, inside as well as out.

"I wandered off among the boulders and trees up the shore, and took a short swim in the icy water off the point, and dried myself in the sun and got dressed and came back. The peace of Tahoe had worked into me, and I felt gentle and clear. Mother felt the same way, I think. She smiled at me, and there was none of that terrible wanting in her look. She was sitting up against a boulder with the blanket across her lap, and had in her hand a few tiny carnelians which she had picked up from among the beach pebbles around her.

"She said, making it sound like a gentle joke, 'I wonder if heaven could be any better than this, Timmy?'

"It nearly broke my heart, and yet it made me happy at the same time. It was as if she had won through to something, or more as if we had made a great, final discovery together, perhaps about the size of things, and the extent of time, and the point at which an individual can let go and stop blaming and urging himself. It's hard to explain the feeling, but you know it. You become just yourself, fitted perfectly into your place in everything, with all the weight off, as if you had discovered what you should always be, but can't because the affairs of human beings keep pecking at you, or there are walls, all kinds of walls, which shut out the greater, non-human part and keep the balance wrong in the mind. Anyhow, it's as close to religion as any experience I know. She had it that afternoon, and it must have been a marvel and a treasure to her, considering the weight of her burdens, and the fact that she wasn't put together to let go and feel that everything was out of her hands. Maybe that kind of ease comes permanently to some very old people, but

Mother wasn't very old, and I doubt if she could have let go if she had been. She suffered for people; everybody's trouble and pain were hers. For her to rest, there had to be a positive feeling, not just that she could let go, but that something much bigger and stronger had taken hold, and for one Sunday afternoon, at least, she believed that.

"I like to think about Mother that afternoon," Tim said slowly. "I like to remember her just as she was, sitting there in the sun with her handful of carnelians, watching the clouds. Great, domed thunderheads had thrust up a mile into the sky from behind the western mountains, and were hanging there, almost unmoved, as if they had established the balance too. They made a shadow upon the hazy mountains and a deep garden of clouds under the water, which was perfectly still. Later in the afternoon, they shattered the sunlight, which streamed up from them in visible rays, and struck off at angles onto the mountains and the water. Mother's face looked rested, and the light from above the clouds glowed on it as from within, the way a colored sunset glows in the desert hills. I remember how thin her wrists and hands were, and how white they appeared, especially the hand holding the carnelians. Yet there seemed to be a peculiar strength, like that of ecstasy, in their quiet, a strength which was equal to that of the water.

"That winter," Tim said finally, "the cancer took hold once more, and she was all twisted out of shape by the pain. The doctors were afraid to operate on her again in this altitude, so Dad took her to San Francisco and she died there, two days after the second operation.

"Dad sent me a wire, but I didn't really believe she was dead. I kept thinking of her as she had been before that last awful stage. The bony, bleached, misshapen creature of the last days, with nothing, or only unintelligent, unfathomable pain, in her eyes, seemed to me like another woman, because of whose fate I pitied the chances of mankind, but whom I could not greatly pity, herself, or even feel strongly about in any way, because she wasn't quite real, and certainly didn't know what was happening to her. It was the reality of Mother which was still alive in the house, and though I knew she was gone, I believed she would be back shortly, and reclaim all the suggestions of herself.

"It wasn't until Dad came home that I really knew she was dead. He had buried her in San Francisco, and then stayed on there for a week, looking up old friends and places, he said, and then had gone down to Grace's for another week. I met him at the train. He shook my hand as if I were a sympathetic stranger. He looked old, exhausted and indifferent. He forgot that he had a handbag, and I had to go back to the platform after it. He didn't say anything on the way home, and that evening all he talked about was the bills. He didn't see how he was ever going to pay for the surgery and the burial. He was bitter. He said you'd think they'd bought her body and soul and he had to ransom her off before she could get any rest. He talked about the price of the hospital room, the burial lot, the stone. Seeing him come in without Mother, and sit at the table in the kitchen with me, and Mother not there, had robbed me of all the comforting ghosts. My senses were wickedly clear, and everything that had been whispering, 'She is still alive,' now said aloud, 'She is certainly dead.' His talk about the bills made me very angry. Mother, who had spent, and spent was the word, all her life on him and the three of us children, and without even the return of recognition and confidence, except from Grace, Mother was dead, and all he could do was fuss about bills.

"But after that, I got to know him for the first time. It was then I remembered and understood about him and Mother sitting on the front porch, or going to a show without any of us, and the way Mother had always been near him and tender, even when he seemed the most discontented and self-centered and cruel.

"Breakfast was the only time I saw much of him. He was at work all day, and I'd started out at the River House with Arty that fall, trumpet and arrangements, so my work began with the dinner hour and went on till early morning. But I used to get up for breakfast, to see a little of him, and once in a while we'd have an early supper together, or both be home for Sunday. I began to see that his talk about expenses was just part of his end-of-everything feeling. He didn't want to have any responsibility for anything ever again. He felt that his life was really done, except dragging through the rest of his time, and that he was wronged by people who insisted upon acting as if he were still a living man.

"For a couple of days he just told me facts about the operation, the funeral, the old haunts he had seen and his visit with Grace. His mind was full of them, but as it might have been full of some dull selections he had memorized years before, and couldn't get rid of, but didn't care about. Then he began to talk to me as if I were anyone he didn't actively dislike, but also I began to understand. All he was doing was remembering. He had wanted to do something entirely different with his life. He had wanted to be a sailor, and, in time, a merchant-marine officer. His heart had been sold to tramp steamers, and, in a ghostly way, it still was. He didn't say so. He just told me again and again about incidents of the seven or eight years he had worked around the San Francisco waterfront and been a sailor on the coastwise freighters, from Seattle to Panama, and I could feel a strange breath of hopeful youth in his words. He wasn't blaming anyone. He didn't see that it could have happened any other way. But there it was. Those seven or eight years made up the time when he had lived. Since then he had been remembering them, but not saying much, until Mother died. Then they came back to the top again.

"When Willis was born, he had given it up, because his advance had been slow, and because Mother wasn't well, and the doctors said, 'Get her away from the sea; get her up onto the desert.'

"All the rest of his memories were about Mother, and he felt guilty toward her. Behind his violence and independence, his discontent and his contenting himself with petty things, there had been, I believe, a great love for her. They had it, and Mother had known it. Yet it had never been joyous or tranquil or fulfilled. It was queer. I would have said, thinking over my whole boyhood, that Mother was the one who had done all the loving and giving, that if Dad had ever possessed anything that big and strong, he had worn it out with fussing. Perhaps that was it, after all, and he knew it, knew that he had worn out something big, for he wasn't merely remembering, but in a degree confessing, when he put his mind in order before me, that all that had been worth while of his life had been the sea, and Mother. I had never heard him talk so much before, except in anger or complaint.

"After about a month, he was different one morning. He had made up his mind. An old friend in San Francisco had offered him a job on the waterfront, and he was going. He didn't want to live in that house any longer. I wanted to stay in Reno almost as much as he wanted to leave, and it didn't take much of an argument to make him leave me. He didn't really care where I went. He only felt that he should have cared, because Mother would have worried."

So a realtor's sign was nailed to the front porch of the house by the race track. The sign looked too fresh and cocksure on the house, for it was glossy white with new, red letters, and the paint on the house had been powdered and blistered by the sun.

Almost everything in the house was put up for sale with it, as:

ITEMS—Back porch: 1 washtub, 1 wash board (rattly), 1 woven hammock, frayed by time, bleached by sun.

ITEMS—Kitchen, downstairs, rear, west: 1 four-hole iron range (1 lid slightly curled), 1 table covered with figured oil-cloth only slightly worn through, 4 chairs (rungs scraped), used kitchen utensils, 1 incomplete set imitation willow ware for 6, 1 incomplete set white china, buttercup pattern, for 6, 14 odd pieces china in 5 patterns, assorted tumblers (including jelly glasses), 1 set picnic silver for 5, odd silver pieces, including 1 child's cup, sterling, engraved Timothy, 1 ironing board for use on 2 chair backs (iron burns on square end), mops, pails, brooms, etc., all used, 1 ice-box, slightly leaky, so additional pan must be used under right rear corner, 19 glass jars of jam, jelly still in pantry; incidentals, including sun-and-leaf pattern on worn linoleum rug at right hour of morning, 1 light as of stained glass through leaves at window at same hour in autumn.

ITEMS—Downstairs, back, east: 1 living-room suite, brown, thoroughly used, sags in right places. Incidental pieces, all loose in joints.

ITEMS—Downstairs, front, east: 1 parlor suite, mohair, blue, good as new, 1 piano, upright, ancient, battered, in very good tune. Incidental pieces, including lamp with hand-painted china shade, beaded fringe.

ITEMS—Downstairs, front, west: 1 dining-room set, golden oak, including glass-faced dish cupboard (in which are arrayed as in a museum) 1 full set for 6, white china with gold band trim, incidental pieces cut-glass and hand-painted china, all practically unused.

ITEMS—Sundry pictures, including boy Jesus instructing learned elders, the challenging stag, tinted photograph of Lake Tahoe, colored print of 2 dead ducks on mahogany panel, feet up.

ITEMS—Sundry trophies of prowess of A. Hazard, including 1 head of mild buck (downstairs hall), 1 Pyramid Lake trout mounted on panel with tag attached saying, WEIGHT WHEN CAUGHT—34 lbs. (dining room above sideboard), 1 stuffed eagle on limb (piano in parlor), 1 coyote, condition poor (attic).

ITEMS—Upstairs: 4 beds, 1 double, 3 single, with accessory bedroom furniture including:

West, back: 1 dark square in faded wall paper above 1 double, from which has been removed an early, enlarged photograph showing Mr. and Mrs. Alexander Hazard, late of Reno, Nevada, in front of the rocks at Pyramid Lake on a sunny day. They are both smiling, not to say laughing. Mrs. Hazard wears a hat with a huge brim, which Mr. Hazard is turning up to show her face. Mr. Hazard wears the cap of a merchant-marine seaman and an appearance of seeing his wife clearly and with affection, and is holding in his outside hand a pair of horseshoes.

East, back: 1 chest of drawers, pine, painted, marked around the edge by cigar burns made between 12 and 3 in the morning, 1 closet still smelling strongly of horse.

West, front: 1 dressing table, pine, stained, varnished, the mirror of which is mystically clouded and discolored by exposure to sunlight excepting small rectangle in lower right-hand corner, once protected by framed photo of Mary Turner, later by framed photo of tall, blond, young man with big grin, in uniform of gas-station attendant. In left drawer, scented powder caught in cracks and lingering reminder of cheap but mild perfume. In right drawer, overlooked by owner, left by Mother, 1 coat-collar ornament, artificial cherries on leaves.

East, front: 1 table, pine, stained, varnished, on which a small, scarred area indicates the former position of a miniature mining mill with a red roof, and very close inspection would discover traces of a great deal of writing in which occurs frequently, in printed letters, sometimes surrounded by crude oriflamme, the name RACHEL. Additional item, in all seasons but winter, constant sound of leaves of poplars to be heard through front window.

Book Two

CHAPTER THIRTY-THREE

*The Dark Age of
Timothy Hazard, an Interlude Including the
Tokens of the Waste Land, the Empty City,
the White Horse and the Paper Prayer, But
Also Including the Sanctuary of the Peavine
Quarter*

THE next two or three years were a ceaseless battle in the soul
of Tim Hazard. It is impossible to fix the lines, or even the time,
of this period. I could select arbitrary dates for its beginning
and its end. Let's say it began the day the real-estate sign was
removed from the house of Hazard, and ended when Tim accidentally met Rachel on Virginia Street for the second time, and
didn't have to run away. Let's say that at 10:47 in the morning
of such a day in such a year, the assistant of the moving-van
driver, watching the tail-gate approach the Hazard porch,
waved his hand and shouted, "Whoa! That's good," and that at
3:19 of such a sunny, windy day in August, of such another
year, in the mouth of Douglas Alley, Rachel Wells, with her
arms full of bundles, uncertainly, half-laughingly said, "Hello
there, Tim Hazard," and Tim looked up and saw her again.
That would sound definite enough for the *World Almanac*.

But when did the dark years really begin? The moving-van
had nothing to do with them. When Rachel closed the door of
the big house, taking in with her a moss-agate she didn't want, a
moss-agate reduced to exactly its visible dimensions and attributes? When Willis closed the front door of the Hazard house
and began to whistle as he approached the corner into the unknown? When Mr. Hazard stepped off the train from San Francisco, and Tim knew that his mother was dead? Or did they
reach even back of any of those to the moment when Tim
turned his head from the humiliation of Sunday Wind at the
barrier, and saw Rachel alone in the sun in her yellow dress?

Or to the moment Tim was born? Or to the moment Mrs. Hazard was born? You see the difficulty.

It is equally great in the other direction. Wouldn't it be more accurate to say that the dark years ended when Tim and Rachel made that peculiarly disembodied but crucial pilgrimage up the enchanted mountain? Or at the moment, after years of preoccupied blindness, when Tim clearly saw Mary Turner as she was, standing at the edge of the Verdi road, nodding good-bye to him and wishing he would hurry? Or when Rachel stood in the doorway of his bedroom in Carmel? Or are they still going on at this moment, in Tim's little daughter, who is already a fledgling in the magic wilderness, darting here, darting there, stopping abruptly to stare at whatever it may be, a trembling leaf, a cloud, a face, a strange pup, a thought?

When I try to think of the dark period in a calendar sense, when I finger dates, get out old letters from Tim, Mary, Lawrence, Helen, and even a couple from Rachel, remember incidents, places, conversations, bits of music, and yet remember also the tremendous gaps between these little realities, the gaps wherein the history really took place, it refuses more stubbornly than ever to hold its shape. At one moment it seems a few frantic, tormented weeks, at the next a lifetime, gray, thin and unpeopled. I can imagine the volumes of that lifetime set up before me, like thick, leather-bound law books, stamped across the backs with their dry titles: Vol. I, TIMOTHY HAZARD vs. MEMORY OF RACHEL WELLS; Vol. II, MUSICAL DESIRE OF TIMOTHY HAZARD vs. IGNORANCE; Vol. III, TIMOTHY HAZARD vs. THE ALMIGHTY DOLLAR; Vol. IV, THE MORIBUND CITY vs. THE MAGIC WILDERNESS; Vol. V, THE DREAMS OF TIMOTHY HAZARD vs. REALITY, etc., on to the end of the shelf at say Vol. XX, TIMOTHY HAZARD vs. TIMOTHY HAZARD.

In order not to become lost in this dark library of the interior, in which Tim himself can no longer discover an accurate temporal sequence, I must resign myself to giving you a brief external catalogue and a handful of token scenes. They will serve, if you remember the comparable period of your own life, the terrible adolescence of the mind, which follows that of the body, the time during which reality gradually emerges streaming from the sea of dreams, but in a primal chaos, an awful birthday of the world.

Tim moved from the house by the race track into a second-floor apartment on upper Sierra Street, the Peavine Quarter. He was still working at the River House, and by the measure of his past and of his small desire for possessions, he was wealthy. The apartment had two rooms and a bath. Tim rented a piano, bought a portable phonograph, and began to collect records, mostly of dance bands, but also Tschaikowsky, Debussy, Beethoven, Wagner and Grieg. He brought his old books with him, but the ones that shone from his hand and lay on the table by his bed, were new favorites, Edwin Arlington Robinson, the plays of Yeats and Synge, Hawthorne, *Moby Dick,* Keats, Shelley, Blake, Poe, a history of instruments and a treatise on symphonic composition. There was always a chess board, with the pieces set up, on the table in the living room. Tim and I were learning chess together, and once in a while Lawrence Black dropped in and played, though usually we had to go to his father's house to see him, or to the narrow studio on the top floor of a downtown building, where he was doing scores of charcoal portraits, delicate as engravings and warm as paint, which were bringing many sitters to him, especially women in whom a certain faith of countenance had been shaken by the border years and the divorce court.

Two of these portraits, one of a girl who was singing at the River House, and one of Tim himself, hung in Tim's living room, with a pale color print of *The Last Supper* and an enlarged, tinted photograph of Belle Isle in the Truckee, before it was a part of the park, both hung there by Mrs. Martin, the landlady. In the bedroom were three more of Mrs. Martin's, a tinted Burne-Jones seeress, and two Sargent prophets, but there were also a panorama of Pyramid Lake in sunlight which streamed from afar out of other-worldly clouds, and Willis in jockey's silks, his legs apart, his hands on his hips, the visor of his cap turned up, and a straw in his mouth. There was also the graduation photograph of Rachel in the gray dress, but it had no permanent place. Sometimes it was on the piano, sometimes on the desk by the west window, where the poplar leaves swam in the sunlight outside, and sometimes, if I arrived in the morning, before Tim was out of bed, I would find it on the bedside table, or standing beside the silver mill on his dresser, whence it regarded him with transitory blitheness over the foot of the bed.

During the first part of this Sierra Street period Tim often talked about Rachel to me or to Lawrence, although never to both of us together. He assumed a detached and amused air of observing his own ridiculous antics of the past, but the ridicule was never aimed at Rachel, and he remembered her words, and amazingly trivial details of every incident, and sometimes these details led him into a mode of recollection that was not at all humorous. Then, if he observed his hearer's uneasiness, he would stop abruptly, even in the middle of a sentence, and get up and go into the bedroom or the bathroom for a moment, and when he returned, start to talk about something else at once. Before he left Mrs. Martin's he had altogether stopped talking about Rachel, and her picture wouldn't be in sight if he'd known beforehand that one of us was coming.

This change spread into other realms also. What had seemed before to be merely a faint and puzzled melancholy, with brief periods of abstraction, from which he could easily be drawn into the eager, explorative talk natural to him, now deepened into a heavy mood. He lost chess games through absent-mindedness. There were long spells when he sat by while Lawrence and I talked, and was not with us. It would take a direct question to awaken him, and then he would lose interest again shortly. Often we would find the room blue with smoke. There would be torn pieces of paper in the waste basket and, with the day nearly ended, he would still be in his pajamas and unshaven, playing his symphony records, especially the *Pathetique*, but not seeming to pay much attention to them either. He would be doing nothing, really, and yet we would have a feeling of intruding which had never existed before. He would refuse to go on the long walks he and I had been taking together, walks which had almost always broken his moods. He came out of this depression best when we ate with Mr. Black at the house in the Court Street Quarter. The drink and the quiet talk before dinner, the house itself, Mr. Black's unfailing manner, seemed to restore him, and when Mr. Black had smoked his one after-dinner pipe with us, bowed his farewell and his invitation to come again, and gone off quietly to read by himself or to complete some long document at the office, Tim would often argue and discuss and tell stories with his old spirit and imagination until it was time to go to work. Yet even at Black's we'd lose him sometimes. A look of great weariness would settle on him suddenly at the table, as if he had come to a conclusion which made him hopeless. We would have to repeat remarks before he heard us, and often he would reply only with a wry smile of apology and a nod or a shake of the head.

The end at Mrs. Martin's came abruptly, though there may have been lead-ups I didn't know about. Tim and I were coming down from his rooms one afternoon, when Mrs. Martin emerged from the shadows of the lower hall, and stood at the foot of the stairs, waiting for us. She tried to smile, and kept patting at her gray hair, which was in perfect order, as all parts of Mrs. Martin always were.

"May I speak to you for a moment, Mr. Hazard?" she asked.

I went out onto the porch and waited. I could hear Mrs. Martin's voice, though not what she said, but Tim's short replies were clear.

"All right," he said when she stopped the first time.

She went on again. She seemed to be pleading.

"I can't do that," Tim said. "It's impossible."

She kept at him. "No," he said once, and then, impatiently, "I know; I know."

He came out. Mrs. Martin followed him to the door. "I'm awfully sorry, Mr. Hazard, but you see how it is. If I don't . . ."

"It's all right," Tim said.

When we were around the corner, he said, "Well, I have to move."

"What's wrong?"

"The noise I make, and coming in that time in the morning."

He walked silently for half a block. It was bothering him.

"It's not Mrs. Martin," he said. "It's the new roomers. Andersons. Mrs. Anderson's home all day. Seems she has insomnia too, and just manages to get to sleep and then in I barge next door and go creeping about in my bare feet and reading in bed and raising all kinds of hell.

"Oh," he said, after a minute, "I suppose it is pretty bad. It's hard to practice a trumpet quietly, you know, and I suppose it's enough to drive anybody crazy to have to sit there and listen to the piano just being pecked at now and then all day long."

Yet he felt the rebuff. He felt that he had become offensive to people and had been cast out. He felt that way too easily, and with increasing ease for a long time to come.

The next day he moved, piano and all, into a single room over on Ralston and farther downtown. It was a nice room, though, on the ground floor in the back, with French windows looking out onto a lawn shaded by elms and cut off from the neighbors by a high hedge. It belonged to a middle-aged couple by the name of Allen. Mr. Allen was a traveling salesman, and was away for days at a time, and seldom home when Tim was working anyway. Tim explained, almost angrily, the noise he would have to make, but Mrs. Allen assured him she wouldn't mind it. She'd be glad of it, she said; it would remind her there was somebody else in the house. She didn't like being alone in the house all the time.

A week after Tim had moved into Allens' he got into a quarrel with Arty at the River House, and refused to do any more arrangements for the band, and was fired. He seemed to be almost relieved, at first. For a few weeks he spent all his time at Allens', writing and tearing up, playing his records, brooding by the window, going to bed at three and four in the morning in a room blue with smoke. Lawrence and I couldn't get him out. Then he had to move out of Allens' because the neighbors complained. He had taken to playing the piano tempestuously for an hour or two before he went to bed. It was the failure of his writing gnawing at him all the time, and without the piano he couldn't get to sleep.

His movement toward the dead center continued at an accelerated pace, a circular movement, a movement like that of a leaf in a whirlpool. He took an apartment on lower Court, but had to let it go because it was too expensive, and he was playing only odd jobs at parties and fraternity dances. He took a gloomy, downstairs room in one of the old houses on Mill Street, like the house where Marjory Hale and her mother had lived. He had to leave there too, and for a while he let his piano go, and slept in a small hotel room on lower Sierra Street. Then he got in with the band at the Cloudland Ballroom, the big public dance hall by the tracks, and moved into a little house by himself, a paintless place with a broken picket fence, on University above Fourth. He missed too many practices of the band. He wouldn't mean to miss them. He would be writing; it would seem to be going. The exaltation would rise in him. Those were the moments that mattered. Just a little more and it couldn't escape him. It always did escape him, though, and when he had torn up the score or the pages of verse, the practice would be over. Cloudland let him go too. Then it was the odd jobs again, and he had to move out of the little house into the single rooms once more, often rooms where he couldn't keep a piano.

It was Rob Gleaman who got Tim into the job he held longest. He met Rob in the Alfalfa Club, a place with a back room, and a door on Douglas Alley. Tim had begun to go there often. He wasn't drinking heavily; he didn't have money enough to do that, for one thing, and for another, he was fighting his troubles, his self-doubts. He went to the Alfalfa Club to sit there over a beer and fight with himself. Mentally he had little mercy for anything in the world then, but least of all for himself. He'd make a beer last an hour while he sat there fighting. Sometimes he'd get another beer and sit there for another hour. Every once in a while he'd get up and put a nickel in the juke box, always picking the smooth, sweet stuff, with bad lyrics like a million other lyrics, the stuff he despised most. Then he'd sit there listening to it, and believing he heard his own habits in it everywhere. He'd remember everything he had tried to write seriously, tried to make say something, all the piano studies, a couple of violin concertos, the songs, the three abandoned attempts at the symphony of leaves, which wouldn't come whole, which always died in the second theme, the Court Street, Wingfield Park theme, and suddenly his stomach would flop over and sink away toward the bottom of everything, and he would want to put his head down on his arms and weep. He wouldn't do it, though, for fear somebody would think he was drunk and couldn't hold himself together. He'd sit upright, looking ahead of him, holding his cigarette in one hand and his beer glass in the other, and believe that he saw nothing in any of that music that had even a promise of being his own. He'd tell himself that if he ever wrote serious music it would be just that, serious, studious, correct stuff, the music of a scholar. He mocked himself for refusing to write for the dance bands, and then going on living by them anyway. He told himself that if he was even honest he would admit that all he was good for was slick arrangements, and would go back to work at them and at playing a good horn. Then he would remember Rachel, and the talking too much and the moss-agate and the despair would spread out into everything, the smallness, the helplessness of mankind, the cruel, worse than animal history it had made for itself with murder and selfishness and stupid prejudice. Everything he was reading then, Darwin, Huxley, Mill, Adam Smith, Bertrand Russell, Jeffers, Marx, O'Neill, Hardy, Flaubert, Dostoievsky, the thinkers who could bear his test of reality, would seem to bear out his despair, and the reason of the scientists and the solitary heroism of Jeffers and the social heroism of Russell, would seem to him futile, like the far-off antics of one man trying to stem a flood by himself. The same futility would wash over the music he was admiring then, Bach, Mozart, Ravel, Stravinsky.

He got into the habit of going to the Alfalfa Club when he fell into one of these sieges, because there he was anonymous. A shabby man was natural there. Most of the customers were miners and lumberjacks, cowboys and railroad section hands, old or out of work or down on their luck or all three. They had troubles enough of their own.

He was sitting in the Alfalfa Club one afternoon, when Rob Gleaman came in and sat down opposite him and told him the Northern Lights was looking for a horn, and that he'd put in a word for Tim with the manager. Rob nearly pushed him into going up there; it was only a couple of doors along the block and up a narrow, rattly flight of stairs. It wasn't quite like playing at the Stockade, on the Line itself, but it was the next thing to it, a dime-a-dance hall where the girls came and made their dates. It was a big, bare room, like a gymnasium, with a glaring light. The band was bad, and five pieces, and happy the way it was. There wasn't much money to be made either, just what the kitty took, but at least it was fairly regular, and nobody cared if he was late or a little off form, so he stayed. He would be there most nights from eight or nine in the evening until the first daylight showed in the three windows high off the floor on the east side. He even started doing arrangements for the band, and trying to pick it up, but the men weren't interested. Then it became like a drug, a habit, just going there and sitting and playing mechanically through the hours. He had short spells of trying to cook up dance numbers of his own, transcribing them carefully and sending them out to publishers. They all came back. I suspect that he did that only when he was lowest, mocking himself, and that the songs he wrote were satires, but Tim says it was accidental if they were, that he was really trying to write the stuff, and couldn't.

He met some old friends of his at the Northern Lights, saw them almost every night, Lucy and Dorothy and Harold Ashby. He says that now the memory of them makes him very glad that he was a dreamy child, content with his visions and the adoration of Mary. At that time, though, they added to his feeling of doom in the seed. They were further proofs of futility, each of them the final product, already, of his grammar-school promise. Lucy was all right; Lucy could still take it or leave it, and she was still clean, sharp, cheerful and witty. Lucy was probably a good friend to a lot of lonely men. But Dorothy and

Harold were also still themselves, only more so, and that was different. It wasn't hard now to believe the stories Harold had told about Dorothy, or about himself with Dorothy, either. Gladys wasn't there. Gladys, Lucy said, was already dead of the sickness, as Lucy called it, still using a gentle vocabulary for Tim.

Yet, even at this time, it wasn't all darkness in Tim. There was something which kept him going, call it what you want, the memory of Rachel, the adoration of Mary, the St. Francis hope, the gift of Mrs. Hazard, the sound of the poplars outside the window of the house by the race track.

There is one picture which stays with me, that seems to mean all this. While Tim was working at the Northern Lights, he made his last move toward the center of the city. He took a top-floor room in an office building on East Second, right across from the Orient, a place where he liked to eat. He got a lot of food for a few cents there, and he liked Ling Choy, the cheerful, heavy man who ran the place, and he enjoyed Ling Choy's hot, pale tea, which was like drinking in a long rest. Ling Choy always sat on a high stool between his cash register and the front window, and Tim could look down from his own window and see the massive head and shoulders of Ling Choy above the half curtain on its brass rod. Tim's room had belonged to an eccentric lawyer, who in his last years had never wanted to leave the building where his office was. It had a bathroom, and was the only living quarters in the whole building, all the other windows having gilt names on them, lawyers, mining companies, agencies. In fact Tim's windows still had the dead lawyer's name on them. He would always see it there, backside to, with the sunlight darkening it, when he woke in the morning. The room was high, and had remnants of the mining-boom kind of splendor, nine-foot doors and windows, a tin ceiling pressed into birds of paradise and a worn, gray carpet that covered the whole floor. The bed was an old walnut, with a high, armorial head, and the only closet was a huge clothes press against one wall. It was a good room for what Tim wanted; nobody cared how much noise he made there, or when. He could croon himself to sleep with a trumpet if he wanted to, or maul a piano for hours, any hours. There was no one else in the building from six in the afternoon until nine in the morning, and that part of town was awake and noisy all night anyway. Tim couldn't afford the room, but he could afford still less not to have it, so he managed to keep it paid for. He kept it for a long time, until well after he was out of his worst period. He loved it, in the way Lawrence, later on, got to love one particular bedroom in an old hotel in Austin. It was his cave, his refuge, almost his world. His clothes were reduced to old sweaters and slacks, except one dark suit he kept for his jobs. He got himself one meal a day on an electric plate in the room, and sometimes ate another at the Orient or the Waffle Shop or had a sandwich and a beer at Benner's. There were even times when he didn't buy any records and pinched out and saved his cigarette butts. The room was the thing he couldn't give up.

It was as monastic as Tim could wish, as far as its contents were concerned, but only once in a while, in a spasm, did it attain the kind of order which had once mattered to him. Most of the time his clothes would be out on the chairs and over the foot of the bed, the bed would be unmade, tin-can lids full of cigarette butts would be everywhere, crumpled pages of scores and of notes or retorts on his reading would be strewn around the table, and his breakfast dishes, still with egg or a little milk or coffee in them, would stand on the window sill all day. There would be dusty heaps of books and records and manuscripts in the corners. For a time the only extraneous thing in the room was that photograph of Eileen Connor on the piano. Toward the end of his worst period, there was one other decoration, the verse to a kind of Indian chant he had written, called *Prayer for the Evil Days*. It was printed out in ink on a big, ragged piece of brown wrapping paper and pasted up on the wall over his bed with adhesive tape. On days when not even the hopeful beginnings came, when the score of the fifth try at the trembling leaves was tied up and thrown in a corner, the top page dusty and yellowing, and Tim would stop work after only a few minutes, and then sit there for hours, slumped down in his chair, staring at nothing, and finally, without shaving or combing his hair, put on his overcoat, and turn up the collar, and go out and walk for more hours, slow and hunched as an old man, or go up to the Alfalfa Club and sit with a beer and his thoughts, during this time, when he avoided even Lawrence and Helen and me, he used this prayer. At first he read it, word for word, out loud, but when he found that he'd memorized it, he began to just touch it, look at it and touch it, like a Tibetan priest using a prayer wheel, and let that do, not even trying for the completed mood. Nevertheless, that prayer shows a little of what I mean, the something that didn't give up.

I stand on the mountain in the dry wind blowing.
My feet on the mountain burn; my eyes burn beholding
  in the valley of my soul, desolation,
  in the hills of my mind no springs.
I am silent. I hear
The rabbit of my heart make his last kick.

Ayee, god of life, god of the deep night,
Stars are the fires of your people; they are many.
Oh, Sun, riding over the day,
Moon that walks by herself, making a long song of love,
The little bird hope
Lies in my hand and cannot flutter.

Raise the tent of clouds over my desert;
Open my tent of clouds upon the west.
Ayee, Sun, stand in its peak like a moon,
Teach lightning to dance where the white dusts walk.
Make my ears happy with rain.

Then are the good days.
The grass comes back in the valley,
There is a noise of happy water in the hills,
On the bank of the full river the willow makes green
  smoke
And the wild duck comes home.

Tim's talk with Lawrence and Helen and me showed what was still alive too. It was almost impossible to get him to go out anywhere now, except to Lawrence's cabin in the Peavine Quarter. We had to come to the room to see him, even Lawrence, who also preferred to stay with his own gods. He wouldn't play chess with us at all. Sometimes he'd play records, and prowl about softly in his socks. Sometimes he'd lie flat on the floor, staring up at the birds of paradise, and let us talk over him. But once in a while, perhaps by praising Wagner, or the old love, Tschaikowsky, we'd get him started. Then he was magnificent, a natural phenomenon, like a volcano in eruption. He would go on for an hour or more, playing bits on records and on the piano, singing and whistling other bits, stalking about, sitting down, getting up, discovering, discovering all the time, illustrating abundantly, with an heroic disregard for fact or authority. When he was in full flow, he would keep addressing me, sharply, with a thin and wicked pronunciation, as "My dear Professor Clark," or "You, Master Footnote," and Lawrence as "Listen, St. Francis," or "My good Mahatma Aquinas." Lawrence seldom replied to him, but sat there, thin, dark, quiet, receptive, taking in the whole show with an air of amused wonder which encouraged it, viewing it as the tremendous creative relief it was. Lawrence never argued anyway. He talked only in quiet give and take, with exact and colorful images that often made me feel that my own mind was working very shoddily. He liked best to let a whole point rest on a single, short parable, usually remodeled out of his own experience. I, on the other hand, was the antagonist. I argued. And it was true that if I meanly pounced upon an error of fact, a date, a title, I could often explode a whole structure. "Ah, Doctor X^2," Tim would say, but then his flow would fall off. After a little, he would be sitting there silent, with the shadows of self-doubt chasing each other behind his eyes. It wasn't that the fact mattered. It was often of no real importance. But Tim would feel it, not as an argument, but as a blow against himself, a revelation of his pretense, a curt suggestion of scorn on my part, although it never was that. He would feel that this scorn was justified, and all his fine, exploratory harangue would shrink before his mind into that old bogey, the instead-of talk. I learned not to do that. The real point is that the unquenchable something stayed alive in those talks.

It showed a little in his books, too. No matter what direction he turned in his quest for the veritable shape of his new world, a world still lifting from the waters, there would be among that clutter of books, astronomy, biology, political science, history, that one little collection of men to whom nature, no matter what shape they gave its god, no matter how they saw men against it, was still mysterious, beautiful, exciting, enough: W. H. Hudson, Tomlinson's *Sea and the Jungle*, John Muir, Joseph Conrad. Tim would never go outside the city with us during this time. I suspect that he felt like a sinful priest, unfit to enter his chosen places, but often we could rouse him with talk about those places, about Pyramid, Death Valley, Tahoe, the Black Rock, the Toyabes, and always his little lake under Mt. Rose.

Even in the darkest manifestations of the depths there was a touch of this something, call it romanticism if you want, call it youth, call it the memory and the hope of the never-was. Whatever you call it, it was there, and it was the saving touch.

Tim had a couple of dreams that may well have marked his lowest reach. I would never have known about them, save that he made them both into music, which shows you what I mean. He made them into piano studies which had a haunting, unsatisfying, memorable suggestion of wanting to be more, orchestral pieces, perhaps. He was playing one of them when I came up to his room one afternoon. I asked for it again, and then he played me the other also. Finally he let me read the dreams which had started them. The dreams had impressed him tremendously, the more so in that they had been repeated, in exact detail, as far as he could remember. Each day, after one of the dreams had come, he had lived more in its aura than in Reno. He had written them out very carefully, some twenty pages for the two of them. When this was done, they had begun to make their own music, *The Empty City Prelude* and *The White Horse Prelude*, he had called them. They speak for themselves of his loneliness, at least.

In the first dream he believed that he was standing on the very peak of a high mountain in a black night. He believed the mountain was Mt. Rose, though he couldn't see its shape, or even a star. He could see only a single faint light, far below him. He was on skis. He was drawn to this light, and fled down toward it, only to find that it was a lantern overhanging a tremendous precipice. He leapt out into the emptiness and, after the terrible fall, found himself walking in a city below. The city seemed to be a fantastic composite of Reno and his reading-imagination of Venice. He wandered in it for a long time, feeling that he was always about to meet someone or come upon a place which was unquestionably familiar, but at last he realized that he was the only person in the city, and that its looming walls and flying overwalks were without doors or windows. Then he went on down the same street, hoping for something beyond a turn which never came, until the dream winked out.

In the other dream, the one I first heard him playing, he was mounted upon a white horse, and brandishing a horseshoe with a green ribbon on it. He rode for miles over an empty, mountainous landscape, always about to become familiar. He changed beings, was now an oaf on a cumbersome plow-horse, now a valiant with a mission, upon a splendid charger. Then, in the central movement, he was looking for someone whom he loved very dearly. This someone was hidden or imprisoned in a vast building with marble pillars, numbered doors and furniture in striped dust covers. He didn't know who the person was, but only that if he didn't find him, the person was lost. Enemies whom he never quite saw multiplied behind the doors and pillars as he explored, yet, sweating and frightened, he went into every room. Then, all at once, he knew that the person was already lost, and made his escape. At last he was riding back over the same mountain, upon the same horse. The sun was coming up, and he was triumphant, although he did not know why.

The strongest fort for Tim against the empty city and the enemy house, the strongest fort for all of us, for that matter, was Lawrence's cabin on the alley in the Peavine Quarter. Lawrence and Helen had been married for more than a year when they moved up there. Tim and I hadn't even known what was going on at first. Lawrence gradually dropped out of our ken. When we went up to the studio, there would be a BACK TO-MORROW sign on the door. When we called his father's house, he wouldn't be there, or he would tell us softly that he would be busy that afternoon, and would see us in a day or two. We merely caught glimpses of him afar, as it were, as he disappeared through strange doors. Then, one night when we were eating at Ling Choy's, he appeared in the world again, and Helen was with him. He introduced her as Mrs. Aikens, and they sat in the booth with us, and we talked and liked her. We were gaining a member, not losing one. They had been out at Pyramid all day, exploring among the needles at the north end, and they were dried out and scorched. Helen kept talking about the light and the bareness, trying to find a way to tell us what it did to her. She had a deep, husky voice, with a strong kind of haste or excitement behind it, a permanent quality, which had nothing more to do with her subject than her hair did, or her hands, that black, wild mop of hair, or the strong hands which she seemed to curb from constant gesturing by will alone. She was all of a piece in this impression, as far as that goes, the energy of her beautiful body, very upright on the bench, the movement and shining and interest of her big eyes, the tipped-up nose, the brown, sculptured face, the wide mouth, curved down at the ends, so that when she was not speaking it seemed quietly set to contain some sadness of her own. She spoke quickly, but her mind ran far ahead of her words, and she was impatient about finishing thoughts. You felt that what she wanted to do was run, jump, shout, get her hands on the things she talked about. She propelled incomplete sentences at us, shooting them just far enough for us to get the drift and then leaving us to finish them, or suggesting the rest with a gesture or a blanket expression. We understood what she meant this time. She was a dazed neophyte in a faith which had been ours for a long time. That was test enough, if one had been able to think of making a test with Helen in front of him.

She and Lawrence were married a few weeks later, and disappeared in the old Cadillac into the wilderness of desert and mountains and mining camps for another month. Then they lived at Black's until Mr. Black retired and went down to the coast, when the gatherings at the cabin began.

We were often together up there in the late afternoons, and sometimes for supper. Helen would scuff about in the dark, little kitchen in her flopping sandals, humming or singing bits of tunes which were never finished either. Through the screen door, and out beyond the vine-covered porch, the sunlight would lie on the back fences and the dusty alley, and the shadows would lengthen across it. We would be in the main room, Lawrence and Tim and I, but even through her pots and pans and her humming, Helen would join in our conversation. Lawrence would show us a new portrait. He wouldn't talk about it. He was at a crossroad too. He saw behind him miles of these delicate charcoal women, and he suspected them of a family likeness and of kinship to the camera. More and more often his subjects were finding signs on the studio door, "Out until some ungodly hour," or "Gone to find a man," or, if he had known them longer, "Sorry. Lawrence." He was beginning to fill these stolen hours by walking Commercial Row and Lake Street, looking for old, weather-beaten and troubled faces. But even these studies were only a kind of temporizing with a growing discontent. In his studio and in the cabin appeared more and more notebook sketches by Leonardo and Rembrandt, and color plates of paintings by El Greco and Michelangelo, or of Italian primitives, which he pored over, delighting in their pure color, loaded pattern and childlike purpose. Blake's *Job*, a huge, gilt-stamped volume, was almost always open beside his bed. The intensity and sense of destination of a lost religious era was enticing to him. Simple, mutable figures for design, like his fish, interested him far more than portraits. He was doing hundreds of quick, flowing sketches with brush and pencil, bits of anything, a hand, the line of a hill and trees, the corner of a room, mobile, faceless figures; he was yearning after a freedom of hand and a simplicity of intent which his complex nature made difficult. He was exploring paints and colored chalks, mixing his own colors, concocting new binders and driers, inventing new, quick ways to approximate the effect of an engraving or a wood cut. He was on the verge of a period of rich, unlivable revolt.

We knew all this; we knew what he thought of the portraits. He would set this one up on a chair and let us look at it. He would move softly, carrying the picture by its edges between his long hands, and set it up as if it were a sacred object, but this meant nothing about the portrait. It was an inalienable trait, like his quiet speech and detached courtesy, and it was aimed at leaving us to look at the picture as if he weren't there, or hadn't made it. When it was set up, he would smile at us, and return without a word to the low stool and table where he was trying some new trick of simplicity with figures of turtles or fish. His thin back, in its dark flannel shirt, would be toward us, rounded intently over his moving hands. He would disown the picture, and we would stand there looking at it.

The steaks would hiss in the kitchen as Helen flipped them over, and their smell would come to us, with the smell of the onion rings she was throwing in with them. Tim and I would be holding tall, yellow beers. Another beer would stand upon the table by Lawrence's elbow. Jewels of sunlight would gleam into the room through the vines over the window, which made a cool, green aquarium of the interior unless a lamp was turned on over the table or beside Lawrence's Morris chair. The backs of Lawrence's few books would shine softly out of the unpainted case. Down the alley there would be the sounds of children's voices in last games before supper. Down the alley, over the whole quarter, strong in the cabin, was the blessing of Peavine.

Under his thoughts about the picture, Tim would feel the kindness of the small west room, where he sometimes slept. The walls of that room were the earth color of an old water olla. There was one window, which opened into the yard with the one aspen and the high, board fence. There was a cot, a low table beside it for a book, and on the wall one picture of

Lawrence's, not one he would sell, but one in which he was try-ing for something. Tim loved that room. When he slept in it, he always woke up feeling at home, and as if he were about to discover something, as if he were on the brink of the secret.

In the kitchen the plates would rattle, and Helen would call, "Did you ever see so many rubber checks in one pair of eyes, Tim? Lawrence is crazy. He thinks—but then, that kind. You know."

Then the talk would go on while they sat in the green room, eating their steak and onions and hard rolls, and drinking their beer.

Tim would come out easily, there in the cabin. Almost at once he would begin to look rested and happier, as if being there and with us was enough, and all the rest could be put away for the time being. He would talk with great energy, branching from idea to idea, not arguing, never even ironical. He would improvise for us on the violin or on the harmonica Lawrence kept by his bed. The bed, with a bright cloth over it, was a couch at these meetings. Helen would sit on it, her back very straight up against the wall and her legs curled under her. Her bright bracelets would click sharply as she gestured. There was a strong, undeclared love dwelling there among us.

Then it would be getting near nine o'clock, and Tim would have to go. And at four or five in the morning, tired but sleep-less, he would go back to the room with the lawyer's name backwards on the window.

Now that you know a little of what it was like in that room, and of what Tim took into it with him, you can see the picture I mentioned, the one that might represent the whole period.

I was standing on the corner of Second and Center, waiting for the light to change, so I could cross to Tim's building. It was late in the afternoon of a day in July. It had been one of those hot, glittering days, with a strong wind in the afternoon. Now the wind had died, and left a coolness and a smell from the mountains in the city. The sunlight was streaming down Second Street from low in the west. It gleamed and burned on the windows, and flashed on the car tops. It picked out all the signs hanging over the sidewalks with a stereopticon clarity. Life was picking up. People were hurrying home from work, talking and laughing. The summer night was before them. The doors of the clubs on Center Street opened and closed, letting out the click of the games, the babel of voices and the beginnings of dinner music, and closing them in again.

I looked up and saw Tim leaning on the ledge of his open window. His shirt sleeves were rolled up and his collar was open. He was leaning out far enough so that the sun concentrated on him, as it did on the signs. He was very bony and white from his night work and the long case of Tim Hazard vs. Tim Hazard. His hair was at the end of a period of neglect, and must have been raked frequently in recent torment, for it curled out in an immense confusion which made his face look even thinner than it was. In one hand, marking his place with a forefinger, he held a slim, black-covered volume. Even at that distance I guessed that it was Eliot's *The Waste Land*. For a long time it, and many of the references that had to go with it, had been lying around in Tim's room, with markers in them.

The room behind Tim was like a black cavern, like the vestibule to miles of caverns, going in and in. On the windows all about him shone the gilded signs. On the sidewalk below, a man was talking to a woman. The man was wearing a wrinkled suit, and his hair and tie were disordered. His body was swaying jerkily through a small ellipse, and although I couldn't hear him through the traffic and the voices and the scuffing of feet around me, I could see that he was arguing vehemently. He was jerking his hands at the woman, and then standing with them wide apart, asking why. The woman was wearing a black velvet evening cloak over a silver gown, and high-heeled, silver sandals. Her silver flashed sometimes in the sunlight, and sometimes glowed softly and turned gold. She was hugging herself with both arms, very white arms, and not answering the man, and not looking at him, but always at one spot in the street, across which the traffic passed unnoticed. An old policeman was standing on the corner and watching them without interest. He was shaped like a pear from his head to his hips, and his legs were short and bowed. The man and the woman and the policeman all looked very tired, but it was impossible to tell whether the man was arguing about something tragically important or about where they should get the next drink.

But Tim wasn't watching the confusion of the crossing, or the three figures below him. The only things he could have seen, leaning out and staring east, as he was, were the trees beyond the middle of the city, and, back of them, the Virginia Mountains glowing in the sunset. When I came up to the door of his room, I knew I was right, for I could hear him softly whistling the trail song from the *Grand Canyon Suite*. When I knocked and he said, "Come in," his voice was very quiet.

CHAPTER THIRTY-FOUR: *Prelude to the Mountain*

THE paper prayer hung on the wall of Tim's room for two years, long past the time when it served even as a reminding ritual. Then, on an afternoon in August of the second year, a touch of the magic wilderness erased it, the finger of God, you might call it, which eventually rubs out all it writes, to make space for new versions.

Tim, nearly incorporeal after a long meditation at the Alfalfa Club, and without any desire except for sleep, was drifting out of Douglas Alley onto Virginia Street. He paused for a moment, dazed by the motion and summer glitter in the street, and by the sudden buffeting of a wind, full of the smells of desert dust and hot pavement. He didn't feel hungry, but he hadn't eaten since five o'clock that morning, so he decided to go on up the alley and get a glass of milk and a sandwich at Benner's before he went back to his room. He crossed the street slowly, and was about to enter the alley on the other side, when the voice spoke which echoed far along familiar corridors of his mind.

"Hello there, Tim Hazard," said the voice.

He was not at once seized by vertigo and breathlessness. He was merely confused because it seemed, for the moment, that he was leading someone else's existence, and that when he shed the error, he would go home to the house by the race track, and Willis would come vaulting down the stairs on his way to somewhere else, shouting, "Hiya, bum?" as he shot past, and Mrs. Hazard would come to the kitchen door and say, "Hello, son. Home already?" This instant of sweet and painful youngness passed, but it had broken his daze. Like one waking in a strange place after a long dream of the too familiar, he became clearly aware of telephone poles, ash cans and fierce sunlight upon dirty bricks in the alley before him, and at the same time of his work shirt and frayed trousers and unshaven face, and the overcoat which he put on whenever he left his room now, regardless of the temperature, as armor against the world. He resisted the impulse to feel his face, and keeping both hands in his pockets, turned and looked at her.

How much she appeared the same as ever, standing there smiling at him, her arms full of bundles and the wind whipping her skirt, and yet there was a difference which he recognized at once. This was a woman's face, not a girl's, from which she regarded him evenly and humorously. Her smile didn't wink out at once, as if it had been a convulsive effort, but lingered, awaiting his recognition and reply. The long battle of Rachel vs. Rachel was over and won, or at least well along and well in hand. He felt before her the reticence of humbleness and inexperience. There passed through his mind, rapidly and without sequence, things he had heard or imagined about her in this time she had been away, the malicious hints of Pauline Chester, the account by better friends who said she had almost killed herself over a broken love affair in college, and that her mother had taken her to Europe, pictures of her moving in settings which his own mind had constructed from, say, Herodotus and Proust, Synge and Homer and Debussy, the Italian primitives and the *National Geographic*. He advanced, watching her face, until he might have touched her.

"Hello, Rachel," he said. "How are you?" he asked.

"I'm fine," she said, and then, "How are you?" as if that were the question which really needed answering.

"I'm fine too," he said, "only I guess I need a shave pretty badly," and finally gave way to the impulse to feel his chin.

"This wind," Rachel said, turning her head from it. "Are you very busy, Tim?"

"No," he said. It was a silly question, when everything else in the world had receded behind her and become a trick animated backdrop, but it was also an exciting question.

"Then you're just the person I'm looking for," she said, and began to walk north. He walked beside her, taking some of the bundles from her arms. Together they bowed into the wind; together they bowed their heads to the dust. "The car is up around the corner," she said.

The car was a roadster with the top down, though not a blue one, but dark maroon. Rachel dumped her bundles into the space behind the seat, opened the door and slipped in under the wheel. Tim put his bundles with hers and hesitated, one foot on the running board, and looked at her. A long cattle train was going by slowly, thumping and clanking on the crossings. The patient, white faces of the cattle stared out in rows from behind the slats which made shadows on them. The crossing bells clinked thinly in the wind, and the traffic piled up at the striped gates. Rachel made a face about the noise.

"Really not busy, Tim?" she shouted.

He shook his head. "Work at night," he shouted.

She patted the seat beside her, and with his heart suddenly playing at double tempo, he went around and climbed in. She glanced back, and saw that she would have to wait until the traffic on Virginia and Sierra opened the street, and then looked at him, smiling with that new easiness, but also with a glint of enigmatic malice in her eyes.

"For a minute," she shouted, "I thought you wouldn't recognize me; I thought you were going right on by without even saying hello."

A light, continuous laughter, not about anything funny, but

about the pleasantness of everything, had been going on in Tim from the moment he had begun to walk beside her. Now it nearly broke out of him in a shout. Not recognize her? Had not his deafened ears, at the first syllable spoken in her voice, opened and heard the wind roaring in the trees of Reno? Had not his blinded eyes, in the same instant, been unsealed to the desolate beauty of sunlight upon brick walls grimy with life of which he knew nothing? Wasn't he, here, beside her, for the first time in ages, cradled in the hand of God? There was also something new in this meeting. He was still Tim Hazard; he wasn't erased by her presence. He was not sure that this was a gain, but his instinct was to defend it. He must watch his words; he must watch his thoughts. A single familiar phrase, one of his old openings, one of his still more habitual thoughts about her, which seemed now just a saving trifle false to what she really was, let go by itself, might release the flood again.

"You surprised me," he shouted. "I hadn't thought of you as any nearer than the Appian Way. I lost my bearings for a moment."

She laughed. The laughter, like the smile, was easier. She bent over a little, but didn't seem to undergo a spasm.

The rumbling of the cattle train diminished, and the roadster stopped quivering from its weight. The caboose passed over the Sierra Street crossing and came by them, bearing upon its rear platform a man who stood with one foot up on the rail, and picked his teeth, and regarded Commercial Row with the detachment of one who has seen so many railroad streets roll past without affecting his snug world that he no longer quite believes in any of them. The striped gates rose slowly and hung pointing up into the deep-blue, windy sky. The two tides of cars, sparkling and flashing, began to pass each other on the crossing.

"I have to go up to the house," Rachel said, "and I want a bodyguard against ghosts."

"I'm better at raising them," Tim said, "but maybe my familiar presence will keep them reasonable." Rachel laughed again.

When they were moving in the traffic, Tim asked, "You going to stay at the house?"

"No. I just want to get a few things. I'm staying with Fay and her husband."

He let the roadster go a block before he asked, "Are you going to be here long?"

Rachel shook her head, lifting herself on the wheel, reaching for the gas like a ballet dancer. "Only a day or two, I'm afraid. I have to be back at work next Monday."

"What kind of work are you doing?"

"Social service; San Francisco. Mother and I have an apartment together."

Only a day or two, he thought. She still had the power to age the world with a few words, to give everything seen a new and almost painful clarity and yet an antique splendor. Nonetheless, he felt no urge to self-annihilation. He was merely touched by melancholy.

They turned onto the drive between the big lawns under trees. The place seemed very old and somewhat strange, as if it had emerged from a hearsay memory rather than a personal one. The caretaker had neglected it for more pressing duties around occupied homes. The grass was long, the gravel in the drive was worn through to hard earth in many places, and vines climbed over the walls and roof of the house, and hung from the top of the porte-cochere and from the eaves and across shuttered windows. It was hard to turn the key in the lock of the front door.

Inside, the house was cool, musty and dim. The only light seeped in through cracks in the shutters, or around drawn curtains. The floors were bare, and the furniture was shrouded in striped dust covers, which seemed to Tim ominously significant, though he couldn't, at the moment, remember why. A fine, gray dust had settled everywhere, dimming such glints on banisters and woodwork as the rays of light could make. Rachel had entered quickly, briskly, as if she meant to accomplish her errand in a minute or two and be gone without another thought, but before she reached the middle of the hall, she was walking more slowly, and at the foot of the stairs she stopped and looked about. Her chin came up. Gradually her face assumed the expression of the little soldier. It was as if all the years between had dropped away when she entered. She spoke as she had always spoken when she looked like that, making an effort to speak at all, and not saying what she was thinking.

"Let in some light in the living room, will you, please, Tim? It's so gloomy in here. There are no shutters on the big window."

"Sure," he said, but waited, watching her.

She ran up to the first landing, and turned and said, "I'll only be a few minutes, if I can remember," and then ran on up. When she disappeared above, he felt as he had always felt in a strange place with her, that he shouldn't let her out of his sight for fear something would happen to her. Or was it that when she went out of sight, it seemed that nothing of importance could ever happen to him again? No, those were the notions he must pinch off when they started.

He went into the living room, his steps echoing, and let up the shade from the big, west window. It was a fine window, a single, huge sheet of plate glass. He remembered how, when you sat back in the room, away from this window, it made a frame for Mt. Rose and her foothills. He thought of the mountain as he had often seen it through that window, snow-covered, austere and so lofty in the sunlight in the blue sky that it seemed to send its own pale, clear light far into the room. The sensation of lost time and changed self, which had been in abeyance since the moment Rachel had spoken to him at the corner of the alley, returned overwhelmingly when he let up the shade, for the window was dusty and stained, and vines hung down across it outside, in a leafy valance and a drape along one side. A single, hanging tendril danced in the wind in the center. He had to stoop to see the mountain, and then the mountain was not white and austere, vaulting up into the blue, but brown and dulled, a great weight sinking wearily into the dark thunderheads of its foothills. The only snow was the tiny patch on the north side, just below the summit. He turned back into the room, and it appeared even more dead and empty with the light in it than it had before. Looking at the furniture in the striped dust covers, he now remembered what he hadn't been able to remember in the hall, that the furniture was like that in the vast building where he had so fearfully hunted for someone in the White Horse dream. He shrugged his shoulders as if to throw off the weakening memory, but already it seemed to him that Rachel had been upstairs for hours. He stood still in the middle of the room, listening, but heard only the creaking of the house when the wind leaned on it, and the rushing of the trees outside, and the tapping of the vines against windows and shutters. An unreasonable fear that something had really happened to Rachel upstairs, the ghost of a belief that he would search this house through also, door by door, with growing dread, and she would not be in it, came over him. He crossed to the piano and turned the dust-cover back. The piano wasn't locked. He opened it, and passed his fingers idly up the keys in a run and a series of light chords. It wasn't badly out of tune. There was only the slightest ringing of the overtones. He took off his coat and threw it onto a chair and sat down at the piano. He was still thinking about the house, and he let his hands play whatever they worked into. The touch of the keys was all he wanted, something going on, a link with reality.

It had always seemed to him that this house was an unhappy one, that Rachel's battle with the world had been, in part, an extension of her life in the house, in much the same way that the old house on Mill Street had maintained a private aura about Marjory Hale, wherever she went; or did he only believe that he had always felt this, having constructed the past after Rachel had gone and her father and mother had been divorced? No, it wasn't entirely an after-the-fact reconstruction. It must have been an unhappy house. He had never known Mr. Wells, even to the extent that a boy in his teens may know a man in his forties, but he had been sure of that one thing, that Mr. Wells wasn't happy. He had seen Mr. Wells only four or five times, excepting those moments which didn't prove anything, when he had stopped to leave Rachel at a party or to pick her up at the tennis courts, or was seen passing through the door that led to the gloomy staircase in the building where he had his law offices, or entertaining clients at one of the clubs. Those four or five times, Tim had been sitting in the hall, waiting for Rachel, and Mr. Wells had come out of the dining room and through the living room and the hall, walking slowly, with his hands in his pockets, his gaze on the floor and a weary stoop to his shoulders, and thinking to the point of detachment from his surroundings, worrying, it had seemed to Tim. His face had been unhappy and absent-minded. When Tim had stood up to greet him, Mr. Wells had always appeared faintly surprised to discover him there. Each time he had glanced at Tim, not really seeing him, nodded, murmured, "Good evening," and gone on without changing his pace, up the stairs or into the study at the other end of the hall. Tim had caught a glimpse of the study as Mr. Wells had opened the door, a glimpse of deep rugs, a big, leather chair with a table and lamp beside it, the corner of a gray-stone fireplace with a stand of brass-handled fire irons, and filled bookshelves reaching to the ceiling. Then Mr. Wells had closed himself in quietly. That was all, really, that he knew about Mr. Wells. Yet Mr. Wells must have been an unhappy man. He had been married to Rachel's mother, and even then, whatever the causes, he had known he was losing her. Rachel and her mother were very much alike. It would have been impossible, then, for any man who had lived with Mrs. Wells all those years not to have loved her almost unbearably. Tim grinned a little, and shook his head, as if arguing with himself, as he realized how that conclusion would have struck him if he had read it in a book or heard it about people he had never seen. Nevertheless, that was the way he felt about it. He remembered Mrs. Wells, with a smile like Rachel's smile now, being very kind and friendly with him while he waited, asking him into the living room when the family dinner was done, or coming to sit with him in the hall while the sounds of silver and china and quiet voices were still going on beyond the opened double doors, making him feel more welcome than Rachel ever had, asking him about his studies, his music, his tennis, probably, as he saw it now, feeling sorry for him because she could see, like reading a map, the state he was in about Rachel, and knew, from a thousand little confidences with her daughter, how foolish and useless it was. How many times, he wondered, making fun of himself with short, sardonic turns and dancing but minor ripples on the piano, but nonetheless not wholly escaping the mortifying unhappiness such a thought would have produced in him at the age of seventeen, how many times had Rachel returned from dates with him, and in the security of her home, the relief at having escaped him, said passionately, the little fury dancing in her eyes, "Oh, that Tim Hazard," or stronger things of the same import? It hadn't been altogether pity, though. Mrs. Wells had really liked him, he thought. He had always, rather ridiculously, he saw now, felt more hopeful about his chances with Rachel after he had talked with Mrs. Wells, probably because she and Rachel were so much alike that it seemed that everything Mrs. Wells thought and felt might some time be what Rachel thought and felt, if it weren't already something they shared.

He thought again of Rachel and Mrs. Wells journeying about Europe and the Mediterranean together, Rachel blind and shaken and despairing, Mrs. Wells with her older sorrow, her much longer, if now less passionate, memories and defeated hopes. Emerson said you found only what you took with you, and that seemed true to Tim, but maybe he and Emerson were both wrong. He had never gone anywhere where people and surroundings were really strange, and neither had Emerson, until he was too set in his habits to admit new thoughts or emotions except as slight, transient and distasteful.

The thought of Emerson brought him to the surface for a moment, and he noticed what he had been playing, a medley of fragments from music he had scarcely thought of for a long time, Mozart, Brahms, Debussy, Chopin, songs of Grieg and Bach. Now he was playing *Footsteps in the Snow*. He deliberately shaped it a little more softly and distinctly.

Hadn't he often known himself, when he did break away from his room and from the city to some place like Pyramid or the little lake under Mt. Rose, feeling dead, feeling that there was nothing left in him, to find, after only a day or two, that there was a great deal left in him, that he could still be moved after all, and even profoundly, toward peace and sane relativity? For him it took those wild and quiet places to do it, but perhaps for others, for Rachel and her mother, new people, unfamiliar streets and buildings and tongues would do it. It seemed to him undeniable that most of human trouble and suffering was human made, that, as Jeffers put it, it arose like an evil exhalation from "the race turning inward," from "the dream festering," but certainly there was no cleavage between human life and the rest of nature, and it was quite possible that his own hunger for solitude and the non-human was quite as much an inturning, a festering of the dream as was an appetite for human activity which seemed to him mostly a monkey-like response to mere distraction. And of course, though it was odd how little he had realized it in school, Rachel had always been a more sociable person than he was. He remembered innumerable evidences of her popularity to which he had given no thought then, although he had recognized them only too clearly. He had gone along blindly believing that Rachel felt just the way he did about everything, simply because he had immediately recognized in her signs of the same terrible shyness he knew so well in himself.

What ugly twist of jealousy, or of malice toward him, he wondered, had led Pauline Chester into inventing those distortions of Rachel's struggle to be liked by others, to escape the influence of her unhappy home? Pauline had been afraid, with him sitting there, his hostility and skepticism probably only too evident in his expression and in the few non-committal words he would say, to make clear accusations, and yet she had been the more driven to torment him with hints that Rachel, even when he had known her in high school, had been far more generous to other boys than to him, and that she had even played the laughing little wanton with mature men at clubs and at drinking parties in private homes and apartments. It had been so easy for him to believe that Rachel could be kinder, freer with others than with himself, considering what he had done to her, that these impossible tales had hurt terribly. He had even wondered, with a pain of loss which became an actual physical agony, if the same blindness which had led him blundering into the mortification of the moss-agate, had also made him blind to what Rachel might do with others. This doubt of the goddess had never lasted long, though, and had always been followed by a secondary agony of repentance because he had even considered such lies. They were incredible when he thought of anything he knew about Rachel, the quick smile, the little, clenched fists, the twinkling walk, almost a run, but seldom gay, the passionate integrity, secrecy, honesty. They were doubly incredible now, looked back on, and with the thought of Mrs. Wells in his mind, like Rachel grown up. He remembered meeting Mrs. Wells downtown, a long time after Rachel had gone away to school, two years, he thought, or more. She had given him Rachel's address. He had felt almost as if she were trying to be an ally. How hard he had worked at that letter. He had wanted a letter from Rachel, the marks of her own hand on the paper. Yet twice he had given way to an uncontrolled outpouring, trying again to tell her everything, before he had, holding himself in an iron grip, testing the outward aspect of each dry, false word, written the polite little note it would be possible for her to answer, as if a chance word from her mother had reminded him of her existence. She had answered him in a note of the same kind, nothing real in it, yet he had carried that note around in his pocket until it was worn out. It had been a sacred talisman to him, he couldn't say exactly of hope, but certainly of life in the world when he had begun to doubt it, of Rachel still her precious, inestimable, secret self, seeing the sun, the ocean, hearing the wind in trees and grass, Rachel alive somewhere.

The mood of unhappy lassitude which was so near Tim all the time now, began to envelop him again. He made a wry, self-contemptuous grin. So he had seduced himself into the idiotic youngness after all. He lit a cigarette and switched into *St. Louis*

Blues. When Rachel came down, he didn't hear her in the hall. He was playing a blues of his own, which he called *Moon in the Street*, and singing it under his breath.

> *Old moon, she's my friend; ain't no friend to know.*
> *Same old moon she's my friend; ain't no friend to know.*
> *My baby done left me;*
> *There ain't no place to go.*
>
> *I keep asking, "Old Moon, how come you look so cold?"*
> *Keep on asking, "Old Moon, how come you look so*
>   *cold?"*
> *Moon she's telling me, says,*
> *"Because I'm getting old."*
>
> *I keep telling old moon, "Go on outa my street."*
> *Keep on telling that moon, "Go on now outa my street."*
> *Old moon she don't care none*
> *Don't I never get no sleep.*

Rachel came in quietly and crossed to the big window and stood looking out at the mountain. Tim stopped singing, but played *Moon in the Street* through once more, slowly and softly, while he watched her. When he stopped playing, she turned.

"I like that, Tim," she said. "Is it yours?" She sat down on the arm of the chair beside the window. She didn't seem to be in a hurry. She wanted to talk. Possibly he had been wrong about what was going on in her when she stopped in the hall to look around. Maybe it had all been in his own mind. Certainly there were no signs of the little soldier about her now. She was her present self, part of the world which had left this house behind. It already seemed impossible that he should have worried about something happening to her upstairs, or that he should have tormented himself about an old letter and old talk.

He nodded in answer to her question, but when she asked what else he had been writing, he found himself reluctant to talk about his music. He was still eager, too eager, that after this meeting he should remain somebody in her memory, and it seemed to him, here, in her presence, that everything he had been doing, his reading, brooding, wondering, arguing, had been concentrated upon one end, the writing of good music, music with his own mark on it, and that actually he hadn't written one note of such music, and would only expose this emptiness to her if he talked or played. However, he did play another of his blues, *I'm Always Thinking Too Many*, and then the *White Horse*, and by talking about them, Rachel led him to discuss some of his ideas, and to play a few brief, illustrative passages, which he broke off short each time, saying, "Something like that," or, "That's enough to give you an idea." When finally he opened up, it was in a manner which surprised him as much as it did Rachel. He had been improvising softly for a minute or two, neither of them speaking, when Rachel started the conversation that set him off.

"Fay says you've been working on a symphony, Tim. Helen Black told her about it."

"I threw it away," Tim said.

"Helen told Fay there were some very lovely passages in the parts she heard."

"It was no good."

"You can't always be sure about your own work, can you, Tim?" Rachel asked softly.

"That," Tim said sharply, "is a superstition with which listeners comfort themselves for ignorance and writers for having let out stuff they knew was lousy."

He looked up, and Rachel was watching him curiously. She seemed hesitant, perhaps even hurt.

"No, that's not always true," he said. "Sometimes you don't know, when you're still close to a piece of work. After a little while you know, though, better than anybody else. I've had time enough."

"Just the same, I'd like to hear some of it," Rachel said.

So he began to play his last version of the Court Street theme. It didn't even occur to him to wonder why he had selected this passage, the one in which he had always begun to fail. It sounded very thin and sad on the untuned piano in the empty house, and he let it dwindle out finally in a series of inconclusive minor chords, and at the very end made two discordant thumps.

"No, what I really am," he said abruptly, "is a horn blower in a honky-tonk band, a very bad honky-tonk band." Then, because that remark sounded like deliberate, humorless understatement, which is really nothing but inverted boasting, he went on quickly to describe the band. His description was funny enough, so she smiled for what was to come, when she wasn't already laughing. He described the five of them sitting there, four of them in a small semi-circle around the feet of Fatso, the huge drummer, who loomed over them like some satiated jungle god, motionless save for his hands and one foot, his third chin resting upon his second stomach, his hair hanging down in two horns over his eyes which were perpetually fixed in a glassy stare upon the far corner of the room, which he never saw. He described his own sensations of being a musical madam, and invented examples of how their music, by creating a great sadness and revulsion against life, a yearning for annihilation, hastened affairs among the dancers and was the greatest power in the business. He said their most successful melody had been *Lover, Come Back to Me*, and gave a detailed account of the reasons for its success, the effects upon certain glands, and in varying degrees of inebriation or marijuana happiness, of given phrases played by different instruments and in different combinations. He illustrated the lecture on the piano, imitating the jerky rhythm and off-beat entries with which the band played *Lover, Come Back to Me*. He imitated the trumpet through cupped hands, the clarinet through a pinched nose, the drum on the floor and the lower end of the keyboard, keeping the piano going between times. He was surprised himself at what he'd got into. He'd never done anything like this before. Rachel was really amused, waiting all the time for what came next, and he became inspired, in a sharp, self-contemptuous way. Beating with his foot, tinkling with his fingers, he went on: "We apply the latest, laboratory-tested methods of business-volume measurement and the sampling of customer reaction. Nothing is left to chance. The elaborate statistical graphs we have developed have been written up in three magazines of nation-wide circulation, including *Fortune*, and adopted in practice by fourteen international business-machine companies, to say nothing of the innumerable private businesses and our special forms for use in the home. Each evening I keep a card which fills the top of my instrument case. This card is divided into columns which we term barometric indices or thermal registers, modes of measurement indistinguishable for our purposes. The columns are headed: Degree of Rigidity of Female, Degree of Reluctance of Male, Alcoholic Content, Number of Steps Taken Per Unit of Rhythm, Emotional-Financial Equation of Male, Expression of Ticket Seller, etc. We strive to take every factor into consideration, marijuana, as I have already hinted, hashish, hypos, even tobacco, weather outside, other activities in town that night, and so on, as well as variation of basic factors above listed at different degrees of light, heat, smoothness of floor, etc. We use outside scouts to check after-affects of each combination according to destinations and distances, as well as means of conveyance. We even keep a personal index on the girls, in order to discover what music will improve individual performance. Let us say, for instance, that Constance, artificial redhead, aged 32 years, height 5 ft. 6 in., weight 153 lbs., bust 38 in., waist 20 in., hips 42 in., evening gown type, appears disconsolate and remains in the dance hall all evening, often not dancing, under a program composed of *Brown Eyes, Why Are You Blue?* played thirteen times, *Mexicali Rose* ten, *Avalon Town* seven. The next evening we will vary the program, say *Mexicali Rose* thirteen, *Avalon Town* ten, *Brown Eyes* seven. It is better, but still not good. Say she leaves at 12:32 with a lumberjack from Lassen who, according to our scouts, has already been rolled the night before and is still in possession of only three or four dollars which he kept in his socks, which were not removed. The next evening we vary the program again, *Avalon Town* thirteen, etc. Results indicate a downward trend. Constance, art. r.h., 32, 5-6, etc., leaves at 1:09 with a waiter from a restaurant which is practically in the business, so that no extras may be expected. Besides, he is probably just taking her down for company while he eats a hamburg with mustard, since he is unfortunately prejudiced by un-scientific deductions of his own concerning the case history. We switch the program, throwing in, let us say, at thirteen first, *Yes, We Have No Bananas*, retaining *Mexicali Rose, Avalon Town*. We try these three in different combinations, as before. Results vary, but nothing positive. At the end of a week, we drop *Avalon Town* and try *Star Dust*. And so on. Remember, the inspiration of science is patience. Then comes the night we try *Wabash Blues* at thirteen, and Constance, art. r.h., 32, etc., leaves at 9:06 with a broker from San Francisco who wears pince-nez glasses and a pin-stripe suit, and was had, according to our scout, at the Alfalfa Club the night before for $1257.50 without batting an eyelash. Good. We have it. For several months, it varies with the girl, of course, we know that we can bring Constance up to par with an injection of *Wabash Blues*. A little further experiment will tell us the exact number of renditions which will market her to best advantage. And so it goes. You perceive the general method. Only its thoroughness is unusual in scientific business practice.

"But there is another factor of our method which is, to the best of my knowledge, unique. Below the factor register and the register of girls, I keep a third in columns extended from those above, which is termed Index of Coincidence of Instrumental Accidentals. The purpose of this register is simple. It is detail which counts, and a sufficient accumulation of detail may in time even formulate a consistent and practical style for the band. It works this way. On the evening when Constance, art. r.h., etc., leaves at 9:06 with broker, S.F., pince-nez, etc., I jot down, at the moment of her exit, the exact passage of *Wabash Blues* being played, and as nearly as possible all the factors involved in the particular emotional and tonal effect of that passage, as, trumpet swabbing out bell of instrument, considering suicide, silent; pianist softly playing *Aloha* with his left hand; drummer using only bass drum and brush for 47 minutes now; saxophone carrying air with strict attention to score, resting on thirteenth vertebra, tapping with extended left foot; clarinet also steady, but peculiar effect attained at moment by coughing several times, rapidly, without lowering instrument. When we are done that night, the merest glance at the data shows me that there was no unusual factor at the moment save the cough of the clarinet. Good, we test it. *Wabash Blues*, other selections. Trumpet playing, sax silent, with same cough in clarinet. Three coughs, four coughs, eight coughs, ten coughs to the measure. You see the method. At the end of a month we are able to send Constance, etc., within five minutes of first noticing that she is in depressed spirits, and never with a companion lower in the economic scale than a blackjack dealer from an in-house.

"It is on the basis of nearly two years of such unflinching research, attention to detail, and application of findings in the co-ordinated indexes, that we are able to say with certainty that, in general, over all the girls, in any combination of temperature, light, alcohol, etc., with any combination of visiting personnel, and according to the best-established tests made independently by the ticket seller and our outside agents, we have succeeded three to one over any other number with *Lover, Come Back to Me*. . . .

"Played," Tim said more loudly, pounding his foot harder on the floor, and illustrating each statement with the suitable sound, "by the piano doing *Aloha* with the left hand, sax carrying the air from score, on thirteenth vertebra, left leg extended, foot tapping, clarinet coughing five times to the bar, drums bass and brush, and trumpet—all of this when we have our full complement, of course—silent except on the last chorus."

He did the chorus as loudly as possible, stamping his feet until the room echoed, approximating *Aloha* with his left hand, and making the muted trumpet noise, a little off key and going as it pleased, wah-wah-wah, and stopping the noises one at a time, not quite together, except *Aloha*, which he played softly with both hands, in a vacant, running, dinner-music way, while he spoke.

"It is true, to be sure, that during that period we played *Lover, Come Back to Me* three times as often as any other number, which might have had something to do with its success."

He stopped playing and sat staring at the keyboard. In the quiet, the frail, sardonic inspiration which had run away on its own, faded out of him quickly, and he was revolted by what he had done.

Rachel laughed. "How long did it take you to work that up, Tim?" she asked.

He looked across the piano at her. "Clown," he thought. "Always everything else but . . ."

"First performance," he said. "Unrehearsed."

She was going to say something more; she was going to compliment him on this spontaneous nonsense. He got up from the piano and went across to the chair opposite her.

"But it will do," he said, grinning, "as a history, with examples, of the musical development of T. Hazard. It leaves little more to be said."

Rachel sat looking at him, seriously and curiously.

"Now," he said, "how about the history of R. Wells?"

"Nothing in particular has developed in the case of R. Wells," she said, smiling, showing a little confusion. It was the quick smile again, although it didn't die into complete seriousness quite so immediately as it once had. It pierced him. He again felt the cold wind of time rushing past.

"What have you been doing lately?" he asked.

"Social service," she said, looking at her hands in her lap. "In the city."

He remembered that he had asked her that once already. He asked her other questions. She began to tell him about the work. Gradually she explained her philosophy of the work. To her, it was waiting; it was a poor substitute for the basic changes which should be made in order that no one need feel like an object of charity. She told of the trouble she had with many of the cases she interviewed, people who resented this dependency, and treated her as the cause of it.

"I'm afraid I'm often inefficient," she said, "because I know that their feeling is justified. Not many of them have any ideas about it. They simply resent me, and I feel guilty. I feel almost like apologizing to them."

After that the talk was easy, all ideas. They searched each other out through thoughts and feelings, with no personal conversation, with almost no words about the past. They bridged the years more really and completely by telling each other what they thought about prominent public figures, about books and music, about theories in politics and economics and education and science. Rachel shook her head over his favorite writers, declaring that she no longer had the courage to read them, though as they talked it became clear that she had read most of them, often more thoughtfully than he had read them. The signs of the knowledge of darkness and pain which she had gained during these years were in everything she said, but she was generally gentle, and even, and a little shy in her judgments. She also defended the romantic and impressionistic composers against him, and Tim found it so easy to talk to her now, and so wonderful to be thus at ease in her presence, that he didn't take off on any of his prolific flights of condemnation, but found himself remembering quietly how the music they were discussing sounded, and often agreeing with her. He guessed, feeling her attitude in everything she said, noting her comments on science and sociology and her bits of first-person philosophy, that she was religious in the same way he was, altogether by desire, without faith in any formal doctrine. She said, smiling, as if embarrassed by a boldness, that she supposed she was nearer a socialist than anything else to which a name could be applied. Certainly she had no faith in a dictatorship, by any class whatever. There was no such thing as a class dictatorship. There was either a representative government, in which the form of national life changed slowly as opinion developed, or there was a dictatorship, which could mean, when you were done quibbling, only one thing, a nation subject to the whim of one man.

Without saying anything about what she herself had been doing or feeling there, for which he found himself listening always, she talked about what was going on in Europe, about the wobbling republic in Germany, about Mussolini and about the troubled, conflicting French politics. She had never talked to him so much before. It gave him a secret joy beyond anything they said, to be so long in her presence without strain. It was almost as if he had succeeded at last in making her his love, though he understood that this was only because he remained himself and didn't experience any urge to violate her mind, her separate presence, beyond the buffoonery at the piano.

His first impression had been right. She had won the long battle of Rachel vs. Rachel. He could feel in the little person sitting before him, with the light of the summer desert on her from the window of a dead house, a depth of sadness which was no longer personal, a reaching of the mind and an embracing of the world, a quickness of perception and feeling that was undiminished, but was not now sharp or defensive. Now the stirrings within her were large and slow and full, and the quick perceptions were only ripples upon these tidal movements. There were no more walls, no more sentries on the towers, no more desperate daring of the world by the tiny one. In the sadness there was no agony, or dread, or expectation of being humiliated. She had come through splendidly, and joined life. Often he felt her beyond him, and was almost jealous. She laughed more easily and more often than he had ever heard her laugh before, and from joy or gentle pleasure, or from amusement, not merely from relief. Sometimes she seemed to him, as he sat there looking at her and listening to her, to have become too big for her little body, which wasn't greatly changed. Then again she would seem physically a larger person, able to contain easily all she had become. She contained herself easily. There, all in one, was the great difference.

Finally, when the sun was low over the mountains, she said, just as if they were old and easy friends, who had always been equals, "I hate to break this up, Tim, but I'm afraid I'll have to." She stood up. "I'm very late already."

But then she went to the window again, and stood there looking out at the mountain.

"You know," she said, "I've never been up Mt. Rose. It's always seemed to me that I should go up there. I used to look at it so much, from this window. I kept thinking about it when I was away. I felt as if I'd failed to do something important in that part of my life."

She turned into the room again, smiling at him. "It was queer," she said, "almost a religious sensation of omission, as if I couldn't know the world and the word until I had looked around from up there. You used to go up there quite a lot, didn't you?"

She turned back to the window. He came and stood beside her, stooping to see under the vines. So near sunset, the mountain was higher and darker and had recovered its austerity. The afternoon wind had died. The air between the house and the mountain was very quiet and golden. The trees were quiet in the golden air, only a few leaves at a time whispering to themselves. When he thought, in this quiet, of being on the peak or in the highest meadow under it, or among the twisted trees in the pass, he felt ashamed of his night-tired body and the weary, undirected wrestling of his mind. Looking at the mountain he felt the joy of being in a high place, of stopping the mind off with the filled eyes and the quiet, fallow spirit that came up there. Then he thought, wryly, that the mountain would probably reject him now. Certainly he was no fit pilgrim.

"There's a little lake up there," he said. "Snow water stays in it all summer. Whenever I come down by that trail, I swim there. It's become a kind of ceremony with me. I haven't been up for a long time now," he said, still looking at the mountain.

"Tim, let's go up tomorrow," Rachel said.

They made their plans while she drove him down to his office building on Second Street. When he got out of the car, she said, "Tim, you really don't mind? Taking me up there, I mean?"

379

He shook his head and grinned. He couldn't have explained to himself why he so much wanted to take her up there, why, for the first time in months, maybe in years, he was excited by a sense of impending discovery. It would have seemed important that he was to be with her anywhere, but that wasn't all of it. He didn't expect any miracles to occur. Or did he?

"Nonsense," he said. "You know there's nothing I'd like better to do. Besides, if you didn't go, I probably wouldn't go at all, and think how bad that would be, just when you have aroused me to the contemplation of such unwonted activity."

"Fine," Rachel said, laughing softly. "And I promise I won't spoil your swim. I'll go and hide my head, so you can take your swim."

He watched the roadster until it disappeared around the corner onto Lake Street. Then he bounded up the stairs, let himself into his room, shaved and changed his shirt, humming *Moon in the Street* with a very gay step-up as he did so, grabbed two new arrangements he had made for the band, and fled back down the stairs. He found Fatso Carmichal, the drummer, wedged in behind the table at a booth in Benner's, eating pig's knuckles and kraut in slow, huge mouthfuls, and left the scores with him, saying he wouldn't be up to play that night; he had to get some sleep. He felt an affection for everybody in Benner's, although he didn't know most of them, and delighted in the place itself, its brown, soupy air, old pictures, worn counters. He ate supper with Fatso.

When he got back to his room, it seemed newly alive too. His books were full of people and places and ideas with which he should revive acquaintance. His scores, even his own in Mss., were full of music aching to be put forth in the air. He bathed, singing *Old 97* at the top of his voice, put on his pajama pants and flopped on the bed with *The Education of Henry Adams*, but after a few minutes gave up the discouraged old scholar, got out his violin, and began to pad about the room with it, playing cheerfully and furiously. It was while he was thus parading that he realized that *The Prayer for the Evil Days* still hung there over his bed. He stopped playing long enough to yank it down, crumple it up, and chuck it into the waste basket.

CHAPTER THIRTY-FIVE: *The Mountain*

THEY left the car under a pine by the creek that came down from the north ridge, and walked slowly out onto the summit meadow, and stood in the sun and looked at the heights around them. It was only a little after eight o'clock, and the air was still cold, but it would be warm enough before long. The sky was cloudless and a very dark blue, and the brilliant, thin sunlight seemed to reach everything. The insects had already begun to sing for heat. Their piercing sound was everywhere, like a radio tone in the bones, or an audible aspect of the light itself. After a while it wouldn't be noticed at all, except for the changes, the sudden clicking or whirring near by. On the north and west, the steep ridges they were going to climb stood up out of the thin forest into the light. They loomed close over the meadow. Far off, on the south slope of the meadow, a big flock of sheep was grazing down toward the hollow. They were scattered wide across the slope and up among the mouton rocks above, and looked like small boulders or bushes themselves until one of the dogs began to race above them, bringing down stragglers. This quicker motion made them real, and then Tim and Rachel could pick out the herder and the burro too. The dog must have been barking, but they couldn't hear him, only the insects and the creek. Rachel looked up at the western ridge.

"I can feel the height already," she said.

"We'd better catch up a little, before we start," Tim said. He could feel his own heart shaking, and the little irritation and flightiness of thought that came from the altitude. He lit a cigarette and stretched out on the grass. Rachel sat down with her back against a boulder and her arms behind her head, and looked up at the sky. They talked a little about the sky and the light and about the flock of sheep, and let the time pass. Only one sound they could hear came from the flock, the shrill whistle of the herder. It came to them as a tiny sound.

"I guess I'm ready," Rachel said.

They went back to the car, and Tim took out a tube of zinc ointment and smeared the ointment on his nose and lips and cheek-bones and the tops of his ears, and gave the tube to Rachel. When she had used it too, he put it into the pack, and slung the pack on, hitching it high, where he liked it, and fastened the canteen onto his belt.

He led the way slowly onto the north ridge, because there was no clear trail at the beginning. He zigzagged across the face of the ridge, gaining a little height on each tack. He was trying to keep his pace behind his pulse until they leveled off and the good feeling came that he could go on forever. Until you found that steady ratio, you were like two people fighting each other. First you got angry and wanted to bolt; then you thought you couldn't do it at all. You couldn't receive what the mountains had to give until the quarrel was over. He looked back twice, and Rachel was coming along all right, and smiled at him.

When he reached a stretch of clear trail that went along the flank of the ridge, through great, heavy-leafed plants that made a musky stink in the sun, and then into the pines, he waited. Rachel had fallen behind. She was climbing stubbornly, and not looking around. He sat down on a rock. When Rachel came up, she sat down too. Her face was flushed, and after a moment she leaned over and put her head on her knees. He could see her whole body stir forward with each beat of her heart.

After a couple of minutes she looked up and grinned. "If I quit, you go ahead anyway, will you?"

"It's not as bad as that," he said. "It was my fault. You go ahead and set the pace where you feel all right."

"If I didn't keep slipping," she said.

He showed her how to climb pigeon-toed, and putting the whole foot down at each step, instead of keeping on the toes.

When she was steady again, they went on. She entered the woods ahead of him, and the sun and shadow slipped down her back steadily, in changing pattern. She was trying to keep inside her pace now, to be ready for the next pitch. This made him loiter, which was all right, except that they wouldn't be together, they wouldn't be in the mountains, until they could get over thinking about how they were walking. Yet against this irritation worked his feeling of cherishing her. Little surges, dangerously like the old adoration, flowed through him often as he watched that small figure going steadily and intently through the chill under the trees ahead of him, in the old brown sweater with the sleeves pushed up above her elbows.

At the top of the first ridge, where the creek cut through and began to drop rapidly in white water, they stopped to drink. Rachel knelt and drank slowly, scooping the water up in her two hands together and sucking at it. She appeared nearly entranced. He was experiencing the same thing, the first other-worldliness of the heights. He lay down, propping himself on his hands, and drank from the running water. They sat down shoulder to shoulder against a big pine, and watched the broken water flashing in the light, and the softly stirring designs of the pine boughs on the old, red needles.

"It's wonderful here, isn't it?" Rachel said dreamily. "You wouldn't believe anyone else ever came here, except for the trail."

"It's only too many people at once that spoil the balance," Tim said.

On the next ridge, Tim found himself, and got the happy, steady feeling, and the hunger to see and remember everything. They were climbing back and forth among big boulders here, and the trees were fewer and smaller. Rachel was very quiet, and stopped often, but on the way down the other side, she found herself too, and when they came onto the meadow beyond, Tim could tell by the lift in her walk and the way she looked around that she was all right. There were small, white butterflies dancing over the meadow, and sometimes glassy dragonflies flashed over the black cut of the stream. These small movements made the meadow seem quick and gay. Then you looked across the meadow, which was open to the west, and there was the wall of the steep ridge, bare except for a few twisted trees in crevices. It was already shimmering with heat. The ridge looked down on the meadow, and the meadow belonged to it, and the heights clearly asserted their strong and religious power.

Tim came forward and walked beside Rachel as they crossed the meadow. He felt happy and childish. He wanted to touch her constantly, not to make love, but just to touch her hand or her arm or her face, or to feel her hair to make her seem more real. Her hair was long and heavy now, and for the climb she had done it up into a braid around her head. It was wonderful hair. But also he liked the feeling of not touching her. It was a full, satisfying kind of restraint, like not letting himself run or whistle or yodel or talk because of his happiness and the altitude excitement.

The ridge ahead of them to the north was a low, sandy whaleback. He wanted to tell her what was coming on the other side of this bare whaleback, but he wouldn't do that either. He wanted more to watch her see it without expecting it.

They came onto the top of the whaleback, and Rachel saw it and stopped, and stood there looking down.

"This is your place, Tim, isn't it?" she asked finally.

He nodded.

"I don't blame you," she said. "It's wonderful. It's queer too. There's not much there, but everything seems to mean something particular. I feel as if I ought to study it, learn the symbols, before I went down."

"It's no use," he said. "I feel that way every time I come here, and I haven't figured it out yet."

Part way down the slope were the three twisted trees, like parts of one tree, and no other growing near them, so that they stood there very importantly with their shadows, and the loose, blackened stones of a fireplace under them. Then, in the hollow below, sheltered on the other side by a steeper wing of the mountain than the one they were on, was the little, dark lake, with the wiry grass standing up in the edge of it. On the east, close above, a steep mountain of white boulders guarded the lake, and much farther away, on the west, was the high ridge. The lake lay still, and they began to see into its shadows. Then the wind came gently from the ridge, and feathered the surface, and it was all the color of sky and the white boulders, and they couldn't see into it at all.

Finally they went down and stood at the edge of the lake, and could see the shadows again, and the murky lights which made the water appear very deep. Frogs leapt out into the water from among the tough grass, and their splashes sounded loud. Somewhere on the north ridge, among the boulders and the dark, crouching trees, a chipmunk was chittering. While they were standing there, a hawk sailed up out of the white mountain against the wind. From a high point directly over the lake, he banked and fled swiftly down across the wind and out of sight behind the north ridge. These small, wild sounds and movements were intensely significant, touching the profundity of the place itself.

When the hawk was gone, Tim knelt and put one hand into the water.

"I always have to touch water," he said, grinning.

Rachel also knelt and put her hand in. "Now I'm initiated," she said.

"Now you're initiated."

While they were climbing the wooded ridge, he said, "Tonight you'll know."

"Know what?"

"If you've really been initiated; if you've been accepted. We'll go back there for supper, and watch the moon come up."

"I'm being given special privileges, aren't I?"

"Very special. But you have to climb the mountain and come back before you understand them," he added. "They're not my privileges; they're the lake's and the guardians'. You're only an acolyte now."

"I suppose I must be," she said, "though I feel as if I'd been here all my life already. At first nothing up here seemed real to me. Now it's everything else that doesn't. I never lived in San Francisco. That was a dream, and a rather empty one."

"You'll be initiated," he said. "The guardians like you. I have to be initiated again myself, for that matter. I've been away too long. I still knew, but it was by rote; memorized prayers. I'd nearly lost the understanding. The guardians don't like back-sliders."

After a long time she asked, "What do you mean, guardians?"

"I don't know," he said, grinning. "It's a secret fraternity, I guess. No mortal's ever let in, and you never quite see them. But if you're all right, and the time is right, you'll know they're there, and they do something which changes you."

They didn't talk again until they came down into the last meadow under the peak. The sod was heavy and wet here and sank underfoot but didn't spring back. Narrow, crooked streams of snow-water worked through it everywhere. The water appeared black, but when you lifted it in your hand, it was perfectly clear. The meadow was full of small flowers in the grass, and hundreds of butterflies blew and fluttered across it. They had come down terraces of stone, like great steps, to get onto the meadow, and trailing, flowering plants grew over the terraces, and red and blue clusters grew upright in all the crevices. Rachel knew all the flowers on the rocks and in the meadow, and stopped to look at each new kind, and often bent to finger them.

They drank from one of the icy brooks in the meadow, and Tim filled the canteen. When Rachel stood up from drinking, she looked slowly all around the meadow, and at the terraces, and at the light on the heights. This meadow was under the care of the great peak itself. It appeared very close and high over the meadow on the north-west, single and challenging and luminous.

"That's it, isn't it?" Rachel asked.

Tim was still holding the canteen into the icy water, which played with his hand. He looked up at the mountain. "That's it."

"My lord," Rachel said softly. "Do you think I'll ever make it?" she asked.

Tim laughed. "It's not as bad as it looks," he said.

He was filled with delight in this place. Her doubt and amazement in the presence of the mountain delighted him. It was nearly mid-day, and there were few shadows anywhere on the mountains or the meadow. The close, thin light out of the very deep blue was everywhere. He was delighted by the light, and by the soft, hollow rushing of the upper wind over the little valley, and by the gentle purling of water all around them.

"It's still spring up here, isn't it?" Rachel said.

"We've caught up with spring," he agreed.

"Do your guardians watch this place too, Tim?" she asked. "I feel as if something were about to happen all the time. Something wonderful."

"No," he said, grinning. "There's another kind here. The direct descendants of all the original gods are in the mountains, you know. In the mountains or in the sea. I suppose there's a hundred kinds in the Sierras alone. Maybe if we really studied the *Golden Bough* and meditated, we could be more specific. We should come on hints, anyway. It would make very exciting reading up here.

"I believe the ones here are very small and quick, and short lived, and I think there must be thousands of them. Some of them are in butterflies, I suppose, and I'm sure there are some in the water glitter. They're a joyous breed. They never wait and pass judgment on you. They're immediately wild with joy to have you come. They can't waste time because their single lives are so short, and they are reincarnated without memories. I suspect that they are even more transitory than the frailest insects. They are born and they die and they are reborn within an instant. That is why you are always delighted here, but never sure what it is that haunts you, so that you are always full of expectation and wonder, which is the best feeling in the world. I've never had any other feeling in this meadow, so that must be it. It's here even at night.

"The guardians back there are old and philosophical, and individually immortal, so they prefer loneliness, and are in no hurry to accept you.

"Nevertheless," he said, fastening the canteen back onto his belt, "they're the ones who really test you. Until you're in with the guardians, you can walk all over the mountains and learn nothing, and return to people as foolish as ever. Until you are greatly moved by the beauty of mountain sadness and loneliness, and for a moment perceive time according to stars and wholly without mathematics or any other intellectual or ritualistic crutch, which is the first-degree test of the guardians, there is almost no use in coming into the mountains, except to exercise your legs."

"Are they sprites or guardians on the peak?" Rachel asked, still looking up at it.

"Neither, I believe," Tim said. "They seem different up there, only a little less than human size, and very lean, surreptitious and hostile. They don't want you up there. You have to be on guard all the time."

"I'd always thought of it as aloof," Rachel said. "Hard to get at, but not hostile really."

"Oh, that's the mountain herself, not her attendants. Sometimes I don't think she wants them. But they're there, just the same. You wait; you'll know. They're like all immortals. You never quite see them, unless you're mad. It's always someone in the past who has seen them. But for a long time there will be nothing there, just you on the mountain. Then suddenly will come a moment when you know they are around, and after that they will be watching you all the time until you go off the mountain. I've seen it happen to as many as five people at once, so it can't be an illusion. Nothing imaginative ever happens to five people at once, because each is up to only one-fifth of his personal intelligence and perception. A crowd is never equal to the intelligence of any one of its members. You know that. In a theatre or at a concert, once in a while, there will be an illusion of super-perception, but that is only because emotion may be massed, and because all of those minds, for the time being, have become identified with the one mind of the playwright or the composer. But these five people, including myself, were not identified with anything. We were all sitting around eating hard-boiled eggs and chattering. Then I thought

I saw something disappear behind a rock, a foot, a tail, a small, scurrying creature; I wasn't sure what. I just caught it out of the corner of my eye. But I knew they were there. I didn't say a thing, but I noticed that at that same moment, everyone else suddenly stopped talking also. When I looked around the group, everyone was looking in a different direction, and all of them seemed to have forgotten what they were talking about. That general conversation never got going again either. There were only scattered, necessary remarks, 'Please pass the salt,' and so on, and single, quite thoughtful observations.

"You'll see," he said, grinning.

They waded across the meadow, and climbed north on the side of the great ridge, the dust caking on their wet boots. When the trail turned west and up into the notch, it was very steep. Below them, on the right, a creek went down, filling the ravine with the continuous sound of its rushing. It was quiet and hot in the ravine. Tim could feel the sweat running down his body under his shirt, and the pack made a sticky patch on his back. There was a warm, pungent smell of brush, and a strong smell of dust and hot rock. Yet now and then a cool breath came down from the top of the pass, and was like a promise. Toward the top of the canyon the trail came among heavy, torn trees, many of them showing the white spirals of their twisted fibers. The rushing of the creek gradually lost out to the roar overhead.

When they came up into the notch, the wind struck them, and then continued to push them steadily. This was where the cool promises had come from. The long ridge ended in a high cliff on the south side of the pass. At the top, against the blue, was a fort of rock, and on the steep slope below it lay the perpetual snow bank that was the beginning of the creek. From the snow bank down across the sandy hollow and up onto the peak, stood the stunted, bent trees, far apart, as if spread in skirmish formation. The Clark crows, like huge jays, flew slowly about among these trees, calling in sharp, querulous voices, chiding and exhorting. Fallen trees lay on the sand in many places. Chipmunks bickered rapidly on logs or from hiding places in the standing trees, but made single, silent dashes across open spaces. Steadily the wind blew from the west, roaring through the trees and bugling among the high rocks. This was the break in the wall, where the storms poured through first in their frontal attacks, day after day, night after night, in the winter. The strongholds of the cliff and the mountain would be held against them for a long time, and their power would be funneled into this pass, where the stubborn trees writhed and tore at it.

Once, in late November, Tim had come through this pass from the west side, with the first blizzard. All the way up the west side, he had felt the snow pelting against his back in wild forays, the wind attacking, and whirling, and falling away. Then he had come up into the notch, and felt the blast suck him eastward. He was in a snow cloud there, the van of the attack which was breaking through to the valley. The flakes had materialized all about him out of a vapor which was also snow. He could see the trees only as fighting wraiths, and only when he was very near them. The flakes clung against the trees and against upright rocks, but on the open ground and in the air they fled on east like smoke. Several times he'd been brought to a standstill, blind and bent, as blasts had swung back at him, turned by the ridge. When he'd finally worked over from the notch into the ravine on the east side, it had been as if, suddenly, many heavy enemies had stopped pummeling him and throwing sand in his face. The clouds and the roaring had passed above him then, and down in the ravine the snow had really fallen, quietly and thickly. Now it always seemed to him, even in August with the sun shining, that the cliff and the mountain and the trees in the notch were waiting for something like that. They didn't believe the truce was for long.

Rachel and Tim sat in the sun on one of the fallen trees and rested, and drank a little from the canteen. Then Tim refilled the canteen under the snow bank, and when he came back, Rachel stood up, and they began to climb the last trail, the long switch-back among the timberline trees on the peak itself. It felt like going up to the sun here. They were closer and closer to the sun and there was less and less of anything else around them. Most of the time they were sheltered from the wind by the peak. They felt the height starving them for air now, as if they had entered another region and their adjustment to the meadows, and even to the notch, was no use to them. The lure of expectation was let down to them also. They kept looking up, in the belief that the very top rocks of the peak would be in sight, but always the great swell of the flank hid them. At each new turn in the trail, they would see higher, but each time the summit was still hidden. In the meadows and the ravine and the notch, they had only drifted toward the peak, happy with what was around them, not feeling pressed to achieve. Now the summit became an enticing goal, and was part of every thought.

Once Rachel stopped and looked down at Tim. "I keep wanting to go faster," she said. "I feel as if the peak were moving too, and we'd have to hurry to catch it."

Tim nodded. "From here the mountain always pulls at you," he said. "It's part of the preparation of the acolyte," he said, grinning. "It taketh away the worldly from the mind. To be on the mountain is all that matters."

They went on up, slowly, toward the realm of the sun. There came an explosion among the trees, which made them both jerk, and then stand where they were. The explosion dwindled downslope in a series of rapid, stuttering reports. After an instant, Rachel looked quickly at Tim, and he pointed at the big, dark bird darting down, left and right, among the trees, which were now only tall bushes. The bird abruptly ceased beating and volplaned down, tilting and swerving from side to side, till it dropped out of sight under the swell. It was a violent, quick-minded, purposeful flight, and yet, in the mountain trance, the moment the bird was out of sight, they doubted they had seen it. It was another spirit of the place; something the mountain created in their brains.

"Good lord, what was it?" Rachel asked.

"The first warning to the ones up above that we're coming," Tim said. "They beat the drums here at the gates. Then the others, up above, will be all set for us. Blue grouse. They're most always up here this time of year."

"I jumped a foot," she said, mildly ashamed.

"They always go off like that."

After that first one, they heard many grouse, and saw most of them. Usually they broke out one at a time, but once two of them thundered up together, close ahead of Rachel, and fled down past, one on the right and one on the left, and then went into the long, dodging slip in different directions.

The trees became yet smaller and one-sided, and many of them lay close to the ground from the roots, and then lifted their outer boughs. More mountain and sky showed between them all the time. When the two came slowly around the mountain onto the west side, all at once there were no more trees. The dome of small, broken rock, almost in mosaic, swept up and east from them in a magnificent, barren, extended curve at the sky. Looked at big, there were only the two colors, the red mountain and the deep, pure blue in which the eye made tiny, darting dazzles of its own, but looked at small, there were many colors, though all mild, secretive, against the two big ones. There were the lichens, microscopic forests on the stone, gray, black, pale green. Close to the ground, their leaf whorls snug against it, were thousands of stubborn, papery blossoms, so small that the observer had to look purposely to see they were there. The rocks were of many colors too, but they all became one on the giant shape of the mountain. Everything was the same way here, the vast one made out of the tiny and infinitely numerous. When they listened closely, the wind wasn't a roar, as it had seemed from below, or might here, if they could think of something else. It was a great, uphill singing made up of the voices of all the rocks, even to the pebbles so small that they could not wholly protect the blossoms between them, which shivered under brief touches of the wind. The two, feeling how small and temporary they were themselves, and yet exalted by the sensation, stood on the open dome and stared west. There the great basin curved steeply down from them, like the slope of one wave, and at last rose again into the blue wave of the distant range, and between were the ripplings of the timbered hills. On the near hills the rock and sand showed through, and the trees were single and black, but up the side of the following wave the forests were unbroken and green, the trees invisible, and then succeeding ripples became paler and paler blue. Very far in the north-west, showed a faint rim of snow mountain, which couldn't be seen steadily, but appeared and disappeared.

In the wind, they had to yell to each other.

"I feel like hanging on with my teeth," Rachel cried.

The trail, faint among the rocks, went on up and around to the north. The wind struck them violently and coldly on the north slope, and they had to lean down in it, and sometimes it made them waver. It was strange to feel the strength of the wind moving them, and yet not to get enough air to breathe. It made the body, and the mind, fanciful with altitude, feel that any law of nature might be broken, that the mountain itself might break loose and sail off, or that the great blue wave of the range on the west might roll forward and break tremendously over the mountain.

On this naked slope Rachel waited until Tim came up beside her.

"They're here," she cried.

"What?"

"They're here," she yelled. "Your hostile spirits. I felt them when we came around on this side."

Tim looked up over the dome. He felt it too, then, the conviction that just out of sight, near any spot he looked at, were bigger rocks, dark boulders, and that the inimical watchers were behind them.

He looked at Rachel and grinned and nodded. "Won't bother us, though," he yelled. "We were passed-on at the lake."

They went on up over one dome after another, feeling increasingly that they wanted to hurry. It seemed that each dome would finally unmask the summit, but then it didn't. When the true summit, capped by its fort of upright rock, was finally revealed, still distant, and high on the right, the disclosure was so gradual that they climbed for a while without realizing that the goal was in sight.

This ending was so quiet that at first it didn't seem conclusive, but left them expecting. But as they stood there, steadying themselves on the rock beside the ruined weather station, and looked into the great distances, the sense of fulfillment grew in them gradually, as if it were their own achievement, and an unfamiliar and powerful content and detachment came with it. Far down in the basin in the west, lay Lake Tahoe, shrunken, and fitted neatly into all its bays and inlets in the wooded mountains. Smaller lakes lay on higher shelves of the mountains beyond it. But it was when they turned east that the world spread out under them, pale, painted, turbulent mountains, range after range toward the sky which curved beyond the shoulder of the world, all of them subdued by sun except the very last, a thin and broken edge of snow. In the north-east, through a distant pass, glittered an illusory sliver of Pyramid Lake. When you had looked east for a little while, and then looked back west at the green and blue basin, and across it, the great middle range of the Sierra, which had seemed so distant before, seemed very near and final on the sky. It was the pale, burning and shadowed east that led the mind out.

They ate their lunch sitting close together behind a wing of rock on the east side. The cold wind was wuthering all the time, but only occasional small freshets of it reached them, and the rest of the time they were in the warm, still sun. The wind was pure, almost sterile when it came, smelling only of snow and cold shale. The height worked on them constantly, begetting a bodily inertia and at the same time a light, nervous happiness. To suck in the wind was like drinking something cold, and yet it left a greater thirst. The oranges Tim took out of the sack tasted very sweet and good. The water had warmed in the canteen in the sun and against his body, but they gulped it eagerly, and it was good too. They ate all the sandwiches, and drank from the canteen again, and lit cigarettes between cupped hands and lay back against the rock. They had to keep the cigarettes covered against the wind flaws, or they burned down quickly, like paper.

"This," Tim thought, vaguely and contentedly, "is what I've been after. This brings me together. This makes me one." He included Rachel with the mountain in his thought.

However, it wouldn't do to touch Rachel; not even with his mind must he ask anything of her. It was the suspension, without desire, without regret, with only the lucid, independent present, which was the gift of the mountain. It was that, if you learned it by being there long enough with a wholly receptive mind, a mind judging nothing and considering nothing, which would stay with you for a long time afterward, and seem to have taken error out of your being. He looked at Rachel. She was sitting there against her rock, all by herself, and looking at the deep valley, and the toy city, and the sea of pale mountains, and then, for a long time, at the glittering sliver of Pyramid. It came on him that he had been foolish for years. He had never really expected to have her. He had never believed that he would either quell or fulfill that yearning. Everything in the world that might be between a man and a woman, between the male and the female of all life, was proven when they joined. Then you knew, and after that, either everything turned stale and the light went out of the world, and you played tricks on yourself, trying to believe that there was the equal of love in power or money or fame or even notoriety, or else the light was there for good, and you fitted into time, and began to know things, instead of merely guessing at them, or remembering what somebody else had said or done. Either you closed yourself and became one of the jealous or ambitious, or you were opened up, and became simply yourself, which was enough. Yet with him, in a way, it was neither. He had never expected to have her. He was dedicated to her. That was it. He would keep what he had of her, and it would be enough. He began to memorize her as she had been all the time that day.

"Tim," she said, "you're not going to stay with that band, are you?"

He felt uncomfortable that this should be mentioned on the mountain, and when he was trying to memorize her. It didn't seem important anyway. It was a trivial accident which was accompanying his life for a time, that was all.

Finally he said, "Oh, I don't know. It doesn't matter much."

"But your music does? Writing it?"

"Yes, I guess it does."

"You know it does. It's been everything to you, for years."

"Not everything. Just being is the main thing. Anything else is extra. Nothing else seems to matter much here, does it?"

She looked out again over the ocean of pale mountains and saw the shining sliver of Pyramid Lake. "No, not here," she said.

After a minute she looked at him again, smiling. "But how do you take your mountain with you?"

He laughed softly. "All right," he said. "The music."

"Then what's the matter?" she asked.

"Well," he said softly, dreamily, also staring at the sliver of Pyramid, "I guess perhaps I don't have it. I've been kidding myself." He said this easily. Everything they'd said had been easy. The mountain made ideas unimportant too. But after he had said it, it struck him suddenly that she had heard the words, and that he had spoken them. It seemed suddenly a shameful utterance, a major blow at himself. It was as if, out of his own flesh, he had admitted physical cowardice to this courageous and adored woman. He had defiled the peak. It must be a good animal to be equal with the wild.

But his words hadn't struck her like that. She didn't know the history of doubt behind them.

"That's nonsense," she said. "You don't even believe it. Tim, why don't you get some other job? In a store, on a road gang, anything, but get washed of that band."

"Oh, it's not the band," he said. He'd often thought it would be better to get another job, but not as if it were really possible to do so. He'd always thought of it when he felt desperate, and as an escape. It had never seemed more than a notion. Now it seemed real and an answer, ridiculously easy.

"I've thought of it," he said.

"You'd feel freer," Rachel said. "A simple job, with hours, and the responsibility somebody else's, so you wouldn't carry it in your mind."

He sat there staring down the mountain. It offended his pride that her will should make this so simple and clear.

"It's none of my business, though, is it?" she asked.

He looked at her, and she was smiling tentatively.

He grinned. "It's all right," he said. "Being you."

Then she was looking at him seriously, searching him, as his mother had done sometimes, as if he had opened up to her a view of something she'd forgotten or had never realized, and of which she wasn't sure now. If she continued to look at him like that, even with that ludicrous mask, that ceremonial mask of white ointment, behind which her face looked small and savage against the rock . . .

"Will you do it, Tim?" she asked. "Being me?" she asked, smiling.

And the weakness was past, and he was looking at the vast map of mountains again, aware of her, and of himself, separately, and of the shapes of the rocks among which they sat. At the moment this felt more like a defeat than a victory.

"I'll think about it," he said.

"No," she said, shaking her head. "Promise."

"All right," he said, grinning. "I promise."

"That's better. You must let me know when they play your first symphony."

"They don't play American symphonies, except once, for charity," he said. "Don't you know that?"

"They will now," she said. They both laughed.

"That's Pyramid Lake, isn't it?" she asked, after a moment, and pointed to the shining sliver.

They sat for an hour, watching the lights change among the mountains and talking quietly and more seriously than they had the day before about Tim's music. Tim was surprised at how clearly and simply he was formulating much of his theory which had appeared confused and difficult in his lonely hours, and at the swiftness with which he diagnosed the weaknesses of attempts he had already made. It seemed to him that as he talked the plan of his future became visible, though less than twenty-four hours before it had been a misty region in which he was doomed to wander by chance, led here and there by the shadows of hope, only to find each, when he came up with it, the mere passage of mist across mist. Now it seemed to him that he had been shaped in his tribulation, and that something in him had never lost sight of the desired end, even when he had appeared to himself most shapeless of intellect and exhausted of will. All that had been needed was this hour in which Rachel's sympathy, and the detachment which the mountain gave, broke his bondage in doubt and let his knowledge up to be seen and known.

He was aware that such lucid intervals had aroused his hopes before, only to prove so illusory when he had worked a few hours that he couldn't even believe he had passed through them. But this wasn't a compelled, inspired outpouring, a passionate teaching of himself as he talked. It was a quiet, fragmentary clarification of much that he had accumulated. He didn't seem to be saying anything new. He wasn't making discoveries about music or himself or the nature of life, three subjects which couldn't be separated, but must grow together. He wouldn't have to test what he was saying. It had been tested. This was a summing up, the definition of a line of action. It was even more than that. He understood that no creative worker could make a plan of his work and follow it, as a traveling salesman might jot down an itinerary on an envelope and work by it, so many places to be visited in so many days, such and such goods to be sold in each place. He had written down many comparable plans in the spirit of a self-reformer about to compel himself sternly to make a change in his life. He had made lists of compositions to occupy as much as two years ahead, even to titles and the approximate time to be allotted to the composition of each. In parallel columns he had written down the technical weaknesses which would be most likely to block each piece of work, and made lists of the readings and exercises he should undertake to overcome each weakness, and of the composers he should study for relevant excellences, and the composers he should guard against because he feared the appearance of their idiom in the work. Often he had gone even further, and written out, to be a kind of spiritual mentor, his own philosophy of music at the moment, his philosophy of life from which the emotional intent of the music must derive, and lists of studies for the clarification of both.

Doubtless these copy-book exercises, these bursts of writing down the rules for salvation, had been of some value in the process of his education. Doubtless he would continue to devote hours to them, even after today. But he knew now that they were of no direct value to the writing. It wasn't an itinerary of that sort he was sketching out for Rachel, but rather a series of facts and ideas which added up to a definition of his own natural tendency, and it was this which he must discover and fulfill. Gradually, as he talked, the feeling that he had debased himself, and that Rachel had been stronger in the recognition of a vital fact than he was, wore off. That the decision to quit the band had been made was all that mattered. He experienced little gusts of the joy of freedom each time he thought he would never go back and sit in the barren glare of the Northern Lights and blow methodical trash, that he would never drag himself out of bed again, dead for sleep, but with half the day gone, only to torment himself for hours over mechanical arrangements for that trash.

When the sun was gone from their niche, Tim made up the pack again, and they went back down the mountain. They seemed to Tim to be closer together now, because of her directness, than they had ever been before. They traveled easily during the descent, and stopped more often to look around them, and talked more about what they saw.

The sun was already well down when they reached the meadow of the sprites. Under the darkening palisade, they began to feel that they must hurry. Tim helped her up over the flowering terraces of rock, and believed that each grip of her hand on his would be something he'd never forget. They passed silently and swiftly over the ridge where the white boulders were tumbled, and the broken trees crouched among them. The slanting sunlight came in here in long and separate beams, lighting single boulders and splintering into halos of dazzle among the boughs. They hurried through each hollow, where the shadows were gathering, and stopped for a moment on the top of each ridge to look back at the peak, where the red, heavy light still burned on the west slope, while night prepared in the meadows below.

When they reached the little lake, there was still light on the peak of the mountain of white boulders, but the water and all the meadow lay in the shadow of the great ridge. They gathered firewood under the last trees on the north shoulder and carried it around the lake and up to the three trees on the sandy whaleback. Tim laid the fire among the blackened stones, and spread the food and set out the frying pan. Rachel went down to the lake and drew water for the coffee. They were quick and happy with hunger and the mountain air and the sensation of the momentous which is enduring in such a place. Rachel began to slice the crusty French bread. Then she stopped and looked at Tim, who was getting the matches out of his shirt pocket to light the fire.

"Aren't you going to take your swim?"

"I guess I'll let it go this time," Tim said.

Rachel put the knife down. "Tim, you're an old prude," she said.

Then she asked, "If I do, will you?"

"Yes," he said finally.

"All right," she said. "You go in, and then I'll come in." She stood up.

"You don't really want to," he said, laughing. His breath was catching and he was trembling a little because of the image his mind made of her, naked and white, wading out into the water in the dusk, and the image which followed at once, in which they sported near each other in the water, and then, half drawn, half by chance, came together and were suddenly serious as he took her in his arms, and they put their wet mouths together, and he felt all through him the wild, delicious shock of her slippery breasts against his body.

"I have to be initiated," Rachel said.

His hands were shaking, and to be sure of himself before he spoke, he finished lighting the fire.

"You go on in first," Rachel said. "When you're in, you call me."

"All right," he said.

Rachel lit a cigarette and went slowly up past the three trees onto the whaleback, and stood there looking west at the great ridge, beyond which the afterglow was drawing in. Tim watched her while he fed enough wood onto the fire to hold until he came out. Then he took his towel and went down through the sand to the edge of the water, and undressed. The air felt cold on his naked body, and the wiry grass was sharp under his feet. He waded out slowly until the water was around his thighs, and then made a short, looping dive. When he came to the surface, he swam hard for a minute to get used to the water. Then he stood up in the middle. The water reached his armpits. He was steady again, and could master his thoughts.

"All right. I'm in," he called. His voice echoed somewhere on the white hill. He watched Rachel come down to the water. She chose a place far from his clothes, and dropped her cigarette and rubbed it out with the toe of her boot. She didn't look at him in the water. She began slowly to pull the old brown sweater over her head.

Tim plunged under the water again, and swam at his end. He rolled over onto his back. In the sky over the white hill, the first stars were showing. He tried to still his spirit to the perfect quiet of the place, but he thought, with gentle thunder, that now she would be standing white in the first dusk, feeling the cold air play with her breasts and thighs and throat, feeling the coarse grass under her bare feet too, and the little, stinging points of the quartz sand; that now she would be wading in slowly, perhaps slowly lifting the cold water against herself with her hands. It wasn't the mountain water which shook his breathing now. He rolled over again, and began to swim and play porpoise. Her presence, their swimming together in this sacred pool, was no violation of his meadow. Rather it was the final dedication. But it must remain that. He mustn't let desire soften him toward her. He mustn't touch her with a look or a word or a thought.

His head emerged streaming from a roll, and he saw her in the other end of the little lake, swimming evenly and easily, with a soft fluttering of her feet. Then she stopped swimming, and let herself down in the water, and he stood up also, and they looked together at the sky and the mountains. The afterglow was dwindling rapidly behind the ridge. The white boulders on the hill were no longer distinct. From their fastnesses in the rocks, the bats came down and softly worked the air over the water. Rachel laid herself quietly out into the water again, and swam quietly, using a breast stroke, and still looking around. She turned toward the bank at last, and when her hands struck in the oozy bottom, stood up and began to wade out. He didn't even feel that he was watching her now, save in a way she wouldn't mind. She was a small, indefinite glimmer going up onto the bank. Her motions as she began to dry herself were like those of a restrained dance in one place. He went out too, and wiped and dressed quickly, and climbed back up to the three trees.

He was feeding the fire again when she came up. She had let her hair down over her shoulders to dry, and the mask of white ointment was gone from her face. Standing beside the fire, smiling slowly at him, she looked like a dreamy child. A terrible tenderness filled him, so that he looked away from her quickly, but the shaking desire was gone.

"Am I initiated now?" she asked.

"I don't know," he said. "You'll have to wait and see."

"I feel wonderful, anyhow."

"So do I."

He broke down the last sticks into coals, and rubbed the pan with a piece of fat, and left the fat in it, and pushed the pan into the coals. When the fat was sputtering, he put the steak in, and set the coffee pot among the coals too. The smell of the steak and of the coffee, when it began to boil, was very good in the cool, dark air. Rachel set out their plates and cups, and put salad and butter and chunks of bread on each plate. She stopped now and then to peer out of the firelight toward the top of the whaleback.

"Won't it be hard to find the trail in the dark, Tim?"

"The moon will be up before long," he said. "You have to see it in the moonlight too. Besides," he said, after a minute, "we still have to find out if you belong."

"Yes," she said.

They sat cross-legged, side by side, to eat. All the time he ate he was studying her face. He didn't realize he was doing this except when she looked up and caught him. She didn't seem to mind, but smiled at him. Tim threw another stick into the fire now and then, and the sparks flew up for an instant, and winked out, and they saw the stars above them. They didn't talk very much. Being here was everything now. The day had worked in them very well, and they were content.

When they had finished eating, they drank coffee slowly and smoked their cigarettes. Tim got up once and filled the dishes with the coarse sand, and took them down into the darkness at the edge of the lake and scoured them. He looked up from his darkness, and saw her sitting there quietly, with the firelight moving on her, and on the under boughs of the three trees, and his content welled up into something that was of the same nature but much stronger. Everything was very good; everything, in the little valley at least, had the mark of the eternal. There were no questions in his spirit. He stood there for a while, when he had finished the dishes, and listened to the singing of the small frogs in the margin. Then he went back up, and put the pack together, and stretched himself on the ground where he could watch her bind her hair.

"I wish we'd brought blankets," he said. "It would be nice to be here when the sun comes up."

"I wish we had too," she said.

After a while he said, "I'm not going to like the idea of never seeing you again."

"Oh, it's never never, is it?" she asked, smiling.

They listened to the frogs, and picked out different voices, and tried to guess what was happening down in that part of the world, by the little splashes and the changes in the chorus. They lay on their backs and hunted for constellations. Tim watched her listening for frogs, and smiling quickly when she detected a change. He watched her lying there, staring up at the stars. Whenever she moved, he would look away.

Once, when he looked away like that, he said, "There. It's beginning."

Rachel sat up and looked.

The first moonlight was creeping down the great ridge on the west. The ridge appeared to grow higher, and yet to move farther away. Stars began to fade out of the eastern sky, only the largest holding out, and the white mountain developed a long shadow.

Then slowly the moon sailed up out of the white mountain. When its light filled the valley, the fire appeared smaller and very red. On the broken ridge across the lake, the shadows were deep, and the boulders were softly shining presences.

Rachel got up and went slowly away from the fire, and down toward the lake. Tim scooped sand onto the fire. When it was banked under, he stood up and swung the pack on. He waited for her there. He was opening up with a slow, solemn joy because of the pale peaks standing about in the moonlight. Everything was slow and full and going to be something. The creative principle was alive in the world, and the quiet mind knew it.

Rachel came slowly back up toward him. She was in no hurry either. Her small face was very white in the moonlight.

When she was close enough for him to hear her, she said, "It's all right, Tim. You haven't sinned. I touched water, and then I knew they were here. Some of them were up here near you."

"That's good," he said. "Only now you'll always want to come back here."

"That's all right too," she said. "To want to be up here is better than to be most places. Or am I a greenhorn to feel like that?" she asked, looking up at him.

"Not unless I am too."

Rachel stood looking down into the hollow for a little while. Then she turned and started up the whaleback. Tim followed her. They both looked again from the top.

They had to pick their way slowly among the shadows of the

other ridges, and most of the time Tim led the way, but they walked swiftly, and side by side, across the moonlit meadows. The air was very cold and still. It felt as if there would be a frost later. It wasn't done being spring up here, and already it was turning autumn. There was no way of knowing in what hour summer had been lost. They talked softly together in the meadows, and were silent among the trees. It seemed to Tim that they were very much together.

CHAPTER THIRTY-SIX: *About Certain Signs of Altitude Hangover, and the Accidental Reunion of the Houses of Hazard and Turner*

TIM didn't go out at once and find the job that was to save him. He didn't forget about it or change his mind, either, as he might have if the idea had been his own, and therefore likely to seem one of the thousands that fled singly through his mind, like a long, thinned flock of birds, whenever he was seized by the juke-box despair. Having emerged as he sat beside Rachel in the niche on the mountain, and having become a promise to her, the notion had the force of a vow. He delayed because of the empty house, the mountain and the lake. The first day after the mountain, he awoke full of a happy anticipation for which he could discover no reason. He wanted to be alone, to protect this fragile excitement. He tried to work in the morning, but his mind was open to birds again, not the dark, one-by-one birds, but flocks of bright birds, white pigeons, perhaps, swinging in splendid formations through a blue and windy sky. It felt like spring in his mind, the way it had felt when he was kneeling beside the brook in the mountain meadow. He went for a long walk by himself, out Riverside, across the bridge by the entrance to the park and on along the old Verdi road to the barn where the trail up Hunter's Creek began. He climbed the trail to the first gravelly clearing, where it crossed the creek, and sat on a stone in the sun and watched the water, and the changing light on the cliffs, and the aspens shivering in the faint, water-chilled draft of the canyon. Everything looked new, and near to making revelations. It was after dark when he got back to his room. He played at the Northern Lights until four in the morning, but even that didn't break his happiness. He danced with Lucy once, and afterward they had a drink together and talked. Lucy looked at him curiously again and again. Finally she stopped in the middle of something she was saying, and laughed.

"What's the matter with you, Tim?" she asked. "You act like a kid in love, like about seventeen. You make me feel like an old hag." And later she asked, still studying him, "You ever see Mary Turner these days, Tim?"

This made Tim feel very young himself, almost the way he'd felt when all the Hazards in the kitchen were trying to find out why he didn't want to talk about Billy Wilson's party.

"I see her once in a while," he said.

"What's she doing now?"

"She works at the Music Box. I see her sometimes when I go in there to buy records or something. She's alone now, you know," he added. "Her father's dead, and her mother moved back to some place in Oregon, where they used to live."

Lucy was still looking at him with the questions she wouldn't ask. It was just like making Mary into a dummy fortification against Willis, except that now he wanted to laugh a little, half at himself, instead of being so thankful, when the attack went wrong.

"You still make me feel old," Lucy said. "About five years older than God."

Tim grinned. That even sounded like Willis.

"It's funny," Lucy said. "Reno ain't such a big place, but I ain't seen Mary once, not once since we was in school. We might as well be in New York or London or some place, for all I see of most of those kids. All you see is just the part you get stuck in, huh?" she added after a moment.

This problem of the time and worlds of Reno seemed to trouble Lucy all night. She was still around after most of the women had gone, which was unusual in itself. She came over to Tim again, when the band was taking a rest. After some talk about how long the time seemed to her tonight, she asked, "How did you ever come to get in a joint like this anyhow, Tim? A guy like you ought to get out of a joint like this. There ain't no future in it. I always thought . . ." And then she talked about Mary again, and about how sad it was the way Jacob Briaski had died, and about the time she had tried to lead Tim astray back-stage in the auditorium.

So Tim still had the day with him, in a way, when he went back to his room.

But in his sleep he had a dream like a few of the stories he had tried to tell himself when he was seventeen. He and Rachel were in one of the upstairs rooms in her father's house. Tim had never been in one of those rooms, yet this one was very familiar, in a sad-happy way, as if he and Rachel had been wonderfully married for years, and this was their bedroom. He was naked, and standing at the window looking out into a moonlit night in the winter. There were no leaves on the trees, and the bare branches rattled in the wind, and their shadows moved on the snow. For some reason or other, he was remembering that all the furniture downstairs was sheathed in dust covers.

The moonlight came in the window at an angle, and made a long, pale window across the floor. He turned, and the corner of this moonlight window was on the bed, and Rachel was lying there waiting for him, filled with a love and a cosmic yearning as great as his own. He wished to cry aloud the pain of his adoration, but he crossed to her very slowly and softly, so as not to disturb a precious balance which existed in the room. But then it wasn't Rachel, but Marjory Hale in his arms.

When he awoke in the room on Second Street, and saw the name of the eccentric lawyer printed backwards across his windows, he was overcome by an almost forgotten kind of heaviness, no mortal despair, like the sinking about his music, but a dull heaviness that would last forever, and keep him from caring very much about anything. He tried to write, and nothing came. He sat in a chair by the window and smoked one cigarette after another and stared at nothing. Late in the afternoon, he fell into a frenzy of despair, and wrote a long, wild letter to Rachel, proving to her in a hundred painful ways that she was all in the world that mattered to him, that even the music could never matter unless he was with her. When he came in from the Northern Lights he read the letter, and was shocked, as if reading a madness poured out of someone else's mind. He tore the letter up, and burned it, piece by piece, in one of the tin-can lids, and went to bed, making a savage declaration of independence in his mind.

The next morning he was restless; something was shaping in him. He moved to the piano and began to write while he was still drinking his coffee. When it was time to get ready for the Northern Lights, he put on pants and a sweater and went down to Ling Choy's in his slippers and called up Jimmy the Needle from the pay booth. Jimmy played the sax in the band, and was called the Needle because of what he used to keep going. He was Tim's best friend, except Lucy, at the Northern Lights. Tim told Jimmy that he was quitting the band, and that Howie Johnson, who was a good horn, had been hanging around the Newark Café for a week with nothing to do, and hung up. Then he drank a bowl of Ling's noodle soup and went back to work. He worked and reworked for ten days, stopping only to sleep for three or four hours toward daylight, and to go over to Ling's when he was hungry. The work developed into an orchestral piece in three movements, The Trail, On the Mountain, and Water at Evening. When he had inked in the last note of the copy, and was still happy about the music, he tried to write another letter to Rachel, telling her what their day together had meant to him, and about the music, which he called *The Enchanted Mountain*, and asking if he could dedicate the piece to her. But the letter went wrong. He tried four times, but sooner or later each letter began to say things he hadn't intended to say. He would start out each time to write like a good friend remembering a happy day with her, but then the first time he tried to recall an incident for her just as it had been—the rest-stop on the creek, filling the canteen in the meadow, their swim in the lake at dusk—a sentimental wildness would over-whelm him. He would begin pouring out as his thoughts at the moment he was describing, all the things he should have said years before instead of going on about basketball, track and the science of putting together a dance band.

The fifth attempt was a short note, telling Rachel that he re-membered with pleasure their hike together, that it had fur-nished the initial impetus of an orchestral piece which he had completed, he believed, with some success, and asking if he might dedicate the piece to her. After much deliberation, he signed this note, "As Ever, Tim." She could make what she liked of "As Ever." He knew what he meant by it. He left this note on the table overnight, and the next day it appeared to him as ridiculous as the others, and even more false, a pompous impli-cation that he had condescended to enjoy her company for a short time, and therefore was willing, if she were properly eager, to dedicate his latest masterpiece to her. He burned that note up too, tied the score of *The Enchanted Mountain* into a bundle, without looking at it again, and threw it into the corner on top of the symphony of leaves.

Even then, if it hadn't been for meeting Mary Turner in Benner's, where she almost never went, he might have delayed still longer before looking for the job. He felt a cool triumph about having passed through this trial without exposing himself, and an urge to go on writing, now that he had at least completed something deeper than a honky-tonk satire.

He went up to Benner's for supper, and the lunch-counter side, where he usually ate, was so crowded that he crossed over to the family side, where the booths were. Most of the booths were filled too, but Mary was sitting by herself in a booth un-der the gloomy, grand-operaish picture of two lovers in medi-eval costume, maybe Romeo and a very well-developed Juliet, locked in an embrace which must have been brought on by trag-edy, to judge by their expressions and by the light of a lurid sunset or a city burning behind them. So Tim sat in across from Mary, and ordered his hot roast-beef sandwich and beer, and they talked.

At first Mary was extremely shy, as if she had never known Tim except by sight, and was judging how everything she said would sound to him. She sat very upright in her neat, blue coat, keeping one hand in her lap, and watching her plate most of the time. When something Tim said made her look up at him, she would seem even more quiet than when she was looking at her plate. She was smiling all the time, intently and gently. It seemed to Tim that their relation had been reversed during all the time since they had been in school together, the time in which he hadn't thought of her very often, and never with any particular emotion except a fondness for the revived memory of the alliance between the Hazards and the Turners. Well, not exactly reversed. Mary appeared to be struck dumb, more by apprehension than by adoration.

Tim couldn't know, of course, how much he had been changed by the long battle of Timothy Hazard vs. Timothy Hazard. He didn't know that he had a thin and savage countenance, a slight but constant frown, a stare in his eyes, whenever he looked directly at anyone, that seemed to promise a sudden onslaught of contemptuous words against any opinion with which he disagreed. He couldn't know, either, that he had gained a reputation among past friends and acquaintances as a ferocious and worldly wise recluse. In many this reputation produced a contempt equal to the contempt they imagined in Tim. They could see no reason for being superior and aloof about playing at the Northern Lights. Mary had never felt any protective contempt, and her doubts about the unknown were aggravated by Tim's visits to the Music Box, and by her memory of him as an entirely different being, not only well within her realm, but even under her sway. She would see him come into the store, tall, a little stooped, bushy-headed, preoccupied, his coat flapping about his thin legs, and her affectionate memory for the past, which seemed so lively as compared with her solitary present, would bridge the time and make her think "Timmy Hazard," with a quick warmth, only mildly melancholy, for Mary was neither old nor a mourner. Actually this warmth would be somewhat transforming the memory of a skinny, dark-brown boy with big eyes, excitedly showing off for her by diving from the white rock at Pyramid, or sitting on the floor of the old Dodge and leaning very lightly against her leg, sitting there all the way home under the fountains of stars, not saying a word, and very carefully not making a move which the car didn't compel him to make. Whenever Mary thought of riding home like that, she remembered two sensations, against her knee the hard, thin shoulder blade of Timmy Hazard, and against her side the padded and comfortable presence of her mother. The past would touch her in this way, and she would prepare to greet Timmy Hazard, and then this tall, thin, young man would not be Timmy at all, but a courteous stranger who remembered her name automatically and had no time to waste. He would get his record, or whatever it was he had come for, and go out. She had been robbed of her past so often in this way that she had become wary of the Tim Hazard who wasn't Timmy Hazard.

Tim, however, found it unexpectedly easy to talk to Mary. When they were done eating, he ordered another beer for himself and another coffee for Mary, and they sat there drinking and smoking and talking for an hour. He even described his room for Mary, making out that he shared it on disagreeable terms with the ghost of the crotchety lawyer. The wariness went out of Mary's eyes. She still sat most of the time with her hands folded before her on the edge of the table, as if in prayer, but she laughed several times, softly, with her head thrown back, and finally she even began to tell him about her life.

She was living alone in a room in the Great Basin Hotel, which was just a block west of Tim's office building, and around the corner from the Music Box. She had a landlady, Mrs. Mott, who ran the Great Basin as a hotel, though most of her guests were permanent, like Mary, or at least long term, like the divorcees who could pass Mrs. Mott's first-week examination. Mary said she had been nearly scared to death of Mrs. Mott at first. Mrs. Mott was a broad, heavy woman, with bobbed hair which was red but turning gray, and a booming voice. She always looked like somebody's respectable aunt when she was dressed to go out, but at home she usually wore a man's shirt and a pair of Levis. The third day after Mary moved into the Great Basin, Mr. Atley had come up with her after work to get some papers she'd been typing in her room. You couldn't know how funny this was, Mary said, unless you knew Mr. Atley. Mrs. Mott had the front apartment, right by the head of the stairs. From her door she could see these stairs, and the first few steps of the stairs to the top floor, and the length of the second-floor hall. This made her doorway a well-placed sentry post, for there was no first floor to the hotel, no lobby. There was a women's clothing store underneath, and Mrs. Mott's sitting room was the Great Basin office. It was simply cluttered with furniture, Mary said, and always too hot for any mortal but Mrs. Mott, and usually the radio in there was going full blast. That was what made Mrs. Mott's sudden appearances so startling at first. Mary and Mr. Atley had come up quietly, having nothing to say at the moment, which was usually the case with Mr. Atley, who was very hard to talk to, and the door to Mrs. Mott's room had been closed, and a dance band going full blast inside. Yet all of a sudden, when she and Mr. Atley were only a few steps down the hall, Mrs. Mott's door had been flung open, so the dance music was much louder, and that voice had boomed out, "Who's that you got with you, young woman?"

When Mary remembered this, she laughed softly, with her head back. Then she shivered her shoulders a little. "I was never so scared and ashamed in all my life," she said. "I hadn't even thought of that before, but I knew in a moment I was trying to smuggle a man into my room. Mr. Atley was even more frightened than I was. I suspect he had premonitions of law suits. He cleared his throat two or three times and looked around, over his shoulder, and kind of smoothed his hair out, like this. I knew he would never be able to think of anything to say, and I was getting ready to explain that the man was just my boss, and we were only going to stop for a minute to get some papers he wanted, and that we would leave my door open, and everything that would make me sound just as guilty as I felt. But I didn't have to. Mrs. Mott knows everybody downtown. Mr. Atley didn't know her, but she knew him. She bellowed out, 'Oh, Mr. Atley, that you? O.K.,' and went back in and slammed the door. Mr. Atley felt worse than ever, poor man. He looked all around to see if anybody'd heard her, and he wouldn't come in my room, but just waited in the door while I found the papers."

Tim chuckled.

"There's really no mystery about Mrs. Mott's hearing, though," Mary said. "When you've been there a week, if she's decided you're all right, she tells you her secret, so you won't bother her any more."

"What is it?" Tim asked.

"I shouldn't tell you."

"I'll never use it, except maybe to sneak into your room," Tim said, "and I'll never give it away."

Mary laughed, but then, suddenly, she flushed too, and looked down, and joined her hands upon the edge of the table. There was a moment of constraint, as if Tim had passed lightly over something which wasn't light. Then Mary looked up, and everything was nearly all right again.

"With that as a promise," she said, laughing again, "I'll trust you. The fifteenth and sixteenth steps are wired to a buzzer in Mrs. Mott's room, so that even if somebody comes up two at a time, he'll step on one or the other. But if you come up on the left side, right next to the wall, fifteen doesn't buzz, and all you have to do is step over sixteen."

Tim laughed.

They talked about the Music Box and Mr. Atley, and about old Mr. Breese, who tuned pianos, and mended instruments and radios down in the basement. Then Tim found himself telling her about the Northern Lights, and about why he had quit there, and was going to try to get a regular day-time job. It seemed to him that while he was talking Mary had stopped looking at him, and that first wary stillness had returned to her face. He wondered what he had said to offend her. He had been very careful about the Northern Lights. It was hard talking to somebody you hadn't really known for a long time. You got to talking as you would to people you saw every day, and all of a sudden you were wrong.

Actually Mary was thinking about something she and Mr. Atley had discussed several times. She wanted to tell Tim, but she didn't know how to begin on it, and she was afraid he would go before she could tell him. He was stubbing out his cigarette in a way that looked final. It seemed to her, for no particular reason, important that she should tell him now.

"You wouldn't care to work at the Music Box, would you?" she asked.

"Is that an offer?" Tim asked, after a moment.

"Well, yes, I guess it is," Mary said, laughing quickly. "That is, it's not official, but it practically is. Mr. Atley has asked me about you several times. He keeps saying we ought to have a clerk who knows something about music and can play the piano for customers who want sheet music. We don't any of us know much about it," she hurried on, looking at him. "I know more about it than Mr. Atley does, really, and I don't know very much. And I'm terrible on the piano. I can't play jazz at all, and that's how they want it played, of course, jazzy. Sometimes I think Mr. Breese knows more about real music than either of us. I don't know," she said, slowing down, "just from the way I've heard him sometimes, on a piano. But he wouldn't say so if he did, and he'd walk out if we asked him to be a clerk. But maybe you wouldn't be interested anyway. I mean, it would still be . . ."

"Yes, I would," Tim said.

"There's really nothing to the accounts and the ordering and so on," Mary said quickly. "I could show you all about that part in no time."

"When could I start?" Tim asked.

"Any time," Mary said. "Tomorrow, if you wanted to."

"I'll be down tomorrow," Tim said.

Mary stubbed out her cigarette with a trembling hand. Tim didn't notice this. He was feeling fine about the idea of working at the Music Box. It would be swell never to hear that band in the Northern Lights again, and to eat at regular hours and have enough sleep and all his evenings and Sundays free for work and a lot of music to hear, even on the job. He wondered why he had never seen for himself the happy land that kind of a job could make. He felt a great, golden affection for life blossoming out from him through the brown rooms of Benner's. It made little high-lights on everything he looked at. Especially he felt this affection enwrapping Mary, who had always appeared to him somewhat golden anyway. He felt that whatever else it was like at the Music Box, Mary's presence would make a center of peace there, a kind of family peace, such as his mother and Grace had made in the House of Hazard. After all, the Hazards and the Turners had been practically one family. He felt about Mary just as he had felt about Grace, when he had stopped to think about her.

"Come on," he said, as he stood up. "We'll go spend my last ill-gotten groat on a real drink to celebrate the reunion of Turner and Hazard."

He left money for both checks on the table, and a fifty-cent tip, which would shock Sam, the duck-footed waiter, half to death.

Outside on Commercial Row, under the immense night and the very beautiful little signs, he cocked an arm at Mary.

"My arm, Miss Turner," he said sternly.

Mary looked at him for a moment, smiling, but with that stillness in her eyes.

"Come, come, woman," he said. "Stand not aloof. This is an honest burgher's arm I offer."

He took her hand and drew her arm through his, and pinned it to his side. Mary laughed a little. They stepped off together, with measured and companionable swiftness, toward Virginia Street.

CHAPTER THIRTY-SEVEN: *About Mr. Atley, Who Was Better Than a Cash Register; Mr. Breese, Who Prayed to Grand Pianos; and the Heckling of Henry Adams, with Other Items Which May Have Added to the Burden of Mary Turner*

MR. ATLEY entrenched himself behind a glass counter full of the small parts of instruments, mouthpieces, strings, bridges, keys, and interviewed Tim for twenty minutes because of a desire to appear thorough and to make it clear that he was the leading figure of the Music Box world. Before the interview was over, Tim was nearly as nervous as Mr. Atley. It was hard to keep his mind on what was being said when Mr. Atley stared at him with such emptiness and deliberate fixity that he wanted to look away to prevent a deadlock in which there could be neither speaking nor hearing. Also, Mr. Atley's hands were constantly busy with his tie or the edge of the counter, or in smoothing back the thin hair which was already glued to his scalp or flicking ash from his cigarette. Tim became so fascinated by the ash of Mr. Atley's cigarette that Mr. Atley had to repeat two questions intentionally. Mr. Atley would light a cigarette, and for a minute or two, before any noticeable ash had formed, he would remove it from his mouth every few seconds and flick the end of it rapidly, three or four times, with his little finger. Then he would forget the cigarette, and it would paste itself to his lower lip and periodically drop its ash upon his vest as he spoke. One of Mr. Atley's hands would rise mechanically and dab at the ash.

Nevertheless, the interview finally attained the crucial point with a last declaration of the position of Mr. Atley. "That being your line, partly, you could probably do quite a bit of our ordering in classical stuff, keeping in mind, of course, that it don't do to overload on such stuff. We aren't any highbrow place. The business couldn't stand that sort of thing anyhow. People don't go for it. You got to remember that. And of course," he added, after a lapse into vacancy, "of course I'll want to check over all those orders."

"Of course," Tim said.

"Now," Mr. Atley said, clearing his throat and speaking a trifle more loudly, "as to the matter of your, er, ah, salary . . ."

He ran down, and seemed to brood upon Tim. There was a suggestion in his eyes that his mind was at last in touch with his problem. Tim waited.

"In a way, of course," Mr. Atley continued, "you are something of a specialist in our line, so that . . ." He fell silent again.

"But on the other hand," he began, with new confidence, "you have no experience in salesmanship itself, so that . . ." This time he was the one who waited.

"No, that's true enough," Tim said.

"And after all," Mr. Atley said, firmly at first, "this is primarily a business. You got to remember that. So I would hardly be justified, at least to start with, in . . ."

Tim waited.

Mr. Atley unstuck his cigarette, leaving a little white tab on his lip. He sucked at the cigarette twice, quickly.

"So you can start at, let us say, a hundred . . ." He paused again, looking at Tim, but since Tim didn't feel anything about the amount thus left in the air, he didn't show anything either. Mr. Atley was disconcerted.

Finally he said, hastily, and not very clearly, "A hundred and fifteen a month."

"That's fine," Tim said. It was, after the kitty pickings.

Mr. Atley was relieved. "And now," he said boldly, making a triumphant pass at his hair, "now that you are one of us, we'll get to work, eh? Miss Turner knows nearly as much about the business as I do. She can show you the ropes. If there's anything you want to know, you just ask Miss Turner."

That, Tim discovered, should have been printed up in big

letters over the door of the glassed-in cubicle in the back corner: ASK MISS TURNER.

It's my guess that it wasn't very long before Tim added another to the burdens which "Miss Turner" carried so quietly and cheerfully, a burden which had nothing to do with the workings of the Music Box. In those, he undoubtedly lightened her load. One tour of the store was enough to tell Tim all he needed to know about the merchandise. The Music Box was small, and its stock was simple, one sample upright out front, a few radios, scarcely more than a sample stock of smaller instruments and parts, an abundance of popular records and sheet music, all of which Tim already knew only too well, and a moderate collection of what Mr. Atley called "high-class but not high-brow," including, for instance, some choir-like renditions of Stephen Foster, John McCormack's *Mother Machree*, and Fritz Kreisler playing *Ave Maria*. There was also a very small collection, five albums, to be exact, of symphony. It took Tim a little longer to master those foreign creatures, the order book, the catalogue, the charge account and the cash register, but they were all fingertip habits with Mary, and by the end of his first week, Tim was at home in the Music Box, and plotting revolution.

No, it was in another matter that he added to Mary's burdens. You can see for yourself how it was with Mary, if I cover most of the Music Box era with excerpts from a few of Tim's long letters to me. You will find other matter of at least equal importance in these excerpts, tokens of the journey of Tim Hazard up from the Empty City. In fact you will find that there is so little of Mary in both the letters and the events of this time, that you may wonder why I think she matters at all. But if you will remember what you already know about the life of Mary Turner, and imagine yourself to be Mary Turner reading these lines, and between them, I believe you will see what I mean about her burdens, anyway.

This first letter came to me some months, perhaps nearly a year, after Tim started work at the Music Box. Tim seldom bothers to date a letter, and I can't remember the exact sequence or time. Besides, it doesn't matter; it's only in their sum that the letters prove much.

No, I still don't finish any sustained work, only a lot of short studies, like notes on what I hope to do; and you know what happens to notes. I've made two more tries at the Leaves since you've been gone, but neither of them took. A falseness creeps in. I float to the surface and labor like a scholar. Perhaps it is ignorance. Perhaps it is the desperate quest of our time for a workable synthesis and a new mode, a quest reflected in the arts as certainly as it is in the daily papers. Perhaps, I tell myself, when the black dog is on me, T. Hazard hasn't it in him to do anything bigger than songs. In fact, there is our whole plight, perhaps, perhaps, perhaps. Sometimes I even blame the job.

On the whole, though, I bless that job. I enter the store in the morning full of a miserly joy about all the treasure that is stored there. There is a cardboard Spanish dancer just inside the door. She is life-size, wears a scarlet skirt, and is dancing with a toothy smile and a pair of castanets. Sometimes, when I've been thinking about something else, she startles me, but I always greet her, "Ah, good morning, Señorita." Mary Turner is back in the office, preparing her mathematical engines for the day. I greet her also. If Mr. Atley is there at such an hour, I greet him. On exceptionally fine mornings, I may even yell down the stairs at Mr. Breese, and wait with a hand behind my ear for his grunt. I hang up my coat and pause to look about and gloat. All about me is material of great spiritual promise. Mary and I have won a slow revolution.

You remember the Music Box as it was. Well, now the one off-center phonograph behind the counter has been replaced by three listening booths under the balcony in the back. In the balcony itself, which used to be a kind of catch-all, there gleam the dark mahogany of a concert grand, the curves of a matronly cello and the golden bell of a big horn. In front of the booths there is a little lounge, with wicker furniture, ash stands, an up-right piano and the radios. I've come to regard this nook as mine, for I often work there at night. The piano is better than mine, the room warmer after closing time, and I am backed by a comfortable library of my trade. Sometimes I'm still there when daylight comes in the show windows, and I dash home for a shave and a cup of coffee before the store opens.

It is in that library that the most important change has been made. Mr. Atley, a financial ritualist to the bone, had a system: ten demands for a given recording before he would stock it. Gradually we have tormented him over into a philosophy of propinquity, and the little tags upon the well-filled shelves, and the new cardboard faces above, remind us of the difference. Along with Pops. Orch. and Pops. Voc., appear tags reading Symphony, Concerto, Ballet S., Chamber M., Opera Voc., etc., and we may contemplate, among the Vallee waves, Jolsen grins and mustaches upon a moon, the intent, cerebral countenances of Rachmaninoff and Heifitz, the leonine dome of Beethoven, the bejowled nudity of Sibelius and the wistful hairiness of little father Grieg, just for instance. Do you wonder I rub my hands?

Also, we're a very smooth-working combination here, having fallen into our departments by nature. I take care of the music, Mary of the business, Mr. Breese of the mechanics, and Mr. Atley of the money.

I've underrated Mr. Atley because he is a man who droops, inwardly and outwardly, the flesh, the garb, the glance and the soul, and I fear my coming has aggravated this unhappy tendency. He will stand in one place and stare at Mary or me for five minutes without seeing us. I think of Ling Choy; I think of Lawrence. How can there be such vast differences in immobility? Then he will remember that he is visible, start slowly away in one direction, come about with falterings, like an ill-handled sailing vessel, go off sideways upon his new tack, and bring up before the shelf of dance-band albums, which he will carefully rearrange into exactly their original order. It is terrible to behold. And yet he has one genius. He never forgets what a good customer has bought. Enter, for the first time in two months, Mrs. Brown with a bulging handbag. At once he lights up, the way a nickel lights up a pin-ball machine, and you can hear him working inside, "Mrs. Brown, March third, eight-

een dollars, seventy-eight cents, Sibelius Fourth, Stokowski, Philadelphia, Columbia; Taylor-Millay, King's Henchman, songs from, Tibbett, Victor; etc." He will recall the non-financial items aloud, a bit at a time, apropos Mrs. Brown's new interests. Mrs. Brown, encouraged to be so remembered in a forgetful world, will buy also three items she didn't intend to and depart with flags flying. Click, the last ball drops, and Mr. Atley's lights go dead. Without Mrs. Brown, he won't remember a single item.

Old Mr. Breese is our troll, our Vulcan below. He hates light. On a sunny day he comes scuttling in, squinting through his bifocals, muttering through his mustache, his cap pulled so far down on his nose that he has to throw his head back to see where he is going, and at once plunges down into the gloom. Down there he crawls around happily inside phonographs and radios, strewing their internal organs over the floor and diagnosing ailments and damning the owners. I suspect that his soul will prove a set of directions for the Lord on overhauling and restoring to divine condition the wiring and the cogs of Lester Breese. I could be wrong, though. He is reverent toward grand pianos. Whenever we have one on the floor, he will stop and run his calcified old hand gently along the top, and sometimes even open the keyboard and finger his way delicately up it, making never a sound, and peering angrily through the top half of his glasses once in a while, to be sure he isn't caught making love. Also, when he goes out to tune a piano, there is a detached look of dedication on his face, though, since he never speaks from out such rapture, we can't be sure that he contemplates anything more than a mechanically perfect action.

Mary Turner keeps a T-square order in her glass fort which not even Mr. Atley's mumbulous fumbling can long disturb, and does it almost dreamily, without becoming in the least like a filing index or a blotter herself. We often lunch together, when we can get off at the same time, and we form a kind of humorous alliance against Mr. Atley, muttering, "What's this doing here?" about something he just put there, or "In God's name, Miss Turner, can't you ever remember where we keep anything?"

Best of all, though, in this new and orderly life, I work much more steadily, and my appetite for being and for music is constantly refreshed. At six o'clock the store closes. Mary and I lock up, I say good night to her, and go forth shouting, "The night is mine." I walk upon the streets and look at all the lights and hum a song. I go to Ling's and slowly drink his tea and ponder happily the problem of his secret, the music within his silence, the gentle, perpetual motion within his immobility. Has he learned the master secret we all seek, and found it so small and simple that he is always amused, though kindly, by the antics of the rest of us? That's my guess. When I'm tired or discontented, or have failed after hours at the writing, I go to Ling's as much to sit in his monstrous and placid presence as to drink his healing draft. It seems to me it would be a fine thing to be Ling, to sit upon that stool for hours, contemplating the outward and sufficient order of his business, and the inward, simple secret. How full of life I would always be, storing it like that, instead of pouring it out forever in evil forms! I go to Ling's when I am going to work that night.

Or I go to Benner's and take an hour over supper, and every man there is a fine man, and doing a strange and interesting work in some corner of the multiple world, a world I yearn to know completely. Or I walk uptown under the quiet trees, peering curiously at every house where my unknown friends are having supper, and come onto the hill at sunset, and go along the alley and rap at the back door and am at once and tremendously rewarded. Helen calls, "Come in, idiot, or there won't be any steak left." I go in, and Lawrence rises and takes my hand as if I were just back from Africa, and says, "Timothy, how are you?" so much the way his father used to that I almost laugh, and gets a can of beer for me, and there is really plenty of steak left. Sometimes I stay all night. They give me the earth room, and there is a new picture of Lawrence's on the wall, and a book that I really want to read on the box beside the bed, and outside the window is the aspen.

From another letter, most of which was about a trip to Virginia City with Lawrence and Helen, comes this excerpt:

Mary Turner is certainly a kind and considerate person. I'm always being surprised by new evidences of how constantly she thinks about others. I suppose my surprise arises in part from the fact that we really see so little of each other, except when working together, when our minds are on something else, that I'm still more likely to think of her in terms of our childhood than in terms of what she is now, so that she seems chiefly a pleasant link with the past. I hate to think what the store would be like without her. She reminds me of my mother in the way, with no particular method that I can see, she holds together our trio of wholly discordant males. She does an inordinate amount of work for Mr. Atley after hours, a lot of it private business. It's hard to find anything to do for Mr. Breese, but she discovered the one thing. He smokes a peculiarly stinking brand of pipe tobacco, fortunately rare, Calgary Roper, or something of that sort, and is always running out of it, and unable to get any. Mary hates the smell he makes, but she found out where she could order the stuff, and always has a packet on hand for him. The thing she started doing for me touched me in an almost sentimental way, though I had to put a stop to it before she tired herself out. It started one night when I stayed on at the store to work. The idea was hot, and I didn't want to wait to eat supper. I thought I'd get things safely under way, and then go out and eat and come back. But you know how such plans work. I didn't get out. About ten o'clock, Mary came by, going home from a show, and saw me in there. She brought me in a milkshake and a ham sandwich. She did things like that several times, even bringing me in a snack at midnight or one o'clock in the morning. Sometimes, when I had a score ready for it, she would stay and work at making the ink transcript for me. She was very good at it, incidentally, her copy being a sight more legible than mine. But I couldn't have her wandering around all hours of the night, just to help me with my personal, and to date rather fruitless, work. Besides, you know how it is; you don't like to have anybody else around when you're working. Sometimes you want to sing to clear something up. Sometimes you want to get up and walk around and mutter and tear your hair, so to speak, and it cramps your style to have company, even as quiet as Mary. In a way I hated to ease her out, though. I think maybe she's lonesome. I don't know much about her private life, but it doesn't seem to me that she goes many places or has kept many friends, in an active way. But still, typing for Mr. Atley or copying score for me would hardly fill that bill.

And I suspect that there must have been some outward reflection, for Mary, from the following short bit out of a letter largely about some occasional piano-recitation numbers he was doing at the Latin Club, and about the other entertainers there.

Apparently an old ghost lurks in me yet. I've thought many times that I ought to write to Rachel Wells to tell her how much better the store job is working out for me, but have put it off because I always have such bad luck with letters to her, and because it's been so long now, anyway, that it seems foolish. She's probably forgotten the matter. But last night I made another try, only to find the same old trouble, a tendency to say thank you in a ten-thousand-word revival of the past. The funny thing was how it got started. A woman came into the store wanting a vocal of Moonlight and Roses. I rummaged around in dusty back corners, and actually found her one, and played it for her. Then, when I was going home from work, I thought I saw Rachel come out of a store some way ahead of me. It stopped me, stopped my feet and stopped my breath. I was full of idiotic confusions and hopes. She came by me, and wasn't Rachel at all, of course.

The next excerpt is long, for one dealing chiefly with abstractions, even though Tim's manner is hardly Hegelian, but I believe the reason for including it will be self-evident.

You know how often I have pored over The Education of Henry Adams *as over a gospel. I mistrust the systematic philos-*

ophers, who, like Kant, take wing from the ultimate cliff, or, like Spinoza, base their whole structure on the dubious premise that the mutable world of idea and being is governed by the arbitrary laws of geometry. I mistrust the standard historians as men who present the inscrutable, slightly molded by their personal bias, not as inductions to thought, like honest story-tellers, but as the facts about mankind. Hence my admiration of Adams, who reminds you at every turn, "This is Adams thinking," reveals to you, as part of his history, the daily and human sources of his thought, and far from coercing life into a shape that would please himself, leaves the Education unfinished, saying that when blind, dynamic forces move outward in a thousand directions, it is impossible to determine at what point, if any, they will draw together. Besides, I've felt some likeness between Adams and Hazard, which makes me hope to discover a valuable personal lead among his many leads. To mention only the most important points, I share his belief that the Dynamo is a fitting symbol for our time, his disbelief that such a symbol can ever prove a sufficient focus, an idol, for humanity, and his great desire to discover the sufficient idol, the goal of pilgrimage, such as he conceives the Virgin to have been in her day. So I return to Adams often, as to a twentieth-century father confessor, who may be trusted, at least, to reveal me to myself in my time, and not stop my mouth with ancient clay and close my eyes with Roman coppers. Yet, this last time I read him, I really squabbled with him.

I hadn't read the Education for a long time, and probably a good many day-by-day indecipherables contributed to the change between us, but there were two unquestionable factors. I had looked up Adams, and learned about the loss of his wife and his sister, and I felt that in his great sorrow, but also not a little because of a caste pride, he had cheated when he left them out of the Education. It was a small cheat considering the scale of his quest, but a big one considering what he had set out to do, present himself as the lens through which we twentieth-century infusoria were to be observed. Secondly, the last time I'd read him, I had been well down in the dumps. It was back before I *quit the Northern Lights, I think. This time I was feeling good. I had just finished a piece of work, a little atonal study, in which I believed I had even gone beyond a lucky catch, and made a discovery. I got back to my room early, took a stiff work-out, so my mind would quit celebrating, and a cold shower, and flopped on my bed to read awhile. The* Education *was handy, so I picked it up and began to read in the last section, where he discusses the divergent forces more generally and directly than anywhere else, searching for that unifying principle he hoped might close the book with a victory.*

Immediately I became, as usual, an A.C. between the Virgin and the Dynamo. I can never open the Education *without thinking about the* Mont St. Michel and Chartres *too. Pretty quick I saw that I was quarreling with him, instead of discussing as with myself. I would read a sentence or two, an idea, and flit back over the wire to his beloved twelfth and thirteenth centuries, and squawk.*

"To speak real, Adams, who was your Virgin of Chartres but that highly unvirginal Blanche of Castile? And who were all those meager, elongate, spiritless saints, martyrs and apostles who, in the mass, made beautiful her porches, save her equally unsaintly relatives and henchmen?

"O.K., Adams, all hail to your anonymous masons, architects, and glassmakers, and to the devotion which led them not to skimp even the darkest, highest corner. But why are they anonymous?

"How do you know how the people felt, Adams? All the records were left by the crowns, the cowls and the helmets, the crosiers, the scepters and the swords, and they didn't seem to find anything in the people worth talking about.

"Which leads us to another point, Adams. Why did the Virgin outshine her son in that age of 'dignity and unity'? Because of a hunger for compassion, you say. Why does anybody get hungry for something, Adams?

"And besides all the details, Adams, weren't you a mite arbitrary in nominating the Virgin, even for her century? If you had looked around as far as you did when you picked the

Dynamo, wouldn't she have become just a kind of local saint, the symbol of one of those same multiple forces? Whose stone were they kissing in Mecca then, Adams? What were the Himalayan bells saying? How did they pray in the Ghettos? And how about the other places, Adams? Up the Nile and the Congo and the Amazon; in the Andes and the Mexican valley, and on the North American plains? Weren't you staking on a sentimental favorite?"

So I heckled the unhappy old gentleman.

I saw what I was doing, and was ashamed. I put the book down and tried to find out why I was assuming this air of superiority toward a man of such great intelligence, integrity and experience. I came upon a number of hints.

Why did Adams fall in so easily with the contempt of his English political friends for Abraham Lincoln? If you will picture Adams condescending to Lincoln, there are a great many things said. For one thing, and it is nuclear, Lincoln, the compassionate skeptic, was a living disproof that the thirteenth-century peasant boy, standing before the stained-glass Virgin, experienced an intensity of emotion of which the modern is incapable. For that matter, why go to Lincoln? I've seen dozens of kids look at new cars the same way.

Why did Adams feel he had failed because he didn't go to the top in politics, when his teaching and his writing exerted an influence far beyond that of any politician save those few, like Lincoln, about whom the people's legend accumulates?

Again, why weren't Adams' wife and sister in the Education?

Why, all through the two great books, is there nothing about a mountain, a river, a tree, a flower, a bird, fish, snake, animal, star, unless they're in stained glass? How, for instance, could Adams wander all over the tremendous west and tell us nothing but what he had thought in Washington, D. C.?

Above all, why is his reconstruction of a feudal age he couldn't experience so enticing and so full of vital and colorful people, when the course of his own life in the most dynamic era of his nation reveals practically no feeling about place or people save a late, mild pity for other disillusioned diplomats of his

427

own age and caste? Yes, that might be just the point he's mak-
ing about the Virgin and the Dynamo, but it might, and much
more easily, be something else.

So I told Adams one more thing, in order that I should re-
member it myself. "Adams," I said, "your trouble, after all,
wasn't that you wanted too big and too soon. You really wanted
the past, Adams, and not enough to go around. You didn't want
out, Adams; you wanted in."

And I asked him one last nasty question.

"Adams, weren't you in love with a stained-glass Virgin?"

That letter is of the greatest importance in the story of the
loves of Timothy Hazard, and yet, for all his identification, I
wonder if he read himself as well as he read the unhappy old
scholar from Boston. I wonder, for instance, what Mary Turner
would have thought about stained-glass Virgins. Or, for that
matter, what she did think about them. Rachel Wells had been
a very good friend of hers in high school, and she had known
Marjory Hale, too.

CHAPTER THIRTY-EIGHT: *In Which the Lives
of Timothy Hazard and Lawrence Black
Become Practically One, Helen Assumes a
Hundred Forms, and Jeremiah Goes into
the Desert*

EVEN before Tim had come to final grips with Henry
Adams, Lawrence Black, sitting in the cabin in the Peavine
Quarter, sitting on a high stool by the window of his darkened
studio and looking out on the roofs of Reno in the moonlight,
had begun to read with desperate seriousness in the Education
of Lawrence Black, or was it in Mt. Peavine and St. Mary's in
the Mountains?

Tim had sensed the first signs, of course. Sometimes, when he came in, there would be an emptiness in the green room of the cabin. Helen would be too quick, inattentive and cheerful. Lawrence would be possessed by a new silence, which set him apart while Tim and Helen played chess or listened to records or talked, a silence no longer receptive, but resistant, filling the room like the ceaseless spinning of a huge motor, too far off to be heard, but on the same foundation. There was a difference in the way Lawrence played with something in his hand, a silver dollar, a round, volcanic pebble from Death Valley. Tim and I had called these toys the grain in the oyster, as if Lawrence's ideas grew about them, layer by layer. Now they were merely distractions. Yet these signs had been so intangible, so often rubbed out by meetings as good as the early best, that Tim had never let them accumulate into a meaning. It was too important to him that the cabin on the alley should go on being the same place forever.

It was Helen, of course, who made him add them up. Lawrence mistrusted an arbitrary decision, or even a definition. His world, moral and external, was fluid, and he preferred to let the inevitable evolve. It was one night at the Latin Club, a little dance-and-eat place with a floor show and a couple of twenty-one tables, that Helen, in her own way, did the addition for Tim.

Tim had been playing at the Latin Club now and then for three or four months, taking over piano interludes in the dinner music, and sometimes putting on a piano-talkie act with the floor show. It was an arrangement he liked. It brought him in some extra money and gave him a change of mind, and there was nothing regular about it. If he dropped in during the evening, they'd put him on if there was a spot, or they'd call him up at the store when they needed him. He had started by accident one night, filling in for the pianist while the band was resting, and doing something he'd always wanted to do, a malicious take-off on dinner music, in which he carried on, above his own piano playing, which seemed to be the usual idle medley, the loud greetings and vacant conversation of one table after another, interlarded with a savage monologue of the pianist's thoughts. The act was popular, and he'd done it several times since, differently each time, and added the one about picking honky-tonk dance numbers, and another, the history of a divorcee (with piano commentary from a wedding march to *Crazy Over Horses*) who, coming to Reno lonely and heart-broken, had been amazed to discover how friendly everybody was, the man who found her a house, the man who brought her an automobile, the men who showed her the town and kept her from brooding, the lawyer who understood perfectly how she would always love her husband, though there were certain beastly things about him which made it impossible to live with him, who, in fact, was so restored to her faith in mankind by all this generous attention that in the end she decided to go back to her husband because anyway it would take ten years, at the alimony she had requested, to pay for the house, the car, the understanding and all the attentions which had accumulated while she was not brooding.

He was doing the Loving Divorcee the night Helen came in with a couple he didn't know, and took a small table back by the wall. He had been writing almost every night, and hadn't seen Helen or Lawrence for more than a week. When the band took over, and the couple at her table worked their way out onto the floor, he went over and sat down with Helen.

"How's it been going?" he asked.

"Fine, just fine," Helen said fiercely, and tossed her head.

Tim looked at her, and then at the table. It was hard to come out of the fool mood of those monologues so fast. "I've been meaning to come up, but . . ."

"I'm not at the cabin any more," Helen said. "I've got a job. I moved down to the Allbright Apartments to be near my job."

Finally Tim asked, "What are you doing?"

"At present," Helen said, very distinctly, and with her chin up, "I press the dingus on a cash register at Arley's, but I'm planning a future." That seemed to be all she was going to say.

"Is Lawrence up there now?" Tim asked.

"I don't know where Lawrence is," Helen said, the same way.

"I came home three nights ago, and found a note on the kitchen table. He's gone away to think." She stared at Tim angrily, and blinked hard, and tossed her hair back. "He couldn't think in the cabin because it reminded him of me. So," she said, holding one hand out, palm up, "like John the Baptist, or whoever it was, in the wilderness, or something.

"I pray the Lord my soul to keep," she said, as if it had no connection with what she had been saying. "I left a note in exactly the same spot on the kitchen table, and went to the Allbright.

"Well," she said sharply, "don't you even want to know what I said?"

"What did you say?" Tim asked.

"I said, 'Darling Saint Lawrence, I have moved to the Allbright on California to be near my cash register but it is a double bed and no matter what you think the cash register doesn't sleep there or I will come up to the cabin and cook supper with all my love, Helen.' That's what I said. And that's fair enough, isn't it?

"I got the job ages ago," she added suddenly, as if that explained everything.

Tim thought how long Lawrence would stand there in the kitchen, with the one weak light bulb hanging down behind him, reading that note.

"Oh, Tim, I don't know," Helen burst out. "Timmy, it's all kinds of things, little things, all the time, and—oh, I know it's probably mostly my fault, but . . . Tim, you know how he is. If we could have a decent quarrel, but he just sits there, looking at me and smiling, and then I yell. He makes fun of my job. He calls me 'Calculator.' He can't stand it that I'm . . . Oh," she said, pounding her knee softly and rapidly, "If he'd only say something. Timmy, I love him so goddam much. You have no idea how much," she said suddenly, her eyes filling with tears again. "But he gets me so goddam mad, and I yell all that at him, and he hates yelling, but I can't help it, and the first time I take a breath, he says, 'Hello, Calculator.' Well, somebody's got to make some money," she said fiercely, "and it's all right with me, only . . . Anne Farling," she began again. "You've met Anne Farling."

Tim shook his head.

"It doesn't matter. We went to school together. Her family and mine were old friends. We used each other's kitchen doors in the summer, up on the Cape. Anyhow, she married money too, and she's practically gilded, and she's here for the cure. I met her down at the City House. I don't care," she said, tossing her head as if Tim had argued against her. "Anne's swell, and it was like old times. You can't just forget everybody you ever knew. Anyway," she said, turning on Tim, "Lawrence isn't like that. You know he isn't. He doesn't care what anybody has. Only, maybe, just now, thinking about my family." She shrugged.

Tim realized that this was the first time he had heard anything about Helen's life before she came to Reno.

"No," he said, "that wouldn't make any difference to Lawrence."

"Maybe not," Helen said, "but—well, anyway, Anne had seen some of the portraits, and she was crazy about them. She wanted to know if he was my husband, and I was proud, goddamit, Tim, I was. Her family was painted by Stuart and Copley and Sargent, and—it isn't the money, Tim. He looks at me, thinking that . . . Tim, I don't, do I?"

"Not that I've ever noticed," Tim said.

"Oh, to hell with you too," she said, and finished her cocktail at one draught.

"What about Anne Farling?" Tim asked.

"She wanted him to do her and her boy. He's a nice kid, Tim, and beautiful. Five hundred dollars. She told me he ought to ask that much anyway, and then he'd be cheated. And you know how long it takes him. In one afternoon . . ."

"He hasn't done any portraits for a long time," Tim said.

Helen stared at him. "That's what he said."

"Well," Tim began, not knowing what he was going to say.

"But for a friend, Tim," Helen pleaded. "I took her up there myself. He used to do it for nothing, Tim, lots of times. If they like them . . . I couldn't look her in the face."

"He didn't slit her throat or anything, did he?" Tim asked.

"You bastard," Helen said, sighing. "You're both bastards, and I love you. You know how he is. She never knew what killed her. We got outside again before even I knew he wasn't going to, and she looked at me, and I could have cried. When Anne told him how much she liked that portrait of Paula that's up at Dr. Land's, he said he'd done that a long time ago, but he thought the frame and mat were as nice as any he'd ever put on."

Then Helen's friends came back, and Tim excused himself. He was bewildered and full of foreboding about Helen and Lawrence. He went home to his room. He'd meant to work, but now he just played for a little while, and then stood in the window, looking down at Ling Choy sitting there behind his half curtain.

He went up to the studio the following noon, and up to the cabin in the evening, but Lawrence wasn't back yet. It was a week later that he went by the Music Box early in the afternoon. He didn't come in, or even look in. He went by slowly, very thin and vertical in his dark flannel shirt. His face was burned almost black, so he had been out in the desert somewhere. The bright shuttle of the street in the sun moved behind him, but he didn't know it was there.

After work Tim went up to the studio again. The door was closed, but there was no sign on it, and somebody was moving about inside. Tim knocked, but there was no answer except that the moving stopped, and when he knocked again, Lawrence's voice said, "Yes? Who?" very quietly, but with something behind it Tim had never heard before. Usually he would just touch the door, and Lawrence would call, "Come."

"It's just me; Tim.'

"One moment," Lawrence said. The key rattled, and he opened the door. Tim had never known him to lock the door before, either.

"I'm just cleaning up a bit," Lawrence said. "How are you, Timothy?"

The studio looked bare, and there was a big wire waste basket in the middle of the floor, already half full of the torn pieces of portraits and studies. There were still two piles of the portraits and the photo prints of them on the draughtsman's table under the east window.

"I'll be done in a minute," Lawrence said. He smiled. "Then we'll go have a drink." He picked up four or five of the portraits together, and tore them across one way, and put the halves together and tore them across the other way, and threw the pieces into the basket and picked up another four or five. He didn't seem to be angry or in a hurry. There was only that distance between him and Tim that hadn't been there before. He hadn't wanted Tim to see him tearing up the portraits. He had wanted to get it all done, and then come and find Tim for a drink, and never say anything about it. There was nothing to do now, though, but sit there and watch him tear them. Everything else in the studio was piled up neatly, the paints and chalk and charcoal in boxes, the bottles of binder and thinner and dryer in other boxes, a portfolio and a few canvases on the floor, with cigarettes, ash trays and a pocket bottle of whisky on top of them.

When the portraits were all torn, Lawrence opened the door and picked up the heap from the floor. "Do you want to take some of these?" he asked, nodding at the boxes.

When they were on the stairs, he said, "We'll go up to the cabin and have our drink there, shall we?"

It took two trips to get all the things down. On the second Lawrence pulled the studio door shut, with the lock on. The old Cadillac was out front, covered with white dust. They loaded the things into the back, and climbed in front.

When they pulled in beside the cabin, though, there was light shining out through the vine leaves, and a smell of steak and onions coming through the back screen, and when the motor was turned off, they could hear Helen shuffling quickly about in the kitchen and humming, and sometimes singing a few words. Lawrence sat there for a moment, still holding the wheel, and looking up at the stars coming out. There was no way to guess what he was thinking, but Tim suddenly felt that it was more beautiful up here in the alley, with the last of the sunset dying between the houses, than anywhere else in the world.

Some time that winter, though, one of his letters included this:

I'm afraid you're only too right about what Lawrence doesn't say in his notes to you. Helen seldom goes up to the cabin now. She has a new job with a real-estate company that's cutting up the south side, and out of hours has become a determined woman about town. Lawrence buries himself at the cabin for days at a time. He eats almost nothing, and the pint whisky bottle is always out on his table. He calls it his father confessor, and says that without it the world would be intolerably clear. He reads Swedenborg, Havelock Ellis and The Golden Bough, *but the book that is always out beside his bed is that little, leather pocket copy of Buddha. Helen protests almost tearfully that she could keep them going, if Lawrence would let her, and would work happily and stop knifing her about her jobs. But he can't. I think he is constantly mistaking the tread of his own enormous conscience for a following of mockers. Helen knows this, and cries at me that Lawrence must sell his work, but with him she will only repeat praise for things he has already sold. He won't believe that it isn't the money she wants, but himself as he used to be, and she can't see that he must sell only what seems to him good, that an arbitrary decision of any sort would be fatal to him now. And intervention, my friend, is futile. I made the mistake of trying to tell them about each other. You know Helen. When she is steamed up there are no neutrals in her mind. "Oh, damn you, Tim," she said. "You're another." Lawrence listened to me for a time, with a faint gleam of malice, and then said, "How about a little game of chess, Hazard?" So I keep quiet, and we play chess, or I get out the guitar and imitate Segovia on Bach very badly, or Gomez on the tarantella not quite so badly. Helen moves outward fiercely, and Lawrence sits there in the green room and moves softly in-*

ward. Helen greets me brightly and sharply in passing, or occasionally reveals to me, defensively, a past of pink-coated fox hunters and Parisian sojourns I had never suspected, and later probably wishes she hadn't. Lawrence accepts me most of the time as a not unpleasant shadow circling afar in the fluid universe about him, but sometimes the vast distances will dissolve, and he will be sitting there, a few feet from me, staring at me quietly, and judging me, without a word, to be among the impatient mockers. There is no answer I can make. The real war is going on, not between Lawrence and Helen, but within Lawrence himself, and its peace, whether by solution or dissolution, may emerge only slowly, according to his master dictum. When we are twenty moves into the chess game, his hand will hang poised above his beloved queen like the bill of a diving bird, and he will smile across the board at me, and apologize by repeating this dictum, "Everything will work out in time." He does not mean this loosely, or as a mere put-off. He means just what he says. He has faith in time. I'm afraid of it.

Probably the fact that Lawrence had to sell the old Cadillac had something to do with the purchase of Jeremiah. Tim introduced Jeremiah to me this way.

I have at last fallen among the legless plutocrats, and bought a car. Yet I haven't altogether deserted my kind, for he is a very old car, high-wheeled, low-nosed, topless, grumpy and sturdy, a car I'm proud to be seen with, who hides his multiple histories from none, and shows forth wherever he passes, his faith in ultimate oneness. Originally he was a respectable black. Next he became an electric blue. Then he fell into the hands of some high-school kid, who finished off several used cans on him, green, yellow, red, purple. His last owner before me, a prospector, reduced his gears to a comfortable limberness and gave him one thin all-over wash of gray, which softened his emerging pasts without concealing them. The result is a work of the Master Cartographer of Tomorrow, continents and islands, nations and principalities, clear to be seen in their shapes, but in happy redistribution, obviously without regard to politics, creed, economic pressure or any other known form of prejudice. I call him Jeremiah, for, lo, he driveth me from the sinks of iniquity, chasteneth my flesh upon the way, drowneth mine idle babble, and leadeth me to meditation in the wilderness. Also, we have managed between us to carry Lawrence into the wilderness several times, where at least he may brood in the sun, until the pebble turns more slowly in his hand.

Later that winter, troubled by the cryptic gloom of Lawrence's notes, I asked Tim to write me about the painting. He wrote me some twenty pages about it, but these bits will serve.

It is the dark region with him, all right, and full of fitful marsh lights. He tries everything. He has cast a model for a new dollar, designed signs for two clubs, done a mural for another, a letterhead for a mining company, and a wall map of the bright spots for a hotel. He won an award on the coast for the first sculptural piece he has ever done, a woman's head carved from, of all materials, tufa. "It took only one night to do it," he says, "with a monkey wrench and a screwdriver, and some day the thing will dissolve into lovely dust. I wasn't even sure it would get there this time. I imagined them carefully, patiently working down through all that crating, and finding a cupful of tufa dust. The Spirit of the Heights, *by Lawrence Black. Wouldn't that have puzzled them?" The idea pleased him. He sat there smiling, thinking about the astonished museum people staring at the "cupful of dust." He has done a score of other momentary things....*

All this must sound as if he were scattering himself cynically. Actually he tries only once in a while, at long intervals, to make things that will sell, and then they're always things which won't cut the main stem. Main stem is not just a figure of speech. I went up to the cabin one night, and there he was thumb-tacking scraps of paper on a piece of wall board which covered one whole side of the earth room. The scraps were an amazing collection, birthday cards, Fisher Body ads, cartoons, pieces of

*wall paper, photos of ball-bearings, magazine illustrations, I
don't know what all, mixed in with prints of Da Vinci, El
Greco, Velasquez, Van Gogh, Picasso, Braque, a hundred
painters. He had a wad of these pictures in his hand still, and
scores more were strewn over the cot. On the wall board he had
drawn the trunk and wide-flung branches of a tree, on which
these pictures hung like leaves. The trunk was still so broad at
the top of the board that one could imagine it going on up
through the roof. Out at the end of each branch, he had printed
a single word, Camera, Abstraction, Sentimentality, Commercial, etc. It wasn't a history. There seemed to be a kind of time
sequence on the main stem, Botticelli, Buonarroti, Leonardo,
Rembrandt, El Greco, up to a garish, angular Picasso with a
question mark beside it. But this order disappeared on the
branches. There was Raphael part way out a branch which
ended in a lacy valentine and the word Cuteness. There was
Hogarth well out a branch to Mutt and Jeff. Lawrence calls
this chart the Tree of Intentions. He plays with it a great deal,
changing the leaves, adding new ones, putting things in his
pocket for it wherever he goes. And certainly some startling
alliances become visible there. Take the limb out to Camera, for
instance. . . .*

*He is also putting all the little technical devices he has been
working on into a kind of exercise book for skills and mastery
of materials. He calls the exercises his Turtles. . . .*

*Still, you know Lawrence wouldn't trust deeply in such con-
scious exploration. His real search goes on in a region as twilit
and instinctive as his brooding. Actually, in the work which
fills hour after hour of his days, and his nights too—well, as
Helen said to me after she had been up there one night, "But all
those misty women, Tim. What . . ." and waved her hand helplessly. Anyway, when I stay up at the cabin now, I get the
green room. Lawrence takes the cot in the earth room, which
has gradually become his studio. Nearly all of the paintings,
and the majority of the dark chalk studies he does in there are
of the women, or the woman. Some of them don't live an hour
after he's painted them. Some last a week or two, in stacks*

against the wall. A few, three or four at a time, will hang a little longer where he can look at them. None of them ever gets out to anybody else. He will talk only about technical points in them, as if they meant nothing else, about a lucent flesh tone here, a warmth and profundity of shadow there, a luminous underglow. Possibly it is not safe to say more, yet they are all related, these women, and by more than details of craft. They are all lovely, weightless, serene—not happy, but serene, and secret. They emerge only partially from a great profundity of shadow. As I said, it is always twilight, late twilight. I come in out of bright sunlight in the alley, and go into the room where these women are hanging, and they are emerging from a twilight. Or perhaps they are not emerging at all. Perhaps they are retreating into that mysteriously moving darkness. There is one of them. . . . And there is something of Helen in every one of those women. They are not portraits, of her or of anyone else, but she is in them all. She was in that tufa head, too, come to think of it. There those women glimmer in their own dusk, and in the real dusk from the alley too, like moths in the edge of a wood. There is one of them still on the easel, nearer the window. They possess the place. Yet Lawrence steps back from the canvas and looks at it for a minute, moves to one side and looks at it again, then sits down beside me, wiping the thumb with which he has been working back through to the face and shoulder, and says softly, "That over-paint is too grainy. It smudges. I wonder what solvent . . ."

CHAPTER THIRTY-NINE: *In Which the Waters Without Time Are Viewed from a Cave*

IN THE next August there came a couple of weeks when Tim was hopeful about Lawrence and Helen again. This time began one Saturday afternoon, when Lawrence came into the Music Box, which was a sign in itself. Tim had seen little more of him than he had of Helen since early spring.

439

Tim was standing at the front window, staring into the street. The scalloped edge of the awning danced and snapped in the wind, and now and then the windshield of a car at the crossing flashed like a heliograph. He had been restless since the long evenings began that spring. He had stopped writing and begun to take long walks by himself after work. He had thought of Eileen Connor. He was fed up with the store, and he had quit playing at the Latin Club because his act had gone bad on him, heavy and angry. He wondered if Eileen still sang with the band at Venice, and thought of hooking on there again. He could get up to Hollywood from there, and hear some of the Bowl concerts. He was hungry for symphony fresh from the strings and the horns. Then he had thought he'd take his vacation in July, hearing the concerts in the Bowl, and the morning rehearsals too. He'd changed his mind about that when he began thinking about Rachel Wells on his walks. He would pass her house, where somebody else was living now, or walk along the river, where he could look across the water at the shadows on the tennis courts under the big cottonwoods, and he would begin to think about Rachel, and even to tell himself stories again. He would imagine how it would really be to meet Rachel again. He found her on a street in San Francisco, and she cried, "Oh, Tim," as if her breath were as short as his own, and held out both hands to him. He came upon her at the edge of the little lake. The lights of his celebration for Rachel Wells would rise quickly and spread wondrously among the trees beside the river. In one moment the futile burdens of multiplicity would fall from him. Then he would perceive that he was voyaging among the enchanted isles again, and he would smile. Nevertheless, he became possessed by the notion that he must finish the trembling leaves before anything else could stir in him, and by the old St. Francis feeling that what he needed to bring it alive was time at the little lake. It would be best at the little lake in the autumn, when there was a stillness of the year too.

He was thinking, as he stood in the window, about undergoing this quiet reincarnation. There was no one else in the store except Mary. He could hear Mary at her typewriter in the shining cubicle behind him. In late September, or even October, when the aspens were yellow in the canyons, he would take his two weeks and go up there with just his food and blankets, a pipe, some paper, and maybe one book of the right kind, like *Green Mansions*. He turned, with the slight impatience that always came now, to serve the customer.

"How are you, Woolworth-Gershwin?" Lawrence said. "Could we have a beer somewhere?" Lawrence never wanted to talk in the store.

"A resurrection," Tim said.

He told Mary they were going out, and they crossed the street in the glare of the sun and the smell of dust in the wind. In the shadowy club they got their beers at the bar and took them into a booth.

"When does your vacation come?" Lawrence asked.

"Any time. I was thinking October, maybe."

"It would be swell at Pyramid now," Lawrence said.

Tim thought of the arc of beach behind the Pyramid, and the tufa castle at the top of the beach, like a desert watch tower against the brown wall of the mountain behind it. That was where the three of them had always gone. The Pyramid was the most important member of the company there. You didn't think about it often, but it was part of everything you thought. Sunrise began with a light on the peak of the Pyramid. You measured the stretching midday indifference of the lake by the Pyramid. The premonition of night emanated from the Pyramid. Its shadow darkened the still channel late in the afternoon, and then pushed slowly up the terraces of white sand, like an enormous prow, but silent. Behind the Pyramid was the heart of silence and time.

"It would be swell," Tim said.

"If you were to take your vacation now," Lawrence said, "we could go out tonight. There's a moon tonight. I'd like to see the moon on Pyramid. When do you get off work?"

"Nine o'clock."

"The stores will be closed then."

"I'm off an hour at six," Tim said. "I'll get the stuff then."

"No," Lawrence said. "We'll get it together. I've been thinking about going to Pyramid for weeks. We can't go into a thing
like that lightly. There's beer, steak, dozens of eggs, coffee,
bacon, pork and beans, raviolas, asparagus tips." He made a
long, affectionate list of the green delicacies for which he hun-
gered. "And bourbon," he said, "and plenty of ice. We'll be
there fourteen days. Maybe we'll never come back."

It was wonderful to hear him so pleased.

"I've got the wood all piled, and the water kegs filled," he
said. "I'll take Jeremiah and load him this afternoon, and at six
o'clock we'll do the food together."

"Swell," Tim said.

They drank beer and considered this voluptuous idleness.

"And it's on me," Lawrence said.

"Nonsense. I'm . . ."

"It has to be."

"At least dutch," Tim said.

"No. There's money I have to spend. I've paid the rent and
the back bills, and bought colors, and still there's money. I took
it all to the bank and got it changed into silver dollars. For three
days I have been sitting beside the kitchen table and building
it up in piles, and spinning it to hear it ring, and counting it,
and thinking exactly what we would get with it. There are
eighty-seven silver dollars, three quarters, a dime and six nickels.
I have been dreaming about a Virginia ham."

Tim stared at him.

"I did a portrait," Lawrence said. "No," he said. "In oil and
just the way I wanted to, and she took it anyway. Also there
were two pictures of the Virginia City house with the crazy
outside stairs. Chalk. They sold the afternoon I brought them
in, so I knew we were going to Pyramid."

It was while they were selecting the Virginia ham at six-
fifteen that Lawrence said, very quiet-faced, and turning the
ham upon one raised hand and studying it like a strange bit of
sculpture, "Helen's coming out for the last week. She'll bring
more ice and butter."

Tim felt so good that when the store was empty for a while

in the evening, he improvised uproariously on the piano. When Jeremiah bleated at the curb, he jumped up and went to the door of the shining cubicle.

"I'll close up," Mary said. "Have a good time."

"Mary," he said, "you're wonderful. You're always there. You are a torch in the dark and devious alleys of my life. You are the star on the hills. Mary," he declaimed, "you are the cedars of Lebanon, and I love you," and he took her face between his hands and kissed her on the mouth. Mary's hands came up from the typewriter keys, but trembled in the air, not quite touching him. He let her go. "In fact," he said exultantly, "I love everything. Even Mr. Atley."

When the blanket rolls were laid out in the old place behind the wing of fallen tufa blocks, and the ice was buried in the sand in its little cave under the separate boulder, with the beer and butter and meat against it, Tim and Lawrence went out into the open at the top of the beach and sat there with a can of beer apiece, and looked at the moonlight on the lake and on the Pyramid. It was always even better than they thought it would be. After a while Tim went back up to Jeremiah, on the ridge behind the castle, and got his guitar. He sang *Tombstone Town* wide open and quavering, so it came back to them from the Pyramid, wonderfully thin and melancholy. Lawrence liked *Tombstone Town* the best of Tim's ballads. He even grumbled along with it part of the time.

> *Tonight in Tombstone Town, I say,*
> *Somebody's going to die,*
> *When the moon comes up as bright as day*
> *And I hear my pardner's cry.*

> *In Tombstone Town last night they shot,*
> *They shot my pardner dead.*
> *He just stepped out to cross the street*
> *And they pumped him full of lead.*

Oh, a man come by on a sorrel hoss,
Said he never had a chance,
Said they shot him down in Tombstone Town
And him with empty hands.

They shot him once to kill him dead;
They shot him five times more,
So I'll have to empty one six gun
To even up the score.

The man in the bar was playing guitar
And singing a lonesome tune
When the shots rang out in Tombstone Town
By the light of the rising moon.

Oh, a man come by on a sorrel hoss,
He said it was old Maguire
And his man called Zed and his man called Red
And they all three opened fire.

My pardner called me on the trail,
Oo-lee-ay-lee-oh,
And I'd hear my pardner far away
Until they laid him low.

Now my pardner lies in a bloody sheet,
He lies on a barroom floor,
And he will hail me oo-lee-ay
By the moonlight nevermore.

Oh, a man come by on a sorrel hoss,
Said he seen him lying so,
Said he seen him laid on the barroom floor
With the red blood coming slow.

All laid out on a barroom floor
With a sheet to hide him too,
But from his head and from his heart
The red blood coming through.

Tonight in Tombstone Town, I say,
While the sad guitar does cry,
While the moon comes up as bright as day
Somebody's going to die.

The six days passed in heat and silence. Lizards skimmed the sands and balanced on the rocks. Gulls rested furled upon the steely waters. At dusk fish leapt in the channel, making sounds like flat stones thrown in edgewise. In the nights the moon shrank and steered ever nearer day.

Tim woke each morning when light touched the peak of the Pyramid, and paraded in pajama pants down to the edge of the water, bearing soap and water, brush and towel. Thigh deep in the water, which was also his mirror, he shaved, a slight motion of his conscience doing penance for the offense of his dead stubble, a sin for which he was absolved by dimension. Then, setting his razor and brush upon his folded pants, he returned slowly into the water until he floated, washed off the soap, scoured his body with sand, and played porpoise till he was limber and happy. When he came up to the rocks again, clean and holy and hymning the great day aloud, Lawrence would be crouching drowsily before the separate boulder, performing the fire rites. The great bubbles of heat broke upward in the blue shadow.

After breakfast, while the shadow shrank around them, they underwent the morning meditation. Cross-legged upon the sand, carving arabesques and equations in the air with his cigarette, Tim ranged the fields of life exuberantly. Thin and black in his white pajamas, Lawrence warmed both hands devoutly upon his coffee cup. Slowly the tide of life returned to him. The cave of his being began to reply profoundly to Tim's surf.

At last the sun would drive them into motion. They explored the hills and the shore. In the midday hours, when the sand was too hot to touch, they retired into a cave which looked out across the channel at the Pyramid, and slept or read or played chess. Every once in a while one of them would say, "How about a beer?" The other would say, judiciously, "I think we should have a beer now," and the one nearest the mouth of the cave would creep out into the glare, rise and disappear. After a couple of minutes he would come back with two cans of beer, still sweating from the ice. Then the sun would let up a little, and they would go far north along the shore to the white palisade, where the water was deep and green, and swim, and bake on the rocks. At sunset, having fed with amplitude and consideration, they would set forth two deck chairs upon the top of the beach, and sit there with pipes and tinkling highballs, feeling the cooling air play with their sunburned bodies, and watching the gulls and cormorants return to Anaho. The habit of the place came back. Lawrence spoke of Helen only once. "When she has been out here a week," he said, and left it unfinished, the way Helen would.

They heard the first faint throbbing of the launch while they were in the cave. They looked at one another solemnly, finished their beers, and went slowly down through the white glare across the white sand to the little cove at the south end of the beach. The launch always came in there because the water was deeper against the sand. Far out they could see the launch approaching with white wings of spray. Helen was perched astride the prow. The orange bandanna on her head came like a tiny ball of fire across the opalescent waters. She saw them standing there together, and flung up both arms in greeting, and they could hear her faint cry, like a gull's. The peace of the place, however, was heavy upon Lawrence and Tim, and the question came with Helen, and also the people from the ranch. Tim waved a little, but stopped quickly. Lawrence raised one hand slowly, like an Indian asking parley, and let it down again. Helen stopped waving.

There were three men and another woman in the launch. It nosed up into the sand and hung there, rocking a little. Helen let herself down onto the sand and stood looking at Lawrence and Tim, while the men began to unload the things from the launch. It looked as if Helen had come for a month. Lawrence and Tim moved down to help with the unloading. They knew two of the men. They had come across with them often, but now they spoke to them politely and charily. They said they would carry the things up to the rocks themselves. Helen cried many loud good-byes, and made promises to meet the people in Reno. When the wake of the launch had died on the cove, she confronted Lawrence and Tim. She tore off the orange bandanna and shook her mane loose.

"My God, what a reception!" she said. "I'm weak. All the cocktails and back-slapping and flowers."

"They love it," Lawrence said softly, smiling. "They love to ride around in that launch."

"They wanted a drink," Helen said. "A cold drink, and ..."

"We're glad to see you, Helen," Lawrence said.

"I'm glad to see you too, you bastards," Helen said.

"We really are, Helen," Tim said. "We've been waiting ..." He tried to explain about not wanting the others right now. Lawrence watched him, smiling.

"We've been here about a hundred years, you know," he said to Helen.

"I'll be quiet," Helen said. She picked up her sleeping bag and slung it over her shoulder. "Anyway," she said, "I've brought two cases of beer, six big steaks, five pounds of onions, three bottles of bourbon and two hundred pounds of ice."

"It's wonderful," Lawrence said, looking at the pile of stuff on the sand. "It's astonishing. But even without it ..."

"Oh, go to hell," Helen told him.

Tim couldn't look at either of them.

"The ice is melting," Helen said. "If you two Franciscans ..." and she marched away from them, up through the loose sand.

After a moment, Lawrence said, "She's brought the pressure stove. We'll take that and the steak and onions in the first load. She'll be happier cooking something. She's hungry."

"The ice is melting pretty fast," Tim said, looking under the wet gunny sacks.

"We'll take that next."

When they got up to the rocks, Lawrence set the stove up against the smudge from the fires, primed it, and laid the meat out open beside it, with a long-handled fork. Helen was standing outside the wing, looking across the lake, but she took this in.

"It's nice to be here, anyway," she said.

"It's very quiet," Lawrence said.

When they brought the next load up, Helen was turning the steaks. When they were sinking the beer from the last load against the new ice, she said, "If you two anchorites aren't fasting..." and put three steaks out on tin plates and covered them with browned onion rings. They ate silently, Helen sitting apart, in the sun. When she was done, she came back to the stove.

"I don't care," she said. "I'm going to have some more."

"I'll take care of it," Tim said, getting up.

"I wouldn't trust you," she said. "You aren't civilized."

When the extra steak was done, though, she cut it into three pieces. She gave Tim his piece first. Lawrence got up and went over to her, and she put his on his plate, and scooped onions over it. He was watching her face all the time, smiling a little, but she pretended not to notice this. Just when she was going to turn away, he said softly, with a sound of great pleasure and surprise, as if he had just seen her, "Hello, Helen." She looked up quickly to see how he meant it. "Hello, you old bastard," she said, and kissed him, and then bent down quickly to fill her own plate, so he couldn't see her face. Tim could see it, though. She was nearly crying.

Tim finished his steak quickly, and went down to the beach, and after about an hour, Helen and Lawrence came down too, and they all went swimming. It was fine among the three of them, as good as ever. Near sunset, Tim went up ahead of them, and started the stove, and pulled his bed roll around in front of the cave, and laid Helen's out in the space beside Lawrence's.

But the next morning, while they were drinking their coffee, Helen began to talk about her work. When Lawrence got out a cigarette, she worked across the sand on her knees, and held a match for him. When he had taken one drag, he rubbed her shoulder affectionately with his hand, and smiled, and said softly, "How are you this morning, Calculator?"

Helen stood up. "Oh, go fry," she said. She poured herself another cup of coffee, carried it out into the sun, and stood there with her back to Lawrence and Tim, staring around and sniffing the air like a hound. Between pulls at the coffee, she began to hum, "Through the dark of night," but then realized what the song was, dashed the rest of the coffee out onto the sand, threw the cup back into the shadow, and marched down to the firm sand at the edge of the water, and then north. Lawrence moved his deck chair out from behind the rocks and sat there, cuddling his cup, sipping the coffee like a rare liqueur, or even an elixir, and watching her. Upon her right hand the mountains loomed, silent and smoky; upon her left the lake stretched forth, silent and shimmering. The tiny point of color which was her bathing suit, dwindled, and then disappeared among the white rocks at the beginning of the palisade. A pelican appeared from behind the palisade and approached through the shining air. He cruised slowly by the Pyramid, stroking and gliding, and was at last swallowed by distance and the morning. Lawrence set his cup down gently upon the sand, rose, paced down to the beach, and also went north. It was two o'clock when they returned together. Tim was in the cave, and Lawrence stooped at the entrance and asked, "May we come in, Hazard?"

So it went the rest of the week, first one and then the other of them needling. Lawrence, out of a silence which Tim had believed amicable, asked, "And how is the old ground-hog?" which was what he called Helen's boss. They sat in a row in the night, watching the bright spraying of the meteors, Tim plucking idly at his guitar and conversing with Helen, who sat in the middle. Lawrence huddled in his chair, cherishing his beer and saying nothing. Helen and Tim were talking about the *Mona Lisa*. There was a silence, and then Helen said, "But da Vinci never married her, did he, Black?" They were in the cave, Helen stretched drowsily upon the pallet, Lawrence drawn up against the wall, with his arms about his knees, Tim seated cross-legged, reading *Seven Pillars of Wisdom* aloud. In the middle of a sentence, Helen said, "Oh, for Lord's sake, Tim, that's too much like a man, lying around brooding about his immortal soul, and doing nothing to cure it. Read something else. Read something . . ." and she waved at the mouth of the cave, to show that he should read something equal to the blazing and indifferent world outside. Tim laughed, and went out and got three beers, and when he came back, started on *The Heart of Darkness*. Lawrence didn't stir or speak, but he understood the attack. Helen never made real generalizations.

The struggle didn't stop when they were apart. Once, when Lawrence had wandered out of sight into the hills, Helen said, pleading with Tim, "He's got to be on his own, Tim. He's got to get where he doesn't have to worry. He does such beautiful things so easily, but . . . Like that oil portrait of Mrs. Emory. And then he says—you want to know exactly what he said, just this morning, before we got up? He said, 'It's all right now. There are exactly thirty pieces of silver left.' My God, Tim, he acts as if it were a crime to make money. He even acts as if it were a crime to know people who have money, or own things that cost money."

"No," Tim said, "only if the money comes first."

"Well, it's a damned common crime," Helen said, and jumped up, getting ready to leave him.

"That's right," Tim said, "and damned is the word."

But the next day, while Lawrence was sketching in the sun, down by the squaw rock, Helen and Tim swam out to the Pyramid, and walked along the wide ledge of the base into the sun, and sat down with their legs hanging over. Lawrence appeared very small from there, stripped to the waist and black with sun, standing at his easel. Feeling the Pyramid loom behind them, they felt no larger than Lawrence looked.

"Tim," Helen said.

"Yes?"

"You know it's not really the money I care about."

"I know."

"But this birds-of-the-air stuff, Tim."

"I know. I just meant the work has to come first, or a guy's no good. I think he's wrong about some of his things too. I've yelled at him that he can't wait for the final masterpiece, and that if he did, he'd only find he'd waited till the sap was dried up, and that his real best was the stuff he'd burned ten years before. But sin's in the man, you know," he said, grinning at her. "It's his work, and he can't sell what he doesn't believe in."

"Tim, if he had money?" Helen asked slowly. "If he didn't have to sell what wasn't good? Would that spoil his work?"

Tim thought about that. There was something behind it when Helen asked a question like that. He remembered the new kind of talk he had been hearing from Helen during the last year, talk about Paris, her father's crash, the art of riding hunters. He remembered the only description Lawrence had given him of a trip east to meet Helen's relatives. They had made the trip the summer Tim was down on the coast with Eileen and the band, and Lawrence hadn't mentioned it until months afterward. Sitting in the green room, palming a cigarette the way he did when he worked outdoors, Lawrence had softly and humorously described his orphaned bewilderment in a huge house where he was always meeting somebody he'd never seen before, where those he had met never remembered who he was, where he fell over all kinds of dogs on stairways and in shadowy halls, and where everybody wore boots to breakfast and evening clothes to dinner, and in the evening the vast living room was filled with neighing. "There was one old gentleman, however," Lawrence had said, "with whom I formed a defensive alliance. He also was merely a husband in the family, though I was never sure whose husband. Everybody just called him Uncle Ned, and rode on over him. Uncle Ned rescued me from the porch full of potted plants, where I had concealed myself. He propelled me into a big study, saying, 'Young man, come in here, where there isn't some goddam horse sticking his head in every window.' We sat in the study and drank. Uncle Ned had a fine rum shine, like old rosewood. Much later I heard him saying in the amicable fog, 'The dirty brute tossed me into a mud hole and broke my shoulder, and then kicked me in the shin as he left, so I told my wife that from there out, if I couldn't share her bed without a horse, she was a widow. I was a liar. Do you know my wife, young man? But how would you? She's the biggest one, the one that looks like Man o' War.' "

Tim smiled, remembering the portrait of Uncle Ned.

"Would it?" Helen asked.

"He wouldn't go at it any differently," Tim said.

He believed Helen had meant to tell him something, but after that answer, she studied him for a moment and said, "Let's climb the Pyramid." So they climbed. The wind was coming up, and when they stopped to rest and gaze down at the surface of the water, they could hear it playing a score of soft, hollow tones around them. On the top it struck them cool and strong, coming out of the north-west. The lake was rippling finely before it, in long curves. From that height Lawrence and his shadow were one dark point upon the beach, but when they waved and he replied, the shadow also raised an arm.

Nevertheless, after each brief duel there was a reconciliation, and all week the intervals of peace became longer and the power of the city became less. On the way home Sunday night, they loudly sang *Tombstone Town* as a trio, and then Tim sang the narrative of another of his ballads, *The Sweet Promised Land of Nevada*, and Helen and Lawrence bore down lustily with him upon the chorus:

> *Oh, this is the land that Moses shall see;*
> *Oh, this is the land of the vine and the tree;*
> *Oh, this is the land for my children and Me,*
> *The sweet promised land of Nevada.*

Helen went back to the cabin with Lawrence that night, and the next day she borrowed Jeremiah and moved her things up.

TIM didn't visit the cabin until the following Sunday, and then he found Lawrence alone. He was in the earth room, working. The shadowy women were gone from the wall. The canvas on the easel was nearly covered by voluminous, dark hills, rolling and rising like the slate-colored clouds which shadowed them. A tiny, white pyramid stood at the foot of the hills, bright as a spearhead, caught in a pale light that shot down from a rift in the clouds. The light lay more softly upon the slope behind the pyramid, dimmed outward and was lost. Helen, Lawrence said, not turning from the easel, not stopping his brush, had gone to Beverly Hills for a week. Her uncle was very sick, the friendly uncle with the rum shine. Lawrence went on painting, slowly and silently, for an hour. Then he put down his brush without looking at the canvas again, and went into the kitchen and got two beers, and they went out into the yard with the little aspen, and sat in the sun. It was warm down behind the fence, out of the wind, but there was a feeling of autumn in the air. Lawrence talked quietly, an idea at a time, with long pauses, about the difficulties of painting the size of Pyramid Lake.

For three weeks after that, every time he went up, Tim found the same note on the cabin door. He was eating supper at the counter at Benner's when he next saw Lawrence. He looked up, and Lawrence was sitting on the stool beside him, smiling a little, as if he had been there a long time before Tim noticed him. In spite of that smile, Tim was frightened. He had never seen Lawrence looking like that before. His face was covered by a heavy stubble of black beard, the blue cotton suit was wrinkled and soiled, and there were still paint stains around his nails and in the wrinkles of his knuckles. His eyes were strangest, though, enormous, weary and unseeing, blind from within. Tim tried to get him to eat some supper, but he wouldn't. He said, gently, that there was so little but rum in his system that he would have to taper back onto food very gradually.

Then he said, "I sold the Pyramid, so I guess I'll travel for a while, Timothy."

"Beverly Hills?"

"Oh, no; no. Old places, quiet places, falling apart, the way I am. I wish to go over things with the dead for a while."

Tim wasn't sure, looking at him, how he meant that. He offered to take a few days off and drive Lawrence wherever he wanted to go. Lawrence shook his head. He was going to bum around until he found a place that felt right.

Tim went up to the cabin with him that night. The cabin was in the most perfect order Tim had ever seen there. There were no pictures or materials in sight. All the books were put away, and all the furniture was formally and exactly in place, and dusted. There was even a fire laid in the stove. It looked already dead and deserted. They slept there that night, Tim in the earth room again, and it was like sleeping in a different place. The little aspen whispered in the dark outside the window, and it made Tim think of other places where he had listened to the leaves, Lone Pine, the creek into Mono Lake, the poplars of Bowers' Mansion, the house by the race track.

Lawrence didn't want to eat in the morning, either. He said he would eat somewhere on the road. He put a razor into a box held together by a rubber band, and put the box and a pencil into a pocket of the blue jacket. Tim drove him out to the east edge of Sparks, where he wanted to start. The poplars, standing in rows across the valley, were yellow. The smokes of Reno rose faintly, like Indian-summer haze, out of the cluster of yellow trees shining in the early sun. Lawrence stood at the edge of the road and looked at Tim.

"Why don't you move into the cabin?" he asked. "Then I could think about it," he said. "Now it doesn't seem real."

"Maybe I will," Tim said, knowing he wouldn't.

"The rent's paid for a month," Lawrence said, "and there are five beers in the ice-box. They will get warm if they're not used."

After a moment he said, very casually, "You might write Helen a note, if you have time. Just a short note. I have her address here for you." He took the slip of paper out of his pocket and gave it to Tim.

"She's not coming back," he said. "Her uncle died." He went on more quickly, afraid that would sound like a curtain line. "I'll write to her myself when the alphabet is more than so many pollywogs in a bowl of rum."

Tim understood that he was to tell Helen that Lawrence would write.

"I'll tell her you're climbing the golden path," he said, "the eight-fold way."

"Do," Lawrence said, chuckling softly. "It would make her furious. She'd feel much better." He stepped away from the car, and stood there waiting. When Jeremiah had turned and started back, he approached the edge of the highway again, and rubbed it with the toe of his sneaker, as if to determine which was less real, himself or the pavement. Then he looked up and around him slowly, at the hills, at the files of yellow poplars, at the mild sunlight spreading upon the valley. This was a place he had never seen before.

CHAPTER FORTY-ONE: *About the Seven Lost Symphonies of T. Hazard, the Life of Lawrence Black on Paper, and the Quiet That Was in Mary's Room*

UNTIL the evening in June when Tim was assailed in the Latin Club by Knute Fenderson of Carmel, California, his next year went by with the evenness of life which is no longer moving. Only its interruptions may be recorded.

In December a letter came from Helen, begging him to argue Lawrence into coming to Beverly Hills, and asking for Lawrence's address. There was everything Lawrence wanted now, she said, freedom, materials, the company of artists and beautiful things, and a ducky little studio on the roof. The whole letter disturbed Tim vaguely, the way that one word "ducky" disturbed him. It contained only what should have been very hopeful news. It was still written in that big scrawl, a few words at a time, separated by long dashes, and it was still shot through with bold and affectionate insults. Yet the profanity, somehow, seemed remembered, and there were fewer statements than usual left unfinished and more which were not written at all. It made Tim feel guilty, as if he couldn't trust Helen to believe him, when he had to write that he didn't know where Lawrence was.

In January Mary Turner wrote to me. I include her letter as much for what it doesn't say about Mary as for what it does say about Tim. At least they are her own words, and Mary seems to have a way of disappearing from the picture in this period, though she was present in it six days out of seven.

Tim asks me to tell you why he hasn't written. He's been very sick, though he is coming along well now, and grows more insubordinate every day. Two nights ago Mrs. Mott found him up, barefooted and without a bathrobe, writing music, the idiot. She bundled him back to bed in short order; she is very fierce in her flannel nightie and leather curlers. And just this noon I found him on the lower stairs with his head in his hands. He had dressed himself and sneaked by Mrs. Mott's room, but that was as far as he could go. He was shaking like a leaf. He said no English sparrow could stand on the window-sill and make fun of him when there was a blue sky. He was a much better patient before he began to improve, except that he was worried about the immodesty of being helped into a chair in his pajamas when I did his bed, and about his beard, which was certainly impressive, and probably itchy. We couldn't shave him for nearly a month, because of the sores on his face. But when we remind him what a model patient he was, he grins and says that was because he was hearing things. He claims that he lay there and was the composer, the conductor and the orchestra for the seven most beautiful and terrifying symphonies ever written, and that it's no wonder he's crabby now, when every attempt to recall that music is interrupted by the ridiculous solicitudes of remorseless females and fat Chinamen. The fat Chinamen are Ling Choy.

Maybe I'm telling you more than Tim would like, but never mind; it's only his vanity. He had measles, and he feels that measles cannot be regarded seriously in a grown man. They were serious enough, just the same. He was delirious for three days, and he lost forty pounds. The doctor was nearly as frightened as we were. Tim has a hide like a walrus, and the trouble was that he couldn't break out. We tried everything, hot-water bottles and tons of quilts, hot drinks, hot poultices, hot towels and hot tubs. Tim was terribly mortified when he learned that Mrs. Mott and I had helped the doctor dunk him in a hot tub. I was going to keep that a secret, but Mrs. Mott is very earthy. She told him with pleasure, and also told him how he had chattered about everybody and everything he's ever known, especially Rachel Wells, in his delirium. Actually he didn't say much that anybody could understand. Just once, when I was with him, he spoke so clearly it made me jump, because I thought he knew what he was saying. He said, "Don't pay any attention to him, Mary. It's only Willis. Don't pay any attention to him." And then, though I'll admit I racked my nosy mind, I couldn't make anything of it. Mrs. Mott, however, is not to be stopped. She makes up whatever she needs and uses it in blackmail for good behavior.

As you've probably gathered from my ramblings, Tim is here at the Great Basin now. He has a top floor room with nice, big windows, and he's going to stay, since Mrs. Mott, who has taken a shine to him, says he can make all the noise he wants. We brought him over as soon as the fever broke and he could be moved. We made quite a procession up Second Street, Ling Choy and that nervous little Chinese cook of his carrying the stretcher, and Mrs. Mott and I bringing up the rear with pillows and pajamas, bedroom slippers, hairbrushes, razors and what-not. Ling Choy has been marvelous. When Tim didn't come to work, I phoned Ling and he went up with me to Tim's room. He got the doctor too, and took his shift watching Tim, and even after Tim moved, he continued bringing hot tea, gallons of it, and special food, and some nasty herb drinks of his own concoction, which he said would soon make Tim "a man with love and strong to play the piano." Poor Ling. He is very kind, and also very stubborn when he gets an idea. He imagines that Tim must be in love with me because I have "seen him when sick," and is disturbed because he knows I heard Tim muttering about Rachel. He assures me it means nothing, that it is "from distantly behind, when a child." Some of his jokes about the feast he will prepare for our wedding are rather em-barrassing. But Tim is very fond of him, and they visit like old cronies.

Tim sits up every day now, in his chair by the window. He's teaching Mrs. Mott to play boogie-woogie piano, and in the evenings, when he isn't too tired, he gives me lessons on his guitar. I think he's still afraid he's being a nuisance, and is try-ing to square the account. He even wrote melodies for some verses of mine. They are quite lovely, the melodies, I mean, and go very well on the guitar.

You don't happen to know where Lawrence Black is, do you? He's been gone a long time now, without a word, and Tim is worried about him.

Write when you can. Tim loves to hear from you. I duti-fully send his very best regards, and of course, my own too.

Affectionately,

Mary Turner

Later I received a letter from Tim, including a long descrip-tion of the pleasure he took in just lying there and waving one hand feebly and bringing forth seven symphonies. He enclosed a note he had received from Lawrence.

Tim—

I have wandered in a great circle, which is as it should be. Perhaps Salt Lake City is the place. I met a grocer there who paints the Wasatch Mountains every Sunday, and he gave me two apples. I will tell you about it some time. I am in the National Hotel. It is very quiet. Your hills are blessed, but so are my steep streets. I taste only the cool beer again, and the turtle has just put out his head and opened one eye.

Lawrence

With this note there came to Tim two brush drawings in sepia ink.

One of them showed a thin, old man, with a walrus mustache and a loose coat, seated upon a straight-backed chair and leaning forward a little, with his hands upon his knees. There was no background, and the figure was suggested by a few simple and flowing lines, save for the hands. The hands, enormous and twisted, were done with great care, every wrinkle and shadow and hair and cracked nail. The eye always came back to those hands. It was a beautiful, satisfying, sad drawing. Lawrence had printed lightly across the bottom of it, *Listening to the Radio*, and signed it in pencil with a minute turtle.

The other drawing showed Lawrence's room in the National Hotel, contorted so that it seemed to have the motion of a racked ship. Lawrence himself was the informing presence in that room. He had just put it off, like the blue-cotton jacket which hung on the wall, like the sneaks standing together under the bed. He had but a moment before set out on the marble-topped dresser, like sacerdotal instruments, the Gideon Bible, the razor and the beer bottle which were reflected in the mirror. His dark dreams still hung above the great iron bed, and his gentle mockery observed the china pot of necessity beneath it, ornamented with floating cherubs and fruit. The center of the drawing and the altar of the room was the tall window hung with frilly curtains and filled with light. In the middle of the window-sill stood a three-bladed cactus. There was no color

459

but the sepia, yet that room was remembered, after one look at the drawing, as full of soft and faded color, touched by winter sunshine.

They were very encouraging pictures to look at, when you were wondering about Lawrence and his pilgrimage.

Tim took Mary out in Jeremiah several times during that year, but only one of these trips turned out to be an interruption. One Sunday in March, when Tim's legs were steady again, they drove out to the last valley before Pyramid, where there stand, upon the right a dark castle of rock, and upon the left a gray table land which we call "the butte," it being a unique formation in those hills. It was a cold, gusty day. Gray clouds sheathed the mountains to their lower slopes and flung down long trains of hail and dry snow, which swept the desert. Tim and Mary walked far back into the hills north of the butte, where Tim had never been before, and then returned and walked across the top of the butte. Tim's senses were still fresh with convalescence, and he could not look around him enough. He sucked in each new blast. He was lured by every canyon revealed for a moment and shut away again. The storm was breaking up under the wind, which became steadily stronger and colder, and he was excited by its tumultuous changes, the increasing range, the beginning of the smoky war of light and shadow. He and Mary stood together on the eastern edge of the butte, and saw, through the distant notch, the waters of Pyramid turn jade green under a sunburst, and the steam of white dust arise from its shores and evaporate south-eastward. They ate lunch in a sheltered crevice part way down the side of the butte, where they discovered that the insects they were watching creep over the gray carpet of the desert below were cattle. This recognition produced a great extension of vision, such as may come to a man who stares upward at the stars until they sink away from their common plane, each to its depth in the infinite well of space. There was a new awe, then, in watching the vast and easy play of the light as it gained, until only single shadows fled it across the hills. As they drove home, the last shadows flew silently into space, and light was everywhere triumphant in a biting, crystal air. Then, as they came over the final rise, there was the clear sunset above the Sierra, like, as Tim wrote, "a chorus of golden horns, blown thin upon one lingering, major note, quiet, piercing, without a tremor."

Tim conceived this adventure as a symphony of Light and Shadow, or Desert Storm, to be done, as he put it, "in one, continuous development, from the first gloomy and gusty depths, screened by the hail of a descending, minor theme for violins, to the last high cry diminishing into the golden horns." But that symphony wouldn't come to please him either, and when one more try at the trembling leaves failed, he burned the yellowed pages he had kept and subsided into brief and fitful writing. He was troubled by his unwillingness to write, or rather by his willingness not to write, but deliberate efforts to break the quiescence failed. I suppose he was still weak from his sickness, but perhaps it was also what he feared it was, resignation to a life which might get easy.

Another note came from Lawrence in April. He was with Helen.

Tim—

I have meant to write for months. Helen came to Austin in February. There was thunder and lightning in my room, and at the center, the still, small voice. We drove back together by way of Death Valley. I can practically hear the Bowl concerts from the studio. There is a grand piano here, in a room by itself, and neither of us can play it. We will look for you this summer.

Tim began to think once more about leaving Reno, and the old restlessness filled him. He and Mary would come back from a show, or from dancing. He would stand in the doorway of her room, looking down at her, and often there would be only a glassy moment, only the thickness of one shadowy idea, between Mary of the shining cubicle and Mary of the adoration, between Mary, the reincarnation of Mrs. Hazard and Mrs. Turner, and Mary, the bird of the wilderness, devouring the apple of life one peck at a time. This glass and this shadow were all that lay between prettiness and beauty, between friendliness and the searching terror, between the things Mary said and the things she might have said, but Tim didn't break the glass or brush away the shadow. He was thinking about Rachel again in these spring nights. He would remember the confessions on a raft in the sky. He would remember that he and Mary had to be at work in the store tomorrow. Mary would see his look change. She would go into the room, leaving the door open, and he would follow her. They would play records, or the guitar, or they would sit and try to talk. He liked Mary's room. It was quiet and gray and orderly, and very clean, and it seemed more spacious than it was. The soft light of three shaded lamps fell upon the two easy chairs and the head of the couch, and picked out the gilded titles of her books on the shelves behind the couch, books mostly of poetry, drama and music, and reference books about birds, trees, flowers, rocks and stars. Mary would curl up on the shadowed end of the couch, and the faint, coppery gleams in her hair would come and go as she moved her head. Tim would sit in the chair by the phonograph in front of the window. When the door of her bedroom was open, he could see the foot of her bed, covered very smoothly by its coarse, tan cloth, and often with her hat and coat laid down upon it. It was very pleasant in Mary's room, yet he seldom stayed long. It was too quiet, motionless as well as hushed. He would begin to hear the street sounds outside. The call of a single voice a block away would work in him like the cry of a gull on a lonely island. It was queer about Mary. It was fine together when they were at the store, or practicing the guitar, or out in the hills in Jeremiah, or when they danced. Mary was a wonderful dancer, the kind who made her partner better than he was. But when they were sitting still together, when they talked, it would be like the first few minutes of that supper at Benner's. He would have to do all the starting. He would feel that he was always about to say something which would offend her, that her silence was waiting to censure his words primly. Sometimes this heaviness would be quickened by a sensation of reverence for her flesh, a light, unadmitted hope which worked pleasantly under his words, under the frail notes of music in the quiet, meeting Mary's secret without recognition. Sometimes, in a passionate revulsion, he would imagine quickly what it would be like to carry her into her room and throw her onto the bed and use her violently, paying no attention to her wishes or her words. Most often, however, he believed that he was bored by an old friend whom he could not desert or injure. Frequently, when he left her, he would go up to his room and play the violin until the first quick and irritated improvisation worked into music for itself. At other times he would go back to the Latin Club.

CHAPTER FORTY-TWO: *In Which Knute Fender-son Demolishes Yesterday and the Dangerous Quiet*

IT WAS at the Latin Club that he met Knute Fenderson. He had performed a new act about dude ranches, too thickly, he knew, but the guests had called for an encore, and he had given them, just because he felt like it, *The White Horse*. He played it straight the first time, but he could feel that it didn't take, so he went into it again, without a pause, syncopating it, aggravating the clumsy gallop of the opening and closing passages, satirizing the fluctuating themes that played over it, turning the haunted hotel into a grotesque parade, a comedy danse macabre. They loved this, and probably believed, he thought gloomily, that the take-off was the real point to having played it straight the first time. Well, maybe they were right, in the Latin Club, and he was wrong. He went back and sat down at the table at the corner of the floor, where Mary was waiting for him. She smiled at him doubtfully, and he tried to smile back, and then sat there, slumped down in his chair, watching the waltz team turn and glide in the blue spotlight, keeping straight faces, like wax dummies.

It was then that the man appeared by the table. Where he came from, Tim didn't know. He was just there, and sat down abruptly across from Tim, with his back to the floor, and leaned forward on his elbows with his hands folded tightly together, and asked, "You wrote that, didn't you?" His voice wasn't loud, but it had more urgency than if he had yelled. That urgency was in his face and body too. It wasn't until he was seeing him every day that Tim realized that Knute Fenderson was not a big, thick man with a heavy and threatening face. Actually he was smaller than Tim, and his face, though wide across the cheeks and with jutting brows, was thin and intense, like the face of a soldier who has undergone fear too long.

"Which, the dude-ranch thing?" Tim asked. If customers wanted to talk about his acts, it was always about those talkie stunts.

"No," the man said, contemptuously. "Hell, no. The last number. The way you played it the first time."

Tim sat up and looked at the man more carefully. "Yes. I wrote it."

"Excuse me," the man said. "My name's Fenderson, Knute Fenderson. I write music too. That piece has something, only you don't get all you wanted. What the hell does Debussy have to tell anybody now? Look, in that last part . . ."

He hummed the return, speeding it up to get it over with, and yanked a big blue pencil out of his pocket. He glared around over the top of the table, and then at the service table against the pillar beside it, but there was nothing to write on. He dashed off a big stave on the table cloth and began to spot notes onto it rapidly, digging into the cloth. Then he whirled the cloth around on the table, so Tim could see what he'd written.

"Like that?"

"Practically."

"It doesn't matter," Fenderson said. "Note for note, it doesn't matter. Now, look."

Again he plowed up the table cloth, in a fury to be done. Once in a while he would pause and stare at the center of the table, and pound in the air with his fist, not in any rhythm, but as if trying to knock down an obstruction in his mind. The waltz ended, and a marimba band struck up *La Paloma*. "Kee-riste," Fenderson said, and covered his left ear while he went on writing. He ended with a wild flourish that made a note as big as an apple, and spun the cloth to Tim again.

"See what I mean?"

Tim didn't know how much of his trouble was the pressure of Fenderson watching him, but he couldn't hear half of what he was looking at, and he was bewildered by the part he could read. He couldn't discover the line of his own theme in it at all. Besides, there were little, interpolated notes which he finally figured must be quarter tones and even eighths, and whole blocks of an incredible vertical notation, running up through three staves, and with no linear development at all, as far as he could see.

"You couldn't play that on any instrument made," he said.

"The hell you couldn't," Fenderson said. "Though, if you couldn't, what of it? Are you a composer or a mechanic? Do you write music, or count keys? You write it. Somebody'll make the fool machine. They got over the lute, didn't they? They got over the celeste, didn't they? Every generation has a wooden ear. In a hundred years they get over it for that music, but then they've got a new wooden ear. That's none of your business."

"I guess I have a wooden ear too. I can't hear it."

Fenderson began to explain, leaning far across the table, his pencil jabbing among the notes, his pressing gaze shifting from them to Tim and back rapidly. Then he just leaned on the edge of the table again, and became more general. He was passionate about creating a better ear, and about something he called a fluid, polytonal screen with the figure worked out in it. "The way," he said, "you can pick a lyre bird out of a tapestry it's woven right into with the leaves and stems, the same kind of lines it has, and the same colors.

"Look," he said, pressing slowly down upon the table with both fists, as if preparing a leverage that would throw him to the ceiling. "Look. Who thinks any more that you have to bother with arbitrary divisions in a symphony, with some asinine scherzo that kills everything you're after? Who thinks you have to stack on a ten-minute peroration that winds up like a grand-father's clock, just so it can spend another ten minutes getting unwound? Then why in hell should we go on being stuck with these mechanical, singing-master scales and rhythm divisions? Oh, these pontifical bulls on the limits of the human ear. They've been turned out by the dozen every day since the first cave-brat whistled through his teeth, and just the same . . ." And he began to throw at Tim a fast, sketchy history of notation, instruments, rhythm, tone range and combination, punching all the points where the growth had stuck and the back-flood had begun, and showing how somebody who could "hear new," as he said, who wanted more room, had always broken the dam down.

Tim was fascinated. Time after time he wanted to quarrel, and he began to, but also he was delighted. He was sitting up and leaning forward too. He was hungry for this kind of talk. The only real talks about serious music he'd ever had before were those first talks with Jacob Briaski and his father. But then the marimba band was done, and the torch singer had finished her wailing, and right over the table, practically, the band burst out on a hot number. Knute raised both hands in the air, as if to choke somebody, and then jumped up.

"Look," he shouted. "I've only got tonight. Let's get shut of this infernal racket. Is there some place we can go where we can get hold of a violin? Two violins," he shouted.

"Sure," Tim shouted. He jumped up too. His face was eager. Then he looked at Mary.

"Does she care about music?" Knute roared. "Bring her along."

They went to the store first, and picked up a second violin, and then they went back to the Great Basin. Mary was walking between them, and Tim held her arm, but he kept talking across her to Knute. When they got up to the hall on her floor, Mary said she was tired and thought she'd better turn in. Tim didn't argue with her. Knute nodded good night to her, thinking about something else, and waited by the stairs while Tim took her to her door and came back, and they went on up.

They didn't go to bed at all. First, making Tim play along with him, explaining all the time how an orchestra would be used to expand the pattern, Fenderson illustrated his tonal screen. Then he made Tim play one thing after another that he'd written, and dig the score out if he still had it. After each one, he'd tear into it with voice and instrument. Yet all the time he was encouraging. He disputed with Tim as one composer with another, and without ever saying it, made Tim feel that he wouldn't have wasted a minute if he hadn't believed the music was there. He kept repeating that Tim would have to come down to Carmel, so they could have some time. At six o'clock they made coffee on the electric grill, and ate canned grape-fruit and toast, without a break in their tempestuous discussion. A little before eight Knute looked at his watch, roared, "God Almighty," and began to throw on his coat.

"Got to catch a bus. Got a suitcase at the Golden. Send it to me, will you? Fenderson, Carmel."

At the door he said, "You'll come down sooner or later. Why not now? Forget about the suitcase."

Tim wanted to. The thought of shaving, and changing his shirt and going to the store was like a small, stuffy room after all outdoors. He grinned wistfully and shook his head. "Not before the end of the summer, if I can come at all."

"If you can come," Knute snorted. "End of the summer. You might as well make up your mind to stay," he said. "What in the seven circles of hell does selling records to a lot of pimps and politicians have to do with music? You come to stay."

Tim heard him plunging down the stairs, three or four at a time, and then, from the window, saw him running across the street and on up toward Sierra, his overcoat flapping out behind him.

Tim sent Fenderson's suitcase to him, and received a card saying there was a fine, gloomy fog in from the sea, nobody ever bothered you in Carmel, and Tim could have the piano all day, because he used it only at night. When another card came in August, saying, "You can't give it half," he made up his mind, and though he told himself that it was only for a couple of weeks, three at the most, he wondered if it might work out for longer. He didn't think any definite time, just longer. He wrote a letter to Lawrence, gave Jeremiah a new coat of blue paint, with yellow arrows on the wheels, and talked about his hopes to Mary. He was going to get the symphony of leaves moving this time. Mary didn't seem at all dull to him now. He was going to miss Mary.

CHAPTER FORTY-THREE: *Wherein Timothy Hazard Sets Out for the Wide World of Carmel, California, Having Heard for a Moment the Bird in the Inmost Thicket*

MARY had breakfast with Tim at the Waffle Shop the morning he left. It was only a little after five when they went into the Waffle Shop, and the light was still gray in the streets. From inside it was periwinkle blue through the steamy front windows. They sat up at the counter, side by side, and Mary said, nearly laughing, "Mr. Atley will be terribly crabby. He always is when you're gone. He's forgotten so much about the shop." They talked about the shop. At the last moment, like this, with Mary beside him in her straight brown coat and her little brown hat with the brass buckle on it, and her narrow brown suede shoes with the high heels, which made it look as if she had dressed up for him, at this last moment, with sad dawn spreading for the how many millionth time over the desert east of Reno, over all the deserts, he thought, over Salt Lake, the Humboldt, the Black Rock, over the Yuma and the Mohave, at this last moment, with his mind going out to run through all the streets of Reno, watching the first light creep among the quiet leaves around the quiet houses where all the sleepers stretched in their beds were beginning to dream toward morning, in this last moment Tim was a little homesick. It was important that Mary was sitting beside him.

"It won't be for very long," he said vaguely.

Mary didn't answer, and he looked at her instead of at the apples in the cut-glass dish in front of the mirror. Her purse was lying across her lap, and she was looking down at it and playing with the hasp.

"Two or three weeks," he said.

Mary looked up, and when she saw him watching her, smiled quickly.

"Don't make up your mind," she said. "You shouldn't make up your mind. Fenderson was right, if you can get what you want."

Red, whom they knew so well, Red, who had served each of them probably a hundred breakfasts, together or alone, at that counter, finished waiting on the three tired-looking men at the other end, and came to take their order. He looked tired too, but he made a joke about their being up so early or so late, and Tim, to fortify them all against the weight of time, ordered fruit and ham and eggs and waffles and coffee and rolls and jam for two. Mary said, "Heavens, Tim," and Red grinned.

Outside a high voice came closer, calling with great range through the dawn, like yodeling in the Alps, "*Journal*. Hey, *Journal*. Get yuh mawning papuh. *Journal*, *Journal* here." Tim went out and bought a *Journal* for a quarter and told the kid to keep the change. He looked all up and down Virginia Street before he came back in, and it was a street he had never seen before, a street in a strange city.

At the counter, he folded the paper and put it between him and Mary. They looked at it while they ate. He would look at her before he turned it over and she would always smile quickly and nod, but he didn't believe she was reading it. She didn't seem to be eating much either. Her waffle was cut up into fifty little pieces, and if he looked at her too long, she would eat a couple of pieces, but there wouldn't seem to be much more gone the next time he looked. The sadness about leaving Reno became also a sadness about leaving Mary. Maybe it was from reading the newspaper so early in the morning. Everything he wanted for the world was always being defeated in the pages of newspapers, and early in the morning it was worse. That was why he saved the sports page till last. At least somebody was always making a home run or a hole in one on the sports page, and the names of race horses were fine. He explained to Mary how somebody had made a home run in the sports page. She smiled, but when he thought about that smile, it made him look back at her before he was ready to turn a page, and when he hadn't said anything to warn her. She was staring at her plate, and she looked very sad, as if she were hearing even more in the morning than he was. "My Lord," he thought, "she doesn't want me to go. She's afraid I'm never coming back, and she doesn't want me to go." And then, because something turned over inside him, and he didn't want to eat anything more either, and because he was going anyway, any minute, he thought, "My Lord, you'd think I was falling in love, or something. It's too early in the morning, that's all. It's too early in the morning, and we didn't get to bed last night, and I've been reading the newspaper, and man is not a bat. He should never have a thought between midnight and sunrise."

Mary finished her coffee and slid down from her stool and went to the slot machine beside the door. He watched her solemnly putting the nickels in and pulling the handle and standing there with her arms straight down at her sides, watching the fruits, the bars and the bells go round, and vague, symbolic notions about the fruits, the bars and the bells going round appeared on the edge of his mind and dissolved without ever taking form. He carried his second cup of coffee over to the slot machine, and stood with his arm lightly against her shoulder, and began to put his nickels in alternately with hers. When the fruits stopped whirling after his fourth nickel, there were three plums in a row, and a clattering took place in the cup. He scooped the nickels out, and took Mary's purse, and put the nickels into it. Then he put his coffee cup back on the counter, and paid Red and said, "So long," to him, and they went out onto the sidewalk. The street was still in shadow, except at the crossing, and on the tops of the buildings on the west side. The shallow river of morning flowed over the crossing. They stood beside Jeremiah for a minute. Tim didn't know what to say.

"I'll ride out to the beginning of the Verdi road with you," Mary said.

"That's a long walk back."

"Well, I have all day," she said, and he remembered that it was Sunday, and she would not be going to work. She would be going back into that gray, orderly and quiet room, and sitting there by herself, and reading the Sunday paper. Maybe she was just dressed up for Sunday.

When he stopped to let her out, where the street jogged and became the highway, he didn't want to do it. It was all wrong to be leaving her there at the edge of the highway, looking at the empty gleam upon the S.P. tracks, and also at the trees of Reno, absolutely motionless at the end of summer, with the new sun looking over them. There were a hundred things which might happen to Mary, besides being alone, which was happening to her, between the Verdi road and the quiet room in the Great Basin. Mary, however, got out of Jeremiah at once. She closed the door, and stood very straight beside the pavement, holding her purse in front of her with both hands.

"Well, take care of yourself, Mary," he said.

"You take care of yourself," she said.

"Well," he said, putting Jeremiah into gear, "I'll be seeing you."

Mary nodded quickly, three or four times.

He let the clutch in very slowly, but nothing happened to change the way things were going, so at last he really let it take hold.

TIM took his time on the way, stopping at Donner Lake and on the summit above the lake, and often on the downslope, at places where he could see, through breaks in the near trees, receding waves of timbered mountains, growing bluer and paler with increasing distance, and the great, still gorges between them. He ate his lunch beside a creek that rushed and twinkled down among alders and willows, and then he lay out in the sunlight for nearly two hours, staring up at the sky and dreaming. He had supper at an Italian place in Oakland, and got into a long argument with the proprietor about Caruso's singing voice and the serious possibilities of the guitar. It was after midnight when he came over the hump of the peninsula from Monterey and saw below him the few street lights of Carmel, leading like far-spaced candles downhill toward the invisible ocean. There was a fog in. It drifted up among the black trees, made halos around the lights, twined about the gables of the stores on the main street, and rained down in a fine, cool mist upon Tim. The scent of wet pines and cypresses was strong. Now and then, from far down in the darkness, came the long, faint shoring of the surf.

There was a man standing on the curb of the main crossing, within the aura of the street light. He was wearing a sweater and blue jeans and sandals. He was short, and had thick limbs and a big head with a huge shock of black hair with gray streaks in it. He was picking his teeth and staring dreamily at the middle of the crossing. Tim stopped Jeremiah beside him. The man's head was wonderful. The shadows of its broad features and heavy brows gave it a gloomy, brooding, Neanderthalish look. It was a head like a lion's, like a Russian novelist's, like Beethoven's. It was a massive, profound and possibly dangerous head, which must be addressed with consideration. The man gazed at Tim from under his brows, stopped picking his teeth, felt them over with his tongue, and smacked his lips softly. Before Tim could speak, he asked mildly, "Out kind of late, aren't you?"

"Kind of," Tim said, and grinned. There was something about this question, emerging from such a face, that tickled him, and made him at once fond of the man.

"Could you tell me where a fellow by the name of Knute Fenderson lives?"

"Oh, my, yes," the man said. "Everybody knows where Knute Fenderson lives. Wouldn't be the same place without Knute."

He put one foot on the running board, and pointed down toward the ocean. "You go down . . ." He gave the directions, drawing a diagram in the air with one finger.

"Place with a big veranda with a canvas over it," he concluded. "Knute sleeps out there, because the canvas sounds like a sail. He used to work on an old whaler, you know. Can't get a wink of sleep unless he hears a sail."

He began to pick his teeth again, and murmured around the toothpick. "Strange fellow, Knute. Delightful in his way. When he first came, he claimed he couldn't sleep without the stink, either. Used to put a new mess of dead fish in the rocks down in front of his place every couple of weeks, so the stink would blow up onto the veranda and he could get some rest. Neighbors didn't like it. Threatened to drown him or burn the place, so now he just puts a little smear of some ointment he's got under his nose before he goes to bed. It works fine. Terrible-smelling stuff."

Tim laughed. "Is there a hotel handy?" he asked.

"Hotel?" the man asked vaguely. "What on earth do you want of a hotel?"

"Well, it's kind of late to go barging in on somebody."

"Oh, good heavens," the man said, "I wouldn't worry about that, if I were you. Fenderson never goes to bed at night. Sits

473

up making a dreadful racket on the piano. Any time I go by there, before sunrise, he's making that dreadful racket."

Tim remembered that Knute had promised him the piano in the daytime. "Well, I don't want to interrupt him when he's working."

"Oh, he loves to be interrupted," the man said. "Makes him miserable, working like that. I interrupt him almost every night myself, if I don't forget." He took his foot off the running board and backed onto the curb again.

"Thanks, I'll try then," Tim said. He began to coax Jeremiah into gear.

The man with the big head took the toothpick out of his mouth again. "I just happened to think . . ." he began.

Tim looked at him, and waited.

"Is Fenderson expecting you?"

"Maybe not tonight, exactly."

"Mmmm," the man muttered. "I'd just be a little careful then, if I were you. Oh, it's all right," he said quickly. "Fenderson loves to be interrupted. Won't do to startle him, that's all. Sort of break in on him gradually."

"Is it that bad?" Tim asked, grinning.

The man nodded. "Impulsive," he said. "Terribly impulsive."

Tim laughed. "Maybe I'd better look for the hotel, after all."

"Good heavens, no. Fenderson'd never speak to you again. Nobody uses hotels any more. Oh, a few strange creatures. See them around once in a while; people with money or important business or ancestors or some dreadful thing they can't recover from. Just don't startle him, that's all. Throw a rock or something through the window first, and wait till he gets over it."

"Thanks," Tim said solemnly. "I'll be careful."

The man nodded. "Well, good night," he said, and again began to pick his teeth and brood upon the middle of the crossing.

Tim found the house without much trouble. He drew up into the salt bushes in front of it, and turned off the engine. Then he could hear the surf rushing up loudly among the rocks below him. A light showed through the red-and-yellow cloth curtains of the front window, and he could see the shapes of fog moving across the light. Inside a piano was being played rapidly and loudly, through long passages of melancholy dissonance and rhythms which shifted so frequently that Tim felt no order in the sequence. He listened for a few minutes. Fenderson didn't seem to be composing, anyway. The piano went right on.

He went up onto the porch, and there was a wide bed there, with a canvas roof over it, and another canvas closing out the sea. He knocked on the door, and in spite of himself, stepped back a little. He had to knock again, much more loudly. The piano stopped.

"Somebody there?" Fenderson called.

"Yes," Tim called. "It's . . ."

"Come on in, then, if you have to," Fenderson interrupted. "Don't stand out there raising hell all night."

Tim went in, and closed the door behind him. There was an upright piano against the wall beside the door, with a clip light over the rack and several sheets of penciled score under the light. Fenderson was sitting at the piano. He was wearing a blue-flannel bathrobe with big red diamonds on it, and he was barefooted. The hair of his head had been wet but not combed, and the great mat of wiry, blond hair on his chest showed in the open V of the bathrobe. He stared at Tim for a minute, and Tim thought he had forgotten him. Then he got up suddenly and padded over and shook hands.

"By God, so you did break out," he said. "Glad to see you. Glad you came. Been wondering about you."

"Don't let me break in," Tim said, nodding at the piano. "If you'll just tell me where . . ."

"The thing's awful," Fenderson said. "You came just in time. Now we can have a drink."

"I've got some stuff out there . . ."

"Later," Fenderson said. "I want a drink. How about some supper?" he asked, stopping in the middle of the room.

"I ate in Oakland," Tim said.

"Not hungry?"

"No, thanks."

Fenderson padded on across the room and through one of two black doors, and switched on a light.

Tim looked around the room where he was standing. It was big, and there wasn't much in it, a couple of mission rockers and one straight chair, a square table, a cot with an Indian rug over it for a couch, a small bookcase with a score of books in it, most of them with library numbers on the back, the rest of the shelves filled with piles of sheet music. Besides the piano light, there was only one central light on a drop cord with a paper shade. A square straw rug nearly covered the floor. There was a violin case on the cot and an old, hand-winding phonograph in the corner, with a rack of dusty records beside it. A pair of wet, black dungarees hung over the end of the cot. They had made a puddle on the floor. The smell and the dampness of the sea were in the room, and Tim felt that they had worked into the dark, unfinished redwood walls like wine into a cheese.

Fenderson came back in with a tray holding a glass decanter of whisky, two tumblers and a heap of rye bread and cheese in slabs.

"I'm starving, anyway," he said. "Haven't eaten since noon. Dug clams down by the point till dark. We'll have them to-morrow."

While Fenderson was pouring out the whisky and passing him the bread and cheese, Tim told him about the whimsical man with the big head.

"That's Steve Granger," Fenderson said. "He's a good guy. Used to be a newspaperman, foreign correspondent. Been all over the world a dozen times. He's writing a huge book now. Been at it three years already. He never sleeps, that I can discover. I don't know when he writes, for that matter. You're likely to find him around anywhere, any time. He drops in here almost every day. He has a little place farther down along the beach." He pointed south. "Place is just like him."

When they had eaten the bread and cheese, talking about the clamming and the swimming and Tim's trip down, Knute said, " 'Nother fellow you'll see a lot of is Teddy Quest. Writes and plays the cello. He has a place down the other end of the village, toward the river, lousy with animals and all kinds of truck. We play quartets over there all the time. We're figuring on you playing the violin with us."

He got up. "Let's get your stuff in."

When the things were in the bedroom, he said, "Piano won't bother you?"

"Lord, no," Tim said.

"Good thing," Knute said. "I thought maybe the first night."

He went out and closed the door, and after a minute the piano began again. The bedroom was dark redwood too, and full of the smell and dampness of the ocean. It contained only an unpainted chest of drawers and an iron double bed, covered by a red-and-blue patchwork quilt. The floor was bare. On the wall by the door was a bad charcoal sketch of a waterfront lined by small fishing boats, and over the bed was a large, framed needlepoint of a three-master at anchor off a shallow bay, with a boat coming in from it. Tim listened to the piano while he got undressed and turned off the light. It began to go only a few notes at a time, with long pauses.

He stretched happily between the damp sheets. The world seemed submerged and melancholy around the cabin. Outside the open window, the fog dripped from the eaves like slow rain. Once in a while came the faint ding-dong of a bell buoy, very far off, which made him think of the limitless reach of the sea out there under the darkness and the floating fog. It was like a homecoming. There is something about the sea which makes coming to it like a homecoming always, even if you have never been there before. It calls way in deep. The house was good too, the way Tim liked a place, with room and just what you need, nothing more. The strong, gloomy man, now listening attentively to each little test he made out there, really wanted music, too. It was fine to be in a house without much in it but this hunger and anger for music.

WITH no job to be using his time from eight to six, six days a week, the clock and the calendar as instruments of coercion faded from Tim's consciousness. A method of life developed by itself in the house, around his working time and Knute's, and the evenings they went over to Quests' to play chamber music. When Tim got up in the morning, they both put on their swimming trunks and labored down over the white dunes, where the wire grass broke through in the hollows, and ran south on the beach to the mouth of the river, and then back. They would finish the run back with a sprint into the surf and long, looping dives over the first roller that made the water deep enough. The water was very cold, and often riotous, and they battled it gleefully, diving under each breaker, rising to snort and puff and yell, and gradually working their way out onto the deep, heavy swells, where they would dive and roll and play porpoise for a few minutes, and then return, trying to catch the breakers right to ride them in. Even when the clouds were low, and went far up into the river canyon, and rain from the ocean roared across the beach and the black cypresses that hid the houses, those were fine mornings. The ocean still felt cold after they had run in the rain.

Knute liked the foggy mornings best, when Point Lobos was hidden, and the trees on the nearer cliff were wraiths, or when the ceiling was higher, and Lobos stood out grim and distinct under it, but the heights of the Coast Range were cut off. Tim liked the clear mornings best, when the first sunlight reached far out to sea and created the ineffable horizon, and southward great cleavers of gold came down through the passes and lit the white rocks off shore.

After their swim they would return to the house and rub down till their bodies burned, and Tim would get into a pair of pants, and Knute into his beloved dressing gown, and they would eat and drink their coffee, one or the other of them usually roaming around, and argue fiercely until Knute went to bed on the porch and Tim began to work.

When Knute got up in the afternoon, he would always drink a whisky, and then they would usually take a long walk, sometimes out onto Point Pinos, where the white sand ran before the wind and the cypresses on the knolls lay out flat away from the sea, and where the little signs among the rocks gave the names of ships which had been wrecked there in storms or fog; sometimes south through the village and across the river valley and out past the last houses on the cliffs to the magnificent, barren headlands, where the dry wheat changed color in the wind on the slopes above. The whole world out there was simple and vast, just the yellow hills shouldering up into the sky, and the blue and glittering dome of the sea. When the rim of the ocean rose to the sun, the hills and the cloven headlands were wild and sad with the last light.

When Tim worked, he was actually settling out what he learned from Knute and Teddy Quest, getting rid of the part that couldn't be his, working the rest into place until it became natural and easy, part of his musical language. This learning and exercising was often a torture, because he believed, until long after he had left Carmel, that he was really trying to compose, and was failing. As a critic, Knute was as hard on Tim as he was on himself, which was very hard. A false passage, a reminiscent motif or chord sequence especially would arouse his wrath. Tim would play something for him, an etude, the first movement of a concerto.

"Whales from the forgotten depths," Knute would yell. "The stink of old funerals. Let Beethoven alone. He likes it dead," or, "Get out of the closet, get out of the closet. Bach is all bones. The bones of Bach have been cleaned for centuries. He's a fine skeleton. You can learn a lot from him, but he isn't music any more. We've got new instruments since Bach, idiot.

We've got a new ear. If you're doing finger exercises from him, all right. If you're just learning the tricks, if all you want is to see how he turns a theme upside down and inside out thirty-four times in fourteen minutes, all right. But don't get it in your ear. It's worse than a flea. When you write, put some flesh on the bones. Pound your chest; believe in life. Now, burn that damned thing up, will you?"

He would swing the ax on Brahms, Tschaikowsky, Mozart, Sibelius, Handel, Haydn, Moussorgsky, the French impressionists, almost everybody Tim knew anything about. "Old fish," he called them. "You don't keep a house you live in full of old fish," he would roar. "Old fish is manure, but nothing else. Spade them under. Don't keep shoving them back under my nose on a platter."

Tim would support a judgment of his own by a remark by Teddy Quest, and Knute would hammer the table and yell, "Teddy Quest's dead too. Powdered wigs in candle light, hoop skirts and fiddle squeaks. The age of reason, faugh! Jehovah of the seven seas, when did reason ever have anything to do with music? Don't pay any attention to Teddy Quest. He is the great-grandfather of music. He ought to be conducting a church choir. He has a heart like a Gregorian chant—wah-wah-wah," and he would give a nasal imitation of a monotonous and dirgelike melody.

He would rise abruptly and stride about the room in his bare feet, roaring about how bad and habitual Teddy Quest was. Then he would suddenly cross the room and confront Tim, with his hands spread out beseechingly, with an air of being superhumanly patient and reasonable, and say, "Teddy knows how to play the cello. He is wonderful on the cello, and he knows even more than he can do. Pay close attention to everything Teddy does on a cello. But that's all, absolutely all, just what he does on a cello. He could still be a great concert cellist, if he wanted to; the greatest. But a composer? Somebody should tell him."

Then he would begin to illustrate his condemnations of Tim's work or Teddy's, on the violin or the piano. He had a quick ear for any mannerism or echo, and a prodigious memory, so that often he could display similarities with devastating effect, although, in such a mood, he had a tendency to allow his playing to make two passages sound more alike than they were. At other times, to illustrate his positive points, he would play from the moderns, or put on records, dozens of them, playing only the pertinent fragment of each. Some of them were recordings made privately by men Tim had never heard of, men Knute had turned up everywhere on the globe in his furious ransacking of the world for a new vocabulary in music.

Usually he was like that, as if he could never tire, and would never approach any topic except at full speed, and with the purpose of clearing the whole field of similar practices at the same time he demolished the specific instance.

Once in a while, however, a great gloom would descend upon him, and he would hardly speak. They'd eat breakfast at the little table in the kitchen, in silence save for the sound of their chewing and the rattle of their forks and cups, and now and then a great, dismal sigh from Knute, as if he were wrestling ceaselessly with despair, and not having the best of it. Other times, he would rise from the table frequently, and pace around the room with a savage scowl on his face, and then come back and sit down, full of darkness and silent uproar, and drink another cup of coffee, and sometimes two or three whiskies, and chain-smoke cigarettes, and at last stalk out to his bed on the porch without having said a single distinct word. These were the mornings when he wouldn't want to go swimming, and when Tim would find many sheets of unfinished pencil score balled up and lying in far corners.

Knute attacked Stephen Granger even more often than he attacked Teddy Quest, although there was no musical incitement. This was because Stephen dropped in to see them so often on the evenings they were home. He wouldn't knock, or call from outside, but just open the door and enter slowly, and sit down carefully on the cot or in the big chair by the side window, and fold his thick hands between his knees, as if to warm them. If Knute was padding around, swinging the ax, Stephen would peer at him from under his apish brows, his great, dark eyes apparently full of wonder or mild bewilderment. Knute, turning around to march back from one of his elocutionary excursions, would see him sitting there, and would yell at him, when Stephen hadn't opened his mouth, "Shut up. Don't you say a word, you mocker, you feeble skeptic." Then he would roar at Tim, "This man is the most God-awful liar. He's an evil influence. He's a bad deed in the memory. Lies, lies, lies. He can't help it. It's a sickness. Everything in the world bores him, so when he tells anything, even how he goes to the can at night, he has to fix it up, make an adventure out of it, so it won't bore him. The worst of it is, you'll believe him. Everybody, except the damn fools, believes him. Oh, they don't believe what he says. Nobody could believe anything he says. But they believe what he means, and that's worse. When you see him coming, go away, or stuff your ears."

Stephen would watch him, and nod slowly at everything he said, as if he were carefully thinking it over, and unfortunately finding it true. Then, without changing his huddled position or his owlish gaze, he would say mildly, "The world is too much with me. I must consume whisky. I must get roaringly drunk, perhaps."

"Now?" Knute would yell.

"Not now," Stephen would murmur. "Later, perhaps."

"Bah," Knute would exclaim. "Always later. Always perhaps," and he would go back into the argument Stephen had interrupted.

In the middle of the discussion, ten or fifteen minutes later, Stephen would suddenly say, softly, "Let's have a beer."

Knute would break off at once and glare at him. He would point at him, and roar at Tim, "You see? What did I tell you? He comes in here shouting and moaning about he wants to get drunk, roaring drunk, and forget about this terrible world. Then he says, 'Let's have a beer.' He's not a man you can trust."

Then he would go and get the beer.

After a while Tim saw that Knute really loved and admired Teddy Quest, too. They went to Teddy's twice a week to play

482

chamber music. It was a small house, at the south end of the village and back from the sea, near the point where the road descended into the river valley and passed the old mission. It was surrounded by mountain oaks, and buried in vines, so that from the outside it appeared to be hiding, and inside, in the day-time, there would be a green gloom, like that of Lawrence's cabin in the Peavine Quarter of Reno. The inside, in that gloom, also appeared to be a hiding place, a place where a soul from another century had decided to secrete itself until the uproar of trains, airplanes, cars, radios, jazz, fly-paper thinking, Napo-leonic table-thumping and headline emotions, had worked itself out. If Knute's house had so little furniture that it resounded like a barn, Teddy's had so much that it was like the storerooms of an old hock shop in which an indifferent proprietor kept just enough stuff scooped out to make lanes in which he could get from one place to another. The living room was small, and made smaller by deep bookshelves, shoulder high, on three sides. On top of the bookcases stood plaster busts of Beethoven, Bach, Rousseau, Goethe, Heine, Mozart, Shakespeare and Tolstoy. There were several small, dark paintings of the ocean shores and ruined medieval castles on the walls behind the busts. The shelves were crammed full of books in many languages, and all kinds of bindings, from news-stand paper covers to rusty old leather stamped with gold leaf. Other books were laid on their sides on top of those standing on the shelves, and scores of pamphlets and notebooks, too wide to fit evenly into the rows, projected here and there. There was a phonograph in one front corner, an upright piano beside it, set across one window, two heavy, mahogany tables with ball-and-claw feet, one in the mid-dle of the room, and one under the other front window, both of them laden with books, papers and magazines, ink stands, paper cutters and figurines. There were four big chairs, two of them Morris chairs with worn and hollowed velvety cushions in dark green and wine color. There was a carpet, now worn bare in spots, which had once been thick and brilliant. Most of the bare patches were covered by small rugs. Four lamps with painted china shades, two of them with bead fringes, hung on triple brass chains from the open rafters. There was a fireplace let into the bookcases on the west wall. On the mantel above it stood a brass clock, wooden figures of a sandaled priest with a burro, and an Italian boy with a violin, a Hungarian doll with a scarlet jacket, a voluminous skirt and patent-leather boots, a pair of brass candlesticks and a rack holding six pipes. The mail of several days was always lying up there too. A big basket of roots and the brass-handled fire irons stood on the hearth, and whenever Tim came on a foggy evening there would be a small fire of the roots, as slow and steady and comfortable as a peat fire, burning behind the andirons, which were two dancing bears.

In the dining room, besides a big, battered, oak table and its chairs, and a gigantic, ornamented sideboard on which stood a row of old steins with pewter caps, there was another bookcase, full of phonograph records, bound scores and piles of Mss. score, the cello in its case in one corner, five music stands and a violin and a viola in another, and usually some tools, a rake, a hoe, a shovel, clamming forks, an ax, all together in a third, often with a couple of pairs of muddy rubber boots. On the walls hung a Japanese brush painting of a little tufted duck upon silver-rippled water in a mist, the enlarged photograph of a distinguished-looking man with white hair and mustaches and a high collar, and a plaster plaque of a Greek tomb decoration in which a father and two children mourned the wife and mother, and brought her gifts.

Only the kitchen had plenty of room. It was big and dark, with a sloping, board ceiling. When the sun was out, the door onto the back porch would be open, but even then there was only a faint and broken light admitted because the porch was covered by a bougainvillea vine which climbed all over that side of the house and up over the roof on the kitchen end. Teddy's wife, Pearl, kept the kitchen for herself, and Pearl liked room. Everything was around the sides in the kitchen, and everything was in order, so there didn't seem to be nearly as much stuff there as in the rest of the house.

Chaotic abundance took over the yard again. It was enclosed

by a high, untrimmed salt hedge. The live-oaks roofed most of
the rest of it, and the pale wild wheat and weeds grew around
thinly but freely under them. There was a pig called Otto, who
lived at large in the yard, with a saturnine and ancient ram called
Voltaire for company, and in one corner was a chicken house
built from old boxes and roofed with flattened tin cans. The
chicken house had a small yard of its own, but this was always
open, so that the chickens were out too, scratching under the
trees and pecking around the kitchen doorstep. Many of them
roosted in the oaks at night. A long vegetable garden was laid
out along the salt hedge on the east side, more or less fenced
away from Otto and Voltaire, and flowers grew in tumult all
around the house and the chicken house, and even out in accidental patches, where they had seeded themselves in ground
kept moist because the running hose was so often forgotten.
Probably these survived because Voltaire had worn out his
teeth, and had to be fed on soft, warmed mash now. There was
a dog, and there were a great many big orange cats. Tim was
never sure how many cats there were. He would see them
everywhere, in the house, on the back porch, lying wonderfully
red in the dry wheat, curled contentedly on the black limbs of
the oaks, on the roof of the house, snuggled against the chimney, and coming back along the edge of the dusty road, from
hunting gophers and field mice and ground squirrels in the river
valley. They were Pearl's cats. Teddy liked them, which was
a good thing for him, but they were Pearl's. Pearl and the cats
understood each other. Pearl had big, green, predatory eyes,
like a cat's, herself, and she was as silent as a cat. The dog, who
was shaggy and gentle, and so old that he was failing, so that
when he wandered uptown he would often forget how to come
home, was Teddy's. Probably no decision had ever been made
as to who owned which animals. They were all simply loose
there, and the division happened by nature.

Tim never saw the bedrooms, but he supposed that this same
freedom existed in them, and was probably even exaggerated.

Such a riot of animals, plants, things, and articles which had
the vitality of creatures, like books, music and instruments,

seemed to Tim, with his spare nature, as unmanageable as Knute Fenderson when he was excited. Yet before he had been there many evenings, he discovered that there was a fine inner order in the Quests' house. The group would meet to play a quartet, and it would seem impossible to make enough room for them. Yet there would be only a little moving, and they would all be comfortably seated where their scores were well lighted by two of the hanging lamps. The other two lamps were over the Morris chairs in the front corners. On the shelves beside the Morris chair nearest the fireplace were the books Teddy most often wanted to read, Shakespeare, Goethe, Schiller, Heine, Rousseau, Chekov, Anatole France, Rilke, a volume of translations from the Chinese sages. Beside the other Morris chair were the books Pearl read most, D. H. Lawrence, Synge, Dostoievsky, Swinburne, Proust, Poe, Beaudelaire. The rest of the books were in an orderly arrangement, not by sets or authors, but by kind, poetry, drama, novels, essays, biographies, short stories, history, music. There were reference books handy on the bottom shelf beside each Morris chair, dictionaries in several tongues, encyclopedias, texts on music and art, and bound collections of prints and reproductions. Teddy could reach his pipes without getting all the way up from his chair. There was also writing material within reach on the table. Ash trays were strategically placed. The lamp that illumined Pearl's chair also served her piano. The tools and boots were in the corner nearest the kitchen, where Pearl and Teddy came in from clamming or working in the garden. The instruments and the music stands could be reached from the living-room door. The record albums and scores had their own places. Teddy never had to fumble for one. Teddy did most of his composing on the dining-room table, without an instrument, and everything he wanted was within reach, in the music cabinet. Everything was like that, ready for use.

Pearl hated housework, except getting meals. She would let the dishes stack up, and have one huge washing of them every two or three days. She liked to work outside, go clamming, fish in the surf with her overalls rolled up above her knees, and take long walks by herself, up the river canyon or south along the coast road. But she could get a huge dinner for eight or ten of them in half an hour without any trouble, and even when the dishes piled up, they were all off on one board reserved for that purpose, and were never in the way.

Just after Knute had been roaring against Teddy, he and Tim would walk along the dirt streets, under the pines and cypresses, to this orderly house, and play quartets until twelve o'clock, and Knute, playing first violin, would never protest the classical scores which necessarily made up most of their repertoire, and would observe strictly the unorthodox leadership of Teddy's cello. Teddy would appear mild. Teddy would appear to be in a dream over his beloved cello, or during his rests he would be staring up into the shadows above the lamps, his head tilted a little to one side, apparently vaguely enjoying the thin sweetness and interplay of the two violins and the viola, which was played by either Christine Hardy, a tall, white-faced, red-headed, big-handed girl, very shy and uncommunicative, who came up from one of the ranches way down beyond Big Sur, or by Mr. Greever, a thin, stooped, gray little man who ran a chicken farm up the valley, and who always counted audibly through his rests. Yet suddenly, in the midst of a passage, and while they were all playing along happily, Teddy would strike a sharp discord across the strings, and then rap twice upon the body of the cello. At once there would be a complete silence, and if the sinner did not admit his error, and show that he knew better, Teddy would tell him what was wrong, and make him play it alone before they went on again. He would do this not only when there was a note or phrase misplayed, or a rhythm broken, but when any one of the instruments, in volume or modulation or phrasing, departed in the least from its place in the ensemble. All the little concerts were like hard rehearsals for a professional appearance. To each of these corrections or interpretations of Teddy's, Knute would listen intently, and when the first quartet was over, and Pearl, who sat listening to them in her corner, had brought in coffee or tea and cake, and the conversations began, Knute would also listen intently to anything Teddy said about music, the writing of it as well as the playing.

It made Tim feel happy, and in the midst of what mattered, and great with love for all these people, to sit out on the edge of his chair, his violin raised, and await with keen, restrained excitement, the nod of Teddy's head which started them off. It was just as good to begin the second quartet at ten-thirty or eleven o'clock, when the empty cups and plates were put by, and everybody's hands and attentions were rested, and Pearl sat down at the piano again, and struck the keys while they tuned, and watched each in turn out of her great, predatory eyes. Pearl had straw-colored hair done around her head in braids as thick as big rope. She struck the notes sharply, as if stabbing with a knife, and told each player when his turn had come, merely by shifting her gaze to him. If he were not yet paying attention, which seldom happened, she would speak his first name sharply, once, "Timothy," or "Christine," or "Albert," for Mr. Greever, and then strike the note of the lowest string. If a player, even Teddy, did not come to tune at once, she would say crisply, "Flat," and strike the key again.

Distinctly there was order in the house of Quest.

CHAPTER FORTY-SIX: *In Which Tim Hazard Prolongs His Exile from the City of Trembling Leaves, and Begins a Double Life as a Musician*

TIM learned a great deal from both Knute and Teddy, and under their influence was compelled to put in order much that he already knew in a disorderly way.

The two men taught by methods as different as their natures. Learning from Knute continued to be a process of battling for every inch of ground. Knute was always attacking him, calling him a many times profane romanticist, asking him if he hadn't heard the impressionists were dead, shouting at him to know how in hell he thought he was going to write music for the twentieth century, for a time full of speed, idiocy, uproar, bloodshed, concrete and steel, if he kept thinking in terms of a harpsichord and of Debussy played in pastels by Gieseking.

"What are you doing," he'd roar, "subduing the itch of a syphilitic Borgia, or stimulating the ditch-water in the veins of an Esterhazy? Nobody listens to music nowadays, you hopeless innocent. How in hell could they? Bangety-clatter, bam-bam, honk-honk, whooo-wooo, beep, peep, bong, yammer, yammer, yammer. Be rough on them. Make it new. Make it tough. Make it hurt. Make them listen. A composer has to be a prize-fighter to live these days."

Tim fought back with equal volume and ferocity, producing and elaborating a hundred proofs of his belief that what the twentieth century needed from its arts was an antidote to its slavery to mechanism, tabloid emotions and the Napoleonic appetite, and demonstrated that all the modern composers were really doing, for all their cult of "pure music" and their cant about Bach, was seeking, intellectually in serious music, and emotionally in jazz, a musical idiom for their time, a process essentially as impressionistic as that of Debussy had ever been. To talk of pure music, he argued, was to talk pure nonsense. The thoughts and emotions of a musician were as subject to the movements of the world as those of any other man, usually more so. If they weren't, he'd never even be moved to write any music in the first place. He would be a void, a vacuum, in which nothing, not even a sense of number, could germinate.

"That there are certain inherent attributes of music to which a composer must accede without regard to any image or program which may have stirred his emotions, goes without saying," he argued vehemently. "Is that anything new? The crumbiest imitator in Tin Pan Alley, a man without a theory, an idea, an ear or a skill, can't help but write music according to music. Something comes before. Something comes after. The sequences have different results. One bunch of sounds comes together here, another comes together there. The effects are different. One rhythm pattern has one result, another has another. But how do you recognize any of the differences, whether you're Bach or Bill Bungler? By the way you feel, that's all. And what makes the differences in the way we feel? Some mysterious divine attribute? Some little, separate psyche of pure music, omnisciently guiding some, and left out of others? Clap-trap. Only two things, the differences in our physical makeup, and the differences in our lives, where we've been, what we've seen, heard, felt, thought, done. There's no rule of music. There are no laws of music, in any permanent sense.

"If all you mean is that you are more moved yourself by the music of men who feel that life is tragic than by the music of men who feel that life is not that important, why, all right, I agree with you to this extent, that I feel the same way. But if you mean that there is some inherent difference, some native superiority, in men whose musical judgment is formed by big cities, factories and express trains, as over against men who prefer clouds, oceans, wind, snow-storms, mountains and the moods of humanity, then I say you're crazy. And if you mean that music can be made an entirely independent experience, then I say you're crazier still. Not even learning the alphabet can be that. The most dehydrated architect of a traditional fugue who ever warmed his long, cold nose over a cup of ginger tea can't listen to a C Major scale without feeling something, and what he feels is a little offshoot from the sum total of everything he has ever felt."

And he would demonstrate the impressionism of one intellectual modern after another. Knute was delighted by this resistance. They had many long, fruitful squabbles. Knute brought home all kinds of volumes, technical and theoretical, and when Tim had devoured them, the arguments and demonstrations would begin again. Knute insisted on propelling Tim through an intricate history of music, with abundant examples, telling him he couldn't know when he was born until he knew who had already died. Consistency wasn't one of Knute's weaknesses.

Teddy's teaching seemed much more accidental. It was a

matter of moments, a general remark during a pause between movements of a quartet, or during a brief visit at Knute's house that seemed to have occurred to him as he was going by. The remark was usually a simple one about some small, specific matter, the bowing or fingering of a given passage, which would be found later to have a much more general application, or, conversely, a seemingly vague generality which would actually throw light on many details of practice. It would as often be a remark about something outside of music as about anything in music itself. Music and life, both viewed gently and largely, flowed back and forth through each other in Teddy. What Teddy said never seemed to bring on argument, but to rest by itself. He was constantly affording Tim mysterious glimpses, as of a spot of light in a copse of the magic wilderness, and then leaving him to find his way back to it. He would ponder aloud about there being so much Debussy in a certain Gershwin piece. He would tell a short anecdote about the philosophy of Beethoven or the activity of Mozart. He would quote from a letter by Rilke or a sonnet by Michelangelo. Tim would get the scores or listen to records, or read the letters or the poems. He felt himself gently expanding under this teaching, which made everything his own discovery. It was not until long afterward that he realized how many of these germinal hints had been made for him, and how much of that inner order of his was present in Teddy's teaching.

Teddy would come in with a score under his arm, sit down in one of the rockers, hang his cap on the post of it, and wait until Tim turned around from the piano or looked up from his book.

Then he would ask blandly, "Well, how goes it today?"

If Tim said, as he did most often that year, "Terrible," Teddy would nod solemnly and say, "Good, good. That's fine."

After that they would sit there together, each with his own thoughts, Tim like a lost army fighting in the dark, his mind full of quick lights, explosions, and little, sudden deaths, for each of which he mourned, and Teddy apparently in benign meditation. Or they would talk for a few minutes about a clambake Pearl was planning for them, or a trip back among the redwoods in Teddy's Ford, which was even more venerable than Jeremiah, or a quartet they were preparing to play in the community theater.

Then Teddy would get up. "Well," he would say, "I just dropped in to see how it was going.

"Oh, by the way," he would say casually, when he had reached the door, "I brought over your score for that quintet we were talking about. Thought you might like to go through it a couple of times."

He would leave the score on the piano and go out. It would be terrific. It would make Tim feel like a mass of undisciplined thumbs.

If Tim said his writing was going, however, Teddy would carry the score away with him.

It took Tim a long time to see how much order, both in composition and in instrumental skill, there was in the scores Teddy chose to leave for him. They made a developing series of lessons.

Also, it was Teddy who fixed things so Tim could extend indefinitely the stay of two or three weeks he had vaguely in mind when he came. Tim had stretched it a bit by himself. Here he was always on the verge of a discovery. Always in a few days more he would have something he could carry away with him, something which would grow by itself. He would know. Then two letters came in the same mail. One was from Mary. It didn't say much about the shop, except that Mr. Atley was fuming more persistently than usual. It didn't say much of anything about what she was thinking, except to hope that Tim was getting what he wanted with Knute, and having a good time besides. It was a very careful, uninformative little letter, written, apparently with some hesitation, on a page and a half of gray note paper, and signed, "Affectionately, Mary." Tim, searching it for some personal expression, hardly understood why she had written, until he opened the other letter. It was from Mr. Atley, and was more exact and businesslike than Tim would have thought possible, even to the usual pompous vacuity of business courtesy.

*As we have already been put to considerable inconvenience,
due to your insistence upon so ill-timed a holiday, and as that
holiday has already been extended beyond the time we understood to be intended, and as we are in serious need of an
additional assistant, I must ask you to return at once, offer an
adequate explanation of your delay, such as illness or other un-
avoidable accident, or consider your relationship with us ter-
minated. In any case, I deem it no more than reasonable to ask
that we be informed of your intention in this matter at once.*

Yours Very Truly,

Marvin T. Atley

M.T.A./m.t.

Mary had only wanted to soften that letter. She had only
wanted to hint, without seeming to interfere, that Tim should
do what he thought was best for his music. Then it seemed to
him that her own careful little letter was quite forlorn, that it
was down under the bar, like her m.t. under the M.T.A.

He felt bad about both letters, for that matter. Mr. Atley was
right, of course. He couldn't hang on down here indefinitely
without deciding one way or the other. Mr. Atley must have
felt greatly injured and angry to dictate such a letter, and there
was no reason why he shouldn't. Tim's conscience said he owed
it to Mr. Atley to go back at once. It also seemed to him like
an enormous task to find another job. They weren't easy for
anybody to find in these depression days, and musicians especially were on their uppers. Yet he was terribly depressed at the
thought of breaking off this exciting exploration and comrade-
ship, in which he had scarcely made a beginning. Merely to
imagine himself in the store again made him uneasy and gloomy.
He felt the virtue ooze out of him at the thought, and caught a
glimpse of himself, years down the trail, a bleached and spiritless clerk in whom the strains of great music made only mechanical echoes of satisfaction. Still, there was Mary. Suddenly a
strong desire to see Mary entered into his melancholy indecision, and he knew that behind her great care in writing the

letter was a loneliness and a wish to have him back, which she wouldn't express.

When Knute got up in the afternoon, Tim told him about Mr. Atley's letter.

"Thundering Jove," Knute said, "I thought you were over that notion. I told you when you came down here that you were going to stay. Here you are, just beginning to shake the dust out of your mind and the molasses out of your soul, and you want to go back and sell Bing Crosby to drunkards and waitresses."

He wouldn't say anything more about it, either.

But he must have spoken to Teddy, for that evening, when the quartet came to the coffee and conversation, Teddy came over and took a seat beside Tim.

"Knute says you play the trumpet?"

Tim nodded.

"I need a trumpet in my band at the inn—three nights a week, Wednesday, Friday and Saturday."

"Band?" Tim asked, incredulous.

"Didn't you know I had a band?" Teddy twinkled a little out of his seeming quiet indolence. He was a short, heavy man, with a head almost as large as Stephen Granger's. He always seemed to settle into his baggy clothes for an indefinite stay, whenever he sat down. His hair was blond, beginning to get gray, very thick in the back, and permanently creased by the cloth cap he always put on when he went out, even when he was going no farther than the back yard to scatter grain for the chickens. His face was expressionless, and when he spoke you usually had to wait a while to be sure he was talking to you, and not just thinking half aloud. He liked to sit hunched down, with his hands folded upon his stomach.

"Oh, yes, I have a band," he said. "A good band. We play what they call jazz, I think."

"He thinks," snorted Knute, who was sitting on the other side of Teddy. "He knows damned well it's jazz. He even writes some of the stuff."

Tim looked at Teddy.

"Why not?" Teddy said. "It's the American folk music. Nobody can write any kind of music for a country if he doesn't understand its folk music. We're going to rehearse two of my latest tomorrow. One of them is called *Moonlight on the Dunes*, and the other is called *Sweetheart of Monterey*. Those are good titles, I think. Not too original. Everybody will believe he has heard them before."

It was usually impossible to tell just how much Teddy meant by what he said, how much, or even what. You had to think about it.

"He's got a salon orchestra at the Inn too," Knute said. "The orchestra plays upstairs in the lobby. The band plays downstairs in the cocktail lounge. He runs back and forth between them, and becomes a different man on the stairs. Downstairs he is Paul Whiteman, except the mustache, all smiles and fat affability. Upstairs he is as gloomy as Beethoven. Even looks like Beethoven. You should see it."

"Would you like to blow a trumpet for Paul Whiteman Quest?" Teddy asked.

Tim said he sure would, and all during the second quartet, he alternately marveled at the picture of Teddy undergoing his transformation on the stairs, so that he even grinned from thinking about it, and felt surges of quick joy because he was going to stay, and because Teddy and Knute wanted him to.

He wrote a short letter to Mr. Atley, saying that he was sorry for his thoughtlessness, and even explaining why he believed he should stay, although he thought that was probably useless, and a much longer one to Mary, telling her all about Knute, Teddy and Stephen, about the swimming and the hiking and the music, and the job with the band. He was happy at the way things had turned out, and he felt very affectionate toward Mary while he was writing to her. He wrote both letters that same night, and the next day he joined the band for its first turn at Teddy's new numbers, which turned out to be real enough, and named just exactly what Teddy had said they were named.

AFTER a month with the band, Tim also began to play the violin with Teddy's salon orchestra. At first the rapid changing seemed like a prank, but then, as he tried to put himself more fully into both kinds of music, it became like living over again in the flesh that long war of the mind which had preceded his pilgrimage to the mountain with Rachel. He often felt as he had when he was sitting in the back room of the Alfalfa Club. Sometimes he even experienced the old sensation of despair, as if he were faint and weak from lack of food. Even the two rooms in which the band and the orchestra played made each other unreal.

The basement cocktail lounge, in which the band played, was called the Marine Room. The dance floor was made of glassy, black tile, in which were staggered, at irregular intervals, figured tiles showing sailing vessels, breaking waves, spouting whales and fish. There was a deep-piled, black carpet before the bar and under the tables. The tops of the tables were painted to represent tide pools full of seaweed, crabs, tiny minnows and anemones of gigantic size and violent color. Frosty mermaids and dolphins were cut into the mirrors behind the bar, and the walls, lit whitely from below, were a shallow and sunny sea wherein, before cliffs and grottoes of scarlet, orange, blue, green and purple coral, there balanced contrasting shoals of tropical fish. This ocean bottom was crowded and noisy on dance nights. Most of the crowd was young, and though there must have been just as many young men, it seemed to be made up chiefly of beautiful, tanned, long-legged girls with highly brushed hair curled upon their shoulders, crimson mouths, arched brows and huge smiles, so many of them that they were like multiplications of each other in mirrors. These girls had made a fatherly idol of Teddy. They steered their partners to a place below him, and danced there, back and forth, with tiny steps, swaying as if they were actually rocked by a tide in the Marine Room. Their partners, somehow, looked helpless and unimportant among them. The beautiful girls turned up their faces to Teddy and smiled and laughed at him and teased him, and made him promise to play the numbers they wanted. Then they would let their partners dance them away, and still they would be smiling and laughing back at Teddy. Teddy stood on the edge of the platform, most of the time with his back to the band, his baton moving gently up and down, and twinkled solemnly at them. Each of the girls, as she rocked there, pleading with Teddy for the number she wanted, would seem wonderful and inimitable, a wild creature only playing tame, possessed of the secret of the quick edge of the magic wilderness, the eternal region of the sun among the leaves, a secret which could endure through whatever the newspapers had to say about stocks and bonds, diplomacy, power-mongers and the destinies of nations. They had the idle confidence of sharks in teeming and lukewarm waters. Yet, for some reason or other, when they had danced away out of the light of the bandstand, it was impossible to remember them individually.

Teddy never paid any attention to their requests. "It is simple," he said. "One of them always asks for what I have decided to play next, unless it is a new number. Then I tell them it will be a new number, and that is what they want most of all."

There was only one of the young women whom Tim could remember distinctly. She was a thin ash-blonde. She moved with a smooth, formal flowing which reminded Tim of the way Marjory Hale had walked. There were many things about her which reminded Tim of Marjory, but always with the difference that the memory of Marjory ambled indistinctly through the gray miasma of her spirit, while this girl proceeded distinctly through a clear, cold air. She stared, unabashed and unchanging, at everything about her, as if judging life with mathematical certainty and with no emotion, excepting, perhaps, a slight distaste. Whatever she looked at, the dancers, the bartenders, the fish on the wall, or nothing at all, her gaze had that same surgical clarity. He imagined she would speak that way, too, coolly, briefly and finally. Even her body seemed subject to the same control, and appeared to make no accidental movements. She sat as upright as she stood and walked. She accepted invitations to dance with no change of expression, and her partner was compelled to dance with the same vertical equanimity with which she crossed the room alone. She was never one of those who gathered below Teddy and played favorite. She went by calmly and distantly, looking right before her, over her partner's shoulder. Most of the time she sat by herself at the same table in the corner. Sometimes she would signal to a waiter, but more often she would rise and make a slow and stately passage among the tables to the bar, and order her own drink, and bear it back. She drank in neat, single sips, and, after each, set the glass down again exactly. She never required more than one stroke to light her match, or more than one drag to light her cigarette. Tim imagined that she must have a soul like the works of Euclid. She was the organization of science in the chaos of the material world. She was the order of reason in the wilderness of the spirit.

Teddy knew this young woman, who was not a seasonal visitor, like most of them. Tim had said nothing about her, but one night Teddy led him over to her table and introduced him to her. Tim couldn't remember afterward how much Teddy had twinkled while making the introduction.

"He plays the trumpet, doesn't he?" she asked Teddy, while dissecting Tim.

"Oh, he plays everything," Teddy said. "Composes too."

"Ah," she said. "Versatile."

"May we sit down?" Teddy asked.

"If you like," she said, turning her head slowly, and beginning to dissect him.

Teddy seemed to believe that this was an invitation. Tim sat down because Teddy did.

"Have you written anything lately?" Teddy asked her.

"Doris is a poet," he said to Tim.

"I am not a poet," she said distinctly, "and I have not got anything written in months. Does it matter?"

"Not if you still want to," Teddy said.

Then he left them alone, saying he wouldn't need Tim for the next number. When the number began, Tim asked Doris if she wanted to dance.

"No," she said clearly.

She rose and picked up her glass.

Tim rose too. "May I get you a drink?"

"I'll get my own, thank you."

Tim waited by the table, feeling conspicuous and foolish. Doris returned at her unvaried pace, set the glass carefully upon the table, and stood there for a moment, staring at Tim as if he had said something which she must consider in order to be sure whether or not it was an insult. Then she began to sit down. When she was nearly down, her knees gave way, and she dropped into the chair with a thump. She looked at Tim.

"I am very drunk," she explained in a clear voice. "This will be my ninth whisky sour. I had no supper. It is ridiculous, of course."

Tim didn't know what to say. There never seemed to be anything to say after she had spoken.

She drank, set the glass down, and looked abroad upon the glittering drift of the Marine Room.

"Where," she said, as if pronouncing a formal judgment rather than asking a question, "where is it all going to?"

Tim didn't attempt to answer this question. Neither of them spoke again until the dance was over. Then it was time for Tim to change his jacket and go upstairs to join the orchestra. He never spoke to Doris again, although she was there almost every evening the band played, but she remained to him a personification of the Marine Room. Whenever he saw her, he would think, "Where is it all going to?"

He and Teddy left their white jackets with the hat-check girl of the Marine Room, and she handed them out their black coats. Tim had an old tuxedo jacket which he had borrowed from one of the hotel waiters. Teddy had a much older set of tails. It was worn green in places, and Teddy had colored some of the buttons with ink where the fabric had been rubbed through. They put on these coats while they ran upstairs. The arms and the tails of Teddy's coat flew out about him as he struggled with it, like too many wings. At the top of the stairs, Teddy would wait, and Tim would go in and take his place with the violins, and the orchestra would take this as their sign, and sit at attention. Then Teddy would enter, slowly and with great dignity. As the clapping began, he would bend his head slightly toward the audience, without smiling or pausing in his progress. He would take his place upon the podium, bow once, face the orchestra with his arms raised, wait till the clapping had ceased, and at once start the orchestra upon its meticulous course. There, in the great, shadowy hall, in a semi-circle behind their lighted stands, the players would regard with strict attention the restrained gestures of his baton, most of which couldn't have been seen by anyone sitting behind him. Tim would feel himself change, trying to become part of something very like what Knute had described. Sitting there, poised for his entry, watching Teddy's hand move above him, and still full of the confusion and throbbing of the Marine Room, he could easily imagine that he and the other players wore satin knee breeches and long coats carefully parted to fall from the chair, and curled and powdered wigs, and that their music rested upon lyre-shaped racks of ebony, beneath the soft and flickering light of many candles.

The lounge was an enormous room, with a ceiling out of sight in shadow. Excepting the little points of light on the racks, the only illumination came from a few shaded floor lamps, set far away along the walls. The small audience was scattered about in the gloom, upon davenports and easy chairs. When Tim wasn't playing, he would rest his violin on his thigh, keep his ear open for the point of his re-entry, and look out across his light. The audience would appear only as small, pale patches. Within sound of a warning whisper, within sight of a raised finger, there were always children, usually upon stiff, high-backed chairs, girls in white dresses, small boys in flannels, with their hair wet and combed slick, wriggling through the long and tedious strangeness, and adolescents, writhing more slowly and dreaming more often. All about, upon the walls, hung huge, somber marine paintings, their deep, gilded frames gleaming in the light from the floor lamps. It was like playing in the night empyrean, like making a faint, sweet, intricate noise in the heart of a void in which the stars were faint, distant and meaningless points. A cough from those shadows, when Teddy's hands were lifted before the first note of a movement, was as startling as a shout. Waiters pussyfooted over the deep carpets among the davenports, bearing trays of gently tinkling glasses, and bent deferentially to hear whispered orders.

It seemed all the stranger to come into this divided world after riding over from Carmel with Teddy. Teddy's old Ford had no top. The stuffing peered out of both seats in many places, rust from the fog had attacked it like a plague, and in back, besides their instruments, there would always be other tools of the Quests' life, the clamming forks, fishing tackle, wet gunny sacks smelling of fish and eels and clams, tin cans full of earth in which stood plants Pearl had dug up on the hills, or in the ferny gorges, a box of kindling for a beach fire, a sack of potatoes or sweet corn for roasting.

Over the noise of the engine, Teddy would shout, and yet seem to be speaking as quietly as if his hands were folded upon his paunch, always with that gentle twinkling.

"What America needs," he would yell, sitting there comfortably, with his hands limp upon the lower half of the wheel, "is chamber music it can like, music families and friends can get together and play at anybody's house, instead of playing bridge or the radio."

Or he would shout, "Do you play for people? That's what counts, the audience of four or five. Then everybody is a musician. Then you don't make the music; it grows by itself. Everything good grows. Anything that is not shared is dead."

On the way home, the night Tim met Doris, Teddy said, "Doris is having a hard time getting born. She is afraid of love."

Then, after a moment, he added, nodding cheerfully, "But she gets drunk for the world, not for herself. She'll be all right."

Another night he said, "Don't be afraid of sentiment. It's better to be a fool once in a while than all the time."

They would come over the ridge of the peninsula, and see the lights of Monterey around the bay, and a service station shining at the crossing below. They would work out of the light onto the dark, curving drives to the hotel. There would be the smell of the sea, and the melancholy clanging of a bell buoy. The hills reaching inland toward Salinas would loom heavily through the fog. The black cypresses, the fog collecting upon their boughs and dropping slowly, would close around the old Ford. In Teddy and in the hills lay the quiet seed. It was like that. For ages yet, maybe for centuries beyond man, the rain would turn the hills of Monterey green, and the sun would turn them white again. There was no hurry. The seed was always there. Tiny, abundant life nobody saw went on all the time in and around the roots of the grass on the take-it-easy hills. The fogs passed silently over in the nights, in the lowering afternoons when the surf was hidden, and the abundant life took new hope. The night, the hills, the fog, Teddy, Tim himself, would blend into one being, and Tim would feel spaciously comforted. He would discover in himself quiet and durable hills, like those of Salinas and Teddy Quest, and the fog of doubts and despairs would break around them and make a gentle rain to quicken the seed in their slopes.

Then they would reach the hotel, and start racing up and down the stairs between the Marine Room and the lounge, changing their coats as they ran. Downstairs Teddy would smile blandly and watch the dancers, and let the band go pretty much as it chose. Upstairs he would be solemn and exacting, listening intently, hurt by the slightest deviation from what he had expected to hear. It took Tim a long time to understand that these two parts did not change Teddy, any more than he was changed when he left the table, in the dining room of his inwardly ordered house, covered with the score upon which he had been writing earnestly and quietly, and wandered uptown in his bedroom slippers and ancient smoking jacket, his cap pulled down over his nose, smoking his curved pipe, jingling a chain in his hand, and asking everybody he met, "You haven't seen my dog, have you?"

The whole answer was revealed to Tim one night; though, of course, that was only the beginning of the lesson, the bringing to consciousness of what he had long experienced. For once they had come out of the Marine Room with time to walk up instead of running. They had even stood in the cloak room and changed their jackets without hurrying.

As they went up the stairs side by side, Tim asked, "How do you manage to keep switching back and forth like this? It's hard enough just with an instrument. How do you do it with the whole score to think about?"

"Ah," Teddy said, stopping on one step. "It's what we're coming to." He spread his arms so that one reached toward the Marine Room and one toward the lounge. Then he waved them rapidly back and forth across each other, and shook his head. Last, he stretched them out before him, the fingertips of his right hand pointing toward the fingertips of his left hand, and brought them slowly together until the fingers dovetailed, when he nodded. Throughout this pantomime he was twinkling brilliantly, but without the trace of a smile.

After that Tim noticed how often Teddy made this sign, though in a less dramatic way, of everything coming gently together, of opposites becoming one. It was his totem, like Lawrence's turtle; it was his charm, his rabbit's foot, his lucky coin. A good sign must be a very simple thing which reminds you easily of a big truth, and can encourage you in low moments. Teddy's was a very good sign. It applied to everything, music, ideas, feelings, people, nations, species. It was the promise of union and the refutation of despair and haste. You could see that Teddy thought of it that way, by the slowness with which he brought his fingers together, by the manner in which, when he sat in the midst of foolish talk and argument, he would fold his hands upon his stomach, and look down at them, and twinkle.

THERE was also a kind of inner order, an inalienable character, in Stephen Granger, though its manifestations were accidental, as its growth must have been accidental. His own nature transformed all the accidents, that was all, so that when enough of them were known the whole world would assume a unity of a sort, the unity of the nature of Stephen Granger. He would drop in just to sit with Knute and Tim for a while, never with any other purpose, such as the music lessons Teddy gave, and when he departed he would leave behind him a nostalgic encouragement about mankind, and often a ponderable tale.

It was in this way that Tim heard the life of Knute Fenderson one afternoon. Knute was up after his sleep on the porch. He was opening and closing cupboard doors in the kitchen, looking for something to eat, and grumbling ferociously about the idiocy of trying to write music in a world where nobody thought you had a tune unless it was some spavined, staggering, jungle thing to which you could get out and shake your rear end. "Hind-end music, that's what they want," he muttered. "No brains, no soul, no beauty, just a big, fat, wobbly hind end."

Stephen was sitting beside the table, playing meditatively with Knute's chess pieces.

"Did I ever tell you," he asked Tim, "how Knute became a hermit?"

"No. How was that?"

Knute came to the kitchen door and stood there eating doughnuts and drinking cold coffee.

Still slowly moving the chess pieces, Stephen began:

From the time of his earliest childhood in a Norwegian fishing village, Knute Fenderson, composer, violinist and incendiary, gave promise of both the originality and the indifference to difficulties which were to characterize his entire career. His father, a man of remarkable perception for one of his calling, which was that of landed proprietor and conservative politician, presented the child with a half-size violin on his third birthday, but Knute rejected the gift in favor of an old double-bass he had found in the attic, and within a few days had transposed Rimsky-Korsakov's *Flight of the Bumblebee* into a range suitable to this instrument, and had mastered its intricate fingering, despite the fact that his small stature made it necessary for him to move from the floor to a chair to a table and back with such rapidity that he became all but invisible and the sound of his movement formed a not unpleasing accompaniment to the piece. His father accepted this decision gracefully, and indeed, for four years carried the boy about from drawing room to drawing room, exhibiting his skill and calling attention to his visibility before he began. The practice was then abandoned because Knute had grown sufficiently to play the *Flight of the Bumblebee* from one position on the chair, and so had lost interest in his accomplishment.

It chanced that there lived in Knute's village an aged and poverty-stricken musician, who may have been truly great, since he not only composed during his spare time, but also played the organ and the flute, conducted a children's choir, and was considered a harmless idiot by most of the villagers. To him the boy went for advice on his next move.

"What's the hardest kind of music in the world to write?" he asked.

The choirmaster removed his bifocals, wiped them meditatively with the end of his beard, put them on again, and examined the past for some time. Finally he said, "Eh?"

Young Knute repeated his question.

"Ah," said the old man. "Mmmmmmmmmmmmm," he said. "Probably," he answered at last, "for the unaccustomed Western ear at least, or perhaps, considering the limitations of my own experience, I should say for the Norwegian ear, or, even more confidently, for musicians of my own locality, long subject to Christian hymns and the rigors of the sea, which have been at the same time our mothers' breasts and our sorrow, probably for musicians so situated . . ." He paused in thought. "What was that now?" he asked.

"What's the hardest kind of music in the world to write?"

"Ah, yes," said the old man. "Chinese, I should say."

Knute applied himself to composition in this medium with such success that at the age of eleven he had completed a two-hour orchestral piece which it was impossible, at that time, to have performed anywhere in the Western Hemisphere, for lack of suitable instruments. He then presented himself before the village banker.

"Outside of the arts," he asked, "what is the hardest way in the world to earn money?"

"I'd have to think about that," the banker said. "I've never approached the problem in exactly that light before," and for an hour he studied the small ledger in which were set down the losses of his firm through unsound loans. "Of course," he said, closing the ledger at last, "this is strictly between us. If it weren't that your father . . ."

"I understand," Knute said. It made him very uneasy to have his father's influence mentioned.

"In my official capacity," the banker said, "I should feel it incumbent upon me to point out that with the money market what it is these days, and the lamentable tendency of our people to prefer parsimony to a moderate and lucrative indebtedness, to say nothing of the inroads made by the insurance charlatans, there is no occupation more uncertain in its rewards than that of the banker himself. It can be shown by statistics that . . ."

"Unofficially," Knute said.

"Unofficially," the banker said, "whaling, for the common hand."

Knute found himself a berth as cabin boy on a declining whaler commanded by an old man who had turned strongly to religion in his later years, and there he might have remained, contentedly misused, for the rest of his days, had it not been for an unfortunate conjunction, in his seventeenth year, of his own peculiarities and those of the captain.

The vessel was anchored one moonlit night in a lonely fjord, and Knute was left alone on the middle watch. The dismal splendor of the scene aided his contemptuous meditations, and for an hour the time passed pleasantly enough, but then he became conscious of being repeatedly disturbed by certain multiple sounds and movements in the darker regions of the fjord. At last the cause of this disturbance entered the path of the moon, and he saw that it was a sizable school of whale. He lowered a boat and set off in pursuit, and so inspired was he by his irritation and by the problems which he encountered that when he returned to the vessel at dawn, he left four of the leviathans bleeding and blowing their last upon the rocky shores. The captain insisted upon turning over to Knute the price of the smallest of the four whales, and thus, put all at once in possession of a sum more than adequate for his purpose, there was nothing for him to do but return to his home, because, as he confessed years later, "Who the hell would imagine there could be any interest in any kind of serious music, let alone a new kind, in a little dump like that?"

By the work of his own hands he constructed a concert hall in the mountains, some miles distant from the village, and accessible only by way of a narrow and precipitous goat-path. He then turned his attention to assembling an instrument which would sound like a small, Oriental orchestra, a task which he accomplished with discouraging ease, due to the manifold skills he had acquired as a sailor and a carpenter, and when he was twenty, there remained no further excuse for delaying his debut.

In making the final arrangements, he sought the advice of an established composer and concert artist in Oslo, who had taken an unfriendly interest in the young man's work for some time, having himself made a considerable reputation by arranging Hopi ceremonial dances to be played on two dry sticks and a willow whistle. Knute found this celebrity reading his autobiography, and interrupted him at once.

"How can you make a reputation out of one concert?" he asked.

The composer looked up. "You are Fenderson?" he inquired. "I am."

"I've heard of you. They say you are mad, but whether or not there's anything in that remains to be seen. Is your stuff any good?"

"It's terrible," Knute said. "The worst you ever heard."

This statement shook the composer's confidence profoundly. He pondered his answer, covertly eying the young man now and again. Finally he said, "You're not to mention my name. I can't afford a reputation for helping people, especially indigent musicians."

"It's the last thing I'd think of," Knute said.

"With that understanding," the composer said, "I give it you as my considered opinion that the most certain way to make an immediate impression is to secure for your opening performance . . ." He paused and studied Knute. "I take it your music is something quite new?"

"Absolutely new," Knute assured him. "I have successfully violated every precept since the time of Palestrina."

"Ah, so?" said the older composer. He was evidently stimulated by the thought of such an achievement. "As I was about to suggest," he went on, "you could do nothing better than to gather as your first audience all the critics of our own country who are well seasoned, let us say over fifty years of age, especially those who have formulated systems of appreciation."

"Thank you," said Knute, and turned to leave.

"By the way," the composer said, "I have drawn up a list of such men for my own abuse. You are welcome to it. And I might add that it wouldn't be a bad idea to invite a number of the veteran German critics. They have enormous prestige in the larger centers of music."

Young Fenderson accepted this advice in the spirit in which it was given, and determined to act upon it. After nine months of diligent study among the back files of innumerable magazines and periodicals, he sent out personal invitations to all the

Scandinavian critics, in which he stated, with specific illustrations and comparisons, that the work of Knute Fenderson as far surpassed that of the favorite composer and concert artist of each critic as did the work of the composer and the artist that critic most heartily detested. He varied this approach only in the case of the German critics, to whom he sent a circular merely stating that the music of Knute Fenderson was incomparably greater than that of any German.

In spite of these preparations, however, Fenderson was discouraged as the moment of his concert approached. For five hours there had not been a break in the file of music lovers climbing the goat-path, and several hundred who had been turned back at the door, stood outside in absolute silence, listening attentively for the first strains of the music. Peering from the wings, Knute saw that not only were all the invited critics there, but practically the entire population of his own village as well, and that almost everyone appeared cheerful and filled with the liveliest anticipation. There was, however, one group of dour and skeptical faces, well down front in the center. Fenderson recognized them as critics and musical biographers who had once been composers or performers, and pinned his hopes on them.

"As for the rest of these fools," he muttered, "just wait until I begin to play. I'll change their tune fast enough."

Nevertheless, as an additional precaution, he began with a long lecture on the history, influences, forms and instruments of Chinese music, using Chinese terminology throughout, and interlarding a substantial number of quotations in the more obscure Oriental dialects. The critics all leaned forward with expressions of intense interest, and at one point, when he was explaining in ninth-century Chubi-Chubi, an extinct dialect of the south-west Gobi region, the influence of certain constructional peculiarities of the prehistoric Easter Island hand drum upon the rhythm choirs of the second Ming Dynasty, an old fisherman who was sitting in one corner with his hand behind his ear and a red stocking cap still on his head, said loudly, and with evident pride, "He knows a thing or two, he does."

Fenderson at once broke off the lecture, with a gesture, half contempt and half despair, and took his place in the center of his instrument, an amazing construction which filled the entire stage, rose in places to a height of thirty feet, and required the utmost agility and stamina in the performer, being covered with a great variety of gongs, wires, cymbals, mouth-pieces, keys, pedals, levers, lights and control boards, arranged upon different levels and connected by ramps, ladders and hanging ropes. Fenderson threw his whole body into the performance. The instrument poured forth without interruption a bewildering succession of single, minor and discordant twangings and pipings, many of which I could hear distinctly from my place in the center of the hall.

Stephen paused and looked up, and Tim asked him, "You were there?"

"I am always there," Stephen murmured. "It is a vice against which I have struggled for years without success. There is a morbid region of my mind which has developed an almost telepathic awareness of crises in other people's affairs. It gives me no rest. On this particular evening, however, I was merely obeying orders from my editor. He thought an international incident might develop out of Fenderson's invitation to the German critics."

Stephen went on:

Fenderson arrived at a pause, the end of a species of movement, I suppose. He was sweating profusely, his hair was in disarray, his garments in shreds and his hands and arms lacerated. He leapt out of the instrument and confronted the audience from the apron, his fists doubled and planted upon his hips, his feet apart and his face lit by a furious scowl. His reception was appalling. Even I, with my moderate concern about musical activity, shrank from its implications. The critics, even the ex-artists and the delegation from Berlin, rose as one and applauded thunderously. The villagers stood on their seats, leaped in the air, tossed their caps, skimmed their hats through space, and shouted "bravo" repeatedly. Programs, torn to bits, snowed down from the gallery, accompanied by a hail of corsages, coins, invitations to dinner, offers of marriage and requests for loans. Everywhere people embraced each other, their faces streaming with tears.

Poor Fenderson was stricken white and speechless. The agony of death stared from his eyes. It was in that terrible moment, I believe, that I first felt a kind of affection for the man, and decided to interview him at the first opportunity.

At last his senses returned to him, and his conduct became almost irrational. He began to tear his instrument to pieces and fling it at the heaving multitude. They were enchanted. Fragments were snatched up and pressed to worshipping bosoms. At intervals Fenderson was compelled to rush out and kick off the admirers who were trying to climb onto the stage in order to touch him or present him with bouquets. At last they became too many for him, and in this extremity he tore his score from its fourteen racks, converted it in a moment into a blazing torch, and rushed out into the house, setting fires at every possible point, drapes, carpets, coat-tails, petticoats and hair. When the concert hall was a bedlam of flame and voices calling his name with the confidence of martyrs, he staggered out onto the open mountain and stood there shaking his fists and cursing until he fell senseless, and was borne off tenderly and triumphantly by his fellow villagers.

I went round to his quarters the next day, taking with me a young American composer who had recently undergone the first performance of his work in Boston. We found such a multitude that at first we couldn't approach the door. My correspondent's visa and pass were of no avail. I retired with the young American to a convenient bar, and, while we revived our strength, drew up a couple of very creditable imitations of American diplomatic passes. These also proved useless. Finally I hit upon a very simple expedient, which should have occurred to me, of all people, almost at once. I made us two badges, with ribbons attached, such as are worn at all conventions, and inscribed upon each, Representative of the Standard Oil Company. When we returned with these, there was made for us a passage so wide that one might almost have felt the deference to approximate trepidation.

We found Fenderson, exhausted and discouraged, pacing around and around the living room, cursing his fate, occasionally overturning a table, statue or bookcase, and kicking his way through newspapers, all of which had been thrown down open to the music section. He was carrying in one hand an Oslo paper marked with red pencil, and now and then he would pause, glance at the marked column, break into a terrifying groan, and resume his pacing more rapidly than before. At last he caught sight of us in passing. He halted in the middle of the room and glared.

"Who are you?" he roared.

"American press," I said. "If we . . ."

"Get out," he roared. "Is there no degree of suffering for which you hired vultures have any respect?" He took up his pacing again, as if we had already gone. "Reporters," he muttered, "correspondents, columnists, critics, the pulp-wood brains of the century. Is it any wonder there is no peace, no home without its murder and incest? Is it any wonder diplomacy is in a hopeless confusion, finances are more obscure than ever, labor is discontented, literature has disappeared and the arts are on the greased slide? All night creeping in my windows, sneaking down the chimney and up through the cellar, insects, reptiles, germs, prolific and legitimate offspring of Hearst, McCormick and Gayda. Every time I move, more of them, hauling out their damned pads, flashing their infernal cameras, presenting me with their abominable cigars and flowers and candy and liquor."

At this point I ceased to follow him, and must have muttered some inadvertent word of doubt. Fenderson swung around.

"You still here?" he roared. "I thought I told you . . ." He stopped and looked at me more attentively. "Well, what did you think of it?" he asked.

I confessed that I had never seen such a spontaneous reception.

"I don't mean that, idiot," he roared, rather impatiently, I thought. "The music, you fool. What did you think of the music?"

"Frankly," I ventured, "I thought it was lousy, but then, I'm no . . ."

But Fenderson himself prevented me from spoiling the impression I had made. He rushed to me and embraced me. "My friend," he cried. "At last, a man of some judgment." He began to walk about excitedly. "You will write for me. You will tell them how it really was. You will be unmerciful. You will persecute me. You will become a musical monomaniac. In time an anti-Fenderson cult will gather about you. I may yet be great." He continued for some minutes in this strain, paying no attention to us or to the cries of the crowd outside, until his eye chanced once more to notice the paper he carried. He came to a halt. His gloom returned. "But no," he said. "You cannot do it; with the best will in the world, you cannot. Already I am hailed everywhere. I am established. You would only be ruined, you, the one sane and friendly person I have encountered in the last eighteen hours. I cannot let you do it. If you truly understood—but no, that is impossible. No journalist can be expected to understand true fame. They are compelled by their calling to give their entire attention to superficial and annoying persons, dictators, financiers, armament manufacturers, movie stars."

I assured him my greatest difficulties had always arisen from a disinclination for such people, but he shook his head. "It is too late," he said. "Have you seen this?" and he held the Oslo paper out to me.

I took it and read the marked column. The young American composer read over my shoulder. It was not hard to understand why Fenderson was so upset. In several different ways the column hailed the concert as the greatest triumph within the memory of that particular critic, and stated that Fenderson was a genius of the first magnitude, both as composer and as artist.

"And that," Fenderson lamented, "that unspeakable detraction, is the nearest thing to a measured evaluation that I could cull from this mass of offal," and he kicked furiously among the papers.

I ventured to guess, privately, that his own judgment might not be of the soundest at such a moment, but glances at a dozen of the scattered sheets forced me to conclude that he was not far wrong. The Oslo critique, indeed, began to assume its true place as censure of a local prophet. Most of the articles verged on the extravagant, and one Berlin paper spoke with complete immoderation, saying, "This is a music the German people could be proud to call their own. Its clear Aryan tone would have to be confessed even were it known that Mr. Fenderson himself were not of Nordic extraction."

Fenderson bore down upon us from the farthest reaches of the room. "Is there any place in the world where such things cannot happen?" he roared.

"Yes," said the young composer, "America."

"It is possible to insult Americans?"

"They are automatically insulted and enraged," said the young composer. "They form splenetic organizations by the hundreds, and write letters to periodicals and congressmen. They gather in mobs and pay no attention. They hang people without trial and shoot citizens down with machine guns out of passing cars. They will despise you because you do not eat the same things they eat for breakfast. They even apply indifference."

Fenderson stared at him for a moment. Then the light of a terrible joy emanated from his countenance. "How I shall suffer!" he cried. "Why don't people tell me these things?" he cried, and started for the door.

"The crowd," I reminded him.

"True," he said, "the crowd," and sank dejected into the nearest chair, and commenced, inattentively, to wrench its arms off. Such hopeless inaction was not long possible in one of his temperament, however. When I began, "If you will wait until tonight," he leaped up, crying, "Tonight? Endure endless hours more of that fulsome mass out there? I had rather live to be ninety and be elected to an Academy. The next boat; I must take the very next boat, I tell you."

We all walked about with our hands behind us, considering the problem. Suddenly Fenderson cried, "I have it. A disguise."

I was skeptical, but having thought of nothing else that would serve immediately, I joined in the effort, and at the end of two hours we had him wonderfully stained and attired as a maharaja. It was as I had feared, however. The crowd at once penetrated this disguise, and we were fortunate to be able to get Fenderson back in and force the door closed. He was in a pitiful condition, stripped nearly naked by souvenir hunters, his right hand wrung into a limp and bleeding mass, and all the exposed parts of his person covered with lipstick.

At last an idea occurred to me. I cleared my throat. Fenderson was leaning gloomily against the piano, cutting its strings one at a time with a pair of pliers. He looked around.

"If you would assume an expression of calmness," I suggested.

After some practice, he managed reasonably well, and we passed through the crowd unhindered and arrived at the dock, where we booked passage for New York. Fenderson immediately retired to his cabin and commenced the composition of a symphony based on Eskimo drinking songs, and the construction of an instrument suitable for playing it, and had completed his task before we sighted the Statue of Liberty.

But even then he was doomed to disappointment. He filled Carnegie Hall five nights running. In Boston the police had to form cordons to get his car through the streets. All the movies in Philadelphia closed their doors during his stay. In Chicago the dance halls remained empty for a month after his departure. These disasters multiplied westward, and Fenderson fell from wrath to indignation to spitefulness to irritation to discontent to melancholy to meditation, and when San Francisco, at the end of three months of unbroken ovation, offered him a house and a pension if he would only make that city his home, he saw placidity staring him in the face, and came at last to Carmel,

515

where his only neighbors were other artists, and he could be reasonably sure of the neglect he so desperately needed.

CHAPTER FORTY-NINE: *The History of the Hanging Tree, by Stephen Granger*

STEPHEN often dropped in at Quests' while the quartet was practicing. Usually he would enter silently some time during the first number, stay for the coffee and conversation, and drift out again before the second number began. One evening, however, he came just as they were starting the second number, a quartet of Teddy's which they were preparing for a village concert. He moved a chair out to the edge of the darkness in the dining room, and sat there with his hands braced upon his knees, his arms akimbo, and his face, like that of a gigantic gnome, bearing upon the quartet in puckered abstraction.

When the last, tremulous, blended sounds of the strings had died away, Pearl asked, "Have a beer, Stephen?"

"No; no, thank you, I guess not," Stephen said absently. "That yours, Teddy?" he murmured, turning his head slowly and really looking at Teddy.

"It's his, all right, damn him," Knute said. He was petulantly wrapping his violin in the rubber jacket it had against fog and sea air, and stuffing it into its case. His part in the quartet was a dominant one, and difficult, and he hadn't been playing well. There seemed to be something else, probably from his writing, which he couldn't get out of his mind. Teddy had stopped several times to let him correct passages and play them alone, but it had been no use. He had never really led the quartet.

"It's tremendous," Stephen murmured. "It makes me very sad. What do you call it?" he asked Teddy.

Knute grunted as if the question were an insult to him, and went out onto the porch, leaving the door open. He stood out there, smoking a cigarette with deep drags and looking up at the sky, in which there was a full moon riding over toward the sea. Christine wrapped her viola carefully, in agony lest she should make a sound now that Teddy was about to speak. She was happy because after a passage of hers in the quartet, his own quartet, and when the score was about to call him in too, Teddy had nodded at her and said, "Good, Christine."

"Opus 137," Teddy said.

"Or *Quartet in F Major, for Strings*," Stephen murmured.

"D Minor," Pearl said.

"Of course, D Minor," Stephen murmured, not looking at her. "Isn't he amazing?" he asked Tim mildly. "There he sits for days at that table, in the torments of the damned, scribble, scribble, scribble, wonderful strings sawing and pecking away in his head. At last he emerges, unshaven, inky, worn out, just in time for supper. 'Here it is, world, Theodore Quest, *Quartet in D Minor, Opus 137, for Strings*. Embrace it tenderly, world. Open your soul to the healing of *Quartet in D Minor*. Weep gently for the sad humanity of *Opus 137*.' Heavens, such prodigality."

"What's the matter with it?" Pearl asked sharply.

"Nothing, nothing, nothing; not a thing. It is beautiful. It is profound. I am deeply moved by Thedore Quest's *Quartet in D Minor, Opus 137*. Deeply."

He crossed one knee over the other, gripped it with locked hands, and brooded downward.

Ages back, he began, before the word propaganda was understood by anyone outside the Vatican, and I was a young fellow who believed that politics was a matter of occasional larks everybody got in on, I lived in a little town in Montana. It was a typical cow-town; you know, a few shacks, a general store with a false front, a hitching rail, a watering trough, a haystack and fourteen saloons, in the middle of any quantity you wanted of knee-high brush, and dust and sun and blizzards. It was named after a self-appointed colonel who had wiped out quite a number of half-starved Indians somewhere in the neighborhood, and had an oil portrait of himself up behind the bar in the biggest saloon. Let's call it Oliver City.

Well, there was one nice thing about Oliver City, besides the fact that there was freedom of speech for the fastest shots and no newspaper. During its earliest days there'd been a sort of mad female living there, who didn't understand minding her own business to mean what most of Oliver City took it to mean. She liked trees, and Oliver City was short on trees, so she just went ahead on her own and planted cottonwood cuttings whenever she felt like it, and wherever, and then hiked around in a sun-bonnet the rest of her life, carrying two buckets and watering her shoots. It was a harmless enough idiocy, and nobody minded much. In fact Bucket Bridget furnished quite a bit of amusement in Oliver City, where life was generally a little slow. When she got to lugging her buckets, all the men would come out of the saloons and squat on their heels along the edge of the boardwalk, or hoist themselves onto the hitching rail and balance there, and start making bets on how long it would take her to reach the next shoot, or how many buckets she'd lug by four o'clock, or even long-range bets on how many years she'd last, or how long it would be before her hands hung clear down to her ankles.

By the time I came along, though, the excitement was all over. Bucket Bridget was years dead, and her cottonwood cuttings were big, spreading trees that practically made a roof over Oliver City, and everybody sat around in the shade and thought nothing of them. A cottonwood tree was just a cottonwood tree, that was all. If you wanted to meet your girl under a cottonwood tree, you had to tell her which one by talking about something else, the cottonwood in back of the Oliver Saloon, or the cottonwood east of the haystack, or something like that.

Then, one day, the vigilantes hung four men from one of the cottonwoods out on the edge of town, and everybody got into the habit of calling that particular cottonwood the Hanging Tree. They'd say, "I'll meet you under the Hanging Tree." It got so that tree looked different to us, some way, and whenever anybody said Hanging Tree, all the rest would look up and begin to take an interest. Pretty soon it got to be known even outside of Oliver City. People from all over the territory, who'd never even heard of Oliver City before, would keep dropping in at the Oliver Saloon and asking which one was the Hanging Tree, and then they'd go out and pass up all the other trees, and stand under the Hanging Tree and take on a solemn, thoughtful look, and stare up at the historic limb, and then gaze all around too, as if the whole country looked different from under the Hanging Tree. Most of the other cottonwoods were a lot bigger, finer trees, too, because the Hanging Tree was so far out that Bucket Bridget hadn't been able to get to it as regular as she did to most. After a while we began to get visitors from San Francisco. Then they came from Chicago. Next they were coming from St. Louis and New Orleans and Charleston. Finally they were even dropping in from Paris and London and Moscow and all those places. Every week some Sunday supplement would have a wonderful story about the Hanging Tree. In the second year alone, the Sunday supplements hung two hundred and fifty-three men from that tree, for different crimes, and had pictures of them all, too.

Oliver City began to build hotels like they have in Saratoga, and spread out over the desert in every direction, and had three banks, an Opera House, a race track and twenty-nine clubs, besides a lot more ordinary bars and a jail. One old lady even put in a public library in her woodshed, and some of the visitors used it, too.

One night, in the fifth or sixth winter after it was named, the Hanging Tree blew down. You'd think that might have hit the town pretty hard, but not a bit of it. The name had got rolling; it had an influence of its own, and nothing could kill it. In fact, you might say things went into a new boom, now that the limitations were off. Right away the Chamber of Commerce picked another cottonwood to be known officially as the Hanging Tree, and to carry on, just as if nothing had happened. There was some thought given to the matter this time, of course, and they picked a lot better and more central tree than the first one. Another group of public-minded citizens got together and formed an arbor club to see to it that there were a certain number of new cuttings set out every year, so the succession wouldn't be broken.

Besides that, there was a new business took hold that pretty soon was the biggest in Oliver City, even ahead of the bars. It began the night the tree blew down. The word got around, the way it does, and by sunrise there wasn't a piece of the tree left in sight. Everywhere you dropped in for a neighborly whisky and a hand of stud, somebody'd show you a piece of the Hanging Tree. They were all off the historic limb, too. The owners could show you the rope marks. That was how the idea of Hanging Tree, Inc., got started, I suppose. Anyway, a fine new building was put up in a kind of park next to the new Hanging Tree. It had a main hall, or museum, that went straight back from the front door, and a wing out at each side where you could buy things. It was a very impressive building. I used to spend hours in the museum myself. It was a high, gloomy room, and as you went in, you saw a big window at the back end, right ahead of you, with the Hanging Tree and its four victims painted on it. Under the window was a long glass case, always lighted and guarded, and in it you could see the original historic limb, intact, with the grooves made by the four ropes showing as clear in the bark as if they'd been cut there by hand. The window and the limb were set back in a kind of deep bay, and on the sides of the bay, under glass and well up, were the original nooses, two on each side. Under the nooses on the right side was a life-sized statue of Bridget, a very beautiful girl in a satin gown and a cloak, and holding her buckets, and on the left side were statues of a judge from Butte, and the leader of the vigilantes. By then it was pretty generally accepted that there'd been a regular trial, though some busybody from a neighboring town had dug up some pretty convincing evidence that the judge they were using hadn't been born yet when the hanging took place. Outside the bay, two on each side, were life-sized bronzes of the victims, with their hands tied behind them and the ropes around their necks. The floor in front of the bay was paved with big squares of marble of different colors, and under it were buried, according to the plates set in the marble, Bridget, the judge, the four desperadoes, most of the vigilantes and the jury. The existence of a jury was pretty well substantiated too. There had been plenty of written evidence to prove it since Hanging Tree, Inc., got under way. There were a lot of benches down the middle of the room, where visitors could sit while they looked around and thought it all over, and along the walls were cases containing the weapons of the desperadoes, the weapons of the vigilantes, four barrels the desperadoes had stood on and one the judge had used for a desk, and so on, and up over these reminders were small statuary groups of all the incidents leading up to the hanging.

When you'd seen all this, and worked up an interest, you could go out into the wings, and there were shelves of books and pamphlets about all phases of the matter, and glass counters full of souvenirs modeled after the exhibits in the museum, and little hanging men on necklaces and bracelets and ash trays and hats and balsam pillows, and all that sort of thing. The most important case, though, was the one that held the few original souvenirs that were left for sale, pieces of the tree and of the ropes and the barrels and the saddles and such. Those went for pretty high prices, of course, and were bought mostly by speculators and wealthy collectors and institutions.

After that building was put up, it was hard to tell how far the influence of the Hanging Tree spread. It was the greatest thing that ever happened to the West. There are a few signs I know about, though. The Metropolitan bought a plaster copy of the statue of Bridget and a twenty-four-by-fourteen painting of the hanging. An agent of Hanging Tree, Inc., told me that he had sold over twenty-seven hundred polished mahogany cubes from the Hanging Tree in and around Los Angeles alone, and that, although business wasn't quite as good as that in other places, it wasn't bad anywhere. He told me that sales in the rope were even better, and I could believe him. I knew one old man in Salt Lake who used a piece of it to cure the rheumatism in his neck, and a spinster in Pasadena who used it for her headaches, and quite a number of vaudeville hoofers, and even a couple of ballerinas, who carried bits of it as pocket pieces.

There was more than this little personal carry-over, too. Forty-six other towns in the Great Basin designated hanging trees of their own, and did pretty well, and there were hundreds of thousands of cottonwoods planted in the region, with an eye to the future. You can see them there any time. Even the mining towns started in trying to keep a tree or two each alive. An editor in Miles City, an old friend of mine, told me that the last time he'd checked the vital statistics for the area, he'd found that every third female child born during a period of thirty years after Hanging Tree, Inc., was set up, had been named Bridget, and in some places the enthusiasm had gone even further. There was a little Indian girl from Pocatello was called Two-Bucket, and there was a minister in Cody named his seventh daughter Hanging-Tree. I remember her pretty well, because I got caught up in the excitement about her myself. Hanging-Tree Doright, that was her name. By the time she was fourteen her father had been forced to give up his church and settle down with three secretaries to take care of the proposals that came in by mail. I made her a proposal myself, but I was way down the list, and by the time she got around to reading my offer, she'd already made up her mind to go on the stage. She wrote me a very nice letter, though, with her own hand, saying she'd been deeply touched, and would have given me serious consideration if her duty to the public and her new position as a representative extraordinary for Hanging Tree, Inc., hadn't made it necessary for her to maintain a more or less virginal status. She invited me to come and see her, too, and I did go to Oliver City the day she was showing there, but I couldn't even get close enough to tell which one she was, there was such a mob around the building.

Stephen descended through murmurs to silence.

Teddy grinned and folded his hands slowly upon his stomach. Pearl leaned forward, staring intently at Stephen, and trying to understand the murmurs. "What did you say?" she asked.

Stephen looked up as if startled out of reverie. "Eh? Oh," he said. "Oh, nothing. Cottonwood east of the haystack. Quest,

Opus 137. No," he murmured, wriggling with mild discontent, "even a haystack . . . Cottonwood 137."

IT WAS about a month later that Tim first visited Stephen's place, a little, shingled cabin, gray with weather and set among a few scrawny cypresses on the waterfront street. It was the evening the group played a piano-quartet of Tim's, *The Smoky Bar*, for their second number, and Stephen dropped in to hear it, as he had dropped in to hear the "Haystack" quartet. Knute played his lead very sharply and clearly this time, but there was something he wanted to get at. During the intermission he hadn't talked or eaten anything, but just sat in the same place behind his music stand and made notes on a folded piece of paper, which he put into his hip pocket when they started to play. As soon as *The Smoky Bar* was over, he went home. So Tim walked home with Stephen. Walking with Stephen was a slow, discontinuous performance. He strolled in a wavering line down the middle of the street, and stopped often to peer into the darkness under the trees. Tim knew, however, that in traveling the half or three-quarters of a mile from Teddy's house to his own, Stephen was actually traveling thousands of miles back and forth across the globe and out into space, at a speed greater than that of a meteor, and that he was pausing to examine strange sights in places as far apart as Glasgow and Hong Kong, so he didn't mind. He also stopped, automatically, each time Stephen stopped, and continued to hear certain doubtful passages of *The Smoky Bar*, sorting out those in which he believed the playing had been at fault, and hunting for the trouble in the others.

The two of them made a final, silent stop in front of Stephen's house. There was a high fog over the shore and the village, and not even a star showed, so that Carmel too seemed to be alone with its thoughts, but gradually the cracking and rushing of the breakers brought Tim and Stephen back to the place where they were standing. Tim didn't expect to be asked in. Stephen kept his company abroad; even Knute and Teddy seldom visited him. Tim began to dig up the words for a good night, but Stephen spoke first.

"Dangerous thing to stand listening to the ocean like this," he murmured. "Bottomless indifference. Deep calls to deep; no answer. Besides, Fenderson's in a state, and you'll never be able to sleep in the racket he'll be making. Better come in and have a drink."

So they went in, and Stephen closed the door, and the sound of the breakers became faint.

"Better wait a minute," Stephen said. "There's usually quite a lot of stuff in here. Have to know your way around." Tim heard him bumping into things and muttering, until he found a light in the corner and switched it on. The room that was revealed reminded Tim of his bedroom in the house by the race track, way back when it had been a museum of the magic wilderness. The light stood on a roller-top desk, and under it there was a small orderly area, a green blotter with a thin pile of manuscript set exactly in the middle of it and held down by a ceramic St. Francis with a bird on his hand and a cat rubbing against his leg, and beside the manuscript, a bottle of ink and a pen. Beyond this area, far back into the shadow, was chaos. The pigeon-holes of the desk bristled, around the blotter were piles of papers and books and a litter of pens, pencils, sea-shells, pebbles, evergreen cones and nameless oddities, and on top of the desk were more piles of books and papers, a miniature of an Easter Island stone head and another of the Eiffel Tower. The bookcase beside the desk was crammed, mostly with reference books, from Bulfinch to the *World Almanac*. All around the room, against the walls, were boxes, piles of books and bundles of bound newspapers. There were papers strewn over the floor like leaves in a wind, and fallen among them were shoes and socks and a shirt. The bed was unmade, and on the pillow lay a tin flute. On the small table at the head of the bed were piles of opened letters, a couple of ash trays full of butts and matches, an unwashed coffee cup, three books and a small bronze dragon. On the corner of the open closet door, hung a pair of trousers and several neckties. On the walls were a few strategically hung useful objects, a bathrobe, a towel, a damp bathing suit, a fly-swatter, a beer-can opener, and also more trophies of the random researches of Stephen Granger. Beside the door was a small reproduction of an Alpine shrine, the crucified Christ, emaciated, white, and dripping with red, under a gable of dark wood. From a nail beside the bookcase hung three Indian cere-monial masks with real hair. In other places were a Damascus scimitar, a pair of Japanese clogs, a Navajo doll with a velvet jacket, baskets, jars, gourd rattles and a black figurine of an African warrior with a shield. The walls behind these reminders were almost completely papered with signed photographs of people of many races, prints, and little ink drawings, some of them tinted. Over the desk hung a gigantic caricature of Stephen himself.

Stephen stood in the middle of the room, looking around. "Sometimes I wonder if there isn't almost too much stuff in here," he murmured. "Might be a good idea to clean some of it up before too long. Well," he said, "you can sit on the bed while I get us something to drink." He went out into the kitchen, and Tim could hear him opening and closing the ice-box and clinking glasses. Tim went over to the nearest of the many little drawings.

In faint and wavery lines, creating great distance by sugges-tion, it showed the Grand Canyon, with a tiny, black figure, recognizable by its stockiness and its profuse mane, standing upon the brink. Tim moved around the room, looking at the others. They all had the same motif. The stocky, hairy figure, tiny and alone, stood at the end of a statue-lined, flag-draped avenue, and looked across a wavery crowd at a still tinier black figure, standing with raised arm upon a balcony. It stood before a pagoda, an elephant, Brooklyn Bridge, a streamliner, a China Clipper, an immense dollar, upon which the wavery Liberty was winking, the ten commandments on a billboard, a wine bottle, a factory whose smoking chimneys appeared to become ghostly minarets, a baby who had assumed the lotus seat, and many other interesting objects. It appeared also before the big caricature of Stephen himself. Stephen came back with the drinks while Tim was looking at this one.

"Those are my prayer beads," he said. "If I can't get something out of my head, I draw one of those and put it up where I can see it all the time, and then I forget it." He gave Tim one of the glasses, and sat down in the swivel chair by the desk. Tim sat on the bed.

Stephen appeared, for a time, to brood upon something not in the room, and then woke abruptly, raised his glass to Tim, and they took a swallow or so together. They began to talk about the music at Teddy's, and went from that to *The Smoky Bar*. Teddy had remarked that *The Smoky Bar* sounded like a symphonic poem reduced to a piano-quartet, and they started there. Stephen was easy to talk to, and curious about everything, and Tim took *The Smoky Bar* apart for him. He admitted there was something in Teddy's criticism. That was just the trouble he'd had while he was writing, always hearing more and different instruments than he had to use. Stephen agreed with him that this difficulty had perhaps only strengthened the total effect, the harassed, minor dissatisfaction Tim had wanted to express. Tim told how the writing of *The Smoky Bar* had worked for him, anyway. When he was done, he had felt a knot in himself untied, an internal closeness aired, the recurrent numbness of the double life worn off, so that he had been unified, quiet and happy. It was as if his spirit, for a long time slightly near-sighted and blurred of vision, had put on satisfactory spectacles and seen the world and itself jump into focus. Not that this clear state was permanent. Even when he was playing with the quartet, the orchestra or the band, he didn't so much break bondage as ignore it, with the latent fear that he would be bound again the moment he stopped concentrating upon the work of his fingers and let his mind range out. But having several times experienced that clarity, calmer and more enduring than the wonderful ascents into exultation or descents into furious despair, he had his touchstone, and was coming more and more to trust his judgment in that mood and to rework his writing or develop his uninspired transitions with calm and mathematical confidence. Not, he maintained, that this clear state could be a substitute for the exultation, but it could sustain the work through lapses which would have been fatal before, and it could set him soaring again after shorter periods of the terrible self-doubt.

Then they argued about whether the sensation of catharsis in the writer himself could be a test of the work. Tim believed it was the only test. He couldn't remember that it had ever failed him, admitting that the quality of inspiration, and so of catharsis, was a relative matter, the same as everything else was relative. Stephen was gently skeptical. They went back to particulars in *The Smoky Bar*, and decided that it had worked for Tim because it had projected a troublesome portion of his past, and even more because it had successfully resolved jazz forms into a serious intent, and so had brought about at least an armistice in his long war with himself. It was a good talk, and cleared up many remaining confusions in Tim's mind.

"But maybe you're right," Stephen said, after a few moments of thoughtful silence. "I mean about catharsis being the test afterward, and ecstasy while you're working. I remember one of my little experiments . . ." and he went on to tell about a temple dance he had watched in Bali. He appeared, as usual, to be an accidental, preoccupied gnome in his own story. He had been on his way to interview an attaché of a French consulate about a local crisis precipitated by the latest of the fortnightly changes of government in Paris, when he had found himself part of a great crowd of natives, which increased as it went along. At first he had been fretful over the delay, but finding himself unable to pass the crowd, the road being narrow and fenced by jungle, he had finally resigned himself to drifting with it. Once he was resigned, the day became beautiful, a matter he hadn't noticed before, and the people who blocked him, instead of being a collective, heathen nuisance, became unusually charming and interesting individuals. He listened to their soft voices. He gazed upon their rapt and gentle faces. He was fascinated by their delicate and informing gestures. He had been in that part of the East for two years, he said, but until then he had always been in trouble with the officials because he insisted, with naive, cow-country democracy, that he was unable to discover any essential difference between the natives and the representatives of the various commercial and political empires. Now he saw how wrong he had been. He became so happy in this revelation that he forgot all about his appointment with the attaché, and followed the multitude all the way to its goal, which was the open court of a gray stone temple in the jungle. Here, and in the neighboring village, he had remained for seven days, in a condition verging upon trance, and possessed of such a content with life as he had never before known. It required the seven days to witness the entire cycle of the temple dances, which were performed by a score of very young maidens, attired in miniature replicas of the temple itself, with lofty, spiral headdresses like the towers. He described the dances, slow and continuous maneuverings in pattern, many of them performed in a sitting position, only the snaky arms and hands dancing, and all of them as angular and restrained as Egyptian wall paintings. Only when the last dance was over, and the crowd of pilgrims had dispersed, did he emerge from his happy daze. Then he was in a panic. What had he done? He had betrayed the trust of his paper and of the waiting world. He rushed away in a great sweat, twenty-seven miles through the jungle to the nearest railway junction, and telegraphed for instructions. Unfortunately for his career, he had taken the reply very much to heart. It read, "Two changes of government and four diplomatic crises while you slept, stupid. Affairs now in the same state as previous initial crisis. Interview no longer news. Return." So he had returned to the city on the coast from which he had started, and had gone to his hotel room. There, seated cross-legged upon the floor, he had attempted to imitate the temple dancers with his arms and hands, and to approximate the music to which they had danced by whining through his nose, at the same time seeking a religious state of mind, in order to discover how the dancers had felt while performing.

"But, my goodness," Stephen said, running his hand through his mane from the back, raising his great eyebrows into peaks, and narrowing his eyes into slits of puzzlement, "they were lovely, pearly-skinned little thirteen-year-old girls, supple as water. Besides, they ceased to exist normally when they danced, and I couldn't even ask for a gin-fizz in Balinese, let alone enter into sacred meditation. I felt like a stuffed sausage, sitting there on the floor and trying all those things, and the idea of the attaché I had missed kept buzzing around inside my head like a fly in a closed room.

"So maybe you're right," he said mournfully. "Maybe I just can't get the feel of inspiration. Certainly those girls were inspired." He lapsed into dismal contemplation of his failure.

Tim understood the story, but he couldn't resent it, any more than any of Stephen's appraisals could be resented. He kept chuckling, remembering Stephen illustrating his bodily experiment in the dance.

"In fact," Stephen murmured, "I believe it was that incident which first planted in me a seed of doubt concerning my occupation, or at least concerning my fitness for it, a seed which, only twenty-three years and five months later, was to mature in a conviction which led me to retire and start work on the story of my life as it should have been lived."

"Is that the book?" Tim asked, nodding at the desk.

Stephen roused himself. "What? This?" he asked, putting a finger on the manuscript on the desk. "Oh, great heavens no, no. Only wish it were. Boxes of it; dozens of them," and he waved his hand at the boxes along the wall. "Man's insane to start writing a book. Leads to trying to tell the truth, one way or another. Fiendish torment. Breaks up all a fellow's normal, sociable habits. Never would have started it if I hadn't contracted malaria on my last departure from an assignment. Had time to think then. Thought over everything I'd written, and it was always the same. Only good things I could remember were about accidents like the dancing girls, and nobody'd use them, or else there was nothing left of them by the time the censors got done and the editors finished revising them to suit their hypothetical public-taste and the aims of a publisher who wanted to be President of the United States one day, and a deep-sea diver the next. Began to really think about Teddy Quest then, too. I'd met him years before, when he was a concert cellist in Europe, but I'd been too busy to think then. Inquired around and learned he'd come to Carmel. Came myself, and after a while began to write the book. Only trouble is breaking my old habit of hurrying. Very, very hard, after years of rushing around meeting deadlines and important politicians."

He subsided into thought again. After a minute or two he reappeared.

"This Teddy Quest is a wonderful man," he said. "Can't fool him out of a good thing. Can't hurry him. Try it. Get him rushing around as fast as you can, his mind is still out strolling on the beach on a fine day. He was always like that." And for an hour, Stephen told Tim little stories about the small, calm, gentle and important judgments of Teddy Quest in the whirlwind of the world.

CHAPTER FIFTY-ONE: *Traces in the Heart of the Wilderness*

IT MAY seem, from what I have told you so far, that Tim, during his year in Carmel, was so constantly with his three friends, or so busy exploring the larger world they opened to him, that he couldn't have fallen into his old brooding, or even into the easier restlessness of the Music Box. Actually this wasn't so. Knute, Stephen and Teddy, all considerably older than Tim, had long since cleared their glades in the wilderness and built their solitary huts. For minutes and hours with them, Tim had hours and days by himself, and often, even when he was with them, they would be withdrawn beyond reach into their own labors and ponderings. Gradually, as the place and the friends became familiar, and he settled into the routine of his work, long moods of heavy melancholy overcame him, the more intolerable in that they seemed to him throw-backs to the years before the pilgrimage to the mountain. Often, when he put his books and papers aside, or laid down his pencil and closed the piano, and went out on long walks, he would find himself envying, as once he had looked down from his window on Second Street and envied the complacent Ling Choy upon his stool, the men he saw doing some simple and objective work, truck drivers, ditch-diggers, cowboys on the coastal hills, fishermen in Monterey. It would seem to him that, like Ling Choy, they stored some secret essence of life which informed their every necessary gesture with a kind of vital grandeur, their deep voices and direct looks with a force and independence which he, drained by his excruciating and fruitless labors, could not equal.

His continual failure, even now, when all his time was given to his true work, to write anything which seemed to him clearly marked with its own singular nature, was doubtless the most potent cause of this dark restoration. Only one other piece besides *The Smoky Bar*, another single-movement orchestral work, which he called *The Stone Woman*, seemed to him to have life of its own, and that, as you will see, he was compelled to destroy. Both were born out of an unpredictable labor of self-loathing and despair, *The Smoky Bar* out of the second and most prolonged of five more failures at the symphony of leaves, and *The Stone Woman* out of an act which he regarded, though with some wonder at his attitude, as the vilest of his life. That is, both impressed him as the minor and accidental results of falling far short in attempts to wrest his two major answers from life. *The Smoky Bar* offered at least one consolation. He had done the re-work and the orchestration on it coolly and dispassionately, which seemed a hopeful gain in control. *The Stone Woman* didn't offer even that reassurance. It seemed a wholly isolated upheaval, and for some time, even a vileness in itself, serving, as it had, in the place of a true act of atonement. In reality, probably, *The Stone Woman* was the monument to the crucial hours of all Tim's time in Carmel. It was in that act that the last two wavering traces out of the hundreds in his Matto Grosso came together and led him up one of those isolated hills which rise bare above the dense foliage, affording an open view of the charted sky and a distant sight, across the plain of top-leaves, of the great, blue-hazy rift that marked the course of a major river.

To reach this hill ourselves, however, we must still follow an obscure track through all the months in Carmel up to the second July. Fortunately Tim left a record of this wandering in the greatest number of letters he had ever written to one person in his life, all of them to Mary Turner. None of these letters, in itself, would be evidence of more than the mood of the moment, but in their succession they seem to me to indicate a great deal.

At first he answered most of Mary's short, careful notes with others scarcely longer and wholly factual and external. "I'm getting a new look at writing for strings by playing in a quartet which meets a couple of times a week at Teddy Quest's. Teddy has written a good many quartets himself, but even more important, he was a concert cellist and also the cellist of a concert quartet for years. I learn something new from him at every rehearsal." Items of that sort, scribbled rapidly and rather largely, and seldom over more than one side of one page, and signed, "As Ever, Tim."

Gradually, and most markedly after he had burned the symphony the second time, his letters became more frequent and longer. Some of them were very long, twelve and fourteen sheets of typing paper (he never used any other kind) covered closely on both sides by the small, vertical writing which came when he was thinking hard and setting the results down slowly. These letters took hours, sometimes a whole day or night, to write, but they must have disappointed Mary bitterly. Imagine her coming home to her quiet and orderly room after supper and finding one of these fat letters on the floor, where Mrs. Mott had squeezed it under the door. Imagine her delaying the reading in order to prolong her anticipation. She has confessed such deliberate ceremonials to me. She would turn on the lamp at the end of the couch, and place the letter on the table, upright against the base of the lamp, where she could see it from the bedroom door. Then, half believing all the time that this was the letter in which there would be the paragraph, the sentence, the change of one word in the greeting or the close even, that would make all the difference, she would take a shower and dry, stand before the mirror and comb out her hair until it was sleek and shining, sit upon the white-enameled toilet seat and give herself a quick manicure and pedicure, and then, back in the bedroom, put on her house-robe and neat, blue-leather mules, powder her nose, touch up her mouth with lipstick, and finally draw onto her left wrist the Navajo bracelet of heavy silver with three large turquoise stones, which Tim had given her for Christmas, the year he came to the Music Box. Sometimes she would still further prolong the delay by setting out beside the letter the brass ash tray with a raised dragon on it, which was a present from Ling Choy, and her carved teak-wood cigarette box, and by making coffee or pouring herself a little glass of sherry. Only then, pristine of body and devout of spirit, and with a hope as unquenchable as Tim's had once been in a like cause, would she curl up on the end of the couch, taste of her drink, light her cigarette, and take up the letter bearing upon it her name in the hand which could stop her heart for a moment, even when she came upon it on an old sales-slip in the glass cubicle. Imagine her, then, thus prepared, drawing out the many pages, unfolding them reverently, reading again, "Dear Mary," and again at the close, often more than an hour later, "As Ever, Tim," or sometimes just, "Tim," or even, "Sincerely, Tim." And save for commonplace and rather stilted acknowl- edgment of remarks in her letters, it was rarely, through all the lengthy meditations and discussions between those salutations, that she would find herself anything but the impersonal audi- ence for the debate of Tim Hazard with Tim Hazard over the history, the nature and the destiny of mankind in general and of music in particular among its works.

The most readable passages in these philosophical essays were those in which he escaped his bondage while setting down for her one of Stephen Granger's stories or a description of silent and embattled breakfast with Knute, or of a meeting of the quartet at which Mr. Greever counted with unusual faithfulness, or of a pilgrimage into mortal time by way of the old mission in the river valley, or into immortal time by way of the mouth of the Big Sur, where the tiny gulls glittered in the air around the lighthouse rock, and the tide, slow and shining, crept up across the bar.

Even the rare personal interludes could scarcely have been more comforting to her than the rest, for though they might quicken her breath for a moment, and draw her back to reread, her sensitive ear could not have been deceived by any strained and overly lyrical recollection of their stormy day at the butte, or of her kindness and patience when he was sick, or of their evenings together with the guitar. Often, when she had gone to bed after reading a letter which contained such a passage, she would lie awake, listening to the city noises and the sounds of coming and going in the halls and rooms around her, and watching the light of the café sign across the street appear and disappear on her ceiling, while she explored the paragraph or page over and over, and also the incident which it was recalling, and then others to which that one led. But even when she succeeded in believing what she wanted to before she fell asleep, she would know better in the morning, and would again comb out her hair and powder her nose and touch up her lips, but with no lift of anticipation at all, but only the small, energetic urge of duty or of habit, sustaining a routine a trifle heavier than it had been the day before. And when, that evening or the next, she answered the letter, it would be as carefully as ever, admitting, at the most, what records she had brought home to play or what book to read in order to understand what he had been talking about in the rest of his letter.

That may sound as if Mary were carefully protecting her pride, or even as if she were adhering to a deliberate and long-term plan of conquest, but, if that was the case, it was so only to the degree to which the little imp of independence in her could manage without her knowing it. Her letters were as much the result of her nature as Tim's were of his. Where Tim had to struggle, even against hostility, as in his letters to Rachel, in order not to pour out all he felt, Mary could never have begun to write what she felt until she was released by the knowledge that her love was wanted. There was in Mary, quiet and gentle as she was, a good deal of that hoarded essence which Tim sensed so longingly when, inwardly exhausted, he walked the coastal road and met a Mexican cowboy, with eyes like wet obsidian, drawing his horse after him up the steep bank of a creek, through the laurel brush, or when he stood on the weathered wharves and watched the Portuguese fishermen, their teeth gleaming, their oily hair shining in the sun, bartering with the cannery men over the catch.

Perhaps it was a gradual perception of this inviolate power in Mary, reaching Tim, by other routes than thought, as he read her letters, and as he remembered in more truthful hours the scenes he rather wildly evoked in those letters, which brought about the next change in his writing. You still couldn't say with certainty that he wrote love letters, though he did occasionally sign them "Love, Tim," and sometimes opened them with this rather important transposition of the same two words, "Mary, dear," but he gave less and less space in them to abstracted meditations, and more and more to memories of which Mary was a part, and there were, once in a while, pages of a tenderness not at all strained and dangerously close to declaration. It was as if he had finally discovered, sitting alone in Knute's dark, bare living room, staring out the window at the fog, or at the blinding sea in the sunlight, or around him at the records of his hopes and defeats, that it was also possible to desire Mary. At any rate, for the first time, the alliance of the Hazards and the Turners was pushed back into its true perspective, and he spoke to the living Mary in the present moment, so that Mary's replies changed too, became longer and easier and even gave way to some brief recitals of what she thought about and felt in her room.

Then, in July of the second summer, there came another change in Tim's letters, so sudden but unmistakable that it must have bewildered Mary. They became fewer and far shorter again, and the crowding passion, which had given them a peculiar and, to Mary, an exciting intensity, was gone. Yet they weren't like the first impersonal diaries of his activities, either. They were quick and gay, obviously dashed off in a few minutes, and often illustrated with hasty, ludicrous cartoons of the life of Tim Hazard in the wide world of Carmel, California, and with bits of music and spontaneous verse. They should have been the easiest of all to answer, but they weren't. They were almost always signed, "love," but the word had undergone an amazing change. It meant now just what it had meant the evening Tim and Lawrence had set out for Pyramid, when Tim had kissed Mary in the glass cubicle, and said that he loved her, and added that he also loved Mr. Atley.

It is probable that Tim was not even aware, beyond the fact that he wasn't writing such long letters, of this last change, which so mystified and disturbed Mary. It wasn't a matter of decision with him. It simply happened, at once and of itself, in the first letter he wrote after that night in the second July. He walked into the Marine Room slowly that evening, and with his head down. He didn't feel like playing dance music, or even like touching a trumpet at all. He was preoccupied with the score he had been wrestling over all day, and with premonitions of an uneasiness he hadn't known since he left the Music Box. He walked in this blind way, paying no attention to anything around him, almost to the platform where the band sat, and then looked up, and at once stopped, and stood there, his face growing hot and everything he had been thinking gone from his mind. Eileen Connor, in a stiff, sea-green evening gown, which would rustle when she moved, with her shining copper hair heavy upon her very white shoulders, and with the same delightful little constellations of freckles upon her nose and cheeks, was leaning on the piano, smiling, very ready to laugh, talking to Rod Carman, the pianist.

In the moment before Eileen felt Tim's presence and his stare, and turned and looked at him, he remembered a great many things from that summer three years previous. Eileen was walking beside him on the beach, her hands deep down in the pockets of her shining slicker, her laughter coming to him in little gusts as the wind struck them with freshets of rain, and she had to turn her head from it. Eileen was standing on the end of the long, dark rock, where the white spray leaped about them, her bare feet, almost as white as the spray, gripping in the crevices, her hair flying and the westering sun making her eyes as blue and sparkling as the sea. Eileen was lying on her stomach beside him to watch the slow flowering of the translucent, pastel anemones in a tide pool. There came over him, as with the memory of a long-lost state of blessedness, a slight physical renewal of the easeful pleasure, the cleared vision of both his eyes and his mind, which had almost always come to him when he was with Eileen for any length of time. He remembered many things which were not Eileen, but might as well have been, because he always thought of them when he thought of her: a clear sunset over a sea that clamored softly all down a long, curving beach toward a headland blue and misty with distance, save where the light gilded its seaward face; white Spanish houses looking out to sea from among an infinite variety of leafy color and form, which buried the steep hillside and mingled and parted with marvelous, slow graciousness as the soft wind played up through it; a moon, saffron and full to almost overflowing, rising from among the low, round hills where the insects sang all night in the aromatic brush and the dry grass.

There were other recollections too, less eternal but more immediate, as if they reached back no further than last night, as if they were even happening to him again in that moment of standing. He and Eileen lay side by side on the club raft, out beyond the surf, in the darkness after one o'clock, when the dancing was done. He drew at her shoulder, and they turned to each other, and their wet, cool bodies and their wet, cool mouths were together. They were standing on the shadowy esplanade in an intermission. He was unhappy about his music, and deeply puzzled and grieved about life, and at just the right moment, Eileen laid her head against his shoulder and took his arm under hers and pressed it gently, and slowly and surely his immense and tragic wilderness was transformed by a redeeming splendor. It was rarely, indeed, that he had even begun to fall into such a mood during that summer with Eileen. Eileen had seldom fully understood what he was talking about, when he launched forth on one of his inspired harangues, still less when he groped unhappily after the great pattern and the great answer, but she had always understood what he was feeling, and known what to do about it.

Only the last day he was there, she had surprised him. She had come to his room to talk to him while he packed. She had been as gentle and happy and real as ever, an apparently unfailing state with her, that gave to her face and body alike a kind of serene radiance that sometimes led him, though he usually thought of her as entirely a perfection of flesh and senses, to see her for a moment as just the contrary, a fleshless perfection of spirit encasing itself in an illusion of body in order not to startle darker and more transitory animals like himself. She had packed his clothes, saying with soft laughter that they would be wrinkled beyond recovery the way he was folding them, and she had talked with him cheerfully about their near and separate futures, and their more distant but more important future together. Then, without any warning, just as they were about to leave together for the station, she had suddenly clung to him, not kissing him, not making love to him, just holding him and weeping softly, but so inconsolably that she hadn't been able to go to the station with him after all, but had run back to her own room and plunged into it blindly and closed the door.

And all the time these memories worked in him, Tim, standing there in the Marine Room, was also remembering, as if by some other, conscious, and somewhat more real process, the tenderness of Eileen's letters to him, and that last, cruel letter he had written to her, full of indirections, full of false-sounding repetitions of an affection which was actually real and enduring, though not deep and preoccupying when he was away from her, a letter which nonetheless said only that nothing more could come of their wonderful summer together because he had caught a passing glimpse of a girl she didn't know, but of whom he had thought a good deal, some years before.

Tim considered turning and walking out of the Marine Room again, before Eileen saw him, and then felt a little sullen anger against her because of that impulse, the resentment of the one humiliatingly in the wrong. He didn't know how he would act when he had to meet her in this crowded room. He only felt sure he would fail miserably to act in a natural and casual manner. He didn't dare to look around, and already, so much longer did his pause on the floor seem to him than it actually was, he believed that fifty people must be watching him and noting his confusion.

Then, actually after only a very few seconds, Eileen turned her head and saw him. She wasn't surprised, and she made it very easy for him. She came quickly and smoothly across the stage and quickly and lightly down the steps, before he could do more than move a pace or two toward them, and she took both his hands and pressed them warmly, and smiling, almost laughing, gazed up eagerly at his face, then directly at his eyes.

"How are you, Timmy Hazard?" she asked softly, intensely, and then said, before he was forced to speak, and taking his arm to draw him up the steps with her, "I saw your picture up in the lobby. At first I couldn't believe it was you, but I asked the hat-check girl, and she said it was. So then I didn't know whether I ought to run away before you came, but instead I asked Rod if you couldn't play the piano for me, the way we used to." She laughed a little, and perhaps the least bit breathlessly. "So you'll have to come up, Timmy, and see what I'm going to sing."

Maybe that was all an act. Probably it was. He couldn't remember Eileen as ever having been quite so quick and stagy. But it was a good act, and he felt very grateful to her. He even, and quite spontaneously, returned the happy, affectionate pressure of her arm.

So Tim played the piano for her on those numbers where the whole band wasn't behind her. Then, when he had to go up into the lounge, to play with the salon orchestra, she laughingly helped him into his tux jacket, and ran up the stairs beside him, tickled by this crazy transformation, and then entered the lounge as casually as he did, and drifted away into the lofty darkness to sit by herself and listen. It was as if they had never been apart, as if she had forgotten, or rather as if he had merely imagined, a life to make up the time between, which had now lapsed into proper unreality.

Yet perhaps she did remember, and was only deliberately making it possible for them to work together, for after that beginning, she was no more attentive to him than to any other member of the band, and when she had sung her last encore, she said good night personally only to Teddy, waving a general good night to the rest of them, and went out by herself, though the band had several numbers yet to play.

CHAPTER FIFTY-TWO: *His Heart with the Sun —or A Very Short Biography of Eileen Connor*

NEVERTHELESS, Tim felt light and happy and expectant the next morning. He sang as he and Knute were going down over the dunes to the beach. He challenged the waves with a loud voice and tumultuous energy. The world understood. There had been a clear sunrise with a gentle land wind. Now there was a sea wind from a spotless horizon. The sea was blue and it danced and sparkled. It was good of the world to understand. Tim's mind leapt up from him like a golden dolphin from the sea. It took to the sky like a gull. Like a well-grazed stag it ran upon the shoulders of the lighted hills.

While he was drying himself on the beach, he did a little dance to the air he had been humming and singing as he came down. All at once he realized that he hadn't heard the air before, that it was his own, bubbling up by itself to relieve him of his excessive happiness, and that although it was a canticle, a song of praise, it could easily be made to dance. As they returned to the house, he made it dance, humming most of the time, but occasionally letting it out loud and free. The words began to come with it. It was a song about a returned lover.

He and Knute took turns getting breakfast, and it was his turn this morning. He continued to work on the song in his mind, while he made coffee and toast. When he had put the meal on the table in the living room, Knute came in with his bathrobe bound tightly to him, and his hair combed down slick. This was a bad sign. When Knute had worked lustily, his hair would always be left uncombed and tousled, his bathrobe loose and baggy. Then he would utter a half-dozen stentorian ukases on the important matters of life, such as the annoyance caused by females, the vileness of slavery to money, and the hangover of a sterile idiom in modern music, roar bits of song himself, gulp his breakfast down without sitting still for a moment, and go out, roll into his bed, and fall asleep at once. When he combed his hair tight and bound his bathrobe to him like a dress uniform, which was much more frequently the case, it meant that he was unhappy and was defying the world.

Usually Tim looked for these signs, but this morning he didn't even notice that Knute hadn't spoken a word. He put music paper beside his plate, and while he ate, he wrote out the melody. It seemed to him that the notes danced upon the page. He began to add the words. With his mouth full of toast, he hummed the air in order to match the words to the rhythm and to the mood.

Knute sat huddled over his coffee, silent and dark. He sipped the coffee instead of gulping it, and drew only at long intervals on his cigarette, but then drew deeply and quickly, and expelled the smoke suddenly and fiercely.

Tim sang a couple of lines aloud, words and all.

Knute stared at him murderously. "My God," he muttered, "what makes you so revoltingly cheerful? And do you have to take it out like Bobby Burns in a honky-tonk?"

"Have to get it down," Tim said, paying no real attention. He didn't realize himself the simple reason why he felt so good, after the pedantic cosmologies, sociologies and fatalisms which had been the ideas of his discouragement. So far as he knew, the whole world had looked very bright and shining from the surf this morning, and a happy love song caught the mood quickest, that was all.

Knute finished his coffee and stood up.

"Who and what were your parents?" he asked.

Tim looked up, a little puzzled. "What?"

"Every time you fall into happiness," Knute said, "I can see it all written out like a damned pedigree: Jazz Prince, out of Mae West by Paul Whiteman."

He went out onto the porch and slammed the door behind him. Through the window in the upper half of the door, Tim could see him out there, sitting tensely on the end of the rail and staring at the morning sea beyond the dunes. He sat there for a long time before he finally got slowly into bed and pulled the covers clear up over his head. Knute hated a bright morning after he'd had a bad night.

Tim worked happily all day. When he'd finished the song, he broke it down into a dance rhythm, and wrote a lyric for that version too. Before dark he had even completed the orchestration for the dance number. He called the ballad *My Heart with the Sun Arising*, and the dance number *Get Up with the Sun*.

The quartet was playing that night, and he took the songs over to Teddy's. Eileen was there, and Teddy made them try the songs. Eileen had a little trouble bringing the dance number up to tempo. It talked as quickly as it sang, so that it was almost a patter number. Tim played it twice through on the piano for her, and even sang part of the chorus, to show how the words should be hit. She caught it then. In her clear, tender voice, it didn't sound the way Tim had imagined it. It came out more full-toned and overflowing; it was happy, not excited. He wasn't sure of it that way; it didn't have edge and pace enough, but he tempered the accompaniment to suit. Teddy liked it well enough, and made them practice it, ready to give the band a start. Then they worked on *My Heart with the Sun*. That was better for Eileen. She sang it just the way Tim had imagined it.

They took so long on the songs that Pearl brought the coffee in when they were done, and the quartet was cut to one number.

While the quartet was playing, Eileen and Pearl sat out on the porch, surrounded by the great yellow cats, and watched the constellations proceed slowly over the river valley toward the sea. Whenever the music allowed, Tim looked out at Eileen sitting there. The music was Debussy's *Quartet in G Minor*, which was about as far a cry from the songs as anything could have been, but it seemed wonderful and easy and natural to Tim. He had no trouble at all making the change.

He drove Eileen home in Jeremiah. She was living in one of the cottages in the woods behind the inn. They sat on her doorstep and talked for a long time. They could see the stars in places, through the tops of the pines. They could smell the ocean, but there was no wind, and the air stayed warm and heavy among the trees. It was a night to breed thoughts and hopes of forever. They could feel the ground and the thickets full of life getting born, full of the promise of everlasting and abundant life good enough for itself. All over the hills beyond the woods, the crickets sang, and the cicadas were omnipresent. They made little watch-fires of sound in counterpoint, changing tone with distance. Tim became possessed by the unreasonable notion that this kind of night returned with Eileen, that wherever Eileen went, this kind of night emanated from her, and the kind of daybreak which had started him on the song.

They talked about what they had been doing since they had last seen each other. They talked carefully at first, but after a few minutes it was all right.

Eileen had been singing in all kinds of places, on a cruise ship to Honolulu, in a club in San Francisco, in Chicago and Cleveland and Boston and New York. She had wanted to sing opera, and had gone broke in New York studying for it, but had never reached the stage except in a couple of choruses. She didn't have volume enough or range enough. It wasn't only opera, either. There was something wrong with her voice. On sentimental dance lyrics, and simple songs, people seemed to like it, but even on such stuff, she said, and laughed softly, she would never make a real headliner. She didn't seem to carry over and stay in people's minds. She could understand. She had sung in one club in Chicago where she was double-featured with a Mexican girl who had a very sharp, strong voice, and she had always felt, when she went on after the Mexican girl, as if she were singing Stephen Foster to a room full of drowsy old people. The difference showed even in their pictures outside the club. They were framed together, two big, shiny pictures with an ad for the orchestra. She found that she always had to look at the Mexican girl's picture. Her own wouldn't seem to be there. She'd look at it, and then she would be drawn back to look at the picture of the Mexican girl again, and her own would disappear from her memory. The Mexican girl flashed and shone, and was dark between. It was hard to look away from her picture. Eileen didn't resent the discovery.

"I don't have glamour, I guess," she said. "I can't even seem to figure out what it is." She laughed softly.

"You surround glamour," Tim thought, "as the hills at night surround an overlit city. You encompass glamour the way the sky holds the moon.

"Just the same," he thought, "all the popular tunes are about the lights and the moon."

It was late, and Tim was very tired from writing so long, although not at all sleepy. At times waves of the love of everything, and floods of Eileen, which were nearly the same thing, poured over him, and he wanted to go into the cabin and lie with her in this teeming night she had brought back. He thought, as one might dream of a cure for a terrible malady he had been enduring for years, of relaxing and falling asleep afterward, with his face in her shoulder. He didn't touch her, but it seemed impossible to leave her and go home, and sometimes his voice shook when he was saying the most ordinary things. He was lost in her, but happily. In the streets of the city of trembling leaves, which were everywhere now, he was a boy running and running under the arc-lights toward joy.

When, in the gray light, with the sounds of birds waking in the trees, Eileen held herself to be kissed good night, he couldn't disguise his desire. Eileen turned her mouth away from the kiss, and pushed him off gently, but held onto his arms, as if she wanted to draw him back. She looked up at him, and her face was very sad. She didn't like to feel at war with herself this way. He was used to it. He was always at war with himself. To Eileen it was a wrong way to be. She didn't understand such battle, and didn't like it. He had never seen her face so sad. It wasn't Eileen at all, sad and tired, staring up at him, trying to figure out how he wanted her. She had cried in his arms the day he'd left her, ages ago, in their first summer, but even her crying then had been easy and full of life, like everything else about her. She hadn't looked sad in this terrible, strained way.

She let go of his arms, and took his face in her hands, and kissed him quickly and lightly, and went into the cabin.

When he got back to Knute's, Tim said he didn't want any breakfast, and went into his room and closed the door, to be hidden from Knute. For a long time he stood at the window and stared out across the dunes at the blue dome of the ocean. He wasn't really thinking, but just waiting rigidly until the confused storm inside him went down. He heard Knute go out to bed, and gave him time enough to fall asleep. Then he went out into the living room and wrote down the melody and words of a blues which had started to come by itself as he grew more quiet. He scribbled the title across the top, *Why Do I Always Do Wrong?* and sat there and heard the chorus through in his mind, behind a muted trumpet, and then he knew he could sleep.

In the month following that first night with Eileen Tim wrote six more songs, *The Ships of Monterey*, *When the Long Tide Sweeps Pinos Rocks*, *Cypress in the Fog*, *The Waves in Shining Storm upon This Shore*, *I Bought a Bracelet of Painted Beads*, and *I Heard You Sing by 'Dobe Walls*. Eileen sang all these, and *My Heart with the Sun*, with the salon orchestra, and in the Marine Room she sang the dance versions he wrote for three of them, and *Why Do I Always Do Wrong?* Her hit for the summer was *Why Do I Always Do Wrong?* and Teddy used a few bars from the chorus as the signature music of the band. During all that time, Tim scarcely thought of the symphony of leaves, nor did he try any other serious or prolonged work. A day or two was enough to complete any one of the songs. He had a great deal of free time, and he and Eileen spent most of it together, swimming and sunning on the beach, driving back into the redwood canyons in Jeremiah, taking long walks around the peninsula or down the coast road. Tim couldn't have said whether or not he believed he was in love, but they didn't talk about love, or about the past. The weather was brilliant, too constantly brilliant, and they were happy together, and that was enough. The time went by lightly and without pressure, and with a sameness that made it seem, in retrospect, like no time at all, until well into August.

CHAPTER FIFTY-THREE: *The Stone Woman*

BEFORE the end of August, this long spell of clear weather became a drought. The wind blew steadily and gently, but brought no rain with it. The hollow sky drank up the fogs before they could come in from the sea, and remained cloudless. At night it was filled with stars too big and too distinct, which the waters, stirring only sluggishly and with little moanings against the shore, made even larger in reflection. The dry grass on the hills leaned always the same way, and whispered continuously. The river lost the strength to cut the sand-bar at its mouth, and sank away into stale pools on which the green scum spread vigorously. Boulders emerged from it into the light, and, where all the water was gone, the drying mud cracked into squares, and dead fish and turtles stank. Plowed fields turned to dust, and the dust settled upon the leaves of the motionless brush along the roads. Everything alive began to suffer from the suspense. The gulls huddled at the top of the beach more than they flew, and even the seals lay in the sun on the rocks off Lobos for hours at a time and were less noisy at their sports in the channel. Knute declared angrily that no man could work in such weather, and went off to San Francisco to see what was going on there, swearing he wouldn't return until there was a long rain.

Eileen and Tim talked less, and with wandering attention, on their walks, and the walks became shorter. Often they just strolled until they found a secluded spot with a clear view of the sea, and then lolled in the shade of the cypresses, still without much to say. As the bright, slow, idle days passed, Tim found himself struggling more and more unwillingly against a sultry desire for her which was more completely physical than any he had ever known before, and which made it nearly impossible for him to talk with her sensibly, or even playfully. Stretched out on the dead needles, his chin on his arms, he would gaze at her as she lay against the slanting trunk of a cypress, her head back, her eyes half closed against the dazzle of water below, and his eyes and his mind would enumerate the promises of her body, her mouth in its full and classical repose, her round throat and shoulders, her firm, wide breasts and thighs, drawing the thin linen of her dress tight and making her appear larger and heavier than she was. His heart would begin to thump slowly and heavily, as if it were clogged, stirring his whole body, and it would seem to him that the happy gentleness of spirit which had sometimes made her appear without substance lacked power in this long heat, or even that it had never existed, that she had always been ripe for unpretending passion, needing only the first touch to awaken and become insatiable. Perhaps she didn't even need the touch, but was already impatient at his stupidity or childishness which kept her waiting. Yet he couldn't tell her he loved her. Often he was about to, the first words, a mere prelude to the rush of desire behind them, shaping on his tongue, and then he would remember that letter he had written her, and roll onto his back and stare at the bits of sky showing through the boughs above him, and struggle, even by means of such tricks as thinking of a chess problem, or of some clear and passionless Bach fugue, to rid himself of the smoky, aching wish to hold her.

It was one night in the last week of that August that he could no longer let her alone. They were sitting on the steps of her cabin in the grove, Tim a step below her, lying back upon his elbow, so that his shoulder was against her thigh, and his head, if he hadn't held it away from her, would have rested against one of her breasts. Once in a while they spoke, idly and about unrelated things. The night was warm and motionless, and full of the singing of insects. As once before, but far more urgently now, Tim thought of the room behind them, and of the bed, faintly scented by the sweetness of Eileen, which was all around him there, until his desire seemed to fill the night and become the meaning of all the waiting under the enormous stars.

"Eileen," he said, softly, but it seemed to him loudly and hoarsely.

Eileen didn't answer, but stirred a little, leaned over him as if drawn without volition. He pulled himself up to the step she was sitting on, and took her in his arms, and she pressed to him eagerly with her body, with her mouth. But when he forced her back until they were lying nearly across the steps, and yet was increasingly importunate, she was frightened. She didn't repulse him, but she became almost inert, and her silence seemed to deepen, as if she had retreated far within, away from this clamor upon her. He drew down her evening gown with shaking fingers, and pressed his face to her breasts, and kissed them, and she didn't resist him, but neither did she make any response, by movement or by word. He began to kiss her mouth, her eyes, her cheeks, her throat, wildly, and between caresses to whisper to her rapidly and insistently, pleading openly for her desire, and then even for resignation as enough. He made a fierce, irresistible music of his whispering, like the incessant, piercing cry of the millions of insects, praising her beauty and her wonder, telling her swiftly, his lips against her face, how he ached for her, how terribly desire was scalding him, and strove to break her dread with visions of the loneliness and brevity of life. He scarcely knew what he was saying to her or doing to her, but the pressure of his desire was unrelenting, and Eileen had no defense against it. When, at last, he stood up and drew her to her feet, and would have led her at once into the cabin, she resisted for a moment, but as if resisting herself, not him, falling away unsteadily against the door-frame, her head back, her eyes closed, and whispering his name once, like a protesting cry. When again he put his arm around her and drew her gently from her support, she straightened up, and moved out of his arm, and went in ahead of him, slowly.

Now that she had surrendered, even thus silently and doubtfully, his insistence was transformed into a shivering tenderness. He followed her in, full of things to say which he couldn't say. He wished her to know that he would be gentle, that he would never in the world hurt her. She was standing still in the darkness, and he touched her, and then turned her to him very gently and kissed her very gently. She returned his kiss, but only as if it were automatic that her lips should move when his touched them. Yet even then he couldn't quell his rage for her, his strident expectancy. He couldn't let her go. He kissed her again, and stood away from her, trembling, just touching her with his hand, but waiting, still applying the pressure of his presence. At last, but without even turning to him the faint, pale oval of her face, she drew the already loosened gown yet farther down, and unhooked it, and let it slip to the floor. In the same slow, nearly unconscious way, she stripped herself, drew back the blankets from the bed, crept silently in under the sheet, and lay there waiting for him. When he came, her hands met him, but half as if to keep him away. Even as he turned to her, he heard some insect, a beetle or a great moth, beating frantically against the screen of the window at the head of the bed. Whether it was inside and wanted to get out, or was outside and wanted to get in, he couldn't tell, but the sound appalled him, as if, in some inexplicable way, it came from Eileen herself. And when he drew gently away from her, his desire done, and yet no true union achieved, but only one of the flesh, and that in estrangement, the soft, frantic beating was still going on. He kissed Eileen's shoulder, more in penitence then anything else. She didn't move. His mind shied away then, from what he had done, and darted here and there in the dark. He wondered what time it was, and thought that it must be very late. He had made that disgusting love to her on the steps for a long time, and it had been nearly two o'clock when they left the Marine Room. He wondered, for a foolish but dreadful instant, if Eileen was dead. He wondered if he should get up and leave her alone now, even though there hadn't been a word of understanding between them. He couldn't bring himself to do that, or even to ask her if that was what she wanted him to do. He took wider flights, to the songs he had been writing. He loathed them now. They appeared to him the worst of substitute trash. Yet a couple of them had already been recorded by Teddy's band, with Eileen on the vocal. He thought of Rachel. He thought of Mary. He thought of himself and Lawrence at Pyramid or on some of their desert trips, without any woman around to stir up unclear feelings and keep them stirred up. He wanted to find something to say that would bring Eileen back, but his thoughts flew out farther and farther, into tremendous realms of time and space, where the little violence to Eileen was of no importance. Suddenly the beating on the screen ceased. The creature, whether outside or inside, had given up. Tim's mind expanded and slowly became one, vastly enclosing this trivial moment. He lifted himself onto his elbow, and began to speak to Eileen.

When the first light entered, showing the shingles of the roof over them, and their clothes lying together on the one chair, and Eileen beside him, the sheet drawn up only to her waist, so that her throat and shoulders and breasts, as glossy and cold as marble in that colorless clarity, were still exposed to his gaze, he was talking the way he wrote music when it came by itself, when he couldn't write it down fast enough. He was telling her about everything in the world he wanted some time to get into his music. He was creating, with words, a tremendous symphony of mankind in which all borders were erased, a symphony of glad, free humanity, singing in one tongue, dreaming one dream of unending strength and clarity, joyous over a world it had attained to again, by the mind, after long and bitter centuries in which the mind had mostly tricked it, drawn it away from the strength of instinct and fed its new hungers with lies and fables which lingered after their time and made hatred and division and death. He could feel Eileen's warm flank against his thigh, but she really lay by herself, staring up at the shingles, and there was no answer, in her face or in her body, to anything he said. She was a white stone over which he poured the ocean of his inspired and hopeful words. The visions streamed down from her in a receding wave, and the stone emerged into the light unchanged.

It was only when Eileen moved for the first time, drawing the sheet up to her chin, as if she were cold or had just noticed the light, that he suddenly realized she wasn't listening. He was hurt, feeling that she had pulled up the sheet to hide herself from him. His words faltered and then the vision failed. He was back in time, and in the bed in the cabin beside her. He stopped talking. It came to him, like a blow on the mind, that even when he had been begging her so wildly, even when he had turned to her naked in the bed, he hadn't once told her he loved her. He'd told her only the too strict truth: that he wanted her. He saw he'd known this all the time, that it was the reason he'd started to talk. Eileen hadn't listened to him, but she'd listened for the words he hadn't said. Even then, though seeing it her way a little, he couldn't make himself say anything real to comfort her. He lay there looking at her for a minute, and then leaned over and kissed her cheek, very gently. She didn't look at him or move. His mind turned numb. After a few minutes more, he got out of bed and dressed himself, slowly. Then he came back and sat down on the edge of the bed and kissed her again. This time she glanced at him for an instant, and smiled a very little, and touched his face with cold fingertips, as if to say that she wasn't angry, but made no other move and said nothing. He stood up. It was getting daylight, and he'd have to go before somebody from the hotel saw his car here. This feeling of sneaking, hurrying, made things all the worse. He stopped in the doorway, and looked back, and for a moment the numbness broke a little and he was frightened. Eileen seemed as still inside as her body was, stretched there so circumspectly beneath the sheet which her hands held up against her chin.

"Eileen," he said.

After a long time, she said, "Yes?"

"Are you all right, Eileen?"

There was another wait, and then she said, tonelessly, "Yes, I'm all right."

He came back a step or two toward the bed. "Eileen," he said again, more strongly. He couldn't leave her like this. He'd tell her he loved her, and if it wasn't true, he'd make it true. He'd ask her to marry him, if that was what she wanted. "Eileen," he repeated, but still she didn't answer him. He stood there, not knowing surely what he hoped, and the numbness closed on his mind again, and finally he went out very quietly, closing the door very quietly too, as if she were asleep.

The numbness continued all day. The sun wasn't up yet when he got back to Knute's house, and the air was still cool from night, but the distinct outlines of the ocean horizon, and of the headlands to the south, promised another hot, cloudless day. He was tired; his eyes burned in his head, and sometimes deceived him in a first glance, but he wasn't sleepy. His weariness was strung up to a high, nervous twittering; he'd found no more relief in his flood of oral composing than in the unkind embrace with Eileen. It had been only the old, detestable talk again. He thought of eating, and the thought was repulsive. He thought of making another start at the symphony, working at something serious to counteract this conviction of sin, but abandoned the notion as soon as it occurred to him. Even these thoughts didn't seem to be his own, but rather to be light, winged creatures of no significance flying off in all directions from the immovable rock of his mind. He sat down at the piano, but couldn't pay attention to what he was playing. It was just so much far-off noise in his ears. At last he changed into old clothes and set out to walk himself free, but even the walking turned out to be sleep-walking. He found himself on the end of Point Lobos, which had been a favorite haunt for him and Eileen, without knowing how he'd got there, yet with no memory of anything distracting taking place in his mind either. He remained on the point all day, sometimes lying, for an hour or two, staring down at the hypnotic glitter and surge of the water in the stone channels, and sometimes walking about aimlessly among the rocks and the cypresses, seeing them and the sea and even the looming coastal hills, blazing in the afternoon, as an artificial back-drop. Still the catalepsy didn't break. He had no real feelings, and the flitting ideas seemed all platitudinous and ineffective, sometimes like Byronic gesturings of magnificent sin, and sometimes like the contradictory whisperings of an aged and scientific cynic, who reminded him that marriage was merely a social convenience which had nothing to do, at least not necessarily, with either love or passion, but was more often than not the graveyard of both, that, moreover, there were two billion such accidental morsels as himself and Eileen Connor on the globe, and that far greater stars, for that matter, were both innumerable and indifferent. No great pattern was going to be much upset by the chance rutting of two rabbits in a bush. Even the passing realization, in a voice that was neither of these, that the wonderful idea, the symphony of the world which he had poured out to Eileen, wasn't necessarily false because it had come out at a false moment, didn't seem to him any more important or any more his.

It was dusk before he started home. At one point, after he had come out onto the highway, he felt a brief rage against his stoniness. Even this slight inner activity felt good, and he tried to encourage it by striking himself hard upon the face and by calling himself at one moment a damned puritan and at the next a romantic posturer, either of which epithets, from another, would have enraged him. He spoke the words aloud, with a violence which was startling, because he didn't feel it, but in the immense, sterile night of the drought, against the interminable, shrill sheen of the insect song, they immediately became tiny and ludicrous. He compelled himself to start running, and then to run faster and faster, until his knees gave way under him and the starry darkness was blotted out by flashes in his eyes, and he fell. Yet when he rose he felt no change except that he was a little and indifferently tremulous and sick.

When he reached the house he still didn't feel hungry, but he took a drink of Knute's whisky to stop his shaking, which was violent now, and, when he was steadier, made coffee. When he had drunk the coffee, he became aware of the gnawing in his stomach, and ate two slices of dry bread. Then he wandered into the living room and turned on the light, and sat down at the piano again, more out of habit than intention. But gradually the mere sounds, single meaningless notes, reached him. He began to shape their sequences into small, exploratory themes. To the hopes of these orphan themes, never fulfilled, faint stirrings began within him. The exercising became more distinct, more deliberately restrained, and as he played, he began to remember Eileen in the cabin the night before. He realized, now, the weight of her silence and her inert resistance. He understood, now, that she might have breathed quickly, almost sobbing, when he touched her, not because she was wildly expectant, but because she was dreadfully afraid. He began to feel it all as he believed Eileen must have felt it. Finally there came a moment in which the understanding was so clear that a startled revulsion against himself jerked his hands from the keyboard. He sat there on the bench, huddled down, with his hands gripped together in his lap, and thought rapidly, almost with terror, of one thing after another in the night with Eileen. This was what he hadn't done all day, become Eileen enduring silently the shame and misery and annihilation which had almost nothing to do with what happened to her unskillful, half-forgotten body. The accumulation became unbearable. He perceived tremendous import and bitter torment in her slightest movements and sighs. He got up quickly and walked about the room. He struck his fist softly against the wall, against the piano, on the table.

But all the time there was a part of his mind that wouldn't surrender to this futile attempt at penance without action. It kept toying with one of the fragmentary themes he had fingered out. The bit of melody had no end, and led into nothing. He couldn't discover where it was going. He went back to the piano. He hunted up and down from that little motif. He inverted it and reversed it. He changed its key. In one major key it became astonishingly triumphant. He began to play with both hands. Still he couldn't develop the phrase. Always it came back by itself. Yet the music which it interrupted began to assume a continuity. Suddenly he saw its shape entire. He sat motionless and tense for a moment, his hands poised above the keys, examining what he had caught. It was no mirage. It was there.

He got up quickly and went to the table. There was clean paper lying there. He picked up a pencil without knowing it, seated himself, waited a moment, and began to scribble furiously.

Upon a sullen, throbbing background, with violins whining above, alternating two faint, persistent notes, that major theme emerged and died and came again. It increased in volume and tempo and dominated the orchestra. Even the shrilling of the violins became less broken, moved toward a separate unity of its own, and blended into the theme as it was renewed. Only the moody percussion, resisting the rhythm, and then, softly, a single, muted trumpet, entering irregularly, prevented fulfillment. The trumpet grew louder, disagreeing with the violins. The entire orchestra broke into tremendous, discordant union. In the turmoil the woodwinds strove to regain the never-completed theme, let go of it, tried again, and gave up. The violins were lost. Only the trumpet, a half note higher, went on straining through the uproar. The volume and incoherence increased about its piercing monotony. The drums hastened, lost their resistant pattern, ran into thundering riot. For a moment the trumpet was lost also in the chaos, and then, abruptly, it was alone, whining on like a ringing in the ears. Only an unrhythmic fluttering of drums interrupted it now and then.

Softly, under the trumpet, the woodwinds began to attempt their theme again, but each time it diminished prematurely and fell away into silence. Gradually, at first hesitantly, then as persistently as in the opening passage, the intervals were taken over by the mutinous drums and the insect violins. At last the woodwinds failed to come back. The drums ceased abruptly.

Suddenly began in full force a triumphant and regular and

stately major theme, half march and half deliberate dance, in the brass. It absorbed the trumpet. The violins gave up to it. The stubborn drums began again and moved toward its pattern. It was very near to succeeding, when the woodwinds interrupted it with the first theme. The brass choked them off loudly. The choirs entered into an increasingly rapid alternation, the brass breaking in more quickly each time, and compelling surrender. A transformation crept over both themes. The woodwinds changed key. The brass became macabre, satirical, and at last swept the woodwinds into silence and went on alone, but now in a minor travesty of what it had set out to announce. Just when this passage had assumed the complete regularity of a spectral dance, it too broke off incomplete. Twice, like mortal crying, the trumpet hunted for the woodwind theme by itself in a great silence. The second cry faded out half blown, and came back in the unbroken, monotonous whining. The whining swelled. Softly, in a different key, the violins resumed their irregular, high chirping. Their dissonance, like little points of fire, became louder. The trumpet fell off a note, making an instant of harmony, faded, and gave up. The violins finished alone, playing their two high notes, a half tone apart, the higher tone softer, but both growing fainter, until the higher note, the distant note, the far reply, was not heard at all, and the one tone dwindled into a whisper whose death could not be detected.

When the last note was written, Tim closed his eyes and sat there steadying himself. Colored lights flew behind his lids, disks of hot color flowing through and past each other in overlapping, rotating patterns. He had a moment of feeling that when he opened his eyes and looked down, he would find that there remained of him only bones strung loosely together at the joints. He waited until the lights swam more slowly and their colors darkened toward purple and blue. Then he opened his eyes, slowly set above the last note a long > of diminishment, and after it the mathematical sign for infinity. Finally, with a hand so tired that he drew the letters, and that with difficulty, he wrote across the top of the first page: *The Stone Woman.*

He piled the sheets neatly, and set an ink bottle on them, and stood up. He wasn't happy, but he was empty, physically exonerated by the music. The day of brainless wandering seemed months long, and done with years ago. He went into the bathroom, undressed, and washed himself all over with cold water. It was nearly four o'clock when he turned off the lights and got into bed. Before his eyes the sunny waters in the channels of Lobos danced and shook, and out beyond was the wide glitter of the sea. The vision faded, and he fell heavily asleep. He didn't wake until two o'clock in the afternoon.

CHAPTER FIFTY-FOUR: *In Which the Revelation of the Stone Woman Is Considered, and Mary Turner Receives a New Kind of Letter*

IT WASN'T long after the night of the Stone Woman, that Mary Turner began to get long letters from Tim again. There was a difference, however, between these letters and the earlier philosophical essays. Mary couldn't have pointed out, sentence by sentence, exactly where the difference lay, except that Tim seemed less concerned with the ravages of Alexander the Great, the sufferings of Beethoven and the moral temperature of interstellar space, and more troubled by what he deemed his failure to comprehend objects and people close about him. Yet the difference, indecipherable though it was in its parts, less tangible than thought, more quiet than silence, became a great power at work in Mary's orderly room at the Great Basin Hotel. To begin with, after she had read one of these new letters, the words "love, Tim," using the same letters, placed in the same position, and taking up much less space than when they had been scrawled at the end of the short, gay notes, seemed filled once more by a meaning which did not include Mr. Atley. Something of this meaning went with her daily to the Music Box, and was strengthened daily upon her return. It was present when she lay on the rug in the evening, listening to the records she had brought home. It was there when she took her shower and dressed, so that she often caught herself singing under the beating water, or dusting the end of her nose with the powder-puff in a manner quite new and flippant. It was always there, waiting for her, catching her by surprise, just as that sudden sensation of nothing at all, of falling through space, had caught her not so long before. It was only occasionally, now, that she became convinced, as she lay in bed watching the café light wink on the ceiling, that she was making something of nothing, and fell asleep unhappy, and in the morning light, that melancholy would, in its turn, appear to be the illusion. While her coffee bubbled on the percolator in the living room, she would ply the comb through her hair with no nudge of duty at all, and would lightly touch the lipstick to a mouth already shaped for it by whistling *Get Up with the Sun.* The goal and the distance were as yet uncertain, and she wouldn't ask herself about them, but, nonetheless, Mary Turner felt definitely that the life of Mary Turner was on the way to somewhere. In her quietest hours, the power was there most strongly. As she sat curled on the end of the couch with a book, it would all at once surge up, a sad, enormous joy, for a reason no clearer than the power itself, and because of, say, some single sentence describing daybreak at sea or wind about a lonely house, and she would have to look up from the pages, and take a deep breath, as if defending against a physical pain, and search herself for profound but darting meanings, and search the world for their sources. It often appeared, like the fragmentary gift of someone else's mind, in the little poems she wrote and kept instead of a diary. She no longer felt betrayed when she read one of Tim's letters after her ceremony of preparation, but instead felt as if Tim had been sitting beside her all the time, his arms crossed on his knees, staring at the floor, speaking quietly, perhaps unhappily, but always naturally, to her, taking comfort in the syllables of her name. For the first time, she also began to write long letters without trouble, and to end them with "love."

All this sounds as if *The Stone Woman* had been an end in itself, and its creation enough to terminate Tim's affair with Eileen Connor. In a way this was true, although it was some time before Tim knew it, and then it wasn't the success of the writing, but what he had learned as he wrote, that marked the end. *The Stone Woman* itself went out of existence. When Tim woke, the day after he had written it, the catalepsy broken, his mind intolerably clear after emotional exhaustion, the music appeared to him only as a celebration of his cruelty, and he carried it down into the same sacrificial hollow in the dunes where he had already burned four attempts at the symphony of leaves, and set fire to it one page at a time, and buried the black tinsel in the sand. For several nights after that, he slept little, and for several days walked a great deal by himself, or brooded in the big chair by the window in Knute's living room, or, in order to stop his circling, repetitive thoughts, set up chess problems with Knute's pieces, only to leave them unfinished too, as the unfinished question returned. In Eileen's presence he often wavered, telling himself, as he had in her cabin, as he had a thousand times during that day on the point, that even if he didn't love Eileen, he could marry her and learn to love her, which wouldn't be hard for any man. When he was alone, however, it would suddenly come to him, out of all the confusion of pity for her, and self-loathing, and all the innumerable thoughts they led to, clear as a blue break in a foggy sky, that that wasn't the answer. In fact it didn't even touch the real question. It wasn't marriage Eileen wanted, any more than it was the mere act of his body against hers that was his crime. Already that embrace, that moment of exploding nerves, had become nothing, as if it had never been. He couldn't even remember it with any reality. But he couldn't forget the approach to her as she lay there waiting in the dark, silent and withdrawn, and above all he couldn't forget that moment afterward, at daylight, when she drew the sheet up to her chin, and he saw what he was doing with his talk. Every detail of those moments still came back clearly, and stung him with shame. And if there, in her arms, he had been unable to say the word that would bring her out of hiding, if even there, when his mouth was against hers, some small and canny monitor sitting in a cold cranny of his brain, some tiny monster of misplaced honesty, of dry and ancient knowledge, had forbidden him the word, when could he say it? And that word was all that mattered to Eileen, and Eileen would know unerringly when that word was truly spoken and when it wasn't. So he had nothing to give her. When he was alone, he knew that the monitor was still on duty. He would tell himself contemptuously that he was making an excuse of something which no longer existed. He would think of Rachel, and she would seem to him exceedingly remote, a love he had imagined, a creation of one of his adolescent sagas. Nonetheless, the monitor continued to sit there, lifting his wrinkled and knobby finger, saying, "Remember."

With enough repetition, these moments of perception became a conviction. Tim didn't see Eileen except when they worked together, and then neither of them mentioned the night in the cabin. Conversationally it might never have been on their calendar. Silently, however, in their every glance, in the movements of their bodies when they were near each other, it was as if nothing else of any importance had ever happened. Tim wanted to plead with her not to let it matter, not to let it change her, but he would remember again that letter in which he had said such things, and be unable to say even that much.

When he was full of this speechless wondering about what he had done to her, the same uncertainty would encompass everything he saw and heard. A commonplace remark by some man at the bar, a half-joke from the hat-check girl in the Marine Room, would seem not to mean what the words said at all, but to echo far back, one echo fainter behind another, into a dark and hollow core where the answer to everything, surprisingly small, wholly unimaginable, stirred, but never quite woke. He would look at the enormous, ugly, lovable face of Stephen Granger in the open sunlight on the beach, and be amazed that he had ever dreamt he knew the man. Even the trees and the dunes would appear to him in the same way strange, intricate, profound, incomprehensible, not to be tampered with even by a thought. It was as if the whole universe, animate and inanimate, were held in so light, close and interdependent a balance that there wasn't the fraction of an inch or the fraction of a moment to spare for error, so that he must start all over again to learn truly even the little he had believed he knew, and must not, until his knowledge was certain, touch anything or speak to anyone, lest he make the minute error that would send the world flying apart as it spun. In this state, when he was, as he himself puts it now, "a kind of moral Roderick Usher," his mind, alternately seeking relief and seeking meanings, was drawn ahead of his body out of Carmel. He began to think often of Reno, the desert, the mountains, the house by the race track, of Lawrence and Helen and Mary. This retrospection was not often nostalgic. Rather it was restless and investigative. He was taking possession of his own past. It was then that he began writing the new letters which so encouraged Mary.

CHAPTER FIFTY-FIVE: *Family Reunion*

IT WAS then also, on a clear Sunday, when a steady, cool wind blew in from the sea, that he finally drove to San Francisco to visit Mr. Hazard. He had been putting off this visit from week to week ever since he'd come to Carmel, telling himself always that he'd go the next Sunday, when this rehearsal or that portion of his study or writing was behind him. The truth was that it seemed to him it would be far easier to visit a total stranger than to visit his father. The few letters they had written to each other, short letters, proceeding by unrelated bits, labored of language and stiff with the difficult diplomacy of minds with nothing in common except an exterior past which they couldn't discuss, had only increased the distance between them. Yet that diplomacy of conciliation had been practiced as much by Mr. Hazard as by Tim, and Tim believed that he had also discovered in his father's letters an increasing tone of loneliness, only the more disturbing because it seemed beyond his power, or that of anyone living, to alleviate. So he went.

The house with Mr. Hazard's number on it was one of a cluster of narrow, wooden buildings out beyond the last wharf toward the Golden Gate. It stood in the first rank, on the waterfront street, and like the others beside it, and tier upon tier above it, stared out at the bay through tall windows under flat brows, and yet appeared not to see the bay, but to be wholly taken up with memories of the brief and uproarious past which it defended from the encroachments of the modern city. There was only one bell-button beside the narrow, double door, and no cards telling who lived there, so Tim went into the hall. There the past seemed to take hold of him too. The hall was high, narrow and shadowy, only a faint, colorless light coming down the stairwell from far above. The stairs, covered with a worn runner, went up against the left wall, and there was a light in a red globe on the ceiling. Or was it that the doubtful, rather unhappy excitement which came on him now that he was about to see Mr. Hazard, made him feel that he had walked into this hall off Mill Street in Reno, Nevada? For there was a difference; there was a door on each side of the hall instead of only the one door on the right. Just the same, Tim went to the door on the right, and although the card said Mrs. A. L. Jenson, he was half expecting, as he rang the bell, that when the door opened, it would reveal a room with dark corners, smoky, old portraits in gilt frames, bow-legged chairs, and ornate tables covered with little boxes and figures.

The woman who came to the door didn't belong to that kind of a room, though. She was tall and white-haired and flat, and she wore a blue-and-white cotton dress, and a pair of steel-rimmed spectacles, through which she looked at Tim with pale-blue, direct and incurious eyes.

"Yes?" she asked.

"Is Mr. Hazard in?"

"I don't keep watch of my people," she said, "but I expect

he is. He generally tells me if he's going out Sunday. You can go up and see. Top floor; room 402."

"Thank you," Tim said.

The woman nodded, and closed the door.

Tim went up the steep, creaking stairs and along bare, clean halls into increasing light. On the fourth floor, with the skylight directly overhead, he came into a clear whiteness, almost without shadow, and found 402 at the front. There was no answer to his first knock, but after the second there came a sharp thump, as of a chair being set back irritably. There were slow steps across the room, and the door opened. For a moment Tim thought he had made a mistake. The man was tall and broad, but he was bony and gray too, with a gray mustache, and he wore glasses and had a scrupulously clean, pale, dry and powdered look. Also, he had on a freshly starched white shirt, and neatly pressed black trousers with narrow black suspenders, and a pair of black-leather slippers. He held the door open grudgingly, like a man interrupted at important work. He was holding part of a deck of cards in his free hand.

"Did you want to see me?" he asked, and the voice ended Tim's doubt.

"Hello, Dad," he said, smiling uneasily.

The old man, who still seemed like a clean and feeble imitation of Mr. Hazard, blinked and really looked at Tim for the first time.

"I didn't know you," he said. "I wasn't expecting . . ." Then he tried to be more hearty, saying, "Well, well, Timmy, this is a surprise. Come in, come in," and managed to get hold of Tim's hand. They were both nervous and smiling. Tim came in, and Mr. Hazard closed the door, after one try which didn't succeed. Tim stood uncertainly in the middle of the room, looking around. The room didn't seem to belong to Mr. Hazard. Except for a freshness which hadn't given in to the past, it reminded Tim of his old room in the office building on Second Street, or even more of hotel rooms in old mining towns like Virginia City and Austin and Eureka. It was high, and perfectly square, and had the same kind of pressed-tin ceiling, and two tall windows set close together in a square, shallow bay. There was no closet, but only the familiar, enormous wardrobe, and there was no bathroom. But its difference from most rooms of its kind seemed to be what one would expect from Mrs. Jenson, if that had been Mrs. Jenson on the first floor. It was as if the room, or Mrs. Jenson, had made the change in Mr. Hazard. It was a scrupulously clean and orderly room, full of light and cool sea air, and there wasn't much furniture in it, only the wardrobe, a big iron double bed, a high dresser beside the door, a flat desk against the opposite wall, and two chairs, a Morris chair by the windows and a straight chair pushed away from the desk. All the woodwork and all the furniture except the Morris chair was painted with shiny, white enamel. The wall paper was white, with a faint yellow pattern; the cushions of the Morris chair were covered with clean, faded yellow and white chintz; and there was a yellow and white striped coverlet on the bed. There were starched white curtains beside the windows. The pattern-shadowed rose of the worn carpet and the blue of San Francisco bay showing through the windows were very strong colors in that room. There were only three pictures on the walls, a framed needle-point of the *Flying Cloud* over the bed, and over the desk the photograph of Mr. and Mrs. Hazard which had left the unfaded square on the bedroom wall in Reno, and another photograph, taken by Mr. Turner, showing the Hazard family and Mrs. Turner and Mary grouped upon a blanket between two juniper trees in Antelope Valley. This picture had been taken at a time when Timmy wore knee pants and Mary's hair hung long down her back. A fourth picture, of Mrs. Hazard by herself, stood on the desk. This Mrs. Hazard looked much younger than Tim could remember her ever having looked, with a frail, eager youngness that made him feel old and unemotional himself. She had on a long-skirted white dress, and was standing at the rail of a ship, facing into the sun and wind and laughing with a tremulous, shining love of everything, such as seldom comes except from some great love which isn't nearly so inclusive. Tim had never seen this picture before, and it embarrassed him, as by a gross and personal incongruity, to think that this saintly-laughing girl was his mother, that in her was predicted the twisted, wasted creature who had passed beyond his knowing in the south-west bedroom in the house in Reno. It embarrassed him to think that probably it was this thin, gray man in the room with him now, this man who wanted to be left alone to play with his cards, who had called up the shining in that face. The room became as old as any in Virginia City, despite Mrs. Jenson and her white enamel. There was a small, irregular piece of gray wood, which looked like driftwood, lying in front of the picture. Mr. Hazard's solitaire game was laid out on the desk too.

"I was just having a little game with myself when you came," Mr. Hazard said.

"Go ahead and finish it," Tim said. "I'll watch."

"Oh, it doesn't matter," Mr. Hazard said, but since he hadn't put down the rest of the pack yet, he looked again at the cards that were laid out. "Well, it won't take a minute," he said. "I think it's coming out, too."

He sat down and began to play, and Tim stood behind him, solemnly watching, as if Mr. Hazard were signing a document of great importance to humanity, or completing a vital experiment, and actually, since that game didn't work out, Mr. Hazard went on playing and commenting about the cards and the luck, until the fifth game did work out.

Even the sensation of hard-earned victory, however, though it made Mr. Hazard feel much better, didn't make the conversation easy. Tim sat down in the Morris chair, and Mr. Hazard turned his chair around and began to argue about all the kinds of solitaire he played, Canfield, four-cornered, thirteen, idiot's delight and others, and about their relative chances of working out, and which cards in the first showing were likely to afford the best start. He had played three of the games a thousand times each, in order to determine the relative chances of winning them, and he made a detailed report on the project. Tim tried to pay attention, but his mind wandered off onto questions of the work of time, and occasionally he even had to look away from the face of his father making this instead-of talk. There was a pile of Western and adventure magazines, a detective novel and the morning paper on the window-sills. There were four more detective novels, an almanac and a pilot's handbook between sailing-vessel book-ends on the desk. The plume of Mr. Hazard's shaving brush showed above the edge of the dresser, and the foot of the white iron bed was reflected in the white-framed mirror over the dresser. Out on the very blue bay, in the brilliant sunlight, small, white launches skittered like water-bugs, small, white sails turned and balanced and slid slowly off upon new tacks, and the blank wall of Alcatraz stood up alone, an island in the water and in the mind. Far beyond it dreamed the low, wilderness hills of the Berkeley shore. Most often, because he could see them without turning his head, he looked at the pictures over the desk, and at the young Mrs. Hazard on the desk, and at the piece of gray wood in front of her. It reminded him of the moss-agate in its open case in front of the graduation picture of Rachel Wells.

A black freighter passed purposefully among the hovering sailboats toward the Golden Gate, its smudge thinning and disappearing in the bright air behind it. Mr. Hazard watched it, and his discourse upon the science of solitaire died in a void. Tim also looked out the window again.

"It's a swell view you have here," he said.

"Yes," Mr. Hazard said. "Mrs. Jenson's been after me to take a room down on the second floor. Says I should leave all that climbing to younger men." There was a familiar rumble in his voice for a moment. "But I tell her I like it up where I can see a real stretch of water. You'd think I was on my last legs, to hear her fuss."

Then he answered the question Tim had wondered most about.

"I wouldn't live anywhere but San Francisco," he said. "Of course, when your mother was alive . . ." He sat there, staring out the window. "But now all you kids are grown up and I've only got myself to think of . . ." he began again. And then, "I took my vacation down with Grace last year, you know, and she was after me to come and live with them. I told her maybe I would when I retired, but I wouldn't. I have everything fixed to suit me here. A man gets tired having kids around all the time, and then you can't make any plans for yourself, either. I don't care for it down there, anyhow. They're living in Bakersfield now, you know. So hot all the time you can't hardly breathe, and that flat valley. I like it where I can smell salt water."

After a minute he said, as if afraid Tim would think he was scorning Grace's life, "They have a nice enough place, as far as that goes. Her husband's working with the highway department now, you know. Grace writes to me regular, every week," he added, and then stared out the window again.

Finally Tim asked, "Do you ever hear from Willis?"

"Willis isn't much for writing, I guess," Mr. Hazard said. "He wrote me last Christmas, I guess it was. He writes Grace once in a while, though, and she sends his letters on. Do you ever hear from Grace?" he asked.

"Not very often," Tim said, "but it's my fault. I'm as bad as Willis about letters."

"Grace is quite a lot like her mother, some ways," Mr. Hazard said. "She'd kind of like to keep the family together still."

"I guess that's pretty hopeless."

"Well, when a family grows up," Mr. Hazard said. "That's what I used to tell her. Your mother, I mean. Grace has enough to do with her own family. Four kids now, you know." He began to describe the activities of Grace's children.

Tim had received announcements of the births. He had answered them too. He had sent a silver mug with the name engraved on it when one of the boys had been named after him. Thinking of Grace with four children made it seem that a great amount of time had swept by him almost unnoticed. He and his father sat there, like two well-meaning strangers, trying to talk on the outer edge of time. And yet that was human time. There was the bay out there. Its endurance mocked them, changing water that was yet always the same, had been the same before the city was here, flight above flight on its steep peninsula, white and shining in the sun, a skeleton mountain of shining points at night, imbued with the tragic beauty, the distant wistfulness of human time. The bay had been there when all this was only dunes and marshes where the gulls flocked and the herons waded in the shallows. It had been here long before the gulls and the herons, for that matter. It would be here still when there were only dunes and marshes again. You couldn't believe that when the city was all around you, when you could hear it through the walls and feel it shaking the floor and looming above you, but it had happened to some big cities before this, and left almost nothing but guesses. There were many Troys, one upon another, and Nineveh, and Carthage, and empty Petra cut in the rose-colored stone, all within some kind of recorded time. There was the magnificent civilization, more than a city, a whole national, maybe racial, history, which had mothered the Incas and the Aztecs, and was now only an hypothesis for footnotes and appendices. The trouble was that your own time wouldn't let you believe the effects of bigger time, where the lives of single men winked in and out like the glitterings on windy water. And yet, didn't man and the bay use the same time after all? The waters changed, but the water was still there. The tides pushed up the dunes and the cities and left them for the wind to play in, and pushed up more, and sometimes came back. Troy sat upon Troy unknowing. The error lay in what the eye beheld outwardly. Even the stars . . .

He realized that Mr. Hazard wasn't talking about Grace's children any longer. He was saying, "but someways Willis has changed quite a bit, I guess. He was up to see Grace about a month before I was down there. He had a load of horses to bring up to the coast, and took a few days off. He's doing all right, I guess, training quarter-horses for some man in Texas. But Grace said he'd changed a lot. He was more quiet like, not so sure he could lick the world."

In the same way Mr. Hazard spoke of many things, the connections lost in his silences or in Tim's lapses. He talked about Mrs. Jenson, whom he admired. She was the widow of a sea-captain, and over seventy, though you wouldn't guess it to look at her. He asked how Tim was fixed now, and that worked into insurance. He explained to Tim at length why he should start taking out insurance now. After the next silence he spoke bitterly of the depression and the waterfront strikes, which he seemed to regard as aimed against the peace of himself and other men like him, who hadn't much time left in which to make enough to keep them. Mr. Hazard was a checking clerk in a waterfront warehouse, and the maritime strikes and lay-offs had involved him. Then, because one of them, Mr. Nelson, had been involved too, he spoke, in disconnected memories, of his three particular friends. He feared Mr. Greeves' eyes weren't what they had been. You couldn't mention it, because the old man was touchy about his failings, but it was beginning to show in his horseshoe pitching. Mr. Nelson's son, who lived in Kansas City, had just had a boy, and to hear Mr. Nelson talk, you'd think it was the old fool's own work. Captain Williams had got into trouble with his last batch of beer. It had turned out black and heavy, and they'd had to buy some store beer while a new batch was working.

The paragraphs about these three friends had been the best in Mr. Hazard's letters, and gradually Tim had come to know the men. Occasional Sunday adventures with them made up Mr. Hazard's social life. All four of them had been connected with the sea in some way, and three of them still worked on the waterfront. Captain Williams, who had owned his own tugboat, was retired, and had his own house now, just a couple of levels above Mrs. Jenson's. Below the house there was a small yard enclosed by a high salt-hedge, and on most good Sundays the four gathered there and played horseshoes. They had come to form a legendary brotherhood in Tim's mind, the four old men slowly tossing their horseshoes on Sunday afternoons, bickering happily about the score, stopping to pull at their beers, discussing the weather and the harbor conditions and the modern idiocies. He thought of their names together, as you might think of the three musketeers and D'Artagnan or the four Marx Brothers. He always thought of them with their titles, though, Mr. Hazard, Mr. Nelson, Mr. Greeves and Captain Williams, to keep them from sounding like a firm of lawyers or undertakers.

Somehow, out of last Sunday's game, in which he and Captain Williams had badly defeated Mr. Greeves and Mr. Nelson, Mr. Hazard was all at once supposing that Mrs. Jenson, for all she was so well preserved, couldn't be expected to last forever, and then someone else would be taking over the place, or it would be torn down to make room for some showy modern apartment. He was keeping an eye out for a place to go when that happened, but he hadn't seen anything that suited him yet. They didn't make them as good as Mrs. Jenson nowadays. She kept everything ship-shape, but did it all while you were out, and you knew she wouldn't be nosing around in your things, either, or misplacing them. Then he gave a detailed account of how he spent each day, what time he got up, how he took his turn in the bathroom, how he ate at Ned's Diner, down the street, and Ned put up his lunch for him. Mrs. Jenson wouldn't have help, except one woman who did cleaning for her, and she'd given up trying to serve meals before Mr. Hazard had moved in. He liked it better at the diner than at a boarding table anyway. There was a choice, and the time was your own. After work he always came home and bathed and changed and went down to the diner for supper too. There was a movie just a block beyond Ned's, and he went to the show every Saturday night, and sometimes on Wednesdays. Other evenings he just came back to his room and wrote letters or played solitaire or read until it was his regular time for bed. He liked detective stories better than any other kind. They weren't always telling you a lot of things you didn't want to know and couldn't remember anyway, like most books. Charlie Chan was his favorite detective. He'd been to Honolulu a couple of times in his youth, and he knew San Francisco, of course, and that made the Charlie Chan stories more real. He was in the middle of a Charlie Chan story now. He liked to leave a story in a good place, so he'd have it to look forward to for the next evening. He began to tell Tim about the Charlie Chan story he was reading now. Tim looked at the picture of the Hazards and the

Turners between the juniper trees of Antelope Valley. The picture had been taken in bright sunlight, and all the Hazards and Turners were squinting and grinning. Nevertheless, it reminded him of a great many things. He felt a pang of desire to be with Mary now, in this very moment, in any place, in order to check the sad, empty, reckless flowing away of time.

Mr. Hazard was on his feet, looking at his watch. Tim got up too.

"It's a quarter to six," Mr. Hazard said, putting his watch back into his pocket. "I generally go out for supper about this time. You'd better have supper with me, Tim. No sense to start back empty." He sounded much heartier, now that there was a break in the talk, and he was about to do something to which he was accustomed.

They took turns in the bathroom down the hall, and then Mr. Hazard put on his black Sunday shoes and his tie, vest and coat, and a yellowed Panama hat, which made him look more than ever like a retired bank clerk.

On the stairs, he asked, "Do you like sea-food?" but the question was rhetorical. Before Tim could answer, he went on, "There's nothing like good sea-food. I know a place . . ." and while they walked along in the sunset shadow of the city, he described for Tim all the wonders of this sea-food palace where he sometimes took friends, or went for a special treat to himself. He had taken the visit into his own hands now, and it had become a party.

The sea-food palace was a big place, all of shining white tile and glass and metal. The floor was tiled, and the tops of the small tables by the windows were white-enameled metal. The lights were glaring, and the silver rattled on the tables, and voices and footsteps echoed. Men with red faces and hands, in white jackets, stood behind glass counters and great bins of ice, ready to prepare the sea-foods chosen by the customers. Mr. Hazard conducted Tim on a tour of the place, showing him everything he had already told him about, the deep, salt-water tanks where shadowy fish swam slowly about, the tables heaped with cracked ice, where the benumbed, green lobsters lay as they had been placed, and sputtered softly and made vague, hopeless gestures with their long antennae, the thick cuts of giant swordfish in the refrigerator case, the heaps of clams, mussels, abalone and shrimp. He made loud, salt-water jokes for the men behind the counters, who laughed and joked back, but then, after he had passed, grinned at each other in a different way.

Mr. Hazard and Tim sat facing each other at one of the tables by the front windows. The suppertime traffic went by close outside, with a noise of motors and horns. Whistles and bells from the bay sounded clearly through the open door, and people walking home came in to buy at the counters, or stopped at the farther window to look at the lobsters on the mountains of ice. Mr. Hazard described everything on the menu, and then practically ordered Tim's dinner for him, too, in his eagerness that Tim should taste the best in the sea-food palace. He made more jokes with the plump, blonde waitress who served them, and the waitress smiled at him patiently. Mr. Hazard's jokes had about them a flavor of long use, but not long enough use to make them quaint or individual.

When they had finished their shrimp in red sauce, Mr. Hazard felt so much relieved that he even inquired how Tim's work had been going. He was very much pleased to hear that two of Tim's songs had been made into a record. He asked how much money things like that made, and was again pleased to hear how much Tim had already received. He even led Tim to talk about some of the serious music he had been writing, and at the end of the meal, he gave Tim a cigar, and lit a cigar himself, and they smoked the cigars and drank an extra cup of coffee apiece, and Mr. Hazard said, "I never had the time to pay much attention to such things, but your mother had an ear for them, and she always said you could make it go. She was a remarkable woman, your mother. It's too bad . . ." and finished that thought to himself, staring out the window into the gathering dark, where the waterfront lights were beginning to appear.

So even there, they didn't quite get together, and what they thought moved along secretly behind their words.

Mr. Hazard looked at his watch again, when they reached the entrance to Mrs. Jenson's rooming house. "I could step around the corner and get us a couple of beers," he said. But Tim could feel how far away he had gone. His duty was done, and it was his usual time to go in. He wanted to be alone in his room, perhaps to finish something he had begun to remember, perhaps to test further the mathematical probabilities of Canfield, or to continue the adventures of Charlie Chan.

"No, thanks, Dad. I have a hundred miles to go, and Jeremiah's no infant. I guess I'd better get started."

"Well," Mr. Hazard said. He came to the curb, and stood there while Tim climbed into Jeremiah. "Well," he said again, "I'm glad you came up, son."

He appeared peculiarly small at the edge of the wide street, now almost empty of traffic, with Mrs. Jenson's old white house standing up behind him in the slanting light from the corner.

CHAPTER FIFTY-SIX: *In Which Tim Hazard Receives a Visitor at Dawn, and Hears a Far Cry*

POSSIBLY the visit to Mr. Hazard had something to do with it, but whatever the cause, the fact remains that two mornings after the trip to San Francisco, Tim awoke with the symphony of leaves working in him once more. The mysterious happiness of the little aspens of the outskirts was already nearly audible. He lay motionless in his bed for half an hour, his hands folded under his head, his eyes staring at the dark roof but seeing, one after another, pictures of Reno which moved in him a profound yearning to return there. Several times he felt, looming behind these familiar scenes and their beginning motifs, the big themes of Mt. Rose and Peavine. At last he could lie still no longer. He got up and took a cold bath, put on a sweater and a pair of ducks, and combed his hair, moving quickly, as if there were a limit to how long this hope could last unrecorded, but very quietly also. He believed that the entire symphony was taking shape in him, one great movement, flowing strongly and evenly through all its changes from the little aspens out to the little aspens again. He didn't want to eat. He made a pot of coffee, and took it into the living room with him, and started to write while he drank. He was tight as an E string, but from this tension the first movement began to emerge thin and lucid and spacious, just as he wanted it. It was Tim Hazard, aged twenty-six years, seated alone in the dark living room of Knute Fenderson in Carmel, California, who slowly, meticulously, filled those sheets of barred paper which piled up beside him, but the music sprang from the adoring, racing spirit of Tim Hazard aged, let us say, sixteen years, running on the yellow hills behind the stallion of his hope, and Tim Hazard aged thirteen, sitting in front of Billy Wilson's house at sunset, in conference with the little tree on the lawn, and even Timmy Hazard, aged not more than ten, riding home from Pyramid Lake with his shoulder against Mary Turner's knee.

For three days Tim wrote, begrudging every moment that he wasn't at the table with the pencil in his hand. He begged off from one rehearsal of the quartet. He got his meals quickly, mostly from cans, and ate them while he wrote. When Stephen dropped in, late in the afternoon of the second day, Tim got out two beers, and sat talking with him, but the conversation was an illusion and he often lost track of it. The symphony was coming this time; it was coming. Yet he controlled himself. He wouldn't let it race, run itself out too soon. He made himself go swimming at the end of every afternoon. He made himself stop every evening, when the music began to come too fast, to be loose and excited.

Even so, it didn't come, after all. In the middle of the third afternoon, well into the Court Street theme again, the impulse began to lag. Tim Hazard, aged twenty-six years, sat alone in Carmel and no longer projected of necessity, but endeavored to remember or even to construct. The music ceased to come of itself, quite separate from the city and the mystery, and became tricks, little traps, devices set to capture the nature of memories which wouldn't flow together. The melancholy time-lessness became dismal and heavy and time-bound. Tim struggled, floundering in a quicksand of despair, but when he had misbegotten the same brief transition a dozen times, and when the succeeding theme, which he had believed, only a little while before, to be clear and sure ahead of him, dissolved and seemed to have been a deception, he furiously drew a great X across each of the last three pages, and then sat motionless for nearly an hour, his eyes closed, his head bent, his hands clasped behind his neck. Finally he got up, and went out of the house and slowly down into the white dunes. He sat on the seaward side of one dune, bowed as in sackcloth and ashes, and even the sun appeared to him to be of false coinage, casting a baleful light over a world which desired darkness and the distance of stars. He wanted to run, as the young Tim who had deserted him had once run, until he broke out of bondage and attained the exaltation of successful prayer. But the music lay on the table in the empty house behind him, like the body of a loved one, and he couldn't leave it. At last he had to go back to it. He read it over, and then the light seemed gone from even the little aspens. They didn't tremble by themselves for any secret in the still air of the sacred Truckee Meadows. Their leaves were dry foil. No, they didn't even rustle; their leaves were cut out of limp green felt for a pool table. Tim took them back down into the sacrificial hollow and burned them, and again sat there, with his forehead on his knees.

It was long after dark when he returned, like a somnambulist, to the house. He didn't think of eating, but in order to stop the fatal searching within him, got out Knute's chess set, his habitual refuge in confusion, and began to work through a game from the book. After half an hour, during which he had been forced to begin anew three times, he abandoned this distraction, leaving the pieces where they stood on the board, and went to bed. He lay awake for a long time, fighting off recurrent tides of despair, listening to the soft rushing of the summer sea, but at last, spent with defeat, began to drowse off and at the same time to remember, disconnectedly, but for themselves, many of the things which had come back so vividly with the music.

The next thing he knew, he was lying there in the dark, full of that joyous expectancy again. It was a steady, single emotion now, though, and so intense that he held his breath for fear he was going to lose it. There was some single reason for his excitement, he thought, something he must remember, and it was very near him, and it wasn't music. Then, suddenly, he recalled what had just happened. A very familiar, very dear voice had spoken to him. He couldn't recall whose voice it was, and it had spoken only his name, very softly. Or had it said something else too? He lay holding his breath in the dark and listening. It was important, more important than anything else that could happen, that he should hear that voice if it spoke again.

Then it occurred to him that he was in the dark only because his eyes were still closed. He opened them. The gray light of early morning was in the room, and he was looking into Rachel's eyes. She was standing at the foot of the bed. He could see her small, thin-fingered hands closed over the foot rail. She was wearing a dress with a plaid skirt and a velvet jacket with many buttons, and her hair was cut in the short, straight bob. Tim was tremulously, speechlessly happy. Nothing else in the world mattered, not even the music. He was afraid to move or to speak. He was telling himself, and thinking it in a whisper, "She thinks I'm still asleep. If I sit up, I'll frighten her away." He lay there carefully motionless and looked at her, his heart and his hopes racing.

It seemed to him that she spoke, but that he was too excited to understand what she said. But he had heard her voice, and it was the voice which had awakened him, and this certainty came to him like a reassurance and a promise. She smiled at him, not quickly and in spite of herself, but gently and steadily. She was his very dear friend. The world was just as he wanted it. There was no need to say anything. Very slowly, he began to raise himself toward a sitting position. He felt faintly humiliated to be lying in bed before her, but he must rise and approach her very cautiously and attentively. If even so much as his hand were to move quickly, or he were to look away from her for a moment, she would be gone.

When he had lifted his shoulders from under the covers, he remembered that he had nothing on. He wanted to tell her that if she would wait in the living room, he'd get something on and be right out. It embarrassed him to think of trying to tell her this, and it worried him to think of her being out of his sight for one moment. He didn't realize that he had looked away from her then, but he must have, for when he looked back, she was gone. His happiness began to crumble with terrible rapidity, but then he saw that she had just moved into the doorway of the living room, and he was tremendously relieved. He gazed at her as if he would draw her back just with his eyes.

Then Rachel spoke softly. "It's all right, Tim," she said, quite distinctly, and was gone from the doorway. He heard her heels tapping lightly and quickly across the floor of the living room. He leaped from the bed, and called to her that he would be right out. Rachel didn't answer, but he was sure she was waiting out there. She couldn't have left the house without making the whole place feel different. Remembering the sound of her heels, a memory poignant enough by itself to stop his breath, he guessed that she was sitting in the chair by the south window, where Teddy usually sat when he came. He dressed quickly but very quietly. He still felt that he must be very quiet about everything he did. He was worried because his hair was all awry from the pillow, and so stiff he couldn't comb it without water. He didn't want to go out there and face Rachel with his hair standing up like that. There was nothing else to do, though. Well, what did it matter? His mind was still singing madly because she was there. Even while he was worrying about his hair, it didn't stop singing. He went out into the living room quickly, barefooted and with his hair on end.

She wasn't there. At first he couldn't believe this. He had been prepared for an incredible fulfillment. Just what it would be, what she could do or say, he couldn't have guessed, but it was going to answer all the questions of his life. Never before had he been so wholly and exaltedly happy. Always before he had approached Rachel with his rapture alloyed by some fear of offending her, of making a fool of himself, and this fear itself had always betrayed him. This time there was no such fear. Therefore she must be here somewhere.

He stopped in the middle of the room and looked all around, thinking he might have missed her in his first excited entry, but she wasn't there. The early sun cast a slanting beam through the window and across the big chair. The chair was empty. He felt very strongly that she had just been sitting in the chair. He looked down at the chess board beside his hand on the table. He couldn't remember exactly how many pieces he had left on the board the night before, or what their positions had been, but he believed they had been changed. The white queen appeared to him to be standing on a different square. He touched the white queen with his fingertips, as if by this contact he might learn whether or not Rachel had touched it. He called her name softly, "Rachel," and more clearly, "Rachel." He listened, expecting to hear her answer, or the little, quick steps returning. The only sound was the rushing of the sea down beyond the dunes. It sounded peculiarly loud, though, and he could smell it in the room, not the stale damps of a room that has been closed all night, but the fresh salt smell and the morning wind. He saw that the front door was standing wide open. He never left the door open at night. He hurried out onto the porch. The smell and sound of the sea were much stronger there, but the porch was empty. He went out into the center of the street and looked up toward the business blocks above, but there was no one in sight. There was only the soft dirt street in the early sunlight, and the low black trees along both sides of it, and the small houses still asleep under the trees. He went into the house again, and looked in the kitchen, but she wasn't there either.

How long it was before he began to understand, he couldn't have said. Finally he moved dreamily across the living room. He intended to sit down in the big chair in the slanting beam of sunlight, but then, because she had just been sitting in it, he remained standing in front of it. There was no question that he was awake now. Then when had he awakened, if not when the monitor first heard her speak? He could remember distinctly how the happiness had begun even before he opened his eyes. And when had he opened his eyes, if not when he remembered opening them and seeing her there at the foot of the bed?

He never found an answer for those questions, so that the visit remained as real to him as any event of his life, but it was finally a very simple fact which convinced him, against the belief of his whole body, that Rachel hadn't been there. She had been wearing the dress with the velvet jacket, the dress she had worn to Billy Wilson's party, a dress which must have disappeared from the world years before. When he understood that, he perceived that he too had been very young, as he lay there to receive that visit, a forgotten boy, almost a stranger, capable of a kind of ecstasy which no longer existed, and at the same time terribly troubled about his nakedness and disturbed that he should have to appear before Rachel with his hair uncombed and his feet bare. All that day a kind of illusory happiness from the dream stayed with him, but at the same time Rachel, with that ecstatic boy, sank further back in time than the life of an old man could have made possible. It was as if he had been forgiven his past, and might move without it. But at the same time, the answer about Eileen became final.

It was five days after this visit that the letter from Helen came, which made Tim leave Carmel in the flesh also. It was the first time he had heard from Helen since he'd left Reno. The few huge, scrawled words completely covered the one page of heavy note-paper. *"Tim Darling, for God's sake chuck whatever you're up to—no matter what—and get down here—I have to see you— Lawrence is probably cutting his throat now in some unspeakable dry-wash— Honest—Timmy—I'm scared to death— Love—Helen."*

Tim packed Jeremiah hurriedly, just tossing his things in, gave the house a cursory cleaning, took a last swim and dressed. He wrote a note and left it on the piano for Knute and locked up the house. He stopped at Stephen's cabin, but Stephen wasn't there, so he scribbled another note, and shoved it under the door with Knute's key. At the Quests', he found Pearl out watering the garden. She had to water it every day in this drought. When she saw all the things sticking up out of Jeremiah, she tossed the running hose down under the oak and came to the gate. Voltaire walked behind her, shaking his beard and threatening to bunt her, but not doing it.

"You look like you're going somewhere," she said, and when Tim explained, said, "Well, come in and see Teddy for a minute. He's just finishing his breakfast. He worked most of the night."

It was impossible to leave the Quests with only a word, so Pearl and Tim had coffee again with Teddy. Teddy sat there beside the table in his pajamas and bathrobe, the gray whiskers still on his face, the thinning hair on his dome rumpled, the night's weariness, but also the gentle humor, in his eyes, and petted one of the big yellow cats while they talked. It was all right about the band. The season would end in a week or two now, anyway. The quartet would miss him, though. Yes, he would say good-bye to Eileen for Tim, though he doubted if it would be quite the same thing. He set the cat down and came out onto the porch with Tim, and stood there, squinting up at the sun, and then watching Tim climb into Jeremiah and start the engine. Pearl came out and stood beside him. Teddy brought his hands together slowly and let them rest upon the bulge of the red bathrobe. "Come back some time," he called, and twinkled, and nodded two or three times, slowly.

CHAPTER FIFTY-SEVEN: *In Which Tim Hazard Is Becalmed in the Sargasso Sea of Beverly Hills*

TIM was so surprised by Helen's house, when he found it, that he stopped Jeremiah in the street below it, and stared up. He always remembered houses by the way he felt when he was in them, which is a matter of people, not of buildings. He realized now that he had thought of Lawrence and Helen as living here in a somewhat more commodious Peavine alley cabin, of Helen as still shuffling around in her sandals in a small kitchen, and of Lawrence's words about a music room and a piano as mostly figurative. Yet here before him was this huge white mansion, a cross between a Spanish mission and a Versailles palace. It sat upon a small, terraced mountain of shrubbery and lawn, guarded along the base by a row of lofty palms with tiny heads, and shielded behind, and beyond a white diving tower, by the shadowy wall of a eucalyptus grove, whose stately and feathery domes stirred slowly on the sky. He looked at Helen's letter again, but the address was right. He forced Jeremiah up the steep, crescent drive, and left him in the parking space outside the porte-cochere.

A thin, gray maid crept ahead of him through the shadowy hall to the door of the living room, announced him in a voice which had the effect of a whisper, and disappeared in the gloom without another sound. The living room was very long, and had a low, raftered ceiling. At the nearer end, a life-sized, globular Buddha of bronze maintained the lotus seat with ease, and gazed enigmatically through space at a huge fireplace. Across from the door was a wide, shallow bay, lined with glass shelves upon which perched, as if suspended in air, chalices, vases, bowls, round-bellied flasks, bottles and figurines of colored glass. Afternoon sunlight, entering through the bay, picked out gilt titles on the rows of handsome editions which lined the inner wall, gleamed upon five separate arrangements of chairs, lamps and tables covered with more ornaments, and made patches of cathedral window color upon rugs already richly dyed. So great was the impression of multitude in the room, that Tim didn't recognize the man and woman on the couch under the window as living creatures until they put down their cocktail glasses and cigarettes upon the low table before them and stood up, the woman quickly, the man reluctantly. Even then he wasn't sure the woman was Helen until she came at him with her hand out, crying, "Tim, you darling." She was much heavier, and her brown skin had faded to a parchment yellow, with purple patches, which couldn't be powdered out, under the eyes. Even her quick walk and the sound of her voice crying his name affectionately weren't right. It had cost her an effort to play the old part. He felt that he hadn't really been expected after all, and that he had entered at a bad moment. He had to look away from her eyes.

The man by the coffee table was obviously waiting for the time when he might sit down again. He was a short man with a round body, a round face, thin legs, thin lips, thin hair and a long, thin nose. He didn't move forward to meet Tim, or speak when Helen brought Tim to him, but very slightly inclined his spherical body, permitted Tim to shake his limp hand once, and looked to see if Helen was sitting down yet.

Helen said to Tim, "Mr. Hule is an old friend of my family," but to Mr. Hule she said, smiling apologetically, and speaking with too much energy, "This is Tim Hazard, an old friend of Lawrence's from Reno. He's a composer. You remember Lawrence speaking of him?" Tim got the impression that this meant more to Mr. Hule than it did to him.

"Ah," Mr. Hule said, bowing slightly toward the space between Tim and Helen, and sat down slowly in his corner of the couch, carefully lifting his knife-creased trousers. Helen dropped into the other corner of the couch and picked up her cigarette.

"Get a chair, Tim, and join us," she said, and then called, "Maddie," and when the creeping maid appeared through the swinging door in the dining room, which was a deep alcove in the book-lined wall, said, "Another glass for Mr. Hazard, please, Maddie." While Tim was drawing a chair up to the coffee table, she went on, "Timmy, you simply must admire this set. Mr. Hule . . ." and she waved at an open, velvet-lined box between them. "You must be nearly starved. Did you have lunch on the way? Dinner will be ready in half an hour, though. I counted on you. It's Louis XV," she said, leaning over the box again. "Don't you love all those . . ." She wriggled her hand in the air to indicate the ornamentation of the set. "It's incredible luck, really it is. No one but Mr. Hule . . ." and she smiled at Mr. Hule, with her head tilted a little.

Tim obediently looked at the intricate, silver toilet set. Its bulby fruits, babes and blooms were forced into preposterous relief by the tarnished channels that looped among them.

"Mr. Hule's a magician," Helen said.

Mr. Hule didn't seem impressed by his own powers. "It's badly in need of cleaning, of course," he murmured, and slowly drew a silver cigarette case from his pocket and opened it, although there were cigarettes in an open box on the table. He held the case out to Helen, then to Tim, then took a cigarette himself. The maid appeared at Tim's elbow and set a glass on the table. Tim was startled. He had heard nothing to suggest her approach. He looked at her face in the moment she was leaning over. It was a narrow, melancholy face, which looked as if it ran with tears whenever she was alone. She withdrew silently, and Mr. Hule poured a cocktail for Tim.

Helen must have decided not to talk about Lawrence in the presence of Mr. Hule. She began to relate the history of the toilet set, which was long, and economically amoral. Then she and Mr. Hule discussed other objects Mr. Hule had bought for her, or for others, or for himself when he believed their value would increase markedly within a reasonable length of time. Helen did most of the talking. Mr. Hule merely nodded, or said, "Ah," and once in a while told an extremely short, dry story about one of the treasures, in order to correct an error of Helen's. While Helen was rapidly and vaguely reciting the history of an "incredible" porcelain tea set, he rose without a word, walked meditatively across the room, and disappeared in the hall, to return in the same manner during the Odyssey of a jade cat. Mr. Hule, it appeared from Helen's sketches, was an expert in all manner of things, furnishings, objects of art, first editions, musical instruments, weapons, important letters and documents, real estate, stocks and bonds, and intrigue of a private or speculative nature. He was also an adept in clothes, dining, and comfortable travel. He had helped her in nearly all of these matters. Nevertheless, Mr. Hule appeared bored, as if he had passed beyond real interest in any of his skills. He traversed, in a series of confessional footnotes to Helen's monologue, the entire map of Europe, and most of the Orient, without showing any emotion save a slight amusement that anyone should attempt to compete against his knowledge and connections, and an imperturbable contempt for the artists and craftsmen who furnished his toys. Gradually it came over Tim that Helen wasn't merely being diplomatic in the presence of a difficult ego. She was truly fascinated by the theme, if not by Mr. Hule himself.

When Maddie finally announced dinner in that voice like a dismal whisper, Mr. Hule went slowly out into the hall again. Then Helen turned to Tim as if really speaking to him for the first time. She was so glad he had come; she had been worried sick. Still, she didn't know what they could do about it. She hadn't the faintest notion where Lawrence was by now. Lawrence seldom bothered to keep her informed about little matters like that. He'd been gone for days before his letter had come, two days ago, and then he had said nothing about where he was going. But then, she didn't suppose, after all, that Lawrence would really do anything idiotic. It was only that she'd read the letter late at night, and had been feeling so incredibly low herself that she had written to Tim at once, in a panic. Still, it had been an incredible letter. But then, it wasn't the first time she'd had a letter like that from Lawrence, practically threatening that he'd kill himself, and trying to make her feel that it was all her fault. Tim knew how Lawrence was, didn't he? never coming to the point, always leaving you guessing what he meant? Just the same, this letter had been the worst ever, so incredibly cruel and insulting. Helen's lip trembled, and there were tears in her eyes. She wanted him to read that letter for himself tonight. They couldn't very well talk about it in front of Mr. Hule.

Didn't Tim think Mr. Hule was simply incredible? She explained that Mr. Hule was an old friend of her family, and incredibly wealthy. She really hadn't sought his services or attentions or whatever they were, but under the circumstances, what could she do if the man chose to practically live on her couch? He had the most incredible attitude about women, too.

She had never known a man, at least an American, and after all, Mr. Hule was completely an American, with such an attitude about women. It was simply fascinating; incredibly medieval, or something. On Helen's face, when she considered Mr. Hule's attitude on women, appeared a pale shining which wiped away years. Mr. Hule returned before she could explain this attitude, but she promised Tim, by a private glance, to explain it at the first opportunity. Mr. Hule looked at them both, as if to discover what they had been saying about him, but not as if he cared. Possibly he wished to store more useful information.

Following the route charted by the journeys of Mr. Hule, Tim found the bathroom. It had a sunken, green tub, and green-tiled walls upon which swam inlaid tropical fish. When he had washed, Tim filled the basin with cold water, immersed his head and pummeled it savagely. The treatment was a failure. When he entered the dining room, he still felt that he had only to sink one level deeper into the trance which had begun, in order to start asking permission of the furniture before he moved or spoke or even developed a private thought.

At the table Helen tried to bring Tim into the conversation by opening with music, but she didn't succeed. She didn't really want to talk about music herself, and Tim was unable to emerge against the informed and skeptical inertia of Mr. Hule. Mr. Hule wouldn't argue against theories which didn't appeal to him; he contradicted them as if they were misstatements of the morning quotations on Standard Oil or Anaconda Copper. When he was caught by a statement of fact which he couldn't contradict, he would say, "Ah," and continue to eat slowly and rhythmically while he waited for quiet. Even Helen seemed temporary in her own home, as if it were actually possessed and understood only by Mr. Hule. Tim finally felt that he couldn't speak without sounding angry, and settled into a silence deeper than Mr. Hule's. Maddie crept around the table, performing a silent and unpleasant sleight of hand with plates and glasses and serving dishes, and Helen smiled with strained eagerness, first at one of her guests and then at the other. The table was lit by four tall tapers, which guttered whenever Maddie passed through the swinging door, and tossed about the enormous shadows of the three diners upon the walls and ceiling. The conversation began only with the dessert, when Mr. Hule complimented Helen upon the dinner. He made it clear that excellence in such matters was relative, but Helen was tremendously grateful. She fixed upon Mr. Hule, and in time drew from him speeches as much as four or five sentences long. Together they traversed the map of Europe once more, and even the map of the Eastern United States, this time eating and drinking.

After dinner they returned to the living room and resumed their identical places around the coffee table, and partook of coffee and of a liqueur Mr. Hule had approved. Gradually conversation began again, with only one minor difference. Mr. Hule, having discovered by means of a direct question about a Viennese café, that Tim had never been in Europe, no longer said, "Ah," if Tim made a remark, but merely leaned forward and studied his glass or a corner of the coffee table until Tim was done, and then, after an interval of silence to serve instead of a transition, started to talk to Helen about something else. Yet this did not seem like deliberate condescension, but more like a careful husbanding of the remnants of his emotions, in order that they might be applied to more important topics. There would be the pause, without a thought on the part of any of them, and then Mr. Hule, as if merely breaking an awkward silence, would ask Helen, "What have you done with that white gown you wore to Tamara's reception?" and he and Helen would discuss women's dress. At first Helen offered some opposition to Mr. Hule's very definite judgments on this subject, but gradually they entered into an accord, based upon similar views of the purpose of women's clothing, which went far deeper than design or color or material seemed to account for, and Helen's face again shone with that translucent youth which Tim had already seen when she spoke of Mr. Hule's incredible attitude about women. From women's clothing, they progressed to smuggling women's clothing, and then to smuggling other objects. Twice more, in the course of the evening, Mr.

Hule arose and walked meditatively into the hall. During one of his absences, Helen again promised revelations about him, and during the other she again tearfully protested that she was bewildered by Lawrence's incredible conduct, and pressed Tim to stay with her at least until they had decided what they had better do.

There was only one brief discussion which drew Tim out in spite of himself. Mr. Hule spoke with admiration, tempered, of course, because of certain incidental manifestations, which could only be temporary, of what Mussolini was doing for Italy, and so might do, by example, and in the course of time, for all of Europe, at least. He indicated numerous signs, particularly in Germany, that this latest Italian renaissance was already spreading. Then Tim spoke hotly against him. He spoke of Machiavelli, militarism, racial falsehood, Napoleonic appetites, medievalism and false heroics. He spoke of dictatorial limitations of education, of the suppression or falsification of truths which had been centuries in emerging from an older superstition, and of the end of free expression, which in time could mean only the end of thought and a return to a mental night even worse, considering the engines it would have to play with, than the one they had come out of. He stated fiercely that he did not consider a few highways, a drainage project and a punctual railroad sufficient substitutes for these lost values, and that, all resounding, ill-medleyed, oratorical plagiarisms to the contrary no matter, no man could, save such a man as hoped to gain by the establishment of a new, chiefly economic, aristocracy, since that, and even that temporarily, was the only possible end of the present course. As for him, he didn't even believe the project could mature. It was impossible, in this age, to create and maintain a sufficiently widespread ignorance to form the base.

Mr. Hule watched him for a time, with a mild, amused surprise, and then patiently eyed the liqueur glass cuddled in his lap, and waited. This once, however, he did reply. He admitted that there was a great deal about these early stages and about the Ethiopian war which was like a badly staged carnival, but asserted that, nevertheless, a salutary tendency was already emerging, under the curb of the church and the hereditary nobility, and that, in time, when the inevitable hoodlumism of the initial period had been overcome, and the few really radical tendencies of the fascists, which were merely expedient, had been modified or removed by success, he ventured to believe that Italy would exhibit to the world the first shapely civilization of modern time, a civilization once more guided by a sense of values and maintained by an orderly and stable social hierarchy. Then, before Tim could reply, he indicated that this topic was closed, by extending his cigarette case to Helen, and asking her if she remembered the remarkable midnight entertainments at the home of Madame Chauvrille, which led them in time to similar entertainments of a more professional nature, and eventually to the multiple love affairs of several mutual acquaintances in Paris.

CHAPTER FIFTY-EIGHT: *In Which Tim Watches His Friend Lawrence Swimming Wearily in Small Circles in the Sargasso Sea*

WHEN Mr. Hule departed at midnight, Helen brought out whisky and bigger glasses, and became at once less incandescent, though she began the conversation by declaring again that Mr. Hule had the most incredible ideas about women. The fascination of these ideas was in part due, as nearly as Tim could make out, to certain ideas about religion which Mr. Hule also possessed. Only two years before, in Paris, Mr. Hule, until then an agnostic, if not a downright atheist, had joined the Catholic Church. Helen was intrigued by the veiled processes which had led to this act, and reviewed them for some time, exhibiting a considerable intimacy with Mr. Hule's external past and a method of exploration as obscure as the conversation itself. Having got Mr. Hule's head to holy water at last, by way of ritualistic aestheticism, she was led to explain how essentially religious she had always been herself. Wasn't it true, she inquired ecstatically, after many examples of her childhood tendency toward God, that the Catholic Church still made much the strongest appeal? Didn't Tim think that the appeal of the divergent faiths was terribly attenuated? Take, for instance, the drab performances of the Baptists, with their lack of ceremony and tradition and even of a real clergy. And then take the faith of the Middle Ages; well, he knew himself. "When you go into one of those wonderful old cathedrals over there, with the great vaults above you, and the wonderful windows, and the shining altar and all the pageantry and chanting—well—it just does something to you." She described the mystical changes which had taken place in her during each of several such visits, and poured two more drinks.

"So I think I can understand what happened to Mr. Hule," Helen said, "but even so, such ideas about women, in this day and age, are practically incredible." She related how Mr. Hule had spent a whole evening demonstrating to her, with the entire weight of an orderly civilization behind his argument, that there were only two proper realms for a woman who was both good and attractive, a protected home, where she could bear her husband unquestionable children, and a nunnery. "Did you ever hear of anything so medieval?" Helen cried excitedly. "And he actually put both his own daughters into a nunnery in Italy only a year ago. He actually did, Tim. They were only seventeen and eighteen, and they didn't know a thing about the world. Even before he turned Catholic himself, he sent both of them to a convent school, and when they were home, they never went anywhere without a kind of duenna. Oh, he didn't force them to take the veil, or anything. They were very religious themselves. He said they were so lovely he couldn't bear to think of them being soiled by the world. And still, you heard him talking about those peep-shows. Isn't he the most incredible person? And another thing he said. He said no man should have intercourse with his wife except to beget children. Tim, he really did. He said no chaste woman ever felt any compulsion toward sex, and that a good husband should seek his diversions elsewhere, with women better suited to provide them. And there is a kind of mad consistency about that, isn't there? His orderly world. You know, Tim, sometimes I think he's actually trying to convert me, or reform me, or something. It's perfectly ridiculous, of course, because I can see through him like a pane of glass, but still it's kind of touching, in a way. He practically did everything but write out a set of rules for me, everything a man has a right to expect of his wife."

"Does he have a wife?" Tim asked.

It seemed that Mrs. Hule was dead, but that they had been divorced several years before her death, before Mr. Hule had entered the church, in fact. A good deal of Mr. Hule's philosophy about wives might have developed because of Mrs. Hule, Helen thought, and began to examine the unfortunate marriage of the Hules.

When finally Lawrence appeared, it was still by way of Mr. Hule. Mr. Hule agreed with Helen that what Lawrence needed, besides study in Europe, especially Paris, where art was—well— and the all-indicative hand. "But you know, Tim," she said, making the tragic mouth, "I've tried to suggest, I don't know how many times, that we go to Europe, and Lawrence just keeps saying, 'That would be very nice, some time.' Oh, damn him, if only he'd . . . It would be so good for him, Tim. You know it would. Paris especially. We could get one of those . . ." and she began to imagine how they would live in Paris, all the fascinating people Lawrence would meet, the artists he could learn from, the gorgeous old cathedrals and paintings he could see, to say nothing of just being there, which did something for you all by itself. It was true, and she admitted it gladly, that Lawrence already knew an incredible amount about that life; he remembered all sorts of little things he heard and read, things she could never remember. But still, that wasn't at all the same thing as being there, was it? "But he won't even talk about it, Tim. Sometimes I think if he'd only say something . . ."

But even if they couldn't get Lawrence to travel, she said, with an air of getting down to business, they simply must find a way to make him sell his work, produce and sell, produce to sell, in fact. If he could only make some real money of his own, it would give him such confidence. Mr. Hule, she said, which was what she had begun to say before, agreed with her that what Lawrence needed was to sell. He had even taken the trouble to talk to Lawrence about it himself, but—well—sometimes she thought. Mr. Hule had offered to buy several of Lawrence's paintings, in fact. "You know how well he could have placed them, Tim. And Lawrence was positively insulting. Really, he was, Tim. He said the paintings weren't for sale, and got up and walked out of the room. And that same evening he destroyed them, Tim, burned them, every single picture we'd been talking about. Oh, Tim, sometimes I don't know," she cried tragically.

"And the next day he ran away again. Up to Austin, and in the middle of the winter, too. Oh, this isn't the first time. You know that as well as I do. And it is running away, Tim, it really is. And always to some place like Austin, always. There's something unhealthy about the way he loves those old, dead mining camps, Tim. He feels at home in them. He loves to sit around in those old bars and talk for hours with any kind of bum who wanders in. He's like a saint in a way, and yet he's not. It's more like a saint complex. It's rotten. It's unholy. He's in love with failure. He's always going back to those terrible old places because they're done, they've failed. That's what he likes most about them, no matter what he says. And the people. He knows every bartender of a run-down joint, every old, out-of-work miner, every hopeless, baggy, middle-aged whore in the State of Nevada, Tim. Really, he does, I think. They're failures too, you see. He doesn't have to compare himself. They don't know anything about art, and they wouldn't care anyway. They don't care about anything any more. But if I bring people here, interesting people, painters, sculptors, movie actors . . . And he was gone two months, Tim, two months. And for five weeks he never wrote me a word. That was just last winter." She tossed her head and made the tragic mouth. "I tell you, Tim, a fellow can stand just so much."

Tim stared at his glass and nodded, and then asked, "Did he paint anything while he was up there?"

"He brought back a dozen canvases," Helen said. "He sold some of them to get money to go away with this time. Why does he have to do things like that, Tim?" she cried. "It's just like a slap in the face. I'd give him anything he needed to go away, and it's all right with me if he wants to wander around by himself, but why does he have to act as if there's something poisonous about my money? And why does he have to sneak out every time, or act as if he were leaving for good? And then, all of a sudden, after weeks without a word, and when I've been practically frantic, he writes me that he loves me, that he misses me, that he wants me to come up and stay with him. He wants me to see some wonderful old bar. He wants me to meet Jakie, the sheepherder. He's sure that if we're there together a week or two, out of this house, that's what he says, Tim, out of this house, everything will be better. So I race up there in midwinter, and live in that old, creaky hotel room, with no heat but one little, tiny wood stove in the corner, and then, after a few days, it's just the same as ever. We fight like cats and dogs. He won't even speak to me. And I've got to sit there in the same room. I tell you, Tim, sometimes I think I'll go mad. I don't know . . ."

"Some of the pictures are still here?" Tim asked.

"Yes. They're up in the studio. Five or six of them, I guess. And that's another thing, Tim. It's a beautiful studio. I had it built just the way he wanted it, and he didn't work in it more than two or three months. Then he went downtown and hired that dreadful, gloomy loft. He'd stay down there all night sometimes."

She dropped ice into the glasses and poured two more drinks.

"What are the pictures like?" Tim asked.

"Oh, they're just his, you know. Not like anything in particular. They're done with that black over-wash and then worked back through to the color, a kind of an old-master glow effect. Nothing so special. But they're all Austin, and he told me they were to be left alone; I wasn't to sell any of them. It's the *place* he loves. But he needn't worry. I took Mr. Hule up to see them, and he said he doubted if there'd be any market for them, except at give-away prices such as Lawrence himself asks.

"One of them's different, though," she went on. "He never did anything like it before, and it scares me, Tim, it really does. It's a kind of a nightmare thing. It's crazy, I think, really, quite mad. He put me in it, up in that awful little Austin room, only I'm a kind of fiend, or at least a ghost. Not that I care," she said quickly. "Oh, it hurts. I won't pretend it doesn't. After I've tried to make my whole life over just to suit him. It isn't my kind of life, Tim. I like people. I like to go places and see things. And then he acts as if I were some kind of a female Dracula. But I don't matter. It's Lawrence I'm worried about. He could be a great artist. But when he begins to paint that sort of thing . . ." She tossed her hand, palm upward, to throw "that sort of thing" into space, and shrugged her shoulders. "It's so petty, Tim, even if it isn't really insane. It's not like Lawrence to be so petty, Tim, you know that, but almost ever since we've been down here . . ." and she began to give examples of the sinister outcropping of the petty in Lawrence. She admitted repeatedly that she wasn't perfect, that she was no angel; she knew that. But she tried so hard to make a life he would like. She had people in all the time, not the kind she would choose for herself, but people who would interest Lawrence, people who came to see him, not her, and most of the time he would just sit there in the corner as speechless as a dummy. Sometimes he wouldn't even come down from the studio when she sent word up to him that he had guests, and just to save face for him, she would have to lead them up all those stairs. She tossed her head against the brimming tears again.

"A fellow can stand just so much, Tim."

It had been wonderful when they first came down. Lawrence had planned the whole house, just the way he wanted it, and they had bought everything together. He'd been a wonderful lover, too, so kind and thoughtful. It had been just like starting all over again. All her friends had adored him. They'd been invited everywhere. Almost every night, they had gone out to dinner, or had friends in. It was a new life. It had seemed that everything was working. She had been so happy, and Lawrence had too. And then, after he'd been working just a little while up in his new studio, it had all changed. Finally he wouldn't even come near her. He took to sleeping in another room, and then he got that gloomy place downtown, and sometimes he would stay down there two or three days at a time, unless she went down and dragged him out. And it wasn't that she had interrupted his work. She had just tried to keep him from working so long that he got into one of those terrible, depressed moods. He wasn't really working, anyway. God knows what he was doing. He would be down there three or four days, and then he would bring things home for her to look at, and it was always the same kind of thing, little, useless experiments, no real painting, not even any real sketching, just tricks.

There had even been trouble about clothes. She described the huge closet full of clothes that she had bought for him, just the kind he liked. And they were still upstairs, most of them never worn. He would wear only what he could buy with the money from the few pictures he would sell. It was most humiliating. They would have friends in for cocktails, and he'd appear in some dreadful old work shirt and tennis shoes, like a walking declaration that she was stingy. And it wasn't as if he really liked that kind of clothes. He loved to dress well. He loved the best of everything. Tim knew that. Yet even in his work, he would treat her like that. She would take particular pains to find out what kind of paints and brushes and everything he needed, and then she'd get him the very best there were, and he wouldn't use them. He'd waste days trying to concoct some cheap substitute. He would buy a five-cent child's brush at the dime store, and make those beautiful little sketches in iodine, or something equally idiotic, that would fade to nothing in a week. She cited many examples of Lawrence's rejections. He wouldn't even accept presents from her, she declared, things he really wanted, which he needn't have considered any insult to his precious independence. She'd bought him a handsome electric razor, for instance, and he'd never once used it. She had found him, one morning, shaving with that same disgusting old stump of a brush and that same old safety razor, and when she had looked, there was the new razor, still in its box and still with the tag on it, pushed way back on the closet shelf. It was like a slap in the face. And just a month ago she'd had a special bag made for him, a handsome little leather bag for his trips. There was room in it for his clothes, and a special place for his toilet articles, and a division just for his painting things, with little pockets for the tubes, and containers for brushes, and a place for the palette, and, oh, everything. And where was it now that he'd run off again? Up in his closet, just where it had always been. "And it's so silly, Tim, so foolish, just playing tricks on himself, petty tricks. He still lives in my house, doesn't he? He eats here, doesn't he? He's glad enough to read the books I buy and drink my whisky. And still he'll walk all those miles downtown, or take a street car, instead of using one of the cars. And he'll smoke the smelliest, cheap cigarettes that he picks up God knows where, Alvara Street or somewhere, with the house full of his favorite brand. It may just sound funny to hear it, but after a while it isn't, when you live with it day after day. He acts as if I never thought of anything except my money, and actually, Tim, he's the one who thinks about it. He's a hundred times more money-conscious than I am."

She poured two more drinks, and stood up. "I want to show you that letter," she said. She got the letter from a big bowl on the sideboard in the dining room, and brought it back.

"You tell me about it," Tim said.

"There's nothing in it he'd mind your seeing," Helen said bitterly. "You read it. I want you to see for yourself. I don't want to say a thing about it until you see for yourself." She sat upright and defiant as Tim slowly drew out the letter and began to read. It was a long letter, for Lawrence.

Dear Helen,

I wander and I look, but as yet I see nothing clearly. I tell myself aloud where I am. I am in a cabin in a tourist camp. I have forgotten for the moment where the camp is, but it doesn't matter. The manager is a wise man. He deals only in the tangible and necessary, houses, food and beer. In the morning he will tell me where I am. For now it is enough that there is a big bed in here, and dark hills behind the camp, and a light in the courtyard over that reassuring sign MANAGER. There are innumerable moths dancing around the light. They seem happy, but they aren't. They are possessed. The ground is already covered with their dead. I brought one of them in with me, a very large, beautiful one, with antennae like infant ferns. He lies on the bed beside me, and I look at him. Perhaps I will learn something. Other insects make a perpetual whirring in the hills. Or is that, and all the rest, in my head? No, the moth is still there. I hold out my hand and regard it. I try to remember where I have been.

This afternoon I went for a walk, and the manager's dog went with me. I am sure of that much, because the dog is here on the floor by my feet now, and he is jerking and whimpering in his sleep. He is a foolish, excitable mongrel, but very friendly. While I walked, he chased jack rabbits, yipping in a high, frenzied voice. Sooner or later, every rabbit would dodge behind a bush and shoot off at a tangent, and the dog would run straight on for a quarter of a mile before it came over him that he was pursuing nothing. At last he had an inspiration. He chased the next jack past five bushes, and then tore off on a left tangent himself, his voice full of hope. The jack sat down and watched him depart. They know him here, I guess. How happy that poor dog would be in a whippet race, if only he could believe in mechanical rabbits! As it is, he has these dreams.

Tonight the dreams must be the worst he's ever had. On the way home, he started a cottontail on a flat where there was very little brush. He was sure his moment had come. I was excited myself, and ran after them. The cottontail made it to the first big bush, and plumped out of sight. The dog's hope lifted him to genius. He stopped running and yapping and approached cannily. He cocked his head at something he heard in the bush. He circled the bush slowly, settling to spring as carefully as a cat, his tail quivering. Then he sprang, but straight up in the

air, and with a panic-stricken yelp. Traveling low, his tail be-
tween his legs, whimpering pitifully and looking back at the
bush, first over one shoulder, then over the other, he passed me
on the way home. He nearly bumped into me, in fact, but even
then he didn't see me.

I also circled the bush cautiously. There was nothing. I as-
sumed the dog's point of view, and peered under the shaded
side. I wanted to jump straight up too, but my legs are not as
good as the dog's. There, where the cottontail had disappeared,
was a side-winder, his coffin-head balanced back and waiting,
his forked tongue testing the air. His deadly little eyes stared at
me unwinking, exactly where I had expected to encounter the
large and terrified eyes of the cottontail. But this is the thing
that bothers me. It wasn't until I was halfway back to camp that
it occurred to me that there had not necessarily been a trans-
formation. I bought the poor dog a pound of hamburger for his
supper. He ate it, but merely out of courtesy, and with many
long and haunted pauses.

> *Damn your things, my love,*
> *Lawrence*

Tim kept his head down, as if still reading, in order to consider the implications of the letter before he had to speak. But
Helen couldn't be deceived long. He had only begun to see
how little authority Helen's commission would give him in this
desert, when she interrupted.

"I'm sick at heart for him," she cried sharply. "I'm scared to
death, and he writes such cruel, insulting nonsense."

Tim lifted his head and stared at her.

"Damn my things," she cried, the tears welling up again. "I
don't care about the things, Tim. All this was for him." She
waved her hand contemptuously at the room behind Tim. Once
more she tossed her head angrily. Then she picked up her glass,
emptied it without pausing, and set it down again with a finality
that told Tim that she was also hurt by his silence. Yet he saw
no way in which to break out of this silence. The Helen of
two years ago would have understood the whole letter. Helen

picked up a cigarette, lit the match with a jerk, drew deeply, and blew the smoke out in a short blast through her nostrils.

"So I'm a snake, am I?" she cried. "So I was his rabbit, was I? Well, I'm neither his snake nor his rabbit, if he cares to know. Why should I be his anything?"

"But he didn't mean just you, Helen," Tim began.

"Oh, didn't he?" Helen asked. "The hell he didn't," she declared. "If you think I don't know Lawrence after all this . . . Why doesn't he say what he means?" she cried, and after a minute repeated, in miserable anger, " 'Damn your things.' The bastard!"

"But also 'my love,' " Tim said, "also 'my love,' Helen."

"Oh, you're another, Tim Hazard," Helen said, but not exactly the way she would have said it once. Tim couldn't grin.

" 'Dear,' " Helen said fiercely. "Dear anybody. Why didn't he say 'Dear Mrs. Black'? And look at the address. Now, I ask you . . ."

Tim looked at the address. It looked all right to him.

"Helen Black," Helen said.

"I don't see anything . . ." Tim began.

"You don't?" Helen asked. "Well, he knew *I* would. He never addressed me as just Helen Black before. Never."

"He always writes to me just Timothy Hazard."

"It's not the same. He means something, all right. He always used to write 'Mrs. Lawrence Black,' Mrs., as if he were proud of it. Now I'm not, don't you see?"

Tim stared at her, unbelieving.

"You think it doesn't mean anything? Well, it does. I know him, Tim. But he wouldn't say it right out, in plain words, would he? Always little tricks; needling, needling, always needling. It's just the same when he's here."

Tim wondered. Had it really come to this with Lawrence? How much could he guess of the day after day in this house, of the work of the things and the money and the Hules on Lawrence with his pride and his yearning for peace? He was sure of the big desires in Lawrence, the desires which established a direction and couldn't change. Whatever the difference in their combination, weren't they also his own desires? Wasn't the mutual recognition of these desires, which was always immediately present, making a single something, a love and an alliance greater than the sum of the desires, and needing no words, when he and Lawrence met and shook hands after a day or after a year? Lawrence would always desire to understand; Lawrence would always desire to believe; Lawrence would always desire that every man be himself, not unchanging, but not outwardly compelled to change. Lawrence would always desire, above all, to record these desires greatly, to oppose them, like established truths, against the dark wilderness. Yet the dark wilderness was never finally conquered. It broke different men at different times, and often it was by little things, the stumbling on a root, the cloud of insects, that it finally broke them. Certainly the humor in that letter was near to self-erasure. And it was the little things that Helen was remembering and remembering, the very little things, the Mrs. or no Mrs. But nevertheless, with those desires . . .

"No," he said to Helen, "no, he's just trying to leave room," and he began to explain to Helen what he believed about Lawrence. It was no use. He felt the futility almost as soon as he began. He seemed to himself to be making the truth, the great desires, the important direction, into foibles or even pretenses. He faltered, and then sat there silent, slowly putting the letter back into its envelope. He saw that the postmark on the envelope said Barstow. Well, that was something to go on. That was a direction, at least. That's all anything was, a direction.

Helen stood up. "You must want sleep," she said, and held out her hand for the letter.

It was nearly three o'clock when he got up to his room. It was a quiet room at the back of the house, with a French window opening onto a balcony that looked across the pool to the eucalyptus grove. Helen had been very thoughtful about the room. The reading lamp over the bed was burning, and the covers were turned down invitingly. On the stand beside the bed were cigarettes, a life of Mozart, the score of Copland's *Piano Variations*, and a volume of Chekov's stories. There were no ornaments in the room, but only two of Lawrence's pictures from years ago, a dark, brownish pastel of an old Virginia City mansion, twisted and gloomy and loaded with memories, and a larger pastel, also somber, but with sunken color and powerful as oil, of the rooftops of downtown Reno in the moonlight, with the neon glow of Virginia Street rising out of the crater. Tim looked at these for a long time. When he was ready for bed, he looked at them again, for a minute, and then turned out the light and went out onto the balcony and stood there for some time, watching the stars over the eucalyptus grove and in the water. His thoughts remained confused and melancholy, mostly fragmentary memories, but they wouldn't let him alone. He went back in, turned on the reading lamp again, propped himself against his pillow, and read Chekov until there was a haze of light over the feathery treetops showing beyond the balcony, and the birds were making their first faint chirpings.

CHAPTER FIFTY-NINE: *In Which the Perturbed Spirit of Ancient Mariner Black Is Encountered Lingering Over the Sargasso Sea, and Mariner Hazard Catches a Wind at Dawn*

TIM woke by habit after three or four hours, feeling that even this short sleep had been shallow and unpleasantly active. He heard no movement in the house yet, and tried to sleep again, but couldn't. He lay there looking at Lawrence's pictures, while his mind roved loosely and his body grew restless. Among the more ghostly creatures of his mind, of whom Helen had already become one, less real than at any time during the two years he hadn't seen her, Lawrence arose real, and filled him with fear. Mary Turner also appeared, and he endured a longing for her like the homesickness of a mountain dweller exiled to a flat land. He told himself that all he had to do was to get out of there and find Lawrence, but he knew it wasn't as simple as that. This new Helen had tentacles of need which would let go only when she had satisfied or abandoned some desire of which he wasn't yet sure. Well, there was one thing he must do. He must see the paintings Lawrence had told Helen to keep.

When he came down to the living room, which seemed simpler and more spacious, with no sunlight in it yet, he found the breakfast table set, and the morning paper on the cleared coffee table, but no one there. He sat down on the couch and opened the paper. Two voices were talking in the kitchen, a robust voice, and a whining, monotonous voice, which he felt sure was Maddie's. The news was the same as ever, page after page of apparently random activity, mostly selfish, reported in a flat and inattentive prose, a mass-production prose, in which the writers were allowed to exercise their skill only in presenting editorial or owner bias as unbiased fact by means of emphasis, omissions and occasional modifiers. On the front page were two photographs, one of Mussolini jumping through a fiery hoop and one of the legs of a Philadelphia heiress who was being sued for support by her ex-husband. On the first inside page was a picture of the Bryanish-looking founder of a new religious sect in Los Angeles, who, the caption declared, was seeking funds for a temple, and had declared that God still existed, although He was displeased by avarice and atheism. The voices in the kitchen became louder, the whining voice going on most of the time, with occasional interruptions from the bolder voice. They worked up to a crash of metal pans and a shout from the bolder voice, "Get out of my kitchen, you sneaky little spy; go on, get out." Maddie entered the dining room with a pitcher of water and a wry, secretive smile. When she saw Tim, the smile gave way to the old, lugubrious look. Silently she filled the glasses, set down the pitcher, and came across to the coffee table to inquire, in a whisper, hinting that it would come out badly either way, whether Tim would have breakfast now or wait for Mrs. Black. When it had been established that Tim would wait, but would have coffee in the meantime, Maddie faded into the kitchen again, where the wrath broke out anew, but was quickly silenced. Maddie returned with the coffee, and confided that it might be an hour before breakfast. Mrs. Black had told her to expect Mr. Hule for breakfast at nine o'clock. Tim didn't want to sit there enforcing that silence behind the swinging door. He drank his coffee and went back up to his room and tried to write to Eileen. It wouldn't come, not even anything which sounded honest. He made three starts, wadded them up and threw them into the waste basket, and went out into the hall. The stairs to the studio must start here somewhere.

The opening of the first door revealed a linen press. The second door opened into Helen's bedroom. Helen lay asleep in front of him, her face to him, her cheek on her arm. His irritation about Maddie, Mr. Hule and the letter left him. Helen's unguarded face appeared older and more weary and formless than seemed possible. The stains of weeping were still on it, and its marks of multiple wants, indecisions and grievances made it pathetic in comparison with an old portrait of Helen which hung on the wall behind the bed. Tim remembered that Lawrence had done that portrait even before Helen had begun to appear in the many mysterious women. Helen and Lawrence had been really living together then, in the Peavine cabin. Bars of morning light from the Venetian blind lay across the glass, but Tim could see enough of the face to remind him. It was the face of an undivided Helen, tragic but firm of mouth, with great, challenging eyes, and flesh as tight and clear as bronze. It emerged from a resounding gloom, and from the more tangible darkness of the hair, like the prow of a vessel coming into wind and light at the same time. Tim looked at the sleeping face again, and closed the door softly.

The third door he tried opened into a narrow stairwell which led up toward a clear, gray light. He entered and closed the door behind him and climbed the stairs. He was as disappointed by the bareness of the studio as if he had expected to find Lawrence himself there. Nothing was there except a small pile of canvases leaning against one another, face to the wall, the empty draughtsman's table along one side, an empty set of shelves at one end, and an easel erected against a post in the center. There wasn't even a window, but only a closed door across from the stairs. In the uniform clarity from the skylight, the room appeared even larger than it was, and as impersonal as an empty exhibition room or vault. Yet it was also as if he had come upon the secret of the whole house. The mind of the house had died up here, and below, in the monstrous body, the cancerous agents of the dissolution still multiplied.

He crossed to the door and opened it and stepped out onto the roof. The studio was a small, separate house on the roof. He stood in the sun, where Lawrence must have stood often, and looked down on the lawns and the pool and the eucalyptus grove. The sounds of the birds were clear. When he went in again, he left the door open.

He set up the paintings on the picture rail which ran around two sides of the room. There were eight paintings, seven small, and one as tall as he was. He knew at a glance that it was the large one Helen had talked about, and he set it up at the end of the room, by itself, and saved it for last. The others he set up in a row along the side.

They were all studies painted in Austin. One was of the interior of that same hotel room Lawrence had done before in sepia ink, the room with the Bible and beer and potted cactus. Another was of a brick church by itself against a dark mountain. The rest were designs made up of clustered roofs and walls and empty windows, or solitary fragments of buildings among wild grass and sagebrush and under the looming, dark mountains and dark, tumultuous skies. They were distinctly outlined and simple, and there were no figures in any of them. The blocks and planes of the buildings, the angled lines of signs and telephone poles, the patches of snow, the curves of hills and streets and the ominous, portentous movement of the skies and of areas of light and shadow were erected in single and ascending designs of great power. In the lighted areas vivid color glowed up out of the subdued hues in the shadows with an intensity not their own, as if there played over the Austin of Lawrence's mind long, shifting floodlights of winter sun. A section of brick wall bloomed like a rose. The steeple of the church rose into the darkness above the mountain, but the light struck it, and the fish which was its weather-vane swam glittering and alone. There was Austin, all right, and all the other old camps like it, but greatly enriched, their fierce, brief pasts moving and whispering within them, the grief of nameless humanity deeper over them than imperial history over the ruins of Rome. The power and detachment of the paintings were encouraging, but they didn't answer any personal questions. Tim turned back into the middle of the room and faced the big painting.

For a moment he couldn't discover what he was looking at, save that deep within a surrounding darkness, and widening upward, was a softly lighted landscape dotted with buildings and figures too small to be recognized at that distance, done in clear, affectionate, patient, playful detail, like the work of one of the first exuberant discoverers of perspective. Then he found his viewpoint. He was looking down, from one corner of the ceiling or higher, upon that same hotel bedroom. The landscape was outside the window, so that it had somewhat the effect of a stained-glass window with the light behind it. The tilted and exaggerated perspective gave the room the depth of a bottomless shaft, and made the landscape steep and far-reaching, so that the longer he looked, the more he felt himself a disembodied, omnipresent observer, who might, if he chose, rise higher and higher, while the room dwindled below him, or, by a slight effort of will, dissolve the shadowy walls and extend his vision infinitely in all directions. The objects in the room appeared to float near the top of the bottomless shaft, and they were not sufficiently substantial to stop the eye at any level. The faded blue jacket and trousers swung out from the wall, the tennis shoes dangling beneath them, and it was almost as if the body hung there in familiar garments. There was the ghost of a silver dollar in one pocket of the trousers, and the phantom of a package of cigarettes in one pocket of the jacket. The china pot was faintly visible through the one corner of the bed which reached up into the light of the window. Through a pinch bottle, a Bible and a palette on the dresser, and through the top of the dresser itself, showed one lonely pair of socks in a closed drawer. The heads of nails and the cracks between the floorboards showed through the rug, and up through all of these things, from level to level, rose the darkness of the shaft, denied complete victory only by the light reflected from the landscape.

Gradually Tim perceived that there were also two figures in the room. Upon the bed, dead, or asleep as if formally laid out in death, feet together, hands crossed upon his breast, lay the narrow and naked figure of a man. His head was sunk toward the darkest corner of the canvas, and the light struck clearly only upon one foot and upon the uppermost hand, the right hand. Beside the window and partly across it, stood the elongated figure of a woman, in part mingled with the shadow of the room and in part, like her several bright bracelets, with the light and color of the window. The woman's gaze, from far aloft, seemed bent upon the figure on the bed.

As Tim moved closer, to see what the window showed, the woman gradually ceased to be. Her dark, wild hair and the caverns of her eyes, became shadows in space. Her body disintegrated into the pattern of the wall paper and the shapes of the illuminated landscape. Tim could see now that the lighted hand of the man on the bed was Lawrence's long, narrow hand with its big knuckles. As he continued to approach, the room increasingly lost substance and form, until it became merely a deep, dark frame for the landscape.

Now that its details were clear, the landscape, strange and ancient in its total effect, proved to be a wonderfully familiar assembly. It was as if one had just been awakened by this glimpse to the timeless beauty of things he had looked at all his life. The awakening was sharpened almost to apprehension for Tim, by the four figures who stood close under the window, with their faces raised and expectant. The four were Tim himself, Helen, with the bronzed face of the portrait in the bedroom, the narrator of these lives, and, a little apart from and beyond the others, beneath the breast and arm of the phantom woman, so that her bracelets became his bright shirt, Lawrence. Behind the figures, and diminishing across the window, rose a range of soft and interfolded desert hills, studded with tiny juniper and pinon trees. Over the lower reaches of these hills, and sometimes higher, or drawn back into the canyons, extended a city, partially hidden by the four waiting figures. Even at this close range, it first suggested an old, Mediterranean hill city, watched over by its cathedrals and forts. Examined one at a time, however, the forts became mining mills, and the spires those of the Austin church, with its gilded fish, and of St. Mary's in-the-Mountains. On the right outskirts, showing from behind Lawrence, was the Peavine cabin. Elsewhere along the near edge of the city, among poplars and cottonwoods, appeared the studio-building in Reno, the Crystal Bar and Piper's Opera House from Virginia City, Luigi's Bar in Tonopah, where we all liked to stop for a drink and a talk with Luigi and his sad, gentle and beautiful wife Maria. From among the leaves in the center of the city, rose the dome of the capitol in Carson. There was the university campus along a hillside of its own, and here were Bowers' Mansion, the Goldfield Hotel, the Latin Club, the Copper Club, Stokes' Castle and Wingfield Park with the river flowing through it and out onto the plain below, where it became a desert river, cut in barren earth. At the left edge of the city, where it curved around the nearer hills into a pass, was the Reno race track, and a single, peaked, white house, which might have been any house, but which was, Tim knew, the house of Hazard.

A white road wound up through the pass and out onto a desert of lesser hills between saw-toothed, snowy mountains which converged toward the top of the window. Along the road moved a tiny and scattered Canterbury pilgrimage of mounted cowboys driving their cattle, prospectors and burros, open cars, and Indians in worn wagons. Just beyond the city, a flock of sheep spread wide from the road, under the pale mist of their own dust. Far up, and away from the road, two other little clouds showed where other flocks moved. Upon the tops of many of the round hills were castle-like rock formations.

At the very top of this window paradise, in the extreme and mystical distance, and much the brightest region, so that all the light on the landscape and the little which penetrated the room seemed to fall from it, shone Pyramid Lake.

This window aroused a turmoil of memory and hopefulness in Tim. Everything was there, and in the soft serenity of a golden age. It was the most careful and loving work he had ever seen from Lawrence's brush. Still, he could make up no answer from it. The two Lawrences made it as ambiguous as the letter. He drew back until the landscape became once more a lighted window and the shadowy woman took form again. At least the Lawrence who had painted this wasn't tired of painting, and that might answer everything. He felt that it was a lead. He was upon the verge of important intimations. Then he heard the door in the stairwell open, and Helen's voice call, "Tim, are you up there?"

After a moment he said, "Yes."

It seemed to him that Helen looked at him suspiciously, even a little resentfully, as she came up out of the stairwell, but perhaps she was only trying to guess what he made of the paintings. She came over and stood beside him, and looked at the large painting.

"I hunted all over for you," she said. "Maddie told me you'd been up ages and hadn't had any breakfast yet. Then I remembered you'd asked about the pictures. I'm sorry I kept you so long. He called that thing *The Promised Land.*"

"Did he?" Tim said, grinning.

"Just the same," she said, "I don't like it. I don't like it even as much as I do the others. They're all morbid, but it's so morbid you can practically smell the decay. It makes my flesh creep, like those old saints that were all bones and green skin. Even if he hadn't . . ." and she showed with her hands how the phantom woman loomed beside the window. "Didn't I tell you I was a ghost? Only it's more than that. It's . . ." She raised her hands above her head and shaped them into threatening claws. "A vampire or something. And these were the only pictures he wanted to keep. He didn't want me to forget they were up here; especially this one. Well, if that's what he wanted, he got it. I don't know how often I've come up here, when he wasn't home, and stared my eyes out at that infernal monstrosity. I loathe every brush-mark on it. But I'm done with that, or anything like it. I'm not going to bat my brains out over his double-tongued nonsense any longer. And I don't give a damn whether he wants to come back or doesn't, and you can tell him so for me, when you see him. And you can take these damn things with you, too."

Tim looked at her. "All right," he said. "I'll pack them after breakfast."

"I didn't mean it that way, Tim. You know I didn't. I want you to stay. I thought perhaps . . . It wouldn't be any use anyway," she went on. "There's no knowing where he is by now. Come on down, doleful. Mr. Hule's waiting for his breakfast. He's taking me to an auction at Malibu. We thought maybe you'd like to come along. Sometimes . . ." she began, discontentedly, but then said, "Oh, never mind."

Tim followed her into the stairwell. "Were these the paintings Brother Hule thought were no good?" he asked.

"Yes," she said, without looking back, and as if she didn't want to hear any more about the pictures. But at the bottom of the stairwell, she stopped and looked up at Tim. For a moment, in that lowest glimmer, and darkened by Tim's shadow, her head, with the hair thrown back, had the fierce, emergent beauty of the head on the wall in her bedroom. "Oh, Tim," she cried, "what are we going to do with him? What are we going to do? He's such a fool. Here he could have everything he needs, everything he wants, and he won't take it, because it's mine."

Tim got used to that refrain, and to the others, "A fellow can stand just so much," "incredible," and a dozen others which didn't seem to belong to her even as much as those. He stayed almost a week, and each evening, after Mr. Hule had departed with Helen's incandescence and joyous, vengeful glances, the long, circling talk about Lawrence would begin again. It seemed to Tim that they never got deeper than the whirling periphery, and gradually, at first because he began to hear statements of his own returned to him as original coinage, he realized that he couldn't find Helen herself in anything she said. Hour after hour she put forth to him, with the seriousness of discovery, attitudes, ideas, and even exact expressions, often mutually contradictory, in which he recognized Mr. Hule, and others of the too many and too frequent guests, and sometimes Lawrence himself. Even her profanities were falsified by the loss of the only real power they'd ever had, the power of spontaneous humor and affection which wasn't in the words. It appeared to him at last that behind all this hock-shop display, he could discover only one unswerving characteristic, an inordinate desire to possess and to control. Lawrence's failure to seek recognition, at whatever cost, troubled her most because it lessened the value of one of her possessions. It even became clear that all she really wanted of Tim was another possession, a henchman against Lawrence, not an intermediary. It didn't help much that this urge to devour was unconscious, and even pitiably fearful. Indeed this made it only the more impossible to reach any remnants of other qualities in her, for against Tim's slow hardening, her fears increased, and strengthened the urge, and the conviction that her intentions were altruistic to the point of martyrdom.

Tim began to beg off the innumerable shopping and visiting expeditions with the excuse that he had to work, but then he couldn't work. He couldn't even feel a desire to work. Most often, when he could get by himself, he lay in the hammock outside Lawrence's studio and tried to think it all out. He couldn't do that either, for Helen was still Helen, by memory, and his pity led him to confuse, or to hold in abeyance, what he already knew. In this prolonged indecision and rotation of emotions, in this suppressed resentment, short sleeping and long drinking, a physical sloth also crept into him. It became an effort to put on his trunks and go out to the swimming pool. And as ever, in such doldrums, his conscience became grossly tender, painful and active, a kind of moral tumor, eating out all his strength in futile regrets and self-condemnations about Eileen, to whom he started a dozen letters without finishing one, about his work, even about his old shame before Rachel. The gloom spread out into all creation. Mankind became nothing even to itself. In short, he fell into another dark period. Only two lights remained constant before him, Lawrence, who must be found, and Mary, who had never been touched by this darkness. He began to look forward to speech with Lawrence and to the embrace of Mary as one might to heaven after an ill-managed world. He became Ecclesiastes on the hoof, minus the bitter pleasure.

His escape came suddenly. One evening Mr. Hule stayed later than his customary midnight, and partook of whisky with them, which increased the number of his pilgrimages, but also made him more communicative, and the topic he and Helen fell upon was Lawrence's work. They had enough regard for Tim's presence to avoid direct deductions upon Lawrence's character, but that, after all, would have been superfluous, for in the work they finally left only the smallest vestiges of originality, power, promise, intelligence or technical proficiency. They reduced it, at last, to three attributes, a certain superficial skill of the hand, an incipient dilettantism, and a lamentable pleasure in morbidity. Helen, it is true, rebelled at points, and declared that Lawrence was a very intelligent and sensitive man, and a true artist, and that you might even say that the two strongest contributing factors to his failure were commendable characteristics. Those two were, she declared, a destructive desire for perfection, which led him always to see only what he had failed to accomplish, and an obsession with originality which led him to regard praise as a proof of commonplace work, and to regard the use of the slightest hint from others as a reasonable artist might regard deliberate imitation. Mr. Hule agreed with her suavely, but then demonstrated that those were just the characteristics which in time begot the dilettante, through over-refinement and through destruction of the will to work.

The very fact that there was some justice in these observations, and also that they might equally have been applied to himself, for the line between feckless amateurism and scrupulous artistry was still unclear to him, led Tim to break out at this point, after having silently weathered so many obvious injustices. Just as he had feared, his defense was more angry than apt. He came closer to proving that the only criteria Helen and Mr. Hule were capable of applying to any work were market price and established reputation, and that Mr. Hule's technical knowledge of painting didn't extend beyond counting cracks in old pigment through a magnifying glass, than he did to establishing Lawrence's genius or justifying Lawrence's attitude. Even Helen made some headway against his tirade, while Mr. Hule damned it by silent and amused waiting, and then, for the sake of the amenities, changed the topic to the ideal rose garden, and after a decent interval, departed.

The outbreak did, however, prevent the post-Hule dissection of Lawrence, and made good-nights prompt and merely formal. Tim went up to his room with his head still cleared by resentment. He turned off the light and went out onto the balcony, as he had the first night. His resentment ebbed in the presence of stars and the night quiet, and after it came real clarity and the strong desire to move along. He didn't have to simplify all the moral intricacies. Right and wrong, guilt and innocence, were relative and transitory. They were living fish in a net of starlight. Let them alone now. Life and death are the certain things. There is no mistaking life and no mistaking death, and it works all up and down the scale. If he himself was so nearly dead inside after one week here, less than a week, what about Lawrence, who had been here two years, and far more deeply involved?

He went back in, turned on the light again, changed into his old clothes, and packed. Already he felt happier. He felt the strength coming back. He sat down at the little bedside table and scrawled a note to Mary.

Mary—
I love you. I have kept bumping into that fact for a long time now, in the middle of the night, in the middle of the day; in the middle of crowds, in the middle of nobody; in the middle of talk, in the middle of silence; in the middle of music, in the mid-

dle of me. I am all barked up with it, so I am sending it to you for a while. Don't believe it right away, but don't disbelieve it either. Just keep it around until I get there. Here is another. I want to marry you. No, don't say anything. Just keep that around too. I am coming home to argue with you about it. The world is too big and too foolish without you.

It will be a few days yet though. I'm at Helen's house in Beverly Hills, and I have to find Lawrence. He has wandered off into the desert again, looking for God. But I'm an old saint hunter. I know all the water holes. There is Len's in Vegas. There is Stovepipe Wells. There is Luigi's in Tonopah. There is the upstairs room in Austin, over the little dark bar with the cobwebs in the window. I will crouch behind the beer-tap till he comes. Then I will bring him back to Reno. I won't bring him to the Great Basin for a while, though. Keep listening, now: I love you, Mary. I want to marry you.

Tim

He sealed the note into its envelope, put a stamp and address on it, and put it into his breast pocket. Then he wrote a note to Helen, thanking her, and telling her he was going to look for Lawrence, and would write to her when he found him. He started to leave this note on the table, but he thought of Maddie, and went out into the hall and pushed it under Helen's door. Then, padding about in his socks, with a flashlight, he brought Lawrence's paintings down from the studio, and packed them into Jeremiah. He returned and put on his shoes and got his suitcase, put that into Jeremiah too, and climbed in himself.

He dropped the letter to Mary into the first mail-box he saw along the boulevard. Then, in a fine contentment with motion, he pushed Jeremiah along the empty pavements toward the first glimmer in the east.

ON THE edge of Barstow, where his route changed from 66 to 466 and became eager for real desert, Tim found what he believed was the right camp. There were two rows of cabins, with a dusty lot between them, and on the edge of the highway a diner with a big sign, ICE COLD BEER. The cabins had been painted white, but now they were gray with dust, and the paint was beginning to flake off them in the sun. There was a dog with a coarse coat like a coyote's, lying asleep on the shady side of the diner. He was making little, excited moans in his sleep, and his front paws were twitching. Maybe he finally had that cottontail out in the open, away from all bushes.

It was near noon, and the heat was rising from the earth so that the cottonwoods over the town and along the cut of the river wavered like seaweed.

Tim went into the diner, and let the screen close quietly behind him. The flies came back onto the outside of the screen, buzzing and beating against it. There was only one man inside the diner, a small man with a gray, walrus mustache. He was asleep in a chair tilted back against the end wall. His big hands were lying palms up in his lap, and his chin was down on his chest. Tim went back and swung the screen door so that it banged. The old man's head came up, and he let the chair down slowly, and rose, and went around behind the counter.

"Hot, ain't it?" he asked.

Tim said it was hot, and ordered a beer.

"Have one with me?" he asked, when the man had scraped the head off with his stick, and pushed the glass across.

"Thanks just the same," the man said, "but I guess not. It's a rule of mine I don't take a beer till after the sun's gone down. Then it'll stay with me for a while. If I was to take one now, I'd want another in about ten minutes."

Tim took a couple of long swallows of the beer, and set the glass down and lit a cigarette.

"Those your cabins out back?" he asked.

The man nodded.

"You don't remember a fellow staying here a week or ten days ago, do you? Looks like a thin Indian, and has a deep kind of soft voice?"

"Lots of people stop here nights," the man said. He sounded wary. "They all come in about the same time, generally, nine or ten in the evening, when the heat's let up a little, and it's late to get on to the next place. I'm so busy just getting them fixed I don't usually notice much about them except if I think they're the kind I'll have to get up before daylight to see they don't steal the doors off the cabins. Lots of them thin and dark, too," he added. "Most of them. There's a lot of thin, dark men in this country."

"If it's the fellow I mean," Tim said, "he probably stayed here longer than overnight."

The man looked at him, but there was no way to guess what he was thinking, except that he was being careful.

"What kind of clothes would he have on?" he asked.

"A kind of a blue-cotton suit," Tim said, "faded blue, like old overalls that have been washed a lot."

The man shook his head. "There's a good many of them in suits like that too."

Tim nodded. "I suppose so," he said.

He drank the rest of his beer while he tried to think of an approach. He knew nobody would forget Lawrence if he had been around for two or three days. People remembered Lawrence if they'd only talked with him for a few minutes. He felt sure that Lawrence had been there, and that the man with the walrus mustache remembered him. He wondered if anything had happened that the man didn't want to admit knowing about. He stood up.

"He's a friend of mine," he said. "I'm trying to catch up with him. I just wondered if you'd noticed him."

He went out and stood on the step, squinting up the highway into the white light that came from the hills where he was going. The man with the walrus mustache came to the door behind him. When Tim stepped down onto the ground, the man asked, "Is that your car there?"

"Yes," Tim said. He stopped and waited.

The man was looking at the car. That seemed to make up his mind for him.

"There was a fellow here might be the one you were looking for. Stayed three nights. Left nearly a week ago, though. Seemed like a nice fellow, but you never know," he said. "But I wouldn't want to get him into any trouble. He come over here to the diner every night and drank beer and we talked. The dog took to him," he added. "The darn dog pretty near lived with him. Looked all over for him the day he left. He ain't got over it yet, having him go off like that."

"Did he say where he was going?" Tim asked.

The man seemed to hesitate again. "Not that I remember," he said. "Not exactly. He was going east, though."

"Thanks," Tim said. "I'll ask along, I guess."

The man seemed to want to say something more, but he didn't until Tim was climbing into Jeremiah.

"Would he draw something like this?" he asked. He was pointing to a place beside the door. Tim couldn't see what was there. He came back to the steps and looked. The man was pointing to a turtle about the size of a quarter, drawn in pencil beside the door.

Tim grinned. It made him feel very good to see that turtle. It made him feel as if this camp had been his home also.

"That's his sign," he said.

"I only noticed it day before yesterday," the man said. "I been wondering about it. Looks kind of funny, just a turtle right there, like a doorbell, or something. But it's drawed pretty good. I thought maybe he'd done it. He was always drawing something. At first I didn't know. I thought maybe it was a mark like the tramps use, or something. But I watched, and nothing like that seemed to come of it. Oh, I don't mind a hand-out once in a while, you know. There's a lot of guys out of work these days, good, honest guys, just drifting, trying to pick something up. They get off the trains here sometimes. First place out of the desert, you know. But I can't afford to get a mark for it. There's too many of them now."

"No, that's just his mark for good luck," Tim said.

"Good luck?" the man asked, looking at the turtle.

"Well, for a good life, for peace."

The man seemed pleased. "I hope you find him," he said.

When Tim was in Jeremiah, the man called, "Maybe you better take the dog with you. He's lonesome as hell now; just pining away." He laughed. He even came out onto the step and waved as Tim drove off.

The heat and the glare increased. The last green things were left behind, and there was only the bleached brush and the awful light on the mountains. Nevertheless, this was coming home. Tim felt something in him waking up which had been drowsing for a long time.

He stopped in Baker to eat. There was a crossing there about which he had to make up his mind, if he couldn't learn for sure which way Lawrence had gone. Route 466 went on across the great valley and up into higher mountains. Route 127 went north into Death Valley. Over the swell of the Valley floor he could see the walls of the mountains in the north wavering under the sun, as if it would take just a little more to make them melt and run down and create a molten sea. Everything in Baker glittered, the sheet-metal roofs, the motionless poplars, the radiator caps of cars along the edge of the road.

In the cross-roads restaurant the fans whirred steadily, stirring the heat into a dry draught. When Tim sat up at the lunch counter, the fans dried his shirt, although he could still feel the sweat starting under his arms, and gliding down quickly over his ribs.

The man behind the counter was leaning back with folded arms and half-closed eyes. Up front, the man who ran the cigar counter was lazily shooting dice out of a leather cup against a heavy, gray-haired man wearing high-heeled boots, and a Stetson pushed onto the back of his head. An oil-truck driver was playing a pin-ball machine on the other side of the front door. He stopped playing to put a nickel into the juke box. When the juke box began its mechanical digestion, he went back to the pin-ball machine.

At a table under the north window sat a fat, white-haired man in a striped silk shirt with short sleeves. He hadn't shaved today, and his placid, folded face had a gray stubble all over the cheeks and jowls. He was sweating slowly, and devouring slowly, with great contentment, a meal of pork chops, mashed potatoes and gravy, corn on the cob, apple pie and coffee. Outside his window, between two still poplars and set way back, out of the picture, Tim could see the melting mountains. In the corner beyond the fat man was an old nickel-in-the-slot upright.

All of this felt good and real and musical after the Sargasso Sea. Nobody was lively here, but probably nobody had it in him to be lively at this time of day. But even that was good. The heat made weariness and tempers, but it also made great friends because it was a constant, common enemy which wasn't human. Everybody here would be waiting inside for the evening, when the sun would go off the desert, and they could sit outside with their chairs tilted, and watch the early-evening wind stir the tops of the cottonwoods and poplars. They were all allies under siege.

Death Valley gave an even stronger cure of the same kind. In Death Valley the little things were shed, and great, simple and ancient shapes emerged in the spirit. Lawrence loved Death Valley because of this. Tim thought, sitting here, that it might very well be Route 127 he wanted.

The juke box burped, settled into itself, and began to play. The drowsy waiter came to the counter and stood there, looking at Tim.

"Salmon salad and a beer," Tim ordered.

The waiter repeated the order through a sliding panel above the back counter. Then Tim, who hadn't been paying any attention to the juke-box, except to notice that the tune was familiar, began to listen. It was the vocal chorus which made him listen. It was Eileen singing *Get Up with the Sun.* It was the recording they had made in San Francisco. It troubled him deeply to hear Eileen's voice there.

The waiter put a bottle of beer and a glass on the counter. Tim sat still until Eileen was done. Then he asked the waiter if he'd seen a hitch-hiker come through in the last few days, a dark man who looked like a thin Indian and probably wore a faded blue denim suit and a pair of tennis shoes.

"Would he be a guy that wanted to draw pictures for his meals?" the waiter asked.

"He might," Tim said, "if he thought you wanted the pictures as much as the price of the meal."

The fat man, holding a pork chop up with both hands and gnawing at it contentedly, was watching them and listening to them.

"Would that be a picture of his?" the waiter asked, looking at the fat man and grinning, and pointing at a picture which hung on the partition between the cigar counter and the lunch counter. Tim got up and went over to look at the picture. He felt suddenly that this was all much more serious now. Perhaps it was partly the way the fat man was watching. Perhaps it was just the way Eileen's voice got him, as if there were no going away in the world, as if you took everybody with you, and were responsible for them all. The picture was a brush drawing, like the Austin one of the old man listening to the radio. It was a picture of the fat man, asleep in his chair, with the chair tilted back and his hands folded upon his paunch. The hands, like those of the old man by the radio, were the most important things in the picture. They were as important as the folded hands of Teddy Quest. Under the fat man, in Lawrence's big, drawn script, was the one word *Evening.*

"It's his," Tim said.

The waiter was about to say something when the fat man spoke. "He stayed over at my place," he said. "Those cabins across the street. That was about a week ago. You looking for him?"

"Yes," Tim said.

"He can sure draw," the fat man said. "He did four little drawings for me, the badlands down in the south end there, and everything."

"Which way did he go?" Tim asked them both.

The waiter looked at the fat man. "Vegas, didn't he?" he asked.

"Yeh, Vegas," the fat man said. "He got a ride with a truck." He had stopped eating, and was studying Tim. It was that suspicion again, just like the man at the first camp.

"Funny you should ask," the waiter said. "He sold one of his pictures at the hotel, and then he came in here and drank beer and kept playing that same tune that was playing when you asked." He nodded toward the juke-box. "He sure liked that tune. He must of put twenty nickels in on that tune. Funny, I mean, it was playing when you asked."

"He went to Vegas a week ago, then?"

"Five days ago," the fat man said.

"Funny guy," the waiter said. "These are bad times for the picture-drawing racket. Hardly anybody wants pictures. But he acts like everything is all right. He's a nice guy to talk to. But it was funny. He sat right there." The waiter pointed to a table up front. "He drank one beer after another, and every time that tune stopped, he'd put in another nickel and play it over again. He must of spent a dollar on that tune. You'd think he could of learned it easier."

The fat man was still studying Tim.

"Did you want him for anything special?" he asked.

"No," Tim said. "I'm a friend of his, that's all. I haven't seen him for a long time, and I heard he was moving this way. He drifts quite a lot."

"There are a lot of people looking for people these days," the fat man said vaguely. "There are a lot of men drifting around. Everybody's in trouble. The world is getting to be a hornets' nest. He was a nice young fella," he said to Tim, but didn't seem to intend to say anything else.

After a moment Tim said, "I wrote that tune he was playing so much."

"You did?" the fat man asked politely. He didn't say anything more.

"Only this is the way it should go," Tim said.

He went over and sat down at the piano, and tried the keys. Then he played *My Heart with the Sun* with full volume and in the straight ballad rhythm.

"Boy, you really rocked it," the waiter said.

The cigar-counter man and the man in the boots and Stetson had stopped shooting dice to listen. The truck driver had stopped playing the pin-ball machine, and was standing by a nearer table looking at Tim. The sliding panel behind the lunch counter had opened, and the Chinese cook looked through. The service-station attendant had come in from outside, and was leaning against the wall by the door. None of them had paid any attention when the juke box played, but now even the heat couldn't suppress their interest. Tim played *Get Up with the Sun* this time, and stepped it up. He turned around on the stool and looked at the fat man.

"That's good," said the fat man. He revealed only this weighty and judicious interest.

Tim wondered as he had at the first camp, but with more fear this time, if something had happened to Lawrence that the fat man was hiding. If something had happened while he was sitting around up there at Helen's . . .

"Give us another," said the waiter. "If you feel like it," he added, to show that he didn't mean to butt in.

Tim turned back to the keyboard, thinking what to play. He looked over his shoulder at the fat man. "Is he in any trouble?"

"No," said the fat man. "No, I guess he's all right."

Tim began to improvise softly on the keys, thinking about how to open up the fat man, and feeling for a tune to begin under his fingers. It came out *The Painted Bracelet*, up to dance time. The truck driver and the station attendant came and leaned on the cabinet of the piano. The waiter folded his arms on the counter and rested while he listened. Tim followed up with *Why Do I Always Do Wrong?* as blue as he could roll it, almost barrel-house.

He turned back and faced the fat man. "I wrote both of them too. I'm no cop. His name is Lawrence Black, and he signs most of his drawings with a pencil sketch of a turtle."

"He didn't tell me his name," the fat man said, "and I hardly ever bother to look at the register unless something comes up. I don't know his name. But I guess you're all right."

Then he said, "Your friend was back here night before last. We didn't lie to you. He went to Vegas; but he came back here night before last. He was going up into the Valley. I told him it was crazy, walking. Not many cars go up there this time of year. But he wanted to go up there for some reason; had his mind all made up. I don't usually argue with guys. What a man does with himself is his own business, even if he kills himself. But I argued with this friend of yours. I don't know, there's something about him. He listened to me. He was very polite; I never met a guy so polite. But I could see what I said didn't make any difference. He had his mind made up. So I got him to wait for the bread truck going up to the Ranch. He went up early yesterday morning."

"About six," the service-station man said.

"Why I'm so careful," the fat man said. "It's these state cops; deputy sheriffs especially. Sometimes they're plain-clothes men. You don't look much like one, but a guy never knows nowadays. There's so damn much law crawling around for one thing and another, you gotta draw breath by regulation. Going east, he would be all right, but coming into California again, and hitch-hiking, and with no money much." The fat man shrugged his shoulders. "They've been prowling around again. End of the summer, you know. And all these Okies on the road too. I mind my own business strictly," he said angrily, "but your friend seemed like a nice guy. No harm in him anyway. Soft-spoken and friendly. But I didn't know anything about him, except he could draw."

The feeling in the restaurant changed while the fat man was talking. Just that much about the Okies and the people who came ahead of winter made a difference. The music was gone. Nobody wanted to say anything. Tim himself felt uneasy about the man in the boots and Stetson. Still, the fat man must know about him, or he wouldn't have said even that much.

Tim began to finger *Why Do I Always Do Wrong?* again, while he thought about how the fear any part of the human race had to suffer spread around so that sooner or later everybody felt it. Finally he really played *Why Do I Always Do Wrong?* and then the *Moon in the Street Blues*. The truck driver bought himself a beer, and he and the service-station man pulled chairs over near the piano, and sat there watching Tim's hands and listening. The waiter brought the fat man a fresh cup of coffee, and then stood behind the fat man, with his arms folded, and they both listened too. A man and a woman with two young children came in at the front door. The children were discontented and unhappy. Their hair was pasted to their foreheads, and the little girl had been crying. The man and the woman were dazed and tired, and their eyes were red from the glare. The waiter went over and filled their glasses with water and took their order, while Tim was playing a couple of dance numbers the truck driver wanted. The man in the Stetson and the cigar-counter man were shooting dice again. The man in the Stetson was paying no attention to the piano, but the cigar-counter man was rolling the dice as if he were bored by an old habit, and kept looking over at Tim. The service-station man stayed where he could see his pumps, and once he went out to take care of a car, but he came back in as soon as the car had gone on. Dishes came through the window from the kitchen onto the back counter, and the waiter went around behind the front counter and picked them up and carried them to the tired family. Tim was troubled by the sad, weary face of the woman. He realized, while he was thinking about her, that he had started to play *Rhapsody in Blue*. He paid attention to what he was doing, then, and tried to make the *Rhapsody* as sharp and incisive as the old piano would let him, until he came to the sad, sweeping passage that everybody knew, and then to roll it out, reaching, like the dawn over city roofs it always made him think of, until it broke up again into the chaotic jargoning of full day. When he looked around at the woman, she was sitting with her hands in her lap and a far-away look in her eyes, but after a moment she saw him watching her, and then she smiled quickly, and nodded her thanks at him quickly too.

The waiter brought over Tim's salad and another beer, and put them on a chair beside him. Tim fingered out a little motif, light and quick, with his right hand, while he ate with his left, then went to work with the left hand too, and built the motif up into a kind of jazz fugue. When he played it the last time through, with a jerky, paralytic syncopation, it was funny. He grinned himself, a couple of times, and thus relieved the truck driver and the service-station man of their courtesy, and they laughed out loud. When he ended with a series of descending dissonances which sounded like falling downstairs, the woman laughed too, and clapped. When Tim looked around, she shaped the word "bravo," with her mouth, without saying it out loud. Her face looked rested and amused. Her husband was grinning a little too.

The fat man ordered another cup of coffee, and lit a cigar, and moved over to a chair beside the piano. They were all with him now, and Tim felt good, ready to try anything. He mocked a riotous overture on the piano, and then began to sing very loudly, imitating a quarrelsome conversation between an operatic baritone and a soprano, ending with a tremendous shriek and thump. This time everybody laughed and clapped. Even the man in the Stetson was laughing and clapping. They all looked at each other and nodded their heads or shook them, to show how fine they thought that was.

Tim asked the fat man and the truck driver and the service-station man if they knew *Frankie and Johnny*. They all did. He began it, and they all joined in. Other men came in from outside, to see what was going on. Everybody was singing *Frankie and Johnny* by then, and the new men joined in, softly at first, so as not to seem intrusive. Then everybody did *Home on the Range* and *The Man on the Flying Trapeze*. Tim went from that quickly into a little improvisation to show how good he felt, and to take all the noise off the hour, so it would last better, and ended with "that's all" on the piano, and stood up. They all clapped, and called the names of songs to him, and laughed when he made a formal bow to the right and to the left, but finally they let him go.

He went over to the lunch counter to pay the waiter, but the waiter said it was all settled. He looked so pleased about this that it was impossible to argue with him more than twice for politeness.

"I want a tub of cracked ice and two dozen bottles of beer to go out," Tim said.

The waiter looked troubled. "Gosh," he said. "I don't know. We're not supposed . . ."

The fat man had come over. "They're for his friend," he said. "Give him two dozen bottles of beer in a tub of ice. If Braley crabs when he comes back, I will sit him right there," he said, pointing at his own place by the north window, "and make him drink two dozen himself, without stopping."

"It's all right with me, you understand," the waiter said. "I just . . ."

"Give him two dozen bottles of beer," the fat man repeated, "and put them on my bill."

Tim protested this, but the fat man said, "That's the only way he can do it. I've drunk them myself. Are you going to tell me what I can drink?"

The waiter disappeared into the kitchen. The fat man walked to the side door with Tim. "You'll find him," he said. "He told me he was going to stay in the Valley quite a while."

Tim got gas and oil from the service-station man, who also let some of the air out of his tires, which were getting too hard in the heat.

While the attendant was cleaning the windshield, he said, "You oughta have a top on that jalopy, or anyway a hat. It doesn't get any cooler where you're going."

"No top; no hat," Tim said.

He was a little afraid of the heat himself. His face felt stiff and sandy from the sun in the morning, and now the glare and the heavy burning, like hot metal pressing on the body, were so fierce that a man had to make up his mind every time he stepped out of the shade into the open.

"You wait a minute," the service-station man said.

While he was gone, the waiter and the Chinese cook came out, carrying a large, wooden tub between them. The tub was full of cracked ice, and the bottles were buried about in the ice, with their necks sticking up at the sky. Tim dug out a hole in the back end, and they let the tub down into it. The cook scurried back in.

The service-station man came out of the garage with two straw sombreros, with grease on them, and a few holes in them too.

"Your friend will need one," he explained.

He wouldn't let Tim pay for them.

"I just hope you find him," he said.

The Chinese cook returned with three sopping wet gunny sacks. He put these over the ice and bottles.

"Sun keep them cool now," he said, grinning. "Hell of a sun, huh?"

"Hell of a sun," Tim said.

As Tim drove out, the fat man raised his hand in solemn farewell from the screen door.

Jeremiah couldn't be pushed in the heat. He was boiling most of the time as it was. Tim could feel his own back scorching through his shirt, and he had to squint, even under the brim of his sombrero. Acres of shallow water kept appearing across the highway ahead of him, and evaporating or withdrawing as he came nearer. Where the pavement didn't look wet, a thousand sharp little points of light glittered in it. The wavering mountains on both sides grew higher and drew closer together as he went north, and the pale floor of the Valley wavered too, and wouldn't stay in focus.

It was four o'clock when he reached the Ranch. The shade under the trees was wonderful, and there was a sound of water somewhere. He would find Lawrence here. Lawrence would stay with the trees and water. But Lawrence wasn't at the Ranch. There was almost nobody at the Ranch, and the man remembered. Yes, Mr. Black had been here, but he'd paid last night, and gone on this morning before anybody else was up.

"He didn't walk?" Tim asked.

"Holy mackerel," the man said. "I hadn't thought of that, but he must have. Nobody else has gone from here."

Tim looked at him, and the man said, "Holy mackerel," again, as if he'd thought of several unpleasant things one after the other. "It's been a scorcher, too," he said. "It was a hundred and twenty at eleven o'clock this morning. I haven't looked since, but it hasn't got any cooler, that's a cinch."

"Has anybody come through who might have picked him up?" Tim asked.

"Nobody, all day, I guess," the man said. "This time of year . . . Yes, there was too. One car," he said, as if he had made a happy discovery. Then his cheerfulness about this passed off too. "But that wasn't till about an hour ago," he said. "Not till about three o'clock. Mack said they stopped for water and then went right on."

CHAPTER SIXTY-ONE: *The Well*

TIM drank deeply, bathed his face and neck, wet down the sacks over the beer, filled Jeremiah's radiator, and drove on. What had been only an occasional worry about Lawrence before was now a constant fear, which sometimes rose almost to panic. He cursed himself for having stayed so long in Baker. That adventure would make the kind of story Lawrence loved, a story of encouragement against all the headline thinking, the Napoleonic gluttonies, the Sargasso Seas of the spirit. It wouldn't seem trivial to Lawrence, but now it seemed nearly a betrayal, at best a good passage in the wrong place. His imagination, in spite of him, began to scour the Valley, finding Lawrence roving mad, or fallen, or missing him behind the warped mirrors of the heat. He remembered tales of the suffering and doom of people much better fixed than Lawrence was to fight the Valley, and the hot, arid wind beating in around Jeremiah's windshield, the pummeling of the sun, the blinding light which ricocheted from white earth made the tales real. There were the pioneers who had named the Valley. They had slowly followed their bad guide across the worst deserts of Nevada and into this trap. They had come out on the other side at last, but on foot, with their boots torn, their eyes nearly boiled in their heads, and carrying nothing but their firearms and the strips of evil, dried meat which were all that remained of their animals. The wagons had been burned to cure the meat, and the bones, and the iron hubs and rims, left behind in the dunes. The Valley had been unknown then, of course, but much later the drivers and swampers of twenty-mule borax teams, men who knew the Valley like the palms of their hands, had died in the sun, and their animals with them, or gone mad and attacked each other. And someone had told him about two men who had tried to come up the Valley on motorcycles, before the road was paved. The next travelers to take the road had found the motorcycles, their tires exploded and their paint scorched and flaking off. Then, far apart in the barrens, they had found the two skeletons, as clean and ashy as if they had been there for a century. Probably the vultures first, and after that the sun. One claim of the old timers kept coming back to him with a peculiarly terrible force, because it was easy to believe that Lawrence's imagination might do that to him. The old timers said that heat-crazy wanderers had been trailed by their clothes, which they peeled off and left behind them, and had been found wading naked, sometimes even making the arm motions of swimmers, through their visions of deep water. It was hard to believe that such things could happen now, with cars, and paved roads, and the water-holes marked, but everything in this wilderness of light said they could. Even at this hour, when the sun was well down toward the western mountains, Tim jumped if his elbow touched the metal of Jeremiah's door, and great areas of the Valley floor were invisible behind the heat waves. High and near on the east rose the crenelated cliffs of the Funeral Range, black and dull red, like slowly cooling iron, and with long, gray strata tilted across them. The cliffs were softened, as if by smoke from smoldering fires along their bases, and purple shadows were beginning to give them form behind the haze. Jeremiah couldn't be pushed any faster, though, and besides, it wouldn't do to hurry through the dunes. If there were footprints leading out into the dunes, he mustn't miss them.

Still, as the minutes passed, and the dunes flowed smoothly by, showing only their clear and lovely wind-ripples, like the water marks on a shallow beach, and the shadow of the western range extended its slow blessing, Tim began to feel relieved and glad. Some car they hadn't seen from the Ranch must have come through and picked Lawrence up. Lawrence was probably sitting in the shade at Stove-Pipe Wells Hotel right now, with a cold beer in one hand and a pebble in the other, thinking and watching the light change and the shadows come. Better yet, he didn't have a beer. He was sitting there thinking that in a few minutes he would go and get a beer. Then Tim would stagger up to him, lugging the magnificent tub. He would set the tub down before Lawrence without a word, and watch Lawrence's face as he came to understand what was in it.

This was such an engrossing vision that Tim didn't realize he'd seen the tracks until Jeremiah had gone a hundred yards past them. The dream-success vanished, and the fears returned and multiplied. He backed Jeremiah to the point where the tracks began, and stopped him, and got out slowly, his knees shaking. Yes, they were the tracks of one person, going in a widely wavering line up the high side of the dune before him and out of sight over the top. He didn't like that wavering. It might be just the result of climbing switch-back in the loose sand, but it might not, too. He knelt by the first tracks and examined them closely, but the sliding sand had left only smooth indentations. Anyone might have made them. He climbed to the top of the first dune. A sea of dunes came into view beyond it, and the tracks went on across them, disappearing in each trough, and reappearing, much smaller, upon the flank of the next dune, until they dwindled into a single, fine thread and ended on the crest of another high dune. At least the tracks were going somewhere. The points at which they topped the dunes lay along a nearly straight line.

Tim stood staring across the dunes, trying to think what to do. There was no use following the trail off into the sand at this hour, with no idea how far it went. That was what he felt like doing, and he felt like trying to run, too, which would be equally foolish. He looked all around, as if he might see something which would give him an answer. Nothing moved except, very slowly, the shadows of the dunes, and the tiny shadows seeping in behind the ripples. Repeatedly, he peered ahead at the point where the tracks disappeared. The silence over the dunes rang like bells in his head. He stared beyond the dunes at the mountains, and was suddenly profoundly discouraged and frightened by their immense indifference and by the distance to which they had retreated when he thought of walking toward them. But it was looking at those mountains which gave him the answer. The pass went up through there, through Boundary Canyon, to Beatty. He remembered that he had passed the junction with the Beatty road not far back. He thought where he was, and knew that Lawrence had headed off across the dunes to reach the wells.

He ran back down to Jeremiah and climbed in and started him off. It wasn't far across those dunes between the road and the cut-off, anyway. If Lawrence wasn't at the wells, and the tracks didn't come out there, he could return to where the tracks began, and follow them as far as he had to before it got dark. He came to the cut-off and swung into it. When he saw the sign and the stand-pipe, he stopped Jeremiah at the edge of the road. A man was there, squatting on his hunkers, like a desert Indian, near the stand-pipe. He had a faded blue jacket drawn up over his head and shoulders, and his arms dangled over his knees, so that his long hands touched the ground. Beside his right hand there was an open tomato can with a fresh label on it. While Tim was climbing over Jeremiah's door, the squatting man realized that he had heard a motor, and had heard it stop.

He drew the jacket slowly back from his face and looked at Tim and Jeremiah. The red sunlight shone directly against his face, making a glitter in the deep eye-sockets, and showing up the stubble of black beard, the swollen lips, and the sweaty shine of the skin, like polished dark wood, or wet metal. It was the face of a desperate, perhaps a dangerous man, but just the same, it was also Lawrence's face.

Lawrence rose slowly as Tim approached, but stood where he had been squatting. Tim saw that he was barefooted, and that his feet were packed in wet sand. His tennis shoes were laid in the shadow of the stand-pipe, one behind the other. When Tim was close enough, Lawrence reached out, and their hands gripped fiercely.

"Lord God, Tim," Lawrence said, "I thought you were a mirage. I've just been waiting for the mirages to begin, the kind I would believe. I had to touch you." His words were thick, and he smiled only a little, because of his mouth.

"Those tracks of yours gave me a scare," Tim said. "On the dunes," he explained, "where you left the road."

"Beautiful tracks," Lawrence said. "They made me feel like a beetle. I kept looking back at them, expecting to meet myself coming, an enormous black beetle, with his mandibles working like butcher-shop cutlery." He gestured slowly toward the stand-pipe. "Will you have a drink of mineral water? It scalds you when it first comes out, but after that it's like drinking your bath. I seem to have finished the tomatoes."

"Let's have a beer," Tim said.

"Beer?"

"Beer. A tubful of it, in ice."

"Lord God," Lawrence said again. He appeared to meditate briefly. "Yes, we might have a beer," he said. Tim went back to Jeremiah and got two bottles out from under the sacks, pried their caps off on the edge of the door, and returned with them. He and Lawrence squatted side by side, and took long pulls at the bottles. Then they looked at each other, and Tim grinned, and Lawrence tried to.

"Just the same," Lawrence said, holding his bottle before him

and looking at it reverently, "this is worth it." Thus he confessed that he had been foolish, and felt better.

"It's a present from a friend of yours," Tim said. He told
Lawrence how the fat man and the old man in the auto camp
in Barstow had been so sly about telling anything.

"Which reminds me," Lawrence said. "I've been accepting
you as an act of God, but what started it?"

"Helen wrote me a note, and then your letter to her was post-
marked Barstow. When I got there, I hunted for the dog."

"Oh," Lawrence said, and let it go at that.

Tim went out to Jeremiah and got two more beers, and then
told Lawrence about the music at Baker and about the turtles.
Then Lawrence told how he'd come by the tomato can. He
didn't know what time it was when he had reached the wells,
except that the mirages were everywhere and his head was full
of wool, or perhaps gun-cotton, and his voice was a croak. He
knew it was a croak because he'd tried it out now and then, to
keep himself company in the sand-hills, and to prevent the
growing belief that he was a mirage himself becoming
complete. He thought it had probably been about two o'clock.
He had squatted beside the pipe ever since, waiting for sunset,
and moving only to get another drink or to soak down the
jacket or the sand around his feet again. He had gained a new
insight, he declared, into the well-known fact that the body
was about ninety percent water. He had left Furnace Creek
with only a half-pint bottle of water on his hip. He excused this
piece of desert improvidence by saying that he had left before
the sun was up, and there had been birds singing at the Ranch,
so that he had been blithe and full of a migratory confidence
that there would be cars along. The half pint of water had been
nothing but a torment. He had drunk the last half of it in the
dunes, a trickle at a time, merely to keep his tongue working,
and had arrived at the wells with a body which couldn't have
been more than fifty percent water. He had been busy ever
since keeping it up to fifty. About an hour before Tim came,
he thought, a car with a man and a woman in it had stopped

where Jeremiah was now. The man had left the motor running, and jumped out with a canteen in his hand. Then the woman had spoken in a low voice, and the man had stopped, a few feet from the car, and looked carefully at Lawrence.

"I stood up and pulled the jacket off," Lawrence said, "and tried to explain that it was not my well, and that I didn't even think it was. My voice was still like something from under a pile of quilts, and I used signs to make myself clear. The man approached slowly, keeping an eye on me all the time. The woman called out to him once. I found the experience encouraging, in a way. I had never made anyone afraid before, that I could remember. Also I was feeling quite happy. My feet and I were about to be rescued. Ah, how those remaining miles dwindled, which, only a few minutes earlier, had stretched before me like the march of Moses. I praised the inventor of the automobile. I praised this particular, shining example of automobile before me. The man reached the stand-pipe, and before he would bend over to get water, he asked me where I had come from. I must have been a little woolly still, or the excitement was too much for me. Anyway, I remember that I grated out, most cheerfully, "Over the dunes," and waved an airy hand at my tracks. The poor man glanced at them, and then back at me, quickly, and kept on the far side of the pipe, reaching around it, all the time he was filling the canteen. He even backed off ten or fifteen steps, when he returned to the car, before he risked turning around. He talked to his wife. I had maintained an idiotic grin of conciliation in his presence, and now I prepared a gracious and reassuring speech of acceptance. The man came back carrying this can full of tomatoes and newly opened. I remember thinking vaguely that his conduct was queer, and wondering if the sun had got him, but even so I was more interested in the can. The muscles of my throat worked busily, just imagining that cool and acid juice trickling into me, and my teeth were on edge to sink into those magnificent red pulps. The man set the can down on the far side of the pipe, and it was only then that I knew they were going to leave me. I asked the man, in my most terrible voice, if, by any chance, he had some salt for the tomatoes. He almost ran, getting back to the car, and they both kept staring around at me as they drove away."

Tim laughed. "You haven't seen yourself," he said. "There was a minute there when I wished I had a gun myself." He got out cigarettes, held the light for Lawrence's, and then lit his own. Lawrence drew deeply, and raised his head and let the smoke stream slowly and blissfully out of his nostrils.

Tim finished his beer and stood up. "Is the hotel open?" he asked.

"The man at the Ranch said so," Lawrence replied. He rose also, but very slowly. "I've been putting this off," he said.

"Putting what off?"

"Getting to the car."

He drew one foot out of the wet sand, and Tim stared at it. The foot was an ugly, dark red, and so swollen that the toes were sunk almost out of sight in the distended flesh.

"It looks like a sow with farrow, doesn't it?" Lawrence said. "I was going to wait until sunset, and then crawl on my hands and knees. I was trying to figure out how I could carry the tomato can full of water in my teeth without spilling." He essayed a couple of steps, but then said, "If you would bring my sneaks, please," and let himself down onto his hands and knees and began to crawl toward Jeremiah.

Tim started to ask if he could carry him, but then thought better of it. He picked up the beer bottles and the tennis shoes. The soles of the tennis shoes were very thin, no tread left on them anywhere, and there was a large hole in one of them, patched with a piece of folded paper on which showed a few lines of a smudged sketch. Tim waited until Lawrence had nearly reached Jeremiah, then went ahead and threw the shoes and bottles in back and opened the door. Lawrence pulled himself up into the front seat and sat there, breathing heavily and staring ahead.

They didn't talk on the way to the hotel. All across the Valley the shadows built up fantastic shapes of rock and sand where there had been nothing an hour before. The distances appeared greater, and mystery filtered in by the side-canyons. A tall and ludicrous shadow of Jeremiah and passengers slithered along over the dunes beside them.

CHAPTER SIXTY-TWO: *In the Time of Mountains*

THE hotel was shuttered up, and there were no cars and no people in sight around the row of cabins on the naked rise behind it. The stone water-tower stood above the whole community, under a mountain like dried and crumbling mud. There were only the barren earth and the long shadows. But when Tim and Lawrence drove up in back of the cabins, they could see that the doors and windows were open behind their screens, and when Jeremiah stopped, a man came out of the power shed and stood looking at them. He had curly white hair and a big white mustache, and wore only a pair of soiled duck trousers and heavy boots. His round and sloping torso was burned nearly black.

"He looks like a walrus," Lawrence muttered.

"You want something?" the man called.

Tim got out of the car. "You open yet?"

"Well, sort of," the man said, and approached them. He spoke quickly, almost impatiently, and walked as if he were in a hurry too, leaning forward and scuttling with short, stiff steps. When he was closer, he said, "What you want?"

"A cabin and supper."

"Take your pick. All them cabins in the front row's ready. I'll get you some ice water and see what Puss can rustle up for you. There's nobody here yet but Puss and me, gettin' the place ready." He scuttled off toward the screened dining room at the end of the row, and Tim drove over behind him. They took the cabin next to the dining room, so Lawrence wouldn't have so far to walk. This time Tim offered to carry Lawrence.

"If you had some shoes I could get into," Lawrence said, ignoring the offer. Tim found a pair of old moccasins in his duffel bag. Lawrence couldn't get them on, but he worked his toes carefully into them, and shuffled around and into the cabin. In the cabin were two beds covered with blankets with bright Indian designs, and on the walls three tinted photographs, one of the main falls at Yosemite, one of the rapids in the Trinity River and one of Lake Tahoe. There were huge, billowing white clouds in the Tahoe and Yosemite pictures, and snow on the mountains. Lawrence eased off the moccasins and lay down on one of the beds and closed his eyes after staring at the Tahoe picture for a moment. Tim brought in the duffel bag and some books.

"I'll go see if I can get something for those feet," he said, but before he could leave, a woman knocked at the screen, and entered when he said, "Come in."

"Here's your ice water," she said, and set the pitcher on the small table in the corner. She was a blonde, and no girl, with a pale face and pale-blue eyes which looked as if she had just been weeping, though it was probably from the glare. As she turned back, she saw Lawrence's feet, and said, "Oh, my God," before she could think, and then said, with a little, pained twitch of her mouth, "Gee, those must hurt."

Lawrence opened his eyes and looked at her. "I do it once a year," he said, "for my soul." He closed his eyes again. The woman started to go out, but then paused in the doorway, looking uncertainly at Lawrence.

"Supper'll be ready in about fifteen minutes," she said. "Maybe he'd like it in here, though, huh?"

"Thanks, I'll come over," Lawrence said.

"Well, all right," she said. "Oh," she added, "be careful when you turn on the shower. It comes out pretty hot at first; the pipes."

Tim went out after her. "Do you have anything we could use on his feet?" he asked.

"Gee," she said, relieved, "gee, they look terrible, don't they? Does he really do that? I mean every year, like he said?"

"No, he was just joking. He was out in the sand-hills too long."

"Gee," she said. "Poor guy." She stopped on the dining-room

steps. "Wouldn't he really rather have his supper in the cabin?"

"No, he'd rather come over."

"I don't know," she said, shaking her head. "He could be sick with those feet. His face too," she added. "He got it bad, didn't he?" She became silent, and stared out over the Valley, but not seeing it. "It was hot today, too," she said dreamily. "Oh, I've seen it lots worse, but it was hot enough. I wouldn't want to have been out in those sand-hills. Not me. I stay right in my kitchen. It's not so bad in the shade; makes a little breeze, kind of. Pop don't mind it, though. He's been here all his life, mostly. In the Valley, I mean, or up in the Panamint, which ain't much better. Can't stand it any place else any more. He went down to San Diego last summer, and he came back in just three or four days. Said he pretty near froze to death. Not me, though. I like the coast. Trees," she said dreamily, "and fog sometimes. I love the fog." She trailed off into her memories.

"If you have something . . ." Tim reminded her.

"Gee," she said, "excuse me. I get to thinking. What do you want?"

"If we could have a dishpan and some ice and some extra towels."

"Sure," Puss said, "soak 'em; that should be good."

Tim followed her through the dining room into the kitchen. The Walrus was getting a drink of water out of the refrigerator.

"Could you get out some more ice for the boys, Pop?" Puss asked. Tim explained. It was clear the Walrus thought they were too stupid to be worth saving, but he didn't say so. He said, "Sure," and broke off a block of ice and set it in the pan Puss had put on the table. Tim went back to the cabin with the pan and towels and a dish of lard. He turned on the shower and let the steaming water run off, and then filled the pan. When the ice had made the water cold, he soaked a couple of towels and wrapped Lawrence's feet in them. Lawrence held a wet towel to his face also. The towels dried and turned warm, as if freshly ironed, in a few minutes. Tim kept putting on new ones until the Walrus called them to supper, and after supper they went on with the treatment. At ten-twenty-five the Walrus called in that the power went off at ten-thirty, and scuttled away to make his prediction come true. Then Lawrence rubbed the lard, which was a pool of oil in its dish now, into his face and feet, and Tim turned out the light. It was only after they had lain quiet for half an hour, each with his own thoughts, and hearing the night air stir softly through the cabin, and sometimes a moth tapping at a screen, that Lawrence finally asked about Helen and the house. He began by asking, "Was Hule still around?" and he asked only a few questions, none of them about Helen herself, and Tim just answered the questions he asked.

A bit at a time, as the days passed, one morning an anecdote about Mr. Hule's judgment of painting, the next evening an example of the noiseless omnipresence of Helen's maid, Lawrence let Tim know how it had been with him in the Sargasso Sea. He told more about his sojourns in Austin, though there too his inner life had to be inferred. In much the same way Tim presented Knute thinking at breakfast, the hands of Teddy Quest, Pearl's meals and cats, and the immense and gently skeptical biography of Stephen Granger. These little sketches were the points of departure for their real talk, discussions of work and the world which went on for hours, and gradually brought to both of them, despite Lawrence's silent war with himself, and Tim's restless sieges of longing for Mary and the sacred meadows of the Truckee, the deep contentment of knowing that their big desires were still the same, their alliance stronger than ever. Most of their conversations took place at night, as they fell into accord with the reversed time of the Valley, in which dawn was an end and sunset a release and a beginning.

It was in the early morning that Tim was most restless. He always woke at first daylight, often two or three hours ahead of Lawrence, and was overcome as he lay there by the terror of passing time. His mind raced down the past and up the future, and hurled ideas and hopes and fears madly about, until he got up and dressed and went down to walk in the dunes, looking at the lovely little trails of tail and leafy feet the lizards and mice had made in the night, or climbed the mountain to some high crest or cliff from which he could watch the conquering light send down its first swift columns through the passes. When the heat began to sing on the stones, and the swallows had abandoned the air and were silent in their cliff city, he returned to the cabin, his mind quieted, and often refreshed by discoveries, to find Lawrence still lying there, outwardly motionless, but awake, his eyes glittering fixedly between half-closed lids.

Lawrence would emerge from his thoughts monosyllabically and dress while Tim shaved, and then they would creep, at Lawrence's pace, to the dining room. Lawrence looked like a crippled and passionate lunatic, thin as a wraith, blackened, unshaven and unshorn, as he shuffled along, rigidly upright and silent, between the two canes he was carving from sticks the Walrus had brought to him. After breakfast they would sit for a while in the shade of the open dining room, with cigarettes and extra coffee Puss left for them when she went down to the main building. She and the Walrus worked in the main building during the hottest hours. Then Tim would break out another chunk of ice, and they would creep back to the cabin, and Lawrence would begin on his feet and face again. The terrible day would roll slowly over them, and they would sweat it out. Lawrence spent hours carving carefully on the two canes while he went on discussing the life of Lawrence Black with himself. Wherever the Walrus had found them, cuts from discarded furniture, perhaps, the two sticks were mahogany, and Lawrence was carving climbing serpents upon them, on one stick, more slender than the other, a cobra tapered like a lash, its small head and half-raised hood making the handle, on the other a rattlesnake. When the shapes were clear, and pleased him, he went on carving the innumerable scales. Sometimes Tim read aloud to him from Herodotus, while he carved. More often Tim read to himself, in Renan's *Life of Jesus*, which assumed a new and potent validity in this desert halt, or in Montaigne's *Essays*, or in the Butcher and Lang *Odyssey*, which he sometimes revised into unwritten passages of his own poetry. Occasionally Lawrence would put the canes by, prop himself up in the corner of his bed, under the window, and read one of Tim's books, or the pocket copy of *The Dance of Life*, which he had carried in the blue jacket. Toward noon their minds would thicken over the printed word too. Often, then, they wouldn't eat any lunch, but drink a beer apiece, and stretch on their beds and sleep heavily, with the sweat running in little streams on them.

Twice in the late afternoon, when the mountains began to rise and take shape again, a wind blew down the Valley from the north, like a last, desperate foray by the losing forces of the sun. It brought no relief from the heat; instead, it came like the blast off a furnace, so that any creature which couldn't find shelter from it seemed doomed to curl and grow light and blow off, like a leaf in drought. Even so, it made some sound in the oppressive silence and some motion other than the perpetual wavering. Doors and windows in the cabins banged, and the cabins trembled. The Walrus emerged from the main building and scuttled along the row, closing the doors and windows that hadn't blown shut, to keep out the dust that came charging along the side-hill. Far across, between the dunes and the mountains, spasmodic, white dusts rose like the smoke from concealed batteries, and blew together, and thinned away southward. Then Tim and Lawrence would sit together in the closed cabin, watching and listening to the skirmish until the light began to change, and the wind dropped off and they could open up and breathe again.

In the quiet afternoons, Lawrence always moved his canvas chair out onto the shady side of the cabin and resumed his carving and brooding, and Tim wrote letters in the cabin. He wrote every day to Mary, long letters which came easily, and usually made him feel happy and complete when he was done. He wrote the note he had promised to Helen, and a letter to the Quests, mostly about an idea he had for catching in a tone poem the coming and the passing of sunset on the Grapevine and Funeral Mountains. After three more failures, he at last completed a letter to Eileen also, and before he could change his mind, sent it off with the Walrus when he went for supplies. He still wasn't easy about that letter, but at least it was better than the others, for he had become certain in this meditative quiet, that there was no way to write a pleasant letter about an irremediable offense, so that he simply tried to tell her, as truthfully as he could, what had happened in him during the night of *The Stone Woman* and the days following. At least it would answer her questions, and that was the beginning of forgetting.

The day the Walrus mailed that letter, he came back with one for Tim. Tim and Lawrence were just coming out from supper to watch the sunset when he scuttled up and thrust the letter at Tim, saying, "Old settlers now, by golly. Mail," and went on in to give Puss her mail. Lawrence continued to hobble, by himself, down the slope toward the place beside the main building where, because there was nothing in the way, they always sat to watch the sunset. Tim stood where he had received the letter and read it. It wasn't a long letter, but it took him some time to finish it, because after he had read the first few words, he didn't understand much of the rest of it, and had to read it through again.

Darling—I love you too, and yes, yes, yes. I'm shouting, Timmy. Hard as I tried, I couldn't just listen to what you wrote. In the first place it made me so champagne-headed I was afraid you'd been champagne-headed when you wrote it, and I wanted to get in ahead of the sober dawn. In the second place, I wanted to shout right away, and I didn't know where to shout to. Now your second letter has come, and it isn't a sober dawn after all, and I'm shouting. I know I shouldn't. I should keep you dangling. But I don't want to, and besides, I have my little conceit, which keeps me from feeling like a light gift. I'm perfectly sure I'll make the best wife in the world for you. No, I won't tell you why. Who in the world could keep you without a secret?

I'm so glad you found Lawrence, and give him my love, but do tell him to heal those poor feet as fast as possible. No, not really. You must stay there as long as he wants. It's so long since you've seen each other. But then hurry. No, don't. Oh, this doesn't make sense. I must do some grave penance, cut off all

*my hair, or something equally shameful, that will keep me from
looking like the canary who ate the cat when I go out. I will
end very darkly, so you'll really know what you got into. Darling, it is not possible for anyone else in the world to love even
you as much as I do.*

Mary

It is true that this bubbling little letter made Tim very sober.
It was as if he had put out his hand to penetrate the texture of
a dream and had encountered the body of Mary herself. He was
filled with a thousand misgivings, mostly about himself. He
wasn't even sure he knew Mary. He saw her eyes gazing steadily at him, testing him, now humorously, now sadly, with
changes like cloud shadows, but always enigmatically. Nonetheless, this was the specious sobriety of a self-contained drunk.
He looked up and saw Lawrence leaning on his canes down
there in the shadow of the main building, and at that little movement his head was in a whirl. He wished to embrace Mary in
particular, of course, but also the mountains, and the sky beyond them, and the whole wide world, which was in a hell of
a mess, but it would all work out. Instead, he walked to the cabin
carefully, like an amateur on a tight rope, and got the canvas
chairs and carried them down to where Lawrence was waiting.
They sat down side by side and regarded the vast, slow deepening and rising of the color upon the naked walls and peaks,
where already the shadows of the western mountains were beginning to creep up and blend with the blue rifts and the purple
passes. This was the great hour of the day, the tranquil and
enormous celebration of the coming of night, and the playing
of the cosmic clavichord was no less wonderful tonight than it
had been the night before, but Tim could only half attend to it.
In spite of himself he said at last, with careful quietness, "I'm
going to get married."

At first he thought Lawrence hadn't heard, but then he
turned his head and looked. "Married?" he asked, and then said,
"Married. My God. I have been missing something, haven't I?"
and waited.

641

"Mary Turner," Tim said.

"Mary Turner," Lawrence repeated, "that child at the Music Box; the one with the eyes."

"She's older than I am, a little," Tim said.

Lawrence shook his head. "You and I tasted the worm with the nipple, Hazard," he said. "And when does it happen?"

"As soon as I can make it," Tim said. "She sends you her love."

"Does she?" Lawrence said, grinning whitely in his beard. "I call that underhanded, just when we were beginning to get a little peace here. Well, we will pack tonight."

"No. We're to stay until your feet are well."

"She said that?"

"She said that."

Lawrence rose slowly and picked up his canes. "This calls for a little something," he said. "No, let me." He paused for an instant, balanced between the canes, and looked over his shoulder at Tim. "Did she say all that in one letter?"

Tim nodded, grinning.

"My God, what a woman," Lawrence said. "My God, what a letter. I would have had to read it over for a week." He hobbled up toward the kitchen.

He came down again after a few minutes, with Puss behind him, smiling across a tray of glasses and a bowl of ice. Then the Walrus came out of the kitchen and hurried down the slope after them. He was carrying a dark bottle in one hand, and a silver syphon in the other, and he was wearing a fresh, white shirt. Lawrence sat down in his chair. Puss and the Walrus put down the makings beside him, and he mixed the drinks and passed them out. Then he stood up, using only one cane, and holding his drink in the other hand. They stood there in a little circle, while the last light was winking up off the peaks, and drank, first to Mary, and then to Tim. Later, when the stars were out, they moved up in front of the cabins, and Tim got his guitar and sang.

After that Puss and the Walrus came out every evening for music and to talk. Usually Puss came first. She would come gliding softly along the walk, and sit down on the steps above Tim and Lawrence, with her chin in her hands. Sometimes, if the Walrus hadn't come yet, she would tell her stories, which began nowhere and ended nowhere and ran together. They were very young stories about a dim and mildly magic wilderness in Santa Anna, where she had lived until she was twenty. They were populated by dozens of Bills, Toms and Hanks, Maries, Gracies and Alices who moved fitfully and blissfully about by Ford-loads among schools and football fields, fruit picking and movies, public dance halls and sunny beaches, but always among orange groves, flowering shrubs, and lawns. Besides this inexhaustible cycle, Puss had only one story, a short one. She had been in Yosemite for three days, two years before, and she still only half believed that she had seen the great, snowy peak, far back against the sky, or the falls dropping from the lofty edges of the canyon, or the herds of deer grazing as tamely as sheep in the river meadows. She confessed that when the cabin Tim and Lawrence had was empty, she often went in to look at the picture of Yosemite Falls. There could be no question that when Puss paused in the middle of the dining room, as she often did, even when she had a load of dishes, and seemed to have gone out of herself toward the grim and smoking moun-tains, or in the kitchen stopped cutting bread with the knife halfway through the third slice, and appeared to be giving her soul sadly to the cream pitcher on the shelf in front of her, she had really returned to the leafy glades of seventeen in Santa Anna, or to the awful paradise of the Yosemite.

Even the Walrus seemed to understand her trouble. When he came barging into the kitchen for a drink of something, any-thing, tea, ice water, milk, cold coffee, soda pop, beer, as he was always doing, and discovered Puss thus returned to the green wilderness, he would gulp down whatever liquid he found first, say, "Here, Puss, let me do that for you," finish her loaf with a dozen violent strokes, and be gone again, slamming the screen behind him, before Puss could finish saying, "Thanks, Pop." A minute later they would see him, far up the hillside, scuttling along with his serpent of hose stirring the dust behind him. Where you saw the Walrus one minute didn't mean a thing about where you would find him the next.

In spite of this working sympathy, though, Puss would never tell her stories after the Walrus came. The Walrus would sit there, slowly and energetically puffing at his big, curved pipe, and listening to the songs, or to the Spanish dances on the guitar, which he liked best, and when a number was over, and an impressive moment of silence had followed, he would remove his pipe and say, solemnly, authoritatively, "By golly, that's *good*." Then Puss would murmur, "Gee, yes, that was swell." Puss never said much more than that when the Walrus was there, but for that matter, neither did the Walrus, although Puss declared, in his absence, that he was as full of swell stories about the Valley as an egg is of meat. Perhaps she made up the stories herself, after she had accumulated a lot of the Walrus' short facts. That was all Tim and Lawrence heard the Walrus release, facts, unembellished and unassembled, like a new tourist-guide working out of a poor catalogue. Even so, the four became a community when they were thus drawn forth by night, and it was an important act, an unveiling of the face of humanity, when the Walrus lit a match and held it to his pipe, and for the time of three or four puffs his craggy, deeply lined face was revealed in the darkness of the eternal.

At ten-twenty-five every night, the Walrus would haul out his watch, peer at it closely, say, "Ten-twenty-five. Power goes off at ten-thirty," knock out his pipe and scuttle off. A few minutes later Puss would say, "Good night now," and slip away almost without a sound, her white uniform glimmering more and more faintly in the starlight. It was then, beer bottles in hand, the weight of the day slipped off the mind, that Tim and Lawrence would start their explorations.

On the ninth day, Lawrence finished carving the serpents, and polished them, and made ferrules for them out of some metal scraps in the Walrus' shop. On the tenth day he walked to breakfast without them, and when he returned to the cabin, he shaved, washed all his clothes in the hand basin, hung them on the bed and the chair, and lay down with a towel about his loins, and stared at the ceiling and was smiling. At supper that evening, he presented the canes to Puss and the Walrus. Clearly he had made up his mind about something, though he didn't say what. Even so they might have stayed a day or two longer, but that night, after Puss and the Walrus had gone to bed, a breeze came up. It wasn't strong, but it was cool enough to make Tim and Lawrence go in and get their shirts, and when they went to bed, whole constellations had disappeared high in the sky. From his bed Lawrence said, "I think we should spend an evening at Luigi's, don't you?" and Tim, shaken again by the nearness of Mary and Reno, and the Truckee Meadows, nevertheless said, "We couldn't pass it by."

CHAPTER SIXTY-THREE: *An Evening with the Arts at Luigi's*

WHENEVER Lawrence, in his long search for Helen, came to Tonopah, he went to Luigi's bar, because it was a place in which no drink, not even a short ginger ale, was ever offered to you without a silent and gentle understanding of your part in the bewilderment of humanity. There, in the middle of a plain which is almost as white in September as it is when snow has fallen, rears up a solitary mountain, like an old volcano, and in its topmost creases hides Tonopah, which is very old for its years, having more memories than hopes. To the wanderer coming in there, whether by the south road or the north, or the east, it reveals itself only at the last moment, and if he has been long in that land, and is feeling very small after its uninterrupted instruction concerning astral time, geological architecture, and the insignificant history of mankind, it will open its gates between rusty dumps and old mine tailings, with the splendor of ancient Nineveh or Tyre. At sunset, however, its own smaller loneliness will assert itself, and then there is Luigi's place.

In Luigi's there is a bar with a row of stools in front of it. Behind the bar stands Luigi himself, with his short cigar, which is always out, and with a white apron bound uphill over his belly. Luigi is always worried because, "I don' digest my food so good any more," or because, "I don' sleep so good any more in the night; I am all the time awake in the night, thinking. I am not a young man. I don' change so easy now. All this time, twenty years, I been right here in my place, but pretty quick now nobody come to Tonopah any more. Then what do I do? I don' know anything but this."

There is also Luigi's wife, Maria, the madonna of the middle years, who regards all lonely people as her children, and deeply shares their losses and their sorrows without saying a thing about them. Maria is no longer pretty, but so beautiful with understanding that her guests are more surely restored by watching her face than they would be by joy. Nearly all her guests have a good many reasons for knowing that joy is a brief and often deceptive thing, while the peace of Maria is not upheld by any foolish expectations. Sometimes, when Luigi worries out loud about what will happen to them when "the fellows don' come no more," Maria will say, "Luigi, you shouldn't worry so much. Something is always happening. Maybe there will be something big in Silver Peak, the way they talk now. You don't ever know. And we have many friends, Luigi. All the boys come here." This sounds like foolish expectation, but somehow even new guests in Luigi's, people just passing through, people from the orange groves of California or the small, green farm hills of Iowa, where all the animals grow fat, people to whom Tonopah is a curious and ugly town, dying of boredom and exposure, know that Maria is not really depending upon anything that may happen in Silver Peak.

If it is a time when any number of people come to Luigi's, Sunday afternoon, or sunset, or night, Bill and Nicky will also be there, to make music. Bill plays the old piano in the back corner. He starts suddenly, without any preliminary fingering or thinking, and plays hard and decisively, mistakes and all, going faster and faster as he gets toward the end. Nicky sits on a high stool beside the piano, leans against the back wall, and plays the fiddle, starting a little behind Bill, but always catching up, and sometimes even passing him. He does this with a dreamy look upon his red and unshaven face, as if he were really thinking about something else entirely. In the daytime, with the same expression, Nicky sweeps the main street of Tonopah with slow and measured strokes. He seems never to go to bed, and every morning, for breakfast, he eats a huge, royal-purple onion cut into slices an inch thick. He does this so that his breath won't smell of whisky.

It was early evening, just after the supper hour, and the wind still blowing and the clouds still gathering when Tim and Lawrence came into Luigi's. There was Maria, with her graying hair braided like a wreath about her head. She was wiping a glass and keeping some long thought to herself. When she saw them, she smiled and put down the glass and the towel, and in turn gave each of them her hand across the bar. "I am so glad to see you again," she said. She poured a tall glass of beer for each of them, scraped off the foam with her paddle, and set the glasses before them. They asked about her life, and she asked about theirs. She asked Lawrence, "Did Mrs. Black come with you?" It was difficult for Maria to believe that a wife could be far from her man. Lawrence understood this, and said that Helen couldn't come this time.

"She is not sick?" Maria asked.

"No," Lawrence said. "No. She is busy with the house."

"I am sorry not to see her," Maria said. "Luigi and I often talk about the last time you were here. We had such a good time. She was so beautiful, your wife, and so gay. You remember how she made even Luigi dance? I laughed so."

This was not strictly true. Maria had only smiled.

"Luigi will be sorry she didn't come, too," she said.

When Luigi had finished serving a customer at the front end of the bar, he came to greet them also. Luigi didn't like the look of the world. He had a sign up over the cash register, explaining that he was an American. On the walls, among Johnny Walker, the White Horse, the whiskered goat and naked, cardboard blondes, were little silk banners saying, "God Bless America." Luigi said, "When they talk good about this Mussolini, I always tell them, 'If you want to talk good about this Mussolini, you go somewhere else. What do I care about this Mussolini?'

"I don' care for these kind of man," Luigi explained. "Always pushing somebody around. I don' wan' any trouble. I got trouble enough of my own. Everybody got trouble enough, without these men pushing around making big trouble.

"Like these," he said, nodding toward the front of the bar.

A thin, blonde girl in a fur coat was standing there. She kept her hands on the edge of the bar. They were soft, white hands, with crimson nails, and there were two big, cheap rings on each hand. She was standing between two men in dark suits, who were talking to her quietly and persistently, and sometimes looking around with shame in their faces, and a little challenge. Most of the time the girl just stared at the bar between her hands, and shook her head against what they were saying, but at moments, for which only she knew the cause, she would become very confident, and look up, and stare around with her chin raised, and conquer the world in a few ill-chosen words which everybody could hear. At other times, just as unexpectedly, she would begin soap-boxing because Luigi wouldn't give her anything more to drink. "You old wop bastard," she would declaim, proudly and shrilly, "who the hell do you think you are? I said I wanna drink." She would also call Maria names, and sometimes, suddenly, she would call everybody in the place names, saying they were all against her. Then she would be quiet again, staring at the bar, appearing to fall asleep where she stood. The men would start talking to her once more. They were trying to get her to leave. In the middle of their argument she would begin to laugh, and, still laughing, would loudly tell them a bad joke she had just remembered. Tim was startled each time the sounds began to come out of her again, because when she was quiet, staring at the bar, she looked very much like the proud, blonde poetess who had sat by herself in the Marine Room and wanted to know what it was all coming to.

Two short, stocky, tired-looking men in working clothes, leaned on the bar up front, where it curved into the wall, and held beers in their hands. They were trying to talk to each other. When the blonde's voice became like that of a huge parrot, they would both stop talking and look at her with a kind of frightened fascination. Whenever one of the men who were trying to coax her saw them watching like this, he would shake his head at them, as if asking them to share his helplessness and embarrassment.

In a chair in a corner by the front window, there was an old man asleep. It was amazing that the offended oratory of the blonde girl, or her blasts of humor, didn't waken him, but they didn't. He sat huddled down, with his ancient and threadbare overcoat hanging to the floor about him, like a skirt. His bearded chin rested upon his chest, and his huge hands, folded one within the other upon his belly, rose and fell slowly with his breathing. His beard was dry and bushy, like steel wool, and yellow tobacco stain divided it. His hands and his boots, which were stiff and white with alkali dust, appeared to be made of the same stuff. He wore a straw sombrero, which was pulled down over his face, so that only the beard showed from under it.

Once Maria herself went up behind the bar and spoke gently to the blonde girl. The girl appeared astonished, and was silent for a moment, staring at Maria. Then she broke out loudly, "What the hell do I care? What the hell business is it of mine if he can't sleep? What does the damned old fool want to sleep in a place like this for anyhow? I been thrown out of lots better places than this."

At once the two men beside her began arguing with her again, quietly and diplomatically. They looked at Maria to make a silent apology now and then.

A very tall young man, who appeared even taller than he was because he was so extremely thin, came in and took a place at the inside end of the bar. Maria returned and poured him the beer he wanted. She shook her head sadly at Tim and Lawrence when the blonde began to sing. The tall young man had appeared to be deep in a rather melancholy thought of his own, but now he also stared at the blonde, as if trying, laboriously and carefully, to figure out exactly what made her like that.

Two women came in together. Both of them called out

loudly and cheerfully to Luigi and to Maria, and the blonde stopped singing and stared at them in almost the way the tall young man was staring at her. One of them was a gray-haired woman, whose face and body hung down in folds. She was wearing a brown dress like a sack, men's work shoes, a brown leather coat and a hairnet made out of string, which didn't begin to keep her hair in. She had a large, terrible and jovial face, which was powdered in patches. Tim and Lawrence knew her. Her name was Veronica, but they called her the Fury. Her friend was not a girl, like the blonde, but she wasn't as old as the Fury, either, and she looked very neat and well organized compared to the Fury. She wore tight, little, high-heeled, short-toed pumps, which glittered when she walked, silk stockings as snug as her skin, a neat, black suit and coat and a prim little black hat.

The two stood up to the bar, and ordered their drinks, and made jokes with Luigi. The one in black was next to Tim.

Bill and Nicky came in. When they saw so many people, they went back to their corner at once. Bill set out upon the floor, near the piano, a white wooden pyramid, which was the kitty, and sat down at the piano. Nicky took down his violin from the top of the piano, and climbed up onto his stool, and tuned the strings, one after the other. They began to play suddenly, without warning. It was a terrible noise, but it made everybody feel better. Even the blonde girl was more quiet, and let Maria bring her a cup of black coffee from the back room.

The woman in black spoke to Maria.

"Where's your lead ball, Maria?" she asked. "It's time we got up a pool on the lead ball again."

Maria smiled at her, and took from the back shelf, beside the cash register, a ball made of many layers of tin foil from cigarette packages and chewing gum. It was bigger than a baseball. She gave it to the woman in black.

"Here you are, Francine," she said. "I put some more on it just today."

"Who wants to bet on the lead ball?" Francine asked everybody. "Got paper and pencil?" she asked Maria.

Maria gave her a paper and a pencil. Francine took the ball in her hand and looked up at the ceiling, and hefted the ball judiciously. Then she put it down, and wrote something on the paper.

"One pound, nine ounces," she announced.

"A nickel in the pot," she said, and put a nickel on the bar.

The Fury hefted the ball, and said, "Two pounds, one ounce."

Francine wrote down the Fury's estimate and name under her own.

She tossed the ball and caught it two or three times. "This is the world," she announced to everybody. "That's what we call it, weighing the world. Ain't it, Maria?

"What do you guess the world weighs tonight?" she asked Tim. "Everybody guesses, and puts in a nickel, and the closest guess wins the pot."

Tim weighed the ball in his hand. It was astonishingly heavy, and quite warm from Francine's hand. He made his guess, and told her his name was Tim. Francine wrote them down, and then she went to everybody along the bar, giving them the ball and writing down names and guesses, and bringing back nickels to put in the pot. Everybody at the bar made a guess, except the blonde and Maria, and one of the two embarrassed men made a guess for the blonde, and wrote her name down and put in her nickel. Maria still refused.

"I hold it all the time, to put on the foil," she said. "It's not fair I should guess. I know. I'll hold the stakes."

They all insisted that Maria guess. The game was no good without Maria in it.

"All right," she said. "You make me." She shrugged her shoulders and apologized with her smile. Then she held the ball very still in her hand for a moment, not tossing it the way everyone else had.

"I pretend for the game," she said, smiling at Tim and Lawrence.

"Two pounds, four ounces," she told Francine. "I shouldn't bet. I know all the time."

Francine read all the names aloud, Francine, Veronica, Tim, Lawrence, Al, Buck, Doris, Ted, Jerry, Angelo, Luigi, Bill, Nick, Maria, and counted a nickel for each name.

"Everybody's in," she said. "Everybody except Pop, and he don't care what the world weighs. He don't have no truck with the world any more. I'll go get it weighed. Maria, you keep the names and the bets."

"I'll watch they are all right," Maria said, smiling.

Francine went out quickly, happy about doing everybody's business at once. Bill and Nicky launched relentlessly into *Tea for Two*. One of the men with the blonde walked over and dropped some coins into the slot at the top of the white pyramid. They clinked and rolled on the bottom, and Bill looked around and nodded, and turned back and began to play harder than ever.

After a few minutes, Francine came back. She put the ball on the counter, and slapped a second piece of paper down beside the one that had the bets on it.

"Two pounds and four ounces," she said. "Exactly two pounds and four ounces. Look. Morris wrote down the weight. I made him sign it."

Everybody at the bar except the blonde and Maria made signs or sounds of cheering.

Maria looked happy because everybody was cheering for her, but said again, "It's not fair. I hold it too much.

"I tell you," she said. "We give it to the kitty for all of us."

Bill and Nicky were just sitting there then, not playing, but when Maria dropped the nickels into the pyramid, Bill began to play *Columbia, the Gem of the Ocean* at once, as if the nickels had been dropped into him. After a moment, Nicky caught up with him.

Veronica was talking and laughing with one of the men who were guarding the blonde. Francine began a conversation with Tim. She began it very tactfully by asking him if he could find the man on her package of Camels, and telling him, when he couldn't, that the man was around behind the pyramid relieving himself. She said that, too, relieving himself. Then she told Tim not to worry, she wasn't that way any more. She patted his hand, and said that anyway she was old enough to be his mother. Tim assured her that he wasn't worried, and that she certainly wasn't old enough to be more than his sister, and then they were like old friends.

Francine talked about her own life the way it was now, in Tonopah, as if Tim knew all about the way she had lived before too. You couldn't go on forever like that, she said. She had her own man now, just one. He worked in the mines. He wanted somebody to keep a house for him, somebody to make him happy in bed and keep him comfortable, and get his ham and eggs and coffee for him. That was all he wanted, so he loved her fine. They weren't either of them kids any more. They liked having a place together, and they got along fine. Tim bought drinks for both of them, and Francine asked him what he did, and he began to tell her about his music.

Suddenly the blonde started screaming. She was screaming words which were almost impossible to understand, but the sound was terrible. It was a sound of hungry and desperate rage. It made the muscles of Tim's back crawl. Everybody stopped talking and stared at her. Every face showed a little fear or anger, or contempt, which was just anger being held down. The blonde was accusing the Fury of making a play for one of her men. She was calling the Fury terrible names, worse than any she had called Luigi or Maria, and was trying to get at her to scratch her face. She began to weep wildly, while she screamed, because the two men were holding her away from the Fury. The Fury stood there with her hands on her hips and looked at the girl. Finally the girl was just weeping wildly, and not trying to say anything. She seemed to have forgotten the Fury. It was practically everything in the world which made her feel bad now. The Fury turned back to the bar, and winked at Luigi, and picked up her drink again. The two men got the girl out, and the sound of weeping was gone. Only Bill and Nicky had paid no real attention. They had looked when the first screams came, but then they had gone right on playing, only more loudly.

Maria said sadly, "It's terrible, a young girl like that."

The old man in the front corner got up slowly and stiffly, and pushed back his hat, and went out without looking at anybody. He didn't seem to know that anything in particular had awakened him. Perhaps he didn't even know he'd been asleep. Tim saw him outside creeping past the window, buttoning up his coat as he went, and hunching himself against the wind.

Luigi came over and leaned on the bar in front of Francine and Tim, and looked at the window from which the figure of the old man had disappeared.

"That crazy Doris," he said. "She woke up Pop. That's no good. When Pop wake up, he can't go sleep again all night. He forget where he is, but there is something he can't forget. I don' know what this is, but there is something. He doesn't sleep good anyhow, but when he wake up like this, then he don' know where he is. Some time we got to send somebody to look for him. He is older than he look; an old, old man, Pop.

"Anyway," he said cheerfully, with a sad face, "tonight is no moon. No snow, either.

"Once," he explained to Tim, "we hunt everywhere for him, me, and my wife, and Francine here, and Bill and Nicky and Veronica, all of us. We are plenty scared for him. It is in the winter, a bad winter. Everywhere in town the snow blows off the mountain, whoooo-eeee." Luigi illustrated with both hands how the snow rose before the wind. "Fly way up; make the lights in the street little, and no good to see. It is cold. The snow cries when we walk on it. Then there is that moon; it make me feel lonesome. I don' like to go out at all. I look up, and there is the mountain up above, like it lean over me, all white in the light from the moon. The mountain is lonesome too, and cold. I don' like this.

"At three o'clock in the morning we find him over in the shanty town. He is in a little place with a roof made from these big tin can. No light, no fire, no nothing. I have a flashlight, Bill have a flashlight, Francine here have a flashlight. We go all over that shanty town looking for him, yelling 'Pop, Pop,' all of us. You know how this shanty town is, made from pieces of everything, old beds, wagons, boxes, tin cans, signs; nobody in it any more except sometimes in the summer, and everything go rattle-bang when the wind blow. Yelling that way, we make all the dogs bark too; all over town they go yap-yap. Some of them go wooo-woo-woo-woo, you know, like they do when the noon whistle blows they can't stand in the ears. Maybe we wake them up and then they see the moon, or that mountain. I don' know. But all this noise, and Pop, he doesn' hear anything. I go in one place, in another, in another. No, Pop. I don' feel happy, but we gotta find Pop. Then I go in this little place like a box, where the door go flap-flap. Leather hinge, you know, and when they go away, they don' even bother to close the door, just let her wave. I come in this place, dark as anything, the window all dirty so the moon don' hardly show, and there he is. He is sit in the middle of the room on an old chair has no back. This is all is in the place, Pop on this old chair. The wind blow; the tin roof is loose and go slap-slap all the time. God, he scare me to death for a minute when I see him sit there and look at me.

"We make him come back with us. He is pretty near froze. With his hands, with his feet, he don' feel nothing. I give him a drink, and Maria, she give him some good, hot soup like. After a while he feel better. Then he tell us it is all the moon make him do this. He tell us the moon know something about him and keep looking at him and say, 'Pop, you done it.' He is go in this dark place so the moon don' see him. He says if the moon look at him too long, it will kill him. Did you ever hear anything so crazy? He is crazy, all right, but he is a good old man. It is just he is so old. He don' ever do anything to anybody. He just think that way when the moon is out."

Luigi was silent, thinking of the effect of the moon on Pop. Finally he said more cheerfully, "Anyway, that damn Doris is gone. She is no good. She is no good for anybody. She wants everything. She thinks somebody is trying to rob her all the time. If she was come in here with fifty men, it is just like to-night just the same. Some girl talk to one of her men, and she begin to call everybody names and scream and cry like this way. I don' like she should come here. I don' let her have any-thing to drink any more when she come here. Then she get drunk some place else, like tonight, and come in here anyway. I don' like it, but what can I do? This is a public place. Anybody can come here. Anyway, it's all right now. Everybody feel better. It is nice and quiet when she goes."

It was true that everybody was feeling better since the blonde girl had been led out. Bill was furiously playing "There's a long, long trail a-winding," and Nicky wasn't far behind him. The Fury was leaning on the piano and singing loudly and huskily and a little off key. Everybody else was talking, and beginning to laugh sometimes, except the tall young man, who was slowly drinking a second beer, and attentively watching Bill and Nicky and the Fury, the way he had watched the blonde, as if there were a difficult reason behind what they were doing, and he had to understand it before he could rest.

"What does Pop do?" Tim asked Francine.

Luigi was saying loudly to the tall young man, "Buck, you go get Pop and bring him back here, huh? He don' freeze to-night, but I get scared thinking about him. Some time the old fool will fall down one of the old shafts and break his neck."

"He won't fall down no shaft," Buck said. "Pop knows all about them shafts." He wasn't protesting his mission, though. He finished his second beer more quickly, and went out. His face still looked as if he were attempting to discover the diffi-cult reason behind everything. It was probably a permanent look.

"Oh, Pop don't do anything much now," Francine said. "Just boards around and sleeps where he can, and keeps waiting."

"What's he waiting for?"

"Sometimes it's one thing, sometimes it's another. One day he'll tell you he's waiting for times to get even worse, so he'll have to go to work at something, and the next day he'll tell you he's waiting for nineteen hundred, when the boom starts here in Tonopah, so he'll have a good reason to get out."

Tim shook his head, as if to clear it after a staggering blow. "Waiting for nineteen hundred?"

"Oh, time don't mean anything to Pop," Francine said. "Hasn't, for years. Night or day, now or eighteen-eighty, it's all one to Pop. It's the wind does it. He says the wind makes everything seem the same to him, only always kind of late. But about getting out when the boom starts," she added, "he means that. He's made the first strike for a dozen booms, big and little, and had plenty of trouble about it every time, and always lost everything he had to some claim-jumper or because he couldn't get money to develop and some big outfit took over when his claim ran out. He's too pig-headed to sell, Pop is. He says he can't see taking a few thousand for something that turns out a couple of million or so. I can't say I think he's too crazy there myself, but all that happens, of course, he winds up without even the few thousand. He says that's why he quit prospecting a good many years back. He was sick of living out that way and locating fortunes for other guys."

Luigi came over in front of Francine and leaned on the bar.

"Francine's telling me about Pop," Tim said.

"Ah, that poor Pop," Luigi said. "He's not all there in the head any more. If we don' bring him in and put the food right in front of him, he would forget to eat even. And always he is starting out walking, thinking he is going somewhere again, Austin or somewhere. But he is good old fella. No harm. Just he is so old and crazy with the moon."

"It's the wind," Francine said.

"I don' wanna quarrel," Luigi said. "The wind, the moon, what does it matter?"

"It matters plenty," Francine said. "The moon only comes around once in so often. The damn wind blows all the time here."

She and Luigi began to argue about whether Pop was crazy all the time or only in the periods of the moon. They also argued about how old he was, and when he had started prospecting and when he had quit prospecting, and before they were done, Pop had made all the famous strikes in Nevada, from the Comstock down through the second boom at Tonopah and

Goldfield, besides a number of smaller ones that Tim had never heard of.

While they were arguing, three more men came in. Two of them were gray-haired, weary and sad-looking. The third, a young man in the uniform of one of the oil companies, seemed more cheerful and able to get out of himself, but he was just as tired and red-eyed. Maria went to the front of the bar and gave them their drinks and asked about their recent lives. Her presence worked upon them, and they began to look as if they had come home after a long and hazardous wandering which had left them with memories they didn't care to mention. Lawrence moved over into the chair Pop had left, and with a bread board and paper on his knee, started to sketch the unutterable trio, which was now rendering *A Bicycle Built for Two*. The Fury appeared to be facing a huge audience behind Lawrence, and was shrieking to the gallery and wringing her hands in operatic agony.

Luigi made another drink for Francine, and they went on arguing. Tim listened to them. Finally Francine said, "Nope. I'm just saying if he is a little touched, it's the wind does it, that's all," and spun around on her stool. "Now what goes on?" she asked. Tim looked around too.

The young man in the oil-company uniform had made a quartet out of the trio, and the quartet was singing *The Cowboy's Lament*. The Fury was no longer an opera star. She and the young man had their heads together, and were doing close harmony. Lawrence had come back to the bar, and was having another beer. Maria was looking at the sketch, which Lawrence had given her for the house. She turned it so that Luigi, Tim and Francine could see it too. The expressions on Bill and Nicky and the Fury were wonderful. They got under Tim's ribs at once, with a kind of mournful tickling. There was a "forever more" feel to the group. He couldn't figure exactly how Lawrence had captured it, but he could feel it. There were only the three figures in the back corner of Luigi's, and the old piano, and the stool Nicky sat on, and above, in a kind of faint apex, like a dream above the three heads, the calendar picture which was actually over on the side wall, a picture of an improbably blank, fruity blonde about to finish putting on or taking off a black robe which didn't matter anyway, preparatory to rising from or lying down upon a bed on which she was doing nothing definite at the moment. That was all there was in Lawrence's drawing, and yet somewhere, probably in the faint something which wasn't wholly ludicrous in the expressions, and in the pattern of light and great shadows, there was also all that Luigi's place meant against the meaning of Tonopah under Mt. Butler in the night, and against the white desert which lay around the mountain, and the other valleys and mountains stretching away, one beyond the other, until the mind, considering them, changed time. The great outside came in through the walls of Luigi's. The whole drawing had the fine, ascending pattern that Lawrence always wanted, so that Nicky and Bill and the Fury, and even the piano, were as light as clouds, rode a sky quite free of the street of Tonopah, like the flying sacred figures of El Greco. The drawing was signed with a turtle, and was entitled, boldly and within the pattern, *Recital at Luigi's*. Tim understood that this was not just a token of his affection that Lawrence was leaving with Maria and Luigi, but a beautiful present, the best that he could do to show them how important they were in the world.

Maria was quietly marveling over the drawing, while she held it for the others to look at. Her face was very happy, and she kept saying to Lawrence, "It is so nice."

The *Lament* ended, and Luigi called to the quartet, "Come and look at this."

The quartet came, and the men from the end of the bar came too. Everybody looked at *Recital at Luigi's*.

The Fury was astonished. She stared, and then, all of a sudden, her eyes filled with tears.

"I don't look like that," she declared. "Do I really look like that?" she asked Lawrence.

"No," Lawrence told her softly. "No, of course you don't. I

never make anybody look the way he really looks. I do it to make the picture more fun. It's not you. It's not anybody in particular."

The Fury continued to stare at the picture and blink.

"You must have a drink with me," Lawrence told her. "I used you to draw from, so I owe you a drink." When she had the drink in her hand, he began to explain to her how intent and composition were superior to mere reproduction. Francine and Maria and Luigi and one of the older men listened too. They were fascinated by the quick little sketches which Lawrence drew to illustrate his points. The Fury kept sniffing now and then. She tried to make the sniffs sound angry, but they weren't. However, Lawrence had his work cut out for him. She had been mortally hurt in her ideal. Luigi, however, seemed to feel that the value of the picture had been increased by this incident. In the middle of the lecture he set up drinks for everybody, to celebrate the acquisition of an original Lawrence Black. Tim wandered over to the piano with his new beer. He sat down and began to finger softly through part of *The Smoky Bar*.

Francine came over too, and stood by the piano with her drink. "Veronica is feeling all right again now," she said. "He's a good guy, your friend, isn't he?"

"A very good guy," Tim said.

"You play the piano too?" Francine asked.

Tim nodded. They began to talk about songs Francine liked. While they talked Tim played *Why Do I Always Do Wrong?* like the far-away echo of a blues. When he stopped, everybody clapped. He looked around and saw that they had really been listening to him. Bill was right in the corner beside him, squatting on Nicky's stool. The Fury came over with her drink, and Lawrence came with her. While they were arguing about what they wanted Tim to play now, the tall young man came in with Pop.

"Here he is," he said to Luigi. "He was down across the railroad track, clear down the hill past the monument. He was headed for Hawthorne, I guess. Hikin' up the middle of the road, like he owned it."

Luigi looked at the old man, who was standing right where he had stopped behind the tall young man, and was looking directly ahead at nothing in particular.

"Good," Luigi said. "It's good you found him. Where were you going, Pop? It's getting late."

"I don't like that wind," the old man said, not looking at Luigi.

"You see?" Francine said to Tim.

The old man started to go to his chair in the front corner. Maria came out from behind the bar and began to coax him. "You come back in the kitchen now, and have some hot soup, Pop," she said. Maria's slow and careful speech, in her voice, had something like the moving sonority of sacred Latin, without its pomposity. Pop looked at her and listened. "Some hot soup, Pop," she said again. "Then you get some sleep." The old man went with her into the back room, nodding his head slowly as he went, about something in his own mind.

Everybody felt better because Pop was back, but Luigi especially felt better. He made the tall young man a huge drink with his best whisky in it.

"It *is* a funny wind," the tall young man said. "It smells like rain. The sky's all clouded over black; hardly any stars; and it smells like rain. If I didn't know it never rains here, I'd say it was going to rain."

"If it does anything, it will snow," Luigi said. "It snows easy here. What do we care?" he asked, as if to comfort himself for a thought he'd just had. "We should get sad thinking about what the weather will be, maybe. That is outside. You boys make some music. Maybe Francine and Veronica like to dance, huh?"

Tim started to get up, but Bill said, "You keep it. Play something." He looked very earnest, almost savage, sitting there staring at Tim. He wore thick glasses, and his eyes were enlarged by them until they looked like the predatory eyes of a huge hawk.

"Sing something," the Fury said. "He says you can sing."

661

She pointed to Lawrence. Lawrence had moved the old man's chair over behind the kitty, and was sitting there, playing with the top of the pyramid. He looked up.

"*The Sweet Promised Land of Nevada*," he said.

"Is that good?" the Fury asked.

"It's fine," Lawrence told her. "He made it up himself."

"Everybody in on the chorus after the first time," Tim called, playing through the chorus loudly. Then he set off.

> *Oh, the Lord, He had labored both earnest and long*
> *Five days and a half, and was still going strong,*
> *With the sweat on His brow, but a-singing His song,*
> *When He came to the land of Nevada.*
>
> *Oh, He'd laid out the world just as neat as He'd planned;*
> *Save a few little boners 'twas smooth as His hand.*
> *There was plenty left over to finish this land,*
> *The last land, the land of Nevada.*
>
> *Oh, He leaned on His shovel and looked at the stuff*
> *He had piled up there handy to make the first rough.*
> *"My work has been good, but it's not good enough.*
> *I'll do better the land of Nevada."*

"Chorus," Tim yelled, and thumped it out deep and regular.

> *"Oh, this is the land that old Moses shall see;*
> *Oh, this is the land of the vine and the tree;*
> *Oh, this is the land for My children and Me,*
> *The sweet promised land of Nevada."*

He gave it to them twice, and took up the tale again.

> *"Oh, Himalayas and Andes I piled up too high,*
> *They are colder than death, and they trouble the sky,*
> *And the poles are all icy, I still don't see why,*
> *So the sun it must shine in Nevada.*

"Oh, the Congo's a place I neglected to drain,
The Amazon swamp I intended for plain,
While England, though better, is all fog and rain,
So I'll keep down the damps in Nevada.

"Oh, the deserts of Gobi are uncommon dry;
I forgot the Sahara and left it to fry;
Arabia's sands are as empty as sky,
So the waters must flow in Nevada."

"All together now, chorus," he yelled. They came in uncertainly on the words, but with plenty of volume. They all knew the tune now. Then Tim went on alone.

So He started to dig while He thought up the rest
Of the little details that would make her the best,
And the vision He had made Him dig with such zest
That He turned up too much of Nevada.

"Oh, I'll bend her hills round so they'll keep out the blast;
A nice, even warmth she shall have till the last,
And her storms shall be dew, and no land of the past
Shall flower and fruit like Nevada.

"Oh, the creatures of earth they shall multiply there;
The children of men shall be gentle and fair;
They shall all live together without want or care,
In the wonderful land of Nevada."

Tim signaled the chorus again, and this time it shook Luigi's place. Luigi himself, and Maria, who had come back from the kitchen, joined in from behind the bar. Tim took up the solo again, making a long, groaning slide into the "Oh."

"Oh, the best of it all is the waters I plan."
He leaned on His shovel this vision to scan
Of the lakes in the hills and the rivers that ran
To water the land of Nevada.

"Oh, all these small rivers make big lakes below,
And all these big lakes into two rivers flow,
Which northward and southward, majestic and slow,
Shall go out to the seas from Nevada.

"Oh, one shall be green, and flow softly around
The green hills of Nevada to reach Puget Sound,
And the other be blue as the sky till it's found
Its way down to the Gulf from Nevada."

Tim just nodded his head once, and the chorus came this time.
Everybody was thumping a foot too. It thinned out to Tim's
voice again.

Oh, the Lord, He dug deep where the lakes should be
laid,
And threw up the tailings on what had been saved.
With the utmost of care, the first rivers He made
That would water the land of Nevada.

Oh, He started to pick at the mountains at last;
The sun was down low, and He swung it right fast,
But He didn't get done, for the five-o'clock blast
Whistled over the land of Nevada.

Oh, He shouldered his tools. "I'll be done in one day.
I can't work tomorrow; I've made it Sunday."
So He tucked in the rivers. "I'll finish Monday."
But He never got back to Nevada—No-o-o-o-o,
He never got back to Nevada.

Even Pop had come to stand in the kitchen door and listen. On
this chorus he seemed to be saying the words to himself, but he
was nodding his head to the rhythm. Tim quickened the tempo a
little, going into the last three stanzas of the narrative.

So the hills are in rows, and they're piled up too high;
They are colder than death, and they trouble the sky.
Though at night you may freeze, yet at noon you will
    fry
In the unfinished land of Nevada.

So the lakes are all dry and the rivers all flow
Underground and no green thing will venture to grow,
And all the sweet breezes that come there to blow,
Will tear off your hair in Nevada.

So, with rivers and lakes that forever run dry,
The Lord's only creatures that can multiply
Are the rattler, the jack and the little bar-fly,
The little bar-fly of Nevada.

"So," he roared, with that trombone slide down, to start them, and they went into the last chorus full blast.

"So this is the land that old Moses would see,
So this is the land of the vine and the tree,
So this is the land for My children and Me,
The sweet promised land of Nevada—O-o-o-o-oh,
The sweet promised land of Nevada."

There was great applause. They had it now, and they wanted to do it again. The tall young man and the young man in the oil-company uniform whistled shrilly through their fingers. Nicky was saying over and over through the din, sounding very anxious, "You got the words to that some place? You got the words to that?" So they did *The Sweet Promised Land of Nevada* over again, and this time Tim, not having to watch the choruses, put in all the trimmings, a different voice for the Lord, a fine slide on all the introductory ohs and sos, big changes of tempo, and a long, down-gliding murmur on the last lines that were repeated. It was as much of a success as it had been first time.

He gave them *Tombstone Town* for an encore, and then Bill took over the piano and began to rattle off a dance number while Tim got a piece of paper from Maria and wrote out *The Sweet Promised Land* for Nicky. He wrote out the tune on the back of the paper too. Nicky folded the paper carefully, and put it into his shirt pocket, and buttoned the flap of the pocket. "Thanks," he said, "thanks," and shook hands gravely. He was full of plans for *The Sweet Promised Land*.

Pop disappeared again, but everybody else was staying. Tim and Nicky became part of the orchestra. Tim borrowed Maria's washtub from the kitchen wall for a drum, which made Maria almost laugh. He whittled down a couple of sticks of her stove wood for drum sticks, and sat down on the floor beside Nicky and played the drum. Sometimes he played the tom-tom or a bass drum with his hands or fists, and sometimes he played the snare with the sticks. Then they would trade around, and he would take the piano or the violin while Nicky or Bill took the washtub. When one of them wanted to dance everybody else wanted to take the drum, so there was no trouble, and sometimes the Fury would take the piano. She played it just the way Bill did, only harder, so that it rocked, and with more misses, but she looked so happy and fierce when she played that it made everybody laugh, while with Bill it was still a serious business, the second most serious in the world after mining, of which he wasn't doing much these days. When she wasn't playing, the Fury danced most often with Luigi or one of the older miners, but a couple of times, with loud protestations of the lowest intentions, she dragged the tall, young man with the puzzled look away from his safe place at the end of the bar and whirled him around and jiggled him up and down with great energy. Whenever the dance tune was one she knew, she sang the chorus loudly. Lawrence danced with her once, and it was easy to see that she had forgiven him entirely for the picture.

Francine danced with everybody. She and Bill danced furiously, and she and Tim improvised a couple of numbers so spectacularly that they got to be solos before they were finished. Even Maria danced twice, with Lawrence. She couldn't dance at all, but that didn't matter. They made a stately progression slowly around the outside edge of the floor, where they were not in the way. Every now and then the Fury would yell that she was getting winded, and they should have a song for a change, and then, if Tim wasn't already at the piano, she would push him over to it, and plump him down on the stool. Only Nicky didn't sing and didn't dance. Whenever Tim was free, Nicky would ask him things about the violin, and then try them. The rest of the time he was playing the violin or the washtub, or listening to one of Tim's numbers which he didn't know, listening very closely, as if once through would do it for him, although it never did. Luigi or Maria kept the glasses full on the bar, and nobody cared much whether he got his own or not, as long as it was nearly the same thing in it.

Francine was the first one to leave. "I gotta get home," she announced. "My old man hates a cold bed, and he'll be getting back any time now."

To Tim and Lawrence she said, holding each of them by an arm, "I love you both," and then fled out the door, calling good night to everybody. It seemed to Tim very satisfactory and important, in a general way, that Francine was so pleased with the way she lived now.

When Tim and Lawrence left, it was two o'clock. Luigi called good night and to come again, but Maria went all the way to the door with them, as if they were guests in her house, and said gently and exactly, "Thank you so much, boys. You will come again some time, no?" They stood upon the hollowed doorstep of Luigi's, and this customary question, in Maria's voice, wandered through labyrinths within them and echoed at every turn. Luigi's was no longer enough in itself, but a small place at the bottom of the main street of Tonopah, Nevada, and Tonopah on its mountain was surrounded by night, and filled with the rattling lamentation of the wind.

They told Maria that they would come again. When she had gone away from the door, Lawrence went back and drew a turtle beside it.

IN THE morning the clouds had closed their ranks and darkened, and the wet-smelling wind was still blowing. The shadow lay over the face of Luigi's place as Jeremiah passed it. Only one upper corner of the window, with Luigi's name on it, caught a faint gleam and lost it. On the desert north of Tonopah, the white dust raced through the brush so that when Tim and Lawrence just saw it out of the corners of their eyes, they would look to see what was running ahead of it with such great speed. There was never anything. Sometimes the dust reared into a slender column and spun furiously, but bent slowly and gracefully as it gathered speed across the vast flat.

Jeremiah rolled through Hawthorne and made his ceremonial stop beside Walker Lake, while Tim and Lawrence went down to the shore and stood in the wind and looked wide and listened to the pounding water. Tim touched water, and Lawrence picked up some sage-green pebbles to play with in his hand. They went on, passing through Schurz, where the Indians' gray corrals stood among the yellowing trees, and through the low, painted hills and the alkali earth and into the ranch land of the Carson Sink. After the southern desert, this seemed a country of abundance and of human permanence. Red cattle and bands of horses grazed over the plain. Then dykes of dry earth, smoking in the wind, and rows of yellow cottonwoods and poplars, showed where the canals flowed, and tractors and big horses moved slowly across the fields, pulling deep-bellied hay-wains, built to protect their loads from the wind. When the sunlight broke through, the sleek rumps of the horses shone, and unpainted parts on the tractors gleamed largely, though far off. In near fields, and in the bare yards around the ranch houses, turkeys stepped high and proud, their plumage flickering in the wind.

Jeremiah turned west in Fallon, and Tim felt himself quicken toward the gorge of the Truckee, and the late afternoon, when he would break out of the western end of the gorge and see the shining haze over the shining trees of Reno. He forgot the clouds, and thought of the Truckee Meadows as he always did, as filled with late and tranquil sunlight. The two gods of the valley would stand there, the sunlight streaming across them, close in the north-west, dark and brooding Peavine, the earth god, the lover of multiplicity, and far upon the south-west, Rose, the white woman, the lover of sky, the one who reached for unity. In the late afternoon it was always easy to understand that the sacred Truckee Meadows contained the city of adolescence as easily in time as they did in space, that they would never check the trembling of the leaves.

The trees around the ranch houses and along the highway bent and rushed in the wind, and their fallen leaves fled along the pavement. Flocks of sheep moved slowly under their own dust in the shorn fields between the highway and the river. When the sun broke through here, the dust became luminous, and a soft, revealing splendor descended upon the flocks. The highway passed the fields and came into the sloughs. The water was protected by reeds and cattails, but it was rippled into slaty darkness, and each diving bird made a small silver splash, as if something had fallen where he went under. Red-wing blackbirds flocked and twanged over the cattails. Then the sloughs passed also, and the gray, round hills closed in. Lawrence was watching all this silently and intently.

In the evening, Tim thought, when he had cleaned up, he would climb the dark stairs of the Great Basin Hotel, carefully stepping over number sixteen, and go along the carpeted hall to Mary's door. He would stand there for a moment, and then he would knock. He would hear Mary inside, walking across the room to the door. She would open the door. That idea kept making a dramatic climax in the music of the return. He wished that Jeremiah had it in him to go a little faster.

But when Jeremiah came up onto the Reno to Salt Lake highway, Lawrence said, "Let's stop in Wadsworth for a beer."

For an instant Tim was impatient with the thought of such a delay, but then he knew it was not just a beer that Lawrence wanted. He pulled up in front of a little place that had a beer sign, and they went in. Tim ordered the beers, and while the bartender was drawing them, Lawrence asked him, "Where does the Salt Lake bus stop here?"

"Place with the newspapers out front, couple of doors down," the man said, nodding his head in the direction he meant. "There's a Greyhound sign."

"Maybe you could tell me," Lawrence said. "Is there another bus for Salt Lake today?"

The bartender nodded. "Hour or so, I think," he said, combing off the beers and pushing them across.

"These have to be mine," Lawrence said.

"O.K.," Tim said.

Lawrence put a silver dollar on the bar and took his change. "There was a nice bench outside," he said.

They went out and sat down on the bench, and looked at the wide street, almost a plaza, where the highway went through, and at the trees swinging in the wind and the clouds still racing up out of the western hills. Lawrence took a long pull at his beer and then leaned forward, his elbows on his knees, and held his glass with both hands.

"Did I ever tell you about the grocer in Salt Lake City?" he asked.

"You wrote a note about a man in Salt Lake, when you were in Austin that time, on the eight-fold path, but you never told me the rest."

Lawrence smiled and studied his beer. "You should know about him," he said. "I liked Salt Lake City. At Elko I'd gone off rum onto bourbon. By the time I reached Salt Lake I was on Scotch, and feeling much better. I could see large, permanent objects quite clearly. The first morning, I even saw a lovely band of pigeons come down on a beam of sunlight in front of a great, gloomy building on the main street. I was so grateful I made a sketch of them. In the afternoon I remembered how the Wassucks loomed up behind Salt Lake. I liked the Wassucks too. I decided I would walk up through the city and see if the Wassucks were really the way I remembered them. Up toward the outskirts, I came to a neighborhood grocery store. I'd over-looked lunch, so I decided to get a couple of apples." He paused.

"It was the kind of a neighborhood where the camera would succeed," he went on, "all little, quiet bungalows, just alike, with little lawns just alike, and the same number of the same kind of trees out in front of each. It was like a running border for wall paper. The grocer was also small and quiet and just alike. He had gray hair and gold-rimmed spectacles and a big butcher's apron, and not enough spirit left to say good after-noon.

"When I had my apples, I thought I should leave him at least a touch of amazement, so I told him that Salt Lake was a beauti-ful city, and asked him if there were any artists there. His polite, gray wistfulness departed. His eyes opened fully for the first time, and gleamed almost fanatically behind his spectacles. I thought for a moment that he had known an artist once, and was about to spring at me. Instead, for fifteen minutes without stopping, he told me about art in Salt Lake City. There were some artists there, he said, but not nearly enough. Everybody in Salt Lake wanted to buy paintings or learn how to paint. In fact, he said, very apologetically, he even painted some him-self. Oh, he was no good, but just the same, he went up into the Wassucks every Sunday and painted, because that was what he liked to do. He had a tremendous collection of his own works. He didn't suppose he could sell them; he had never tried; he didn't want to sell them. They were his autobiography; they were the notebook of his life when he was living the way he wanted to. But he also bought other people's paintings, when he had any money to spare, and there were a great many people like him in Salt Lake. He told me all about the painters in Salt Lake who sold pictures, and about all the places that handled their work and sold art materials.

"I had to do something for such a man, but also I knew he

would be terribly honest, so I asked him if he would like a little sketch for the two apples, instead of the dime, and I showed him the pigeons. He was overwhelmed. He made me feel like a reincarnation of Rembrandt, which was not such a bad way to feel, after the way I had been feeling. His hands actually trembled as he took the pigeons, and he carried them over to the window, and pored over them in the light. When he looked up, I thought he was going to cry, and do you know what he said? He said, 'My God, you are good. You are so good it makes me unhappy. I will never be able to paint a picture as good as that little drawing.' Then he was afraid I would misunderstand, and he hurried on to explain that it was not because he would never do as well that he was unhappy. It was the picture itself which made him unhappy. And it was not bad to be unhappy that way; he didn't mean that either. It was better than any happiness. It was the unhappiness of beauty, for which there are no words. That is exactly what he said, 'the unhappiness of beauty, for which there are no words.' "

Lawrence took another pull at his beer. "After that," he said, smiling, "we got along fine. The little grocer said that I could not be allowed to give away such a beautiful drawing for apples. He said, 'Instead, I will pay you twenty dollars for the picture, not because that's what it's worth, but because that is all I can afford right now, and I don't know any other way of deciding a fair price for a picture that makes you unhappy.' "

"And you gave him the pigeons," Tim said.

"No, I couldn't do that," Lawrence said. "You can see I couldn't do that. The way we finally settled it, I swapped him the pigeons for one of his smallest oil paintings of the Wassucks, and I took the apples, and he took the dime. Two entirely separate transactions."

They watched the trees and the clouds in the wind again, for a minute or two, and each of them took a long pull at his beer. Then Lawrence said, "I'd better go and find out about the bus." He left his beer on the bench, and went down to the store with the newspapers and went in. When he came back, he held up his ticket for Tim to see.

"An hour and twenty minutes yet," he said. "You don't want to wait here an hour and twenty minutes. Mary will be expecting you. Why don't you go on?"

Tim said, "Why don't we go take a look at Pyramid, instead?"

Lawrence thought about that. "Fine," he said.

So they drove in through the round, gray hills, and up the west side of the lake until the road was near water, and then got out and went down to the edge, and stood looking across at the island and the Pyramid. The wind made the brush around them jump, and the dust like steam was rising from the south shore, and scudding and thinning out so the hills showed through again. The water was jade green and purple in patches, and long serpents of foam slithered across it. Twice, while they were watching, the smoky cloud-shadows parted upon the far side, and the Pyramid stood up white in a sunburst, and then faded back into the darkening mountains.

"I wonder how those turtles are doing?" Lawrence said.

For a moment Tim couldn't remember, but then he remembered the two thin black boys burying the big turtle and her brood in the ring of tufa, and squatting to wash the sand and clay from their hands where the weeds like bright green hair waved in the water.

"We could find out," he said. "We could stay at the ranch tonight, and you could go to Salt Lake tomorrow."

"No," Lawrence said, "no, we'd better let them alone."

They went back up to Jeremiah. Tim had to push Jeremiah on the return to Wadsworth, because they had looked at the lake and the Pyramid longer than they thought, but they got there in time. They were waiting at the curb when the bus appeared in the west, out of the gloom under the gathering storm. It had its lights on already. When it came closer, they could see the lighted sign above the windshield, SALT LAKE CITY. The bus drew up in front of the store with the newspapers, and the driver jumped out and ran into the store. They got out of Jeremiah.

"What about your pictures?" Tim asked.

"You keep them."

"I'll keep them for you."

Lawrence looked at him and smiled a little. "All right. Keep them for me."

"There'll be a room for you too," Tim said, "wherever it is."

"Not with the pictures in it?"

"No, just a room. No pictures in it at all."

"Fine," Lawrence said.

The driver came running back out, and jumped into the bus again. Tim and Lawrence shook hands, and Lawrence got in, and the door closed wheezily behind him. He took a seat on Tim's side and looked out, and when the bus began to pull away he held up his hand, like an Indian making formal farewell. Tim stood looking after the bus until all the lights on the rear end of it dwindled into one bright point, and then until the point winked out in the gathering darkness on the desert.

The first big drops of rain were falling when he got into Jeremiah again, but the rain only made it better than ever to think of coming to the door of Mary's room in the Great Basin Hotel.

CHAPTER SIXTY-FIVE: *In Which the Circle Closes*

MARY TURNER and Tim were married early that October. The wedding took place in Mary's room, and outside of the people from the Great Basin Hotel itself, only Rob Gleaman and Ling Choy attended. Mrs. Mott's eyes watered, and she blew her nose loudly. She considered the wedding an outcome of her own work. Ling Choy knew better than to assume credit for any of the obscure accomplishments of the human heart, but nonetheless he looked on with the satisfaction of one whose judgment has been sustained. He also remembered his promise to Mary, and after the wedding, everybody went to the Orient Café, from which the public was excluded for two hours by a sign reading Closed—Chinese Holiday, and devoured an excellent and abundant wedding feast. Ling Choy had prepared the feast with his own hands, but he caused it to be served by others, in order that he might sit with his guests. He also connived at an escape for Tim and Mary, who were let out his back door, one at a time, murmuring something about too much tea, while he held the remaining guests with an ancient tale of love in his old country. Tim and Mary went to Pyramid for two days.

At first, when they returned, Tim just moved downstairs into Mary's room at the Great Basin, but he had nearly six hundred dollars from his music, and Mary had saved over two hundred from her wages. They decided they'd work at what counted as long as the money lasted. Rob Gleaman let them use his cabin on a mountain above Lake Tahoe. Rob didn't go up there very often himself, and never after the first snow fell.

It was a fine cabin, all one big room with a huge stone fireplace. There was a sleeping loft at each end, and a big window in front that looked out through the tops of the pines and across the lake at the sharp peaks in the south-west, which still had snow in their crevices. The windows in the other sides looked into the woods. From the eaves outside and the rafters inside, hung yellow pine cones a foot or more long. It was as nearly like being outside when you were inside as anyone could get. The whole mountain about them smelled of pine, fir, and balsam all the time. Its gray rock thrust up through the forest floor and made presences. Manzanita grew like a small forest itself on the open slopes, and the strong squaw-carpet clung to the earth among the rocks and trees, remembering winter. When Mary and Tim were out in the woods, they could smell their own fireplace smoke among the trees too, a sharp, autumnal smell in the chill air, that quickened their minds.

In the first few weeks there wasn't much time for anything but their love. It was impossible to explore each other enough; everything was new now about their bodies and their thoughts. That Mary was shy didn't mean that she was frightened, but only that there was always something more to discover about her. She became quite wise during these weeks, and even learned to tease a little. They used the wide double bed in the loft that looked toward the lake. Sometimes they lay there for two or three hours after the sun had come up over the mountains and the yammering of the jays and the twitting of the smaller birds had awakened them. When Mary tried to get up to start breakfast, Tim held her there, laughing at her, and filled himself with the delightful awe about her light, supple body. The blue shadows of the morning would be under her thighs and breasts and in the little cup at the base of her throat. She had beautiful hands and feet, narrow and shapely and strong, and a habit of warming them on him if he kept her out from under the blankets too long in his worship. It was cold in the mornings, with white frost on the ground outside, and no fire in the cabin, and Mary loved to be warm and easy. Mary never did as much about this love making as Tim did, but her eyes and mouth always drew him back when he went too far with just admiring her. She looked at him enigmatically, storing her secrets for the moment when the two of them suddenly became deeply serious and unable to stay apart. She tugged at his hair with a tight little fist, and looked at him, and waited for him to kiss her, and said not a word all the time he was praising her, and then the moment came, and she was as fierce as he was, whispering his name over and over in his ear, as if that were her only word.

Sometimes Mary was still asleep when Tim woke up, and then he lay there, propped up on one elbow, and looked at her, and that was enough in its way too. After a few minutes he'd get out of bed, go down the ladder, start the fire and hang a kettle of water on for their coffee. Then he'd come back up and get in beside her again, and wait until she woke up.

They stayed together during the days too. In the mornings Tim worked at splitting, sawing and gathering wood to stack in the shed out back for the winter. He gleaned all the fallen wood out of the forest around the cabin, and then went far up and down the mountain, with his sledge-hammer and ax and wedges, and towed the wood home with a rope. Mary went with him. While he was swinging the ax or the sledge, she sat on a rock and talked to him. When he was dragging bigger wood in to split, she gathered dried branches for kindling and broke them into even lengths and made piles they could pick up later. They filled the shed up to the roof, and then piled wood outside the cabin and even inside, along the walls. In Jeremiah, they made trips to the store in Tahoe City and brought back supplies that would keep. The car track up the mountain to the cabin was full of sharp granite ridges and deep pockets where the yellow dust settled lightly and then exploded when Jeremiah fell into it, and they worked on it too, hammering off the ridges and filling the pockets with the chips.

In the afternoon they stopped work and went down the mountain and across the road and through woods again and came out in a little cove between gray rocks. They could swim there without suits on, or bring soap down and wade out knee-deep and cover themselves with suds, and then toss the soap back onto their towels and plunge into the water and rinse themselves clean. On days when the sun was warm, and the wind wasn't right in from the water and the snow mountains, they lay on the sand side by side, and listened to the soft slapping among the rocks, and sometimes fell asleep. When the wind blew they had to dance on the sand to keep warm. Tim improvised barbaric music for this hopping, and once in a while it developed into a real dance, which they kept up for a half hour or more, studying out their movements to give the dance shape and meaning.

When the days got colder, they bathed out of a bucket in front of the fireplace and dressed in flannel shirts, cords and boots and walked back through the woods slowly together, exploring the hollows and the upland meadows. Even then, though, they sat out on the front porch at night, with their heavy reefers on. It was a small, square porch with no roof over it, and no branches hanging over it either, so they looked up the well of black trees into the stars. Mary would lie back in her chair, with her hands deep in her pockets, and look at the stars, and Tim would softly invent things on the guitar until his hands got too cold, and sometimes, when the wonder of the stars and the dark, strong-smelling forest and Mary there with him, got too big to hold in, would sing aloud. He sang big, as he had to, but softly, held in. He made only one direct love song to Mary in this way, but she understood that the canticles he made about everything else on the mountain and the lake were meant to say the same thing.

The times he really opened up were those nights when they walked back through the woods, where they could see a star only here and there through the branches far overhead, until they came into a clearing where there were rocks and brittle grass, and a whole field of stars opened above and even made a faint light in the clearing. Then Tim always felt his love of Mary and of the place, and his hope all expand in him too suddenly, just like walking out from under the trees into the starlight, and often sang wide open, like his old imitations of Spanish and Italian operas. He cut off the last notes sharply, and they heard his voice come back, clearer and sweeter, from some wall of rock or horn of a hill, sometimes two or three times, each softer and farther away than the last.

Tim didn't write any of these songs, or even learn them to repeat for Mary. Each one was for just its time. It wasn't until the snow came that he began to work.

It snowed a great deal that winter. They'd wake up in the night, and turn a flashlight out the window, and there would be the big flakes still softly coming down. Sometimes the snow didn't come down so softly, but rode in on a fierce wind, so that even through the roar of the forest they could hear the brittle flakes strewn like sand against the windows, and they lay there, very glad to be in their bed and together. The storms made being together even better. Once the snow fell for ten days without stopping. When finally it thinned out to golden flakes one morning, and then stopped, the snow was up to the eaves of the cabin. Tim had been shoveling every day, to keep the doors and the porch and the south and east windows free. The sun coming in at the windows over the banks he had thrown up and packed, made a clear, weightless light in the cabin, such a light as comes from a crystal, or a glass bowl holding motionless water. The great banks of snow against the north and west walls of the cabin, where they had closed the windows and put shutters over them in the first storm, made the cabin warm inside.

That day, after the big storm, they both worked on the roof with snow shovels. The roof was very steep, and had long eaves which hung down over the windows to protect them. When the snow gave before their shovels, they sometimes went down with it, but that didn't matter, except that it was hard to climb back out of the drifts. When they were done with the roof, Tim dug a trench out to the woodshed, and finally the walls of his trench went up higher than he could reach with his shovel. The air was perfectly still, and great burdens of snow remained on the branches of the pines. At midday the sun became warm on the mountain, and the snow sank and grew heavy, but there was nothing up there to make it dirty. The world was white with the black tree trunks and the brown gable of the cabin standing up in it. From far below the lake showed through the trees, bluer than the sky.

On clear days, when Tim was done writing, he and Mary went into the forest on their skis, or on their webs if the snow was still too powdery for skis. When there was a moon, they went out at night too. Tim would break the track, and Mary would come along behind him. Their skis, sliding slowly and rhythmically, made a pleasant, soft, rushing sound, and their voices were clear and important in the silence. When they came out into a clearing in the moonlight, Tim would stop and look back. He liked to watch Mary coming nearer and nearer through the patches of shadow and moonlight, and then see her, suddenly much nearer, out of all the shadows, her face clear and of inestimable dearness in the thin, cold light.

When they came back from skiing, they built up the fire, and lit the kerosene lamp, and played chess on the floor in front of the fireplace. The two tall glasses of beer stood there beside the chess board, and the firelight shone through their amber prisms. Once in a while Mary just stretched on the floor with her chin on her arms, and Tim played the guitar softly. Usually it was chess, though, or one of them read out loud. Tim didn't feel like playing the guitar when he was writing on long things. He didn't even want to hear other music.

Once a week they took a day off and went to Tahoe City for the mail and food they wanted fresh, like bread and vegetables and butter. The road from Tahoe City to their track up the mountain wasn't kept plowed, so it didn't matter how they went. They found a new way almost every trip. When they reached the store they stood their skis and poles in a drift, went in and talked with the store people, or anybody else who was in there, and this seemed good too, something to take back with them as much as the food was. When they had talked about the news, about Japan in China and Mussolini orating about empire and looking for excuses in Ethiopia, and about the beer-hall revolution in Germany and the W.P.A. and the depth of the snow now on the Donner summit, and their hampers were packed, they went back out and put their skis on, hoisted their hampers and got them slung right, and started the return trip, which took a long time, because it was almost all uphill, and they had to do a great deal of it by making switchbacks. When they reached the cabin the sweat would be running down their faces, even on cold days. Tim stripped and ran out into the snow and rolled in it and scrubbed himself with it. When he came in, Mary would be standing in front of the fireplace, bathing herself with warm water out of a big enameled pitcher. The firelight danced on her body and shone in the long hair over her shoulders, making it as red as copper in places. Mary never did her hair up any more, except when they went to the village, and it always pleased Tim to see it down again. It was good going to the village and talking to the people there. It broke the daze of writing sometimes, when even the skiing couldn't. But it was even better coming back. He would shout at Mary that she was wonderful, and then come over and whisper to her and interfere with her bath.

Even after his writing began Tim was always full of awe and wonder about having her. He worked at a table by the window. Outside the window they had a place trampled down in the snow around a big tree on which they always kept a bacon or ham rind or a piece of suet nailed up. When Tim looked up and saw Mary out there feeding the birds, he always felt the perfected prayer because of her. If he had come to a place in the writing where he could wait, he sat there and watched her through the entire ceremony, though he never told her he watched, and pretended to be working if she turned toward the window. Mary stood with her back to him, facing the woods, and slowly sprinkled crumbs and grain around her on the snow. Then she put a few grains on each shoulder, and on the top of her head, and held some in the open palm of each hand, and waited motionless, with her hands out. It was like a very slow dance, wooing timidity into trustfulness, a ritual in which it was necessary to touch the head and the shoulders. By means of this silent patience, she summoned the wilderness to her. It was astonishing how many birds stayed in the mountains even after the deep snow came. That was the heaviest winter in years. During the long storm, the snow sheds on the Donner Pass caved in, and the open cuts filled with drifts a hundred feet deep, so that the big railroad plows churned into them and were stalled and buried. Thousands of men with shovels had to load trains which carried the snow down the mountains and dumped it in the desert. The highways were blocked until late May or June. Yet Mary would stand there, waiting, and the birds would begin to gather, chickadees, nut-hatches, woodpeckers, red-helmeted flickers, sparrows, the loud, political jays. As soon as the snow stopped falling, they gave life to the woods. They flashed and cried in the clearings. They were eager and hungry and sharply attentive on the packed snow of the feeding circle. A week after the long storm, forty or fifty of them were coming every day.

The jays were bullies. If the crumbs were just scattered, and nobody stayed there to watch, they drove the other birds off and gorged themselves. Only one of the small black-and-white barred woodpeckers was too much for them. He darted out of the air, stuck like a burr on the big tree, and then marched down it, making a soft bickering, and suddenly launched out into the middle of the circle. The jays scattered and watched him from high limbs, squawking their resentment, and the other birds returned and fed with him. This champion, however, didn't always come when food was scattered, and he never stayed long. As soon as he left, the jays flocked back down and took over. So every day Mary remained and performed her ceremony. The jays wouldn't come down when she was there either, and she would wait until the other birds had picked up their share and then walk away slowly and quietly, and leave the rest to the jays. Before the deep snow had been on the ground two weeks, she had won what she wanted. While she scattered the grain and crumbs, she whistled and cheeped in a soft way of her own. Then she waited with the grain on her head and shoulders and hands, and within two or three minutes birds were all around her and on her. When, at last, she let her arms down and turned to come in, even the most timid birds fluttered only a little way out of her path, and many of them followed her to the door. Before the winter was over, she had only to open the window and hold out the grain in her hands and make her thin, little whistle, and at once sparrows and chickadees and even some of the woodpeckers came to her. She had a lovely slow grace among the birds, and when she turned out of the circle after the feeding, her face had a wonderful stillness. Watching her face, Tim would again be lifted by an access of love and awe.

Often this ascension came on him unexpectedly too, when he had emerged from the store ahead of her, and was putting on his skis, and looked back and saw her coming out of the shadowy doorway into the sunlight in her bright-blue ski jacket, with the cowl thrown back so that the light glinted on the heavy braid wound around her head, or in the morning when he woke before she did, and raised himself on his elbow and looked at her sleeping face in the widespread hair, or when she went into the gloom of the kitchen end of the room and came back with the two beers, and he looked up from the chess board and saw her face with the firelight on it. He couldn't tell when it would come. She might be doing anything, and suddenly he would seem to see her new, and the wonder would lift him. Even when he was very tired from writing, so that his face was changed, and he fell to staring blankly and lost faith in the ultimate, the coming-to-be, in anger or despair over the news, and was tricked badly in their chess game by her bishops, whose sly, diagonal ways she loved, even after an evening like that, he thrilled as with the accomplishment of a high and long-desired music, when he lay in the bed under the roof peak and felt her light, hot body, shoulder to shoulder and hip to hip with him, and her hand in his.

It was in those ways only, however, that he would make love to her. He didn't want her often. The music used all his desire.

Mary laughed at him about this. When he rose from brooding over his coffee in the morning, and turned toward the table by the window, she'd ask, "How is your wife, Tim? Do you ever dream about getting back to her?" She didn't expect him to answer, except by grinning at her.

When he was displeased with himself for having been away from her for days in his mind, she came over and sat on his lap and kissed him, and held his face between her hands and looked at him mockingly and tenderly.

"You never married me, you know, Tim," she said. "You couldn't marry anybody. Anyway," she added, beginning to make love to him with her body, "I'd rather be your mistress on your days off. It's more fun."

He was sure after a little while that she really didn't mind. She liked being alone too, and knew it made being together better. When she was done with her work in the morning, and had finished copying the last pages of score for him, she took a long time feeding her birds and walking about reading their tracks and looking at the lake and the mountains. At noon she put his lunch on the table beside him without saying a word, only stopping to kiss him if he dared to look up. In the afternoon, she curled up on the couch under the other east window and read or worked her way silently, but with little singing movements of her throat, through the manuscript he had finished, or the new scores that came in almost every mail. One of her favorite books was always lying there on the wide window-sill, the poetry of Emily Dickinson, Tyndal's *Sound*, *Plutarch's Lives*, the *Essays* of Montaigne, one of the meandering novels of Trollope, *The Boston Cook Book*, or anybody's book about mountain climbing, an Arctic expedition, or stars, stones, trees or birds. If the afternoon went hours along, and she saw Tim wasn't going to stop working, she went out and drifted back through the woods on her skis by herself. Then, at supper, she always had something to tell him about this quiet adventure.

By the middle of December Tim had finished the *Shadow and Light Symphony*. It was what he wanted, all of one piece, continuous from the dark storm which hid the hills, through the war of clouds and sun over the earth, to the last cool, piercing notes that settled into the mind like silence and space and were winter sunset beyond the Sierra. After that, in less than two weeks, he wrote a concerto for piano and orchestra, which he called *Ghost Town*, and three or four songs, one of which, *After Snow the Shining Peace*, is still Mary's favorite of all his songs.

When these were done, he became possessed by a silence and absence so complete that Mary was finally troubled by it. For days he didn't write anything, or play or sing. When Mary looked at him, he wasn't looking at her, or at anything in the room, but staring at the fire and seeing other things. If she spoke, he roused himself a minute or two later, and asked what she had said. When they were out making their thin tracks through the woods and along the mountainsides, sooner or later he always began to move faster than she could, and grew small ahead of her in the white, cross-shadowed aisle of the forest. She would follow his tracks at her own pace, and perhaps an hour later would come on him sitting or standing on some high place where he'd remembered her, and waited, but when she came up he'd look at her and smile as if he had been waiting only a moment. Often he went out by himself, and was gone for hours, and when he came in he spoke to her softly and distantly, like a courteous stranger. In the mornings when she woke up, stretched like a cat, squinted at the light of sun and snow on the window, and turned to him, he'd be lying there with his hands under his head, staring at the ceiling, and after she'd watched his face for a little while, she'd know he'd been lying that way for a long time.

Out of this spell there came back in Tim, finally, the inner trembling and expectancy. One morning in January he woke before the sun was up. The cold and silence and darkness surrounded the cabin, and were proven now and then by the slow, straining crack of one of the pines as the frost touched it too deeply or a breath of upper wind bent its overburdened top. Tim couldn't lie still, but got out of bed and dressed in the dark and went down the ladder. He built up the fire and put on water, more out of habit than anything else, and then lit a lamp and carried it across to his table, and sat down and began to write at the symphony of the leaves again, and this time it came.

He wrote intently and eagerly, day after day. Mary says that sometimes she'd look at him, and he'd be sitting there staring fixedly at the paper, his pencil poised but not writing, and that an hour later she'd look again, and he'd be sitting in exactly the same position, without a note written, but it seemed to Tim that he was writing furiously all the while. At other times he did write furiously, his pencil rushing softly along, hour after hour, marking off the time with little dots and dashes like the working of a miniature telegraph. Then there was such an eager happiness and distance in his face that Mary felt almost jealous and took herself off into the woods or into the Arctic with Peary or Stefansson or Nansen, returning only when the blue dusk came down about the cabin and Tim lay stretched and silent on the floor in front of the fire.

During this time Tim thought often about Rachel. She brought the Court Street passages with her, and the islands in the river, and the white peak that was the symbol of oneness, the height toward which the music always reached, and she wandered in and out of all the rest. Here he glimpsed her in the tides that flowed between classes in the halls of Reno High School. There he saw her in her seat in the last row beside the window on the morning when the sun broke through and the ice went out on the Truckee and spring came into the class-rooms with the sounds of dripping gutters and sparrows along the edge of the roof. He turned his head and saw her in her proud place in the box, but quite alone and fiercely sending out her best wishes to Sunday Wind being shamed at the barrier. He saw her waiting for him in front of the house by the race track in the morning light in the yellow fall. He saw her with her arms down straight and her fists clenched, coming bravely up the walk to Billy Wilson's house. He burned anew with the shame of trying to give her the moss-agate. He sat beside her again in the niche on the mountain, smelling the sterile wind and the stone and snow, and looking out across the desert ranges. He knelt at the flashing brook in the high meadow. The canteen glittered in the ripples, the water was icy breaking around his wrist and tugging at his hand, and he looked up, and she was standing there gazing up at the peak, and the brilliant sun burned in stray threads of her hair. She stood in the door of his bedroom in Carmel, and said something which he could not remember. Yet in all of this he stood apart from her, and watched the shameful and beautiful antics of another Tim Hazard in the expression of his adoration, and such pain as he felt was like the bearable pain which was half joy and which had always lifted itself toward ecstasy in the stories of Tristram and Isolt which had come to life in the bedroom with the poplars outside the window. Like the face of Isolt turning to-ward him on the sea wall of Tintagel, her face was lifted above the edge of the pool at Bowers' Mansion, to watch the moon rise out of the mountains in the desert. All the other people of this story moved around her, but they too were apart and made music at last; they all stirred in him a love which it is difficult to let go, the searching, impossible desire to pour out to each crea-ture of all multiplicity the adoration which may be given to only one at a time, the yearning to know constantly that final answer which is sometimes, for a few rare moments, almost understood; the whippoorwill in the orchard, history accord-ing to the poplars of Bowers' Mansion, the chess piece that wasn't moved, the room in the Austin hotel, the fire of crickets, the smile of Maria, wife of Luigi, the feeding of the birds. The music arose from these, but it led itself onward, and told no stories. It was whole, circular, complete, and in the last rustling notes the question was there as much as in the first. There was no answer, but the question didn't die.

When the final notes were written, toward the end of March, and Mary had made the last transcription, and the manuscript was sent off to the publisher, Tim was like a dead man for a few days, like a Lazarus leaning against the tree in the desert dusk, watching with pity and a little dry mirth, the blind, habitual activity of the living. Then slowly he was filled again. When the warm spring days came, and brooks of snow-water chuckled everywhere on the mountains, he and Mary were together as they had been in the fall. A child began in Mary, and often she looked at Tim with a new wisdom and secrecy. Tim again wrote long letters to Lawrence and to me.

Postlude

THE last time I saw Tim, it was spring in Reno, and that winter at Tahoe was six years behind him. I was sitting beside him on the front steps of the house halfway out Plumas Street. The sun hadn't quite set yet, but the sky behind Mt. Rose was filling with its gold. The mountain itself was still white with snow, and high and aloof, and its influence lay upon Reno and the Truckee Meadows, though the trees of Plumas Street were in full, new leaf. In less than an hour I would have to catch one of the trains which cried through the valley at night, and both Tim and I were full of things which couldn't be said.

I'd been sleeping in the room where Lawrence's big painting of *The Promised Land* was hanging. It hung across the room from the foot of the bed, so that every morning, when I woke, I had looked out on Lawrence's paradise as if through another window in the bedroom. I had heard fragments of the symphony, which Tim had finally called *The City of Trembling Leaves*, and more of an oratorio he was working on at the time, *The Tower to Heaven*, in which he was combining the history of mankind as told by the poplars of Bowers' Mansion, and a version, in which humanity triumphed, of the legend of Babel which had so troubled him in his boyhood. He had managed to give me a good impression of the whole on the piano and the violin, and I had read the poem, but my present recollection depends most, I think, on bits that Mary kept singing around the house. Some of the titles may give you an idea of the progress of the oratorio. It seems to me they start something in the mind by themselves. *At Babel We Went Down*, a full chorus; *Hearken Thy Brother's Cry*, tenor solo; *Man, We Have Ten Thousand Times Thy Blood*, male chorus; *How Many Are the Gods*, tenor and soprano choirs; *In Their Slow, Great Dance the Planets*, full chorus; *Yet Will I Hope*, contralto solo; *Let the Children Sleep*, female chorus; *All the Nations with One Tongue*, chorus; and that final burst of triumph in which the building of the tower is resumed, *Lo, the Sun Returning Striketh*.

I was remembering this music as I sat beside Tim, and remembering other things too. Tim and Mary and I had talked over much of the past. We had gone to Pyramid and Tahoe, to Virginia City and Austin and Tonopah and Death Valley together. I had come to an understanding with their three-year-old son, Lawrence, and had now and then believed that I was going to catch up with what went on in their five-year-old daughter, Mary, although that was something like trying to catch light in your hand, and darkness, darkness too. Now that I had my coat and tie on for the first time in weeks, and my suitcase stood by the door, I was full of these things, but there was no use trying to talk about them.

We were talking about the quartet Tim had got together, which played at his house every Friday night. Tim was holding the hose to water his lawn while we talked. The stream from the hose shone in the last sunlight, and crystals of light fell from it onto the grass.

Only the screen door was closed behind us, and we could hear Mary in the kitchen, clattering among the supper dishes and singing part of the responsive that led up to the final chorus of *The Tower*, "*On the desert of ages the sleepers stir; the wind at the end of night makes a dance of birds in the ash.*"

Only single leaves on top of the tallest trees were touched by rumors of night. There was a small aspen, which Tim had brought down from a canyon on Peavine, and planted in a circle of turned earth on the lawn. Even its leaves didn't move. The shadows of poplars across the street reached onto the lawn, and they were motionless too. Young Lawrence, in a sun suit, was riding a stick-horse back and forth through the bars of light and shadow they made. He was galloping, more on one foot than on the other. Each time he turned at the end of the lawn, he increased his speed for a moment and shouted,

"Giddap, giddap," and laid the whip on with cheerful fury.

Little Mary was sitting on the step below us, beside Tim's knee, but not leaning against it. She was absolutely motionless, with her hands clasped tightly between her legs. I could see only her back, but I knew she was thinking hard about something. Over the stony ground of life, she pursued the fainting traces of previous passage. She was a bird on the nest, and the eggs were working from within.

In the kitchen, Mary sang, *"From his hill the sentinel stares east. He has cleaned his bayonet in earth. Below him, in the dark, the sleepers turn."*

All at once the little aspen on the lawn began to tremble. Then a heavy tremor, making a sound like the rushing of water, passed down all the trees on Plumas Street. This wave died away into nothing, as it had come from nowhere, but the aspen continued to quiver and twinkle. Little Mary jumped up and ran across the lawn in her bare feet. She stopped beside the aspen and looked at it, seriously and steadily. Little Mary was always like that. She never walked. She ran everywhere. Then she stood very still and looked.

In the kitchen, Mary sang, *"Upon the east the slow, white dance begins."*

Tim was watching little Mary, and he gave the response softly, without thinking, *"Upon the west the splendid peaks behold it."*

Little Mary reached up and stopped a leaf from trembling, letting it lie flat against her small palm. Young Lawrence turned his wooden horse at the south edge of the lawn and started to hurry it back again, but broke off in the middle of a shout and stood still to see what Mary was doing. Mary withdrew her hand slowly from under the leaf, and it began to dance again, by itself.